BRAVE STORY

Miyuki Miyabe

Translated by Alexander O. Smith

Haikasoru
San Francisco

Isle of Dragon
Lourdes
Sasaya
Sakawa
Lyris
Lanka
Bog
Fatal Desert
Grandera River
Dela Rubesi
Icy Capital
Undoor Highland
Maquiba
Tearsheaven
Nacht
Swamp of Grief
United Southern Nations

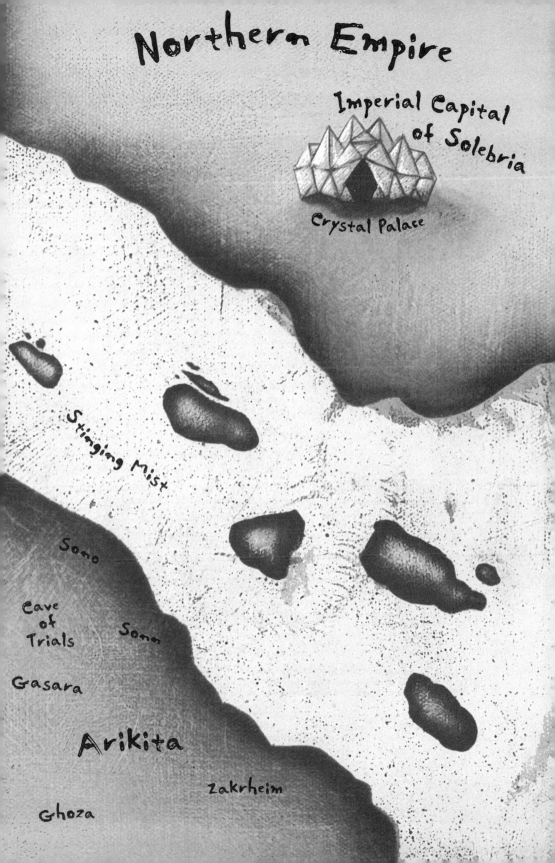

BRAVE STORY by MIYABE Miyuki. Copyright © 2003 MIYABE Miyuki.
All rights reserved. Originally published in Japan by KADOKAWA SHOTEN
PUBLISHING CO., LTD., Tokyo. English translation rights arranged with
OSAWA OFFICE, Japan, through THE SAKAI AGENCY.

English translation © VIZ Media, LLC

Jacket painting and map illustration © 2007 Dan May
Designed by Courtney Utt

HAIKASORU
Published by
VIZ Media, LLC
295 Bay Street
San Francisco, CA 94133

www.haikasoru.com

Library of Congress Cataloging-in-Publication Data

Miyabe, Miyuki, 1960-
 [Bureibu sutori. English]
 Brave story / Miyuki Miyabe ; translated by Alexander O. Smith. -- 1st paperback ed.
  p. cm.
 Originally published: Tokyo : Kadokawa shoten, 2003.
 Summary: With a determined plan to reunite his mother and father, Wataru knowingly enters a fantasy realm inhabited by a goddess who has the power to change
destiny. With the help of the Lizard Boy, the Cat Girl, and the Fire-breathing Dragon,
Wataru faces a series of seemingly insurmountable obstacles on this once-in-a-lifetime
adventure. One way or another, the young hero must reach the Tower of Destiny and
bring his mother and father back together again.
 ISBN 1-4215-2773-1
 1. Japanese fiction. I. Smith, Alexander O. II. Title.
 PL856.I856B8713 2009
 895.6'35--dc22
                              2009027395

The rights of the author(s) of the work(s) in this publication to be so identified have
been asserted in accordance with the Copyright, Designs and Patents Act 1988. A CIP
catalogue record for this book is available from the British Library.

Printed in the U.S.A.
First paperback printing, November 2009
Second paperback printing, November 2009

Contents

Part 1

Part 2

Part 2 continued

You have been chosen. Walk the true path.

Part 1

chapter 1
The Haunted Building

No one believed it at first. Not even a little.

It began right after the beginning of the new school year, and no one knew who started it. Rumors are like that.

Everyone knew the story, down to the last detail. They could even tell you whom they had heard it from, and when. Still, even if you traced the chain of he-said, she-said a hundred people back, you wouldn't find the original source.

"Hey, you know that big building next to the Mihashi Shrine, over in Kobune? They say it's haunted!"

That's how Wataru Mitani heard it, from Katchan, the son of the bartenders over at Bar Komura. Katchan's real name was Katsumi, a girl's nickname. The story went that his parents—expecting a girl—had decided upon the name way ahead of time. The obstetrician told his mother that the ultrasound showed it was "definitely, beyond a shadow of a doubt, a girl." But on that ninth of April, eleven years ago, a healthy baby boy arrived one week ahead of schedule, his wailing cry so distinctive that soon everyone, even the people in the nursing ward across the hall, came to recognize it instantly. It was a funny cry. He sounded hoarse and gravelly.

"My old man says I must've been smoking inside my mom's tummy."

Wataru didn't find it hard to imagine at all. He remembered, with a laugh, the year they entered Joto No. 1 Elementary School together. They walked to class one December morning, both donning their school-issue yellow hats. As soon as they got into the room, Katsumi had run over to the sputtering old kerosene heater and stood there, shivering, even when the teacher came in the room. When he was told to take his seat, he replied as casually as could be, "Oh, don't mind me. Just get on with it, *chop chop, chop chop.*" Wataru had somehow managed to keep from bursting out laughing until he got home, where his parents thought he was making the whole story up. The episode had since become legend, and, even now that they were all in fifth grade, the teachers would say things like, "Doing your homework, Komura? *Chop chop!*"

Katsumi's voice had been hoarse as ever when he told Wataru the rumor about the haunting in hushed, excited tones. His voice broke when he said the word "ghost."

"You've always been into ghost stories, Katchan."

"It's not just me, everyone's talking about it! Some guy was walking by there the other night and he saw it! And when he tried to run, it chased him!"

"So, what kind of ghost is it?"

"They say it's an old man."

Oh, how unusual. "What's he dressed like?"

Katchan scratched his nose, and his raspy voice became even lower. "He wears a cloak. A black cloak, covering everything, like this," he said, swinging his hands up as if to throw a hood over his head.

"So how could they see his face? How would they know he's an old man?"

Katsumi's face wrinkled. Wataru would sometimes run into Katsumi and his uncle at the market or at the station, and his uncle would always greet him with a bright "How are you," his face wrinkling in exactly the same way.

"I don't know, you can just tell. That's the way ghosts are," Katchan grinned. "Why do you take everything so seriously? I swear, your dad must've put a steel trap in your head by mistake."

Wataru's father, Akira, worked at a steel company, which wasn't to say he actually spent time on a factory floor forging steel bars or anything like that. The company ran all sorts of ventures—from foundries to shipyards—continuously expanding as demand for its core product dwindled over the years. At thirty-eight years old, Akira had spent only a few weeks in the company's steel factory, right after being hired. Since then he had worked in R&D, then the PR department, and now he was stationed at a subsidiary company specializing in vacation resort development. Still, Katchan had insisted on calling him Wataru's "steel-workin' dad" since kindergarten and had never tired of the joke.

But Wataru was stubborn. He could never just accept something without a clear logical rationale behind it. It was a trait he picked up from his father.

His grandmother on his father's side had first pointed it out about three years ago. The family had gone to her house in Chiba for summer vacation, and, though Wataru was still shivering from a day of swimming, he had asked his grandmother for a shaved-ice treat.

"Shaved ice? With you fresh from the sea?" she had said. "You'll catch your death of cold." He had protested, and his grandmother had laughed and shaken her head. "Just like your father, always eager to argue a point. Poor Kuniko!"

His mother, Kuniko Mitani (always "that Kuniko" to his grandmother), pretended she wasn't listening.

"In ten years of marriage, that's only the second time I've heard your grandmother say something nice about me," his mother had told him later. She asked why they had been arguing, and Wataru had explained, "She told me I couldn't eat shaved ice after swimming in the sea, so I asked her why she sold it at her shop."

His mother had laughed out loud. Akira Mitani's parents ran a food and drink stand on Ohama beach, on the Chiba Peninsula. A small public beach house was attached to their setup, with showers and places for people to change. During the busy summer months, Wataru's grandmother would be out in back, making shaved ice in a big metal can all by herself.

"That's a good point," Kuniko had said, giving him an affectionate pat on the head, "but your grandmother is right—you do have your father's argumentative streak."

When Akira heard the story days later, he had frowned. "Don't confuse a kid whining for a treat with the argument of a rigorous, logical mind," he had said, as logical as ever.

In any case, Wataru was not the sort of boy to readily believe in ghost stories, especially not one as riddled with holes as this one was.

The building in question, the one next to the Mihashi Shrine, was actually still under construction. It stood in an awkward, half-completed state almost exactly midway between Wataru's home and the school, so he passed it every day on his way to and from classes. He knew its story well, even though the rumors kept getting it wrong.

The building had been under construction for what seemed like forever. A crew had started work on the site during spring break more than two years ago, when Wataru was still in second grade. The eight-story steel framework had gone up first, and everything seemed to be proceeding on schedule, until one day, work stopped, and the whole building was covered in blue plastic tarps. As far as Wataru could tell, there were no construction workers on-site anymore. A while after the heavy machinery stopped coming, somebody removed the old blue tarps and put up new blue tarps in their place. That's when Wataru noticed a new construction company had moved in.

According to Kuniko, the tarps had been replaced once more after that, and the name of the construction company had changed, as well. After that there had been no change to the site at all, and so the building stood there, draped all in blue, not quite a proper building, coldly looking down on the surrounding houses. A placard out in front that had listed a timetable of projected completion dates had disappeared.

"The contractor and the builder had some kind of dispute, so construction stopped. Happens all the time these days," his father had said with a roll of his eyes, and Wataru soon forgot about it himself. But Kuniko's interest was piqued, and she had started asking around.

The Mitani family lived in a large apartment complex with nearly three hundred units. They bought their apartment right after Wataru was born, and moved in right away.

Wataru had several friends among the kids who lived in their building, and they rode the same bus to kindergarten. Kuniko, too, made friends among the circle of mothers in the complex. One of the women she came to know was married to the manager of a local real estate agency. Because of this, she was well informed about all the local properties. One day, their conversation had drifted to the topic of that "terrible eyesore" next to the revered Mihashi Shrine.

"Remember how the temple grounds used to be so large? Well, I guess it was hard to maintain all of that. So, once when they were refurbishing one of the old shrines, they sold off some of their empty acreage. That's where that building is standing."

The company that had bought the land and begun construction of the building was a rental office place called Daimatsu Properties, headquartered in downtown Tokyo. It managed properties throughout the metropolitan area, and while attracting a shrine's business spoke well of the company's pedigree, it wasn't particularly large. In fact, from the sound of it, the whole operation was run by one man with the stuffy-sounding name of Saburo Daimatsu.

Wataru's family lived on the eastern side of Tokyo, or "Old Tokyo," as the locals called it. Years ago it had been little more than a string of factories, but the quick commute to the city center (only thirty minutes or so) made it attractive to residents. Over the past ten years, apartment buildings had sprung up like mushrooms after the rain. With the coming of the apartments and the people who lived in them, the face of the town changed. To long-term residents like the real estate agent's wife, their little borough was like a poor girl who had suddenly married into wealth. "Oh, it's the same old town," she would say, "but now it's all dressed up for a cocktail party."

Wataru's father was born in the countryside of Chiba, and his mother came from Odawara, a coastal town to the west. Being recent imports themselves, neither of them completely understood how the locals felt, but they did sense the town's vitality. It was an easy place to live, and it was only getting better. A quick glance at real estate advertisements confirmed that property values were rising. The price tags on all the new apartment buildings jostling up against each other were comparable to those in other more established parts of town. For Daimatsu Properties, it must've seemed like a great idea to buy the land next to Mihashi Shrine. Apparently, Mr. Daimatsu had paid quite a bundle for it.

"Now, with its neighbor being a shrine and all, they couldn't rent the building out to just anyone. The area is zoned for industry, but it's right up against a residential zone," Kuniko told them at the dinner table, repeating what she had heard from the real estate agent's wife. "Still, they went around to a lot of potential tenants: a coffee shop, a beauty parlor, a cram school. They were going to make the upper floors into rental apartments. Until..."

Days after the building's steel frame had gone up, the first contractor on the job went bankrupt. Daimatsu Properties quickly began a search for another contractor to pick up where they left off, but since starting that kind of work halfway through is much more difficult and costly than starting from scratch, it was hard for the company to find a deal. After a two-month delay, they finally found a new contractor to resume construction. Thus the blue tarps changed for the first time.

"So this new place came, and they got started, and then..."

Unbelievably, after only a few months, the new contractor, too, went bankrupt.

"As you can imagine, Mr. Daimatsu was in quite a fix, and went dashing about looking for another contractor. He finally found a small one interested in the property. In fact, just like Daimatsu Properties, this new contractor was basically a one-man operation."

It was the last job he ever took. Three days after the paperwork was signed, the third contractor died of a stroke.

Kuniko shook her head. "Such a small operation couldn't run without its foreman, and there was no one to take his place. There was a son, but he was still in college. Ultimately, the contract was voided, and so the building still stands, unfinished."

Walking by the building on his way to school every day, even Wataru could clearly see the signs of deterioration on the abandoned edifice. The concrete had dried out and begun to flake at the corners. Exposed steel struts were stained gray by the rain. Inconsiderate passers-by had thrown garbage at the base of the tarps, and stray dogs and cats had taken to using the building grounds as a litter box.

One day in early spring, a strong wind blew off one of the tarps, exposing a steel support post and a steel staircase and landing on the second floor. This was the only part of the building interior visible from the outside. If the ghost had been seen anywhere, that was the place.

Whose ghost was it supposed to be, anyway, Wataru wondered. If it was an old man, then, based on what he knew of the story of the site's construction, maybe it was the ghost of the third contractor who had died from a stroke just after taking on the project. But why would he be wearing a hooded cloak? Wataru couldn't imagine the foreman of a building contractor walking around dressed like that. Even if, for argument's sake, the man had owned a favorite hooded coat, and now wore it as he haunted the empty halls of the building, that still didn't explain why he was haunting it in the first place. Was he concerned about the progress of construction? Did he regret having died unable to fulfill his contractual obligation? It seemed a little dry, for a ghost story. And, if he was in the construction business, surely he would realize that rumors of a haunting would drive away other potential contractors, making things even worse for Mr. Daimatsu, the very client he had promised to help.

Wataru had thought about it all through recess, and when he got back to the classroom and found that everyone was still talking about the haunting, he gave them his opinion. That was when one of his classmates claimed she knew exactly what kind of ghost it was.

"It's a bound spirit," she explained with utmost seriousness. "It's what happens when somebody dies in a car accident or something. They're bound to the place where they died, haunting it."

Of course, that didn't make any sense either. The building stood on old temple grounds. There couldn't have been a car accident there. Wataru told the girl as much.

"Then maybe somebody snuck onto the grounds and committed suicide," she retorted. "There, their spirit wanders, as lost in death as it was in life."

The other girls around her *ooohed* and *aaahed* in approval.

"You know," one of her friends said, "whenever I walk by that shrine I get a weird tingling feeling down my back. Once my knees started knocking together—like I was cold, right? Even though it was *warm* outside."

"Totally! I get that too," another chimed in.

"Well, did you think to check whether there really was someone who committed suicide on the shrine grounds?" Wataru asked. "Did you ask the priest or something?"

Their faces went red.

"Don't be stupid!"

"You can't just *ask* something like that!"

"I don't even want to go near the place."

Wataru continued, doggedly. "But then you'll never know the facts, will you?"

The first girl pursed her lips in a pout. "Look, the place is haunted, all right? And that means there's a bound spirit there. Those should be facts enough for you. You know, this is why everyone says you're so lame, Mitani! Why do you always have to argue about everything?"

"Yeah! Make fun of ghosts, and one of them will end up cursing you!"

"You deserve it too, creep!"

Satisfied, the girls went back to their desks, laughing as they went. Wataru sat quietly in his chair. He was in shock. He was right, he knew he was. What they were saying made no sense. But how could he hope to win when his mind went blank whenever they called him things like "lame" and "creep." The words stuck into him like sharp knives.

On the walk home, Katchan couldn't stop talking about how the Japanese soccer team had given the Iranian team a run for their money the night before. Wataru didn't feel like talking. The trouble at recess was still fresh in his mind. Blissfully unaware, Katchan waxed poetic about his favorite players and gave a blow-by-blow description, waving his fist in the air to mark every kick, pass, and goal. Even if Wataru hadn't seen the match, Katchan's reenactments were always vivid enough to make him feel like he had been there, on the field, watching every moment of the action.

They neared the haunted building. Usually, Katchan would turn right at the corner just before and say goodbye, but today he was so wrapped up in his soccer replay that he seemed to have entirely forgotten about going home.

"Hey, Katchan."

Katchan paused, one leg raised high in mid-reenactment of a critical kick thirty-two minutes into the first half. He looked back over his shoulder at Wataru. "You say something?"

"We're here..."

Wataru stood and looked up at the building. It was a tall, empty box of steel and looked pitiful dressed in its shoddy blue tarps. It was a clear day in May, and the pure blue of the afternoon sky made the grimy plastic tarps look even more miserable. The building was abandoned, lonely.

"What's with the serious face?" Katchan brought down his foot and straightened up, looking at his friend.

"I want to find out. I want to see if there really is a ghost. And, if one shows up, I wanna see whose ghost it is."

Katchan blinked. "How?"

"I'll sneak in at night," Wataru replied, beginning to walk faster. "You've got a big flashlight at your house, right? Lend it to me."

Katchan stood silent for a moment, then came to his senses and ran to catch up to his friend. "Hey! Sure, no problem, but it's kind of hard to get that thing out of the house. Dad says it's for emergencies, and he gets mad when we use it for playing."

Katchan's father had been born in Kobe, in southern Japan. He had lived in Tokyo for years now, since before Katchan was born, but even still, the Kobe earthquake in 1995 had come as quite a shock. To hear Katchan tell it, the level of disaster preparation in the Komura household rivaled that of the metropolitan government offices downtown.

"I'm not playing, I'm serious." Wataru began to walk faster, calling back over his shoulder, "Don't worry about it, I'll make do."

"Wait," Katchan said, hurrying to keep up. "It's fine, really, I'll get it." It was only just dawning on him that Wataru meant every word he was saying. "Why the sudden interest anyway? I thought you didn't care about ghosts."

That's right, he didn't care about the ghost. He was hurt when the girls had called him "lame." Was it so bad being argumentative, even if he had a point? He wasn't trying to be difficult; it was just that the girls' story was so ridiculous. Wataru's mind filled with questions. Was it wrong to say something no one believed, even if it was right? Did he have to just sit there and take it when no one agreed with him? Was he doomed to an existence of being hated, shunned by every girl in the fifth grade?

Of course, he couldn't tell Katchan *that*. Wataru's face twisted into a scowl.

"Hey, what time?" his friend called out to him. "Hey, I'm talking back here!"

Wataru stopped and turned around. "What time...?"

Katchan swung out his right leg as though to kick an imaginary soccer ball floating in the air before him. "What time you going in? I'll go with you."

Wataru was so happy he almost laughed out loud. "Twelve o'clock."

"Midnight, eh?" Katchan laughed. "Good time for ghosts. My dad works at night so I can be there, no problem...but how are *you* getting out?"

Now that he mentioned it, Wataru realized it would be nearly impossible to sneak out of his house that late at night. Officially, Wataru lived with his mother and father, but for most of the year, it was more like he and his mother lived alone. Akira came home late as a rule, and, even on holidays, he always found something to do out of the house. Since he had been transferred to his company's resort development department, he was often gone on long-distance business trips, and they were lucky to see him for two weeks out of any given month.

Akira had not once attended parents' day or the annual sports competition at Wataru's school. He would always promise to go, and then something would inevitably come up at the last moment. He wasn't the kind of father who kept promises.

Wataru didn't mind. Who cared about parents' day anyway? He knew his dad was busy, and it was more important keeping appointments for work. He had a bigger concern right now. His dad would most certainly be getting home after midnight tonight, and that meant his mother would also be up late, waiting for him to come home. She would knit, read a magazine, or flip through the TV channels to see if anything good was on. Sometimes, she would rent a movie and watch that. No matter how late his father was, she would never go to sleep before drawing him a bath, making him dinner, and cleaning up when he was finished. How could Wataru possibly hope to sneak out under her watchful eye?

As he ate dinner, Wataru prayed for a miracle. Maybe his dad would get home early for a change. He'd eat and, saying he was exhausted, both of his parents would go to bed early. Once they were sound asleep, he could sneak out quietly. And, just in case they happened to look into his room, he would hide his stuffed bear under the blankets as a decoy. Akira had won the toy at a company party raffle the year before and given it to him. Wataru didn't care for stuffed animals, but he was glad to finally be able to put it to use.

Miracles were one thing, but reality was reality. He ate dinner with his mother as usual. Later, she told him to do his homework, and she checked over the writing assignment his teacher had returned to him, pointing out the spelling mistakes without even knowing what the assignment was about. Consequently, Wataru was chained to his desk doing schoolwork for an hour or so. Afterward, it was bath time. When he was done, his mother told him there had been a phone call from Katchan.

"It didn't sound like it was all that urgent, so I told him he could talk to you tomorrow at school. I believe I've mentioned before that elementary school students shouldn't be phoning each other after nine o'clock." His mom put her hands on her hips. "Katchan's parents run a bar, so they may see it differently, but this is my house."

It always irritated Wataru when she said this—like she was pinching the thinnest patch of skin on his body with the tips of her fingernails. She didn't have to get all snippy for him to know that she didn't think much of Katchan. He knew she didn't like his parents. All because the Komuras ran a bar, which, as anyone could tell you, attracted the "wrong sort of people," according to his mother.

But Katchan was Wataru's friend. His best friend.

Maybe his father was a bit seedy. Once, he had come to a school function having drunk too much, his face bright red. Wataru had heard the teacher telling him off. And Katchan's mother often wore so much perfume you could tell when she was out shopping by the pungent trail she left—even when she was on the other side of the supermarket. He even said that everyone at the local cosmetics shop knew her by name. Still, none of that made Wataru hate Katchan's parents. At sporting events they would cheer for both Katchan and Wataru, and during spring parents' day in third grade, when Wataru had solved a difficult math problem at the math bee, Katchan's father had shouted out "Way to go!" Even if everyone had sniggered, it made Wataru happy. He had never been praised like that in public before. Even now, years later, that day stood out in his memory like a shining piece of colored glass in a sea of mud.

When his mother looked askance at the Komuras, he always wanted to tell her how good they were, and how nice they had been to him, but somehow the words caught in his throat until they dissolved away into nothing. That he couldn't stand up for them made him feel like he was somehow betraying Katchan and his parents. Yet he couldn't bring himself to contradict his mother on this point. Maybe because he saw the logic in what she was saying. Wataru didn't know much about people who went to bars, but judging from Katchan's comments they weren't the same class of people that, say, worked at his father's company. Once he had asked Katchan if he wanted to take over his family's business when he grew up, and he shook his head, and muttered something about doing some research at a university, or maybe becoming a lawyer. Regardless, the long and the short of the situation was that relations weren't exactly great between the Mitani and Komura households. That much was painfully clear.

Katchan had probably called to see if Wataru really could make it out of the house that night. The only phone in their house was out in the living room, so it was impossible to sneak a call. Wataru felt suddenly guilty.

What if I'm the "wrong sort of people" too?

He sat with his chin in his hands, his elbows propped up on the desk, staring blankly at the chart of class periods he had stuck on the wall above. The first hour tomorrow was Japanese class. They would probably have to write another essay. Katchan was particularly bad at writing, and he was always asking Wataru for help. Of course, if Wataru stood him up tonight, he probably wouldn't bother him tomorrow at all. He'd be too angry.

"Of course he won't be, silly."

The voice was high and sweet—a girl's voice, coming from right behind him.

Every muscle in Wataru's body tensed. He jumped out of his chair, the four casters creaking loudly beneath him. He whirled around. There was no one in his tiny room. He glanced down at his television, a fourteen-inch his parents had bought him after much wheedling and begging last summer. It was turned off.

He looked around some more, then looked back at the desk and sat down. He must have dozed off while he was looking at his class chart. He remembered a scientist on television once saying that the dreams you have when you doze off unexpectedly could be very vivid. Sometimes, so vivid they are impossible to separate from reality.

Then the voice spoke again.

"You *will* be able to leave tonight. Rest up while you can."

Wataru scanned the room. Everything seemed to be in its right place: the bed with its blue-checked comforter, his bookcase filled with reference books and comic books, and his video game console next to the television set. The carpet was depressed where the casters on his chair had sunk in, and the slippers he had been wearing were tossed haphazardly on the floor behind his desk.

There was no one else in the room. Wataru was alone.

"You can't find me by looking, you know." The girl's voice rang in his head. "Not yet."

His heart raced. He felt his blood pumping. He imagined his heart throbbing like Pac-Man, gobbling his way through his maze.

"Wh-who's there?" Wataru stammered. Here he was in his familiar room with its familiar, slightly dusty smell, talking to no one. His voice sounded like a whisper. This was ridiculous. It was stupid to hear voices in his head, and even stupider to try to talk to them. Still, it felt less embarrassing somehow if he talked really quietly.

"Who could it be, I wonder?" the voice said mischievously. "Never mind that now, you should go to bed. If you're going out to play tonight, you'll need your rest. You'll be late for school tomorrow!"

Several possible courses of action occurred to Wataru in an instant. He chose the most childish of them all. He ran out of the room.

"Wataru? Is something the matter?" Kuniko looked up from where she sat peeling an apple at the kitchen table. "Want a slice? Here, have one, brush your teeth, and then it's bedtime."

Wataru suddenly felt weak. He leaned back against the wall.

"My, you don't look well at all," Kuniko said, putting down the knife, then she tilted her head to one side and looked at him closely. "That reminds me, you had a cough this morning, didn't you? Have you caught a cold?"

Wataru didn't answer, so his mother stood up and walked over to him. The skin of her hand was cold and soft on his forehead.

"You don't seem to have a fever…have you been sweating? Do you feel ill?"

Coming to his senses at last, Wataru muttered something about it being a fine and good night. Still floating, he went back into his room, shut the door and leaned against it. He heard the sound of knocking.

"Wataru? What is it? Are you sure you're okay? Wataru!"

"I-I'm fine, Mom. I feel fine," Wataru said, slowly regaining his composure. Thinking of a way to explain what was happening to his mother made him feel even more lost and confused. Finally, the knocking stopped. He moved away from the door and flopped down on his bed. His breathing was shallow, his pulse was racing, and his eyes spun in his head.

"You poor thing," the girl's voice said. "I'm awfully sorry. I didn't mean to startle you."

Wataru slapped both hands over his ears and screwed his eyes shut. He willed his mind to go blank, to slip into unconsciousness. And, though he hadn't imagined he would be capable, he fell asleep. When he woke it felt like he was leaping out of darkness. The alarm clock next to his bed said it was ten minutes to midnight. Wataru shot up in bed, wide awake. He had been sweating when he fell asleep in his clothes, and now they felt itchy and cold.

Quietly, he opened the door to his room, and peered out into the kitchen. The television was on, tuned to some late-night news program his mother often watched. But tonight, she was asleep, her arms sprawled on the kitchen table, lightly snoring.

Katchan was first to arrive at the meeting place, the entrance to a park just south of the haunted building. Katchan always tended to be early, probably a habit he picked up from helping out at the bar.

"S-sorry, I'm l-late," Wataru said, panting to catch his breath. Normally a little running wouldn't make him breathe this hard, but he was still excited by the events of the evening.

"Your mom sounded pretty fierce on the phone. I'm surprised you made it out." Katchan jumped up onto the park's chain link fence and swung from it like a monkey.

"Sorry."

"No biggie. Your mom is always like that to me."

His friend said it like he really didn't care, but it made Wataru a little sad to realize Katchan had noticed his mother's judgmental attitude.

"Did she fall asleep or something? Hey, doesn't she wait up for your father to get home? How did you get out?"

Wataru realized again how odd it had been for his mother to fall asleep. He glanced back in the direction of his apartment.

"She...she fell asleep."

"She sick or something?"

Wataru silently shook his head. Several questions rose in his throat, but none of them made the least bit of sense, so he swallowed them down like a bitter pill. *Katchan, have you ever had everything go black, and pass out, but you didn't fall asleep? Have you ever heard someone talking to you when no one was there? Is that strange? Would it be stranger if it were a girl talking? And has your mother or father ever fallen asleep sprawled on the kitchen table like that? Sleep so deep you could push them and pull them and they wouldn't budge? Or shout in their ear and they wouldn't wake up?* It was almost like a mage from one of his fantasy games had cast a sleeping spell on her. He was afraid.

"Whatever, you made it. Let's get going!" Katchan sprang from the top of the fence. With those words, all of Wataru's questions went swirling away. He nodded and ran.

chapter 2
The Silent Princess

At night, the flat light of the street lamps shining off the blue tarps of the haunted building made it look even cheaper and shabbier than it did by day. The houses in the surrounding neighborhood were quiet. All the porch lights were off, the windows dark. The Mihashi Shrine sat silently in a ring of dark trees, making the gaudy light on the building seem intended to accentuate its miserable appearance.

It felt good to run in his sneakers, even for a short distance, and now Wataru had finally remembered the night's true objective: they were going to see for themselves once and for all whether there really was a ghost haunting the half-built building.

They were past the shrine and nearing the building when Katchan stopped abruptly.

"Someone's there," he whispered, pressing his back up against the wall surrounding the shrine. Wataru reflexively followed suit. He could see no one.

"Where?"

Katchan pointed. "On the other side of the building. See that light down the road?"

"Where? It's just a street lamp."

"Nuh-uh, there's a car."

Wataru squinted his eyes but he still couldn't see anything. He moved away from the shrine wall and began to walk again. "Let's go check it out. We're just walking down the road, anyway—it's not like we're doing anything bad."

So what if somebody had stopped the car there, he thought. As he approached the front of the haunted building one of the blue tarps lifted and he saw a figure standing inside.

Almost immediately, another tarp lifted and someone from inside the building looked out, right at them. They were spotted. "Who's there?" a voice called out languidly. "What are you boys doing?"

The voice belonged to a young man. Wataru guessed he was about twenty years old. With some effort, the man worked his way out from beneath the tarp, and came out to the road. Up close, Wataru realized he was quite tall. He had on a slightly grubby T-shirt and jeans. His hair was cut short, and he was wearing glasses. In his right hand, he carried a flashlight.

From the direction where Katchan had seen a car came the sound of a large sliding door, like that on a van, opening. They heard another voice. "What is it, Noriyuki?"

This new voice belonged to a middle-aged man. Soon, its owner appeared from the direction of the van, a stout, blocky figure beneath the street lamps.

Wataru's mind was racing, though his body was frozen to the spot. Who were these people? Burglars? Night patrolman? Were they searching for something? Were they burying something? Were they trying to set fire to the place?

"Hey, it's just some kids. What are you doing out at this hour?" asked the older man. From his voice, he sounded like he was about the same age as Wataru's father. The younger man called Noriyuki walked over to the boys and looked them over. Then he glanced at his wristwatch.

"You're not going to tell me you're lost, are you?" Noriyuki said, his face breaking into a smile. "And don't try to tell me you're on your way home from cram school, either."

"Urk," said Katchan loudly. It was a familiar sound to Wataru. He had always imagined that if you looked "urk" up in the dictionary, it would read something like "urk: 1. A sound Katsumi Komura makes when he's caught doing something he shouldn't be doing."

Still, at least he had managed to say *something*. Wataru was so flustered he simply opened his mouth and stood there, gaping like a fish. Finally, one thought among the storm of thoughts swirling around his head happened to stray near his tongue, and out it came, launching from his lips like a freshly popped kernel of popcorn.

"I-I'll call the police!"

The two men jerked back. They looked at each other, then turned their gaze back on Wataru. Next to him, Katchan was standing with his mouth wide open. "Why?" he asked after a beat.

The two men burst out laughing.

"Dad, keep it down," said Noriyuki, slapping the older man on the shoulder and laughing. "You'll wake the whole neighborhood."

"My little sir," said the father, waving his arm in Wataru's direction. "There's no need to fear. We're not burglars."

Katchan grabbed Wataru's arm by the elbow. "Really, it's okay. I'm pretty sure they're okay."

Wataru's eyes opened wide and he looked at Katchan. His friend's face gradually broke into a smile. Unable to contain himself, he started to laugh. That was when Wataru realized that it was no longer two versus two, it was three versus one: three people laughing, and one person being laughed at. His face reddened.

"Ah, whoops," Noriyuki said, suddenly turning to run in the direction his father had come from. "We left Kaori by herself." There was the sound of a sliding door around the corner again, and moments later, a light brown van came rolling up. It stopped right before the haunted building.

Katchan nodded appreciatively at the sleek paint job. "Cool, new car. Sure is big!" He sounded impressed. "Must've cost a fortune!"

Wataru noticed something different about the van. Stenciled on the side in large letters was a sign that read: Daimatsu Properties, Inc. He blinked and looked up at the older man. "You...you're Saburo Daimatsu!"

The stern man had been wiping tears of laughter from his eyes. Now his mouth tightened, and he looked down at Wataru. From that one look, Wataru knew in an instant that he was right. Here stood none other than the unlucky owner of the haunted building, the man behind Daimatsu Properties, and his son.

The van door opened. There was a faint mechanical noise, and something like a metal arm extended from within the van. Sliding out along the arm came a wheelchair. The wheelchair slid until it was hanging off the side of the car, and then the arm lowered it to the ground.

In the wheelchair sat a girl with slender arms and a slender neck, her hair tied in a ponytail. Her head swayed with the wheelchair's rocking descent.

"Someone in the neighborhood tell you about me?" asked Mr. Daimatsu. Then, before Wataru could reply, he added, "That's right, I'm the owner of this building. This is my son, Noriyuki."

Noriyuki came toward them, pushing the wheelchair. The girl's head lolled to the side. She didn't look at Wataru and Katchan, or even her father. Her eyes were open, but they seemed to see nothing.

"And this is my daughter, Kaori," Mr. Daimatsu said, walking over to the wheelchair and gently patting the shawl covering the girl's legs. Her hands were hidden beneath the light pink shawl that hid everything from her waist down. If she had reacted to her father's gesture, none of them saw it.

"So you see, we're not burglars. Really," Noriyuki Daimatsu said with a broad smile. From the tone of his voice, Wataru could sense that he was trying to calm them down. He suddenly saw how he must've looked from their perspective: a frightened little kid. Wataru clenched his teeth. He wanted to die, he was so embarrassed.

"We were taking my sister out for walk, and thought we'd stop by and see how the building was doing. As you can see, there's a lot of garbage and strays here. It's quite a mess."

"Oh, I see..." Wataru said, looking down at the ground so he wouldn't have to meet the looks of Mr. Daimatsu, or Noriyuki, or even Katchan. He wanted to swivel around in place, head still facing downward, and run straight for home.

"A walk at this time of night?" Katchan asked, blissfully unaware of his friend's mortification. Before Wataru could jab him in the ribs, Mr. Daimatsu spoke.

"Yes, as you can see, my daughter's not well. She doesn't like it when there're lots of people around."

"So you go out when it's quiet at night," Katchan said, nodding as though it all made perfect sense. When Wataru glanced up at the men, he saw Mr. Daimatsu and his son exchanging nervous looks.

Kaori Daimatsu was a pretty girl. No, she was beautiful. When people around her pointed and said "beautiful," the little fairy herself would have blushed and said something along the lines of "No really, you're too kind"— that's how pretty she was.

In Wataru's eleven years, he had never met someone so beautiful. He had never met a girl so doll-like. Maybe, he thought with sudden horror, she *was* a doll. After all, she didn't speak. She didn't smile. She didn't react at all to the outside world. Her gaze was a blank. The only motion she made was to occasionally blink her eyes. They say that eyes are the windows to the soul, but her eyes were windows to a dollhouse.

"Kaori is in junior high," Noriyuki said, glancing sideways at his sister in the wheelchair. "That makes her only a little older than you. What grade are you in?"

Wataru was on the verge of saying "sixth." Both he and Katchan were short for their age, so they couldn't hope to lie and say they were in junior high. But there was little harm in making themselves one year older.

Katchan dashed his hopes by replying first. "Fifth. Over at Joto Elementary."

"Joto Elementary School? Ah, then let me guess: you must be the paranormal investigators," Noriyuki said, smiling. Next to him, his father laughed so hard his belly shook, and his hand on the arm of the wheelchair shook its occupant. Kaori's head lolled to the other side.

"Paranormal...how..." Wataru sputtered.

"There's a rumor going around that this building is haunted, right? Apparently, kids have been coming out here at night, trying to sneak inside. The Joto Elementary PTA even lodged a complaint with our company."

"When was this?"

Mr. Daimatsu scratched his head. His son answered. "I'd say about two weeks ago."

Wataru was devastated. Someone had gotten the jump on them.

"The earlier paranormal investigators, they came to take photos," Mr. Daimatsu explained. "Like those photos of ghosts people are always showing on TV these days?"

Noriyuki nodded. "They had a Polaroid camera."

"Well, we're not ghost hunters. We didn't come here to play pranks," Wataru insisted. "We came here to find out the truth."

"Wait, I know," Katchan said, clapping his hands together in sudden enlightenment. "Those earlier paranormal investigators, they were from sixth grade, right? Weren't they talking about sending pictures of the ghost to the local television station?"

"Yes, those are the ones," Noriyuki said with a rueful smile. "Their leader—what was his name?—some foul-mouthed kid."

"Ishioka, right? Kenji Ishioka?"

"That's the one! You friends?"

"Not at all. But my old man and Ishioka's dad are fishing buddies. See, he told me that Ishioka's dad was saying something about his son appearing on TV with some sort of ghost photos…if you follow."

Kenji Ishioka and his gang of miscreants were the reigning punks of sixth grade. In fact, they were a terror to the entire student population of Joto Elementary School.

Most students, if asked, would reluctantly agree that the purpose of going to school was to learn. Ishioka's gang hadn't the faintest idea what that meant. They paid no attention in class. They entered and left the classroom as they pleased. They came late, left early, or simply didn't show up—all as a matter of course. They stole other kids' school supplies. They broke things. They bullied their classmates. They took lunch money. They were still in elementary school, but their antics were easily on par with the worst of the high school-level troublemakers.

The sad truth was that, these days, it wasn't unusual to have one or two problem students of this caliber in every class. But Ishioka's gang wasn't confined to a single grade. They had "gone national" during a school festival last summer. Stealing the principal's car, they drove recklessly through the school yard, chasing after younger students. By the end of their five-minute rampage, the festival was in chaos, and three students had been injured.

An emergency PTA conference was called the following day, and the principal explained what had happened. He ended up apologizing for his thoughtlessness in leaving his car unattended. The story went that the principal had broken his reading glasses at home, and had come to fetch a replacement pair from his desk in the teacher's office. He was in a rush, ironically, to attend a teacher's committee meeting on reducing misbehavior in school.

Though the kids actually driving the car had been in the grade above, one of the injured students was in Wataru's class. That's why Kuniko had attended the emergency conference. When she got home she was seething.

"Why was he apologizing? Doesn't anyone find that odd?" she said with a scowl to no one in particular. "I can't believe the principal has the gall to claim it was his fault for parking the car where he did. Parking a car isn't the problem! It's the kids who stole it and drove around the schoolyard that are the problem!"

Apparently, even at the conference, the majority of the parents had looked to the principal to take responsibility for what happened.

"They say that kids are mischievous by nature, and so it falls to adults to watch out for them. Insanity! I even heard someone saying how impressed they were that sixth-grade kids could drive so well! I swear, what is the world coming to?"

Ultimately, the three students' injuries were little more than bumps and scrapes, and so the whole affair didn't get any larger than that. No police were informed, the newspapers didn't pick up the story, and the principal didn't resign. In the end, the net result of the incident was that Ishioka's ranks swelled, and their power over the rest of the school grew.

Still, Ishioka leading an expedition to take pictures of a ghost? It didn't make much sense. Wataru couldn't see the connection.

"Maybe all those sixth-graders wanted was to get on TV?" he wondered out loud.

"Probably so," Noriyuki agreed, glancing sideways at the building. "I even overheard one of them say that if they didn't get good pictures, they would just fake it with a computer." He chuckled.

"No way," Katchan shook his head. "So, did you run into them here too?"

"Sure did. But that time it wasn't just kids. There were two adults with them."

"Reporters, no doubt," Mr. Daimatsu said, his arms folded across his chest.

Noriyuki nodded. "When they saw us, they pretended to be parents, but they had that sort of hungry look you see with people in television."

Wataru looked over at Katchan. "You hear anything more about that from your dad?"

Katchan shook his head. "Last I heard was that Ishioka's father was boasting they were scheduled to appear."

"Did any of you see the program?" Noriyuki asked, an eyebrow raised.

"Nope," Katchan shook his head. "Ishioka's dad doesn't come to the bar anymore—oh, and by the way, my parents run a bar," he said, giving them his best bartender's grin. "Maybe the show got canceled. My dad hasn't said anything about it."

"Or maybe it just hasn't aired yet."

"That's a possibility. Television programs take more time to put together than you'd think. That's probably it."

A wind blew, rustling the blue tarps. They all tensed.

"Look at us!" Noriyuki said with a laugh. "We're as bad as the ghost hunters." Everyone's gaze was turned up at the building. "We of all people should know best that there are no such things as ghosts, and certainly not here. You're looking a bit pale, too, Dad."

Mr. Daimatsu grinned sheepishly and scratched his head. Wataru had seen that gesture so many times this night already that he wondered if it wasn't the scratching that had given Mr. Daimatsu his big bald spot.

"That's right," he said quietly. "If you're going to be scared of something you should be scared of people. They're much worse than ghosts."

To Wataru, it sounded like a perfectly rational adult thing one might say to children afraid of ghosts. Still, Mr. Daimatsu and his son Noriyuki seemed embarrassed. They both looked down at the ground, as though they had said something they shouldn't have.

"Time to go home." Noriyuki walked around behind Kaori's wheelchair, and undid the brakes.

"You get in," Mr. Daimatsu said, waving toward the van. "We'll give you a ride back to your homes."

"We're fine," Katchan said quickly. "We live right over there."

"None of that. It's our responsibility now that we found you out here. It's an adult thing, don't you know," the man added with a wink. "In you go."

Ultimately, Wataru and Katchan were talked into accepting the ride. Wataru got in the van. His seat was right next to where Kaori sat strapped into her wheelchair. He could smell the shampoo scent of her hair. He felt that somehow he was too young by at least five years to be smelling a girl's shampoo in the close confines of a car, but more than some sort of illicit excitement, he felt a pang in his heart. Kaori couldn't move, couldn't smile, couldn't talk. She merely sat like a doll. And yet her hair smelled wonderful. It made it even more painful to see her pretty face, her skin the pure white of soap, and her delicately long and slender arms.

Because Bar Komura was closer, they dropped Katchan off first. Then they headed toward the apartment building where Wataru lived.

"You can just let me off at the corner."

From the driver's seat, Mr. Daimatsu chuckled. "You mean if we drive up in the car, it will make a noise, and someone might notice you snuck out at night?"

Wataru winced. "My dad gets home late every night, and I don't want to run into him at the door."

"But what if you get mistaken for a thief?"

In the end, they let him off on the street in front of his apartment. No one was at the entrance. The entire building was silent. Mr. Daimatsu and his son waited in the van until Wataru had reached the elevator door, then, flashing their headlights once, they drove off.

"You get caught?"

The following morning, Katchan came running up as soon as first period was over. "Let me guess: your mom was up when you got back, and she beat you within an inch of your life?"

Wataru shook his head. He had snuck quietly back into the house to find his mother still sprawled on the kitchen table, and his father not yet home.

"So you were totally safe! How come you look so sleepy then?"

"How could you sleep after that?"

"I zonked out as soon as I got home."

"You amaze me, Katchan."

Katchan gave his best innocent look. "So why couldn't you sleep?"

Wataru had been thinking about Kaori. There was something about Mr. Daimatsu and Noriyuki that made him think they were hiding something. There was more to them, beneath the surface, and it aggravated him to not know what it was. The more he thought about it that night, the more agitated he became, and he couldn't fall asleep until dawn.

"I dunno. They seemed pretty nice to me."

"Oh, they were nice. Too nice."

"How so?"

"Look, normally, when grown-ups find kids running around at a time and place like that, they get mad, right? But all they did was laugh. They didn't even scold us a little bit."

"Maybe they're used to it, what with Ishioka and his gang already having been there."

"It's more than that," Wataru said, staring blankly at his desk. This desk had been his since the beginning of the year. Whatever upperclassmen had used it before had left a present for him etched into the glossy wood finish of the top: the word "EVIL" written in all capital letters. What would possess someone to carve something like that? Wataru didn't see the point.

"I'm sure that Mr. Daimatsu and his son had something far more serious on their minds than kids coming to play ghost hunter. Whatever it was, they were so wrapped up in thinking about it they didn't even have time to worry about a few neighborhood brats. They were nice to us, because they didn't *care*."

Katchan scratched his head—his hair was cut so close it was almost a crew cut—and rolled his eyes in exasperation as if to say "there he goes again." This had happened before. Wataru would be deeply concerned about something, and Katchan wouldn't get it at all. It made Wataru frustrated, and several times he had snapped at his friend. It never occurred to him that, when he did so, his face looked exactly like his mother's whenever she talked about those "Komuras and their filthy bar."

"You think it has something to do with that girl, Kaori?" Katchan muttered. He said it quietly, as though he didn't want Wataru to hear, but loud enough just in case he happened to be right.

Of course it does!

"Of course it does!" Katchan said, beating him to it. "How could it be anything else?"

That was my line, Wataru thought, growing more irritated. *He* was the one who figured it out, *he* was the one who saw behind their kindly façade.

"You think she's sick?" Katchan said, even quieter than before. "It was weird, I mean, she *looked* fine, except she was all limp. I wonder why she doesn't talk?"

Wataru thought. They had said they were taking her for a walk, but that was odd too. If she didn't like other people around, why couldn't they go to a park, or the ocean, or somewhere else? Why did they have to take her out in the middle of the night?

The unsettling thought occurred to him that her condition might have something to do with the haunted building. That would explain why Mr. Daimatsu snuck her out so late at night when they wouldn't be noticed, and brought Kaori to such a strange place.

"Hey," Katchan said, growing restless at his friend's silence. "I asked my old man about Ishioka's dad."

Because of their profession, Katchan's mother and father worked late every night. But they always made sure to get up early the next morning and eat breakfast together. "The family that eats together, stays together," they would say. They loved those kinds of sayings: "One kindness every day," and "Friendship is priceless"—things like that.

"He said he didn't know. Ishioka's dad hasn't come to the bar for a long time."

"Hmph," Wataru snorted in response.

"So, we're done with that haunted building, right?" Katchan said with a grin. "I wouldn't be caught dead following in that jerk Ishioka's footsteps."

Wataru was silent. Katchan scratched his head again, said something about that being the end of that, and nodded goodbye before heading back to his own desk just as the beginning-of-period bell began to ring.

From his desk, Wataru could see the back of Katchan's head. Katchan's father cut his son's hair himself with an electric shaver, and there was always a little bald spot. Every time he had it cut, the bald spot would move slightly to one side or the other, or change its shape. Katchan never complained. His father would laugh while he cut it, talking to Katchan and his mother, threatening to cut off Katchan's ear if he moved.

Someone cut Kaori's hair too. Wataru remembered how it smelled. That fresh, clean scent of shampoo. Someone washed her hair, shampooed it, tied it up in a ponytail. Maybe they talked to her—her face a silent mask. Probably it was her mother. She must be very sad. How horrible it must be to know that Kaori would never answer her. It was like she was dead, even while she still lived.

What had happened to her?

Wataru realized that he utterly lacked the means to imagine what life must be like in the Daimatsu household. He couldn't even make a good guess.

The day passed by in a blur. When Wataru got home, Kuniko was in the living room, having draped laundry for ironing over every available surface. Her hands moved mechanically as she smoothed out dress shirts and pants, her eyes glued to the television the entire time. She didn't have to look, she never made a crease. Akira always said she was the only person he knew who could make ironing a performance art.

Wataru's usual homecoming routine was to call out a perfunctory "Hi, Mom, I'm home," and go straight to his room. But this time he stopped, and spoke to his mom. "Have you heard anything lately about that haunted building next to the Mihashi Shrine?"

"Sorry?" she said, not turning around. It was unlikely she had even heard what he said.

"That half-built building, the one being put up by Daimatsu Properties, or someone. Have you heard that Mr. Daimatsu has a daughter in junior high?"

Kuniko slapped the creases out of a dress-shirt collar while shaking her head. "No, I hadn't heard that." For the briefest of moments she wrenched her gaze away from the television and looked down at her hands. Her fingertips ran along the collar, found a stray thread, picked it up, and threw it to the floor. She looked back to the television.

"Maybe your friend, the one whose husband is the real estate agent, would know something?"

Kuniko didn't answer. She was watching an afternoon soap opera. On the screen, the heroine opened an unlocked apartment door and stepped inside a darkened room. A body was lying on the floor. She screamed and a commercial came on. At last, Kuniko looked up at Wataru. "What? Did you say something?"

Wataru almost went to ask again, but then felt suddenly like he didn't want to. "It's nothing," he muttered.

"Strange child. There's some cheesecake in the refrigerator. You have cram school today, right? You're not going by bicycle. They're doing repairs on Clover Bridge. Did you wash your hands? We're out of mouthwash, but there's a new bottle under the sink."

It was times like this when Wataru fancied that, as long as he said his hellos and goodbyes, he could eat breakfast, go to school, and come back home a slobbering, hairy werewolf, and his mother wouldn't notice a thing. He stood up to snatch his cheesecake and go to his room, when the phone rang.

"Could you get that?" Kuniko said. She couldn't get up quickly from where she was sitting in front of the ironing board. He had heard her telling someone on the phone the other day that she had gained five pounds already this year, and it was hard for her to move around like she used to.

Wataru walked toward the phone hanging on the living room wall and picked up the receiver. "Hello, Mitani residence."

Silence.

"Hello?"

Still nothing but silence. He said hello again, and not hearing a response, he hung up the receiver.

"Wrong number?" Kuniko asked.

"Guess so."

"We get those a lot lately. I answer the phone, and there's nothing on the other end. So I hang up."

Because he was by the phone anyway, Wataru thought about giving Katchan a call. He wanted to apologize for being such a grump today, and for running home without asking if he wanted to walk back together.

The phone rang again, and Wataru quickly picked it up.

"Hello?"

Again, nothing but silence on the other end. Wataru's mood was blacker than it had been in a long time, and a sudden anger took control of him. Holding the receiver in front of his mouth he shouted into it, "If you're not going to talk, than don't call, idiot!"

He slammed the receiver back down on the hook, and saw Kuniko staring at him, eyes wide. She looked more bemused than worried.

Wataru couldn't pay attention in cram school that day, either. Though he was normally an ideal student, he was scolded by the teacher no fewer than three times in a two-hour period. The third time, the teacher asked him whether he was feeling all right.

Wataru couldn't say for sure. He found his mind wandering to the events of the night before. There was Mr. Daimatsu, gently patting the arm of the wheelchair, and Kaori's slender neck lolling her head to the side. Her cheek was pale as wax, reflecting the color of the hastily draped tarps on the haunted building. Everything was permeated with the clean smell of shampoo. The same scene played over and over in his mind. Was she sick? Did she need help, or would she just get better? If she were a DVD player, she would definitely be in need of repair, but did humans work the same way? Wataru couldn't say.

He walked home in a daze, and then it occurred to him to go past the haunted building. Since cram school was in the opposite direction from regular school, it was more than a long-cut. He would actually have to walk *past* his house to get there. Still, he wanted to see it again. He had made it back to the apartment building entranceway and would've kept on going if someone hadn't called out to him.

"Welcome home, Wataru. Back from cram school?"

He looked up to see his father standing a mere ten feet away. He carried his bag in his right hand, in his left, a folded umbrella. Wataru remembered that the weather report said there would be rain showers downtown.

"Hi, Dad," Wataru replied, walking toward his father. Akira turned and made for the entranceway without waiting for him.

"You're home early today, huh?" Wataru looked down at the digital watch on his left wrist, which read 8:43. Beside the big numbers, smaller digits raced on the right side of the watch face, counting out hundredths of a second. The watch was a gift picked up on Akira's business trip to Los Angeles the year before. It bore the logo of a popular U.S. basketball team. Wataru hated basketball, and as a result, he hardly ever wore the thing.

"School going well?"

"Yeah," Wataru said, as usual. This particular exchange had formed the bulk of their conversation over the past year. Even if Wataru said something else, his father would probably just listen in silence. And even if Akira asked something more, Wataru would probably just say "Yeah" to that too. Probably. He didn't know, because it had never happened. Akira Mitani was not a talkative man by nature. In contrast, Kuniko talked up a storm. According to Wataru's observations, the ratio was about ten to one in his mother's favor. If success in daily life and authority within the family were proportional to the amount one spoke, then the one who talked the most would win. In other words, Kuniko wore the pants in the family.

But when the conversation passed from the topics of daily life to more serious matters, things were different. Then, the usually taciturn Akira would become "argumentative," as his grandmother in Chiba called it. The decision to buy their current apartment had been one of those times when he spoke up. So had he done when Kuniko thought to send Wataru to a private school. And again, when they had to decide if Wataru would go to a cram school. And he always had the last say when it came time to buying a new car. At these times, Akira would thoroughly research the problem at hand, think it through, and pick the most logical solution. There were no vague, touchy-feely factors involved, no "I think maybe we should," or "Everyone else is," or "That's what's expected of us." If the subject in question were a new car, fuel economy and safety standards would be carefully scrutinized. If it were an apartment, the contractors, the living environment, all data would be analyzed, and there would be no questioning of Akira Mitani's final decision.

Akira's peculiar way of doing things had received quite a bit of attention ten years ago when his father passed away. The topic remained to this day a matter of discussion among their relatives. Even though Wataru was only a baby at the time, he had heard the story so many times at family reunions that he remembered the incident as though he had seen it himself.

Akira had shocked many of his relatives by refusing to conform to the "way things are done." At his father's funeral, he questioned the order of names on the invitation list. He questioned the gifts some people brought. He questioned everything. Apparently, it was quite a spectacle.

Eventually it was poor Grandma, in mourning because of her husband's passing, who finally spoke to him. "Akira, there will be no more of this," she said tearfully. "At least give your father the quiet funeral he deserves." If she hadn't intervened, their relatives said, the casket wouldn't have left the house for a week.

With that one incident, Akira's reputation was set among their relatives as an "intelligent man, quiet, and gentle enough...but when he gets going, watch out!"

"Of course, I knew that all along," Kuniko would say, laughing.

Akira Mitani was not a scary father. Wataru could not remember ever having been yelled at or struck. So far, he had not even had to face his father's ultimate weapon: the logical argument that others feared so much. Of course, this was partly because his father was too busy to spend time on family discipline.

There were things about his father that Wataru didn't completely understand. But this had never bothered him. The door to his father was simply not open, nor would it probably ever be open, but as long as Wataru cared for whatever was beyond it, and his father cared for him back, that was enough.

Wataru even *liked* his father. In this world, where so many people liked nothing more than to talk about themselves—his friends, people on television, at school—he thought his father was cool to work so quietly all day. Like most children his age, Wataru had an image of his father that was nothing more than the image his mother, Kuniko, had of her husband, Akira.

Even if all Akira did was nod his head and listen, Kuniko seemed to love relating things she had found interesting to him, or things that had angered her. She would even run things by him that had already been decided. Wataru had been like that, too, as a child, always eager to talk. Lately though, he had hardened, like spaghetti prepared *al dente*, and become less a pure child and more something approaching a young adult. This new Wataru could simply say "Yeah," when asked a question, and nothing more. Maybe that was the difference between men and women. Or maybe it was something that Kuniko didn't have, that Wataru had gotten from his father's genes.

Still, tonight, their usual exchange had left him feeling strangely unsatisfied. His thoughts stirred as they walked along the hallway to their front door. He suddenly found that he wanted to say many things to his father. *Were there really such things as ghosts? If everyone truly believes something, and thinks something is interesting, even if it's ridiculous, should I play along? If I don't play along, will they hate me? You don't think I should, do you, Dad? But they never called you names, did they? Even if something's wrong and I know it, how do I do something about it without it turning into a fight? Will I be like you someday?*

And what about Kaori Daimatsu—wordless, cut off from the outside world. Dad, she was just like…like a princess trapped in a castle tower in a video game. I didn't believe such girls really existed. What's wrong with her? Why can't I stop thinking about her? Have you ever felt this way about something?

The words swirled in his head, but in the end they never found a way out, and now they were opening the door and going inside. Kuniko was busily explaining things to Akira, asking his advice, asking about work. It had been a long time since the three of them ate dinner together. His mother seemed very happy, and her happiness was infectious. Wataru hadn't eaten a dinner that tasted so good in years.

Wataru stood to bring his plate and cup to the kitchen when the phone rang. He quickly went to pick up the receiver.

Silence.

"Not again," Kuniko said, her chopsticks frozen in midair.

"Yup," Wataru confirmed, hanging up the phone.

"We've been getting those a lot lately, those silent calls." Kuniko furrowed her brow. "I don't like it."

Akira glanced at the phone. "They usually come around this time?"

"Usually they come during the day, in the afternoon—isn't that right, Wataru?"

"Yeah. We had two in a row the other day."

"Do you answer the phone usually, Wataru?"

"No, yesterday was the first time."

Akira put his cup down and stared at the phone. "Maybe you should put it on the answering machine?"

Kuniko laughed. "It's okay, it's not like it's a crank call, or some pervert. And if it was your mother calling and we let her talk to the answering machine, there'd be hell to pay."

Akira smiled, knowing she was right. Wataru got an ice cream from the freezer, and a spoon from the drying rack, and was about to sit down when the phone rang again.

"I'll get it!" he shouted, flying to answer it. He was going to give the caller a piece of his mind, like he had yesterday. But when he picked up the receiver with a loud "Hello?!" there was an answer.

It was a friendly, hefty voice. "Eh? Wataru? That's quite a way to answer the phone!"

There was no mistaking the voice of Uncle Satoru. Wataru's shoulders relaxed. "Oh, it's you, Uncle Lou."

"You sound disappointed! How you been, kid?"

"Fine."

"You're still going to school, right? You're not playing hooky like those bad kids?"

"No, Not me."

"You're not getting bullied? They taking any money from you?"

"Not even a little," Wataru said, laughing. "You've been watching those dumb news programs again."

"Well, from what I hear, schools these days are worse than medieval dungeons!"

"I don't know what that means, but I guarantee you it's not all that bad," Wataru said, smiling despite himself.

"Well, if you say so. I suppose I shouldn't believe everything I see on television. So, got a girlfriend yet?"

Wataru jerked upright. "Who, me?"

"It's about time. You're in fifth grade, right? You're ripe for finding your first true love! Isn't there any girl around that makes you go all a-tingle up your spine?"

Uncle Satoru always joked around on the phone like this. Wataru was used to the teasing. He usually laughed it off, but the girlfriend comment threw him for a loop. Wataru felt the heat creeping into his cheeks. When his uncle had said "any girl," for the briefest of moments, the image of Kaori Daimatsu flashed through his mind. Those white cheeks. Those big, sad eyes.

"O-of course not," Wataru said quickly, turning his back to his parents at the table. "There isn't a single cute girl in my class."

"Hmph, now there's a tragedy." Uncle Satoru hadn't seemed to notice the wavering in Wataru's voice. "So, is your mother home?"

"She is, and dad's home early too."

He heard an exclamation of surprise on the other end of the line. "Well, miracles happen every day. Get him on the phone, will you?"

"It's Uncle Lou," Wataru began, but Akira was already there, reaching for the receiver.

"Your uncle's name is Satoru, not Lou."

Satoru Mitani was Akira's elder brother by five years. He had dropped out of high school at the age of sixteen to take over the family business, and continued to work there to this day. In contrast to Akira, who went from college straight to life in Tokyo, Satoru would probably never leave the peninsula where they had grown up. He loved the sea, and boats, and fishing too much.

Though they were brothers, their personalities were one hundred and eighty degrees apart. Uncle Satoru talked up a storm, never lingering on one topic for long. His address was far, far away from where logic lived. At times, he didn't even appear to be aware of its existence.

Nor did Akira and Satoru look at all alike. His father was of medium height, and slender, while his uncle was short and stocky. His father's face was long, while his uncle's was round and hardy. At forty-three, his uncle looked much the same as he had in preschool, which isn't to say he looked young. Rather, he had looked like a jolly old geezer as a child, and now his age had finally caught up with his face.

Whether that was the problem, or whether he was merely too self-absorbed, Uncle Satoru had never married. Rumor had it that Grandma had fretted about it for years, but Uncle Satoru himself seemed not in the least concerned. Why would anyone want to get married, he wondered. Still, it wasn't that he disliked children. He always got along fabulously with Wataru, even slipping him money to buy things on the sly now and then.

Wataru had two uncles on his mother's side as well, so instead of just talking about his "uncle," he had to call them all by different names to keep them apart. On his mother's side, he would call his uncles by the place they lived, like "my uncle in Odawara," or "my uncle in Itabashi." But, for some reason, Uncle Satoru never became "my uncle in Chiba." Wataru had called him Uncle Lou ever since he could remember, and continued to do so to this day, his father's occasional reprimand notwithstanding.

Uncle Satoru had been calling about a memorial service or some other serious matter. Akira spoke with him at length, and though Wataru wanted to talk to him again when they were finished, he was sent out of the living room to take a bath before that happened.

His mother always said that she looked forward to baths as a time to relax. Most adults never had time alone, she said. Wataru knew it was the same for kids. Something about being in the tub sent the mind wandering places it couldn't go during the busy day. Tonight, Wataru couldn't help but think about Kaori Daimatsu—the silent princess in the tower. Had someone locked her up? Or was she hiding?

You're ripe for finding your first true love!

Uncle Lou's words played over and over again in his mind until Wataru saw his face redden, reflected in the water of the bath. He slapped at it, destroying the image with a *sploosh* that sent a wave rolling down the length of the tub.

chapter 3
The Transfer Student

He came to town just before spring break started—a silly time to transfer to a new school, all the girls agreed, whispering and giggling.

"I hear he's cute!"

"He gets really good grades."

"I hear he's *fluent* in English!"

"They say his dad worked overseas."

The did-you-hears spread like wildfire until everyone knew everything there was to know, down to the last detail. But none of it was the sort of thing to make Wataru's ears prick up with interest.

The new kid wasn't even going to be in Wataru's class. This meant Wataru would have to go out of his way to find out anything about him, which meant he probably never would, and that was just fine. He also knew that, until the aura of the "new kid" faded and whoever it was became just another classmate, he could be the most simpleminded rube on the face of the earth, and he would look at least three times better than he really was in the eyes of the class.

With the recent apartment-building boom in Wataru's neighborhood, there were always lots of people coming and going. Wataru had seen four transfer students join them in his five years at Joto Elementary. He knew how it worked. The chances of the new kid being as incredible as everyone said at first were roughly equivalent to the chances of being struck on the head and killed by a meteorite while walking down the street. It was certainly nothing to get worked up over. Wataru, for his part, was far more interested in rumors of the haunted building. He hadn't even properly committed to memory the name of the transfer student in the next class.

This was why it took him so long to figure out what they were talking about.

"They say that Mitsuru got a picture of the ghost!"

"Did you see it? Did he show you?"

"I didn't see it myself, but they say it's totally clear!"

It had been a week since his run-in with the Daimatsu family. He shuffled into class that morning, stifling a yawn, to find five or six of his classmates huddled in the back of the classroom, buzzing with excitement. It didn't take long for Wataru to join them. Since that night, when the indelible image of Kaori had been burned into his mind's eye, his ears would tingle the moment he heard anyone say anything that sounded even remotely like "haunted," or "ghost."

"Really? Someone got a picture?" Wataru wedged into the conversation. "When?"

"In the afternoon, two days ago!" one of the girls replied.

"During the day?"

"Yeah, he went there to sketch something for art class."

Art class often had the students tromping all over town looking for flowers and trees to sketch.

"He went to draw the azaleas at Mihashi Shrine," she added.

Wataru looked confused. "But our class didn't go there."

"Like I said, it was Ashikawa who took the picture."

This was when Wataru realized that the subject of conversation was the transfer student from the next class.

"The new kid?"

"Yep. Mitsuru Ashikawa. He grew up overseas, you know," one of the boys said self-importantly. He pronounced the name with all the vowels stretched out, so it sounded like "Meetsooroo Asheekawa."

The girls giggled. "Just pronouncing his name like an American doesn't make him one!"

Wataru couldn't have cared less about the transfer student. He wanted to know more about this picture of the ghost. "You think he'd show me the picture if I asked?"

One of the girls shook her head. "Mitsuru said it wasn't good to cause a fuss over such a thing, so he took it home. They say he hasn't shown the picture to anyone since then."

Wataru secretly rejoiced. Maybe he and this Mitsuru guy would get along. After all, that sounded suspiciously like something Wataru himself would say. In fact, if he had said something of the sort during that argument with those girls, maybe he would have come out looking better in the end. It was something to bear in mind.

"Did anyone in his class see it before he took it home? How about the people that went with him for art class?"

His classmates offered up the names of several people in the other class. Five had gone sketching to the shrine that day: three boys and two girls. One of the boys was the class president, Yutaro Miyahara. A stroke of luck—Wataru knew him.

"I hear the camera belonged to Yutaro. They were taking pictures so they could work on the sketch details after they went home."

Apparently, Yutaro had brought a Polaroid, thinking that each of them could take one photo of the scene they wanted to sketch, so they could work on it at home. Mitsuru had chosen a shot from the shrine that took in the trees lining the grounds, looking out at the haunted building next door. Just as he was about to take a picture, something like a human face appeared above one of the azaleas.

That was how it happened.

"He noticed something weird, and that's when the excitement started," Wataru's informant explained. "Everyone thought it was cool at first, but soon one of the girls started crying, and they all got scared and went home. I wonder what happened to the sketch assignment?"

This was all he needed to know. Wataru waited for the next break, then hurried over to the class next door. He looked in from the hallway to see Yutaro sitting way in the back by the windows, talking and laughing with a couple of classmates.

Yutaro Miyahara was the top student in his class. Joto Elementary had long since abandoned the practice of hanging up report cards at the end of each year so everyone could see who had gotten the best grades, but still, word got around. Often, the students were more aware of their fellow classmates' progress than their teachers were.

Wataru recalled walking in on his parents one day as they were engaged in a debate on education. Akira had been throwing around a lot of rather difficult words, so Wataru only understood about half of what was said. But, out of the jumble of unfamiliar terminology, there had been one thing that was immediately understandable. It had stuck with Wataru ever since.

"The best students, the gifted ones, they don't have to sacrifice their lives and chain themselves to a desk studying all day to be the best," Akira said. "Why? Because they've got *ability*."

When he heard that, the first image that had floated into Wataru's mind, quite naturally, was the face of Yutaro. He was the one his father was talking about, no doubt about it. No matter when you saw him, Yutaro always looked bright, happy, and laid-back. Yet his grades were impeccable. He was good at sports too: first pick in the relay race, gifted swimmer, ace baseball pitcher. At the same time, he was popular because he somehow managed to watch all the right shows on television and knew a ton about video games. The teachers called him "dedicated," and "a hard worker," which Wataru didn't get at all. Sure, Yutaro was a good kid, but he certainly wasn't a hard worker. It was all so easy for him! Why couldn't the teachers see that?

Yutaro seemed engrossed in his discussion, and the classroom was pretty noisy. Wataru figured his chances of calling out softly enough to get his attention without making a scene were close to nil. He looked around for another in, but none of the other faces he could see in the classroom were familiar enough for him to start a conversation with.

In Joto Elementary, if you were in a different class, you used a different water fountain, and that meant students from different classes rarely met. In fifth grade, some subjects like music or P.E. brought multiple classes together, or split them off into boys and girls, allowing a rare chance for cross-class communication, but like an unspoken rule, any friendship that developed lasted only for the duration of those periods, and no longer. Wataru knew Yutaro only because they were in the same class at cram school.

Wataru drifted toward the entrance at the back of the classroom and lingered there for little while. Yutaro was still too involved in his discussion to notice him. Wataru had a timid streak that came to the surface at times like this, and he found himself unable to step boldly through that doorway into unfamiliar territory. Moments later, the bell rang to signal the end of break.

Whatever, I'll just talk to him tonight.

Wataru spun on his heels to make for his own room, and walked right into something large and black looming before him.

"Ow!"

The thing he had collided with made no noise. It smelled faintly of cough syrup. It was a boy in a black sweatshirt. For a fleeting moment, Wataru thought he was looking in a mirror, so much did the boy resemble himself.

"S-sorry," he managed to say, and the illusion faded. The face bore some passing similarity to his own, but that was all. Too bad, because the boy was incredibly handsome. Wataru stood staring, his mouth gaping open. He had something of a reputation as a funny guy and he wore that title like a badge, always turning over a potential joke or a good comeback in the corner of his mind. It was like he had graduated from some sort of comedy boot camp and now, in overdrive, his brain crackled at super speed, turning over snappy one-liners in his head, considering and discarding one every thousandth of every millisecond.

What is this? National Good-Looking Boys & Girls Week? He abandoned the line as soon as it occurred to him. Too smug. Then he noticed the name tag on the black sweatshirt: "Mitsuru Ashikawa."

"…Mitsuru Ashikawa. He grew up overseas, you know…"

It's him! The transfer student!

Before Wataru could think of something clever to say, Ashikawa slipped past him into the classroom. He moved so swiftly that Wataru stood staring at the blank space where he had been standing for a full two seconds before he realized the boy was gone. When he finally turned around to look back into the room behind him, most of the students were seated at their desks, and the period bell (actually a computer-generated tone) tolled over the P.A. system for the last time, its final synthesized note shimmering and fading into silence.

Wataru sprinted back to his own classroom. His heart was racing.

After school, Wataru walked home, and then headed back out to cram school a bit earlier than usual. He knew that Yutaro often came early as well, and could be found quietly studying in a corner.

Kasuga Seminars was a five-minute bike ride away, and occupied the entire third floor of a four-story building. It was divided into three classrooms, and Wataru's fifth-grade class met three times a week in the northernmost corner room. He attended a two-hour class focusing on Japanese and math.

He arrived to find Yutaro sitting by himself, as expected, in his favorite place in the corner of the classroom. He was looking at a textbook, with his handwritten notes on pieces of paper spread out in a strange pattern on the desk around him. It looked like he was studying math.

In the Miyahara household, Yutaro was the oldest of three children. Their father ran a gasoline stand. Yutaro's younger brother was in preschool, and his sister was still in diapers. Miyahara's mother had divorced his father some time ago, and his siblings were children from his mother's second marriage.

Yutaro was studying at cram school because it was too noisy at his house to get any work done. The instructor understood his dilemma, and let him use the room prior to classes. He got special treatment not because he had younger siblings—plenty of other students were in the same boat—but because Yutaro was the only one among them who would actually go out of his way to study. Everyone else just used noisy brothers and sisters as an excuse to goof off.

Wataru walked into the classroom, and Yutaro looked up. He twitched and glanced at the clock on the wall. He must've thought it was time for class to begin already.

Wataru waved and made his way over to the other side of the room. "Do you have a second to talk?" he asked.

"Sure. What is it?" Yutaro said, bluntly.

Wataru paused. Now that he was here, he realized he couldn't just blurt out that he had come to ask him about the picture of the ghost. That would sound too childish. Still, after a bit of small talk, he managed to get around to the topic at hand.

"Oh, that!" Yutaro said, his face brightening. "It's the talk of the school these days, I hear."

"So was it really a ghost in the picture?"

"Nah," Yutaro leaned back in his chair and ran his fingers through his perfectly combed hair. He was still smiling. "Sure, there was something that looked kind of like a face above this one particular azalea. But it could've been anything. We all acted like it was a ghost and had a good laugh about it, but I don't think anyone really believes it."

"You know the rumors that the half-built building next to the Mihashi Shrine is haunted, right?"

"Sure, everybody knows that."

"You think there's a connection?"

"A connection between a rumored supernatural presence and a smudge on Mitsuru's Polaroid? Not a clue!" Yutaro laughed out loud. "I never figured you were the type to fall for that kind of talk, Mitani!"

Wataru's face reddened. Suddenly, he felt embarrassed and defensive. He wanted to shout that he hadn't believed the rumors at all from the beginning. He restrained himself, and instead told Yutaro about the incident where he had won the ire of the girls in his class by insisting they check the facts before assuming anything about the haunting.

"Heh," Yutaro chuckled, nodding. His smile slowly faded. "I don't believe in ghosts and all that stuff either. Those girls were just being dumb. Don't worry about it."

"Easy for you to say."

Wataru was mollified, but the conversation had ended before he heard everything he wanted to know. He wondered if he should tell Yutaro about Kaori Daimatsu. About how pretty she had been, and about how he couldn't get her out of his mind. Yutaro would understand. He wouldn't laugh at him, or tease him about it. Wataru opened his mouth, but the words that came out were, "So what's Mitsuru Ashikawa like?"

Yutaro blinked, plainly startled. "What's he *like*? What do you mean?"

"I saw him for the first time this morning. He looks kind of too perfect, like a…like a mannequin, you know what I mean?" Their encounter that morning had definitely been a "saw" not a "met." Wataru wasn't entirely convinced Mitsuru had even noticed him.

Yutaro shrugged. "He's cool."

Utterly casual. No reservations, no hidden meanings.

"Like a mannequin, heh?" Yutaro chuckled. "You should see the girls in class going crazy for him."

It occurred to Wataru that Yutaro might not welcome this new challenge to his status as most popular in class. "Isn't he a little strange? I mean, taking a picture and calling it a ghost, then taking it home and acting all cool."

"I don't think he was *acting* cool," Yutaro laughed. "If you're curious about him, you should talk to him yourself when he gets here."

"Gets here? You mean he's coming to cram school?"

"Yep. Today's his first day." Yutaro explained that Mitsuru had asked about good cram schools, and Yutaro had recommended Kasuga Seminars. He had obviously wasted no time getting enrolled.

"Good news for the girls, I guess," Wataru suggested with a grin.

"Whatever. Let them get all excited if they want."

"So how's Mitsuru in school? He get…"

"Good grades? Yeah. He's a good student."

Wataru marveled at the utter lack of concern on Yutaro's face. He really wasn't bothered by this at all. There was no show of bravado, no false projected sense of security. He was perfectly natural. Here there was a clear threat to his position in the class pecking order and he didn't seem to mind at all.

It was like he had already given up, or maybe…

He has nothing to lose.

No matter how good a student Mitsuru Ashikawa was, no matter how cool or handsome, it wouldn't affect Yutaro's status. It wouldn't make him stupid or "lame." He would still be Yutaro, still a good student, still a fast runner, a good swimmer, a good-looking guy who could do anything. None of that would change. In fact, having a friend of his own caliber would be a good thing. He wouldn't have to be the only one excelling in class. And they wouldn't have to fight for the title of "most popular." They could sit side-by-side on that throne if they wanted to.

Wataru felt a pang of envy. How nice life would be in a world like that. How different it was from what he knew. In Wataru's world, the more cool, able students there were in the class, the less room there was for people like him. There was a double standard. They could say whatever they wanted, and no one would ever get mad at a Yutaro or a Mitsuru. The reality of it stared him in the face. Mitsuru had taken a picture of the ghost himself, then dropped a line like "It's not good to cause a fuss." Certainly, that was no less cold or logical than what Wataru had said to the girls in class. But no one who was on that sketching trip ever thought Mitsuru was lame for not believing in ghosts.

What's more, he could imagine Yutaro telling the girls, "You know, Wataru's right. Until you go to the Mihashi Shrine and make sure that someone actually died there, you can't say you know whose ghost it is." They would have eaten up every word. It was an absolute certainty. *If Yutaro says so, it must be right.*

How utterly, totally unfair. Wataru's frustration rose in his chest, choking out everything else. A few girls came in, chatting about something, and Wataru retreated back to his seat. Seating in cram school was supposedly on a first-come, first-served basis, but people tended to pick a spot on day one and stay there the whole year. Wataru's seat was exactly midway down the room, on the side with the doors.

Five minutes before class was to begin, their teacher, Mr. Ishii, strode in. Mitsuru walked in immediately behind him. The room was filled with students who were all talking at once. As soon as everyone saw Mitsuru, there was complete silence.

Most of the kids in Wataru's class, however, came from one of three elementary schools. The first was Wataru's school, Joto Elementary. The second school was also called Joto Elementary. Because of the high population in his district, there were several public schools for the area, each with the same name, and a number to tell it apart from the others. Wataru's was Joto Elementary No. 1, the other that shared his cram school was Joto Elementary No. 3. The third school was a private school. For the kids from Joto Elementary No. 3 and the private school, it was their first time seeing Mitsuru, and the excitement was palpable.

The teacher made a few opening remarks, and then introduced Mitsuru to the class.

"This is Mitsuru Ashikawa, who will be joining us starting today. I believe those of you from Joto No. 1 know him already."

Mr. Ishii was twenty-four years old. His real job was doing research as a grad student at a nearby university. Teaching here was his part-time gig. He was an easygoing fellow with a youthful face. He could be mistaken for a high school student depending on how he dressed. Still, he was incredibly smart, and a good speaker, and class was always interesting. The students liked him.

Standing next to each other, the teacher seemed small compared to Mitsuru. He looked mean, meager, and outranked. Everyone noticed it. If they didn't know that Mr. Ishii was the teacher and Mitsuru was the student, it would have been easy to imagine things being the other way around.

"Hello," Mitsuru said to the class. Another student might have been more formal, or given a full self-introduction, but for him, this one word was plainly sufficient. His voice rang clear in the silence.

Mitsuru found an empty seat and sat down. He caught Yutaro's eye, and smiled. Yutaro smiled back. The girls sitting next to Wataru huddled their heads together, giggling quietly and whispering something. Their eyes sparkled.

Mr. Ishii preferred to lecture and then have the students work individually, so there were few group activities. Wataru would have little opportunity to gauge for himself whether Mitsuru was as gifted a student as Yutaro had suggested. Still, from the questions he asked in class, and the way he sped through the worksheets, it was clear he was a student of *ability*. It seemed that, against all odds, Mitsuru was the real deal: the transfer student who was just as amazing as all the rumors said. A meteorite.

Once class ended and it came time to go home, no one left. Yutaro and Mitsuru naturally formed a pair in one corner of the room, and the other kids naturally gravitated toward them. Not just the girls, but the other boys as well.

Wataru still had questions unanswered, but he didn't exactly fancy striding through the crowd and blurting out something about the ghost photograph in the middle of all the excitement over the new student. Instead, he picked up his bag and headed home. He walked at first, then picked up his pace until he was jogging. *Am I running away? From what?* It was a rhetorical question. Wataru knew the answer before he asked it. He kept running, all the while convincing himself that he wasn't escaping.

He opened the front door and shouted out, "I'm home." Through the glass-paned door leading into the living room he could see his mother talking on the phone. When Wataru opened the door she frowned and slammed the phone down violently.

"What's wrong?"

"Another silent call," Kuniko said, snorting with anger. White steam bubbled out of a boiling pot in the kitchen. "That's the third time today. It's almost like they *knew* I was busy trying to get dinner ready…"

For the first time, Wataru realized that his mother wasn't just angry. She was frightened.

"If they call again, I'll pick it up," he offered. He glanced in the direction of the kitchen. "Um, looks like something's boiling."

"Oh dear!" Kuniko launched into the kitchen, and Wataru went to his room and began putting away the things in his bag. As soon as Kuniko had the kitchen back under control, the rapid-fire questions began. How was cram school? What did you have for lunch? Fried rice for dinner okay? Wataru was used to this conversation and he answered everything perfunctorily, but his head was filled with Mitsuru. He found himself just wanting some peace and quiet.

He washed his hands and began setting the table when the phone rang. Wataru flew to the wall and picked up the receiver.

"Hi, it's me, Katchan."

Wataru gave his mother a look that said, "It's okay."

"You had cram school today, right?"

"Yeah. But this is a bad time to talk. We're about to eat."

"Oh, should I call back? Don't want your mom to get mad at me." Wherever he was calling from, there was a lot of activity in the background. It was hard to hear his voice. "I'll call back."

"Sure, thanks."

Wataru hung up the phone swiftly. He knew his mother wasn't fond of Katchan's calls. But what if it was Yutaro calling? He was sure his mother wouldn't frown at *that*. Best friends with Yutaro. Wouldn't that please her? And what if they *were* friends? This was a thought that hadn't occurred to him. Would Yutaro Miyahara be a better friend for him than, say, Katsumi Komura?

Wataru dismissed the idea as soon as he had it. Yutaro was a good kid, but would he be fun to hang out with? If he could find someone as well respected as Yutaro, and as fun as Katchan, that would be perfect.

Yutaro and Mitsuru.

Katchan and Wataru.

As he sat there in a daydream, the phone rang again. It had to be their silent caller this time for sure. Wataru snatched up the receiver.

"Mitani speaking!"

"Wataru?" It was his father.

"Oh, it's you."

"'Oh, it's you'? We need to talk about your phone manners."

"We've been getting more silent calls. Mom's getting scared."

There was a pause. "Today?"

"Yeah, three times this afternoon already."

Kuniko walked over and Wataru handed her the phone. He went back to sit at the table. Dinner was all laid out. He would be eating alone with his mother again tonight.

Kuniko talked for a while. He heard her agreeing to something, saying, "Very well, I'll get it ready," and then she ended the call with her customary, "Keep up the good work, dear." Wataru had grown used to this habit of hers, and never given it a second thought until one day about a year ago, when a visitor came to their apartment while Wataru and his mother were there alone.

The woman was a sales lady for a cosmetics retailer. She had been in the same class as his mother in college and this was a social call—an opportunity to gossip and push some cosmetics. She was pretty enough, but she smelled too strongly of perfume, and it made Wataru's nose wrinkle just to be in the same room. He had made some perfunctory greeting and then shut himself in his room to play video games.

His father had called that day while his mother and the sales lady were talking away. His mother had ended the phone call with her usual words of encouragement, and the sales lady had been astonished. Wataru heard her loud voice clearly through the door.

"I just don't believe it. That *was* your husband, was it not? Heavens! You shouldn't act so obsequious. We aren't living in the Middle Ages, dear."

"Obsequious"? Wataru had leafed through his dictionary. "Full of or exhibiting servile compliance; fawning," it said. Now he was only slightly less confused. He heard the sales lady go on, trying to persuade his mother of this and that. He listened closely, hoping he would figure out what she had meant with her opening remarks.

"Oh, it's good to be traditional," she was saying, "but you can't pamper your husband too much, or he'll just take advantage of you. Once he's married, it's his duty to work and support his wife and children while you run a household. It's a fifty-fifty partnership. There's no need for you to act like an underling."

His mother had laughed and said she wasn't pampering anyone and she was pretty sure she wasn't being taken advantage of.

"Well, you never know what he's doing once he's out that front door," the sales lady replied, chuckling deep in her throat. "My husband and I, we're *very* laissez-faire. I don't interfere with his goings-on and he doesn't interfere with mine. Why, if we didn't have children, I'm sure we'd have split up long ago. The bonds that tie, the gags that choke, am I right?"

Wataru had the strange feeling that the more the woman spoke, the dirtier the air in the room became. It was as though her words themselves clung to the walls and the floor and the furniture that his mother had spent years polishing and made them all somehow *unclean*. This woman had barged in, declared the Mitani household to be a mess, and, quite uninvited, begun buffing things with her own filthy rag.

The sales lady never came back. Wataru was relieved that, apparently, his mother hadn't liked her either.

He finished dinner and called Katchan back. This time he could hear the sound of a television blaring in the background.

"Think you could turn that down?"

"Oops, sorry." The sound of the television faded.

"So, what's up?"

It turned out that Katchan had run into none other than Mr. Daimatsu on his way home from school that day.

Wataru couldn't contain his excitement. "How? Where?"

"Right in front of the haunted building. He was with some construction-type guy in a gray uniform."

Maybe he'd found a new contractor. "Was it just Mr. Daimatsu? His son wasn't there?"

"Nope, just him. Why?"

"Why…" Wataru paused. "No reason."

Katchan had this annoying habit of answering most questions with "Why?" He just assumed there was a *why* to everything. Wataru had always thought it was kind of a simple and refreshing attitude, but today for some reason, it irked him.

"Mr. Daimatsu looked pretty happy. He said they're going to resume construction."

So he did find a new contractor.

"Well, once they finish that building, it'll put an end to those rumors," Wataru said. "It's probably for the best. The longer it sits there, the more people like Mitsuru will go there and take ghost pictures to show off to their friends."

Now that wasn't a nice thing to say. Nor had it been entirely truthful. In fact, Wataru was pretty sure it was a lie. Mitsuru certainly hadn't been boasting to anyone, and Wataru had just heard firsthand testimony that the picture probably wasn't a ghost at all. Still, he knew the shock it would cause on the other end of the line, and it made his tongue tingle with excitement. The sensation was like an exotic spice. Once he got the idea, he couldn't stop. He would probably lie more often if he wasn't so afraid of it becoming a habit.

But this time nothing stopped him. As predicted, Katchan gobbled it up. "What's that? He actually got a picture of a ghost?"

Wataru explained, piling lie upon lie. Katchan hadn't heard about this latest development at all, and every twist and turn of the story elicited fresh squeals of excitement.

"Cool! I gotta see it!"

"I wouldn't," Wataru advised. "The more people that get all excited about it, the bigger that Mitsuru's head is going to swell."

"Yeah, but my old lady says if you don't see a ghost by the time you're twenty, you'll never see one at all."

"Then you're in luck. You can avoid the whole thing if you just hang on for a few more years."

"No way! I *wanna* see a ghost before I'm twenty! Man, how boring would that be to go through your whole life without seeing one."

This was classic Katchan-style logic. One, you only have until twenty to see a ghost. Two, to avoid leading a boring life, you must see a ghost. Ergo, time was short. Wataru felt like telling him that seeing a ghost wasn't exactly a requirement for living the good life, but he swallowed his words. Saying that would just incite Katchan to wax even more poetic about the ghost, and for some reason everything was getting under Wataru's skin tonight.

"Look, I gotta take a bath and get to bed."

Katchan was still talking when Wataru hung up the phone. Kuniko asked him what the call had been about, and Wataru made something up. He went back to his room and closed the door, breathing a deep sigh of relief.

"Liar."

The girl's voice echoed through the room. In his chair, Wataru froze.

chapter 4
The Invisible Girl

Wataru was hearing voices again.

It was the same phenomenon he had experienced the night he met Mr. Daimatsu. His mouth felt strangely dry.

"So you're a liar."

Sure, it *sounded* like a girl's voice, but Wataru knew it was an echo or something, probably coming from the neighbor's TV. That was it. His neighbors were watching some television show with the volume cranked too loud. His father had complained when they moved in that the walls in this building were thinner than had been advertised.

"Ignoring me won't make me go away."

Now she was sulking. *It must be a soap opera.*

"Why did you lie to your friend? Is that the kind of person you are? Was I wrong about you?"

Definitely a soap opera. Wataru hesitantly looked around the room, but nothing appeared to be out of the ordinary. His mother had changed the comforter on his bed. The old one had a blue check pattern, but this one was yellow. The spines of the books were aligned neatly on his bookshelf as usual. The shelf below them held the volumes of the *Children's Illustrated Encyclopedia* that his grandmother in Chiba had given him as a present for being accepted into his elementary school. He couldn't believe it when he had heard the set cost something like ¥200,000. If she was going to spend that kind of money, he wished she would have bought him a computer instead! When he pointed this out to her she had snapped and said the set of encyclopedias was just fine for a kid in grade school. He could buy himself a computer when he grew up, she said. Adding insult to injury, the volumes took up a huge amount of space on his bookshelf.

He scanned the familiar scene: calendar on the wall, rug on the floor, eraser shavings on his desktop, light fixture on the ceiling.

Wataru hunched over and peered beneath his desk, the movement accidentally causing his chair to scoot back several inches. *No one hiding under there, of course.*

He swung around sharply and took a look under the bed. He felt like a special agent searching a criminal's hideout. All he needed was a windbreaker with the big FBI logo on the back, a bulletproof vest, and a gun in a shoulder holster.

The only thing he spied under his bed was a lone dust bunny—a guerilla soldier who had somehow evaded his mother's despotic cleaning tactics, unexpectedly discovered and forced to surrender.

"I'm not hiding," the girl's voice giggled from nowhere.

Wataru stood up and slowly moved back to his chair. His heart shrank to the size of a ping-pong ball and ricocheted around his body, leaving a cold hollow in his chest.

"Where are you?" Wataru asked quietly.

It was weird. He couldn't pinpoint the direction her voice was coming from. It didn't seem to be coming from the ceiling, or the walls, from in front or behind him, or from the floor. It resonated in his head, right where his own voice should be, but distinctly different.

"I'm not hiding," the voice said in a sing-song, "but you can't find me, either. I mean, it doesn't make any sense to look for something that isn't hiding. Why do the things people search for *need* to be hidden? Do they search for things because they're hidden, or are things hidden because they're searching?"

Wataru scowled and, for lack of a better direction, looked up at the ceiling when he answered. "What are you? What are you talking about?"

"I'm right beside you," answered the voice.

Wataru's eyes opened wide. If there was a ghost in the room he wanted to grab his camera and take a picture of it. He sprang from his chair, flung open his door, and sprinted to the living room, the door slamming shut behind him. The family television was happily singing the latest catchy jingle for no one's benefit. He didn't see Kuniko anywhere. She had to be taking a bath—she always left the TV on when she was taking a bath.

Wataru knew there was a disposable camera in the drawer next to the couch. His parents had bought it for a family trip to the zoo last month. There were twenty shots on the roll, but, in classic fashion, they had taken only three or four.

Wataru yanked open the drawer. There it was! Camera in hand, he ran back to his room.

Wait. He couldn't just charge in there and start snapping pictures blindly. He pressed his back to the wall next to the closed door, waiting until his breath returned to normal. He was an FBI man again. And this time, Special Agent Mitani was on his own, without any backup. This would be a solo mission. Gently, he turned the doorknob and began to push. The door opened an inch, then a foot. He slid inside without making a sound.

Holding his right arm with the camera behind his back, Wataru leaned against the door to close it. The fugitive hadn't noticed—maybe. This vicious criminal was wearing a special invisiwave-emitting suit—or something. That sounded silly, but the point was, she wasn't visible to the naked eye. *Heck of a time to forget the infrared goggles, Agent Mitani.*

Taking a deep breath, Wataru whipped out the camera from behind his back and triggered the shutter, an agent squeezing off a shot from his handgun.

Or not. He had forgotten to wind the film.

That was the problem with disposable cameras. Whoever took the last picture was supposed to wind the film right afterward, and they never did.

Well, the cat was out of the bag now. Wataru wound the film like a madman and pressed the shutter button again. He spun around the room, taking shot after shot. His mind was totally focused. He photographed the ceiling, the space under his bed, the shadow of his desk chair. He took photos behind him and he took them squatting down. Not a corner of the room was missed. No comforter was left unturned.

The camera ran out of film. Wataru wiped off the sweat that had beaded on the tip of his nose and took a seat on the floor. It hadn't been particularly strenuous, but he found himself breathing hard just the same.

"Even if you didn't get a good shot, you can always just lie and say you did," the girl's voice teasingly suggested. It sounded like she was talking from the right side of the room.

Wataru tensed, the camera falling from his stiff fingers into his lap.

"And if you did get a good shot, you can always just lie and say you didn't," the voice said from the left side of the room.

"Saying you have something that you don't makes it yours. Saying you don't have something you do makes it go away," the voice whispered right in Wataru's ear.

The next time she spoke, the voice came from the ceiling, each word falling like drops of rain.

"You are everything in the world, because you *are* the world."

Wataru noticed that the tone of the voice seemed to be changing. The sing-song was gone, replaced with a sort of…sadness. Wataru felt trapped and confused. He lifted his head to the ceiling. "Where are you?"

He could feel his heart finally returning to its normal size and place. *Thump. Thump. Thump.* Wataru counted five beats before the voice answered.

"I think you already know."

And then she was gone. Wataru couldn't see her or even figure out where the girl's voice was coming from, but Wataru knew she wasn't in his room anymore. It was like…like the connection had been dropped.

Wataru's neck and back were soaked with sweat. His hands were trembling. Twice he tried picking up the camera he had dropped in his lap, but both times it slid out of his trembling fingers.

I think you already know.

How could he? The voice sounded too nice—nothing like any of the girls in Wataru's class. He would know if it were one of his friends.

Who in the world could it be?

Wataru suddenly felt abandoned. Or was it he who had abandoned her? Somehow, it felt like both.

The money left over from Wataru's monthly allowance wasn't enough to pay for one-hour development for the disposable camera. He would have to take it to a drugstore and pick it up the next day. And since the store wasn't open when Wataru went to school in the morning, he would have to drop the camera off in the afternoon, further delaying the process. This, he thought, was the disadvantage of being a kid.

Wataru had hidden a secret stash of money in an empty cookie tin, which he kept behind the comic books on the shelf next to his desk. He was saving up for *Eldritch Stone Saga III*, the latest installment in one of his favorite video game series, due to go on sale in September. If he dipped into that money now, he could develop the photos more quickly. He slid the comic books from the shelf to reveal the illustration on the side of the tin: a cream-colored bunny happily munching cookies. Wataru stared at the bunny for a while. Finally he shook his head and replaced the comic books. It was the middle of June. If he spent the money now, he wouldn't have time to save up enough to buy the game when it came out.

In the end, Wataru slipped the disposable camera into his school backpack and took it to the drugstore the following afternoon. The slip of paper the clerk gave him said the pictures would be ready for pickup after four o'clock the day after tomorrow. *The day after tomorrow!* He read the slip again and again, his heart sinking. How could he stay in that room for so long without knowing?

Wataru trudged out to the neighborhood shops, finding himself in front of the video game store he often frequented with Katchan. The windows of the small storefront were plastered with video game posters. Peering inside, Wataru could make out rows and rows of game software along with monitor screens advertising newly released products.

A poster for *Eldritch Stone Saga III* had been placed right next to the sliding door at the front of the store. The game magazines had already run images of the main characters and even some screenshots, but the poster featured a far simpler design: fluffy white clouds hanging in a blue sky. In the center of the scene was a sailboat, its sails full of wind, flying above the sea through the air. Wataru had already determined that the boat belonged to the main character.

A handwritten note on the top of the poster read, "On Sale September 20th! Preorders Begin August 20th!" Someone had used a thick, red marker to add the words "Price: ¥6,800."

Wataru considered the price. He knew he had made the right choice by not using the money in the cookie can. He didn't know about other kids, but Wataru thought ¥6,800 was a lot of money. That's why he'd started saving up the moment he had seen the ads in the magazines.

As a general rule, pleading and begging fell on deaf ears in the Mitani household. Promises of future good deeds, such as "I'll do better on my next math exam" or "I'll get up early every day during summer vacation" never seemed to work. It was the same with citing past successes, like "My grades were good last semester!" or "I did well on my last exam!" The one and only exception had been the time his parents agreed to buy the fourteen-inch television for his room. Wataru had celebrated at first. Finally, he'd managed to talk his parents into buying him something. But quickly he realized they had their own motives for buying it.

"We think you're old enough to choose what to watch on your own," they had said, "and we're interested to see what it is you'll choose." If he had to report to his parents about every show he saw, that was no better than sharing a TV!

Akira was particularly strict when it came to money. "I don't want you thinking along the lines of 'I did this much work, so I deserve that much in return' when you make important decisions in your life," he would say. "You've got to work for yourself, not for rewards."

"Wow, your parents are super strict!" was Katchan's comment when he heard about it, and Wataru couldn't deny it. He understood why they did it: if his parents never listened when he pleaded for more allowance, he had to learn to be pragmatic about his money from an early age. The things Wataru *wanted* to buy weren't necessarily the things he could *afford* to buy, so he had to adjust his desires to match reality.

Katchan wasn't the only one who thought Wataru's parents were "super strict." His uncle did too.

"He's just a little kid, Akira! Why not cut him some slack?" Uncle Lou would occasionally argue on Wataru's behalf. "It feels good to get a reward after working hard, just like your friends—right, Wataru?"

"You don't have any kids, so you don't know what it's like to raise one," Wataru's father would say dismissively. "As a parent, you can't always take the child's side. It's irresponsible."

Akira's child-rearing methods weren't the only bone of contention between him and Satoru Mitani. In fact, they saw nearly everything differently. Uncle Lou tended to look at the big picture; Wataru's father was methodical and precise. Uncle Lou didn't have a lot of patience for extended arguments or discussions; Akira would happily debate until his opponent collapsed from exhaustion.

Which isn't to say the two brothers didn't get along. They hardly ever fought, and seemed to enjoy having a drink together during the holidays. By most standards, they had a pretty good relationship.

Wataru noticed, however, that something was changing of late. Normally, his uncle would back down when an argument got too heated. But now, when they discussed Wataru's business, Uncle Lou never gave up.

These conversations made Wataru more uncomfortable than either he or his uncle ever realized. But, he loved his parents and he loved Uncle Lou, so he was confident that things would work themselves out.

Whenever Wataru visited Chiba, his uncle would often slip him some pocket money. "Don't tell your dad," he would say, but Wataru always did. Starting the year before, the amounts had grown to sizes too large for him to feel comfortable keeping quiet about. Whenever Wataru reported another gift to his parents, they would take it and put it in his bank account. Every once in a while, they showed him the balance so that he knew how much he had saved. This tradition had begun when Wataru received his first gift of New Year's pocket money at the age of four.

"We don't want him getting used to carrying around a lot of cash," his father would explain to Wataru's grandparents when he took the gifts for safekeeping.

Wataru's grandmother in Odawara would occasionally give him even larger gifts than his uncle. She was also more secretive about it, as though she were wary of what Wataru's father might think. Regardless, Wataru always dutifully reported the gifts, and they went into his savings account straight away.

All this meant that Wataru didn't have money to burn. Katchan wasn't the only one who was surprised at Wataru's situation. One of his classmates reacted in shock when he heard the story. "I'd flip out on them if I were you," he had advised with all seriousness. It made Wataru uncomfortable because it sounded like code for "you're acting like a total wimp."

One time, Wataru tried asking Kuniko about his allowance. "I don't feel like you and Dad are too strict," he had begun, "but all my friends say you are." Were his parents really strict? If not, why were they so different from everyone else's families?

It had not been the best timing. It was right in the middle of the uproar over the Kenji Ishioka joyriding incident, and Kuniko was furious. Kenji spent money like water. Rumor had it that Kenji got so much money in allowance every month that he could buy *ten* copies of a game like *Eldritch Stone Saga III* and still have some left over. Kenji himself claimed he had no idea how much he spent. There was no need to keep track—his parents gave him money any time he asked for it.

Worse, Kenji's mother was proud of it. "Our son will never have to worry about money," she had boasted during the very PTA meeting called because of her son's wild ride through the schoolyard. To the other parents, the meaning was clear: "our son will never have to worry about money because we're rich, and we'll pay whatever it takes to patch the problem up."

Kuniko had been furious. She couldn't believe her ears. *No wonder their kid is out of control!* But PTA meetings—along with the rest of the country—are run democratically, and freedom of speech is guaranteed. No matter how much you wanted to, you couldn't just throw someone out for having a condescending attitude. Kuniko was unable to take her frustrations out on Mrs. Ishioka directly, so she came home frustrated, seething like a witch's cauldron on the verge of boiling over.

And that was when Wataru decided to ask about his allowance.

"Oh, so you want a big allowance, just like that Ishioka boy?" Kuniko snapped. "You really disappoint me, Wataru."

Wataru didn't know—couldn't know—how he might have disappointed his mother, but he reflexively apologized just the same. Retreating to his room, he felt like a sinking ship, plunging to the bottom of an unfathomably deep sea. He resolved never to broach the subject of money with his parents again.

Wataru was a logical kid; he had his father to thank for that. He knew it wasn't right for children to carry around large sums of money. And he knew it was better to work for himself rather than focus purely on financial rewards. *Okay, Dad, fine, I get it.* Still, it was only natural for him to want some kind of reassurance. All he needed was an explanation, something that he could parrot when classmates accused his family of being overly strict. He never really doubted his parents' good intentions, anyway. A simple conversation would have been all he needed to turn the situation around and wear their strictness as a badge of honor.

As it was, Wataru got sad every time he thought about the incident. It was simply a case of bad timing. It was nobody's fault, but he felt bad just the same. As for his small allowance, Wataru accepted it as a fact of life. Sure, it was occasionally inconvenient, but there was an upside as well. People always said that waiting for something made you appreciate it more, and Wataru was a living example of that. He could walk by the store, gaze at the *Eldritch Stone Saga III* poster, save his money bit by bit and excitedly count the days until the release date. Kids like Kenji would never experience happiness like this, no matter how many copies of the game they could afford with their huge allowances.

Wataru tried to force the mysterious girl's voice out of his head until the pictures were developed. But the more he tried to not think about her, the more real she became in his mind. His every thought veered between rose-colored dreams and all-consuming dark fantasies.

Who is she?

Where does she come from?

What does she look like?

Is she human?

A ghost?

A fairy?

That was it. She had to be a fairy, like the one that was supposed to guide the player in *Saga III*. In the previous game of the series, she was just a minor character who showed up now and then for comic relief. In the first game of the series, however, Neena the Fairy had been a major member of the cast. The hero would never have made it up Wight Cliff without her help. Without question, she had been Wataru's favorite. He had spent hours raising her strength to the point where she could face the last dungeon of the game, but just before the climactic battle, there was a fully animated scene featuring Neena that confounded his strategy.

"This is as far as we fairies can go," Neena said, and just like that, she dropped out of the game. Wataru nearly threw his controller to the floor. In the throes of disappointment, he had called Katchan for moral support.

"What, you didn't know?" Katchan asked incredulously, making Wataru feel even worse. "The last boss monster, the Elemental Guard, used to be chief of the fairies guarding the Kingdom of Toma. If you had her in your party, it'd be fairies fighting each other! Of course you had to get rid of her."

"I didn't know!"

"Well, did you trigger the event at Noru Spring? No? Well, that's your problem. You learn the whole deal there. Looks like you screwed up. Sucks to be you, man."

In the end, Wataru had to start all over again. All the time spent building up Neena's powers had been a waste.

In the world of *Eldritch Stone Saga*, fairies were tiny enough to fit on a child's palm. They wore pretty, ballerina-like dresses and had wings on their backs. Neena fit the typical fairy profile. She wouldn't ever think of doing evil. She talked back sometimes, but she also knew a lot of things. She was chipper, kind, and cute—and always would be, thanks to a lifespan far exceeding that of humans.

What if she's a fairy, like Neena?

Waves of hope and anxiety washed over Wataru. He knew he couldn't tell anyone about the voice, not even Katchan, not yet. It was all too fantastic sounding. If there was anything to see, Wataru planned to show the pictures to Katchan right away. But without photographic evidence, his friend would laugh him out of the room. He might even start worrying about him.

Wataru ran to the drugstore the moment school let out. He found himself checking his watch at every stoplight and crosswalk. *Five to four, four to four, three to four…*

Wataru reached the photo counter at ten seconds to four o'clock.

Only one customer was ahead of him: a plump, middle-aged woman. She was locked in some sort of negotiation with a clerk wearing a white lab coat.

Wataru craned his neck to see behind the counter. He spotted a rack of long envelopes containing finished pictures. There were a lot—maybe twenty total. Each had a tag listing the customer's name. Wataru strained his eyes looking for "Mitani." There it was! The fifth envelope from the front! Wataru's pictures had been developed for sure.

"It didn't work at all," the plump woman pouted, "and I switched medications on your recommendation, even though it was more expensive."

"I understand, ma'am," replied the cashier, lowering her eyes with obvious discomfort. "Maybe you need to give it more time? Everyone's talking about this drug. It's the next big thing. "

"Everyone? Then why hadn't I heard of it until you told me?"

The clerk shrugged.

"Look, all I ask is that you let me exchange it for something else. It's pointless to keep taking something that just isn't working."

"But it's already been opened, ma'am."

"That's beside the point! It doesn't work! We're talking about medicine, here! What don't you understand? I want something new and I want it now."

The woman was brandishing a box of antacids, a brand that Wataru often saw advertised on TV. He peered around the store in frustration, searching for another clerk. It was a big drugstore. Usually there were more people working. For whatever reason, though, nobody was around today. He was growing impatient.

"E-excuse me," Wataru began, hesitantly peeking around the middle-aged woman. "I'm here to pick up my pictures…"

"I'm sorry, but I'm helping this customer," replied the clerk with an apologetic smile.

"Wait your turn!" snapped the plump woman ahead of Wataru.

"Perhaps I can interest you in this brand instead," the clerk said to the woman. She was holding up a free trial package of antacid tablets.

"I don't want a different one," she said, taking the offered box anyway. "Does it work?"

"It's new and based on a Chinese herbal remedy. It's supposed to be highly effective for upset stomachs and digestive problems, and it's got a refreshing flavor."

"I doubt that," said the woman. She lifted the sample to her nose and sniffed. Her nose wrinkled. "Smells funny."

The clerk smiled nervously, saying nothing. Wataru caught her eye and silently mouthed the word "pictures."

"All right. I'll take it," the woman said at last, stuffing it into a huge bag already bulging with other purchases.

Wataru felt as relieved as the clerk looked. But the woman didn't move. She stood in place, stubbornly scanning the racks of medicines displayed behind the counter.

"I'm also looking for some cold medicine," she said. "And not a strong one—I have a sensitive stomach. And I don't want anything that makes me drowsy. Everything you carry always makes me sleepy. Maybe you've gotten something new?" She moved to one side to get a better look at the row of cold remedies. Wataru took the opportunity to gently elbow ahead of the plump customer.

"Um, Mitani. Wataru Mitani. I came here to pick up my photos," he said, stretching out an arm to show his receipt.

The clerk glanced at the plump woman for a moment. Then, with a brief nod, she took a step toward the rack of photo envelopes. Wataru felt a warm breeze on the back of his neck. He spun around to find the woman snorting in frustration.

"How rude!" the woman bellowed, angrily glaring at Wataru. "I told you to wait your turn!"

"I'm sorry. I thought you were finished."

"You've got some nerve, young man! If your parents were here I'd give them a stern talking to!" she seethed, stepping back from the counter. "Didn't they ever teach you to respect your elders?"

The clerk came back to the counter, holding the envelope Wataru had spotted earlier. She slid several pictures out of the envelope and showed them to Wataru.

"These the ones?"

"Yes, they are."

Wataru felt the plump woman glaring down at him as he paid for the photos. He did his best to ignore her. The cashier appeared to be doing the same. He pitied her for having to deal with people like the woman. *A bad customer's still a customer...*

Outside, Wataru ran as quickly as his legs could take him. He looked up after a while to find he was across the street from the haunted building. His lungs were aching, his cheeks burned, and his hands shook with anticipation. He hadn't wanted to open the photos in the drugstore; he wanted somewhere with more privacy. And home was out of the question. He'd used up a perfectly good disposable camera without asking permission—and on a fairy! He couldn't let his mother see the photos.

Wataru had stopped, but his heart was beating wildly. He looked around, trying to catch his breath. *What about Mihashi Shrine? There's a bench and it's nice and bright there. Plus it's always empty.*

Wataru crossed the street and walked through the faded red torii gate. The shrine itself was a small building, with red pillars supporting a green roof. New benches flanked either side. They were always empty...

Someone was sitting on the bench to the left.

It was Mitsuru Ashikawa.

He was reading a book. It looked thick and heavy. The spine had to be at least five inches thick. Wataru gawked at him. That perfect face. That perfect hair. Just like a mannequin.

Mitsuru looked up briefly and then resumed reading. Wataru was nothing to him, a passing sparrow, a dog, a dead leaf or piece of litter drifting in the wind.

Maybe he doesn't remember me, Wataru thought, desperately trying to put a positive spin on the situation. *That must be it.*

"Uh...hi," Wataru croaked. It came out so weakly he almost laughed.

Mitsuru didn't even notice.

Wataru's mouth had half-formed the greeting for a second time when Mitsuru finally glanced up. His eyes flickered over Wataru's face for the briefest of moments before returning to his book again.

Warmth began to creep up Wataru's cheeks. It was strange. Why was he embarrassed? Mitsuru was the one being rude. Wataru was just trying to be friendly.

"Uh...We're in cram school together," Wataru finally managed to sputter. *I'm qualified to talk to you, really. Permission to speak freely, sir?* Mitsuru raised his eyes. This time, they lingered on him. It reminded Wataru of their first encounter outside the classroom. He had noticed Mitsuru's eyelashes then—long like a fashion model's—and now those same eyelashes fluttered over him, inspecting him.

And then Mitsuru was reading his book again. A light breeze wafted down from the temple's roof, gently tousling both boys' hair.

"My name's Wataru. Wataru Mitani. I'm a friend of Miyahara's...and, uh..."

Mitsuru slammed his book shut with a sudden clap. The cover was cobalt blue. It looked quite old.

"So?" Mitsuru asked impatiently.

"I, uh, heard that you were really smart," Wataru continued. "Miyahara told me. And then you did really well the other day in cram school, and…" Wataru lost track of what he was saying.

Mitsuru's perfect face regarded Wataru emotionlessly.

"So what?"

It took an eternity for Wataru to realize that he was being asked a question. But he had no idea how to answer.

"I. Said. So. What?" Mitsuru repeated himself slowly, as if speaking to a child.

Suddenly Wataru felt his embarrassment lifting. *So what, indeed!* It was painfully obvious that Mitsuru had no interest in talking to Wataru, let alone making friends. Whatever it was, it wasn't Wataru's fault. *Why is he so cold?*

"Look, I'm in the middle of reading." Mitsuru sighed, his fingers indicating the cover of his book. Wataru looked but couldn't make out the title.

"Uh…okay," Wataru managed, sounding even weaker than before. Mitsuru rolled his eyes and resumed reading.

Wataru could have turned and walked away. He could have gotten angry. He might even have been forgiven for throwing a handful of gravel at Mitsuru—he was too far away to actually hit him, anyway. The kid certainly deserved it. Wataru was only trying to start a conversation.

But instead, he just stood there, entranced by Mitsuru Ashikawa's strange charisma. The odd combination of adoration and insecurity he felt wouldn't let him write the other boy off as a simple jerk.

"I heard you took a picture of a ghost here," Wataru blurted. Mitsuru's face slowly swiveled up, his book lying open on his lap. His expression remained impassive, but Wataru cheered inwardly. *That got his attention.*

"You said people shouldn't make a fuss about it," Wataru went on. "I think so too." Mitsuru's eyes twitched—a sure sign of interest. Wataru felt a smile creep slowly to his lips. "I know it's not easy for everyone to do, of course. Sure, it's stupid to freak out over a ghost but there *are* strange things out there. That's why you've got to approach them with a cool mind, with…"

"Photographs," Mitsuru said, cutting him off.

"What?"

"I see you have photographs."

It was true. Wataru was still clutching the envelope of photos from the drugstore. That was the entire reason he'd come here in the first place. In fact, Wataru had been about to mention them, but Mitsuru beat him to it.

His embarrassment returned. Wataru's stomach lurched as though he'd just stepped onto a high-speed elevator. "I might, uh…I might have taken pictures of a ghost too."

Wataru hurried over to Mitsuru, his feet lifting across the gravel like he was walking on air. One part of Wataru was furious at himself for acting like some kind of awestruck fool. Another part was jumping for joy that he was actually talking to Mitsuru Ashikawa. Why, they might even become friends.

"I took these in my room." Wataru nervously began fumbling through the envelope with shaking hands. "You know what fairies are, right? Like the ones in *Eldritch Stone Saga*? Well, I think there's one in my room. I heard it speaking…and not just once, but twice!"

As the son of Akira Mitani, man of logic, reason, and rationality, Wataru would rather have bitten off his own tongue and died from massive blood loss before allowing himself to spew such irrational chatter. But, every once in a while, even the most normal of people act in ways that surprise themselves, doing things they might never have imagined themselves doing because they're excited, or they're obsessed, or they're in love…not that Wataru realized any of this. "I took so many shots I'm sure I got it—check it out!"

Hand shaking, he drew the photos he had taken of his room from the envelope and handed them over to Mitsuru. In the process, he managed to drop the thin plastic sleeve containing the negatives and a few pictures from the zoo onto the ground. Wataru quickly scooped them up and placed them in a pile on the seat next to Mitsuru. He would have sat down, but the boy didn't move from his spot in the center of the bench, and there wasn't enough room on either side.

Wataru had taken close to twenty photos. He watched nervously while Mitsuru shuffled through them rapidly like someone leafing through trading cards looking for something valuable. Mitsuru finished and flashed a smile at Wataru for the first time.

"Where is it?"

It took a few seconds for Wataru to realize that Mitsuru meant the fairy.

"You didn't see it?"

"Nothing. Looks like pictures of an empty room." Mitsuru shrugged. His smile was gone. Now he was holding the stack of photographs in front of Wataru's nose.

After a pause, Wataru snatched them back. He started clumsily leafing through them. His hands were shaking. "No way!" Wataru cried, shuffling wildly. Several of the photographs slipped through his fumbling fingers, fluttering down to rest on the tops of his running shoes.

It was like Mitsuru said: pictures of an empty room. The walls, the curtains, even the pattern on his comforter—all were perfectly clear. He could even make out the titles of the textbooks he kept in the little hutch atop his cluttered desk.

But no sign of the fairy.

No golden hair. No flowing robes. Nothing. Zip. Nada.

Wataru slowly raised his head and looked at Mitsuru. The boy had returned to his book again. It was as though Wataru had never even been there.

"I know what I heard…" Wataru began, the words trailing off and disappearing the moment they left his lips. "It was so close. I thought the camera would catch it for sure."

"You had a dream," Mitsuru said quietly, his eyes never leaving the book.

"What?" Wataru took a step closer. He could barely hear what the boy was saying.

"A dream. You had a dream," Mitsuru repeated, flipping a page. "You must've been half asleep. You heard someone who wasn't there."

"Yeah, but it happened to me twice!"

"So you were half asleep twice, then." Mitsuru flipped another page. The next page was blank. Perhaps he had reached the end of a chapter. Mitsuru sighed and looked up. "You'll step on them."

"What?" Wataru's brow furrowed. *What is it this time?*

"Your pictures. They're right in front of your feet."

He was right. The tip of Wataru's right shoe was already stepping on the corner of one of the zoo pictures. He looked down at it. Wataru and his mother were smiling and standing in front of the elephant cage. A zookeeper had just given the elephant an apple.

"I didn't take a picture of a ghost," said Mitsuru as Wataru squatted down to retrieve his photographs from the gravel. It was as though he had been waiting for Wataru to look away to speak. "I took a blurry picture of an azalea. Everyone freaked out and got excited because it's more fun that way. That's all."

"But you said …"

"I said people shouldn't make a fuss about such things. You agreed with me, didn't you? I heard you say so just now." Mitsuru looked a little angry now. His eyes gleamed. "You know, if that's the way you really feel, it's a little weird trying to take pictures of a fairy. Pretty hypocritical."

Now it felt like he was being scolded.

"Look, I know it sounds strange, but I swear I heard a girl's voice and there was nobody around but me." Wataru raised his voice to be more assertive, but it seemed like every sentence came out weaker than the next.

"Like I said, you were dreaming. I wouldn't waste my time taking any more pictures, if I were you," Mitsuru said, cocking his head slightly. "You say people shouldn't make a fuss, and here you are making a fuss all on your own. You're kind of contradicting yourself, don't you think?"

Wataru wracked his brain for a choice retort. He knew he had to come up with something soon, or he felt like he might burst into tears. Quite suddenly he felt a need to use the bathroom.

What was with this boy? Talking to him was like talking to an adult, but worse.

"If you ask me, there's a much bigger problem here than a missing fairy," Mitsuru said, his voice perfectly measured.

Wataru carefully blinked to keep the tears back. His eyes searched Mitsuru's face. "What kind of problem?"

"That depends on your point of view," Mitsuru replied calmly. He raised his book vertically, nestled a bookmark in between the pages, and slammed it shut. Then he tucked the hefty tome under his arm and stood up. A chill went down Wataru's spine. *Is our conversation going to end like this?*

"You're saying I have a problem?"

"I don't recall saying that."

"Yes, you did!" Wataru shouted. Once again he felt like crying. *Now I'm angry.*

Mitsuru cocked his head again, studying Wataru as if he were preparing to dissect some strange creature. "Do you have a father?" he asked, neither his eyes nor his expression changing in the slightest. Only his lips moved.

"What?" Wataru replied in shock.

"A father. Do you have one?"

"O-of course I do!"

Mitsuru blinked. "Does he like having his picture taken?" Mitsuru's questions were getting weirder and weirder.

"What do you care?"

Mitsuru indicated the pictures in Wataru's hands with a jut of his smoothly cleft chin. "Those pictures—your dad's not in a single one."

Wataru looked down. He hadn't noticed if he was or wasn't.

"Check them out yourself after you go home, or you can take my word for it: he's nowhere to be seen. They're all of you and your mom."

Wataru said the first thing that came to mind. "So my dad likes taking pictures. That's all."

"Sure," Mitsuru said smugly, "if you say so." No sooner had the words left his mouth than Mitsuru turned and began walking away. Wataru stood in silence until Mitsuru reached the shrine's red torii gate. He wasn't done with this conversation by far, but Mitsuru kept walking.

"What's your problem?" Wataru called after him. "Why do you have to act like such a jerk?"

Mitsuru disappeared down the street without slowing down. Silence descended over the shrine grounds. Somewhere, a bird began to chirp.

Who does that guy think he is?

Wataru was exhausted. Holding the pictures carefully, he walked back to the bench Mitsuru had just occupied and sat down. He looked up, aware that he was seeing the world as Mitsuru had seen it just moments before. It meant nothing to him. The azaleas had already bloomed and faded. Their petals lay scattered across the ground. Wataru was all alone in Mihashi Shrine.

One by one he checked the pictures, starting with the ones of his room. As he expected, none of them revealed anything about the girl with the voice like honey. He glanced through the photos from the zoo. Wataru mugging for the camera in front of a flock of flamingoes. Kuniko tossing the pigeons some popcorn. It was a bright, sunny day—Kuniko and Wataru were squinting and smiling.

And Akira Mitani was nowhere to be seen, just like Mitsuru had said.

chapter 5
The Incident

This is just my unlucky month.

That was the only explanation for it. Clearly, nothing good would come of this June, no matter how hard Wataru tried. How could so many things happen in one month to make him feel so miserable?

I've just got to lie low until summer vacation starts.

Wataru hated June more than any other month. For one thing, it rained constantly in Tokyo, and the temperature would drop unexpectedly, making his nose run. Then, after that, he was forced to endure an endless stretch of steamy, sweaty nights. He was never sure if he should wear short sleeves or long sleeves, and the humidity meant his favorite clothes took forever to dry after they came out of the wash. To this day it was a mystery to him why his mom never bought a clothes dryer. Since their place faced south, she figured she could hang laundry outside to dry. Wataru reminded her many times that it didn't matter which way the apartment faced. If the sun didn't come out, the clothes wouldn't dry. And he hated having wet laundry hanging inside the house. It felt so…tacky.

"We don't need one," she would patiently explain. "Even during the rainy season, there are sunny days every once in a while."

And so June passed by somberly and, more often than not, soggily. Yes, just letting June mosey on by was the safest strategy. He would just have to retreat into his shell and become even more subdued than usual.

Wataru no longer heard rumors about the haunted building because he had stopped paying attention to them. People tired of such things quickly. He never saw anyone from the Daimatsu family again, and neither did Katchan.

Construction on the building had stopped completely.

Mitsuru continued to prove what a good student he was, both at school and at Kasuga Seminars. When they took the bi-monthly performance tests to gauge their academic progress, he easily scored higher than even Yutaro.

Thankfully, as it came closer to the end of the month, Wataru had something better than Mitsuru Ashikawa and haunted buildings to think about. He would be spending the entire month of August at his grandmother's house near the ocean in Chiba. Since he started elementary school, it had become tradition for him to spend the end of July and the first week of August—prime beach time—with his grandmother. Akira wasn't able to get much time off from work, and Kuniko didn't feel right about leaving her husband to fend for himself, so Wataru inevitably went alone. He had been doing this since he was in kindergarten, so it wasn't a big deal. Not once had he gotten homesick, or cried for his mother. "My little beach bum," Uncle Lou would proudly call him.

This year, for the first time, they were letting him spend the entire month of August there. Of course, because he was going to be there so long, he couldn't just loaf about like a guest. He would be helping out at his grandmother's store, at the beach-house vending stall, with Uncle Lou's work, and however else he could.

"You do good work and I'll pay you a fitting salary," his uncle had promised, making Wataru jump up and down with glee. *A salary!* The word was like magic to Wataru's ears.

After *Eldritch Stone Saga III* came out, another must-have game called *Bionic Road* was due for release sometime in mid-November. It was an action game, not an RPG, but the magazine coverage made it look great. It promised to be just the kind of game that he loved best—a complex, science fiction-based story line, full of mystery, with a cool main character. It would be coming out in a two-disc set. Estimated sale price: ¥7,200.

When he first saw the price tag, he gave up hope of ever owning it. Less than two months after *Saga III* came out? No way could he save up that much money. *Maybe Katchan could swing it.* He might be able to save enough from his allowance in two months to buy the game. His parents were always busy with work, and they gave him a big allowance in an attempt to make up for the time that they couldn't spend with him. They were never overly vigilant about the content of the games that he bought either.

But there was one major hurdle to overcome. Katchan hated action games. RPGs were all he ever played.

"*Bionic Road*? Never heard of it. The hero's a cyborg? You gotta fight alien invaders and save passengers stranded in a colony ship?" Katchan made it sound like a chore. Wataru had tried his best to sell his friend on the game, but it was like talking to a wall. "What, you can't even use magic?" Katchan had asked, incredulously. When Wataru had admitted that, yes, you couldn't, the discussion was over. As far as Katchan was concerned, a game without magic was like peanut butter without jelly. Wataru's plot to convince Katsumi Komura to buy *Bionic Road* and let him borrow it or play it at his house seemed dead from the start.

I really need to get some money, Wataru had brooded. It was just then that his uncle made him the offer: "Do you want to come here for all of August? If you can do some work, I can pay you for it."

"Work? I can work!"

Wataru immediately launched a campaign to convince his parents to let him go. At first Akira and Kuniko had strong reservations about letting their son be away from home for so long. "A couple of weeks, maybe, but a whole month? I don't know," his father had said.

"Out of the question!" his mother chimed in. "If you spent your entire vacation playing at your grandmother's, you'd never finish your summer homework."

"I'll finish all of my homework in July! It's just a bunch of worksheets. And a journal, and an essay—but I can do those in Chiba."

"What about growing those morning glories for your science class?"

"That's even easier to do in Chiba! Mom, you said yourself that you don't want them on our balcony 'cause of the caterpillars!"

That one gave her pause. Kuniko *did* hate caterpillars. In her mind, they were already creeping up the morning glory vines and shuffling over to the laundry that she would be hanging out on the balcony (because they didn't have a dryer), leaving tiny caterpillar footprints wherever they went. Every summer that Wataru had to raise morning glories for science class there would be at least one incident in which his mother, having found one of the little critters getting comfortable in her sheets and pillowcases, would shriek loud enough to earn a few raised eyebrows from their neighbors.

His father was a tougher nut to crack.

"Even if it's for family, I still think you're too young to be working. You're in elementary school! You need to wait...at least until middle school."

"But Uncle Lou said I could!"

"And your father is saying you can't. You're still just a child and shouldn't be working for money."

It looked like a hopeless case. No matter what he said, no matter how much he begged, the answer was always the same. *You're too young.* Wataru almost gave up hope. Each and every day, all he thought about was how to change his father's mind, and what he might possibly say to help the situation. He even lost sleep obsessing over it.

And then, during a late-morning breakfast on the last Sunday in June, from behind his father's newspaper came the answer he wanted: "Wataru, you can spend your summer vacation with your grandmother and uncle if you want." Out of the blue, just like that. Not the bitter denouement of weeks of haggling and pleading, but a casual comment, as though he were asking Wataru to pass the salt. Wataru couldn't believe what he was hearing. Maybe he was still half-asleep. He shot a glance at his mother.

"Honey, are you sure?" she asked, a vague smile on her face. "You know he's talking about spending all of August in Chiba, right?"

"Fine by me." Akira turned the page of his newspaper. "You could go too."

"I can't do that," laughed Kuniko. "Why, it wouldn't be right leaving you here alone while we went off to play on the beach."

"Oh, I wouldn't mind," Akira responded nonchalantly, without even lifting his eyes from the paper. "I hardly see you two, our schedules being what they are. It wouldn't be much different if you were gone. I practically live like a widower anyway."

Wataru felt uneasy, as though there was something being left unsaid, some deeper meaning behind his words. The day before, a Saturday, Akira had been at the office all day, not getting home until late. Maybe something had gone wrong at work, or maybe he was just really tired. That would explain the foul mood.

"That's exactly why I was hoping we could all spend some quality time together over the holiday," Kuniko replied, beaming a smile at Wataru. The look in her eyes was clear. *Private Wataru! Captain Akira has entered "bad mood" status! We need backup!*

Wataru wasn't sure how to respond. He wanted his father's permission to go so badly that he could taste it. How could he take his mother's side with that dangling right in front of his eyes?

"Also, if Wataru spends all of August in Chiba, then he won't be able to visit my parents in Odawara," Kuniko added, rising from the table to fetch the coffee pot. "They would be so disappointed if they didn't get to see him."

Akira remained silent. The newspaper lifted higher, hiding his face. Kuniko's continued protests were met with noncommittal grunts from behind the wall of headlines and weather forecasts. The mood at the breakfast table stagnated until no one said anything at all. From then on, little by little, Wataru's month of summer vacation in Chiba slowly became a reality.

For his time on the beach to be spent as effectively and pleasurably as possible, he would need to finish off the majority of his summer homework in July, while he was still in Tokyo. Wataru was quite meticulous about that sort of thing. He promised himself that during the ten or so days of vacation in July, no matter what distractions the day might hold, he would force himself to get up in time for the early-morning radio exercise program, and other than his twice weekly swimming lessons, would stay at home so that he could concentrate on finishing his homework. Just thinking about it made him ecstatic. To think that June, with its drizzly rain and oppressive humidity, and those unexpected chilly nights that gave him a stuffy nose, could be a time of such unbridled joy! All he had to do was think ahead to that day when the sticky air and gloomy skies blew away, leaving behind a golden summer: polished and gleaming and all his.

"You sure are in a good mood," Katchan observed. He was green with envy when Wataru told him why. "Awww, I wish I could go for a little while too…"

"You want me to ask my uncle if it's okay?" It wasn't an entirely selfless suggestion. Wataru knew that he would have more fun if Katchan were there too. "I'm sure he wouldn't mind."

"Well, I'd sure love to," Katchan began, his expression uncharacteristically clouded, "but I think I better stick around and help with the bar."

"You guys have a summer vacation, though, right?"

"Yeah, but we're going on a trip then. My folks can't take many days off, so that family vacation is kinda important."

"Wow, look at you." Wataru whistled for effect. "Katchan, model son."

"Ya think?"

The two of them laughed at that.

And so the days passed, and June eventually came to a close with only one page remaining on Wataru's daily calendar. He had to go to cram school that day, so he hurried home after classes finished so he could wolf something down before he had to rush out again.

He opened the front door to discover a woman's pretty shoes sitting in the entranceway. There were voices coming from the living room—women's voices. Peeking in, he saw it was his mother's friend, the wife of that real estate agent. He seemed to recall her husband's company having some grandiose name like Saeki Estates. The air was thick with her perfume.

Kuniko spotted him and waved. The woman turned and greeted him. He smiled and asked her how she was doing. With the trip to Chiba this close, he didn't want to risk any mistakes, and, since he wanted to stay on his mother's good side, that meant acting like a respectable little boy. It worked. Kuniko went and got him a plate and gave him permission to go eat in his room. The snack was a gorgeous piece of cake, decorated with heaps of fruit. "Mrs. Saeki brought these for us. Be sure to thank her, now." She smiled at their guest.

In Castle Mitani, it was the law of the land that when Queen Kuniko was entertaining a caller, Prince Wataru's duty was to sit and take tea with them while they grilled him with boring questions about school and his friends. Today's unexpected reprieve from his princely chores came first as a relief, but then puzzled him. His parents were super-strict, after all. *Why the sudden generosity?*

In the living room behind him, Kuniko and Mrs. Saeki were talking in hushed voices. *Whisper, whisper.*

So that was it! They didn't want him to hear whatever it was they were talking about. Of course, the only thing to do in this situation was to eavesdrop. Wataru picked at his cake with his fingers, one ear pressed against the door.

The first low voice he heard belonged to his mother. "So what are the police doing about it?"

Wataru's eyes widened. He licked a stray dollop of cream off one finger.

"Well, they're looking for the perpetrator, of course. I'm sure they must have a good idea of who did it by now."

"Some pervert, I'm sure. No doubt he's done something like this before."

"Well, maybe. But they think it may have been a group of bullies."

"What, you mean like high school students? Surely not any kids in middle school, right? I mean, look at what they did. And at least one of them could drive."

"I suppose, but what about all these children in high school who just stay home and play hooky? It could have been a bunch of those types."

"Just the sort to cause trouble, I'm sure. But, my, this isn't just trouble, is it? It's a serious crime!"

"And that's exactly why I say we need a neighborhood watch program. I only have boys like you, but think about the parents with girls. They must be terrified!"

"One can only imagine!"

"Those poor dears," Mrs. Saeki sighed. "And the Daimatsus too…"

Wataru had just finished eating the cherry from the top of his cake. He gasped and swallowed the seed. The *Daimatsus? The same Daimatsus who own the building?* It made sense that it would be them. It was Mrs. Saeki, after all, who had first told his mother the saga of the unfinished building.

"Their daughter, she was in middle school, wasn't she?"

"That's right. But I hear that the Daimatsus never went to the police—not right away, at least. Then this happened, and they started thinking that it might be the same people who kidnapped her. That's when they finally talked about it. Of course, the police were making the rounds by then."

"Well, I guess I understand how they felt, but I still think they should have gone to the police sooner."

"It sounds like the whole affair was quite a shock for the Daimatsus' daughter…they say she went mute! She was, I don't know, somehow *broken* by all of this."

Kuniko was silent with astonishment. But the one who was truly reeling was Wataru. His ear was still glued to the door, his face as white as the cream smeared on his cheek.

The Daimatsus' daughter...unable to speak...broken.

They had to be talking about Kaori. Who else could it be? That stunningly beautiful girl in the wheelchair with the vacant eyes, her head wobbling on that graceful neck like a limp doll's every time her brother gave her a push. Whatever it was they were talking about, it had something to do with her condition. What had those perverts, or hoodlums, or whoever it was, done? And the police were involved. Mrs. Saeki said something about her being kidnapped. Had someone kidnapped Kaori? Did they do that to her? Did they *break* her?

Wataru's stomach shrank to the size of a clenched fist, then sank down, down, down, finally coming to a rest somewhere near his kneecaps. He suddenly lost his appetite for cake.

Wataru hadn't quite hit puberty yet but was close enough to see it on the road ahead. He had a pretty good idea of what lay in store and already knew twice as much about things as his parents suspected.

He was able to make a decent guess, then, at just what Kaori Daimatsu might have been through to leave her so broken, and what that must have been like for a young girl. Of course, this was all speculation. No doubt the details were a little different—well, very different—but he had an intuitive sense that the whole thing was frightening, detestable, and *foul* beyond words.

It was almost time for him to leave for cram school. He would have to take his plate back to the kitchen and say goodbye to his mother before he could do that, but he wasn't sure if he could pull it off. *Mom, I know that girl! I know Kaori! I haven't been able to think about anything else since the day I met her. She was so cute, Mom...like the fairy, Neena.*

Just thinking about it brought tears to his eyes.

Wataru tore himself away from the whispered conversation, crept out of the room like a ninja, and dashed straight to cram school with an unexpected energy, the wild look in his eyes raising more than a few eyebrows on the street as he passed.

The entire time that he was in class, sitting motionless in his seat, listening to the teacher explain the mistakes he had made on his arithmetic homework, and watching the rest of the class stare in awe of Yutaro's academic abilities, Wataru still felt like he was running...alone. He didn't know where he was going, or why he was running in the first place. He just ran—like a hero on a mission. He didn't have to ask directions, he didn't wonder whom he was supposed to save, or what evil monster he was supposed to vanquish—he just ran.

But the reality of it was that he didn't know where to go, or what to do when he got there. And he was very, very alone.

Class didn't finish until after eight o'clock in the evening. Normally Wataru would be starving, but today he had no appetite at all. He just felt a hollow emptiness in his gut. He hurriedly put away his textbook and his notes, and started home.

As he walked, he felt a desperate need to go back to the Daimatsu building. Something told him that if he went there he would see Kaori again. But it had been much later at night when he first met her there. Midnight, even. There was no way they'd have taken her there for her walk this early. He wasn't even sure if the place was on her normal route. Mr. Daimatsu may have dropped by for a look at the state of his abandoned project on a whim.

Even as he listed all the reasons why it was pointless to go there, he nonetheless found his feet taking him in the direction of the building. This time there was no chance encounter with his father at the entrance to the apartment complex. Wataru walked straight toward the haunted building as if he were on some important errand. Luckily, it wasn't raining that night.

It had already been about two weeks since Katchan had run into Mr. Daimatsu and the man in the gray workman's outfit, but the building showed no signs of any new construction since then. The tarps were draped, as always, over the building's thin steel skeleton, making it look as if it had taken a chill despite summer's imminent arrival.

Nobody was around at this time of the evening. There were always people on the streets when he passed by on the way to and from school, but this was a quiet residential area—the quiet shrine on one side of the building, and houses everywhere else—with no shops or convenience stores. After the sun went down, the area settled into silence.

Wataru stood under a streetlight and looked up at the building. The thick ropes that tied the tarps together had soaked up rain for the past several days, making them hang limp like dead worms. One here, one there—Wataru swung his finger across the width of the building, counting them.

The place that should have been the main entrance was covered with a particularly thick tarp, which was secured, not with a rope, but with a large padlock. Mr. Daimatsu presumably was holding on to the key until he could find another construction company to carry on with the project. He must have opened the lock before Wataru and Katchan arrived on the day they had met, so that he could inspect the interior.

Wataru peeked between two of the sheets. He could just make out some steel beams and what looked like a staircase. The place smelled faintly of mold. He glanced down at the digital display on his watch.

08:19:32

Why would Mr. Daimatsu have brought Kaori here on a walk so late at night? If he wanted to inspect the place, he could have easily done so during the day. Why go to the trouble of coming so late? Maybe he couldn't bear to see Kaori's broken body under the unforgiving light of day? Maybe Kaori herself didn't like going out when it was hot? Or maybe it wasn't the bright sunlight she hated but the strangers who filled the streets. All those people—and not a single one had come to her aid.

Wataru wished that he knew the details of what had happened so that he wouldn't have to suffer through the painful images his imagination dreamed up. Even more, he wished he hadn't heard about it in the first place.

Standing there, he couldn't help comparing this ill-fated, partially completed building to Kaori. A lifeless husk, meaninglessly abandoned to the depredations of wind and rain, wasting away little by little. This wasn't just a building, it was her soul.

For a moment, Wataru was too lost in the sorrow and indignation swirling through him to be aware of his surroundings or to see what was happening right before his eyes. When he did see, he blinked. *Impossible.* Even a fifth grader knows the difference between what should be real and what shouldn't be. This was a fantasy, a phantasm, a…

Somebody was pressing gingerly against the padlocked tarp *from the inside*. He saw a hand. Wataru's mouth dropped open. *It's moving.* The hand was oddly pale, not a woman's hand. It was too wrinkled and dry. It looked like the hand of his grandfather—the one who lived in Odawara.

Slowly, the hand lifted up the sheet, widening the gap between it and its neighbor. Someone was peeking through at Wataru.

"Whoa!" Wataru's delayed astonishment leapt from his mouth in the form of a shout. The hand withdrew, and the tarp fell shut. The padlock rattled.

Somebody's in there!

Wataru crouched and grabbed the bottom of the sheet. It was a lot heavier than it looked, but by using both hands he was able to lift it about a foot off of the ground. He crawled under, into the building, slithering so hastily that his face touched the ground and came up smeared with muck, but he paid it no mind. He was inside.

Wataru got up on his knees, only now realizing how dark the place was. The only light came from thin beams from the streetlights sneaking in through spaces between the tarps. He could see the concrete foundation, rising steel struts, a staircase leading upward to his right—all transformed into blacker lumps of darkness in the dim light.

Wataru heard a noise off to his right. He whirled around. Above him, the staircase twisted up, turning on a landing between the first and second floors, another between the second and third floors, another between the third and fourth floors…and there the stairs ended. It looked like they had built the third landing and then just stopped. Wataru squinted in the darkness.

Someone was climbing the stairs.

chapter 6
The Door

Wataru's mouth gaped. For a moment he could do nothing but stand there, blinking in disbelief.

The figure stood on the landing between the third and fourth floors, so close to the edge that one step farther would have sent it tumbling down. Its black silhouette was thin and tall, and...

That's a hood!

It wore a long-hemmed robe and a hood covering its head. Its left hand lay on the landing banister. In its right hand was a staff, at least six feet long, with a round tip that sparkled and shone.

A wizard.

There were always two wizards in the *Eldritch Stone Saga* series—one on the player's side and another on the enemy's side. In *Saga I* the ally wizard was a difficult and grumpy old man. But at the same time, he was a magus of much power who had once been the master of the enemy wizard.

In contrast, the ally wizard in *Saga II* was a beautiful young woman, the doppelganger of the enemy wizard. The two rivals remained eternally young because of a particularly devastating spell: twisting the aging process to suit her own purpose, the evil wizard had released a horrible plague on the innocent citizens of the Kingdom of Toma. The beautiful ally wizard joined the hero of the story in an effort to stop the plague, despite knowing that victory would cause her to immediately start aging—turning her into an old hag.

According to the literature, *Saga III*'s wizard was once again an old man. Afflicted by an ancient curse, he asked to join the hero's party so that he might find a cure for it. In the preview screenshots and artwork he looked much kinder than the wizard in *Saga I*, less like dark magus and more like Santa Claus.

Though each of the wizards was very different, they always had two things in common: a long, hooded robe and a staff in one hand. This held true no matter what else they wore. For example, the beautiful wizard in *Saga II* wore a miniskirt so short you'd expect her underwear to show, but her long-hooded robe was so long that it dragged on the ground. It was like a mandatory uniform.

And now, in the gloomy interior of a haunted building, standing on the landing of a half-wrought staircase that hung in midair, was someone dressed just like a wizard. What else could it be? The only problem, of course, was that wizards didn't really exist.

"Uh...hey!" Wataru blurted. "Hey, you!"

The figure on the landing seemed to turn. The angle of its staff changed a little.

"What are you doing up there?"

Silence fell. Wataru could feel the hooded figure's gaze upon him in the darkness. "Um, er..." He took a half-step forward. "I don't think it's very safe up there."

No answer. The figure didn't move. An ominous feeling crept over Wataru, enveloping him like steam. What if it weren't a wizard after all, but someone who was a little wrong in the head— someone a little strange? Maybe he had just wandered in here? *Maybe I'm standing in a dark, abandoned building with a madman, and I've just announced my presence for all to hear.* Or maybe it was just some nice old person from the neighborhood who enjoyed dressing up like a wizard.

The figure in the hood took a step forward. Wataru broke out in a cold sweat. *An old man who likes to dress up like a wizard. Right, Wataru. Good thinking.*

Wataru crouched and scrabbled at the plastic sheet to pull it back up, fumbling in his haste, when a man's voice thundered in the air above him.

"Fear not, lad!"

Wataru froze. For several seconds, he couldn't move a muscle. Then, slowly, fearfully he looked back up. The hooded figure remained where he had been before. The staff moved, the sphere at its tip shining in the reflected light of the streetlights that peeked in between the tarps. The voice spoke again, this time in a much gentler tone. "Where did you come from?"

It was asking him a question. The heavy tarp still clutched in both hands, Wataru's mouth flapped open. Nothing came out but silence.

He's speaking to me in Japanese!

"What's your name?" the voice asked. It was definitely an old man's voice, with a hint of gruffness, making it sound like his grandfather in Odawara, the one who smoked.

"Well? Have you no answer?"

The figure above him took another half-step. Wataru's teeth began to clatter. "Um...um...um..."

"Ah, so your name is 'Um,' is it, lad?"

No, no! Wataru shook his head, but his voice was trapped somewhere deep in his throat.

"Tell me, Um, just what is it that you are doing here?"

Wataru slowly raised his eyes to see the hooded figure leaning against the handrail of the third-floor landing. He was looking down at him, his staff held over one shoulder.

Oddly enough, he seemed somehow...friendly.

"Perhaps you heard of this place from your friends?" the figure continued, tapping his staff upon his right shoulder as he spoke. "It seems there's been a lot of talk about this place of late."

His words slowly percolated through Wataru's confused and agitated mind. *Friends. Heard about it from friends. There's been talk.*

"Umm..." Wataru stuttered. The figure cut him off, laughing.

"This isn't the audience chamber of King Midas, young Um, you need not announce your name each time you speak!"

"Umm...that's not what I meant to say." Just finally being able to speak one coherent word did the trick. The curse was lifted. "My name isn't Um, it's Wataru."

"Wataru?" The figure seemed to be cocking his head. His hood slid to one side. "Is that so? Hrm...similar."

Huh? Wataru thought. "Similar to who?"

"No one," the hooded figure immediately replied, "at least, no friend of yours."

The figure shifted the staff to his other shoulder and leaned even more deeply onto the banister. He seemed completely at ease. It wouldn't have surprised Wataru in the least to see him pull out a pipe from his breast pocket and take a leisurely puff.

"And so, Wataru, just why are you here?"

"Well, weren't you…did you look out from behind this tarp just now?"

"Indeed, I did."

"Well, I saw your hand from outside, so I came in to find out who it was."

"I see," the figure said casually. "And why were you here?"

"Like I said, I saw your hand, and…"

A hand slid from the robe's sleeve. The figure raised one finger, and waved it back and forth in an admonishing gesture. "Wataru, that is not what I asked. Now listen carefully. Why were you here?"

Wataru wasn't sure how to respond. "I told you…"

"Perhaps you just happened to be taking a walk by this building? Rather late for someone your age to be out, don't you think?"

Wataru finally understood. "I came here because…I wanted to meet someone."

"You wanted to *meet* someone," the hooded figure repeated in a sing-song voice. "And just where might this someone be?"

It was a hard question to answer, even under normal circumstances, which these were certainly not. How could he begin to explain someone like Kaori Daimatsu?

"Not here, it looks like."

"Not here, you say!"

"No. But we've met here before, so I…"

"Met *here*, before?"

"I know it sounds strange, but I really…"

The hooded figure cut him off again. "And just what kind of person might this someone be?"

"A…a girl. She's a girl."

"A girl, indeed!" the hooded figure sang again, suddenly straightening his back and planting his staff on the landing with a clang, making Wataru start. "It's time for me to be off."

"Uh…wait, I…"

"You seem to be in error, incidentally."

"Me? What do you mean?"

"You should not have come here."

"But…"

"Nor should you have met me. In fact, you didn't."

"Huh? But we're talking…"

"Never mind that, I'll roll back time for you. You were not here. You don't remember anything."

"Hey, w-wait!"

But the hooded figure refused to wait, or heed his pleas. Staff held in one hand, he raised his free hand to the sky. Once again, his thunderous voice filled the space inside the building.

"Chronos, great God of Time! Your faithful servant, emissary of wind, cloud and rainbow, stands in supplication!"

He's casting a spell! Wataru was riveted in place.

"By your will, let time be stopped, be turned back, be purified by the bubbling waters of the Fountain of Forgetfulness!"

The wizard jabbed his staff toward the heavens. "*Dan dalam ekono kros! Hie!*"

For a moment, Wataru's sight was filled with countless silver specks of light, so bright he was forced to blink and then…

"Huh?" He was sitting on the ground, just inside the haunted building's tarps. He scrambled to his feet and looked up, but the third-floor landing was empty. No wizards, no old men playing dress-up.

What was all that?

He blinked.

All that? Wait…I remember everything!

The old man had promised to turn back time, to erase his memories of the encounter, but he remembered it all, down to the last detail. Dizzy, Wataru held one hand up to his forehead. *I must have a fever. Or I was dreaming. Maybe I should pinch my cheek. Here I go. Ouch! Yep, that hurt.*

Wataru lifted the edge of the tarp and went back outside. He looked at his watch in the glow of the streetlights. It must be late. His mother would be furious. What would he tell…

His breath stopped. He looked at the digital display on his watch again and blinked.

08:19:32

No way. Even if it had been a dream, some kind of strange momentary hallucination, just going under that tarp and coming back out would have taken at least thirty seconds, if not a minute.

No time had passed.

I'll just roll back time for you, the man had said. It was like magic. Wataru tried his best to recall the spell. *Something about Chronos, the great god of time? And his emissary...what was it? Something about wind and stuff. Rainbows, maybe. And something like "ramu" and "ekono" at the end...I should have paid more attention!*

It hadn't been a dream, or a hallucination. He hadn't seen an old man who likes dressing up in funny costumes. He had seen an honest-to-goodness, genuine wizard.

What the heck is a wizard *doing in an abandoned building in a Tokyo suburb?*

Wataru jumped up and dove under the sheet once again. His eyes had adjusted to the glare of the streetlights, making the darkness inside the haunted building seem much thicker than before. Nonetheless, it was clear that there was nobody present except Wataru—not on the landing, not behind the steel beams, not under the stairs.

"Well, that sounds kinda interesting, I guess, but it's a bit of a departure for the series, don't you think?" Katchan shifted his yellow umbrella from his right shoulder to his left. A light rain was falling.

"Departure?" asked Wataru.

"From the first two games. Setting it in modern Japan seems kinda lame, if you ask me. And if it's going to start out like that, we probably won't get to ride in that flying boat on the posters until, like, the third disc."

Wataru sighed. "You think I'm talking about *Saga III.*"

Katchan's eyes widened. "You weren't?"

The two were in the courtyard behind school after classes let out, at the top of the concrete stairs just outside the library exit. It had been drizzling

95

since morning, and didn't show any signs of letting up. A large low-pressure front was coming, said the weather report. *Chance of heavy rains in western Japan.*

And wizards.

Wataru had told Katchan everything: the girl's voice in his room that came from nowhere and the wizard in the haunted building who cast a spell on him. He had been bursting to tell someone, and now it came out in a flood of meticulous, vivid detail. And Katchan thought that he was talking about a game.

What could he expect? Would he have believed Katchan if it were him telling the story? Invisible girls? Old wizards? All the stuff of fairy tales and video games. He could insist it was all real as much as he liked, and he would still have no way to prove it.

Wataru felt exhausted, and his thoughts were muddled. He had hardly slept the night before, and he worried he might have caught a cold running around in the haunted building. He sat vacantly watching the rain come down.

"Hey!" Katchan's urgent whisper snapped Wataru out of his sleepy reverie. "Look! Over there!"

Katchan was tugging on Wataru's elbow and pointing toward the library. Through the large glass window they could see part of a single shelf. Somebody was standing in front of it. The figure moved. The window was higher up than they were, so even standing on tiptoe and craning their necks they could see the figure only from the shoulders up. Still, Wataru knew in an instant who it was.

"Mitsuru!"

He was wearing a white, short-sleeved polo shirt—unusual for a guy who always stalked the hallways at school dressed in black.

"It's not *just* Mitsuru," Katchan said, ducking down behind his umbrella so he wouldn't be seen. "Kenji Ishioka's in there too!"

Mitsuru stopped in front of the bookshelf, grabbed a book, and opened it. Kenji moved in, trying to see what the book was, but the other boy turned so he couldn't read it. As they watched, two of Kenji's sixth-grade flunkies came up from behind him, and the three boys surrounded Mitsuru.

Wataru was surprised. Sure, they all went to the same school, but for some reason, he never imagined seeing Mitsuru and Kenji together.

"I've got a bad feeling about this," Wataru whispered, edging closer to the window.

Mitsuru didn't look frightened in the least. From his expression, it seemed he hadn't even noticed Kenji and his crew. His gaze was fixed on an opened page of the book, the angle of his head making the prominent line of his nose stand out even more than usual. Perfectly straight bangs fell down in front of his eyes. For a girl, Mitsuru's hair would have been on the short side, but it was long for a boy. He could get away with that style for now, but not when he entered junior high, where conformity was the rule. Still, it looked good on him, and several of the boys at school had unadvisedly tried to imitate the look.

Maybe Kenji doesn't like his hairdo?

Kenji was extremely sensitive to any perceived attempt to steal his spotlight. Perhaps this had been Mitsuru's inadvertent crime.

Just then, Kenji stuck out his fist, hitting Mitsuru on the shoulder, hard. Mitsuru staggered and fell from view.

"Uh-oh, this could be bad," Katchan whispered excitedly. "Isn't the librarian here today?"

Apparently not. Kenji and his gang would never make a mistake like that. They were meticulous when it came harassing younger students.

"You think we should go get somebody?"

They heard a shrill laugh from inside, probably one of Kenji's goons.

"We gotta go to the office!"

Katchan started to rise, but Wataru yanked on his sleeve. "Shhh! Hang on a second."

Mitsuru came back into view. This time, he was facing Kenji straight on. Kenji had his back to the window, so they were able to clearly see Mitsuru's expression. He was a little shorter than his adversary, but that didn't seem to bother him at all.

Kenji took a step back. The loud, checkered shirt he wore filled up half of the window. Wataru folded his umbrella and snuck right up beneath the eaves.

Mitsuru's lips were moving, but his words were barely audible through the glass. The only thing Wataru caught was, "Just who do you think I am?"

He craned his neck out a little farther, and his eyes met Mitsuru's through the glass. *Uh-oh!* He quickly jerked his head back and leaned hard against the wall below the window. Mitsuru had seen him for sure, and Kenji and his goons wouldn't have missed the look in his eyes. This was bad to the tenth power.

He stood there, pressed against the wall, with the rain falling onto his face and wetting his hair. Nothing happened. Katchan was standing on the top exit step with his eyes opened wide. He was about to say something, but Wataru held a finger up to his lips. Wataru counted to ten, then slowly moved sideways with his back against the wall until he made it to where Katchan was standing.

"You okay?" Katchan whispered.

"They saw me," Wataru whispered back. "Let's get inside. It's dangerous out here." He picked up his soaked umbrella. Katchan folded his and gave it a shake, spraying droplets of water everywhere.

Suddenly, the library window opened and Mitsuru stuck his head out. He didn't say a word. He just looked straight into Wataru's eyes. It was like he was scanning him, reading some hidden information that only he could see.

Several seconds passed before Mitsuru smiled, pulled back into the library, and shut the window.

"Wh-wh-wha…" Katchan stuttered. "What was that all about?"

Wataru clutched the handle of his umbrella. His hands were shaking. He was frightened, and terrified of Mitsuru. It took him a few moments to compose himself, after which they headed into the library, despite Katchan's protests. It was too late. There was no sign of Mitsuru or Kenji and his goons. A few girls were studying quietly in the reading room.

"What do you think they were talking about?" Wataru muttered, half to himself.

"Maybe they were talking about the ghost in that photo," Katchan replied.

Wataru spun around so fast that he startled Katchan into jumping a few feet back. "What photo? The one he took at Mihashi Shrine?"

"That's the one. "

"Why would Kenji care about something like that?"

"Hadn't you heard? Oh, right, you've been too busy daydreaming about summer vacation."

Katchan told him how Kenji wanted the photograph Mitsuru had taken, and had been pestering him about it. "Ishioka wants to take it to the TV station so he can get on that show."

So that's why he wants Mitsuru's photograph so badly.

"Pretty lame, huh? It's classic Kenji Ishioka, though."

It was lame. Wataru couldn't understand why someone would want to be on TV so badly that he would try to use somebody else's story like that.

"Why doesn't he just give him the picture?" Wataru said, disgusted. "Better than getting picked on." He recalled his run-in with Mitsuru at the Mihashi Shrine. The memory was so vivid that, like a fresh scab, he was sure it would start to bleed if he picked at it. He shuddered, recalling the look of sheer contempt Mitsuru had given him. "He doesn't believe the picture's real, anyway."

Wataru was getting angry again. Katchan gave him a perplexed look. Finally, he scratched the side of his head and muttered, "Well, why don't you tell him to do that? You're with him at cram school, aren't you?"

"I'm not *with* him!"

Katchan blinked. "What's your problem?"

"You just won't shut up. Why do I always have to explain everything to you? Not like you even understand. Are you stupid or something?"

Wataru knew that it was wrong to take his frustrations out on Katchan like that, but he didn't feel like apologizing. He started off down the hallway. His friend hesitantly started to follow, but Wataru just walked faster.

"You going home?" Katchan shouted after him. "See ya!"

Wataru continued to walk. By the time he was off campus and well on his way home he calmed down enough to realize how mean and selfish he had been. Oh well, he couldn't do anything about it now. All he could do was plod home alone.

That evening Uncle Lou called just as he was finishing dinner. Kuniko, who was clearing the dishes from the table, flinched when the phone rang and glared at it over her shoulder. When Wataru made a move to pick up the phone, she stopped him.

"That's okay. I'll get it." She tentatively lifted the receiver, but as soon as she heard who it was, her icy expression thawed. "Wataru, your uncle wants to speak with you."

Wataru's conscience had been bothering him ever since the scene at the library. His head was spinning with thoughts about how he should apologize to Katchan tomorrow, and what he would say, and whether Katchan would be too mad to forgive him. Dinner had tasted like paste in his mouth. He wished there was someone else he could talk to about Mitsuru and everything else. When the phone rang, he knew his prayers had been answered. *Uncle Lou!*

"Hello? Wataru speaking."

"Hey!" said his uncle. "Have you had your dinner? What did you have? Hamburgers? Spaghetti? Some of your ma's meat'n'cabbage rolls? Wow, now I'm getting hungry."

Phone calls from Uncle Lou always started this way. Hamburgers, spaghetti, and cabbage rolls—in tomato sauce, not cream—were his favorite foods.

"Hey, Uncle Lou…" Wataru began, but then felt his throat start to tighten, and tears stinging at the corners of his eyes. That was a surprise. He didn't realize he was so worked up about things. "I…"

"Actually," his uncle went on, oblivious to Wataru's predicament, "to tell you the truth, I'm calling because I wanted your advice about something."

Another surprise.

"An old friend of mine got married—he's living out there by you now. Here's the deal: his kid was recently in an accident and is in the hospital." His uncle explained that the boy—a local fourth-grader—was going to make a full recovery, but he had broken his right thighbone, and so would have to be in the hospital for quite some time. "Anyway, I'm going to go visit him in the hospital, but I wasn't sure what I should bring him as a get-well present. A book? Or a game, maybe? I couldn't come up with anything. But I was thinking, since you're his age you might have a few ideas."

Uncle Lou explained that he had several things to attend to, and so wouldn't be arriving until Friday morning, but he'd buy the gift when he got to Tokyo. "Hard to find anything out here in the boondocks that a city kid would care for."

"Are you going to be staying with us?" asked Wataru. "If you're going to the hospital on Saturday, then you'll be spending the night in Tokyo, right? You should come!"

Wataru had his back to the kitchen, so he wasn't able to see the sour face his mother made as she listened to their exchange. She knew Wataru loved his uncle, but she couldn't stand her brother-in-law for his crude ways and lack of manners. Of course, she would never say such a thing out loud.

Meanwhile, Satoru Mitani was turning down the invitation. "No, I've got a lot to do, and I'd be up too late to go visiting," he lied. He was actually far more sensitive to other people's feelings than Kuniko gave him credit for, and he knew exactly where he stood with his brother's wife. "Maybe next time."

"You always say that, but you haven't stayed with us for so long!" Wataru's shoulders slumped in disappointment. "When I was little you used to always stay with us when you came to Tokyo!"

He could hear his uncle laugh on the other end of the line. "Hah! You're still little! Or have you grown big like Godzilla since the last time I saw you? That must be why we've been having so many earthquakes here in Chiba. It's from you stomping around, making the ground shake all the way out here! Whoa, I just felt another one!"

Wataru giggled. Two years ago, his uncle had taken him to see the latest Godzilla movie—the one made in Hollywood and not in Japan. From the very beginning, his uncle groused about how the giant, funny-looking U.S. lizard wasn't the *real* thing. Still, they both loved the scene where Godzilla had come into the city, his pounding footsteps shaking the ground, sending taxis and cars and pedestrians bouncing through the air. They had met up with Wataru's parents for dinner after the show, and the two of them kept acting out that scene, bouncing in their seats on the train, jumping suddenly as they walked, and—much to Kuniko's dismay—leaping from their chairs in the restaurant.

Wataru wanted to see his uncle. He needed to talk to someone about how the girls made fun of him in class, and how he snuck out of the house late one night. He wanted to talk about how he used up the film in the disposable camera and how Mitsuru was rude to him. Uncle Lou wouldn't laugh at him or look disgusted. He wouldn't lecture him either.

"Well, can I go shopping with you?" Wataru asked. "I only have five hours of school and then I'm free. We could go to a department store, or Toys 'R' Us, or anywhere!"

His uncle paused a moment. "Well...that *sounds* like a good idea."

"Lemme come, please?"

"Okay, ask your mother if you can go shopping with me for a couple of hours, and be sure to tell her I'll have you home in time for dinner."

Wataru rejoiced. *I'll have plenty of time to talk with him about everything!* Covering the phone's mouthpiece with his hand, he spun around. "Mom! Can I..."

Kuniko, who had been sitting at the table drinking a cup of tea, answered before he even finished asking. "No."

"Why not? He's coming on Friday! I don't have to go to cram school on that day!"

"Absolutely not."

"Why?"

"Your uncle is coming to Tokyo on business. You'll just get in his way."

"But I'm going to *help* him! He's coming to buy a present for..."

Kuniko placed her mug on the table and let out a sigh. Her face darkened further, until she reminded Wataru of the wicked old witch he had seen once in a television movie. "No means no, Wataru. Give me the phone."

"No, it's okay, Wataru. You can go out with your uncle." It was his father. Startled, both Wataru and Kuniko turned to see Akira standing at the entrance to the living room, briefcase in hand. He was still wearing his suit, and his rimless eyeglasses had slid partway down his nose. He was looking straight at Wataru.

"You haven't seen your uncle in a while." He handed his briefcase to Kuniko, who had approached him with a surprised look on her face, and continued, "It'll be a good chance for you to talk with him about what kind of work you'll be doing in Chiba this summer. Here, let me talk to him."

Akira took the receiver from Wataru's hand. "Hey, Satoru, how've you been? Mom doing okay? Yeah, everyone here is well. So, about getting together with Wataru..."

The cavalry had arrived in the nick of time. Wataru's eyes shone. He could feel his body emitting a happy glow to a radius of at least a yard. Godzilla wasn't coming, but he bounced about the room all the same.

"Hush, Wataru," Kuniko scowled, still clutching Akira's briefcase. "You're father's still on the phone."

You're upset because you just got KO'd, Wataru thought, but he took great pains not to let his unbridled joy show on his face.

Akira finished talking and handed the phone back to Wataru. "Why don't you go ahead and have dinner with your uncle too. That way you won't have to rush your shopping."

"Thanks!" Wataru jumped up and quickly worked out the details with Uncle Lou, who promised to come pick him up at their apartment. Akira confirmed the schedule, then hung up the phone and went to change clothes. When he came back to the table, Kuniko was laying out dishes for supper. Wataru was so happy that he wanted to dance around the room, but one look at his mother's scowl told him that restraint was the wise course of action.

"Thanks, Dad!"

"Don't be a bother to your uncle, now," Akira said, opening the evening paper.

"I won't! I promise!"

"You're home early tonight, aren't you?" Kuniko inquired as she shuttled back and forth between the table and the refrigerator. She was angry and ignored Wataru. "If we'd known you'd be home so early, we'd have waited to have dinner with you."

"My meeting was cancelled."

"Beer?"

"No thanks."

Just as Kuniko avoided looking at Wataru, so did Akira avoid Kuniko, keeping his eyes glued to his newspaper as he spoke. Wataru retreated to his room, mumbling something about having to do homework.

Wataru sat quietly at his desk with his homework spread out in front of him, but there was no way he could immediately shift into work mode. He was too busy imagining how his uncle would react when Wataru brought him up to speed on recent events. *I met a wizard, Uncle Lou! He cast a spell on me to turn back time! It's all true!*

Finally reining in his enthusiasm, he began to tackle his arithmetic and writing homework. When he got up to go to the bathroom, he found his parents sitting on the living room sofa, drinking coffee. Kuniko told him to take his bath.

"Just two more pages."

When he came back, Kuniko was talking about something. Wataru could sense at a glance that the room was still under martial law, so he pretended not to listen and headed back to his own room. He had caught a snippet of the conversation: apparently, someone had again called and hung up several times that day. *Ah, so that's why Mom looked so nervous when Uncle Lou called.* It also explained her unusually foul mood today. Wataru sighed.

By the time he crawled into bed, though, Wataru's mood had picked right back up.

"What's it been, six months since I saw you at New Year's?" Uncle Lou said, grinning as he placed a large hand on Wataru's head. "You sure sprung up! In another six months you'll be up to my shoulder!"

"I'm not growing *that* fast," Wataru laughed. Right now he was only tall enough to come up to the tattooed scar left by a childhood immunization shot on Uncle Lou's left arm. Wataru knew about his scar from the many days they had spent on the beach in Chiba.

His uncle was a big man, both horizontally and vertically. He had long hair and a beard, and both his arms and legs were covered with thick hair. To-day, he was wearing a typically gaudy shirt that made him look like a cartoon bear. If he picked up a banjo and put on a straw hat, no one would be able to tell the difference.

"Sure is hot in Tokyo," Uncle Lou said, wiping his face with his hand. "Muggy too. That's the difference between the heat down here in the city and the heat out on the beach. I would've given up on shopping if I were trying to do it alone. Sure glad you're here to help."

It was almost four o'clock in the afternoon on Friday. Wataru had come home from school two hours before to wait impatiently, fully prepared with a brand-new white shirt on for the occasion. The thing that had been weigh-ing on his mind for the past two days—his fight with Katchan—had been re-solved. The following day in school he had gone up to his friend to apologize, and Katchan had looked at him with his big round eyes and said, "What for?" and the matter had been settled. He was ready to go.

"I don't imagine the rainy season is over yet, but at least today, you're in luck," his mother said, moving to the window and looking up at the sky. It had been overcast all morning, but since noon the sun had been shining with a weak light through the hazy clouds.

"At least we won't have to haul umbrellas around," Uncle Lou said, beaming as he turned to Wataru. "Ready to go?"

"You bet! Later, Mom."

"Be good now. Watch after him, Satoru."

"Aww, he's always a good kid, aren't you, Wataru? I'd have to try pretty hard to be half as good as you are." Uncle Lou cackled as he led the way out. Kuniko saw them off at the door, and apologized for not having been a better hostess. She hadn't even offered him a cup of coffee, unusual for someone who prided herself on propriety. Now that Wataru thought about it, her expression had been a bit stiff and forced that afternoon. *Maybe there were more prank calls.*

Uncle Lou had new intelligence about the boy he was going to visit in the hospital. First off, he had learned that he loved anime about robots. Unlike Wataru, he almost never played computer games, as his mother forbade them. The thing he had wanted most was a portable MD player, but someone had already given him that for good grades on his last report card.

Wataru suggested that they go to the Jinbocho district.

"The place with all the bookstores?"

"Yeah, there's a shop there called Konno Books that specializes in anime stuff. They'll have something on robot anime for sure."

"Good thinking. How do you know about the place? You into that stuff too?"

"Not so much, but a friend of mine from cram school is really into it. If you ever need to know *anything* about anime, just ask him."

Wataru led the way to the train while listening to his uncle talk about news from Chiba. Apparently, the humidity was up, along with his grandmother's complaining. That was okay though, because her gripes were always good for a laugh. There was a new arcade near the beach (which Wataru would have to check out during his visit), and a big debate was going on about whether a man fishing on the pier had really seen a sea monster. Finally, the owner of Wataru's favorite ramen joint had gotten into a fistfight and ended up with ten stitches.

They got off at the station and made their way toward the bookstores, only to discover that the district was so big and there were so many stores that Wataru wasn't sure if they would ever find the one he had heard about. He didn't know the exact address.

"We'll figure it out. Follow me."

Uncle Lou went into a large bookstore facing the main intersection and began talking to a young employee at the register. She was very helpful, handing him a map of the shopping district and pointing the way to Konno Books for him. The encounter put Uncle Lou in a good mood. "You know," he said, "if you listen to the news, you'd think the whole world was going to pot. But there's still plenty of kind folks around, that's clear."

This was Wataru's first time in the booksellers' district, and it made his head spin. He couldn't believe that there were so many books in the world. Who could possibly read them all?

"If I spent the rest of my life trying, I still couldn't read one ten-thousandth of all of the books they sell here," Wataru said.

"I couldn't read one one-millionth!" Uncle Lou replied, his body shaking with laughter. "What I want to know is, who's writing all of them? Whoever it is, their heads must be full of words instead of brains."

Konno Books was a small, three-story building. Uncle Lou pushed his way through the crowd with Wataru following close by. There were rivers of books flowing over display stands, and mountains of books stacked high to the ceiling. After spending close to an hour, they managed to find three glossy, oversize books that seemed to fit the bill.

"Whew!" said Uncle Lou, "talk about a workout!" Sweat was dripping from his brow.

They spilled out of the crowded store onto the street. Wataru was just about to take a deep breath, when someone slammed into him from behind. Caught off guard, Wataru wobbled and fell to his hands and knees on the pavement. A sharp sting ran up his arms and legs. He tried to get up, but his legs were numb. Helpless, he watched as a grimy sneaker came down on his right hand, stomping it into the asphalt.

"Yeeouch!"

Uncle Lou's thick arm snaked around Wataru's chest and lifted him up off the ground. "You okay? Are you hurt?" He was yelling. Numb from the pain in his hand, Wataru managed to nod and slowly stand.

His uncle dashed after a man walking fast in the opposite direction. He grabbed him by the shoulders and spun him around, revealing a very young man in jeans wearing a gray T-shirt.

"What's the big idea, knocking down a kid and stomping on his hand? You didn't even say sorry!"

Even with Uncle Lou's arms on him, the young man's expression didn't change a bit. He looked pale and sickly. His cheeks were hollow, his eyes vacant. *They look like the eyes of a dead fish*, Wataru thought, clutching his throbbing hand to his chest.

"Hey! Do you even know what you just did?" Uncle Lou was coming to a boil. His face turned beet red, and he grabbed the guy by the neck of his T-shirt. The young man remained coolly silent.

"It's fine, Uncle Lou, I'm okay," Wataru called out.

His uncle glanced back at Wataru, and then turned back to his captive. "You trampled that little boy over there and stepped on his hand, and you were just going to walk away like nothing happened? Who do you think you are? What makes you think you can get away with something like that?"

The man's expression didn't change. The muscles in his face were completely relaxed, giving him an angry look.

"You're a grown man! Don't you know that you've got to set an example? Now you go apologize to that boy, and make sure he's not hurt!"

The man's mouth finally moved, but from where he was, Wataru couldn't make out what he was saying. He could see his uncle turn a deeper shade of red, though.

"What was that? Let's hear you say that again!"

The man complied. "Shut up," he said, louder this time.

Uncle Lou blinked. "Did you just tell me to shut up?"

"Man, give it a rest, will you?"

Uncle Lou was so surprised his grip loosened. The man wriggled out of his grasp and started to walk away. "What do I care if he gets stepped on, or run over?" he spat over his shoulder. "He shouldn't be out in traffic."

Satoru's mouth fell open. His face went pale. *This could be bad.* Wataru felt his heart skip a beat. *Uncle Lou, Uncle Lou, stay calm!*

Just then, Wataru heard a familiar voice. "Your uncle's in danger! You have to stop him!"

Wataru was so surprised he stopped for a second.

It's her! Where is she speaking to me from this time?

"Traffic?!" his uncle snarled. "You don't look like a car to me. And what gives you the right to run down children? You think this road only belongs to you?"

"Well, it sure doesn't belong to you," the man said with a sneer. "Out of my face, old man. I don't got time for country bumpkins like you."

Uncle Lou's shoulders rose. *He's going to punch him! What do I do, what do I...*

Wataru threw himself to the ground with a shrill cry. "Ouch, ouch, it hurts!"

It worked instantly. His wild bull of an uncle stopped on the verge of charging and spun to face Wataru. "What's wrong?" Uncle Lou flew to Wataru's side, and the young man melted into the crowd.

"Hey, that was pretty good!" The girl's voice sparkled in his head. "That man had a knife on him! Things could have gotten ugly. I have to admit, you're pretty quick on your feet, aren't you?"

Wataru sat in a daze, listening to the girl's voice. His uncle grabbed him and shook him by the shoulders. "Wataru, are you all right? Can you hear me? C'mon, speak to me! Can you see my face? Wataru!"

"Ungh, ugh, argh..." Wataru managed, dizzy from the shaking. "Y-yeah, Uncle Lou, I can hear you fine."

"You can speak! You're okay!" His uncle looked to be on the verge of tears.

"I'm f-fine so s-stop sh-sh-shaking me!"

"Oh, sorry! I don't believe this...here I am supposed to look after you for just a few hours, and I end up letting you get hurt!"

"It's not bad," Wataru hurried to say, wiggling his stepped-on fingers. "See? Everything works. No broken bones or anything. I'm feeling a lot better too."

The demonstration helped to calm Uncle Lou down a little, but his deeply tanned, leathery cheeks still held a touch of red.

"Can you believe that guy?" Uncle Lou said with a long sigh as he helped Wataru upright. "People like him think the world revolves around them. Never a thought for their fellow man, or all the trouble they cause. What gives them the right?"

Wataru silently watched the afternoon shoppers walking by. Some people had glanced over in their direction when it looked like there might be a fight, but now that it was over everyone was busily pretending that nothing had happened and getting on with their day.

The girl hadn't said anything since praising him for his quick thinking.

"C'mon, let's go," Wataru said, tugging on his uncle's sleeve. "I wanna get away from the crowd."

His injuries didn't seem serious enough to go see a doctor, but his hand had swollen a bit.

"I have a first-aid kit with compresses and bandages," Uncle Lou said "Let's get you back to the hotel and ice down that hand of yours."

Uncle Lou took Wataru back to his hotel, a simple place catering to businessmen near the middle of town. It looked pretty cheap from the outside, but the room was surprisingly clean and had twin beds. Wataru recalled the time that he had spent the night in a hotel with his grandparents from Odawara when they took him to Tokyo Disneyland.

"Whoopee!" Wataru shouted, jumping up and down on one of the beds. "Hey, one bed for me and one for you! Can I stay the night?"

"What about school tomorrow?" his uncle scoffed, but his eyes twinkled. "Staying in twin rooms is a little extravagance of mine. Single rooms make me feel like I'm sleeping in a matchbox."

Uncle Lou had a canvas overnight bag and something that looked like an attaché case. *I guess he really did have business in Tokyo.*

As his uncle wrapped a compress around his right hand, Wataru asked, "By the way, what did you have to do in Tokyo? Are you done with your work? If you still have something to do, I can wait for you here."

His uncle was amazingly deft at first aid. He had emergency response training from his many years as a beach lifeguard. He wasn't one to brag, so not many people knew, but he had saved more lives in his time than he could count on both hands.

"Nope, I'm all finished. Okay, there you go." Uncle Lou finished wrapping Wataru's hand. "No crab or steak dinner for you. You'll only be able to hold one utensil at a time."

"How about macaroni and cheese! We can just go to a Denny's or something."

"You sure are a cheap date, aren't you?" Uncle Lou said, laughing. "Let's take a short break, and then we can wander around and see if we can't find a place that looks good. I think I'll have myself a beer before we head out."

Uncle Lou got an orange juice from the refrigerator for Wataru, who propped himself up against the head of the bed and put up his feet. Sitting in a hotel room like this made him feel like they were on a trip—not just a short errand, but a real voyage to someplace far, far away. It was the perfect time to talk about secrets.

"Actually," Wataru began, "there's something I wanted to talk to you about."

Relating everything that had happened to him recently, and explaining how he had felt about all of it turned out to be no small task. It was about a hundred times more difficult than giving an oral report at school. It helped that his uncle listened intently to every word he said, never interrupting his story—although he did laugh once or twice at the funny bits. Wataru told him everything: the invisible girl with the voice like honey, the wizard in the haunted building, the ghost in the photo at Mihashi Shrine, every event and every detail he could remember.

By the time Wataru had run out of things to say and the energy to say them, his uncle had finished all the beers in the room's mini-bar. He crushed the last empty can with a flick of his wrist, and stared at it for a time before suddenly asking, "That haunted building, it's right near where you live, right?"

"Yeah, on the way from our apartment to the school."

"Well, after we get something to eat, would you mind stopping by there on our way back home?"

This surprised Wataru. "You want to go inside?"

"Sure. Who wouldn't want to meet a wizard?"

This wasn't the reaction Wataru had expected. "Do you think that I'm making all of this up?"

"What? Were you?"

"No, of course not!"

"I didn't think so. Let's go see it."

Uncle Lou stood up from the bed. His face was a little red from the beer, but he seemed to be perfectly sober. His tolerance for liquor was pretty high. "I've never met a wizard before," he said, "and I never play video games, 'cept when you come over. But if there's some strange old man living in that building and giving children a hard time, that bears checking out."

Wataru mumbled something through his teeth. He wasn't sure himself what exactly he wanted to say. He was glad his uncle hadn't laughed at him outright, but this reaction wasn't exactly what he had hoped for.

"I don't think he's giving children a hard time...actually, I'm pretty sure I'm the only one he's met."

"Not likely. A haunted building like that is a kid magnet—there's bound to be others. Didn't the old man ask if you'd heard about the place from a friend?"

"Oh, yeah," Wataru admitted. *I guess he's right about that one.*

"Well," his uncle said with some authority, "that old man is probably also the ghost, not to mention whatever it is that showed up in that photograph the pretty-boy psycho transfer student took. I bet that's why he made fun of you and won't show the photograph to anyone, and why he won't give it to that stupid sixth-grader Ishioka." Uncle Lou's face lit up like a beacon. "Wait a second, I got an idea!" he shouted, clapping his hands together. "What if that wizard guy is Mitsuru's grandfather?!"

Wataru didn't know anything about Mitsuru's family. He didn't even know if he had a grandfather or not. But he did know that the spell cast on him was real, and he didn't find his uncle's theory very amusing. Uncle Lou was laughing so hard his belly shook.

"Wouldn't that be funny? It's well within the realm of possibility. There are people out there that'll do just about anything to cause a stir."

It had taken a long time for Wataru to tell his tale, and it was already after six-thirty. Uncle Lou suggested they try to visit the haunted building around the same time of evening that Wataru had seen the wizard. Their course of action decided, they grabbed a quick dinner near the hotel. Wataru had been hoping to feast on macaroni and French fries and a chocolate sundae while regaling his uncle with tales of his recent adventures, but somehow things never seemed to go according to plan.

As he ate, Uncle Lou watched him, observing carefully, as though Wataru was some sort of extremely delicate object—yet one which was clearly flawed and needed attention—and he wasn't quite sure if he had the necessary tools to handle the job. He told his nephew that he should learn to swim the two-hundred-meter crawl this summer. Plus, he reminded him that work at the beach house would be hard, and that he wouldn't have time to play any video games, since he would inevitably be tuckered out before the seven o'clock news was over.

He didn't think Wataru was making it all up, so, in that sense, he believed him. Still, it was clear he considered everything—except the old man—the result of an overactive imagination.

And why would Wataru be seeing these things? Why, because he was always playing video games and never went outside to play. What this boy needs is some good, old-fashioned hard work. It was worse than if he had called him a liar and laughed in his face for telling tall tales.

Things weren't working out at all in the way that Wataru had hoped. Mechanically, he lifted his spoon and fork to his mouth and chewed on his bitter thoughts. *If he doesn't understand me, no one can.*

Uncle Lou was eager to get to the haunted building as soon as they were finished. If they left now, they would get there just in time. Wataru trudged along behind his uncle.

"You sure are glum. What, you frightened? No worries, Uncle Lou'll be right by yer side!" he said, slapping a big, thick hand against Wataru's back. Normally it would have cheered Wataru up immediately, but today things were different. This wasn't the Uncle Lou that Wataru loved, and even worse, Wataru had a creeping feeling that the events of that night would somehow change their relationship forever.

I shouldn't have told him anything. I should have just kept it all to myself. Serves me right for telling a grown-up.

Uncle Lou bought two flashlights at a convenience store. His back was turned to Wataru as he paid. *What would happen if I ran, now, while he's not looking?* Wataru wondered. He didn't run, of course.

They took a taxi to a spot near the haunted building, an unusual move for his uncle who was normally allergic to wasting money.

He must really want to see the haunted building bad.

Uncle Lou did seem as excited as a little child. "Is this it?" he asked as they reached the unfinished building. He had a look in his eyes like he was the lead actor in a monster movie, or maybe a cop show. This would be the episode in which the hero would be investigating an abandoned building to arrest a perverted old man suspected of doing bad things to little children.

He looked around, making sure that there was nobody around to see them. He then lifted the edge of the nearest tarp. "This where you went in?"

"Yeah, right there."

"Right," he replied, handing Wataru a flashlight. "Be careful, now." Wataru took the flashlight and ducked under the tarp. Inside, Uncle Lou stationed Wataru at the base of the stairs and began scanning the walls with his flashlight. He moved surprisingly smoothly for someone of his bulk, and he didn't bump into or trip over anything. His face was drawn as he searched the first floor. For once, he wasn't making any jokes.

"Let's check out this staircase next," he said, climbing the stairs slowly, testing each step. He kept his flashlight trained ahead of him as he ascended, carefully watching the treads.

"I'd expect to see more trash around here if someone was using this place as a hideout." He stopped on the landing between the second and third floors, scratching his head. "I don't even see any footprints in the dust."

Wataru shone his flashlight down at his own feet. There was a layer of coarse dust and powdered concrete everywhere: on the newly laid concrete floor, on the patches of exposed earth, and on places covered with plywood. Only the staircase was clean, with just a tiny bit of dust and dirt collected in the corners of each step. They would find no footprints there, for certain.

Wait, wouldn't a clean staircase mean someone was using it a lot? They might have been cleaning it with a broom, to keep their feet from getting dirty. Maybe it was the "friend" that the wizard mentioned.

Maybe it was...Mitsuru?

"Hey, Wataru, the stairs end here!" Uncle Lou called down from the third-floor landing. "That old man you saw was standing right here, you say?"

"Yeah."

"It's kinda scary up here," he said, holding on to a handrail as he slowly looked around. "Not a good place for children and old folks to be wandering around. They need to be more careful about keeping people out. You should tell that boy Mitsuru that it's dangerous to play in construction sites."

"Maybe he doesn't come here."

"Of course he does. What about that deal with the ghost photo?"

"Well, I'm not asking him."

He'd just make fun of me again.

"You should talk to your mother and father about this when you get home. And the neighborhood association should…"

Satoru's cell phone rang in his breast pocket. He pulled it out and put it to his ear. "Hello? Huh? Oh, hey, Akira. Wait, I can hardly hear you. Hang on a minute." He nimbly stepped down the stairs with the flashlight in one hand and his cell phone in the other. "Hello? No, I'm getting static here too. What's that? Can you hear me? Hello?"

Uncle Lou looked around for a place with better reception, eventually giving up and going back out under the tarp.

All these steel beams are probably interfering with the cell phone signal.

Wataru headed toward the front tarp, turning off his flashlight and sticking it into his back pocket. He crouched down to pull up the tarp when he suddenly realized it had gotten much brighter inside the building. He could see the heavy stitches in the tarp in front of him. Still in a crouch, he turned his head to look back up into the building.

Wataru's jaw dropped. On the third-floor landing, right where his uncle had just been standing—where he had seen the wizard—was…

A shining gate!

The gate had two doors, their upper halves covered in ornate decorations, with sweeping old-fashioned curves.

It's closed.

The gate was closed tight, outlined by a bright white light around the edges and down the middle seam. Whatever space was behind the gate must be brightly lit. The white light spilled out into the haunted building.

When did that get there?

Wataru stood up shaking. He went to the stairs and began to climb. With each step it seemed that the light leaking in from the door grew brighter. Wataru couldn't look away, even when he nearly tripped on the narrow steps. Relentlessly, he moved toward the door, as if drawn by some force beyond his control. By the time he neared the third floor landing, he was crawling.

As he got close to the door he could feel the light's warmth. Wataru began to smile. As he stretched his hand before him, he thought he could hear a sound like falling spring rain.

The light…so pure, so bright, so gentle…

Wataru reached the landing. Now standing, he reached for the door.

chapter 7
Beyond the Door

The band of light down the middle of the gate grew wider and brighter, almost as if to welcome Wataru.

It's opening!

The door was being pushed open from the other side, from that world filled to overflowing with light. Wataru brought his hands up before his eyes to shield them from the warm radiance that spilled out over him like a tidal wave. It was so bright he couldn't look straight into it. He crouched as if caught in the middle of a rapidly flowing river, barely able to stand.

Then his eyes discerned a form: somebody was walking straight toward him. He was able to make out a human figure through the glow. It emerged from the gate with a leap, abruptly standing before him. It was a boy. It was Mitsuru.

"Just what are *you* doing here?"

He was close enough for Wataru to feel his breath on his forehead. He stood, eyes wide, legs planted firmly. One accusatory finger pointed forward.

"What are you doing here?" he shouted again, but before Wataru could form a response, he spun around and ran directly back into the pearly whiteness of the gateway. In the blink of an eye, the brightness swallowed his form, and he was gone.

Wataru couldn't think. He didn't have time to hesitate or feel scared. The next thing he knew, he was heading toward the gate, toward that light, running after Ashikawa. He crossed over the threshold and, unconsciously, he leapt. Into white emptiness. Into an ocean of light. The warm, flowing air of…

The sky. I'm in the sky.

It was like being in an airplane, looking out over a sea of clouds. Down, down, down he fell. The wind rushed past his ears as he sliced through the sky. Then he was in the clouds. Everything was slow and languid. He felt like an ancient sea turtle, swimming leisurely through tropical waters. He stretched out his fingers and toes, and the light infusing the clouds formed a nimbus about him. When Wataru moved, the halo moved with him. It was like he was dancing in a ring, surrounded by countless particles of light. Slowly, he stretched his body out, and smiled as he spun around. Above him hung a canopy of light, below him rested a sparkling sea of clouds.

Then he broke through the clouds into an azure sky. Far beneath him lay a vast bluish-green grassland.

"Aagh!" Wataru screamed.

I'm falling!

Suddenly everything sped up. He plummeted toward the ground like a stone. Puffy clouds zipped by in a blur. He felt nothing, only brightness. Still he sped downward, his velocity increasing relentlessly. He fell, and fell, and fell...

And landed on his back with a thud, the impact knocking every last thought out of his head. He lay with his back flat against the ground, and his legs sticking straight up into the air.

How embarrassing, he thought at last, and then, *at least I'm still alive to be embarrassed.*

He was looking straight up into an impossibly bright sky. He had never seen such a beautiful, pure blue sky in his life. Except perhaps the photographs on posters in travel agencies, advertising tours to places like Hawaii and Guam. They were all doctored using computers to make the colors appear brighter, his father once told him. No sky is that blue, he said, not even in Hawaii, or Guam, or Saipan.

Except here one was: an unblemished blue sky.

Where am I?

He looked around, but all he could see in every direction was desert. The sand underneath him was coarse and dry, and it trickled through his fingers when he scooped some up.

Did this sand cushion my fall?

The sun shone down on him, hot enough to make his cheeks and the back of his neck prickle. The vast grassland he had spotted during his fall was no-where to be seen. Questions raced through Wataru's head. Had an air current carried him off to this place? He was in a desert, but a desert *where*? All he knew for sure was that he was on the other side of the gate. Which way should he go? How might he find that grassland from before?

And Mitsuru, is he in here too, wandering around?

He stood up shakily and, before he could get his bearings, was enveloped in a swift desert wind carrying a vortex of sand through the air. Holding back a cough, Wataru waved his hand in front of his face trying to see through the flying grit.

Behind him, an inverted cone like an ant lion's trap appeared in the sand. Soundlessly it grew, larger and larger, quickly gathering in the spot Wataru stood. He spun around, and hurriedly jumped back. The edge of the cone had almost reached his heel. Had he reacted a second slower, he would have fallen straight into it.

"What's that?!"

Before his disbelieving eyes, something appeared in the deepest part of the cone: an animal with pitch-black fur. It burst into the air, spraying sand every-where. With effortless grace it vaulted over Wataru's head to land softly upon the sand behind him. The creature had four legs and a tail. It reminded him somewhat of a dog. A cloud of sand flew up around it, and it let out a single yap. Brushing away the blast of sand from his face, Wataru almost fainted in surprise.

The beast had the body of a dog, a sleek, black Doberman, but in place of its head was a...*what are those things called, that thing in the kitchen that Mom uses once in a blue moon to open wine bottles...a corkscrew! That's it! This animal's head is twisty like a corkscrew!*

The monster tossed its screwy head in Wataru's direction and let out a snarl.

Garrrrrraaar!

The thing's head vibrated with the discordant howl, but for the life of him, Wataru couldn't fathom where the sound was coming from.

"How're you supposed to eat me," Wataru asked with a forced laugh, "when you don't have a mouth?"

As if in answer, the monster's entire corkscrewed head inflated and burst, pointed straight at Wataru. The inner part of the screw was a disgustingly moist, red thing, filled with pulsating membranes and surrounded by an array of sharp fangs.

Wataru yelped and began to run. He took three steps away when he realized that a new vortex was forming in front of him. He dodged to the left, right toward another screw-head that came leaping from a sand cone he hadn't seen before. It howled and pounced, instantly closing the distance between them.

Somebody help! I'm surrounded by screw-headed monsters!

Wataru covered his face with his hands, and felt something clamp down on the back of his neck. With a sickening lurch, his body flew up into the air. Peeking through his fingers, he realized that he was flying again. He wasn't up high—it was like being on a ski lift. The only thing different was that his arms and legs were flailing in the air.

Five of the screw-headed dogs ran across the sand below him, howling and jumping up to snap at Wataru's dangling feet. New vortices were forming beneath him as he passed.

They must live below the desert surface, coming up to catch their prey as it passes above them.

"Are you out of your mind?" a shrill voice asked from above Wataru's head. "Jumping down into the middle of a pack of gimblewolves like that. If I hadn't happened by just then, you'd be stewing in stomach juices right now!"

Whatever was carrying Wataru had him by the back of his collar, so he was unable to look up and see the source of the voice—doubtlessly the one who had saved his life. For now.

"Thank you," Wataru managed through the rush of desert wind. "You saved my skin back there."

"Of course I did, of course I did," the voice answered with accelerating pitch. It seemed to appreciate the gratitude. "You're a lucky one. I flew by right in the nick of time."

Another gust of wind caught them, and they dipped suddenly, making Wataru's stomach lurch. "You know," he shouted, "I think we're clear of those screw-wolf-things. Maybe we should go on foot for a bit?"

The thing carrying him snorted through its nose. "Nonsense! I do not slither and crawl upon the dirty ground! I fly, and I only fly! Got it, kid?"

It occurred to Wataru that if the creature became angry, it might just let go, so he refrained from making any further protests. He was being carried along at a leisurely pace, about the speed of a bicycle, albeit one pedaling at the height of a two-story house above the ground. They were still surrounded by desert on all sides, but Wataru could see a rough field of large rocky outcroppings a little to the left of their trajectory ahead.

"Hey kid, just where did you come from?" the shrill voice asked. "You're not some kind of runaway, are you?"

Wataru didn't know what to say. How could he explain the situation when he didn't fully understand it himself? And the word *runaway* gave him pause. *What if I am a runaway?*

"Whatever you are, you sure are heavy." Wataru could hear the sound of his rescuer's wings beating out a slightly irregular pattern. Maybe it wasn't as large a bird as he had first imagined. "Rest break on those rocks," it squawked, and their heading shifted to the left. Their altitude dropped over the rocks and Wataru was let—or rather, tossed—down.

"Hey! Watch out!" Wataru landed on his rear on the rocky shelf at running speed and almost bounced over the far edge. Something grabbed the back of his collar.

"Poor reflexes, kid!"

With much fluttering and flapping, a huge scarlet bird landed in front of Wataru, who was now standing, rubbing his sore behind. The red of its feathers was so pure they seemed to have been dyed crimson. Its wingspan was only about six feet and it had a slender body, but the claws on its legs looked strong and sharp, big enough to easily clamp down on Wataru's head. Just imagining those claws on his collar, brushing up against his neck, sent an involuntary shudder down his spine.

The bird folded its wings, slightly cocked its head, and looked Wataru over. It had a face much like an eagle, but it sported a crest of gold feathers atop its head, like the fronds on a samba dancer. They played gracefully in the desert wind.

"Th...thank you," Wataru said again. His throat felt suddenly dry, and his voice sounded hoarse. *It's a bird! A talking bird!*

"Ah, it was nothing. But, do answer me one thing. This area belongs to us—the karulah. We don't take kindly to other tribes in our..." Suddenly the bird started in delayed surprise. "Why, you're a man-child!"

"Yes…yes I am," Wataru responded, raising an eyebrow. Were humans a rare thing in this strange place?

"And just what is a man-child doing here? How did you get here?" the bird asked excitedly, beating its wings against the rock, forcing Wataru to hold up his hands to shield his eyes against the whipping sand.

"W-wait! Hold on and I'll tell you! Stop flapping!"

"Oh, right," the bird muttered and folded its wings up again. Wataru took a deep breath, and somehow managed to regain his composure. He could feel his heart pounding in his chest. "I came through a gate high up in the sky and fell down here," he said. "That's really all I know."

Slowly the bird turned its large eyes up to the blue sky. "I see," it said at last. "So the Porta Nectere is open…"

"The Porta…Nectere?"

The creature nodded. "Aye. 'Tis the doorway between the Over Here and the Over There—a huge gate, so high its top is hidden in the clouds. None in my tribe has ever seen the top, and because no one in either the Over Here or the Over There has wings stronger than the karulah, that means no one has seen it." The bird thrust out its breast as it spoke. Its long feathers fluttered in the wind. "The Porta Nectere opens only for ninety days every ten years, as such things are counted Over There. I suppose this means that the ninety days have started. I had completely forgotten about it."

Wataru could only gape.

"And so you came through the doorway, stumbling from the Over There into the Over Here, and fell smack down into a pack of gimblewolves," the creature concluded thoughtfully. "I see, I see."

What the creature referred to as the "Over Here" must be where he was now, Wataru figured, while the "Over There" was where Wataru normally lived, the real world. But something didn't fit. The gate that Wataru had come through was certainly impressively large, but nothing like what the bird had just described. Wataru wondered out loud about this, and the bird haughtily replied, "Well, of course. The true scale of the Porta Nectere is visible only from this side."

"I see," Wataru lied. At least his heart wasn't racing quite so furiously anymore. He plopped down on the rock and took a closer look at his surroundings. He could see clearly in all directions, which wasn't saying much. No matter which way he turned, all he could see was desert. Here and there, vague lines interrupted the sand dunes—likely other rocky outcroppings like the one where they sat. One horizon was a dim yellow line that shimmered like a mirage. *A sandstorm, maybe?*

"Well, you look a bit flustered," the scarlet bird said, ruffling its wings in what was apparently a laugh, "but that's to be expected, I suppose. You didn't have any idea all of this was here, did you? First time I've ever picked up a stray. I have heard of other young man-children mistakenly falling through the door, though, so take comfort! You're not the first. Aye, you may be a bit on the dull side, but at least you're in good company."

Wataru decided to take that as a compliment. The creature had saved his life, after all, and he did seem to be a generally decent person—or rather, bird.

"So, um…where *is* this place?" Wataru asked. "Doesn't Over Here have a name?"

"Vision," the scarlet bird replied.

"Vision?"

Wataru remembered a spell in *Saga II* called "Vision Strike." It was a spell usable only by powerful wizards that confused their enemies with magical visions that led them to attack each other.

A vision. An illusion.

"So this whole place is just make-believe?"

"I suppose it must seem that way to a man-child."

"So right now I'm inside a daydream?" Wataru spread out his hands. The sand carried in the wind stung his eyes. "I can feel the wind on my face, the heat of the sun on my neck, and the dust blowing all the way into my throat. Can this all be just an illusion?"

"It can to you, man-child, lost child."

Wataru stood up on the rocky outcropping. All around him were rough stones, and his footing was unsure. "All of this desert that I can see from here? Every bit of it's a fantasy? None of it's real?"

"Well, I've never been to this 'real' place you speak of, so how could I know the difference?" The scarlet bird's head twitched. "You're quite sure that reality and fantasy are opposites?"

"As far as I know."

"Well then if Over There is *real*, that would make Over Here *unreal*. A fantasy, as you say. Regardless, man-child, you must return to Over There immediately, and so the question is rather academic."

"I have to go back?"

"Strays must not be left to wander. 'Tis the law."

"But I followed a friend in here. I couldn't leave him behind."

"From what I've heard of your story, it sounds like this friend of yours isn't lost like you. If he's able to freely enter and leave the Porta Nectere, then he must be a Traveler, authorized by the Gatekeeper. You've no need to worry on his account."

"But…" Wataru began as the scarlet bird spread its wings and took to the air, once again trying to grab him by the back of his shirt. "Wait! I don't want to go back yet!"

Wataru ducked down and ran from the bird's clutching claws. He jumped back to the edge of the outcropping, but his left foot landed poorly on the rough surface and he felt a sudden pain stab through his ankle.

"Ouch!"

Losing his balance, he tumbled down sideways off the edge. For a moment, a blue slice of sky flashed before his eyes, then he stopped falling abruptly and fell flat on his back on another slab of rock. Apparently, another ledge below the top of the outcropping had caught him before he fell all the way down.

Well, that was lucky, at least.

Wataru placed his hand on the lip of the ledge and hauled himself up. A shadow swooped over his head. The scarlet bird was curving about for another pass.

If I don't get out of here quick I'll be back in its claws again.

He would have to move deeper under the ledge. Wataru backed up, feeling his way with his hands while keeping an eye on the skies above him. His right hand bumped into something warm and furry.

That doesn't feel like a rock…

Slowly turning to look, he found himself face-to-face with another screwwolf. Wataru ran screaming all the way to the edge of the rocky ledge. The scarlet bird's shadow approached almost immediately.

So this is what they mean when they say, "Caught between a rock and a hard place."

Wataru looked back fearfully, but the screw-wolf hadn't charged. Wataru shouted at it again, and it didn't move an inch. He looked closer and only then did he realize that he was looking at a screw-wolf's head—the body was nowhere to be seen.

It's dead?

Wataru looked around and saw more heads. Bits and pieces of skulls were caught in between the rocks here, and there, and over there. He looked down and saw bone fragments and fossilized flesh stuck to his shirt and his pants.

"What on earth?"

Wataru brushed the detritus off his arms and legs. Too late, he remembered his pursuer and, when he next looked up, claws caught at his neck, and his legs were dangling in mid-air.

"And now, it is time for you to go home," the bird scolded, sounding for all the world like a strict teacher. "Laws are to be obeyed. I'm sure they taught you that where you're from."

Wataru didn't struggle. He was more intent on getting the rest of the wolf bits off his clothing. "What is this mess?"

"Gimblewolf husks. You found a bone-pile."

"Why would someone make a collection of *that*?"

"We would. Gimblewolves are good eating, for the most part, but the heads are quite inedible," came the answer from above. "They're also a bit violent, as you know. When we catch one, we bang their heads on the rocks to kill them. It's an easy way to do it, and it gets rid of the inedible bits at the same time. Two birds with one stone, you might say."

"You eat those wolf things?"

"We do indeed. That's why we've made this desert our territory," the scarlet bird explained as it steadily beat its wings, taking them higher and higher. Wataru felt drained, as though his batteries had run down, and so he hung limply, allowing himself be carried along.

After they had flown for a while they entered the thick clouds. Soft, fluffy billowing puffs brushed against Wataru's legs and face. They had the light scent of peppermint. *Fragrant clouds?* Come to think of it, Wataru had never been in a cloud in the real world, either. Maybe they smelled like something too.

"Well, here we are," his escort said loudly, with an especially powerful flap of his wings. Wataru shot up through the clouds, and then was released, coming to a gentle landing on his rump atop a cloudbank.

Before his eyes stood a colossal silver wall. Had the bird not explained it before, he wouldn't have realized that it was the gate. It was huge, gargantuan. He felt like an ant looking up at the entranceway to a grand hotel.

"The Porta Nectere," announced the scarlet bird as he came in for a soft landing. "That streak of particularly bright white light running down the center is a sign that the gates are open. When they're closed, you can't see that light at all."

The giant gate's shape seemed to be similar to the one Wataru had come through on his way in. He didn't see any doorknobs or handles.

"The doors will open when you approach them."

Wataru hesitated and looked up at the scarlet bird. Its eyes shone bright with dazzling reflected light.

"Do I really have to go back?"

"I'm afraid so."

"Can I come back sometime? I really want to."

"You aren't coming back," the scarlet bird said harshly. "Only Travelers to whom the Gatekeeper has given permission may visit. You are a child of Over There, a man-child."

"Well, what do I have to do to become a Traveler?"

"I couldn't say."

"Who could say? The Gatekeeper?"

"Man-child, in my world, those who ask too many questions find themselves hurled off clouds."

Wataru's shoulders slumped. He wanted to cry.

Its eyes shining, the scarlet bird spoke again, this time in a gentler tone. "Do not be sad. After you return to Over There you will forget about this place before you see one sunrise and one sunset. You aren't allowed to take anything from Over Here to Over There, not even memories."

Wataru walked slowly toward the door, his head hanging. Just as the bird had said, the gates began to silently open as he approached. It was as if the gate-doors themselves were emitting light. So dazzlingly bright it was that

Wataru couldn't lift his eyes. He moved quicker now, feeling drawn to the widening crack between the two doors.

"Man-child, I wish you a good life." The bird's voice sounded very small, as if it were coming from far behind him. "My name is Gigah of the karulah. Perhaps we will meet again, in the dark of the Over There, in your dreams."

Wataru's eyes were still open, yet he couldn't see a thing. *Or maybe I'm seeing the light...pure radiance.* He didn't even know for sure if he was walking forward or backward. It felt more like he was softly floating. His consciousness faded as the light enveloped him.

Vision...the Porta Nectere...*just what are you doing here...why did you come here*...hot desert wind and Gigah's scarlet feathers...blue sky and green fields...

"Wataru! Wataru!"

Who is that calling me? Who's slapping me...my face...stop...stop!

Where am I?

Wataru opened his eyes and saw his uncle standing over him.

chapter 8
The Realities of Life

"**Wataru!** You're awake!"

"Uncle Lou…" Wataru whispered.

"Thank heavens!" his uncle said, looking as though he might cry at any moment. "Are you hurt? Are you in pain? I didn't know what to do…"

"I'm…I'm fine, really."

Wataru tried to sit up, but a hand reached out and held his shoulder down. "Best not to get up too quickly. Are you sure you're not hurt anywhere?"

It was Mr. Daimatsu. He was smiling.

"Mr. Daimatsu!" *What's he doing here?* Wataru felt lightheaded, and his voice sounded stuffy and far away in his own head. He tried blinking several times.

He found himself in an unfamiliar room. The ceiling light in the middle of the room was square, with a gold frame. It looked expensive.

"Welcome to my home," Mr. Daimatsu said. "To the guestroom, to be exact. I hope the bed's not too hard."

Uncle Lou was standing next to him, looking very distraught. "I found you lying on the ground in that building. Do you remember? I left you in there to take a phone call, and when I came back in, there you were, at the bottom of the stairs…" His uncle began to sniffle.

Mr. Daimatsu smiled and clapped his uncle on the shoulder. "Your uncle was so worried about you I feared he might faint on me too. He dragged you outside the tarps and was about to take you to the hospital when I happened along," he said over the sound of Uncle Lou's sniffling beside him. "I brought you both here."

"I didn't know what to do," Satoru said, wiping his nose, "but Mr. Daimatsu noticed you didn't look particularly pale and you seemed to be breathing normally. You appeared to have just fallen asleep. I'm afraid I was on the phone quite a long time, you see...anyway, it was his idea to bring you back here and give you a chance to wake up on your own before going to the hospital."

"Why, all I could see was a boy taking a rather peaceful nap. You were even smiling. Have any good dreams?" Mr. Daimatsu smiled.

When I was in Vision, my body must have stayed behind...asleep.

"I'm fine," Wataru said, shaking the last of the fog from his head. "Thank you, Mr. Daimatsu. I'm sorry I went into your building."

Wataru's words seemed to snap his uncle back to reality. He immediately began to apologize. "Mr. Daimatsu, I can't tell you how sorry I am that we trespassed on your property like that..."

Mr. Daimatsu laughed out loud. "Like I said, please, don't worry about it. Wataru, I heard the story from your uncle. If there's someone in that building who is threatening children—I don't care who it is—we need to take appropriate action. Don't worry, I'll do everything necessary to make sure that building stays safe." Mr. Daimatsu scratched his head with a thick-fingered hand. "We never really took it seriously when that rumor about the haunting was going around. I thought everything would be fine if we just dropped by every once in a while to check up on the place and make sure no one was getting into trouble."

"That's why he came by tonight, to check the place out," Satoru said, practically cringing with embarrassment. "Good for us. By myself, why, I had no idea what to do."

The relief on his face was evident, but something didn't quite fit. Uncle Lou was a lifeguard with years of experience. He had saved countless lives before. *So why did he get so flustered when it was me? Does that make sense?*

"If you're feeling okay, perhaps we should get going?"

Wataru nodded. Mr. Daimatsu offered to give them a lift, but his uncle politely refused. "It's not far, and I wouldn't dream of imposing any more than we already have. I'm terribly sorry about all of this."

"As you like. Wataru, I'm glad you're feeling better. And you needn't be concerned about that building any longer."

Wataru nodded again, and said he understood—although secretly he was disappointed. If Mr. Daimatsu really did intend to put proper security on the building, it would be more difficult to reach the Porta Nectere.

I have to talk to Mitsuru.

Wataru wouldn't avoid him or run away this time, and he wouldn't let Mitsuru dodge him again. Wataru wouldn't back down, not even if he was made a fool of again.

Was Mitsuru really one of the Travelers he had heard about? How did someone get accepted by the gatekeeper? And what was he doing, going between this world and the other, anyway? Wataru had no shortage of questions wanting answers.

As they left Mr. Daimatsu's and began walking down the darkened road, Satoru held Wataru's hand. It made Wataru feel uncomfortably like a little boy.

"I'm fine, really. You don't have to hold my hand."

Uncle Lou looked down at him, his face drawn. The corners of his eyes still glistened with tears.

Wataru realized he still hadn't apologized sufficiently. His uncle must've been worried sick. "I'm sorry. I am—I must have been tired. I wasn't sick. I was just sleeping, like Mr. Daimatsu said. I wonder when I fell asleep. I must've really been out cold."

His uncle nodded. "No, it's okay. I overreacted." He walked ahead, when Wataru realized something was wrong. He was walking in the opposite direction from their apartment.

"Uh, Uncle Lou, we're going the wrong direction. That's not the way home."

"You're not going home tonight."

"Huh?"

"You'll be spending the night with me in the hotel, Wataru. We'll walk to the main street and get a taxi."

Wataru followed his uncle, looking up at him. Even in the dim light of the streetlamps he could see his uncle's face twisted strangely, like he was about to burst into tears. Then, quite suddenly, he seemed unusually happy.

"That phone call, it was from your father."

He must be talking about the call that came in on his cell phone in the haunted building. "He said you could stay with me for the night."

A problem with that plan suggested itself immediately to Wataru. "But I don't have tomorrow off. I have school tomorrow."

"We'll get up early, and I'll take you there."

"But I don't have a change of clothes…"

Wataru looked down at his shirt and trousers. Suddenly, he remembered the screw-wolves. *Those bone fragments! There's still got to be some on me.*

"Uncle Lou, don't I smell? I mean, smell funny?"

Wataru began frantically brushing at his clothes. His uncle stood quietly, hand over his face. Wataru was so absorbed in what he was doing, he didn't find his uncle's expression odd until he was finished.

"Hey? What's wrong? You feeling okay?"

Uncle Lou talked through his fingers. "I can't do this. I just can't," he said.

Wataru stopped.

"I won't lie to you. And telling you this isn't my job."

"Huh?"

His uncle lifted his face and grabbed Wataru by the hand. Then he pulled him violently in the direction of his apartment. "Let's go, Wataru. It's your house too. You've a right to go home. You've a right to hear the whole story."

"Huh? Wh-what are you talking about?"

"Just come. I'm taking you home."

His uncle dragged him by the hand, walking faster than Wataru had ever seen him walk before. They were practically running.

But when they reached the apartment complex entranceway, his uncle suddenly stopped and hesitated. Steeling his resolve, he dragged Wataru to the elevator. Arriving on the correct floor, he hesitated once more. It was as though his uncle had to battle some horrible monster at every step to advance, a monster that only his uncle could see.

Wataru was scared. Suddenly, he didn't want to go home. Something dark and ominous rose in his chest. When his uncle said they would be staying at the hotel, he should've just agreed. Why did he have to worry about school, or a change of clothes?

Uncle Lou pressed the doorbell to their apartment. The sound of the chime echoed down the quiet hall. Wataru glanced at his wristwatch. It was already past midnight.

He heard slippered feet shuffling toward the door. There was a click and the door opened. The chain was drawn. Akira Mitani's face peered out from behind the door. Wataru stiffened. His father's face was pale and tired. He looked like he had aged a hundred years in a single day.

"Satoru?" he muttered, then he noticed that Wataru was with him, and his mouth tightened.

"Good, I'm glad you're still here," his uncle said in a low voice. "I brought Wataru home. Let us in."

Akira closed the door. There was the sound of him clumsily unfastening the chain, and then they were let in without a word. Ahead of them Akira turned around and went back into the living room. Wataru hadn't even been able to see his face.

The light was on in the living room, but the kitchen and the bathroom were dark. Kuniko was nowhere to be seen. The door to his parents' room was closed tightly.

"Did Mom go to bed already?" Wataru asked, but there was no answer. For the first time, he noticed that his father had taken off his necktie, but he was still wearing his suit. "Did you get home late from work, Dad?"

There was nothing on the table. The dishes were all clean and stacked. Akira didn't answer his question. Instead, he pulled out a cigarette from his breast pocket and lit it.

From behind him, Uncle Lou asked, "Where's Kuniko?" His voice sounded harsh in Wataru's ear.

"Asleep," was Akira's terse answer.

Something was wrong. Everything was wrong! They were acting like his mother was sick. They were acting like someone had died.

"Wataru," Akira said suddenly. "Come over here and sit down." He waved him over as he walked to the sofa. Stretching out a hand, he crushed his cigarette in an ashtray. It wasn't something his father would normally do.

"Akira!" Satoru said, his tone sounding almost threatening. "Your son is home. How can you..."

"Quiet," Akira said, coldly cutting him off.

"But..."

"It's your fault for bringing him here, for making me do this."

Wataru walked over to the sofa and sat. His knees knocked together. He had been so frightened just hours before, when the pack of screw-wolves attacked him in Vision. He was more frightened now.

Uncle Lou stood behind him quietly.

"I didn't want to have to tell you like this," Akira began. His voice was slightly trembling. "I would rather you heard it from your mother later. That's why I wanted you to stay with your uncle for the night."

"That's not fair," Uncle Lou said quickly. "He deserves an explanation."

"And I didn't think I could give it to him," Akira said, lifting his eyes to look at his brother. A faint smile played on his lips. "That's why I asked you."

Uncle Lou was silent.

"Listen, Wataru," Akira said, looking into his eyes. Wataru stared back at him. Deep inside, he could hear a part of him screaming in a tiny voice, *Don't tell me, I don't want to know.*

"I'm going away," Akira Mitani said slowly.

Going away.

"Your mother and I are getting a divorce. You understand what that means?"

Getting a divorce.

"I know this is a horrible thing to do to you, and your mother. But I've made my decision. It took a long time, I thought very hard, but I've made up my mind, and I'm not changing it."

A horrible thing.

"I told your mother tonight for the first time. We've been talking since then, but I think she was very surprised—it came as quite a shock to her."

Wataru opened his mouth. The voice that came out was surprisingly weak, not steady and calm as he had intended it to be. "Is Mom asleep?"

"She was when I checked on her a while ago," Akira replied. "I still have a lot of things I'll need to discuss with her: the house, you and your mother's livelihood…details, many things that need to be decided."

Wataru blinked slowly. He blinked again, and again, but nothing was different. He couldn't change the channel. This wasn't some mistake, some gross misunderstanding. It wasn't a dream. It was reality. *I'm not in Vision anymore.*

Still, the sight of his father telling him he was leaving was somehow more unreal than the screw-wolves on the imaginary desert had been.

There were so many things he needed to ask, so many things he had the right to ask, he was sure—but Wataru hadn't the slightest idea what they were. Like sand trickling through his fingers, the thoughts slid out of his mind before he could complete them. It was like a hole had been opened in the bottom of his heart and everything was draining out.

"Where will you go, Dad?" he managed to ask at last.

"I'll tell you when I'm settled in. I'll reach you by cell phone."

Akira stood. Wataru looked up at him in a daze. Was that it? Was this the end?

Akira stooped and pulled something out from behind the sofa. It was his travel bag, the familiar one he always used for business trips. Wataru had never seen it stuffed so full. The seams were bulging.

"Akira…" Satoru said, his voice hoarse. "You don't have anything else to say? Nothing else to say to your son? Is that all?"

When Akira responded, he was looking at his brother, not his son. "Anything I said to Wataru would only be an excuse."

"Still…"

"You wouldn't understand, Satoru."

Uncle Lou's face went pale. His lips were trembling. Akira lifted his travel bag. Wataru stared at it; he couldn't think of anything else to do. His father's hand clutching the bag. The light shining dully off his fingernails as he turned to walk toward the door.

"Take care of Wataru for me, Satoru," Akira said, his voice no longer trembling.

"You can't ask me to do that," Uncle Lou said stubbornly. "You can't just ask someone to take care of your life. I won't do it for you, that's for sure."

Akira Mitani quietly looked back at his son. "Take care of your mother for me, Wataru."

Then he walked, his slippers scuffing on the carpet.

Flip-flop, flip-flop.

Why am I not stopping him? Wataru thought to himself. *Why am I not running after him, grabbing him, crying for him to stay?*

Because, Wataru realized, *it's no use.* His father was not one to change his mind once it had been set. In the Mitani household, what his father said was law, writ in stone. His conclusions were decisions, and his decisions were final. No amount of weeping or pleading could hope to overturn them. That lesson had been imprinted on every cell of Wataru's body. Being selfish would get him nowhere.

Selfish? Am I being selfish?

Wataru stood from the sofa and ran to the door. Akira was putting on his shoes. His back was turned.

"Dad."

At the sound of Wataru's voice, Akira stiffened.

"Are you leaving me and Mom?"

For a moment, Akira paused. His hand clutching the shoehorn looked white.

Then he went back to putting on his shoes. He put the shoehorn back on top of the shoebox. Then, back still turned, he spoke. "Even if I divorced your mother, I'm still your father, Wataru. Nothing will change that, no matter where I go."

"But you are leaving us?" Wataru said again. *Why does my voice sound so weak? Why can't I talk louder? Why can't I say something more persuasive?* "You're leaving me and Mom."

Akira Mitani opened the door. "I'm sorry, Wataru."

And then he left.

Wataru stood there, watching the door swing shut. His mouth hung open, and his eyes were dry. His stomach ached like he had to go to the bathroom, but was holding it in.

Uncle Lou silently walked up behind him and put his hands on his shoulders. "I'm sorry." There were tears in his voice. "I guess I shouldn't have brought you home. You should've stayed with me at the hotel. I was wrong. I'm sorry, Wataru. I'm sorry."

I'm still sleeping. This is all a dream. I'm still in the haunted building, under those rickety stairs, amidst the scraps of concrete and the dust, hung over a railing, asleep. My uncle will find me and drag me out, then Mr. Daimatsu will show up, and they'll take me to Mr. Daimatsu's house.

I'm sleeping. When I wake up, everything will be like it was before.

Wataru repeated those words to himself over and over, like a spell—a spell powerful enough to defeat the most fearsome monster. A spell to drive all enemies away. A spell to make the monsters vanish.

No. You're wrong. Spells won't work. I'm not asleep. This is reality. This is happening right before my eyes.

Pain welled up from deep inside. What was that spell the wizard used, the one to turn back time? What words did he say? *I should've remembered them. I want to use them now.*

"Uncle Lou," Wataru said quietly, feeling his uncle's warmth against his back. "Did you know? Did you know Dad would be leaving tonight?"

His uncle breathed a ragged breath before answering. "Not until that phone call."

That's why he had been so frazzled, even though Wataru had only fallen asleep.

"It's terrible," his uncle muttered. "I don't believe this. I can't believe he would lay this on you."

Wataru turned silently, and fell into his uncle's arms. Hanging on to him for dear life, he cried and cried.

No matter how confused, how tired, or how sad, every night has its morning. When he opened his eyes, the morning sun shone harsh against Wataru's face.

He'd fallen asleep with his uncle in the living room. Uncle Lou, too large for the sofa, was sprawled on the floor. Wataru had curled up in one corner of the long sofa, a refugee in his own home. When he stood up, every bone in his body made an audible *crack*.

Outside the window was a clear blue sky. The rainy season must be over. There hadn't been a hint of rain yesterday, and the sky this morning was particularly clear. Not a single cloud.

Wataru looked at the clock. It was near eight already. His uncle had his back turned to the sunlight and was sleeping soundly. Even Wataru's muddled head remembered that it had only been a few hours since they fell asleep. If he didn't wake his uncle, he'd doubtlessly sleep for a few more hours.

Not a sound came from his parents' room. He wondered how his mother was doing. Was she sleeping? Was she pretending to be asleep? Did she not want to get up? Either way, Kuniko didn't know that he'd come home the night before.

For a moment he was tempted to go in and talk to her, but eventually he thought better of it. He didn't want to talk to anyone this morning. He didn't want to be seen. Quiet as a mouse, he would run off to school. He'd be late if he didn't hurry.

He washed his face, brushed his teeth, patted his hair down, and changed out of his wrinkled clothes. He had just shoved his textbooks and notebook into his schoolbag when it occurred to him that he didn't need to go to school. He could go anywhere. He didn't even have to come home.

He could go to Vision. He could forget everything.

No, I can't. He would just be caught again by one of the karulah, and that's if he was lucky. He could just as easily end up as screw-wolf food. In the end, he realized he didn't have anywhere else to go but school.

His usual morning walking buddies had already left for school. The rule was firm: miss the meeting time and get left behind. Otherwise everyone would be late. Wataru was on his own today. By the time he reached the schoolyard, he could hear the five-minute bell sounding. He ran for the front gate, just like he had the day before. Nothing had changed. Nothing was different. He had just slept in and skipped breakfast, nothing else.

Unbelievably, class that day was completely normal. Their teacher was even a little more cheerful than usual. She chatted with them about how nice it was now that the rainy season was over. The Mitani household had imploded, and nothing had changed at all. The world went on.

A while ago, somebody-or-other's *Book of Prophecies* had made the rounds at school. They even talked about it on TV. Apparently, the prophecies had originally been written on a stone tablet they found in an ancient ruin, and one of them predicted that mankind would perish in the year 2014. Among the guests appearing on the show was an expert on pyramids. He had annoyed the moderator by saying that, although it was fun to discuss these sorts of things, one shouldn't take them too seriously. Even if you thought the world was coming to an end, there was no good reason to believe this particular prophecy. That makes sense, thought Wataru at the time. He was able to go to bed that night without thinking anymore about it.

The world went on. People could be destroyed, so simply it was almost comical, but the world went on. For the time being.

When the first-period class ended, the teacher called him to her desk.

"Wataru, the principal's office just had a call from your mother. She wanted to know if you were in school or not. I told her you were sitting in class, but I wondered…" his teacher raised an eyebrow. "Is something the matter at home?"

"Mom's been sick," Wataru hurriedly explained. "She was sleeping when I left this morning, that's why."

"Oh, I see. That explains it. You came in all by yourself, then, didn't you? When classes are over, you go straight home so your mother doesn't have to worry too much."

Wataru nodded and said yes and went back to his seat. For the rest of the day, he sat in class, the words around him blowing like a breeze over the smoking husk that was Wataru Mitani's world.

By the time he left school at noon, the sun was hot enough to make him sweat. He heard a voice calling frantically. It made his ears throb it was so loud.

"Hey! Trying to give me the slip, are you? You still snoring there, sleepyhead?!"

It was Katchan. Wataru stopped. It seemed like forever since he had last seen his friend. Ten, twenty years, was it?

"Hey man, you've been totally out of it all day," said Katchan, jogging up to him. "What's up? You get your hands on a demo version of *Saga III* or something?"

"No, it's nothing."

"Huh, too bad. Hey, you should come over after lunch! My dad was out playing pachinko, and he got this soccer game as a prize. I tried it, and it's *totally* addictive. You wanna play?"

Wataru looked at his friend's smiling face in silence. He couldn't think of anything to say. All he could think of was how nice it would be if he were Katchan. *I want to be you.*

"Hey! Why are you looking at me like that? Whoa, there something on my face?" Katchan began swiping at his face with his fingers.

"No," Wataru shook his head. "Sorry, I can't play today."

Katchan noticed something was wrong. His searching eyes stopped a moment. "What is it, Wataru?"

"It's nothing, really."

"You got a cold? Stomach bug, or something? Or maybe...the plague?!"

"No, I'm fine."

Katchan stared into Wataru's face a moment. "Something's wrong, that's for sure."

"Nothing's wrong, really." Wataru smiled a thin smile.

Katchan stepped back. "Well, guess I'll be going home then."

"Okay."

"If, uh, something comes up, you give me a call, 'kay?"

"Okay."

"I'll be home the whole time."

"Right."

"Okay, bye!"

Katchan ran off, pausing occasionally to look back. Wataru resumed walking only after he lost sight of his friend. Other kids who took the same route home passed him by. He walked on slowly. Soon, he was alone, like he had been that morning.

Wataru found himself standing in front of the haunted building. It looked the same as always, blue plastic tarps shining in the afternoon sun. Mr. Daimatsu had promised to beef up security on the building, but nothing seemed different today.

Wataru thought back on what he'd experienced beyond the gate. Oddly, the details of his adventure were getting fuzzy. That big red bird—what was it called again? His memory was fading like an old photograph. It seemed flat, less vivid. What was happening?

"Wataru..."

Hearing his name being called snapped Wataru back into reality. *Who's there?*

It was Mitsuru. He was staring at him from beneath the red torii gate of the Mihashi Shrine. He waved for him to follow, and walked into the shrine grounds. Wataru was exhausted, but as soon as he saw Mitsuru, he remembered the scene by the gate.

What are you doing here?

He ran after the other boy like he had the day before. Mitsuru didn't even look back to see if he was following. "Sit," he said curtly, pointing to one of the shrine benches. Wataru did as he was told. He sat where Mitsuru had been sitting when they had first met at the shrine, days before.

From this vantage point, the shrine interior seemed somehow different. He had looked in countless times as he passed by the front gate, he had even sat right in this spot the other day, but he was sure he had never seen *this* shrine before. It was quiet here, a little world, surrounded by green. Even the old roof tiles of the main shrine, spotted by plaster filling in cracks here and there looked different. It had always seemed shabby before, but now he felt like he had come to some unknown place in a faraway land.

"Enjoying the view?" Mitsuru said, standing ahead of him, his arms crossed on his chest. "This is sacred ground."

"Sacred ground?"

"A place where the gods reside," Mitsuru said stiffly. His voice was harsh, his expression severe. Even the priest who ran the shrine never looked so serious, Wataru thought. A short and cheerful man, he always looked after the younger kids. He would emerge from the shrine every afternoon holding a yellow flag. He wanted to make sure cars would stop for the children crossing the street. He never would have talked about the gods without a generous smile.

Mitsuru looked toward the shrine, furiously silent. Just as Wataru felt like he should say something, anything to break the silence, the other boy spoke.

"So you went?"

"Went where?" Wataru asked, even though he knew the answer. Mitsuru meant that place over there, there...*what was it called again?* He couldn't remember. *Uh-oh.* He was sure that just a moment before he would have been able to remember, but for some reason his mind was drawing a blank.

Mitsuru turned and, for the first time, looked Wataru straight in the eye. "You went to Vision, right? Beyond the gate."

Wataru opened his mouth. Vision? Was that the, that place—right, the desert. Something horrible had attacked him, he remembered that much. Wait, but hadn't that been a dream?

Mitsuru stared at Wataru and took a step closer. His eyes narrowed, and the pupils became hard and focused.

"I...I went into the haunted building," Wataru said with a shudder. "I went with my uncle."

"Yes, I know. We met there." Mitsuru said. "I haven't forgotten. It *was* only yesterday."

"Yeah, but…"

Mitsuru turned his head and spat. Wataru started wondering why he always felt like a fool whenever he met this boy. Still, he heard a voice inside saying that somehow, it was his own fault. It was a little Wataru inside him, shouting as loud as he could, jumping and waving his arms, trying to get his attention, and yet still growing smaller and fainter by the moment.

And then, the second before that tiny, tiny Wataru disappeared, it shouted out one thing with all its strength.

"You will forget about this place before you see one sunrise and one sunset."

Wataru's mouth opened and the words came out, but the voice was not his own. It was a low voice that resonated with power.

Mitsuru, who had been looking off, suddenly whirled around. His eyes were wide. Wataru, flustered, still not entirely convinced the voice had come from himself, put both his hands to his mouth like a giggling schoolgirl.

"I see." The corner of Mitsuru's mouth curled upward. "So one of the ka-rulah caught you, did he."

Wataru looked up at Mitsuru. That handsome face was smiling. He seemed very pleased. He looked as though he might break into dance any moment.

"The officiants do not lie. So," he chuckled, "you're not qualified. You'll forget everything about Vision in a day." Mitsuru went on, sounding immensely pleased with himself. Wataru had no idea what he was talking about. "Your memory won't go away immediately. That would leave a suspicious blank. They allow it to linger for a day—no more. That way if kids think they've had a particularly vivid dream and tell their parents about it, it'll sound like an absurd, unbelievable story. Nothing to worry about."

He clapped his hands together, as if making a grand realization, then, looking up at the sky, Mitsuru began to laugh. Wataru stared at him, wide-eyed. *He's crazy, and I'm getting mad.*

"What do you want with me?" Wataru asked. "Why do you always make fun of me?"

Mitsuru, still chuckling, folded his arms again. He shook his head. "I never made fun of you."

"Sure you did."

"When?"

"The other day. When I asked you about the ghost picture."

"Oh, that?" Mitsuru nodded. "Well, what you were saying didn't make any sense. Sure, I gave you the benefit of the doubt. Yutaro said you weren't a dummy, but when I talked to you, well, you seemed a little childish. It was funny."

"Then again," he added, "Yutaro's a bit childish himself."

Something about that made the bile rise in Wataru's throat. He stood up from the bench. "Yutaro's a good guy!"

Mitsuru was still smiling. "Who said he wasn't?"

"You just said he was childish!"

"Well, it's true. Being childish isn't bad, you know. Why, if it was, kindergartens would be the most evil places around!"

"Now you're being ridiculous."

"Oh? Is that what mommy and daddy say when they scold you?"

"Mommy" and "daddy" were the last words Wataru wanted to hear that day. Mitsuru's way of saying them only made it worse.

"What do you know about my parents?" Wataru flew at Mitsuru. He swung a fist with all his strength and hit only air. The momentum sent him sprawling to the ground.

Mitsuru stood with the tips of his sneakers directly in front of Wataru's face. From this angle, Wataru could see how scruffy the shoes were. For a moment he wondered why this otherwise perfect guy chose to wear such cruddy old sneakers. But now was hardly the time to ask.

Something had caught him in the stomach, and he couldn't stand. He managed to lift his head and look up at his adversary. Mitsuru was no longer smiling.

"Stay out of my way. You annoy me."

Then, in his calm voice from before, "I don't have time to hang out with happy-go-lucky kids."

Happy-go-lucky? Who's happy-go-lucky? Who's a kid?

If Wataru hadn't heard him say that, it probably would have ended there. Mitsuru wasn't his friend, like Katchan. He wasn't a good guy, like Yutaro. Why should he tell him anything?

But now, he had to. He lifted his face, grimy with the dirt of the temple grounds, and spat, "That's *my* line. *I'm* not happy-go-lucky enough to hang out with a happy-go-lucky kid like *you*."

Mitsuru raised his eyebrows exaggeratedly. "Oh? That's a surprise."

"Shut up!" Wataru put his hands on the ground and somehow managed to sit up. The side of his mouth tingled as though it had been cut. "You talk all cool, and look all cool, but you don't know a *thing*. You don't know…you know nothing about me. My dad left us last night, okay? So I'm not—I'm not what you—happy-go-lucky—I'm not a kid. Okay?"

Wataru's fatigue and overwhelming sense of defeat caught the words in his throat.

"Left?" Mitsuru asked, calm as ever. "You mean he divorced your mom?"

"Yeah. What else does it mean?"

"So what?"

The words hit Wataru like a pile driver.

"Wha…"

"I said so what. It's only a divorce."

I don't believe it.

"He left me and my mom, he left us!"

"And? You think being all sad and crying like that is going to help you find someone else to pick up the pieces?" Mitsuru scoffed. "Well, come to think of it, it might be one strategy."

Wataru was speechless.

"In fact," the boy continued in a conversational tone, "It might be a fitting strategy for you and your mom. People will sympathize. Yeah, they'll come running in flocks. You'll get so much sympathy, you won't know what to do with it all. But you won't get any from me."

Wataru merely sat, dumbfounded. He had nothing to say, no ready retort.

Mitsuru looked at him for a moment, then looked aside, and glared at the ground. "Stay away from the building next door. It sounds like you've got enough on your hands. Just worry about that for a while. I live near here, so I'll know if you're hanging around. Got it?"

Even after Mitsuru left, Wataru lingered at the shrine. It felt like some thing was sitting atop his shoulders, weighing him down so that he couldn't stand. *Maybe it's a huge pile of trash.* Debris from a world destroyed. Even when the whole world comes apart, somebody has to clean it up. Someone has to call the waste management company, get them to send out a truck. Somehow, he felt that no one would take on this particular job.

"Hey, you there," an old man called out. Wataru glanced over to see the shrine priest approaching. He was wearing the same outfit he always wore at the annual shrine New Year's celebration: a white kimono with a light green *hakama* skirt. His hair was white. "What's the matter? Did you fall?"

Wataru was covered in dirt.

"You're bleeding! Are you on your way home from school? Did you get into a fight?"

The priest came over and kneeled down next to him. "Are you alone?" he asked. Looking at the nameplate on his school bag, the priest continued, "Mitani? Eh... Wataru Mitani?"

"Yes, that's me," said Wataru. "Say, can I ask you a question?"

"Yes?"

"This is a shrine, right?"

"Of course."

"There are gods at a shrine, right?"

"Yes."

"You pray to the gods, right?"

"I pray and I honor them, yes."

"What do the gods do when you pray?"

The priest gave him a curious look.

"Why do you want to know?"

"I just do," Wataru said roughly. "Because, the way I see it the gods are lazy."

The priest seemed at a loss for words.

Wataru spit. His knee was hurting, but he didn't care anymore. "How can someone who hasn't done anything wrong be so unlucky? The gods must be lazy. They don't care. Why pray to gods like that?"

Standing, Wataru picked up his bag and ran. The priest of Mihashi Shrine looked after him, a worried expression on his face. Wataru never saw it. He never looked back.

When he got home, Kuniko was there waiting for him. As soon as he walked through the front door she began to cry. This was real. It wasn't a dream. He wouldn't wake up. It wouldn't go away. He saw his mother's tears, and everything was painfully clear. Wataru would never cry again. He turned to stone—a little stone in the shape of a boy.

chapter 9
Enter the Tank

On Sunday, Grandma came up from Chiba.

She didn't ring the doorbell, but instead kicked loudly at the door with her foot.

"Wataru!" she shouted. "I'm so sorry! It must have been a horrible shock for you when your father did what he did. But I'm here now, so everything is going to be all right. Don't you worry about a thing. Is Kuniko here?" she asked, the words coming in a rush as she let herself in and took off her shoes. When Wataru's mother stuck her head in from the living room, she received another shout. "Kuniko!"

"What in the world is going on? My heart nearly stopped when I heard the news. Where is my fool of a son? I'll find him and pick him up by the neck and drag him back kicking and screaming if I have to. Tell me where he's gone."

"Mrs. Mitani..." Kuniko breathed, her shoulders slumping, looking more moved than happy. "Thanks for coming."

Kuniko stepped forward and took the bags from her mother-in-law. Wataru noticed that his grandmother's face was bright red, and blue veins were standing out by her temples. She was in full-tilt anger mode.

"Here I was thinking that Akira had finally decided to settle down and become a decent person for a change, and there he goes again. Only now do I realize how remiss I was in raising my sons. One a vagrant over forty and still not married, and the other an incorrigible womanizer!"

"Um...Mrs. Mitani," Kuniko said, with a look at Wataru. Wataru was standing with his eyes opened wide, looking at his grandmother.

"Of course, it's not the kind of talk for a child's ears to be hearing," his grandma said in a loud voice, "but, Kuniko, you have to understand…"

"Thanks, Mrs. Mitani." Kuniko turned to Wataru. "Wataru, why don't you go get breakfast at McDonald's. You could invite Katsumi, if you like."

Wataru headed out the door, a crisp ¥1,000 bill in his hand. His head was spinning. It felt like a tornado had come through their house, leaving it in shambles, and while they were standing there, just starting to wonder how they were going to pick up the pieces, a tank had come crashing through their door.

Wataru went down the stairs outside their apartment, and saw his uncle running up from the parking lot. Wataru called to him from the landing and his uncle stopped and waved—panting to catch his breath. "I came with your grandmother, but she got out of the car while I was looking for a space to park. I had to run to catch up with her!"

Wataru sat down with Satoru on a bench in front of the apartment complex. His uncle was dripping with sweat. He looked pale.

"After you went to school yesterday, I went home. When I told your grandmother what had happened, she demanded to leave for Tokyo immediately. We had to find someone at the last minute to watch the shop, and we left this morning before the sun came up."

"You look exhausted, Uncle Lou."

"You think? You don't look so well yourself, Wataru."

Uncle Lou wiped his face with a handkerchief, and finally relaxed. "You okay?"

"I don't know."

"I don't blame you. Doesn't make any sense. I would be surprised if you told me you were okay."

"Say," Wataru said looking up. "Grandma called Dad a womanizer. What does that mean?"

Uncle Lou looked like he had swallowed something bitter. "There she goes, blabbing about things she shouldn't be talking about."

"Is Dad with another woman?"

Satoru scrunched his handkerchief into a ball, and wiped his nose again. "Do you even know what that means?"

"I think I do."

"You sure?"

"I've watched Mom's soap operas."

"Hmm. I guess you would have. Of course, that's about all they do on television."

His uncle crossed his thick arms. Wataru did the same.

"Did you talk with your mother yet? What did she say?"

"She said she had a fight with Dad. And then she told me he was leaving for a while to get his head screwed on tight. There was no need to worry, she said. He would be home to patch things up soon."

"So, she didn't say anything about a divorce?"

"No. Nothing."

"You didn't tell her that we talked to your dad on Friday night when I brought you home?"

"I did…but I didn't tell her Dad said anything about a divorce." *Because I couldn't say it.* "Because I thought it would make her feel sad."

"Why's that, Wataru?"

"Because…it doesn't sound like he's thinking about changing his mind at all. But Mom thinks he might come back. For sure."

Uncle Lou nodded. "That's probably true. And that's all she said—that she and your dad were just fighting?"

It was all so sudden, she had howled, wringing her frizzled hair.

"Akira has always been that way. He keeps what he thinks to himself, and only says the bare minimum. It drives me crazy. Even the most important things he decides all by himself."

It was unusual for Wataru's uncle to call his brother by his first name. When talking to Wataru, he always used "your father." Wataru's mom was the same way. Always "your father," never his name. Wataru had the impression that, when you grew up, that's the way the world worked. Everyone called each other by their role, never by their name.

For adults, responsibilities and roles were more important than who they were. That was why Wataru did not want to grow up. It was so much easier being a kid. Free.

"So, about your question," Uncle Lou asked, looking at Wataru's eyes. "What would you do if your dad loved another woman?"

"What do you mean 'if'? Isn't that why Grandma's so mad?"

"Yeah."

"Does Dad want to marry her?"

"Get married?? Isn't once enough?"

"Say, why aren't you married? I've always wondered about that."

Uncle Lou's eyes went wide. "What does that have to do with anything?"

Everything, thought Wataru. What was marriage? Why did grown-ups get married? Why did they want to get married again, when they had already been married before? What made them want to do that?

"Well, for one thing, I'm not very good with the ladies."

"Really? But there are lots of people uglier than you that get married…"

His uncle smiled wryly. "You don't go easy on a guy, do you?"

Then, as an afterthought, he said, "I think it's because I'm probably a coward."

"A coward? Does that mean you're scared?"

"That's what it means."

"But that can't be true. You're brave. You've even saved so many people's lives."

"That's a different kind of bravery. Totally different."

Then he rapped Wataru on the head with his knuckles. "I'm just afraid that, if I got married, something like this would happen. That's what scares me. That's why I'm not married."

"'Something like this'?"

"I mean this—what's happening right now." He lifted his hands in a big sweeping motion. "Please don't make me explain it."

"You mean like someone else?"

"Yeah…but, Wataru, that's not the only reason why some marriages fail. That's not the only thing your mother and father have done wrong."

"Really?"

Wataru asked a question that had been lingering in the back of his head ever since his father had walked out.

"Then, it has something to do with me too?"

Satoru stiffened noticeably.

"Maybe I wasn't a good enough kid, maybe that's why my dad left."

Uncle Lou began rubbing his hands furiously through his hair. "Why is it always this way? I dig my own grave every time. I always say the wrong thing.

Man, I'm so dumb." He sounded as if he were on the verge of tears.

"Uncle Lou…"

"You haven't done anything wrong, Wataru. Not a single thing. Your father's the one who's wrong here. Saying what he likes, walking out on you. The way he tried to leave was cowardly too. Trying to sneak away while you were out with me."

If I'm not bad, that means Dad is the bad one. He's the coward. If I'm not bad, and my dad's not bad, I guess that would make Mom the bad one. If neither of us is bad, then the one who's bad is…the one who's bad is…

"Damn it! Who is this woman, anyway?" Uncle Lou spat, trying to get the taste of frustration out of his mouth. "I'd like to see her face. Then I'd like to hit it, really hard."

I know. She's the bad one. The other woman.

As they sat there in a daze, Wataru's grandmother came hustling over from the elevator lobby. His mother was right behind her.

"Mrs. Mitani, please, wait!"

She was running and shouting at the top of her lungs. Wataru's grandmother didn't stop. Her round little body ran so fast it was like she was rolling. "Satoru! What are you doing just sitting there? Come on! Get the car! We're leaving."

Uncle Lou stood up.

"Leaving? Where?"

"As if you didn't know! We're going to talk to that fool, Akira. I'm going to dump a bucket of water over his head, and bring him home."

"I'd love to see you do that, but that won't change a thing. We have to reason with him calmly."

Grandma roared, spitting fire from her mouth. "'Reason'? I'll show you reason! Chasing other women, leaving his wife—LEAVING HIS CHILD. That's no son of mine!"

"Mrs. Mitani…" Kuniko knelt before her mother-in-law. "The whole neighborhood can hear you. Please, be quiet."

Grandma got even madder—and louder. "Who cares what they hear? This is no time to be worried about appearances. You've always been that way, Kuniko. What do you care about privacy or propriety now? Do you even understand that you've been dumped? Can you just stand there and let some strange woman drag your husband into her bed!"

"Mom!" Uncle Lou shouted. Stars flashed before Wataru's eyes.

Chasing other women—dragged into her bed?

"Don't speak that way to your mother!" Grandma was unstoppable. "Look at you, you're as big as they come, and every pound of flesh on your bones is completely useless. Why didn't you stop him when he was leaving?"

Some people stuck their heads out over the veranda to get a better view of the unfolding family drama. His mother was crouched on the ground, holding her head in her hands. She was crying.

"Mom, drop it for now, okay?"

Uncle Lou grabbed his mother's shoulders firmly, but when he saw the look in her eyes, he released her from his grip.

"No good will come from hashing this out here in public." Uncle Lou's voice was kind. "Think of Kuniko and Wataru. We'll go back to the hotel for now."

"I'm going to get Akira," Grandma said stubbornly.

"I'll make sure that happens. Trust me, okay?"

chapter 10
Falling

Eventually, Satoru managed to calm his mother down and get her back in the car. As they drove off, Grandma was still vowing that she wouldn't go home without talking to Akira. Her massive traveling bag sat heavy in the back seat, a testament to her determination.

Wataru and Kuniko went back inside under a pall of silence. As Wataru headed off to his own room, Kuniko called out to him.

"Can we talk?"

She looked horribly tired. Her cheeks were ashen, her hair a tangled mess from when she had wrung it between her hands down in the garden. It was difficult for Wataru to look her in the face.

Mom's sick, that's it. Mom's terribly ill. We should call a doctor.

"I'm sorry," she said at last in a tiny voice. "I'm sorry you had to go through this."

Wataru sighed quietly, his eyes cast down to the floor. They were sitting in their usual dining room chairs, only Akira's chair was empty. It never would have occurred to them to sit there, though there was no danger of its regular occupant suddenly walking in.

This scene, the two of them sitting where they were sitting, right now, at the table, was utterly normal. It was Sunday. Akira had gone out golfing, or maybe he was on a business trip. Nothing was different. Wataru wondered if the day would come when he, or maybe his mom, or someone else entirely, would sit in Akira's chair without a second thought.

"Don't apologize. It wasn't either of our faults. That's what Uncle Lou said," Wataru muttered. "It's Dad's fault, he was the bad one. He and the woman he's with now."

Kuniko sat with her head hung low, wrinkles showing on her forehead. "The woman…"

"He's right, isn't he?"

Kuniko looked up with a wan smile. "I suppose you heard what your grandmother was saying down in the garden. There's no point in trying to hide anything from you now."

No, there's not.

"Wataru, do you know what that means?"

"I think so." Wataru recalled what his uncle had said about that sort of thing happening on television all the time. He said so.

"Soap operas…" Kuniko said with a sigh. "You're right. I used to think this sort of thing happened only on television. Those advice columns, and those radio call-in shows, I thought they were all fake. I never thought…" her voice trailed off. She was talking half to herself. "Those sort of things happen to other people. People who didn't run a good family, people who were lazy, who got into trouble. Not…not us." She shook her head. "Maybe I was too proud, and this is my punishment."

Wataru knew he should say something. *You're wrong. That isn't it at all.* But he said nothing. *Because I feel the same way!*

He only had more questions. "What do we do now? How do we get Dad to come home?"

"I don't know," Kuniko answered quickly, the words coming out in a jumble. For a second, Wataru saw his mother differently. She was more than his mother and more than his father's wife. She was a complete person, someone he had, until this moment, never seen before.

And then it was gone.

"No, Wataru, you shouldn't think about this. It isn't your problem to worry about. It's like your uncle Satoru said, you haven't done anything wrong. This problem is between me and your father."

Wataru's logical brain—inherited from his father, no less—immediately began clicking, constructing a counterargument. Sure, if it was a problem between "Akira" and "Kuniko," then it may very well have nothing to do with "Wataru." But what if it was a problem between his "mother" and his "father"? Then it didn't make sense to leave him out of the equation.

So *who are you? Kuniko and Akira, or my father and my mother?*
What good would asking do anyway?

"Dad told me that even if he—even if he divorced you, he would still be my dad."

"He said that when you came back on Friday night with Uncle Lou?"

"Yeah."

"Your father told you that, did he?" said Kuniko, her eyes filling with tears. "Why didn't you tell me sooner? You only said he told you that he would be leaving and wouldn't come back for a while."

Wataru had lied to her, he remembered. "I'm sorry."

"It's not something you need to apologize for," Kuniko said with her elbows resting on the table and her hands covering her face. "Why should you have to apologize? That's terrible. I..."

She slumped onto the table, and started crying. Wataru whispered that he was sorry. Everything he saw went blurry. He rubbed his eyes again and again but the blurriness didn't go away.

"No, Wataru, I'm sorry," Kuniko said between sobs, her head still down on the table. "The terrible one is your father. Can you believe it? He says that even if he leaves he's still your father—and what are you supposed to say to that? Nothing, that's what. You had to just swallow it all up inside. And then he walks out."

Uncle Lou's voice rang in Wataru's head. Akira had always been that way, keeping his thoughts to himself, voicing only his conclusions. Wataru knew this about his father. Logical thought led to rational decisions, and those, once made, were final. No amount of arguing could dissuade him once he had set upon a course of action.

Rational decisions. For Akira Mitani, the rational decision had been to leave, to abandon his wife and son, so that's what he had done. But how had he come to that decision? What path did his reasoning take? How could Wataru be sure his father hadn't made a mistake, an error in his calculations?

Because Dad never gets anything wrong, never makes a mistake. Until now. This was the exception, it had to be. Somebody had to tell his father that. Somebody had to check his math.

"What did he say to you, Mom?"

Kuniko lifted her head at the question and shook her head. Tears trickled from her eyes. "I don't think you need to know that."

"I want to know," Wataru said, his heart rising in his throat. Kuniko looked at him through teary eyes and smiled a smile so bitter she seemed to be in pain. "Such a good kid."

"Mom..."

"No. No, you don't need to worry about a thing anymore. I'm fine!" Kuniko nodded exaggeratedly. "I'll do it. I'll speak with your father; reason with him. Then, he'll come home. Look, Wataru, why don't you just think of this as an extended business trip? That's really what it is. He had some difficult work to do, and he has to devote his time to it for now. A business trip. Right?"

And what was he supposed to say to this? Nothing—just like it had been with his father. Maybe that was the way it had to be.

"That's right," Kuniko declared. "You're such a good kid, how could *you* lose your father? You can't, of course, and I'll make sure of it."

After that day, his mother didn't bring up the subject again. She met with Grandma in Chiba and Uncle Lou, talked in a hushed voice for long hours on the phone, and called her own parents in Odawara. Oddly, Wataru never knew what was happening, or what she was talking about.

Dad's on a business trip. That's all. A lie, he knew, but he tried to believe it all the same.

When it grew inside him until the pain was too much to bear in silence, he went to Uncle Lou. His uncle changed the minute he brought the topic up.

"What has your mother told you? You listen to what she says, and just, er, live life. Normally."

Huh? Normally?

"Hey," Uncle Lou beamed. "Less than two weeks until summer vacation. You're coming out here in August, right? You'd better, cause I'll be waiting. And finish your summer homework too!"

Wataru's mother had told Uncle Lou not to say anything; that much was clear. He pressed harder.

"What about Grandma? Did she talk to Dad like she said she would?"

"She's getting busier at the store, what with summer coming and all. Don't you worry about that, okay?"

"What do you mean, don't worry?! It's my life!" he shouted.

His uncle's voice got suddenly quieter. "Look, don't give me a hard time about it, Wataru."

"I don't mean to give you a hard time, it's just…"

"You're still a kid! You can't walk around with these adult problems on your shoulders. You haven't done anything wrong, so you don't have to do anything now. Your mother asked me to tell you that there's nothing to worry about. So please, don't worry. For me?"

Something's wrong. Uncle Lou's not usually like this. Why is he siding with Mom and not me?

There was only one thing left to do, and that was to talk to his father directly.

I can't. Not without telling Mom. I shouldn't.

But what was his mother telling him? What was she doing that wasn't hidden from his eyes—in words he couldn't hear? She was trying to clean things up all by herself. It wasn't fair.

I'll do what I think is right. I'll make my own rational decision.

June slid into July, the depressingly overcast days of the rainy season became scarcer, and the sun shone hotter. The bespectacled weather reporter on TV pointed at his weather map and warned about heavy sudden thunderstorms and rapidly fluctuating temperatures. *Careful you don't catch cold!*

Before Wataru realized it, summer vacation was upon him. It was everywhere in the air. Even at cram school, the excitement was palpable. It was like he could hear a whispered countdown in the air:

Five.

Four.

Three.

Two.

One.

Vacation!

In reality, the cram school held classes even during summer vacation—actually, they held them *because* it was vacation—and if you were to attend them all, you wouldn't have much of a vacation left. Still, having some schoolwork to do and having to actually go to school were two separate things entirely.

The former always seemed much brighter and full of hope than the latter.

He sat in his usual chair, but his mind was far, far away. From the outside he figured he looked much the same as always. No one had said anything about him seeming down, or not himself. They didn't get many tests this time of year, so there were no bad marks to raise his teachers' suspicions either.

Of course, there was no fooling Katchan.

"Hey Wataru, why do you always look so angry lately?"

Exactly a week had passed since the Sunday when Grandma Tank rolled into town and blew his world to smithereens. Wataru was over at Katchan's house, playing in his room. It was a small room, with a big dresser, and laundry hanging outside the window. There was a ton of it, flapping in the breeze.

Wataru looked away from the video game and peered at Katchan. His friend sat with a large mug of soda in one hand, his eyebrows raised in an exasperated look.

Wataru's mug sat untouched atop a serving tray, sweating in the summer humidity. The mugs were the same exact ones they used for beer and mixed drinks down in the bar. Compared to a regular soda glass, they were huge. If he drank the whole thing he'd be burping the rest of the day.

True to form, Katchan had already downed half of his, and when he opened his mouth to say something more, a loud belch erupted.

Wataru cracked up, and Katchan joined him. Wataru dropped his game controller on the floor, laughing while his computer-generated opponent proceeded to dice up his character.

Katchan suddenly straightened up. "It's like you're wearing this angry face all the time." Wataru was silently surprised. He had no idea it was so obvious.

For the past week, Wataru had been trying to contact his father every way he could think. He just wanted to talk to him once, just once. But it was proving difficult. It was as if Akira had flown to the moon. What Wataru thought would be so simple was turning out to be so difficult.

His dad had a cell phone, he knew, but Wataru didn't know the number. There had never been a need until now. That Friday night, travel bag bulging, his father had told him to call him on his cell phone, but how could he do that, if he didn't know the number?

There was no use asking his mother. Kuniko wouldn't tell him. Since their talk she had been trying her best to cram Wataru into a box labeled "father on a business trip"—for his own good—and she was desperate not to let him think anything else.

Hoping it might be written down somewhere in the house, Wataru had leafed madly through address books and phone books. He could find it nowhere. He wondered if it was programmed into their telephone at home, and one night when Kuniko wasn't looking, he pulled out the operating manual. There was nothing. *Maybe she knew I would look, and erased it?* It was more than probable.

His next target was Akira's company. But, as Wataru realized with some embarrassment, though he knew the name of the company where his father worked, he knew practically nothing else. He didn't know if his father worked at the main office, some branch office, or even at some subsidiary.

He tried calling the main office's service centers as listed in the phone book, going from the first to the last. That's when he encountered a new problem. At a big company such as the one where his father worked, you could call a number from the telephone book (or from directory assistance), and ask for Akira Mitani—and even if he worked there, they wouldn't just connect you. They always asked for a division or department name, if you were family, or a client, and what your business was. If he couldn't answer their questions they would probably tell him to stop making crank calls, or ask to speak with his mother. He'd be worse off than if he had never picked up the phone.

I'm really Akira Mitani's son, I just want to talk to my dad.

Speaking slowly, Wataru told Katchan everything that had happened from start to finish. The whole time he spoke he didn't tear up once, nor did he get excited. He was calm. Or maybe just exhausted.

Katchan's round eyes went even wider. He listened without saying a word. When Wataru had finished talking and reached out for his mug, he looked up to see Katchan staring at him with his mouth hanging wide open.

"Whoa."

Wataru wasn't sure why, but suddenly, convulsively, he laughed like a madman. "Pretty out there, isn't it?"

Katchan nodded vigorously. "I only know like one other person whose parents got divorced, and that was a long time ago!"

"Me too. Hey, but aren't Yutaro's parents divorced? And I think there's another kid in cram school whose parents got divorced."

"Maybe we're thinking of the same person? Tanaka, that guy in Class Two?"

"No, no, it's a girl, Satoko-something. She doesn't go to Joto."

"I know one kid whose parents died in a car crash," Katchan said solemnly. "I never thought it would happen to someone I knew! I mean, uh, it's not like he died or something, but still!"

Wataru felt the exact same way.

"So why do you want to talk to your old man now?"

"If I don't, how will I know what happened? I don't like this not knowing what went wrong. It ticks me off."

"Yeah, I hear that."

Katchan peered into his empty glass and belched again. This time he didn't smile. "Shouldn't you just leave it up to your grandma? Sounds like she's pretty hardcore about fixing him."

"You think my dad will come home if I do?"

"Sure. Married people are always gettin' into fights and then gettin' back together."

"Who'd you hear that from?"

"Oh, they talk about it at the bar all the time. My dad and mom, they're great at ironing out those marital disputes. Lots of people come to them for advice."

"You mean customers talk about their private lives like that? At the bar."

"You bet."

"Wait, so, even if my dad has this woman on the side, you think I should just wait it out and he'll come back? You can't guarantee that!"

No one could. Katchan chewed his lower lip in thoughtful silence.

"I just don't want to leave it like this," Wataru said at last. "There has to be something I can do."

"You're bright, Wataru. That's why you don't like it when people do dumb things," Katchan said. "If all you need to do is call him, I might be able to help you out."

It took Wataru a few seconds to process what his friend had said. "Seriously?"

"Yeah, seriously. His number's in the call list."

"The call list? What's that?"

Last year their neighborhood held a fire prevention day, with all the local community boards participating. Katchan's dad had been one of the committee members.

"See, we gathered a list of emergency contact numbers for everybody in the town. Your dad wasn't on the committee or nothing, but he was like this emergency contact for when there's an earthquake or fire or something like that, so his name, his company, the address, and the phone number are all on that list. I remember seein' it there."

Wataru grabbed him by the shoulders. "Show me!"

Katchan raced to get the book. It was a sheaf of stapled photocopied pages, with a simple piece of colored paper as a front page. The numbers were there, as promised.

"Akira Mitani...got it!"

The book listed both the name of his division and the direct phone line.

"Can I borrow your phone?"

"Sure, but you won't get him today. It's Sunday. Companies are closed."

Oh, right.

"Come over after school tomorrow. I'll call for you."

"You'll call?"

"Yeah. I'll pretend I work at a shop, and that a Mr. Mitani left something, and get them to the phone. I do that kind of thing all the time. You gotta throw 'em a bit of a curve ball, or they'll just ask to talk to your mom."

"Good thinking, Katchan."

Katchan grinned. "Hey, you share your homework assignments with me and all, but this kind of stuff is my specialty," he said with evident pride. "Also, what if you said you were a Mitani calling, and he didn't even answer the phone?" Katchan looked at Wataru's face and his smile faded. "Sorry. Got a little carried away."

Wataru shook his head. "No, it's okay. It's like you say—I mean, Dad tried to leave when I was out of the house." The likelihood that he would try avoiding any sort of direct contact with Wataru was high. Wataru looked back at his friend. "Let's play a game or something."

Katchan slowly picked up the game controller. The mood was still dark. Wataru's mouth twitched, but he couldn't think of anything to say.

"Come to think of it," Katchan said, a little too loudly, "You go to cram school with that Mitsuru kid, right? Did you hear what they were saying?"

Wataru picked up the change in topic with relief. "What about him? He take another ghost picture or something?"

"Heheh. You haven't heard!"

It turned out he didn't grow up in America at all.

"The story goes that his uncle or something works at a computer company, and got transferred to some place in America—some place no one had ever heard of. Nothing famous like New York."

All Mitsuru had done was visit his uncle for a year before transferring to their school. He was born and raised in Kawasaki.

"No way!"

"But he speaks English pretty good, doesn't he?"

"Yeah. It wouldn't take long in America to get better than us, that's for sure."

Knowing Mitsuru, he hadn't been the one to start the rumor about him growing up in the States—in fact, he was most likely the one who had set the record straight. That the truth had come out now was more a testament to how well Mitsuru was getting along with his classmates. The less people knew about someone, the bigger the rumors tended to get.

Something occurred to Wataru. "I wonder why he was living with his uncle for so long? Maybe something was going on with *his* family?" Given his current circumstances, it seemed like a rational thing to think. Maybe that was the reason Mitsuru was so *odd*. And why he could be scary sometimes...

"So you don't hang with Mitsuru much?"

"Not at all," Wataru said quickly. "We talked a few times, but...he's weird. Kind of stuck up."

The conversation at the shrine—he remembered having talked to Mitsuru at length, but for some odd reason he couldn't remember a single detail of what they had said.

Memories of Vision had disappeared from Wataru's mind. The wizard, the door, Mitsuru running—he had completely forgotten the dire warnings to stay away from the haunted building. He had even forgotten about Mitsuru's threats. In fact, his interest in Mitsuru had waned considerably.

"Maybe he's got issues," Katchan said, gripping the controller. "I hear no one's ever been over to his house to play or anything."

Wataru picked up the second player controller. "Maybe he's not as popular as we thought?"

"He gets along with Yutaro fine. But I don't think *he's* been over to his house, either."

"Where do you hear all this from, Katchan?"

"Sakuma told me. He's in with the girls in class."

"Running-mouth Sakuma? Biggest yapper in school?"

"He wanted to get in with Mitsuru real bad when he first came to school, but Mitsuru wouldn't give him the time of day, so he lurked in the new kid's shadow and listened. You know, like a private eye."

"More like a stalker."

"I wonder what's up with Kenji's gang? Think they're still after that ghost picture? Remember when they surrounded Mitsuru in the library?"

Wataru's memory shuffled briefly, and the scene in the library on that rainy day came into focus. Those eyes fixing on Wataru through the window.

How did he get Kenji and his goons to back off, anyway?

Questions began to bubble up in Wataru's mind like boiling water on the stove—questions he hadn't even thought about asking until now, victims of that strange gap in his memory.

Wataru hadn't noticed anything was missing. The grim reality of his life had risen like a shroud over his brain. When he wasn't looking his memories had begun to slip away.

Vision was getting further away.

"Guess what? I can do the midair combo off the crimson lotus tri-kick now! Wanna see?" Katchan grinned.

"Of course I want to see! Are you kidding?"

"I kid you not, my friend. Check it out!"

The sun set while they played.

Wataru went straight to Katchan's house after classes let out the following day. Katchan's parents were busy getting the bar ready for the evening, and the phone on the second floor was available.

Katchan's number worked like he said it would. When he called, Akira was at his desk. The call went right through.

Wataru took the offered receiver and put it to his ear, hearing nothing but the steady thud of his own heart that seemed to have moved up into his ear.

"Dad?"

Akira Mitani, expecting a phone call about a lost article from some loud bar, paused. Wataru listened intently to the silence.

"It's me. Wataru."

No answer.

"I-I'm sorry to call you at work. I didn't know your cell phone number, and Mom wouldn't tell me. I just...I just wanted to talk to you."

Katchan is staring at me. He's tugging at his ear, nervous, like he knows he shouldn't be watching but he can't help it. He's worried.

"Dad..."

"This...isn't the best place for me to talk."

"What should I do?"

There was a pause. The office where Akira worked must be very quiet. Wataru couldn't hear a sound.

"You don't have anything at school this Saturday, do you?"

"Nope."

"Then how about we meet, just you and me?"

Wataru's heart lurched back into motion, blood surging through tingling limbs with dizzying speed.

"Okay."

"Someplace close by is good. Remember that city library we went to, what was it, last year?"

The library was about an eight-minute bus ride away from home. Wataru's home.

"Yeah."

"How about there, in front of the checkout counter? Noon."

"Exactly noon? You mean, like twelve o'clock? Okay, that should be fine."

Akira told him his cell phone number. Wataru hastily copied it down and memorized it. It was like he had received the secret number to a padlocked cage. *But what's inside?*

"Wataru..."

"Yeah, what?"

"I don't want you to be angry with me, but, when we meet, I'd like it to be just the two of us. You see…"

"No problem," Wataru cut him off. "I won't tell Mom. I wanted to talk to you alone too."

Akira said goodbye. Wataru thanked him, and held the phone to his ear until he heard the click.

"So you gonna meet him?" Katchan asked, leaning forward.

"Yeah, on Saturday."

Wataru's voice sounded strained and thin. For the first time, he realized he was on the verge of crying.

"Alone? What about your mom?"

"It's just me this time. I promised."

"Whoa," Katchan said seriously. "I guess that's how it's got to go down. But hey, great! You two can talk all you want, and you can get him to answer all your questions. Who knows, sounds like it'll probably be good."

"Thanks, Katchan."

"Not at all, man." Katchan grinned. "You just come to me when you need to make things happen. *Chop chop.*"

Wataru was on pins and needles the whole week. Every day things flustered him to the point that his mother started asking him what was wrong, and of course he had no answer. He had even begun to worry that he might say something in his sleep and blow the whole thing.

On Saturday morning, he woke up at five o'clock. Later, when he went out, he told his mother that he was going to the library. Kuniko, not suspecting a thing, gave him ¥500 for the bus trip and some lunch. The bright morning sun shone harshly on her face as she waved goodbye. She looked older than Wataru had ever seen her before.

A washed and wrinkled curtain hung out to dry.

He arrived a full two hours early, so he walked through the open stacks, picking up books on a whim and leafing through the pages. Nothing he read stuck for longer than a passing moment; the rows of text flowed in and out of his head like water from a faucet.

Akira arrived right on time. On this day he was wearing a dark green polo shirt and white pants. His sneakers were sparkling-white new. Wataru had never seen any of these clothes before. He saw too that his father was wearing rimless glasses with small lenses. Wataru knew he was a bit nearsighted, but he'd never seen him wearing designer glasses before.

They looked good on him.

"What, you're already here? Hope I didn't keep you waiting."

He seemed relaxed, quiet, no different from the father Wataru had always known. Gone without a trace were the poorly shaven face, the husky voice, the slumped shoulders of the night he had left.

It was amazing that it had already been two weeks since then. Wataru looked up at him, trying to put his thoughts into words and failing miserably.

His father had lost weight, though not as much as his mom. But he didn't look—Wataru wasn't sure if this was the exact word—quite so *stretched* out. Rather, he looked like someone who, as Grandma was fond of saying, had taken a swig from the fountain of youth.

That's ridiculous.

It was almost an insult to imagine that leaving home had somehow put a spring in his father's step. *An insult to whom? To me. And Mom.*

"No need to stare, Wataru. It's me, I promise," Akira Mitani said with a chuckle. Wataru blinked, but he still couldn't think of anything worthwhile to say, so he said the first thing that came to his mind. "Mom gave me ¥500 for lunch."

"Oh? Well that can be your secret allowance, then. I'm buying today. What'll it be?"

Wataru couldn't think of a single thing he wanted to eat right then. *Anything's good. We can just walk around and go anywhere. As long as I'm with you, Dad, I'm fine.*

"There's a nice breeze today, how about we go for a walk in the park? I came through there on the way here. There's a hot dog stand."

Wataru followed his father out of the library and toward a nearby park. They walked along a lazily meandering path until they reached a central square with a fountain. There were people sitting here and there, but luckily one bench was unoccupied.

"This'll do," Akira said.

The hot dog stand was in a converted van parked by the edge of the square. The proprietors were a fat, smiling couple, reminding Wataru of a pair of snowmen. He asked for two orders of hot dogs and cola, and the man recommended a side of fresh fries. Stepping closer to the van, Wataru noticed a girl—probably about preschool age—sitting in the driver's seat of the vehicle and licking a vanilla ice cream cone. *She must be their daughter.*

Akira and Wataru sat next to each other on the bench and ate lunch. Wataru couldn't care less how it tasted, but biting in, he couldn't help but notice that it really was a delicious hot dog. Akira seemed impressed too. He said he wished there was a vending truck like this near his office. "It's hard to find a good place for lunch."

Wataru remembered there was a time, many years ago, when his father used to bring a lunch to work from home. Later, his division had changed, and he started having more meetings with clients, so he stopped taking a bag lunch.

His father asked him questions in an easy tone. How was school going? How's Katchan doing? Were you happy with your grades from the first semester?

Wataru found himself slipping into a peaceful, familiar rhythm. For a brief moment, nothing was wrong at home. They were just here on a pleasant walk. Back home, Mom was doing the laundry, hanging out the sheets, polishing Dad's shoes, ironing Dad's T-shirts…

The conversation died, and they sat side by side in silence. The fountain splashed noisily in the middle of the square.

"Where did you get those glasses, Dad?" Wataru asked. He knew there was a conversation he should be having right now, questions he needed to ask, but they were all locked up tight in a dark room, and he couldn't find the way inside.

Akira pushed the glasses higher up his nose. "They look funny?"

"No, they look good." A question brushed by the corner of Wataru's mind. *Did she pick them out for you, Dad?* Wataru let it slide, and it drifted off into space, unspoken. "They look good, but you kind of look like a different person. When I first saw you, at least."

"Hmm. Yes, I suppose I do," Akira said, pushing up his glasses again. "I'm not, of course. I'm the same as always."

"Dad?"

"Mmm?"

"Are you *never* coming home?"

An impossible question to ask. *Is that why it had come so easily?*

Akira looked at Wataru through the tiny lenses and then slowly lowered his gaze. Drops of ketchup from his hotdog splattered on the ground, just barely missing his shoes.

"Mom said that if we waited, you'd come home. That there was nothing to worry about."

The park around the hot dog stand was lively with customers. The benches were packed. Children much younger than Wataru were playing in the fountain, splashing water on each other and laughing. The droplets caught the light and shimmered as they fell to the cobblestones.

"So, is she right? Is that what I'm supposed to do?"

Akira took off his glasses, set them on one knee, and slowly rubbed his face with both hands. He looked at Wataru. "I'll always be your father."

The five words ricocheted off Wataru's heart like skipping stones on water. "That's not what I asked. You *know* that's not what I asked." *And Mom thinks you're a coward for saying that,* he thought, but he kept his mouth shut.

Akira turned his eyes toward the fountain, passing over the happy-looking couples and children. For a while he just sat, quietly, as though stupefied.

Then he put his glasses back on and turned back to face Wataru. It was as though he had been on break when he took them off. Now they were on, it was time to go to work.

"If by coming home you mean living with your mother again, then no, I won't. You were right, Wataru. I'm never coming home."

The floor dropped out from beneath Wataru. He reeled. He had asked the question and gotten the answer he expected, and yet he wasn't prepared for the crushing weight of it. Everything—his hope, his father's answer, his soul— went spinning down into a deep, black abyss.

"Remember what I said that night? I struggled with my decision a long time, but now that I've made it, I intend to see it through. I won't be coming home. If there were the slightest chance of that, I wouldn't have left in the first place. I know how hard this is, how deep it must have hurt you and your mother."

Then why?

"You're a smart kid, I should never have tried to talk around it. I should have told you straight from the very beginning. That was my mistake." Akira continued talking, softly yet steadily. "I knew that no matter what I said you'd be sad, and maybe it was too early for you to even understand…That's why I tried to leave without saying anything. I figured even if that made you hate or resent me, well, I would only be getting what I deserved. I was ready for that. I'm ready for it now. No matter how much you may hate me, Wataru, I won't make excuses."

There was nothing Wataru could say. As always, his father was being totally logical.

"Even if you came to hate me and say I wasn't your dad, I would accept that. It's what I deserve, I guess. But Wataru, know this: I will always be your father. That's my responsibility, and, it's the only thing I can offer you now."

Wataru's brain went into a tailspin. He thought he had understood his father's answer, but now the meaning of it had somehow slipped out of his grasp and was gone to who knows where. Maybe it had already hit the ground, beating him to the final impact.

He was still falling, and he was alone, plummeting down a lightless shaft, down, down, the wind whistling past his ears. Far above him, the shaft entrance grew smaller and smaller, and his father, standing at the edge, was already a tiny speck.

"Of course I'll pay for your education. And I'll do what I can to help you and your mother meet expenses. Once I can talk to your mother more officially, I intend to do everything I can to make things easy for her. You can live in that apartment. That belongs to you and your mother now. Everything is taken care of."

Dad's talking about money. Right. Money's important.

"Dad…so, you don't like me and Mom anymore?"

Akira shook his head. "That's not it. The way I think about you and the way I think about her are two completely different things."

"Why? You're my dad and my mom. We're a family, aren't we?"

"Families are…a group of individuals, Wataru. They can live entirely different lives, and sometimes the paths they take lead away from each other."

"You're living with another woman now, aren't you? You like her more, right? That's why you abandoned us, right?" Somewhere along the line, Wataru had gone from asking to accusing.

Akira's eyes grew larger behind the rimless glasses. His mouth gaped. "Who told you that?"

"What does it matter who told me?"

"It matters to me. It's not something you should have to hear. It's not something I wanted you to hear."

"But if it's true, I want to know about it. I don't like lies. You were the one who told me lying is bad, Dad!"

Wataru's voice had grown louder and louder as he talked. They were catching glances from the people on nearby benches. A young couple pushing a stroller nearby stopped in their tracks.

Akira reached out a hand and affectionately stroked Wataru's back. *Don't touch me.* He had to clench both his hands into fists to stop himself from swatting away his father's hand.

"Lies are bad, that's true," Akira said in a low, husky voice. "But twisting the truth and not saying something that's private are two different things. You should understand that. You do understand, don't you? You're a smart kid."

Who cares if I'm smart? Why are you always trying to change the subject?

"Satoru told you, didn't he?"

Wataru was silent.

"Your grandmother? Not your mother, surely."

Wataru jerked his head upward. "I won't tell you unless you tell me if it's true or not."

Akira sighed.

The usual bustle had returned to the fountain square. *All these people have no idea what we're talking about. Everyone in the world is happy. Everyone except us.*

"It is true," Akira said.

The words shot by Wataru, still falling, and disappeared above him. They weren't falling—he had fallen by them. Now he saw they had grown wings, and were flying up into the sky, happy.

"I'm going to start a new life with this woman. If your mother agrees to a divorce, I intend to marry her."

The rumble of tank treads sounded in Wataru's fears. "Grandma's pretty mad. She'll never go for it."

To Wataru's surprise, Akira laughed. "Of course she won't. One phone call was enough to convince me of that. She told me I wasn't a father anymore—or her son. Your grandmother disowned me."

"Disowned? What's that?"

"That means we officially stop being a parent and child."

"So you're not Grandma's son anymore? And Uncle Lou…does this make him not my uncle anymore?"

Akira's mouth curled into a grim smile. "No, Grandma didn't really disown me. But she was mad enough to say she would."

"And Grandma being so mad doesn't make you think twice about your decision? Do you think you're doing the right thing?"

Akira looked into Wataru's eyes. "Do you think it's the right thing to abandon your convictions because someone close to you gets angry?"

"Abandon your convictions? You mean change your mind?"

"Yes, that's right. Convictions are very important decisions, the kind you can't go back on."

So abandoning me and Mom was an important decision.

"So what *are* your convictions, Dad. I mean, Mom is really sad, and Grandma's furious, and all Uncle Lou does is hold his head in his hands and moan. How can convictions be worth all that?"

An elderly couple eating ice cream on the bench next to them had caught a snippet of the conversation and were now peering at them with interest. Akira shot them a withering glare. The two looked at each other and resumed licking their cones.

"What are my convictions?" Akira echoed. "You need to know?"

"Yeah," Wataru said firmly, but inside he was frightened. He had backed his father into this and now he was treading on unknown territory. He was trying to open a door that shouldn't be opened. If only there were a strategy guide for this, like for a role-playing game. *A powerful, secret boss lies in wait behind this door. If you're under level fifty, it's best to sneak past.*

"Your father's conviction," Akira said slowly, "is that you only live once."

You only live once.

"That's why, if you think you've made a mistake, no matter how much you struggle, how much difficulty you face, you have to fix what can be fixed.

There's no time for regrets."

He spoke slowly, saying every word with the proper weight, but the only one that stuck in Wataru's head was *mistake*.

Dad's life was a mistake.

So...what does that make me?

"Are you saying it was a mistake for you to marry Mom? So what about me? Does that make me a mistake too? Is that what you mean?"

Akira shook his head. "No that's not what I mean. I'm not saying that."

"Then what was your mistake? I don't get it."

"Look, this isn't something you can understand right now. Maybe when you're older, when you've lived through some of the things I have. Maybe then you'll understand. Though I'm not sure understanding will make you happy."

Wataru was getting lost in a maze that grew more and more complicated with every word said. His father's explanations always made so much sense. Even when things seemed tangled beyond belief, his father would untangle them, and lay them out flat for all to see.

But this time it was exactly the opposite. Things were simple. *Dad left Mom, he left me—he left our house. He wants to marry another woman. It's that simple.* So why does the explanation seem so complicated?

Akira reached out a hand and lightly held Wataru's shoulder. Rocking him slowly back and forth, he spoke. "There's one thing I want you to remember. No matter what mistakes your mother and I have made, no matter what our failures, it has nothing to do with you. You are your own person. Haven't I always told you that? A child has his own personality; he's not just an attachment to his parents. Even if our marriage has failed, it doesn't mean you're a failure. That's the truth. Never forget it."

Akira's brow furrowed. "If you lift your head and look our marriage in the face, you will see it for what it is. Failures *are* failures. Ours was a mistake from the very beginning. We were just kidding ourselves the whole time."

Mom always kept the house clean. She always made dinner. She hardly ever slept late. She fought with Grandma sometimes, but they always made up afterward.

"Mom hasn't done anything bad. She didn't make a mistake," Wataru muttered. Then he noticed that amazingly, incredibly, his father's calm demeanor had faded and was replaced by a look of outright irritation. When he spoke the words came in a rush, like he was trying to push something back down in its place by sheer force.

"Failure doesn't mean anyone did anything bad. Sometimes people fail even when they only do good things. Or they do what they think is good. Only with hindsight can anyone understand the failures they experience."

The lady on the next bench over had stopped licking her ice cream to stare at them. She was oblivious to the melting rivulet of vanilla coursing off the edge of her cone and staining her skirt.

The old man grunted and nudged her with his elbow. "You're dripping."

Flustered, the woman brushed at her skirt. Wataru watched the scene unfold blankly. *You can hear what we're saying, can't you? Do you understand? Could you translate for me? What is my father trying to say?*

"I don't understand," Wataru said meekly, to which Akira nodded.

"I didn't think you would. You don't have to. This was my mistake…and I think meeting you today was a mistake too. I can't explain it so you'll understand, I'm just hurting you. See? That's what I mean."

"That's what I mean" was his father's code for "this conversation is over." How many times had his questions about everything under the sun been answered, tips been given, advice handed out with those words.

A sigh came out unbidden. He felt like he had been holding his breath this whole time. Like he had swum the length of an Olympic-size pool underwater and only just now reached the edge, his lungs burning.

He breathed, and the reality of it hit him. Then, just like that, the thing he had been thinking from the very beginning came welling up and popped out of his mouth. "So basically, you just like this other woman more than Mom. That's what this is all about, right?"

His father did not answer. Brow furrowed, he tapped his glasses with a finger and looked down at the ground.

Spray from the fountain fell lightly on Wataru's forehead.

"If that's what you want to think, fine. Think that," Akira said. He stood up to leave. "I'll walk you to the bus stop."

"No, that's okay. I want to stay here awhile."

"Don't sulk, Wataru."

"I'm not sulking. I just want to go to the library."

"I can't leave you here alone after all we've talked about."

"I'm fine. I can make it home myself."

Just go home, Dad. I'll be fine. Just go back to your woman. The one who isn't a mistake.

Wataru didn't meet his father's gaze again that day.

Akira stood quietly in front of the hard bench where Wataru sat staring at the ground in uneasy silence.

The wind is blowing water from the fountain and it's cold. I can hear a girl laughing. I hear a baby crying.

"Wataru...This idea to meet me—was this your idea alone?"

"Katchan helped me."

"That's not what I mean. Um, did you come up with the idea yourself?"

Wataru looked up. *Funny, he looks scared.* "What do you mean?"

Akira's lips curled, as he searched for the proper words. He thrust his hands into his pockets and looked away. "Did your mother send you here to do this?"

Wataru didn't catch what he said. "Huh?"

"Did your mother tell you to meet with me and ask me to come home?"

Wataru's mouth gaped open. "No, not at all."

"Okay." Akira nodded, still frowning. "That's fine. If your mother had put you up to this...if she was trying to use you, that would be bad. You understand? I just wanted to make sure."

"Mom wouldn't do that." *She wants me to pretend you're on a business trip.* "She doesn't know I'm here."

Akira's shoulders relaxed. He seemed relieved.

"It's the truth, Dad."

"Right, I understand. Well, I'm going now. You take care of yourself, and go straight home." He began to walk off, then paused. "Call me on my cell phone anytime. If you want to talk, just call. Even if it's just about homework. Anything."

Wataru sat alone, staring off into space when he heard a tiny voice. He was too tired to actually focus on it, to hear what it was saying.

"Sonny?"

He felt a light tap on his shoulder and looked up to see the old lady who had been sitting on the bench next to him. He saw the dark stains of the ice cream in the fabric of her skirt. She was plump, and bent over to the point where she was only about as tall as Wataru. She crouched by the bench and smiled a faint smile. "Where do you live, sonny?"

Wataru was empty. An old shopping bag turned upside down. His voice had fallen out a long time ago to clatter on the floor.

"We could take you home?" she offered.

Behind her Wataru could see her husband sitting on the bench, frowning. Then Wataru's mouth opened, and the sound that came out was alien to him, flat, like a synthesized voice.

"No, I'm going to the library."

"You sure, sonny? You live far from here?"

Wataru repeated himself, then stood.

"Leave him alone," the old man said to his wife. "He can take care of himself."

The lady grabbed her husband's shirt by the sleeve. "But aren't you worried?" Wataru heard her saying. "He's so young…"

He left them and began to walk toward the library building. "Oh, sonny!" the old lady called out. "How about some ice cream?"

He could hear her husband scolding her, but their voices were already fading into the distance as he walked away. All but one sentence he heard as clearly as if the old man had been talking right in his ear.

"I knew there were irresponsible fathers in the world, but that was my first time seeing one."

The old woman grumbled something about men, but Wataru was already too far away.

He wasn't falling anymore. He had gone down as far as he could go, and now he had hit rock bottom. He was so far down he didn't know where he was.

chapter 11
The Secret

If somebody had later asked Wataru how he had spent the next several days before summer vacation began, he would have given them a blank stare and said nothing. He was in a daze. Details blurred and faded in the space of hours. Those days, he lived for nothing, and did even less.

Not that there was much of a change in his daily routine. Uncle Lou visited again and they hammered out the details for his summer trip. Late in the evening, he saw him speaking in hushed tones with his mother, but he wasn't told what they were discussing, or whether they had reached any conclusions.

Kuniko settled into the exact same patterns she followed when Akira was on one of his long business trips. In that respect, what she told Wataru wasn't exactly a lie. They would watch TV together at night and laugh, and if Wataru went to bed without brushing his teeth, she would get angry at him, as always. When Katchan called after nine o'clock at night, she would say, "He has to understand. Our family isn't run like his family." It was the exact same thing she always said. No special treatment. Same old Mom.

When Wataru woke up in the morning before the last day of school, his right cheek was swollen and red. It hurt so much he could barely open his mouth. His mother took a look. "Your gum's swollen," she announced. "You need to go see a dentist. No school for you today."

Not that it really mattered—the classes for the year were pretty much over, and he wouldn't be able to get in the pool for P.E. in his condition anyway. Wataru did as he was told, and before lunchtime rolled around, he was sitting in the waiting room at the dentist's office.

It wasn't a cavity, said the dentist, it was gingivitis. "Don't normally see this in children," he said, and asked whether Wataru had eaten something hard recently, maybe cut his gum? Had his mom said anything about him grinding his teeth at night?

The dentist fixed him up, and though the swelling didn't go down, the pain wasn't so bad. He was told there was a chance that he might run a fever, and sure enough, he was starting to shiver. Even under the hot summer sun he didn't break a sweat.

He got home to find his mother out shopping. There was a note on the kitchen table that read, "Put on your new pajamas and get some sleep."

He wasn't *that* sick. A quick snooze on the couch sounded like a better idea. He had just flopped down when the phone rang.

Maybe it's Grandma? Or Uncle Lou. Or it could even be Grandma in Odawara. The last time she called she started crying right away. Wataru didn't fancy the idea of talking to her right then.

Reluctantly he picked up the receiver. He heard a woman's voice, unfamiliar, maybe a salesperson.

"Hello, Kuniko Mitani?"

He tried to tell the caller that his mother wasn't home, but the swelling in his mouth and the lingering effects of the anesthesia made it hard to say anything coherent. Meanwhile, the woman on the line continued talking.

"I heard from a colleague that you called the office yesterday. I thought we agreed last time that you wouldn't call here...did you forget, perhaps?"

It was a pretty and polite voice, but Wataru could hear a little bit of anger simmering beneath the surface. She was talking a little too high, a little too fast. *What kind of a salesperson talks like this?*

"...This sort of, well, harassment—look, I'm human too, and there's only so much I can take. I don't think that us meeting and talking would be particularly fruitful either, to be honest."

You've got the wrong number, Wataru attempted to explain, when the woman with the strange voice began talking faster, each word hitting the receiver with the force of a punch.

"Akira says that if you insist on carrying on like this, a divorce trial isn't out of the question. He's quite angry. I really think you might want to reconsider your actions. That's all I wanted to say. Don't call the office again. I've already received complaints from my superiors about personal affairs intruding on work."

Wataru sensed that she was about to hang up the phone, so he blurted, "I'm noph my mother!"

The silence that followed rang in his ears. The receiver echoed Wataru's voice.

"Heffo?" Wataru managed through swollen lips. "Thiff ith Wataru. Wataru Mitani."

He heard a faint noise like someone swallowing on the other side. Then there was a click. She had hung up.

The telephone call had lasted only a few moments, but it caused Wataru to break out in a cold sweat.

Without a doubt—that was *her*. Dad's other woman.

That was the woman Akira Mitani was living with. The woman he wanted to end his marriage to Kuniko for. The woman he wanted to marry.

She had a pretty voice—like a television announcer's—Wataru thought. He hated himself for thinking it.

The strength went out of his knees, and he knelt down on the floor. That's when he heard the other voice, sweet and small—a voice he had completely forgotten about.

"Wataru, are you okay?"

Wataru jerked upright and looked around from where he was on the floor. No one was there, of course. That sweet, mysterious girl's voice.

"Don't cry, Wataru. I'm with you now."

The words seemed to come from nowhere. Immediately, Wataru felt the pain in his chest lighten.

"Where are you?" he asked the air around him, and the girl answered, "With you, like I said."

"Then why can't I see you?"

"I can see you, but I'm afraid you can't see me." He heard a light sigh. There was nothing to see, no touch of breath upon his cheek, but he had the distinct impression that if she were here, her breath would smell like candy.

"You've forgotten about me, haven't you, Wataru? You've forgotten what I told you."

This was true. With all that was going on, Wataru had run out of room in his head to ponder the mystery of a girl who couldn't be seen.

More than that, all his memories of that time, the mysterious girl's voice, searching his room for the source, taking pictures—all those memories seemed vague, shrouded in a misty veil. They were there when he thought about them, but they seemed so distant.

"You're right...I-I forgot about you."

"Because the Watchers didn't pass you as a Traveler," the girl said, a sharp edge to her voice. "You came here once, didn't you? But they kicked you out. That's why your memory of me has faded."

Wataru didn't have any idea what she was talking about. It all seemed to make sense in an odd way, but he couldn't imagine why. "Wait a minute, where is 'here'?"

The girl sighed again. "Why Vision, of course. Not that that word means anything to you now."

No, no it doesn't.

"In any case, I'm your friend, Wataru. If you can make it over here, I can help you out in lots of ways. Please, try to find another way into Vision. I know you can do it."

Wataru started to wonder if he was dreaming. Maybe the shock of the phone call had knocked him out. That had to be it.

Wataru didn't tell Kuniko about the phone call from the other woman.

His mom already seemed tired enough as it was. He wondered where she had been out shopping, because when she came home after the long summer day, her shoes were worn and caked with grit.

That night, when Kuniko fell asleep, Wataru snuck outside.

He didn't know where he was going at first. He walked aimlessly, gazing up at the night sky, thinking maybe he would cool off a bit before going back home. He could go to the park and ride on all the swings. He could do whatever he wanted, anything to get his mind off the earlier events of the day.

As he walked he had an idea. *I know, I'll go see Katchan.* Summer vacation was the day after tomorrow. Mr. and Mrs. Komura would undoubtedly allow him to stay. Then they could play *Streetfighter Zero III* all night. His mom wouldn't get mad at him for staying at Katchan's, either. Not now.

He walked, slowly formulating his plan, and when he looked up again he noticed that he was standing in front of the haunted Daimatsu building. Trees at the Mihashi Shrine swayed back and forth in the thick summer night air.

This isn't the way to Katchan's. Why did I come here? He had a funny feeling that someone had called him here.

Someone was inside the building—behind the wall of hanging tarps. It was more than one or two people. They were talking in hushed voices. Actually, they were arguing.

Wataru lifted up a stretch of tarp and slid quickly inside. He immediately bumped into a pair of grimy legs and feet wearing rubber flip-flops.

"Whoa! What the—who's he?!"

The owner of the legs cried out and stumbled back, then lashed out with a foot. Wataru quickly rolled away so as not to be stepped on, but he was too late. A well-aimed kick caught him in the side at full force, knocking the wind out of him. Everything went white.

"One of your friends?" Wataru heard someone saying through a haze of pain. He clung to consciousness for dear life.

"Don't tell me you called him to help?"

"Not much of a backup, heh."

Gradually, the world came back into focus. His side smarted where he had been kicked, and he felt nauseated, but he still managed to sit up.

The area inside the tarps was lit by a large flashlight. The bright light made the shadows of everyone inside long and dark, more real than the people who cast them.

There were three others besides Wataru inside the building. The one holding the flashlight was Joto Elementary's very own Kenji Ishioka, scourge of the sixth grade. It took a nanosecond for Wataru to identify the other two kids. They were Kenji's ever-present goons.

Wataru shook his head and forced his eyes to focus. That's when he realized that a fourth person was also present. This unlucky soul was on the ground with his face pressed into the dirt. One of Kenji's boys was on his back, grinding a knee into his spine.

Most of his face was obscured by a sticky patch of duct tape, but it was still clear who it was.

"Ah!" Wataru yelped, the effort sending a stab of pain through his side. He clutched at his belly with both hands.

Pressed to the ground, his mouth wrapped in tape, and one of the Ishioka gang pressing him into the dirt, was Mitsuru. His eyes were opened wide as he looked back at Wataru. He was asking something. He wanted something.

"Wh-what do you think you're doing?!" Wataru said. He meant for it to be a shout, but he was afraid it would hurt his side too much, so the words came out in little more than a hoarse whisper.

Kenji and his pals laughed until they were practically rolling on the ground. It was harsh, evil laughter. *They'll hear you outside. What about the nice priest at Mihashi Shrine, where is he?*

"You're a funny guy, you know that?" one of them said.

"What are you doing?" Kenji parroted with a sneer.

Wataru found himself unable to stand, so he got up on his knees. Slowly, he was able to move forward on his knee toward the spot where Mitsuru was lying. One of Kenji's crew took a step in Wataru's direction, and kicked him swiftly on the side of the head, sending him sprawling on the ground with a loud thud.

Why aren't any grown-ups coming to help? Can't they hear all the noise they're making in here?

"Bull's-eye!"

"A perfect headshot, that one."

"Let me take a swing. Gotta practice!"

Wataru tried to sit up and lurch aside to avoid the next blow, but his head rattled and his eyes spun. He took the knee square in the back.

Collapsing on the ground, he came face-to-face with Mitsuru. Their eyes locked.

Wataru clung to the edge of consciousness. He felt no pain. He felt nothing but a low burning sensation, like a bad fever. His vision narrowed, and he couldn't tell up from down. All he could see were Mitsuru's big black eyes staring into his own. Somehow, that powerful gaze gave Wataru an anchor, something to cling to, a life rope thrown to a tiny craft on the choppy seas of awareness.

He's trying to tell me something —his mouth is moving beneath the tape. —Take it off.

You want me to take off the tape?

—Take it off, quick!

Kenji chortled triumphantly and slammed a foot down on Wataru's back-side, causing him to bounce. He moved his right hand a little bit.

—That's right, use your hand, take it off.

But I'm losing it. I can't—I can't breathe.

Unbelievably, Wataru saw his right hand move of its own accord, inching toward the tape covering Mitsuru's mouth.

A shadow flew over his head, and Kenji's bodyslam scored a direct hit. Wataru was pressed to the ground, and he was afraid his ribs would snap.

"Crunch!" came Kenji's literal battle cry.

Who knew why they brought Mitsuru here in the first place, or what they wanted from him? It was clear they had forgotten that themselves, but now that they had started playing there was no stopping them. *The brakes are off. They might even kill us.*

Wataru's right hand moved again, grabbing the edge of the tape.

I bet it'll smart if I just rip it off.

He thought for an instant, but his hand moved from right to left without hesitation, ripping off a piece of tape. He took off one layer, then another.

"Hey, what're you doing?!" said one of Kenji's friends when he saw Wataru's hand move. But before he could do anything, Wataru pulled the last piece of tape off Mitsuru's mouth—a sticky mass of goo stuck to his fingers.

Mitsuru's eyes shone darkly. His swollen, bloodied lips opened, and he spoke.

"Great lord of the Underworld, by the Pact I call upon thee. Winged kin of darkness and the dead, by the promise of blood, black and ancient, I summon…"

Suddenly, the flashlight in Kenji's hand went out.

"Whoa! Wh-what the…?!"

Kenji staggered back, his shadow wavering on the tarp behind him.

His shadow. Even though the flashlight had gone out, it was strangely bright inside the tarps. He could see everyone's faces even more clearly than before.

Mitsuru's voice continued in a rhythmic chant. The words were clear, crystalline.

His voice—it's beautiful.

"To those who oppose me grant the eternal sleep of death, and in ice un-melting bind them. *Sacuroz, helgis, metos, helgitos!* Come, Balbylone, Daughter of Darkness!" he was saying. The words were like a spell, and when he was finished, Wataru realized why it was so bright. The ground surrounded by the boys was shining white, casting a pale glow on the space inside the haunted building.

What's going on?!

The glowing area was a circle, a little smaller than a manhole. As he watched, it seemed to rise, swelling. It was almost like something was being born from the ground.

That's impossible.

The otherwise firm-packed dirt looked, in that one shining circle, to be as malleable as clay. And there he saw a head—a person's head—emerging. First the top of the head, and the neck, then shoulders, and the chest with two arms folded across it. It was a slender body, lined in graceful curves.

A woman.

It was a female mannequin made of the darkest, blackest clay.

Kenji and the two others stood with their mouths open, trembling. The dark figure emerging from the ground spread her arms. She was facing Mitsuru. Her breasts were bared for them to see, yet they too were as dark as night.

Then, two eyes split the smooth featureless face—eyes of gold, without a trace of white. The only sign of pupils were thin, jet black lines running through their middle. Like the eyes of a panther.

"Welcome, Balbylone," Mitsuru sang, his face bright. He lifted his head as high as he could from where he lay upon the ground. "I bring sacrifices…sacrifices to your beauty."

Hands still spread, the dark mannequin turned to face Kenji and his gang. They crouched stupidly, unable to scream or even run.

From the tips of the mannequin's fingers, long sharp claws began to grow. At the same time, two black wings, darker still than her body, spread from her back.

Wataru turned his head to stare at the unbelievable sight before his eyes. He wasn't sure whether to be terrified or overjoyed, but before he knew it, he was smiling. He said nothing, and grinned so wide he looked nothing so much like the Cheshire cat from *Alice's Adventures in Wonderland.*

The strange dark woman that Mitsuru called Balbylone walked on long slender legs, advancing toward Kenji and his friends step by step. Her wings had spread to their full span of more than six feet. The claws on her hands were hooked, and they made a clicking noise as she swung them gracefully through the air.

Kenji's group backed up until they hit the far wall of the building. No place left to run, they clung to one another and, like Wataru, stared at the otherworldly creature. They were all pale, their faces bone white, eyes open wide, jaws hanging slack. They looked stricken with fear, and yet at the same time, they seemed strangely happy.

Wataru was looking at the back of Balbylone, while everyone else was staring at her face. Kenji was transfixed as he gazed upon her face—his mouth opening and closing without a sound. But in reality, he was saying something that nobody could hear. His voice was too low, and besides, Balbylone's claws were going…

Snick. Snick.

Wataru suddenly wanted to see her face. What does she look like now? Is she smiling? Are her golden eyes staring at Kenji?

"Okay…" Kenji muttered vacantly, "I'll go."

It sounded as if he were answering a question, like Balbylone had asked him, "Will you come with me?" But no one had said anything. *Kenji's lost it.*

Kenji's face melted into a broad smile. Then he stood up, swaying unsteadily, and began to walk toward Balbylone. His gang remained behind, clinging to one another for dear life, unable to wrest their eyes from Kenji. Their mouths trembled.

"K-Kenji!" one said in a voice like a sob. "N-no! Don't go!"

Kenji heard nothing. He saw nothing. He only stared stupidly up at Balbylone, walking until he stood right before her. There, he dropped to his knees, and spread his arms. "I'll go…"

Balbylone lifted her shoulders. The movement spread down her arms, and then down to the tips of her wings, until her whole jet black body rippled and shook. Somehow, with utter confidence, Wataru knew what was going on. *Ecstasy. She's trembling with ecstasy. Like a beast of prey the second before it makes a kill.*

Her wings extended outward with a taut snap, and like a switch had been thrown, the smile faded from Kenji's face.

Then he screamed. It was a scream beyond conscious thought, beyond his ability to control—a raw, primal scream.

Balbylone launched at him. Two slender black arms writhed like serpents, encircling his body. For a moment, she seemed to be crouching before him, then her jet black head wavered and, like an amoeba, became formless, swelling to ten times its original size. Kenji, wrapped in her arms, was lifted into the air. Flipping him toward the top of her head, she swallowed him whole. Kenji's scream cut off cleanly, as if snipped by a pair of scissors.

One of his sneakers rolled to a stop by Wataru's foot.

Wataru's eyes were stretched open wide. All he could see was the expression of abject terror on Kenji's face the moment before she swallowed him, his last milliseconds of life replaying in crystal-clear slow motion, frame by frame.

After she swallowed Kenji, Balbylone's head immediately shrank to its regular size and shape, and she was once again a goddess of ebony beauty. Her nails clicked and pointed at the remaining hoodlums in front of her.

"No way!" they screamed.

Balbylone flew soundlessly with a single beat of her wings, and scooped them up from where they huddled. Wataru could see their legs jutting out from beneath her wings, futilely kicking at the air.

A gust of wind like a cyclone passed over Wataru's head. Even though he was lying down, Wataru closed his eyes and clung to the ground, feeling as though he might be lifted away at any moment. Then, just like that, it was over.

Fearfully, he opened his eyes and lifted his head to find everything around him in darkness.

From someplace far away, beyond the tarps, outside the haunted building, an intersection away, he heard someone gunning a car engine.

Then a flashlight clicked on only a few feet away from his hand. The bright light hurt his eyes. A hand touched him on the shoulder.

"You all right?"

It was Mitsuru. His face looked terrible. His lip was cut. A line of blood trickled from his right nostril. Yet he moved smoothly and competently, helping Wataru up.

Wataru sat up, and suddenly felt quite dizzy. Then he was lurching backward, sticking out his arms to catch himself. Every bone in his body ached, but the sensation of pain seemed somehow distant, like his body wasn't entirely his own.

Beside him, Mitsuru sat on one knee, rubbing a fist below his nose.

"Wh-where'd they go?" Wataru managed to ask. There was an unfamiliar, acrid taste in his mouth. Maybe it was blood.

"They?" echoed Mitsuru, raising an eyebrow.

"Kenji...and his idiot friends," Wataru said, looking up at him. He felt dizzy again, and his vision blurred. He tried to read Mitsuru's expression, but he couldn't get his eyes to focus.

"They went bye-bye. Hard," he said with a wry grin. "Can you stand?"

Wataru's legs felt like rubber. Still, he tried to get up. His sneakers scraped uselessly at the ground.

"What happened to them?" he asked again. "Where did they go? What was that just now? That creature—the dark woman."

Somehow it all felt unreal. He heard himself saying things he didn't entirely understand, then his voice trailed off like someone talking in their sleep.

"There's no monster," Mitsuru said quietly and assuredly, using the same voice he used when he answered the teacher's questions in cram school. "You were dreaming. It's nothing. Just a dream."

"It's not a dream," Wataru said, with much more confidence than he felt. Unable to stand, his body swayed, and he fell to the ground once again. Or he would have, if Mitsuru hadn't caught him at the last moment.

"Why did you come here?"

"Huh? Why..."

"I didn't call for you," Mitsuru spat. He sounded upset.

"I don't know. I just came..."

"You came even though I didn't call for you—you have nothing to do with this..." Then, suddenly, Mitsuru smiled. "But you saved me."

What is he talking about?

"You really are a handful," Mitsuru said, and he mumbled something under his breath. It sounded like another spell. Wataru felt a warm white light spill down on him from above. The light wrapped around his body, suffusing him, and unbelievably, the pain began to fade. It felt good.

He looked up in a daze to see Mitsuru waving.

So long. Goodbye.

And Wataru slept.

When his eyes opened, he was lying in his own bed and the alarm clock was ringing.

It was seven in the morning. He wouldn't have believed the clock if he didn't see the morning sunlight spilling through the checkered curtains of his room.

It was already getting warm, and his pajamas clung to his body.

"Wataru, time to get up!" he heard Kuniko shout from outside his door. She was knocking at the door now. "Don't be late on the last day of school! You'll be the laughingstock of your class!"

The last day of school.

Wataru cradled his head in his hands. He was here. His head was on his shoulders. He blinked his eyes. He could see. He could smell. Mom was frying an egg in the kitchen.

But what was that? What did I see last night?

Was I dreaming?

Did I stay in last night? Did I only think I had gone out, while I was really here under the covers? Was I only dreaming that I wanted to sneak out to Katchan's house?

And what was that—that monster?

His memory was foggy, but some details were clear. Mitsuru, and the jet black creature in the form of a winged woman. Those golden eyes. The *snick snick* of hooked claws.

Kenji Ishioka screaming.

Wataru rolled out of his room and into the living room. Kuniko, about to set a piece of toast on his plate, gave a startled cry.

"Wh-what is it? What's wrong?"

"Mom, I..."

"What, Wataru?"

Wataru's shoulders sagged. He couldn't tell her. He couldn't put what he'd seen into words. No way. Not going to happen. Impossible.

"Don't tell me you were still dreaming?" Kuniko said with a smile, picking up the piece of toast from where she had dropped it on the table. "Go wash your face. Why, you're covered in sweat."

Wataru nodded, and went to the bathroom. He peered into the mirror to see an average-looking sleepy kid's face staring back at him. No wounds, no scars. Just messy bed hair, and that was all.

The last day of school! A fond farewell to books and classes. Forty days of summer vacation lying in wait. The sun singing warmly in the sky. Don't let us down, make it a hot one, because today is when real summer begins!

The principal had begun his usual address to the entire school assembled out in the schoolyard, and Wataru felt displaced from reality—lost in thought about the dream that wasn't like a dream at all the night before. Around him, his classmates giggled and told jokes, and the teachers frowned and looked stern, and Wataru couldn't care less. Katchan, sitting way ahead of him, would occasionally turn when the teachers weren't looking to shoot some sort of signals in his direction. Wataru noticed, but didn't bother to respond.

At last the principal's speech finished, and everyone began shuffling toward the classrooms. Katchan came running up to Wataru.

"Oh man, can you believe it?!"

Wataru stared blankly at Katchan.

"Yo, sleepyhead wake up! What, don't tell me you were up playing games all night?" Katchan seemed extremely excited, even for the last day of school. "Wait, don't tell me you haven't heard? Oh, well I guess your mom isn't on the PTA, so maybe you wouldn't have—of course neither of my parents are on it either, but my old man's a volunteer at the fire department see—" Katchan rattled on at an incredible speed, answering his own questions before Wataru had a chance to get a word in edgewise.

"So, what is it?" Wataru asked flatly. No matter what Katchan could possibly have to say, it couldn't begin to compare with what he had experienced last night. He could tell him the world was ending, and it would have all the excitement of going to a lizard exhibition after watching *Jurassic Park*.

"You don't know. Wataru. You don't know?!" Katchan looked astonished and overjoyed all at once. *"Oh goody, I found someone who hasn't heard yet! Now I get to be the one who tells him!" Classic Katchan.*

"Kenji Ishioka's gone missing!"

The two boys had just reached the landing of the staircase that went up to the second floor classrooms. Wataru stopped short, and a girl walking behind him smacked into him.

"Oh, sorry, Wataru," she said, giving him a playful slap on the shoulder. "Don't stop all of a sudden like that!"

Wataru rocked to the side. His eyes were fixed, staring at the space above Katchan's face. He looked like he had completely lost his mind.

Katchan stepped back. "Whoa, Wataru, you okay? How hard did ya hit him, Sanae?"

Saying nothing, Wataru took a step closer to Katchan. His friend quickly took a step back. The girl Sanae walked over, a look of concern on her face.

"Kenji Ishioka? You mean *that* Kenji Ishioka?" Wataru asked, barely breathing.

"The very one," Katchan said with authority. "Sixth grade. Mean. You know any other creeps with that name?"

"He's missing?"

"Gone without a trace, since this morning," Sanae joined in. "They called the cops, made a big deal about it. His mom called the school. That's why the sixth-grade teachers are all upset this morning."

"That's right, you live near him, don't you," Katchan said to her. "My dad's a volunteer at the fire department. He says they're out looking for him now."

"If you ask me, they're making a big deal out of nothing," Sanae said, brushing her hair off her shoulders. "Kenji goes out every night. You know Makiko? Her parents own this building by the station, they've got a video game parlor there. They say that Kenji and his gang are there until all hours of the night sometimes, and they won't leave no matter how many times they get warned."

"Sure, he may go out at night, but this is the first time he hasn't come back," Katchan explained. "And today was supposed to be this big day— something about him being in an audition for a television show."

"So there's no way he wouldn't come home?"

"I'm not so sure about that," Sanae said with a sickeningly cute smile. "Maybe he was afraid he'd go to the audition and get cut again, so he ran away from home? There's no way they'd let someone like Kenji go on television, anyhow. He looks like a bulldog."

Katchan was ecstatic. "Totally! He's got the nose for it and everything."

"Like an idiot gorilla."

"You know it. I wonder why no one has ever told him to his face."

"Be my guest!"

"Me? No way."

"Chicken!"

Katchan did his best impersonation of a chicken clucking, and the two burst into laughter. A strange high-pitched voice interrupted the laughter. It took Wataru a split second to realize that it was his. "Is it only Kenji who's missing?"

Katchan and Sanae turned back to him. "Huh?"

Wataru averted his eyes. Mechanically, he repeated his question. "Is only Kenji missing? Did any of his friends go missing too?"

Katchan and Sanae looked at each other. "I don't know..."

"But maybe..." Katchan began, catching the scent of another potential rumor. "If three of them disappeared together, now that would be cause a-plenty for all this fuss."

"Hey, Wataru, what's wrong?" Sanae asked, grabbing Wataru by the elbow. "You look pale."

The school bell was ringing. Students were shuffling into their classrooms. Wataru opened his mouth, saying something.

"Huh? What?" The other two leaned toward him. "What did you say?"

"Mitsuru. What about Mitsuru? Is he here today?"

"Mitsuru? Is he talking about the kid in the next class?" Sanae looked at Katchan. Katchan shook his head. "I don't see what Mitsuru has to do with anything."

"Oh, but maybe—hey, hey, Misa!"

Sanae caught a face she recognized in the crowd of students going by them on the stairs. One of the girls stopped and looked around.

"What?"

"Mitsuru's in your class, right? Is he here today?"

"Nope. Didn't see him at the morning speech, and he's never late to class."

"No kidding. Thanks!"

Misa waved and ran off to class. Wataru's vision dimmed, his skin felt cold, he could barely stand. *Ashikawa took the day off. Ashikawa was gone too.*

So long. Goodbye.

Was that what he'd said?

Sanae's grip on Wataru's elbow tightened. "Katsumi, wake up! Your friend's anemic or something. He's gonna collapse. Quick, get a teacher!"

"No, I'm fine," Wataru said slowly. "I'm really fine. I'm not going to faint."

"Are you sure?"

"Um, Sanae..."

"Huh? What? What's wrong?"

"You're hurting my arm."

Sanae stood flustered for a moment, and then quickly released his arm. "Oh, sorry! Sorry."

"Don't know yer own strength," Katchan said, grinning, as she smacked him on the shoulder.

Still concerned, the two of them got on either side of Wataru and walked with him to the classroom. Katchan looked like he wanted to say something, but Sanae kept him quiet with a stern glare.

Wataru stood in the doorway to the classroom, but his mind was somewhere else entirely. The scenes from last night played through his head like he was skipping through a movie on DVD, jumping to each moment, replaying them in vivid clarity.

The classroom was buzzing. It was clear that Kenji's mysterious disappearance was the topic for the day. Their teacher left the room twice during the first class, returning each time with a clouded expression on his face.

Report cards were handed out, and just before they were released to go home, their teacher was called out again. Left on their own, the students erupted with worried chatter and mounting curiosity. It was the same in every classroom. The sound spilled out into the hallways until it seemed like the whole school was participating in one giant conversation.

When the teacher finally returned, he announced that all students would be going home in groups, escorted by PTA-appointed parental chaperones. They would all go down to the schoolyard in order, so until their class was called, they would have to wait patiently at their desks. Message delivered, the teacher left them again.

The excitement had risen to a fever pitch by this point. A few brave souls sneaked into other classrooms to gather information. Some students had brought in contraband cell phones in their bags, and they called home. Their friends clustered around the desk, trying to hear what was being said.

In the middle of it all, Wataru sat listlessly in his chair, half of his mental energies committed to the sole task of replaying last night's events. Katchan and Sanae got up and went over to him.

"Something is definitely wrong with you, Wataru," Sanae said seriously. "What's the matter?"

How easy it would be if it were something he could explain, something they would believe.

A shriek rose from one of the clusters of students in a corner of the room.

"What?!" Katchan shouted, whirling around. "Don't shout like that!"

The circle broke up, leaving one girl in the middle with a cell phone still pressed to her ear. She was gripping a friend's hand tightly. They both looked ready to cry.

One of the other girls from the group walked into the middle of the room, her face drawn, and told the class, "They found two of the sixth graders."

Wataru looked up.

"Two? You mean Kenji's friends?" Katchan wasted no time in asking.

"Yeah. Collapsed in Senkawa Park."

"Both of them?

"Both."

"Were they dead?" someone asked.

"No, not dead, but it's *strange*."

"Whaddya mean, 'strange'?"

"They weren't hurt at all, but they say they don't remember a thing— where they went the night before, how they got there—nothing!"

Somebody started crying, which set off a few of the other girls. Sniffing could be heard throughout the classroom. A boy looking out of the classroom window shouted, "Hey! It's a television crew!"

A few students ran over and threw open the windows. They could hear the sound of helicopter blades coming closer. Not one, but several.

Wataru stood. He couldn't stay here. Not even for another minute.

Everyone was distracted, except Katchan and Sanae.

"Where do you think you're going?"

"Home."

"Home? You can't..."

"I don't feel good. I'm going to go talk to the teacher."

He brushed them aside and walked out of the classroom. His ears were throbbing. Everything seemed muted, like someone had pushed the mute button on the world. He ran down the stairs, then down the hall toward the back entrance to school, taking care to avoid the teachers' room. Luckily, no one saw him or tried to stop him. They had bigger things to worry about. Wataru went outside, still wearing his school shoes.

In contrast to the heated atmosphere inside, the town looked as normal as ever. The hot summer sun beat down on deserted streets. Wataru didn't pass anyone on his way out. He ran and ran until he was out of breath, then ran some more until once again, he found himself standing in front of the Daimatsu building.

He looked at the blue tarps covering the haunted building. They hung undisturbed as always, a veil shrouding a secret. A closed lid on a jar.

Wataru lifted one of the tarps as he had many times before, and slid quickly inside. He realized this was the first time he had ever come here during the day. The light shining through the gaps lit the inside rather brightly. The tarps gave little shade—in fact, it felt more like a greenhouse.

For a full thirty seconds, Wataru stood still and held his breath. A drop of sweat trickled down the small of his back. His heart was beating wildly in his throat. He swallowed once, then twice, trying in vain to force it back down into his chest where it belonged.

He saw where he had lain sprawled on the ground the night before.

Where Kenji and his goons had pushed down Mitsuru, where they had kicked him.

And that monster—that's right! Balbylone, wings of death, daughter of darkness—that horrible thing had been here.

Wataru took a step, walking closer to the place where Balbylone had spread her wings, where she had attacked Kenji and swallowed him whole, where his scream had ended in cold, abrupt silence. He walked like he had irons chained to his ankles, dragging them with every step.

And then he saw it.

A single sneaker lay on its side on the dirt floor—like it had just been taken off and discarded. Wataru crouched down and picked it up. It was white, with blue and yellow stripes. It bore a famous sporting brand logo. It was brand-new.

Kenji's sneaker.

Wataru screamed silently, and threw the sneaker down. It hit the floor and bounced two or three times until it fell with the laces facing away from him.

He ran.

Ripping up the tarp, he barreled out into the street. He was running so fast he tripped and slammed down onto the concrete. He was startled by the sudden heat of the pavement on his palms.

He had stood up and brushed himself off when he started to cry. Crying wouldn't do any good—he wasn't even sure why he was crying, but the tears fell all the same.

Mitsuru—I have to talk to him, to get him to help Kenji. He can't do what he did, it's not right. He shouldn't call on things like that. Maybe it's not too late…

Tears clouded his eyes, until he could barely see where he was going. He stumbled forward, until he ran into something soft. The soft thing had hands, they were grabbing him.

"What's this? Something the matter, son?"

It was the priest from the Mihashi Shrine. He was wearing a white kimono and flowing white trousers, like always. His round face looked kind, and his bristly eyebrows, streaked with white, loomed closer.

"You—ah, we met recently, did we not?"

Wataru found he was standing at the entrance to the shrine. He could see the red crossbeams of the torii gate just behind the priest. Leafy green trees swaying gently in the breeze. Doves perched on shrine roof tiles.

"Have you…" Wataru began; then a ray of light stabbed through the chaos in his mind. *He can help me.* He grabbed the priest's sleeve tightly with both hands. "Have you seen a boy, like me? He comes here a lot. He's got a pretty face, like a doll. His name is Mitsuru. He lives near here—have you seen him? Do you know where he lives? Have you ever talked to him?"

Wataru yanked on his sleeve, but the short stocky priest stood firm and unmoving—though his expression was one of surprise. Peering at Wataru, he asked, "This boy, he's around your age?"

"Yes, that's right!"

"Mitsuru, yes, I see him here quite often. I've even spoken with him. He lives in the apartment building behind the shrine here. Is he a friend of yours?"

"Which apartment building is it?"

Two apartment buildings stood behind the Mihashi Shrine, one with a miniature red water tower on its roof, the other one taller, with chocolate-colored siding on the walls.

"Now that I'm not sure of. Never asked for his address."

Wataru turned and tried to dash off, but the priest caught him by the arm. "Son, wait. Tell me what's wrong. You look as though you've seen a ghost."

Forgive me, but I don't have a second to lose.

"I'm sorry," Wataru said, knocking the priest's hand off his arm. He ran straight into the shrine grounds, feet pounding over the gravel, and out the rear exit. The priest didn't follow. He probably wouldn't have been able to catch up to him anyway.

Wataru headed first toward the apartment building with the water tower. It was closest. He ran into the main entrance lobby, and stood before the mailboxes. Breathlessly, he checked the nameplates. The name Ashikawa was nowhere to be found.

He checked a second time. Nothing. He ran back outside. The other apartment building with the chocolate-colored walls stood with its back to the shrine, so he had to run down the length of the building to get to the entrance. Sweat ran into his eyes, making them sting. As he ran, wiping at his face with his hand, an ambulance siren sounded in the distance. It came closer and then faded away. It went off in the direction of the school.

He finally reached the entrance, finding a doorman in a moss green suit sweeping the floor by a pair of open automatic doors. He turned and looked over his shoulder, broom still moving, as Wataru ran past.

This building had almost twice the number of mailboxes as the last one. Before he could start checking them, he doubled over and put his hands on his knees, catching his breath. The tiles were so brightly polished he could see his reflection. A single drop of sweat fell to the floor.

The Ashikawas lived in apartment 1005. Wataru charged headlong through the entrance hall, running straight into a set of automatic sliding doors with a loud *smack!* The sound startled him.

This building had a security system. To get to the apartments, he had to go through another set of locked doors, with an intercom for calling people's apartments.

Just my luck!

There was a panel with a button and a microphone directly to the left of the door. Fingers shaking, Wataru punched in the number 1005, when someone grabbed his shoulder from behind. It was the doorman he'd seen on the way in.

"You all right, kid?"

The doorman turned him around, and the man's hand on his shoulder made his legs go weak.

"You ran straight into that door! Look, you've got a bloody nose."

Wataru felt a warm trickle down his lip.

"You don't live here, do you? What are you here for? Shouldn't you be at school?"

As he was talking, Wataru heard a woman's voice come from the intercom behind him saying, "Yes, who is it?"

"Ms. Ashikawa?" Wataru said, turning back toward the microphone. "I'm a friend of Mitsuru's! I'm looking for him. Is he home? Can I see him?"

There was a brief pause, and the woman responded. She sounded worried. "You're in Mitsuru's class? Then, he didn't go to school?"

Wataru felt the blood drain from his face. *If she's asking that, it means Mitsuru isn't at home either.*

The doorman bent down in front of the intercom. "Ms. Ashikawa? This boy here is in elementary school, like he says. He seems to be in a big hurry."

"Show him up."

The automatic doors slid open. Wataru ran through, heading for the elevator. The doorman followed behind him. It seemed like he was going to show him the way, though he didn't seem too pleased about it.

They got to the tenth floor and turned right out of the elevator. A slender woman was standing by the open door to the apartment.

"This is him, Ms. Ashikawa," the concierge said, giving Wataru a push. "I don't know what's going on, but be careful. I don't want any trouble like last time. If anything happens on my watch, it's my responsibility, you see."

The woman in the doorway thanked the concierge politely. He walked back, and disappeared into the elevator.

Wataru stood quietly, looking up at the woman. He could feel the warm trickle from his nose spreading. He was still bleeding.

The woman was very young. Wataru wasn't sure exactly how old she might be, but there was no way she could be Mitsuru's mother. She was really beautiful—a knockout. She wore a white sleeveless blouse and a light gray miniskirt. She was holding the door open with one hand, with the other resting lightly on her hip. A silver bangle shone on her wrist. Wataru was so sure the voice he had heard was Mitsuru's mother that for a moment he stood there confused.

"Are you a friend of Mitsuru's?" the woman asked, looking down at Wataru. It was the same voice he had heard over the intercom.

Wataru nodded silently. He only needed to nod once, but for some reason he kept nodding over and over, like a broken toy.

"Your nose is bleeding," she said disapprovingly. She lifted her hand from her waist to her forehead and stood there for a moment. Then, sighing, she opened the door wider and waved him in.

While not particularly large, the room was bright and filled with sunlight. It was very clean. The furniture seemed like something from a designer's catalog. Wataru's head was spinning, so he couldn't be sure, but it didn't seem like the kind of house that people with kids would live in. He started to wonder if Mitsuru really lived here.

The girl shut the door and followed Wataru into the living room, taking a tissue out of a box on the coffee table and offering it to him. "There. Wipe your nose and tell me what happened."

Wataru did as he was told. "I ran into the door downstairs."

He pressed his nose with a tissue. It throbbed painfully. He hadn't been able to feel it before, but now it hurt so much his eyes watered.

The woman pushed forward a chair on rollers for Wataru, and then sat down on a nearby sofa. Wataru sat in the chair. Sitting, their eyes were on the same level.

The woman looked like she was in even more pain than Wataru. "So Mitsuru really wasn't at school?" she asked quietly.

"No, he wasn't," Wataru answered from beneath the tissue. His front teeth were hurting too. He was too scared to touch them, afraid they might be loose.

"What's your name?"

Wataru introduced himself, and before she had a chance to say anything, he added "Mitsuru and I go to cram school together."

The woman merely nodded silently. She didn't seem suspicious at all. Wataru got the feeling that maybe Ashikawa never talked about school.

"Well, thank you for your concern," she said, still looking pained. "You don't have any idea where he might be, do you?"

"I haven't seen him at all today."

She nodded again. "He left a message. I think he's run away from home."

I suppose you could call that leaving home. So long. And where did he run away to? To some other place, some other world?

"Maybe you heard about me from Mitsuru. I'm his aunt."

That explained her age.

"Mitsuru doesn't talk much about home, so I really didn't know anything. Just the rumors about him living overseas and stuff."

For reasons Wataru couldn't guess at, Mitsuru's aunt suddenly looked even sadder. She put a hand to her forehead again. The bangle sparkled in the sunlight coming in through the window.

"But Mitsuru is really popular, you know," Wataru added hastily. "He's really good in class, and the girls are all over him."

Mitsuru's aunt looked at Wataru sadly; then she said in a whisper, "But he left. Leaving a note I don't even understand."

"What did he write?" Wataru asked, leaning forward. "He didn't say anything about...about going to another world, did he?"

The woman looked up quickly, surprise in her eyes. "How did you know that? Did he tell you something?"

Wataru's mouth snapped shut. He didn't want to have to explain anything. If he could just read Mitsuru's note first...

"You must have been a good friend of his, Wataru." Mitsuru's aunt reached over and touched his knee. Her fingers were warm. "You have any idea where

✳

195

he might've gone? I can't let him do this. I can't lose him…"

"Can't lose him?"

She must think that when Mitsuru said he was "going to another world," he really meant he was going to die. Come to think of it, that makes much more sense than the truth.

"He didn't say he was going to die in his message, did he?"

"No, he didn't, but…" Her face twisted like she was going to cry. Even so, she was still beautiful. Wataru noticed some similarity in the line of her nose with that of Mitsuru's.

"It was about three months ago, I suppose. He tried to commit suicide. Had you heard?"

Wataru shook his head, dumbfounded.

"No, I don't suppose you would have. I'm sure he didn't want to talk about it. It was right after he came here—he was spending a lot of time at home, alone. He must've gone stir crazy. He tried to jump from the roof, but luckily the concierge found him in time."

Suddenly what the concierge had said about "not wanting any trouble like last time" made sense.

"I knew I wasn't cut out for this," Mitsuru's aunt muttered.

It was becoming clear to Wataru that there were a number of unusual things about Mitsuru's family and he was only beginning to scratch the surface. If only he had some clue, some gut feeling of how to proceed.

Relax, Wataru. Just remember the Private Detective Meadows *series.* Wataru wasn't particularly fond of text-heavy adventure games, but he had enjoyed that one. *I'll just pretend Mitsuru's aunt is the client, and ask her questions like Detective Meadows would ask. How could that be hard?* Mitsuru's aunt was perfect for the role of the beautiful, mysterious woman who comes to visit the Meadows Detective Agency pleading for help.

"He said in his note that he was going someplace where no one could find him," she said. "He said not to bother trying to look."

"I-I might know," Wataru stammered. "I might have an idea where he's gone."

Her grip on Wataru's knee tightened. "Then take me there!"

"I would, but, I don't…I don't really know how to get there."

She opened her eyes wide. "What do you mean? Is it far away?"

"Well, not exactly…"

"He didn't ask you to keep it a secret, did he? Is that what this is about?"

That wasn't exactly the truth, but, if you thought about it the right way, it wasn't *far* from the truth. After all, the only people who knew about Vision were Mitsuru and Wataru.

"Yes, he did."

"Well, we can't leave him alone. He'll die! When Mitsuru says he's going to do something, he really means it. The last time he was already crawling up the fence on the roof's edge when they stopped him. If the concierge had come a moment later…"

"Um, did Mitsuru call in absent today?"

The change in subject was so abrupt that for a moment Mitsuru's aunt merely blinked. "Huh?"

"Did he call in absent to school?"

"Well, yes. This morning when I saw his note, I called his teacher and told him he would be absent today. I didn't want there to be any commotion at school."

Now that was odd. She didn't want to cause a commotion at school? Wouldn't that be the first thing she would want, as his guardian? Wouldn't it be normal to call the school and ask for help?

"Did you call the school after that?"

"No, I didn't, why?"

So she hadn't heard anything about Kenji's gang, though Wataru wasn't sure whether that was a good thing or a bad thing.

The phone rang.

The phone was sitting in the far corner of the living room. It was a large unit, with a personal fax machine attached to it. Mitsuru's aunt got up from the sofa to pick it up.

Wataru's vision wavered, and he had a sudden feeling of dread. The summer before, he had gone with his father to a large art museum and seen the painting *Cypress Trees* by Vincent van Gogh. It was a bright, pretty painting, but he remembered being struck by the sky the most. It was filled with strange and crooked swirls. When he left the museum later that day, those swirls still turned behind Wataru's eyes. When he looked up at the real sky, it seemed like it was spinning. And when he got on the train, the handrails were spinning. Everything was spinning! That night, when his dad took him to a restaurant for dinner, he was still obsessed with that van Gogh painting—he could barely eat a thing. That's how it felt right now. If he looked out the window, at the sky, maybe he would see those swirls—a churning, swirling energy, flowing into everything, filling the world.

Mitsuru's aunt seemed to be clinging tighter and tighter to the receiver as she spoke.

Wataru began to worry that maybe, by talking about school, he had tripped a flag.

In role-playing games and adventure games, the story typically followed a set course. Usually, you would have to ask a particular person a predetermined question to advance to the next stage of the story. Programmers set up flags to keep track of which of these turning points the player had passed. Once a flag was up, you were free to go on, but sometimes you could get stuck in the same part of a game for weeks, unable to find the event that would trigger the flag, scratching your head without a clue how to proceed.

That's what Wataru's conversation just now with Mitsuru's aunt had felt like. Wataru knew things and she knew things that neither of them were telling each other. They were talking, but the story wasn't going anywhere...until Wataru, unwittingly, said whatever the key word was that she had been waiting for. It had set off a flag. They were going to the next stage.

Mitsuru's aunt hung up the phone. She looked pale. "Three kids in the sixth grade are missing," she said, her voice trembling. Before Wataru could even nod, she ran over to him and grabbed him by the shoulders and shook him violently. "Why didn't you tell me? Wataru, you knew, didn't you? Kenji and his friends were stalking Mitsuru—that's why you came looking for him when you heard they had gone missing, isn't it? What if Mitsuru did something to them? Well? Why don't you say something? Answer me!" she shouted, then shoved Wataru away. She covered her face with her hands and slumped to the ground. Wataru felt dizzy, but not on account of the shaking. It was the swirling behind his eyes, the swirling in his heart.

What if Mitsuru did something to them?

It was one of the first questions out of her mouth—and she had sounded terrified. Wataru didn't think she was worried about Mitsuru, either. She was worried about Kenji.

Who would think that?!

Did she know he could use magic? Did she know he could chant incantations and summon monsters to harm his enemies? She must. How else would she get the idea that Mitsuru could do anything, three to one, against Kenji's gang. *What do you know, Ms. Ashikawa?*

"There were a lot of television reporters at school," Wataru said in a quiet voice. "A lot of helicopters too. One of the girls in class told us that on the news, they were saying two of Kenji's friends had been found. They were alive, but it was weird…"

Mitsuru's aunt looked at him through her fingers. "Weird?"

"They couldn't remember anything about the night before."

Mitsuru's aunt dropped her hands and stood. "Well, Mitsuru can't do anything like that." She spoke in a flat, even tone, as though she had resigned herself to some fate already and was just waiting for the pieces to fall into place. "But if the television crews were there—then I'm afraid he's finished. They'll find out he ran away, and they'll come asking questions about his family."

"His family?"

Mitsuru's aunt merely shook her head. "I-I don't know what to do."

"Ms. Ashikawa…"

She began to cry. "You're the same age as Mitsuru, right? Eleven?"

"Yeah?"

Wataru felt like crying too. He felt so sad, so sorry for her. She had seemed so perfect, so adult. Now it was like he could see her falling apart, just like Kaori Daimatsu must have. What if she became like her, a delicate, broken thing?

"How old do I look?" she asked, and then answered her own question. "I'm twenty-three. I graduated from college last year, and I just started working at my first job. I've only lived twice as long as you and Mitsuru. I'm no grown-up. I can't—I can't deal with all this."

She walked over to the phone. "I have to tell the school," she said. Then she looked at him. "Wataru, thank you for coming. You should probably go home."

By early afternoon, the news of Kenji's disappearance had gone national.

Wataru recognized the buildings in the television coverage of his school, despite the fact that they tried to blur out the school's name. He could even pick out some of his classmates walking home.

Wataru's mom had heard about the incident the same way Mitsuru's mom had, via the PTA emergency phone network. After that call, the phone had rung several times, mostly calls from worried friends and relatives who had seen the news. His mom told Grandma in Odawara, and Grandma in Chiba, that yes, Wataru was safe at home, and there was nothing to worry about. *He got a little scraped up in a fall on the way home. Yes, he ran back from school scared when he heard the news.*

There was a call from Wataru's teacher, who said that Wataru had forgotten to pick up his report card and that he would mail it to them the next day. He wasn't angry that Wataru had left at all. Apparently, there had been a big panic at the school. That ambulance Wataru heard while running to Mitsuru's apartment complex had been going to pick up a girl from Wataru's class who had fainted. Several sixth-graders had passed out too, until they ran out of ambulances and had to call in help from fire departments in the neighboring wards.

Wataru's mom had tended to his scrapes (thankfully, his front teeth hadn't been broken) and made him chicken rice for lunch. He could barely swallow it. Even though she had basically kicked him out, Wataru couldn't help but think about Mitsuru's young, lovely, sad aunt, all alone in her apartment. She didn't have anyone to make her a bowl of chicken rice. He wondered if Mitsuru's uncle (the one in America) was her brother. Maybe he was still overseas. She would have no one to turn to, no one to come running to her aid.

The afternoon news confirmed that sixth-grader "K" was still missing, and now there were further reports that fifth-grader "M" from the same school had also been missing since that morning. The newscaster added that M had left a note, and thus it was unclear whether his disappearance was linked in any significant way to K's situation.

Wataru's mom spent the afternoon glued to the television, eating lunch during commercial breaks. When the phone rang it was Katchan's mother. She was asking for Wataru's dad to come help the fire department's search and rescue team.

His mom politely explained that her husband was going to be late at work and couldn't come home. Mrs. Komura replied that any time would be fine—they would be out searching until quite late. She was speaking so loudly that Wataru could pick up her words from across the room.

"Of course, if they manage to find him before nightfall, there won't be a need," Mrs. Komura said, sounding as jovial as ever. "That Kenji was a real troublemaker. I'm sure he got mixed up with some street gang and had the sense knocked into him, that's all."

His mom apologized a few more times, then hung up and returned to the television. She seemed lost in thought.

"You father isn't calling, is he?" she muttered suddenly.

"He just hasn't seen the news, I bet," Wataru offered.

"He says they have a television in their company cafeteria."

"Then he doesn't know it's my school. They've been avoiding saying it."

His mom was silent. Wataru kept quiet too. The news stations continued talking about it, and the variety programs were already being replaced by live feeds from the school. Unfortunately, there was no new information.

Sometime around four, while Wataru was lying in his bed, resting, the doorbell rang. Thinking it was Wataru's homeroom teacher come to pay a visit, his mother took off her apron and straightened out her hair before running to answer the door.

But the unexpected guest was Sanae's mom. Wataru knew her from having seen Sanae and her together several times at the mall and the nearby supermarket. Wataru had been nervous around her at first—she wasn't just the mother of a classmate, she was the mother of a *girl*—but Sanae's mom was the friendly sort, and it had been easy to talk to her when they met.

"I heard from my daughter that Wataru wasn't feeling well and thought I'd drop by for a visit. She wanted to come too, but with all the commotion in town I thought it best to keep her at home." She looked over at Wataru who had emerged from his bedroom to say hello.

"Oh," his mom said, "I'm sorry—Wataru's fine."

"But look at those scrapes! And is that a bump on your head, poor child! Were you sleeping? You should go back and lie down, sweetie."

Kuniko quickly shuffled Wataru back to his room, handing him the melon Sanae's mom brought as a get-well-soon gift. Wataru sensed the vibe in the room almost immediately. They were going to talk about something he wasn't supposed to hear.

Of course, Wataru pressed his ear to the closed door of his room and began eavesdropping in earnest.

"Mrs. Mitani, actually, there was something I wanted to talk to you about," Sanae's mom began. "Your son goes to the same cram school as one of the missing kids, right. That Ashikawa boy?"

Wataru jumped. They were talking about Mitsuru.

"That's right," he heard his mother answer.

"I hear he's quite a good student, and handsome to boot."

"I've never met him, actually. He's never come over to our place."

"Oh, is that so? Sanae seemed to think he and your son were friends. Perhaps she was mistaken. Well, silly me, I thought that, if they *were* friends, you might know something about him. That's why I came."

"Know something about him? Such as?"

Sanae's mother's voice suddenly got quieter and more intense. "Well, I'm not one to spread bad rumors, but you see, my husband noticed something a while back. Up until now we had kept it to ourselves, seeing as how it had nothing to do with the children."

What had they noticed about Mitsuru? In Wataru's head, the image of Mitsuru's aunt crying repeated over and over. *They'll come asking questions about his family.* What had she meant by that?

"Four years ago, there was this horrible incident at an apartment building in Kawasaki, you see. A company man, age thirty, killed his wife and her lover, then committed suicide. Well, it just so happens that this man's last name was Ashikawa, and they had a son in the first grade."

Wataru's mom was silent. Wataru held his breath.

"They had another child, a baby girl—she was only two or so. The father killed her along with her mother. I suppose he couldn't bear to leave the child behind with her mother gone."

Sanae's mom continued in an excited whisper. "Now, the story went that Mr. Ashikawa discovered his wife's lover was coming to their house while he was away at work. So one day he came home at lunchtime and caught them in the act. He killed the three of them on the spot. And, after that, he waited in the apartment for the son to get back from school. He was going to kill him…"

"Please, stop this at once," Wataru heard his mom say loudly. "I don't want to hear this story anymore."

"Oh, I'm terribly sorry," Sanae's mother replied, "but I'm not just making idle chatter here, you know." She continued. "You see, the neighbors noticed something was wrong, and before the son came home, the husband escaped. He was on the run for a few days until he turned up someplace—Shizuoka, I think it was—dead. He had thrown himself into the sea."

Wataru's body froze. Was the boy Mitsuru Ashikawa? Was he the lone survivor?

Hearing no further protest from Kuniko, Sanae's mother went on. "Now the Ashikawa boy in our school was living overseas for a while, but before that he lived in Kawasaki, and he's not living with his parents now—when Sanae told us that, my husband and I knew he had to be the one. We wished the best for him then—really, we did. But with all the goings-on today, it's starting to sound like the Ashikawa boy is tied up with Kenji's disappearance somehow."

"They don't know that for sure," Wataru's mother said. "He could have just run away from home."

"Well, I wish it were a simple coincidence too, but I'm starting to think it's not."

"But…"

"So I talked to my husband. Of course, the school must have known about the Ashikawa boy's past from the beginning, right? They knew and they didn't tell us, and now look what's happened. Well, we think they should tell the PTA, they owe it to us. Other parents might have put two and two together by now too."

Wataru's mother was quiet for a while, then she finally asked in a weak voice, "And you wanted to talk to me why?"

"Well, when Sanae said your boy was friends with the Ashikawa boy, I thought maybe you had noticed something too, so I came to talk to you first. Of course, it sounds like they aren't friends at all. I'm afraid I've made quite a mistake."

"I've never heard Wataru talk about the Ashikawa boy. I'm sorry."

"No, no, I owe you an apology." Wataru heard the sound of a chair sliding. "I'm sorry to have taken up your time. It's just, it didn't seem like the sort of thing one could talk about on the phone, and you live so close. I'm sorry. I'm off to the school. Good night, Mrs. Mitani."

Sanae's mother was halfway out the door when the phone rang again. His mother picked it up. Then, after a few tense words, she hung up. Wataru heard her walk over and knock on his door.

"Wataru?"

Wataru opened the door and looked up at his mother. He wanted to say something, but he couldn't find the words.

"They found the missing sixth-grader. They found Kenji Ishioka."

He had been discovered lying down on the lawn behind his own house. Wataru's heart thudded once in his chest, loudly.

"He was unharmed. Not a scratch. But something...apparently, something was wrong. He doesn't respond when spoken to. I'm not sure this is the right way to describe this, but on the phone they were saying it was like his *soul* was missing."

His soul...missing?

"But the two kids they found first are fine besides that amnesia. Maybe they'll be able to learn more from them. Wataru, there's been an emergency PTA meeting called for tonight, so I'll be out. I want you to stay here, inside, okay? You should lie down. You look pale."

His mother fretted over him a few moments, then picking up her bag, she walked outside and locked the door behind her. He could hear her calling someone on her cell phone, probably the next person on the emergency contact list.

Kenji had come back. His friends too—with only a little memory loss to show for it.

But not Kenji. He lost his soul.

No, he didn't lose it. Balbylone ate it. That's what it was, Mom. I know what happened. I was there.

And it was Mitsuru who did it. I know.

Mitsuru, the little boy who lost his mother and his baby sister when his dad went on a killing spree. Mitsuru Ashikawa, the little boy who'd been next in line to be murdered. Mitsuru Ashikawa, who tried to commit suicide.

Wataru curled up in a ball on the floor. He couldn't control his shivering. His whole body shook until the bookshelf behind him was rattling.

So long. Goodbye.

Wataru knew now why Ashikawa had gone to the other world. He didn't have a place in this one. Vision was his home now.

chapter 12
The Witch

A day passed, then two, then three, and Mitsuru didn't come home.

Kenji's friends went back to being their normal nasty selves, although they still had no memory of the night they went missing. Kenji was the same as he had been when he was found: vacant, soulless. His eyes were open but saw nothing. Shake him and he would fall over, ask him a question and he would respond with silence.

Wataru heard the news from his mother, and couldn't help but remember Kaori Daimatsu. Just as quickly, he forced the connection from his mind. Kaori and Kenji in the same thought was just too weird.

What happened to Kenji and his friends? And where was Mitsuru? Was he even still alive? Everyone wanted to know, and everyone was worried. Only Wataru knew the answer—Wataru Mitani, the only person on earth who knew everything that had happened.

But when he went to bed that first night and then the night after that, even those vivid memories began to fade. Everything about Vision, about what really happened, was slipping away. Like before, it didn't disappear completely or suddenly. Instead, the memories wore away like a watercolor painting abandoned in the sunlight. The pigment becomes washed out, the lines blurring into indistinct shapes. The memories were still there, but they had become slippery, elusive things, impossible to grasp.

But the emotions remained. Fear, and anxiety—as though he had to find something, or someone, before it was too late. In contrast to his failing memories, those feelings of impending doom grew stronger with each passing day.

Wataru was confused. He was quick to anger. Sometimes, he would wake with tears streaming down his face, and during the day he was turned completely inward, not caring about anyone or anything around him. During mealtimes he would only peck at his food.

But there is a limit to how much a boy Wataru's age can take, and he reached it on a morning exactly one week after summer vacation began.

Being afraid of the dark, he had crawled under the bedcovers the night before. He made doubly sure to keep the lights on. The moment he closed his eyes, darkness pressed in around him and he plunged headlong into its dreamy depths. That nightmare was swift in arriving. A winged monster was bearing down on him. Running, he screamed, but no one came to his aid, and there was nowhere to hide.

He ran and he ran and when it felt like his chest might burst from exhaustion, he heard a voice calling his name. *Mom!* He shot out of the dream, like a shell fired from a cannon.

His mother's face slowly came into focus. She was ghostly pale, and she was covered with scratches. Her lip was cut, and there was a bruise under one of her eyes. Her hair looked like a bird's nest. She was wearing a short-sleeved pajama top, and her bare arms were covered with scratches.

"Mom—what happened?"

She began to cry deep sobs of relief. "Oh, Wataru, you're back. It's you, it's you," she said, rocking him in her arms. She was holding him like a baby. Wataru looked over her shoulder and gasped.

My room...

The bookshelf had fallen over, and the window was cracked. His comforter had been ripped to shreds, and there were tufts of something white floating in the air—the remnants of a feather pillow. The books and papers on his desk had been ripped and torn until they were barely recognizable. He counted at least three dents where someone had kicked or punched the walls.

But who?

Me. I did this.

"Mom? Did I do this?" he asked, dreading the answer.

"You were dreaming, Wataru. You had this horrible dream and you went wild. You didn't do it on purpose. It's not your fault," his mom said, wiping away her tears. She patted him on the head, and gave him a firm hug. But then

Wataru realized something else and his body went stiff.

The scratches on her arms. Her face. I did that too.

—*Wataru, you're back.*

I'm going crazy.

I'm going crazy, and I hurt my mom.

"I-I'm sorry," Wataru whispered, and his mom sobbed again, and assured him it wasn't his fault at all. "We've put you through so much—this is my fault, and your father's too. I'm so sorry. Please forgive us."

No, Mom. I know something, something you don't know; something terrible. That's why I'm going crazy.

"No, it's not you or Dad," Wataru said. "My friends—what happened—I got scared, that's why I…" Wataru spoke in short, clipped half-sentences. Suddenly, he realized his whole body was in pain. *Bruises. Scrapes. I did this too.*

"Of course you're scared, after that horrible thing happened to your friends," his mom said, sniffling. "But it was our responsibility to see you got the support you needed at home, and we could do nothing. We *did* nothing. I'm so ashamed. I let you down."

Calming down at last, his mom went and got the first-aid kit, and treated both of their scrapes. Wataru thought she should go to the hospital, but no matter how much he pleaded, she only smiled and said they had enough medicine at home—they'd be fine.

Fine at home, with no doctor to look at her scrapes and bruises. No doctor to ask what happened, to see the truth. I did this to Mom. That's what she's afraid of.

Wataru left his room, and lay down on the bed where his father used to sleep.

"At night, I've heard you moan in your sleep," his mom called in to him. "Did you notice?"

"Not at all."

"You must not be sleeping well at all. You look so pale, Wataru. There, you try to sleep. I'll be right here."

He didn't feel tired in the least, but he pretended to sleep for his mom's sake.

While he lay on the bed, eyes half closed, his mom made several phone calls. One of them was to school. She was talking to his teacher. Since the incident with Kenji and the others, all the teachers had been stuck at school, summer vacation notwithstanding. He couldn't hear exactly what she was saying, but he caught the word "counselor."

She talked to his grandma in Odawara too. Then she cried again. The next call was to Uncle Lou. This time she didn't cry, she was angry.

Wataru let his mind drift, and watched a dark winged thing slowly glide through the depths of his memory. A strange, pungent odor seemed to waft past his nose.

"If you won't come, shall I go to her office? Is that what you want?!"

His mother was shouting. She was on the phone again. *Who is she talking to?* Wataru sat up and listened, but his parents' room was farther away from the living room than his own, and not as convenient for eavesdropping.

"Come...see...yourself. I don't...how hard...Wataru."

From the few snippets he caught of what she was saying, it was clear his mother was furious. About thirty minutes later, the door opened, and his mother walked in. "Did you get some rest?" she asked gently.

"Yeah."

"I'm glad. Do want to eat anything? I can make you an omelet."

"Yeah, thanks."

His mom smiled.

"Your father's coming this evening. We'll have a talk, the three of us."

Surprised, Wataru looked up and immediately saw from her expression that the questions he wanted to ask, questions like "Really?" or "Did Dad offer to come by himself?" or "Was that Dad you were yelling at on the phone?" would be ill-advised. His mom was quiet, but it wasn't the tranquil quiet of someone calm and composed. She wasn't at ease, or relaxed. She was wound up tightly in a ball. The brightness of her smile could only be measured on a scale with units that hadn't been invented yet—that's how bright it was.

His mom spent the rest of the long afternoon by herself in the kitchen. She was cooking. Wataru stuck his nose in once to find that she was making all of his and Dad's favorite dishes.

Wataru's chest hurt. He was short of breath. He had to stop and take deep breaths or he felt like he might collapse. His mom was cutting vegetables, frying things, and grilling chicken until a delicious smell permeated the apartment. Wataru's feet felt cold. He knew something terrible was going to happen, and worse, he knew that half of him was actually waiting for it. Not that he wanted it to happen, but he was waiting all the same.

His heart pounded.

Maybe I'm wrong. Maybe nothing bad is going to happen at all.

Dad's coming home.

But the tiny Wataru, deep inside him, lurking down at the bottom of his heart, was cupping his hands together like a megaphone and shouting: *Calling Dad now, like this, is a mistake. Nothing good will come of it. Can't you see that? Can't she see that?*

No, thought Wataru. *No, we can't.*

His mom worked furiously, her back turned to him. Wataru had been so absorbed in himself lately that he hadn't paid any attention to her. She was so thin. While he was busy going crazy, his mom had been weeping, raging, trembling, screaming, and sinking, and he hadn't noticed a thing.

The doorbell rang.

Wataru gulped loudly, and reflexively looked at his watch. It was exactly seven o'clock.

His mother turned off the stove and looked at Wataru. "It's your father. Get the door for him." Her voice had an unnaturally high pitch.

She's nervous. Almost as nervous as I am.

Wataru made his legs move mechanically, one in front of the other, to the front door. He grabbed the doorknob and his heart throbbed in his fingertips.

He opened the door to find a woman he'd never seen before standing there.

It's not Dad.

Maybe she was a salesperson. He breathed a sigh of relief, and then she spoke.

"You're Wataru, aren't you? Is your mother home? Tell her it's Rikako. Rikako Tanaka."

Her voice was somehow familiar. *The phone—I spoke to her on the phone.* It was the woman who thought he was his mother, who had kept on talking when he didn't say anything.

It was her: the other woman.

She stared unblinking at Wataru. She was tall—about three inches taller than Mom, he guessed. She was wearing a light blue suit, and the collar of her blouse shone pure white. She had on a silver necklace. She smelled like perfume. It was the same smell as the women going home from work that occasionally got in the same elevator with him at the department store.

She wasn't as young as he had imagined. She looked very pretty in her makeup, and she was very well dressed, but he guessed her age wasn't all that different from Mom.

Wataru stood, stunned. His mother came up behind him.

"What are you doing here?"

Her voice had risen to a higher, wilder pitch than before. Wataru was too scared to turn around.

It's Mom. How can I be scared of Mom?

"I came in Akira's place," said the woman. She was looking over his head, directly at his mom. Even when she stopped talking, her mouth trembled, and while he couldn't imagine why she would smile, he caught a glimpse of white between her lips.

Like Dracula, he thought, *or maybe a saber-toothed tiger.* He recalled an artist's reproduction drawn from fossilized remains that he had seen once. A vicious, long-fanged tiger from the distant past, long since extinct, standing outside their apartment.

"I called my husband," his mother was saying. "He said he would come. He was worried about his son, and he said he would come. Why isn't he here?"

Rikako lowered her eyes and looked at Wataru. "I'm sorry," she said. She still hadn't blinked once. He saw her teeth. *Saber-teeth.* "I hear you're not feeling well. Did you go see a doctor?"

His mom quickly stepped in front of him, putting Wataru behind her back. Wataru swayed, dizzy. He put a hand on the wall to hold himself up.

"Don't talk to my son. And don't act like you care. Just whose fault do you think it is that he's not feeling well?"

Rikako didn't blink. It was weird. How could someone keep their eyes open for so long?

"Of course I'm responsible—in part. But, Kuniko, I'm not the only one doing this to him. It's all three of us. And right now, you're the one pushing him into the middle of this. Not me."

Wataru saw a shiver run down his mom's back. The hem of her apron rippled as though blown by a gentle breeze.

"Me—I'm pushing him?"

Rikako Tanaka drew back her jaw, like a thug getting ready for a brawl, and stared his mother down. "Aren't you? Using him to get to Akira. Don't you see how cowardly that is?"

"I'm *using* Wataru?" His mother growled, her voice breaking. He had never heard her talk like this before.

"You use Wataru as a shield, because you know it's your trump card. Oh, Akira can be as certain as he likes, but how can he win against that? That's why he said he would come, you know. You used Wataru to force him to. Why, if I hadn't stepped in…"

His mom reached behind her and, grabbing Wataru by the shoulder, thrust him out in front of her. "Look at him. Look at his face. See the scratches? His arms, his legs—he's covered with them. He moans in his sleep and thrashes around. And this, he does in his sleep! It's so sad, so…"

His mother swallowed, just like a child trying to be brave, and reined in the tremble in her voice. "That's why I called my husband. He said he would see Wataru and talk to him. Make him feel better. Wataru's *our* child. When a wife and husband separate they may become strangers, but the bonds of parenthood are different. I can't help Wataru all by myself. Wataru needs his father."

Rikako looked over Wataru from head to toe. Then, with a flash of brilliant white teeth, she asked, "Wataru? Did you do that to yourself? Really?"

Wataru couldn't answer. His tongue was tied with fear—fear of saying the wrong thing, fear at what he had done.

"What do you want from him?" his mother interjected.

"I want *you* to be quiet. I'm asking Wataru a question," Rikako replied, never taking her eyes off the boy. "Did you really hurt yourself? Or did someone else hit you? You don't have to protect anyone, you know. You can tell me the truth."

"Someone else?" his mother said, stepping forward. "Are you suggesting that I hit my son?"

Rikako said nothing.

"How could you even suggest such a thing?"

Rikako thrust out her chin and looked up. "I'm his mother, I'm his mother, is that all you can say? I'm a mother too, you know."

She has children? Wataru shrank, looking up from Rikako's slender legs. *I wonder what kind of mother she is.*

"I know. A daughter with your first husband, was it?" his mother said breathlessly, her face as white as a sheet of paper. "And you just thrust her upon Akira, didn't you?"

Rikako sneered. "There was no thrusting upon anyone. Akira was quite happy to become Mayuko's father. He said he always wanted a daughter."

"He can hear you!" his mother shouted in outrage, clapping her hands over Wataru's ears.

"It's over, Kuniko, you know it as well as I do. No amount of plotting and crying will win Akira's favor. He sees through all your ploys. So, go ahead, tell your lies. You're only digging a deeper hole for yourself."

Rikako continued, relentless, taking a half step closer to Wataru's mother. "Don't think I've forgotten for one day the lie you told—the lie that destroyed my and Akira's dream. We were practically engaged when you came butting in and made up that story about being pregnant. We were in love, and your lie tore us apart."

"Stop it. Stop it!" Wataru's mother cried, clapping her hands over her own ears this time.

"No," Rikako said, stepping into the apartment's hallway, her shoes still on. Pushing Wataru aside she came up so close to his mother that their faces were almost touching. "Akira and I lived separate lives, we had to. But nothing could make us forget each other. When we met again two years ago, when we realized that we were still in love, that our feelings hadn't changed, we made a decision. We'll never be able to get back the time you stole from us, but we can live the rest of our lives the *way we want*. Together."

Wataru's mother swayed and fell into a crouch on the floor. Rikako loomed over her, as if picking the spot where she would drive the final stake.

"You can't fool us anymore. If you are going to abuse Wataru just to get at Akira, then we'll take him from you, even if we have to go to court."

Wataru's mother was moaning, clutching her head in her hands. Wataru stood with his back to the wall, wishing desperately to become a piece of wallpaper, to disappear for all eternity.

He was scared. He had never seen someone hate another person so openly. Animosity seemed to come rolling off Rikako's body in tidal waves, smashing into his mother, driving her to the floor.

Rikako stepped back into the entrance hall and opened the door. As she made her way to leave, she stopped and looked back over her shoulder. "Oh yes, onc more thing," she said breathlessly, a boxer just out of a close fistfight. "Mayuko isn't our only child, you know."

Wataru's mother hands stopped moving, fingers tangled in her hair. Wataru had no idea what she was talking about, but the woman's latest revelation seemed to have a profound effect on his mother. "We're expecting next spring," Rikako continued, lightly touching her hand to her belly. She exhaled. "Too bad you'll never see how happy Akira is." And then she began to walk out through the open door.

That instant something large and black rushed before Wataru's eyes with all the energy of a tsunami wave. He didn't realize it was his mother until he saw her collide with Rikako. The two women tumbled into the open-air hallway.

Wataru's mother swung her fists at Rikako's face and upper body. The other woman desperately tried to defend herself. Grunting and snarling, their screams echoed down the hall.

Before Wataru could run out, there came a shout of surprise from the neighboring apartment unit and the sound of running feet approaching. He heard voices. "Ma'am, Ma'am, what's the matter? Please, stop! Oh no, someone call the police!"

Wataru whirled around and fled into his own room. *I can't run away. This is no time to hide. I have to stand up to her, to all of them. I have to be on my mother's side, I have to protect her...* His brain was screaming at him to do something, but his body wouldn't listen.

Slamming the door behind him, he dove under his bed. But he couldn't escape the commotion in the hallway. A woman sobbing. The old lady from next door shouting something.

Wataru covered his ears. He began reciting every spell he knew from *Saga II*—the damaging, offensive spells—one after the other. He knew nothing would happen. He did it so he wouldn't have to think, wouldn't have to feel.

"Wataru, you can come out now." Uncle Lou lay with his body pressed flat against the floor, looking in at him. "It's all over."

Wataru was curled in a ball under his bed. He had no idea how much time had passed. It could've been an hour. It could've been half a day.

His uncle's eyes looked red and tired, like he'd been crying. Wataru wondered whether Uncle Lou was sad about what had happened, or whether he was sad to see him under the bed.

"Where's Mom?" Wataru asked in a small voice.

"Asleep. Sedatives. She's out like a light."

So she was home. That was good.

"Did the cops come?"

"The cops? Of course not."

"The lady who lives next door was saying to call the police. I thought I heard sirens…"

Uncle Lou sighed as he lay pressed uncomfortably to the floor. "That was an ambulance. They had to take that Rikako lady to the hospital."

"Was she hurt?"

"Just some scratches on her face was all I could see. But she made a big deal out of it."

"Do you know about her?"

"What about her?"

"She's pregnant."

Uncle Lou blinked. With one of his eyes pressed to the floor, it came across as a wink. The effect was bizarrely comical.

"When did you get here? Did Mom call you?"

"No. I was supposed to come here today. Your mom knew…she hadn't told you?"

"Nope."

"Huh. I came to pick you up. I figured there's no need to wait for August, you could come to Chiba now. A bit of sea air would do you good. I heard the shouts when I got in the elevator on the ground floor."

"Umm…what time is it?"

"It's night already. Past nine thirty."

Wataru lay under the bed awhile, staring silently at the dust bunnies. How does dust gather in places like this, Wataru wondered. His mom vacuumed every day. Yet it still builds up, when no one's looking. Even if they don't see it, it's there, making the room dirty.

"Are they going to take Mom away?"

"Why would they do that?"

"She hit that lady."

"I don't think they're going to arrest her for that."

"But what if her baby died? It would be Mom's fault, wouldn't it? And there's no way she would be quiet about it. She's going to go to the police and tell them to put Mom away, I know it."

Uncle Lou inched closer. It looked like he was trying to hide under the bed along with Wataru.

"I'm sure the kid's fine." His muttered voice didn't sound terribly confident.

"Mom would never hit me. She's not abusing me."

His uncle lifted a curious eyebrow.

"That's what she said—that lady. She said that I got my scratches from Mom hitting me. She said if my mom was abusing me they'd take me away from her. Please don't let them do that."

Uncle Lou rubbed his face with his hands. "She said that? Now I'm starting to wish I took a swing at her too."

"She said Mom lied, and she wouldn't be fooled again—but my mom would never do that! She wouldn't lie to anyone. That woman's the liar."

"Wataru…how about coming out from under there now? I don't like seeing you scrunched up in such a tiny place. Come out, for me? You and I can go to Chiba. We'll go down to the sea every day. We'll swim, catch fish, build a campfire, and eat 'em. I'm a terrible surfer, but I've got some good friends— we could learn together. And I'll teach you how to fish like a pro. Once you're good enough, why, we can travel all over Japan to hit all the great spots. I'll save up some money and get a cruiser so we can do some trolling. Then, I'll make you captain. We'll go wherever we want to go…"

Uncle Lou was talking like a machine gun, tears trickling down his cheeks.

He's crying. Things must really be bad.

"Yeah," Wataru said quietly. "Let's go to Chiba. But let's take Mom with us. You wouldn't want to leave her here alone, would you?"

"Of course not," Uncle Lou said, wiping his nose. "We'll take your mother.

I'll teach her how to fish too."

Just as the late-night news programs were beginning, Grandma arrived from Chiba. She was breathing heavily, and hefting two giant supermarket bags.

Wataru had crawled out from under the bed, taken a bath, and was busily packing his clothes. Grandma said she would make dinner and went straight to the kitchen. Moments later she called Wataru, complaining that she had no idea where anything was. He showed her what he could, and she sent him back to his room. As soon as he was gone, she began talking furiously to Uncle Lou, but they were too quiet for him to hear what they were saying. His mom was asleep the whole time, and never came out of her room.

The three of them sat around the table and ate. Grandma always used way too many spices, she had no idea what Wataru liked, and she cooked the rice too long so it was all mushy. It was terrible. Still, Wataru ate quietly, wary of the fearsome glares he got whenever he put down his chopsticks.

"Satoru—about Kuniko. I don't think it's a good idea to take her to Chiba," Grandma said just as they were finishing up. "Oh, you should come, Wataru, it'd be good for you. But your mother still has lots of things she needs to do here. Isn't that right? We just can't take her."

Wataru looked at Grandma and found himself speechless.

Grandma, the tank.

"But Ma, I don't feel right leaving her here by herself," Uncle Lou protested.

"She could go to Odawara," Grandma snapped.

"But we can't separate her and Wataru, not with things the way they are."

"Oh? I think this will be good for the boy. That Kuniko is running him ragged."

The debate was on. Just from hearing them talk, it was clear to Wataru that this was merely one of a long string of similar debates that had taken place between the adults in his life over the past few weeks. They had told him nothing, so he knew nothing.

"I think it's pretty clear the two of them are split for good," Grandma was saying. "Things can't go back the way they were before now."

"Ma, please, not in front of Wataru," Uncle Lou said, looking severe.

"What's the problem?" she fired back. "You can't hide things from Wataru forever."

"But…"

"We can talk about it until we're blue in the face—Akira won't change his tune. He'll still want a divorce. You ask me, there's no redoing this, not now. Things get this bad, it's best for everyone to just end it quickly. Kuniko isn't so old that she can't start again, you know."

"Like it was that easy."

"No one's saying it's easy. Why, I never dreamed I'd reached such a ripe old age, only to receive *this* as my reward. I wanted to spend my golden years in a little peace."

Wataru was staring wide-eyed at his grandmother.

"What, you don't want to deal with it, so you'll just stand by and let Akira do as he pleases?" Uncle Lou roared. "Well, I won't stand for it. He calls himself a man? I'm ashamed to have him as a brother."

"Selfish…yes, he's quite selfish," Grandma admitted, grabbing a napkin and wringing it in her hands. "But Akira isn't the only one at fault here, hmm? You heard what *she* said. I remember her too. Of course, I didn't care for her much back then, but she was dating Akira for quite some time. They were in love, those two. I had already gotten used to the idea that she would be his bride. But then along comes this Kuniko and six months later they're married. A hare caught by a fox, that's what it was."

"Quiet, Ma," Uncle Lou said with a glance at Wataru. "That's all ancient history now."

"It's not history if it's going on right now. Kuniko conned Akira, no two ways about it. I knew there was something fishy about how she suddenly got pregnant, and then, once he'd agreed to marry her, she had a miscarriage. I never did believe that one."

"Ma!" Uncle Lou shouted. "Wataru doesn't need to hear this!"

"It's okay," Wataru heard himself say. "I already know that story."

Grandma wiped away a tear with her napkin. "Akira is a fool, that much is certain. A big, dumb fool. But no matter how foolish he may be, he's still my son. When a man his age wants something so much, why not give him a little happiness? If Kuniko says she won't give him up, then I'll just have to beg her. I'll go down on my knees if that will satisfy her, I'll do anything."

Grandma began to weep openly.

"What about Wataru?" Uncle Lou said, his voice barely a whisper.

"We'll take him in," Grandma said decisively. "He *is* the only heir to the Mitani name. And it'll make things easier for Kuniko to remarry, won't it?"

Wataru felt dizzy. He was afraid he wouldn't be able to sit in his chair. He felt like he was going to fall on the ground.

Just then, the bedroom door opened, and his mom walked out, drifting like a ghost.

"Go home, please," she said, staring straight at Grandma.

Wataru's mother looked like she had shrunk to half her weight in only half a day. But her voice was firm. "This is my home, and Wataru is my son. Go home."

"Kuniko?" Grandma said, standing up. "This is no time for you to be coming in here and telling us what…"

"I won't let Wataru go," she said firmly. "I'll raise him—and I won't divorce Akira, either. We are a family. You have no right to impose your decision on us."

Grandma thrust her crumpled napkin down on the table. "Who's imposing? You know what's happening here? You're reaping what you've sown, Kuniko. You brought this on yourself. Akira said you tricked him. He knows!"

Wataru's mother faced Grandma without fear. For all her fiery resolve, the older woman took a step back. The air swirling around Wataru's mother seemed to have dropped twenty degrees.

"I have been a wife, and a mother, for twenty years. If I had really tricked him into anything, how could it have lasted so long? It would've fallen apart years ago. That's not what this is about. Akira's dredged up this old story to justify his infidelity. That's all it is: an empty justification. You know as well as I do how he works. He has to have a reason for everything, even if it's the wrong one."

Grandma scowled. "That's my son you're talking about. No wonder he's run off to another woman, with you saying things like that!"

Wataru's mother stared her mother-in-law down. "Go home. Leave this house. Now."

Grandma moved to step toward Wataru's mother, but Uncle Lou stopped her. "Ma. Kuniko. Stop this. There's been enough fighting today."

Grandma waved a fist in the air. "Satoru, we're leaving. You come too, Wataru."

Wataru's answer was crisp and firm. "I'm staying here. I'm staying with Mom."

Grandma looked pained, as though she'd been stuck with a knife, and Wataru had to look away.

"Right. Kuniko, we'll leave for tonight," Uncle Lou said, grabbing his mother by the arm and walking toward the door. "But, please, think about this when you've had a chance to cool down. I don't want anybody to do anything foolish. Okay? Wataru, I'll be back tomorrow."

Wataru and his mother were left alone, the house seeming quieter than it had ever been before.

"Wataru, go to bed."

His mother's voice was flat and emotionless, just like it had been when she was speaking to Grandma. It was an order.

"I'm going to bed. Get some rest, and we'll talk about things tomorrow. Okay?"

Wataru was left with nothing to do but go quietly to his room. That woman who came earlier—Rikako Tanaka—had seemed like an ugly witch to him when he first saw her. But now, his mom was the witch. A witch, dressed all in black, spitting curses as she stirred a bubbling cauldron of poisonous stew.

Wataru sat with his back against the side of his bed, holding his knees close to his chest. He was suddenly very sleepy. How could he sleep at a time like this? But already his vision was dimming. His body, and his heart, wanted to escape from this reality.

Yes, sleep. Sleep and leave all this behind.

As he drifted, he heard the sound of a phone ringing.

What time is it? Who could be calling?

The ringing stopped. *Did Mom answer it?* He could hear someone talking. Now someone was crying. Or maybe they were angry.

Sleep. He didn't want to hear any of it. No more crying, no more shouting. All he wanted to do was sleep.

Wataru drifted off, sinking into a great dark abyss.

Time passed.

Someone was standing right next to him, shaking him by the shoulder. They weren't shaking him hard, but they were very persistent.

"Wataru, wake up."

Someone was talking to him. *Whose voice is that? So familiar, yet so strange.*

Wataru drifted up from the depths of sleep, the voice leading him to the surface. "Wataru, snap out of it. Quick."

Wataru opened his eyes. He couldn't focus. Everything was black. He looked up and saw a figure, darker than the dim background.

Mitsuru!

He was wearing a black cloak that looked like a wizard's robe. Underneath, he had on a black shirt and a pair of black, loose-fitting trousers. On his feet were knee-length boots tightly wound with leather cord. A leather belt was wrapped around his waist, and from that belt hung a short knife sheathed in a scabbard.

In his right hand, he held a staff—a black staff, topped with a sparkling gem that shone with an eerie light.

"Mitsuru..."

Wataru's mouth shot open, and he looked around.

chapter 13
To Vision

Where am I?

Wataru was in his room. It was dark with the lights out, but there was no mistaking it—he was lying in bed in the same position he had been in when he fell asleep.

Wataru threw himself at Mitsuru and grabbed onto the edge of his cloak with both hands. "Mitsuru! Where did you come from? Where have you been? What are you doing here?"

Mitsuru gave a sad smile and, resting his staff beside the bed, he bent down on one knee. "I don't have time to explain everything at length," he said, peeling Wataru's hands from his cloak. "So I'll be brief. I came to save you. You might say I owe you one."

"You owe me? You've come to save me? What are you talking about?"

"Take a deep breath," Mitsuru said, looking up at the ceiling. The fine line of his nose seemed to shine even in the darkness. "Smell something?"

Wataru snorted. He started coughing. *He's right, it stinks in here.*

"Your mom turned on the gas and let it run."

Wataru was too terrified to be surprised. Fear shot from the tips of his fingers up to his head like an electric shock.

"She wants to die—with you. She must not know that municipal gas isn't poisonous enough to be fatal."

"I-I have to stop her."

Mitsuru put his hand on Wataru's shoulder, keeping him from standing up. "There's time enough for that later. First, you must listen to me."

Mitsuru lifted his hands to his own neck. He seemed to be wearing something like a pendant—two of them, in fact. He took one off and handed it to Wataru.

It was a tiny silver plate on a black leather strap—very light, and very pretty. "This is a Traveler's Mark," Mitsuru said, closing Wataru's fingers around it. "This will let you travel freely in Vision. Go to the Watcher first and show him this, and he'll prepare you for your journey. Like so." Mitsuru spread his hands indicating his own traveling clothes.

"Vision—you mean that place? That other world?"

Mitsuru nodded. "Your memories should be returning to you. Remember? You've been there once. There is a doorway hanging in the space above the staircase in the haunted building. A Watcher waits there for you now. Don't keep him standing around for too long. Go before the star of morning rises."

*Vision...*That strange world, like the fantasy world of *Saga II*—only this was real.

"So it wasn't a dream," Wataru whispered.

Mitsuru smiled. "No, not a dream. Vision exists. In fact, I just came from there. I've already begun my journey, but when I looked into the Mirror of Truth, I saw you here. I could have left you to your own devices. But..." Mitsuru chewed on his lower lip. "Like I said before, I owed you one. And, we are alike, we two. We carry the same burden. I suppose that's why I wanted to give you a chance."

"A chance?"

Mitsuru stood, brushing back his cloak. "We created Vision—us, the people in this world—with our imaginations. Our thoughts create the energy that makes Vision what it is. It will always be there. But the way in, the Porta Nectere, opens only once in a decade—and then only if there is a place suitable to make the connection. There also has to be someone nearby who wants to change his fate more than life itself—to get back something that was lost. Only then will the gates open."

Mitsuru took up his staff.

"A suitable place?" Wataru repeated.

"Yes. Like the staircase in the Daimatsu building," the other boy said, his voice ringing loudly in the rank air of the room. "Staircases are often excellent routes for passage into other worlds. A lot of famous ghost sightings happen on staircases, did you know that? It's in their nature. Stairs cut through space vertically and make a handy passageway for all sorts of spooks."

Wataru sat dumbfounded.

"The staircase in the Daimatsu building was made, but it goes nowhere. That's why the way into Vision opened at its end. That's where I found it. That's why the Porta Nectere opened..."

"You...wanted to change fate?"

"I did," Mitsuru said, showing not a trace of doubt in his voice. He nodded deeply. "You know what happened to my family? You heard, didn't you?"

This time, Wataru nodded. Mitsuru's father had killed his mother, killed her lover, killed Mitsuru's sister, and then lain in wait for Mitsuru to come home from school.

"I want to change my fate," Mitsuru said, his voice quiet and crisp. "That's why I went to Vision."

Gripping his staff, he slid it beneath his cloak. "Vision is a vast place, with much danger, and fearful monsters. But if you can find the Tower of Destiny, the way will open to you."

"The Tower of Destiny?"

"That is where she lives, the goddess of fate. She listens to the pleas of those who come to her. That's where I'm going."

For the first time, Mitsuru's voice showed a wavering trace of emotion. "And if—and if I'm not strong enough, if I can't save my parents, then at least, I will save my sister. I must bring her back. She was so small..."

Beneath the folds of his cloak, Mitsuru wrung his hands as he talked.

"I want to go too. I want to go to the Tower of Destiny," Wataru said, standing up, reaching for Mitsuru's hands. "Please, take me with you."

"That I cannot do," Mitsuru said, stepping back. "Each Traveler must find the path to the Tower of Destiny on his own. If you do not reach it by your own volition, the Goddess will not see you. You cannot rely on anyone else for this journey."

"But that's—that's too much. We're just kids!"

"Kids trying to change fate. Did you think it would be easy?"

For a moment, that familiar disdainful sneer returned. The old Mitsuru. Wataru had almost forgotten he existed.

"I have to go," Mitsuru said, taking another step backward. "Once you've made up your mind, go to the Porta Nectere. If you're scared to go, that's fine.

Just wait until dawn, and the gates will disappear, never to appear for you again."

Then it seemed to Wataru that Mitsuru's outline suddenly blurred. Silver light spread from some unknown source and enveloped the boy standing before him.

"Of course, if you don't go, your fate will never change. It might even get worse."

Think about it— Mitsuru's voice said. But Mitsuru was already gone.

For a while, Wataru sat on his knees, staring at the space where the other boy had been. Then something fell with a clink on the floor.

The pendant—the Traveler's Mark. The silver plate, only about as large as his thumbnail, was shining. Wataru's fingers had relaxed, dropping it to the floor.

As he stared, the plate gave off a sudden rainbow-colored light. It was so bright that Wataru had to shield his eyes.

And then from somewhere, a deep voice spoke.

"You have been chosen. Walk the true path."

Wataru picked up the pendant and stood.

The gas stove was turned on full. Wataru turned it off and opened the door to the veranda. It was a hot, soupy night outside. The air hung like a mantle over the town. Yet the sweat on Wataru's forehead wasn't caused by the heat.

He put the pendant around his neck, and headed toward his mother's bedroom. When he got to her closed door, he stopped.

I'm leaving, Mom, but I'll be back. Wait for me.

I'm going to change my fate. I'm going to make it so Dad doesn't do what he did, so you don't have to hear those words, so that Rikako Tanaka woman never comes into our lives.

I'm going so our family can live in peace, the three of us.

I'm going to change my fate. Then he thought, *No, I'm just going to take this tangled mess and set it straight. The way it was supposed to be.*

Outside, Wataru walked beneath the summer night sky, taking a direct path toward the Daimatsu building. His sneakers kicked lightly at the asphalt. When he ran, he could feel the pendant swaying at his neck.

The Daimatsu building came into view. Draped in blue tarps, its silhouette seemed somehow more mysterious than it had ever been before—a giant street sign, its meaning known by only a select few, pointing the way to another world.

He went through the tarps in the usual place, crawling under until he was inside.

It was bright. Tiny particles of light flitted about, like countless fireflies. The particles stuck to Wataru's body, and when he waved his arms, and stomped his feet, they danced in the air around him.

At the top of the staircase to nowhere, he saw it—the gate. White light ran in bands around its ancient form. Rays spilled out into the stairwell, making the steel rail almost too bright to look at.

Wataru climbed the staircase. One step at a time, each foot placed with utmost care, not once taking his eyes from the gate.

As he walked, his hands moved of their own accord, gripping the pendant at his neck.

Wataru stood before the gate, and the white light grew stronger. A band of rainbow-colored light circled counterclockwise along the edge of the door's frame. The pendant in Wataru's hand shimmered, as if in reply.

Slowly, the gates opened. The light pressed upon him. Wataru squinted, lifted his chin, and spread his arms wide, bathed in the light.

And then, he stepped through the gate.

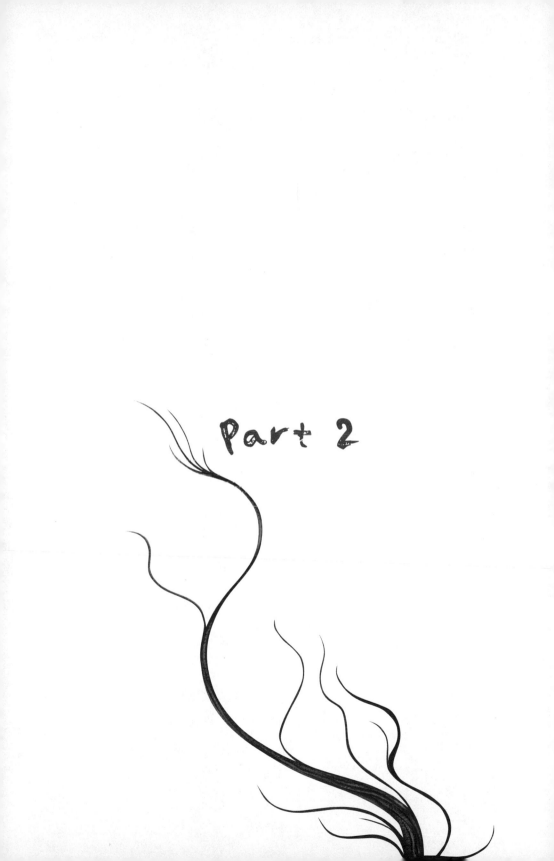
Part 2

chapter 1
The Village of the Watchers

Wataru walked through brilliant light for an indeterminate time. Then, just like that, the light faded and he found himself in a deep forest. A cool breeze brushed across his cheek.

The forest grew thick with massive trees that seemed tall enough to touch the sky. He looked up until his neck became stiff, finally spotting a patch of blue sky peeking through the canopy far above.

There, in the middle of that sky, hung a golden sun.

Fwee! Fwoo!

Wataru heard something—like somebody blowing a whistle. He looked around, and then as quickly as he could, he spun on his heel. There was nobody in sight.

Fwee! Fwoo! Fulululu!

He heard the sound again, and then a bird with brilliant orange feathers came flying out of the bushes directly in front of him. *It must've been that bird singing.*

Wataru turned his attention back to the forest. He'd never seen woods so deep and vast. The thick-growing leaves and branches intertwined above his head, making everything pleasantly cool. Oddly enough, it wasn't as dark under the boughs as he would've expected. *Probably because the sun is so high in the sky,* he thought. *It must be nearly noon.*

The ground beneath his feet was soft, and comfortable to walk on. *Humus, that's what it's called. Dad taught me on a camping trip when I was in first grade, was it?*

The ground was covered with rich green moss, and low, leafy plants with pretty white flowers. Grass was growing everywhere—soft and thick, it felt like velvet to the touch. He looked closer and saw traces of a path worn by the passing of many feet. It wound off through the woods, heading into the distance.

Wataru took a deep breath and began to walk down the path. He heard another birdsong, like a whistle, off somewhere in the woods. Wataru whistled, trying to mimic it, then waited. The bird replied, the end of its song lifting as though in question.

Fwee, fwoo, fololo?

Wataru mimicked the call again. For a moment, there was silence. Then the bird answered. *Fwee-fee, fwolololo fwee! Fwee fwololo fwee fwee fwoolulu!*

He shook his head and laughed. "Okay, okay. You win. There's no way I can do that."

The bird gave a satisfied-sounding chirp.

Walking further, he came to a place where the path zigzagged through the undergrowth. There was a clearing ahead.

In the open space sat a small hut, with a red roof and stumpy chimney. Behind it was another, and another. *A village.*

Wataru walked up to the nearest structure. He now counted five houses standing in the forest clearing. They looked practically identical, with one exception: smoke was rising from the chimney of the nearest hut. Wataru climbed three steps of cut logs to stand before a small log door.

"Hello?"

There was no reply. White smoke drifted lazily from the chimney. A pleasant smell of burning wood hung about the house. Wataru sniffed at the air.

"Is nobody home?"

Suddenly the door swung out with a bang. Wataru was so surprised he lost his balance, slipping on a step and falling on his rear in the grass.

An old man wearing a long robe stood holding open the door. "Foolish question, boy!" he snapped.

Without thinking, Wataru pointed at the old man. "You!" *The wizard from the Porta Nectere!* The color of his robes was different, but there was no mistaking that voice and wizened face.

But his eyes looked menacing, and he seemed much grumpier than he had been when Wataru met him before. He glared at Wataru, and began to frown.

"Were nobody home, how could they answer? Tell me that! Wasted words, boy."

"Um…" said Wataru, still squatting on the grass.

"More waste!" the old man shouted to the heavens. Wataru feared that the spray of spit flying from the old man's mouth would fall on him. "If you mean yes, say yes. If you mean no, say no. What kind of a word is 'um,' anyway? And why would you say it, but to follow with a proper answer directly afterward? More waste!"

"Um, but I…" Wataru began, stopping short when he saw the old man's face go red. He began clawing at his breast with wrinkled hands, spitting furiously.

"No, no, no! A criminal waste of words! Stay where you are, miscreant, and I shall mete out proper punishment!"

Robes swirling, the old man dashed back into the hut. As Wataru stared, dumbfounded, he returned, swinging a heavy-looking cane with both hands. "Prepare yourself!"

Wataru shrieked, shot to his feet, and began to run.

"Wait! No running!" Protesting, the old wizard gave chase. Wataru ran in a circle around the standing huts, like he was playing a schoolyard game of tag. The old man seemed incredibly lively for his age, and his anger never seemed to lessen, nor did he run out of breath. Wataru was afraid he might actually be caught. Panicked, he ran to the edge of the clearing, up against the forest and stopped. There was nowhere else for him to go. He was cornered.

He glanced to the side to see the back door of the rearmost hut directly to his right. Dashing past the fuming wizard, he ran for the door. The small log door opened smoothly inward, and Wataru tumbled inside the hut.

He saw a small chair, a table, and a thin blanket on a hard-looking bed. No sooner had he taken stock of his surroundings than the door behind him swung open again.

"I said no running!" screamed the wizard, charging in. Panting, Wataru flew across the hut and out the front door.

What am I supposed to do? How did I get into this mess?

Mitsuru had told him to go to the Watcher first. If this grouchy wizard wasn't the Watcher, Wataru couldn't think of who it might be. He *was* the one who he had first seen standing by the Porta Nectere, after all. *Why is he chasing me?* It didn't make any sense.

Wataru thought as he ran, looking for a hiding place, when suddenly he realized he was no longer being chased. *Huh?* Maybe his pursuer had tired at last.

Wataru turned around and looked at the village. Something was slightly different about it, but he couldn't quite pin down what it was. It was like one of those find-the-mistake puzzles.

The chimney. The white smoke coming from the chimney.

When he first arrived at the village, smoke had been rising from the first hut. Now the smoke was rising from the furthest one—the one he'd just run through.

It occurred to him that, though the wizard had chased him into that particular house, he hadn't seen him come out.

Walking cautiously across the soft grass, Wataru approached the front door of the farthest hut. He put his ear to the wood. Nothing.

Wait...is that someone humming?

"Um...excuse me, is anybody home?"

The humming stopped. Soft footfalls approached the door.

The door opened, and the wizard from before stuck out his head. He didn't seem angry at all. "Well now," he said, spreading his arms. "Perhaps you might be the new visitor Mitsuru has told me about?" His voice was kind and gentle. "What's going on here?"

"Um, Mister..." Wataru began. "You're not mad at me anymore?"

The old man opened his eyes wide. "Me, mad? At you?" But he lowered his arms and peered at the space between his hands, as though he were looking for something. "Why would I be angry with you?"

"Why—but just now—you sure you aren't angry?" Wataru pointed at the first hut. "When I met you over there, you were grumpy from the first minute. You said I was wasting words, and you were going to hit me with your cane!"

The wizard inserted a long slender finger into one nostril. "Me? I did that?"

He's gone senile.

"You did," Wataru said, rather forcefully. He feared he was being toyed with.

But then it occurred to him that perhaps this was a sort of test—a trial for new Travelers to Vision. You had to placate the Watcher to pass. If that was the case, Wataru better play it serious. "Um, I am a Traveler here, actually," he said, pulling out the pendant. "Mitsuru Ashikawa, he gave me this. He told me to show this to the Watcher in Vision, and he would prepare me for my journey. Are you the Watcher?"

The old wizard thrust his hands into the folds of his robes and brought out a comically large device resembling a telescope. Then, yanking Wataru's hand closer, he examined the pendant through the scope.

"Hrm, yes," he said. "You are the second Traveler. What is your name?"

"Wataru Mitani."

"Too long. Here, your name will be *Wataru*. It's an odd enough name, and no one should be mistaking you for anyone else as it is."

Wataru nodded, not wanting to make a fuss and risk raising the old man's ire again.

"Well, come in, come in," the wizard said, pushing open the door and waving Wataru inside. "Sit on that chair by the table. I'll get the map."

Wataru did as he was told, sitting at the simple table. His heart thumped in his chest.

The old wizard shut the door and shuffled over to a little bookshelf in the back of the room, from which he pulled out several books. To Wataru's surprise, he then tossed the books aside and thrust his hand into the empty space where they had been.

"Here it is," he said, pulling out what appeared to be a long scroll. It looked exactly like an item, the merchant's map, he remembered from *Saga II*—even down to the slightly yellowed edges.

In the game, the merchant's map wasn't a complete map of the Kingdom of Juma. As its name suggested, it was a map used by merchants to mark places of trade, and, as such, showed only the main routes and population centers. To win the game, you had to go to the Land of Faerie. Once there, you needed to add further land and sea information to the map. Then, if you could win the hundred-man bout in the capital city of Jumarang, you would get the Adventurer's Map. All you had to do after that was place the two maps together to reveal the location of Balbalan, Isle of Enchantment, where the final labyrinth in the game awaited.

The old wizard sat across from him at the table and spread out the map. He had to hold the edges down to keep them from curling back. The wizard's hands were so thin they looked almost skeletal.

"This is the map to the Cave of Trials. Follow this path, and even the greatest fool in the land could find it," he said with a significant look at Wataru.

Wataru looked over the map, and felt an immediate and profound sense of disappointment. The map in *Saga II* was a work of art. This looked like a kid's doodle. Even a sketch of the way from Wataru's apartment to the nearest train station would have been more complicated.

"So, this is where we are now?" Wataru asked, pointing to a picture of five huts in a circle.

"Precisely."

"So I just need to go into the forest to the north, straight from here?" A single road led northward on the map.

"Precisely."

"That's all?" Wataru said with a laugh. "I didn't need a map to find that!"

"Yet you need a guide to climb a great mountain—even though the only way to go is up," the wizard said solemnly.

"Climb? I have to climb somewhere?"

The wizard gave Wataru a swift slap to the forehead. "It was a metaphor," he barked. "I said you're going to the Cave of Trials. You don't climb a cave, boy."

Wataru sighed. "Right. So, why do I have to go to this Cave of Trials, anyway? Is there something there?"

"What, Mitsuru did not tell you? That is where you will prepare for your journey."

"Here?" Wataru said, stabbing at map where Cave of Trials was written. "But it's just a name. Don't you have a map of the cave itself?"

"Of course not. It wouldn't be much of a trial if I did, now would it?" the wizard said, rolling his eyes. "Listen, you will go into the cave, and then you will have your map. When you come out, you will be ready for your journey. That's how it works."

I get it! Wataru clapped his hands together. "So the dungeon has, like, a global positioning system feature!"

Slap! went the wizard's hand on his forehead. "I've never heard of such a spell. And there is no such thing in Vision as a spell of which I've not heard. Foolish words, spoken by a foolish mouth."

"But I've played all the games in the *Saga* series, I know all about role-playing games! You see…"

Wataru trailed off. The old wizard was scowling at him in ominous silence.

"Now, go," the wizard said, pointing out the window. "The Northwood is that way."

"Right, I'm off," Wataru said, standing. "Wait, don't I get a weapon or something?"

"Weapon?" The old man lifted a bristly white eyebrow.

"Yeah, like a sword or staff."

"We have no such things here."

"Nothing?"

"No," the wizard answered crisply. "Now leave."

"But what if I get attacked by a monster?"

"Then run."

"Well, if I can, sure, but…"

"Just run fast."

"Right. Got it. Great advice."

The wizard glared at him again. Wataru turned and headed for the front door. Just as he was about to step outside, the wizard added, "If you are that worried, you might try picking up a stick in the Northwood. Find one sturdy and strong."

Fine. Great. Wataru left the hut, cutting across the soft grass that grew between the houses, toward the thick green forest to the north.

A stiff wind blew at his back, lifting his hair. He could hear a birdsong, *fwee fwee*, like a whistle, carried past him on the breeze.

Chapter 2
The Cave of Trials

The air in the Northwood seemed somehow cooler than it had been in the woods Wataru had passed through on the way to the village. He could still hear the beautiful birdsong but couldn't see a single creature—not even a butterfly flitting around the white flowers that grew by the path.

Nor could he find a convenient stick such as the wizard had advised him to pick up. The only things on the ground were flower petals and pine needles.

Wataru was all by himself, and that made him feel very small and vulnerable.

As promised, the path really was as straight as it looked on the map. But in places it was overgrown with grass and brush, making it hard to see. Sometimes it would disappear altogether for several yards, and he would have to search between the trees to find it again. Wataru assumed that few people knew about this route.

After he'd walked about ten minutes, he came upon a large mound of gray rock sticking out like a boil from the ground. This, he guessed, was his destination.

So where's the cave?

Wataru looked around. The village was far out of sight. He turned three hundred sixty degrees, and all he could see was trees. A light breeze blew, rustling countless leaves.

Wataru scratched behind his head. Then he stepped forward and placed his hand upon the rock. Above him, he heard a bird singing.

Here-for-trial? Here-for-trial? Here-for-trial?

Wataru looked up and answered, "Yes! I'm searching for the Cave of Trials! Is it here? How do I get in?"

From the trees around him he heard a sound like many ocarinas blowing in beautiful five-part harmony.

If a trial you would take, guard your life.
For every question, an answer.
For every answer, a question.
The Wayfinder's yawning.
Hop on home.
Never will you solve it—not in a thousand years.

When the birdsong died down, the wind started up again. The ground beneath Wataru's feet began to rumble. And before his eyes, the lump of stone split in two.

The entrance!

It was a dark, narrow hole, barely wide enough for Wataru to pass through.

I'm supposed to go in here?

Suddenly, he was frightened. *Why do I have to go into this place, anyway?* he wondered. *That wizard better not be tricking me.* He couldn't remember anyone in a *Saga* game having to go in a place like this.

As he hesitantly stood by the entrance, a gravelly voice spoke to him from the depths of the cave. "Fret out there, and it'll close," it said.

Wataru jumped back, away from the cave.

"I said stay out thar 'n it'll close. Don'tcha understand what I'm sayin', boy?"

The voice was accented, a southern sort of drawl—just like the old man at the fishmarket in Wataru's neighborhood.

"I ain't got no time to stand 'round waitin' on a whelp like you all day. Hurry it up, or I'm liable to tell the ol' Finder."

"Are you...from the south?" Wataru called down the cave.

Here? In Vision?

"Either yer comin' in, or yer not. Which is it?"

"This is the Cave of Trials, right?"

"If I said it weren't would ya leave?"

"Well, I'm not saying that, but…"

"Then leave. Go home, boy. If y'can't trust the Finder, there's no point in ya comin' in here. Ain't got a lick of sense, do ya?"

A lick of…what?

"Fine. I'm coming in."

"'Bout time. If ya plan on doin' sometin', next time, do it quicker, 'kay? Dumb kid. C'mere."

Wataru took a half-step forward. Suddenly, from within the dark cleft in the rock, a large, filthy hand snaked out and latched onto the top of Wataru's head, gripping him like a claw.

"Augh!"

His scream echoing through the woods, Wataru was dragged into the dank cave. Now gone, Wataru was unable to hear the bird's new chorus.

Who has come?
A Brave has come?
Who has come?
A Sorcerer's come?
Who will come back out?

Through the woods, beneath the singing birds, the old wizard arrived. He carried a staff in one hand and an ancient tome of magic in the other. He walked slowly. Coming to stand before the cave that had so recently swallowed Wataru, he stretched his wizened frame.

"I've a feeling this newest arrival will take a bit more effort than Mitsuru. Quite a bit more," he said with a sigh, leaning his staff against the rock and rubbing the small of his back. "Well now, to business," he muttered, then picked up his staff and began to utter an incantation. Suddenly, his form disappeared, leaving a whisper of dim smoke in its place. The smoke lifted on the wind, assuming for an instant the shape of a bird, then it, too, was sucked into the cave.

Wataru was falling through thick darkness, down and down a hole that seemed to have no end. He screamed until he ran out of breath. Then silently, he continued to fall. He could have taken another deep breath and started screaming again, but he was falling feet first and the sensation wasn't all that unpleasant. Strangely, he soon found himself relaxed. Come to think of it, he wasn't going all that fast—he was almost floating.

So instead of screaming, he started to look around. It was pitch black, of course, but he had a sensation that he was not falling through some vast chamber. Rather, he seemed to be falling down a very slick tunnel. If he moved his arms and legs, he found that he could adjust his fall slightly. When he tried sticking his arms out like wings, he felt something touch the fingertips of his right hand. It might've been the wall.

Where am I falling to?

As he fell, he noticed a wind blowing up from below him. Warm and thick air blew up his sleeves, making his shirt billow out. As the wind blew harder, the speed of his descent began to slow. Soon he was going no faster than an elevator, then the speed of an escalator, and finally he was going no faster than if he had been walking down a flight of stairs.

Directly beneath him, something like a shining white pedestal came into view. It was wide enough for him to land on. *That must be the spot.*

Wataru spread out his arms and legs for balance, and landed directly atop the pedestal. Breathing a sigh of relief, he saw that the pedestal was made of stone. He got down on his knees and touched it with his hands. It was smooth and reminded him of the faux marble counters in his kitchen back home.

He looked up and saw something in the darkness. It was not a door exactly—more like an opening, Rather, it was a crack in the rock similar to the one that had sucked him into his current situation. He would be able to walk through easily. But what he saw beyond that was more darkness.

Be brave. Walk forward.

Wataru took a step, and then another. Suddenly, his surroundings changed dramatically.

I'm in a temple. No, wait. It's the corridor of some castle.

The ceilings were high and vaulted—about the height of a three-story building. Both floor and walls were made of stone, with large round pillars placed at ten-yard intervals. Countless sconces lined the walls, their fat tallow candles shining like stars. Still, the corridor led into a darkness that Wataru's eyes could not penetrate.

As expected, when he turned around, the entrance he had just passed through had disappeared. All he could see was the same sort of passageway as the one that led in the other direction, stretching into the distance.

Okay, pull yourself together. Egging himself on, Wataru began to move forward. Shortly, a large statue—a one-eyed giant—came into view. It was made out of the same sort of stone as the building. Wataru examined the statue. Great armor plates hung on the figure's bare skin, and his exposed arms were covered with the sort of tattoos Wataru assumed were meant to ward off evil. He carried a large axe over one shoulder.

As he stood, staring up at its face, the ground beneath his feet began to rumble, and then that rumble turned into a voice.

"I am the Dawn-God, Ward of the East, servant to the Goddess of Fate. Answer my question."

Wataru steadied himself.

The voice continued. "What do you ask of me and the dawnkin?"

Wataru's mind went blank. *How should I answer?* As he stood there, wondering, he remembered something. That's right, wasn't there something like this in *Saga I*? At the very beginning of the game, you had to make a request of one of three gods that ruled the three lands in the game. There were many choices: "wealth," "honor," "bravery," "beauty," "wisdom." Depending on which you chose, your character's abilities would be slightly different.

Wataru took a deep breath, and then in the loudest voice he could muster, he said "I want—I want to be brave. Give me bravery!"

A moment later, the weighty voice answered, "Then bravery you shall have. You may pass."

The single eye on the statue flashed red, and then the statue simply disappeared. Behind it, the corridor continued, lit by the flickering lights of ten thousand candles.

Wataru walked farther, until he came to another of the statues. He stopped.

"I am the Dusk-God, Ward of the West, servant to the Goddess of Fate. Answer my question."

"I will," Wataru said.

"What do you ask of me and the duskkin?"

"I want wisdom."

"Then wisdom you shall have. You may pass."

The giant's single eye flashed blue, and the statue disappeared.

He walked farther, until he came to the third one-eyed giant statue.

"I am the Snow-God, Ward of the North, servant to the Goddess of Fate. Answer my question."

This time, Wataru asked for health. He wanted to make sure he survived the long journey in Vision.

After he asked, the giant's single eye flashed white, and the statue disappeared. Wataru went on.

As expected, the fourth statue was the Sun-God, Ward of the South. Here, Wataru wished for happiness. No point going on a journey if it wasn't going to be any fun, right?

"Then happiness you shall have. You may pass."

The single eye shone gold, and the statue disappeared, but this time, there was no passage beyond. Wataru stood facing the wall. A dead end. Only candles flickered on its surface.

Then Wataru noticed a candlelit staircase descending from where the statue stood. Without hesitating, he proceeded down the steps. He felt elated, with not a shred of fear remaining. It was like he really had become the main character in a game of *Eldritch Saga*.

At the bottom, the stairs opened out into a wide chamber. Curtains of crimson velvet hung covering windows. There was a line of chairs with high backs sitting against the wall. The floor was polished, so that Wataru could see his own face in the reflection. Here and there were set tall candles in clusters of three. Everything smelled of wax.

Wataru looked up to see numerous paintings covering the ceiling. But the light from the candles was too dim to make out the details. He saw the vague forms of animals, flowers, and trees—*wait, that thing with the strange corkscrew head! It's a gimblewolf!*

Wataru was standing there, mouth hanging open, when a voice called out to him from a distance.

"Wataru, this way."

Startled, he looked around, and then saw, at the far end of the chamber, the old wizard seated at a candlelit desk.

"Wizard!" Wataru ran over. It felt like he was meeting an old friend. He was so happy he almost wanted to give him a big hug. But when Wataru approached, the wizard slowly lifted one bony hand and said, "Fool."

He smacked Wataru on the forehead.

"Wizard?"

"Tsk, tsk, tsk. This won't do."

"Huh?"

"Your performance. You're faring far worse than Mitsuru did. Far worse."

Why? Wataru fell silent in confusion. He thought he had answered the four Wards' questions quite well.

As though he had read Wataru's mind, the old man said with a pained expression, "That was merely average. You lack originality."

"O-originality?"

"Yes. And you were wrong to hesitate at the entrance to the cave. Times like that, you have to move quick. I'd say you lack decisive power, that's what."

No way! Wataru staggered and sat down on the floor.

The old wizard produced a long quill pen and a clipboard from somewhere. Wataru blinked, sure he must be seeing things, but no, it was a clipboard.

"Let's see, your total score is…"

The quill pen—it must have been nearly a foot long—moved swiftly and precisely in the wizard's hand across the paper.

"Vision Suitability Percentile…thirty-five percent. Special Ability: Zero. Constitution is average at best. And for Bravery…the lowest possible score."

"Th-th-that can't be!" Wataru said, clinging to the wizard's bony knee. He received another loud smack on the forehead.

"As a result you have been assigned the rank of Novice Brave, Prototype I. Your equipment will be provided."

The wizard tucked the writing quill behind his ear, and with his empty hand he gave Wataru a pat on the head. Something like a firecracker went off, showering sparks on the floor.

"Stand."

When he stood, Wataru found his clothes had changed. He was wearing a long-sleeved shirt of undyed silk—without collar or cuffs on the sleeves. His trousers were dark blue and baggy. His boots were sturdy and laced with leather straps. Only those resembled what Mitsuru had been wearing. Everything else was definitely a grade down, if not several grades down. Instead of a leather belt around his waist, he found something like a hempen cord had been wrapped around him several times.

"This...is my equipment?"

"That it is. Congratulations."

"What about my weapon? Even a Novice Brave must get a weapon."

"When you return to the surface, yes."

The wizard put pen and clipboard away inside his robes, and then with an audible exertion, he stood up from his chair. "I will be leaving for the surface now."

"Leaving? What about me? Is there another trial?"

The wizard scowled. "You do know that for every request, there is a price?"

"You mean like, money?"

"Not all prices are measured in coins. Sometimes you must offer something larger to receive."

Again, Wataru felt a tremor run through the ground. It was still distant. But it was getting closer. Something big—no, huge—was coming this way.

"I've heard your request, and the price they ask is a game where the stakes are your life," the wizard said simply. "Should you escape, you win. You'll have your life, and your wishes. Should you be captured, you'll lose. And your wishes will not be granted. But that will be the least of your worries."

With a thunderous crash, the walls of the chamber came crumbling down in four spots. The four Wards! They had destroyed the walls with their axes, the way a child destroys a sand castle on the beach. *They're coming for me!*

"There are many exits," the wizard said, pointing around the room. Wataru noticed numerous doors lining the far walls.

"Find the exit and make your escape."

"But how will I know which one is the right one?"

Axes raised, the four Wards charged.

"Good luck," the wizard said with a grin. "Remember the song of the birds in the Northwood."

Then the wizard disappeared, leaving only a thin trail of mist where he stood. The mist formed into the shape of a white bird, and was swept upward toward the darkened ceiling.

"W-wait!"

But there was no time. The four Wards were upon him. Wataru screamed and ran for one side of the room, but his legs were like jelly, and he tripped and fell. Where he had been standing moments before, the great axe of the Snow-God came crashing down, biting deep into the stone of the floor. A jagged crack shot through the floor like a lightning bolt.

"Help me!"

Wataru had always laughed at the people in movies and comic books who screamed for help when it was painfully obvious that no one would hear them, or even think of coming to their rescue. He now realized how little he knew. At times like this, you had to scream.

He struggled to his feet and lurched out of the way as another axe—this one belonging to the Dawn-God—smashed into the floor where he had fallen. Even in such dire circumstances, he could tell the statues apart by the color of the single shining eye in the middle of each statue's forehead.

Okay, run away. But to where?

The chamber was long and rectangular, and the sides were lined with countless doors. He had no way of knowing which one of them was the exit. *Do I have to open every single one in order?*

Wataru ran in a panic, and the four Wards gave chase, the floor shaking under their massive feet. Where they stepped, the floor stones broke into shards and scattered everywhere. Wataru saw the destruction out of the corner of his eye and it made his hair stand on end.

Still, as he ran, he noticed something. After one of the four Wards charged and swung his axe, it took him time to change directions. Not only that, but it seemed like the one who charged set the target for the other three. Where the first statue's axe fell, so too would follow the weapons of the other three. If he could just avoid the first axe, he would have plenty of time to run around before the next attack.

Right! Wataru ran for the far wall of the chamber, the four Wards bounding after him. The heavy armor they wore clanged and echoed off the walls. Wataru only dared look around once, to find they were right behind him.

Only a few feet away from the far wall, Wataru spun and jumped toward the line of doors along the side of the room. The Dusk-God's axe swung down, aiming for the place where Wataru had been seconds before. While the axe was coming down, he was picking himself up and grabbing the doorknob closest to him.

The door opened easily. He ran into a small, square room, lit by a soft glow, like moonlight. There were no features in the room, save a bronze statue sitting in the very middle.

Wataru breathlessly approached the statue. He tapped it. It was metal, and very cold to the touch. It looked like the statue of a fawn. *It looks exactly like Bambi!*

What's a statue of Bambi doing in a place like this?

There was no exit that Wataru could see. He groped around, but all he could feel was the cool, seamless stone of the floor and walls. There was no ladder to the surface or rope hanging down from the ceiling. He had to assume that he had chosen the wrong door. It was time to try the next one.

Wataru opened the door a crack and cautiously peered out into the chamber. The four Wards, having lost their quarry, stood in a circle at the very middle of the room. Their eye-lights were dimmed. Wataru took a moment to catch his breath. Then, summoning his courage, he slid out through the door. But the moment he took his first step back into the chamber, the eyes of the statues flashed bright, and the chase was on again.

Wataru ran close to their blades, dodging aside at the last moment, then took the few moments while they regrouped to try another door. He did this again and again, but every door he opened was much the same. They all led to small, square rooms with the statue of an animal—each one different. He saw an elephant, a tiger, a great fish, a bird, an ox, a snake, and even a frog.

As he left each room he would leave the door open. He didn't want to visit the same room twice by mistake. As he ran around, Wataru began to falter—and not on account of nerves. He was exhausted. It was getting harder each time to avoid the swinging blades of the four Wards. If this went on much longer, he would collapse.

By now he had opened every door there was to open. And, he was sad to discover, there was no obvious exit.

This isn't fair, he thought, gasping for breath. He stopped running for a moment, feeling dizzy, and the Wards immediately turned and charged toward him. *They don't get tired at all. The longer this goes on, the bigger their ad-*

vantage. What do I do?!

—*Remember the song of the birds in the Northwood.*

The wizard's parting words of advice. Wataru remembered the pretty song of the birds, like ocarinas playing in harmony.

Desperately, he tried to remember what they had said. *Something about questions and answers…I think I'm past that part, though. And the Wayfinder, yawning. And what was that about going home? Hop on home? What an odd thing to say…*

And then it hit him.

Hop.

A light went on in Wataru's head. *The frog! The frog is the way home!* He forced his weary legs to move one last time, jumping away from another blow of the Wards' axes, and running up the side of the room, staying close to the wall. *Where was it? Where?!* Wataru breathed ragged breaths as he ran, checking the contents of each room he passed.

Found him!

In the last room to the right sat a statue of a massive, plump bullfrog. Wataru leapt into the room and rolled to the statue's base. *Bong!* went his head on the bronze foot of the frog. Sparks flew before his eyes. "Ouch!"

Wataru was holding his pounding head in his hands when he heard a heavy clunking noise. The base under the statue began to slide forward. He looked closer and saw something very interesting—where the base was a moment before there was now a large opening. He could see the rungs of a ladder descending into the darkness.

I found it! Wataru rubbed his head and began to climb down the ladder. It wasn't that long, ending before the twelfth rung. Wataru stepped off the ladder onto soft, damp earth.

He was surrounded by darkness. Above him he could see something like a cave mouth, and through that—*stars!* Wataru looked up to see something shining like hundreds of stars above him. Occasionally they would flit from one side to the other in a seemingly random fashion. *Fireflies?* Perhaps these were the fireflies of this world.

By the wan glow they cast, he could see that the cave continued on, deeper. The walls were of jagged stone, and the floor was wet here and there with rivulets of water coming out of the rock.

The cave twisted and turned but eventually began to climb. It seemed to be heading for the surface—which gave Wataru much hope. He began to walk faster. At last the cave tunnel ended, and he found himself in a small courtyard paved with flagstones. In the middle, a single ray of light stabbed straight down from above. It seemed to be centered on a blue symbol of some sort drawn on one of the flagstones. Wataru felt his body grow lighter. He seemed to be walking on clouds.

Then, he blinked. He was standing in the middle of the forest, back in front of the entrance to the Cave of Trials. He could hear the birds singing. The sun shone through the trees at an angle, and a faint blue mist was beginning to creep through the woods.

The entrance to the cave was already closed, leaving only a featureless lump of rock in its place. He touched it. No rumbling in the ground. No southern accent. Nothing.

Wataru followed the path back through the woods to the place where the five huts stood. The wizard was nowhere to be seen, and Wataru saw smoke rising—not from the first hut, nor the second, but from the chimney of the third one.

Chapter 3
The Novice Brave

Wataru walked straight up to the door and knocked. Immediately, he heard the sound of approaching footsteps. The door opened and the old wizard stuck out his head. Wataru gasped. He was crying.

"Y-you've come home at last!" the old man said, sniffling. He wiped away the tears with one hand, and waved Wataru inside. "It took you quite a while to solve the riddle, didn't it?"

Wataru sat on a sturdy chair hewn from a single tree stump, and watched the old wizard sit down and brush the tears off his cheeks.

At the first hut, he was angry. At the second, he was kind, and now...

"Um, Wizard?"

"What? If you're wondering about your weapon, I was about to explain that to you."

"Well, before that..."

"Ah, yes, an introduction is long overdue. My name is Lau. You may call me Wayfinder Lau. Though I suppose I'm more of a way-shower than a wayfinder, but no matter. Yes, I am a wizard by trade, but my role here is to serve as a guide to Travelers such as yourself. You've been through the Cave of Trials, you've passed the test, so you may call me Wayfinder...actually, why don't you call me Lord Wayfinder. Yes, I think that will do quite nicely."

"Yes, Lord Wayfinder," Wataru said, speaking quickly so that he wouldn't be cut off again. "Just let me ask one question. Does your mood change depending on which house you appear in?"

Wayfinder Lau stroked his narrow chin with a bony hand. "What, you just realized this now? You *are* slower than Mitsuru."

Wataru winced. That one hurt. "But I'm right, right?"

"Quite, yes. That is the way of this village. The Watcher is bound to guide travelers to the best of his ability. Should I let my own emotions get the better of me, and become lax in my duties, then Travelers would needlessly suffer. That's why each hut is set with its own mood. That way I'll never be confused. I know I'm to be mad when I'm in the Hut of Anger, I know I'm to be kind when in the Hut of Kindness. And…"

"Let me guess, this is the Hut of Tears?"

"No, Wataru, the Hut of Sorrow." The Wayfinder blinked glistening eyes. "Tears can fall even when one is joyous, no? One can even cry from laughing too much. No, I cry in sorrow—because you disappoint me so."

Wataru sighed. "Sorry."

Wayfinder Lau walked across the room, his robes dragging behind him, delicately picking up a woven basket from the corner. He placed it on the log table before Wataru. "Your weapon is inside. Open it."

Wataru's heart beat in his chest, and his hands began to tremble.

The lid of the basket was light and opened easily—there was no lock or fastening to bother with.

A sword sat askew at the bottom of the basket. It was sheathed in a worn, grimy scabbard. The blade was no more than a foot in length, maybe shorter. The aged leather straps wrapped around its handle were so loosely bound they seemed ready to fall off at any moment.

"The Brave's Sword," Wayfinder Lau said, looking up.

"This…is my sword?"

The Brave's Sword? More like the Coward's Pig-Sticker.

"What, you find it lacking?"

"It doesn't look too, um, powerful."

"Of course not. And neither do you. A fitting match, I'd say."

Wayfinder Lau sat across from Wataru and rested his hands on the table. "The Brave's Sword is no mere blade. It grows together with its wielder. As it is now, it is merely a reflection of your own ability and preparedness—or should I say inability and lack of preparedness. As the sword is weak, frail, dull, and altogether unattractive, so too are you weak, frail, dull, and displeasing to the eye. So you see, Wataru, it's not the sword's fault."

The old man gave Wataru a sharp slap on the forehead. "Take it in your hand, look at it closely. See the design on the hilt?"

The Brave's Sword was even lighter than the basket it came out of. *A light-weight…like me.* The blade seemed to drift in his hand, unreliable, without purpose. *Like me.*

The hilt bore the same star-pattern he had seen at the entrance to the cave. At each of the five points of the star small holes about the size of a tablet of aspirin had been bored into the hilt.

"This mark—I saw it on the entrance to the Cave of Trials."

"Ah, so you did notice. Knowing you, I was afraid I was going to have to point it out."

Wayfinder Lau explained that the star pattern was a sigil—the symbol of power of the goddess who ruled Vision. "If one of due strength completes the sigil, then they will be able to work magic, create powerful Wards, fly through the air, and command the powers of water and wind. You will encounter this sigil in many places as you travel through Vision. Remember that when you wish to use the Mirror of Truth, you must be at one of these locations with the sigil for it to work."

"The Mirror of Truth?"

Wataru seemed to remember having heard that word before. *Mitsuru…*

—When I looked into the Mirror of Truth…

That's right! When he came to get me from Vision, he talked about using a mirror…

"It seems you know of it already."

Wataru mentioned what Mitsuru had said, and Wayfinder Lau nodded deeply. "Travelers from your world can use the Mirror near a star sigil to create a link between Vision and the other world—a Corridor of Light. Travelers may pass along the corridor to go back to their world, but only for a very short amount of time. Should they not return to Vision before the way is closed, then they will not be able to return home, nor will they be allowed back into Vision. They will be stuck forever in the Vale of Eternity—the gap between two worlds—lost vagrants in time."

That explained why Mitsuru had been in such a hurry to leave. *The Vale of Eternity? Vagrants in time?* It seemed like there was still much more for Wataru to learn about this place.

"Okay, I think I understand. So how do I get a Mirror of Truth?"

"What, Mitsuru didn't tell you?"

"No."

Wayfinder Lau smiled. "You need not search for your Mirror of Truth. It will come looking for you. It shouldn't be too long before you're found."

"Huh?"

"The Mirror of Truth knows when Travelers have arrived in Vision, only then does it appear. It's really not that complicated a concept."

Wataru wasn't sure. The number of things it seemed like he was expected to remember was dizzying.

"You're confused. It's understandable." The wizard wiped away more tears from his eyelashes, and gave Wataru a kind look. "I don't expect you to understand everything about this world, your world, and the Vale of Eternity anytime soon. Most come to an understanding over the course of their journey, and that's really the best way. For now, I'll tell you only the things that you must remember, the things that are most important."

Lifting the Brave's Sword from Wataru's hand, Wayfinder Lau pointed at the star sigil engraved on its hilt. "Look. See the holes at each tip of the star? These are not mere holes, mind you. They are settings. In your travels through Vision, you must search for five gemstones. These stones will fit into these settings."

"Gemstones? You mean, like diamonds?"

"Something of the sort. When all five gemstones have been placed in their settings, only then will this tiny, worn blade reveal its true nature. It will become a true Demon's Bane, fit to cut a path to the Tower of Destiny."

A Demon's Bane?

"Around the tower where the Goddess of Fate presides lies a thick mist made by the demons. Only the Demon's Bane blade can hope to cut through that barrier and open the way to the tower. Thus it was named. So, no matter how frail it might look now, do not show it disrespect, young Traveler. Understood?"

"I think so," Wataru said, feeling a kind of confident strength welling up inside. He gripped his hands tightly. "Where will I find these five gemstones? What do they look like?"

Wayfinder Lau gave Wataru a sharp slap on the forehead. "If I knew that, I wouldn't have asked you to search for them!"

"What, I don't even get a hint? I have to search all of Vision?"

"You do. But should you find yourself near one of the gemstones, it will call to you in a fashion. Follow the call, Wataru."

This is ridiculous. Wataru felt what little confidence he had draining away.

"You...do not seem prepared." Wayfinder Lau lifted his hand, as though to deliver yet another slap, but then he changed his mind, and instead covered his own face. "For many long years have I been a Watcher, but never have I found myself so lacking in faith in a Traveler as I am now. And to think you might be the Half...I fear rough times ahead."

"The Half? Half of what?" Wataru asked, wincing at yet another term to learn.

Wayfinder Lau jerked back, as though surprised. "N-never you mind about that. I swear, if the rest of you was as exceptional as your hearing, you'd be a force to reckon with."

He rubbed irritably at his face, then he lifted the sleeve of his robe and wiped at his nose. *Eww. His sleeve is filthy.*

"As for the gemstones, there is another important thing you should know," the old man said, looking calm again. "It has something to do with the Mirror of Truth."

There was a connection, the wizard explained, between the number of gemstones and the number of times the Mirror of Truth might be used.

"Find a single gemstone, and you will be able to use the Mirror once. Find another, and you will be able to use it once more. Of course, should you find a gemstone but have no need of the Mirror, you can save it up for later. The Mirror doesn't charge interest, you see.

"A moment ago," Wayfinder Lau continued, "I mentioned that one may use the Mirror only where there is a star sigil to be found."

"Yes, I remember."

"Now these places with the star sigils—I have no idea where they are. That is for you to find. What I do know, though, is that where there is a star sigil, a gemstone will not be far away. And that is your hint."

Wataru turned the Brave's Sword in his hand. "But Lord Wayfinder, I don't think I will want to use the Mirror of Truth—not like Mitsuru did, at any rate. Do I still have to look for it if I'm not even going to use it?"

There was no answer. Time passed. Wataru lifted his eyes from the Brave's Sword, and looked at the Wayfinder. The old man had his hands at his waist, and his face was twisted in a scowl. He was mad again. Only his eyes were still filled with tears. *This guy's screwy.*

"Wayfinder Lau?"

"What about your mother? You left her behind in the other world. Are you not worried for her?"

Wataru was surprised. "My mother?"

"Do not think that time stops in the other world just because you are here in Vision. Don't you wonder what has become of your mother? Don't you think your disappearance has caused her terrible pain? Don't you want to show her your face, tell her you're okay?"

It was as the old man said. Wataru had been so distracted by all the new sights and information filling his eyes, he had completely forgotten about everything he had left behind.

"Of-of course I'm worried about her. She's why I came to Vision in the first place."

The old man took a deep breath and shook his head slowly. "Then you too will need to use a Corridor of Light after all. And for that, you must seek the sigils."

"Then that's what I'll do. I'll find the sigils."

Wayfinder Lau stood up from the table and peered out through the window. "The sun's gone down," he said. "You will stay in the village tonight, and leave in the morning. You may use any of the unoccupied huts. There's only one bed in each, you see, and I'll be staying here. I'll bring you food later."

"Thank you," Wataru said. He bowed deeply and walked toward the door.

"Ah yes, one more thing," Wayfinder Lau called out. Wataru turned to find the old man staring at him, a stern expression on his face. "You must not seek out Mitsuru."

"I know. Mitsuru told me. He said you had to reach the Tower of Destiny on your own—that two Travelers couldn't walk together."

Wayfinder Lau walked over and placed both of his hands—like withered branches—upon Wataru's shoulders. "That is not all," he said. "You see, you could not search for Mitsuru even if you wanted to—because your Vision and the Vision through which he travels are not the same."

Startled, Wataru clutched the Wayfinder's robes. "What do you mean? There's more than one Vision? You mean, this isn't the same place he was talking about?"

"It is, and it isn't. Vision changes for each person who comes to it."

That's right. Wataru vaguely remembered Mitsuru trying to explain the peculiarities of Vision to him.

"I see. This is good," the old man said, with a satisfied nod. "So then you must realize that part of the energy that creates Vision comes from Travelers, like you and Mitsuru. Because you have come here, your energies have a far more profound effect on Vision. This is why the Vision that Mitsuru sees and the Vision that you see are, by nature, quite different."

Wataru scratched his head. He understood when two travelers came, their energies would be added to the world—that part was easy to get—but he didn't quite see why they would have to be separate.

Wayfinder Lau gave Wataru a final slap on the forehead. "In any case, as you yourself said, no two Travelers may travel together. Do not search for Mitsuru, for it would be in vain. That, and he's much farther along the path than you."

"Well, of course he is. He came here a lot sooner."

"Yes, and he's a sight smarter too," Wayfinder Lau added bluntly. "Mitsuru has used the Mirror of Truth once on your behalf. That means he's found at least one of the gemstones. You'll have to hurry to catch up."

The wizard helped Wataru fasten the Brave's Sword to his belt. Somehow he managed to get it to stay.

"You don't look half bad."

Wayfinder Lau hustled him out of the hut. The forest surrounding the tiny village was already dark. The grass beneath Wataru's feet seemed damp. He heard no songs—the birds must have already gone back to their nests.

The sky above his head was studded with stars. He stared up at them until the back of his neck began to ache. He could find nothing familiar—no Orion, or Big Dipper. The night sky in Vision must not be a reflection of the real one. For that matter, there didn't even seem to be a moon.

Wataru decided to stay in the Hut of Kindness. Much to his surprise, the moment he stepped in the door, a flame lit in a small fireplace. An oil lamp atop the table sputtered to life as well. *The old wizard's doing, no doubt.* Alone, he found he was suddenly very tired. Throwing himself upon the bed, he was soon deep asleep.

Wataru woke early the next morning. He was starving.

He stepped outside to find smoke rising from the Hut of Sorrow, as it had the night before. Master Lau was already up and eating at the table, tears streaming down his cheeks.

"G-good morning," he sniffled.

"Good morning."

"Come here and sit. You slept so well last night I didn't wake you for supper. You must be famished. Here, eat."

Wataru felt like he was on the brink of starvation. There was round bread with a crunchy crust, and tea that smelled of peppermint. There was a yellow fruit that looked something like an apple, but it was far more rich and sweet tasting. Everything was delicious.

"Food for the road," the Wayfinder said, passing Wataru a bulging bag of simple cloth. "There's enough for your lunch in there, but that is all I can give you. After this, you're on your own."

On my own? For a moment, he didn't understand what the Wayfinder meant. *Wait, so I have to get my own food and find a place to stay? What did the characters in Saga do, anyway?* In all the games he had played, save for some event scenes, he had never seen a character eat. And money to stay at an inn was easy to come by—if you could kill monsters.

Suddenly, Wataru felt very alone. He had never been on a trip by himself before. Once, he had gotten on the express train to visit his grandmother in Chiba, but even then his mom had gone with him all the way to Tokyo Station, and Uncle Lou had been waiting for him at the ticket gate when he arrived.

"That's right. But don't you worry. Stay on the path, and you'll reach the town of Gasara a little after noon. Gasara is a lively place, and a center of trade—the largest in these parts. All you need do is ask around, and I'm sure you'll find work."

Work. Right.

"Um, can't I kill monsters to get money or something?"

Wayfinder Lau opened his eyes wide. "Are you mad?"

Something told Wataru that his travels here would be quite different from adventuring in the world of *Saga*. He felt defeated, and sat slumped at the table until Wayfinder Lau prodded him to his feet.

"The way out of the woods is there. Good travels to you."

Wataru walked off with hesitant steps, looking back again and again at Wayfinder Lau. The old wizard stood in the village clearing, thoughtfully rubbing his chin as he watched Wataru leave.

"Well, Lord Wayfinder, I suppose I shall leave too," came the sweet-sounding voice of a girl. The old man brushed back his robes and looked down.

"I'm not down there, silly," the voice said with a laugh that sounded like the tinkling of tiny bells.

The Wayfinder grunted. Still looking down, he said, "Well, Lady Onba, you certainly seem to have taken to our young traveler. Not that I can fathom why you'd do such a thing."

"But he's so cute, so young. All Travelers should be cute, I think," the lilting, enchanting voice said. It was the same voice that had spoken to Wataru in his room—the one he called a fairy.

"The other Traveler, that Mitsuru, he's a handsome lad, no?" Wayfinder Lau said, then quickly clapped a hand over his own mouth.

"Hmph," the sweet voice said, pouting. (Or at least it sounded like she was pouting.) "Really, Lord Wayfinder. You needn't be concerned about *that* anymore."

"Erm, yes, well, my apologies all the same. But, Lady Onba," Wayfinder Lau added quietly, "feelings aside, it does not do to intervene too deeply in Travelers' affairs. You wouldn't want to incur the Goddess's wrath again, would you?"

"Oh, that trollop can thunder and fume all she likes! I'll do as I please, as I always have. I'd reconsider my unwavering support of her too, if I were you, Lord Wayfinder."

The old man lowered his head and said nothing. He stood there motionless for a while before realizing that Lady Onba had departed—most likely to follow Wataru.

"Dear, dear…" the Wayfinder muttered under his breath. His face was dark. "I knew only trouble would come from Lady Onba's delvings into the other world."

Wayfinder Lau walked over to the window and looked out. As one, the birds of the forest resumed their song, as though they had been waiting for him.

Good morning, Wayfinder. Good morning.

"Lo, my friends," the old man called out smiling. He leaned on the windowsill and, listening to their song, sat for a long while deep in thought.

chapter 4
The Endless Field

Wataru continued walking in the direction he had been shown. Suddenly, and dramatically, the deep forest changed.

"Whoa!"

Before him stretched a vast field—a sea of grass as far as the eye could see. It seemed to stretch all the way to the horizon.

A refreshing breeze washed over Wataru's face as he stood gazing out on the waving grass. Here and there, bleached rocks jutted out from the greenish towers. Here and there, the grassland dipped and rolled with little hills and valleys. In other places it was dull and flat. The sheer distance he could see was breathtaking.

—*Walk toward the rising sun.*

So had Wayfinder Lau instructed him. Only one sun rose in Vision's sky, and it was quite similar to the one in the real world, except that you could look straight at it and not risk hurting your eyes. It wasn't very bright. Wataru remembered that in *Saga I*, there were two suns. The story went that one of the suns burned too hot, until it threatened to destroy the very world. *Not a problem here.*

Wataru walked out into the field. There were no roads to speak of. Nor could he hear any birdsong. Occasionally he would spot insects, like tiny white moths, that would flutter about him. But otherwise, he had no other companions.

For a while the pleasant view lifted his spirits, but as he walked through the seemingly endless plains, he began to realize the harsh reality—or perhaps here he should say the *fantasy*—of his situation.

I'm going to be walking forever. I have no other means of transportation. No car, no train. Nothing to rely on but my own two legs.

Well, he thought, hoping to cheer himself up, *every RPG I've ever played begins with the main characters walking.* It didn't work. Games were games. When he played the last dungeon of *Saga II* with Katchan, their characters had to walk forever through treacherous terrain, but the hero never said, "I'm tired." Wataru and Katchan, for their part, were sitting on the floor, or lying on their sides, drinking as much cola and juice as they pleased.

The thought of a cold drink made him suddenly thirsty. It occurred to him that, though the Wayfinder had given him a lunch, he hadn't said anything about drinks. Wataru had to find a source of water, a river, or a lake. And he had to find one soon.

He walked on a while, and when he felt he'd gone a substantial distance, he looked back over his shoulder. The forest was still close behind him, looming thick over the grassland. *How depressing. I must walk slower than I thought.*

He continued on in silence with no one to talk to. The sun beat down hard and hot on the unchanging field. Wataru was sweating. He forced himself to keep up the pace by counting steps, *one, two, three.* This seemed to help. It occurred to him that part of his unease was because he was unable to count the passing of time with any accuracy. Then again, he hadn't wondered what time it was once since his arrival in this world. It didn't seem to matter.

When he'd counted nearly a thousand steps, he spotted a small, round copse of trees ahead and to the left. It was as though someone up in the sky had gathered a bundle of trees and stuck them straight into the ground. The cluster of trees seemed very tall above the flat of the plain.

Wataru stopped and wiped the sweat off his forehead with a hand, and began to walk toward the woods. He counted his steps again, starting over with *one.* With trees growing like that, he thought, there might be water—a sort of oasis in this desert of grass.

Water...water...cool water. He repeated the words to himself like a mantra, approaching the oasis, until at last he saw something like a roof poking out between the trees. He caught a glimpse of tiles as the tree branches swayed in the wind off the grasslands. *Somebody must live there.*

At about fifty paces away from the stand of trees, Wataru noticed a thin line of white dust rising on the horizon. He stared at it, and saw that it was moving from right to left, a little at a time. In fact, it seemed to be coming this way, heading for the oasis.

Wataru ran for the copse. As he drew nearer, he could hear leaves blowing in a stiff wind. There, in the middle of the trees, he could see a low wall of round stone, above which hung a bucket on a rope. *A well! It really is an oasis.* At least, he thought it was a well. It was Wataru's first time seeing the real thing. He walked over to the rim and looked down to see water glimmering in the half-light below.

The tiled roof stood above it, supported by four sturdy wooden posts. *Probably to keep rainwater out,* Wataru thought, *if it ever does rain here in Vision.*

Wataru drew water from the well, and putting his lips to the edge of the bucket, he drank in deep gulps. It was cool and delicious. A loud sigh of relief escaped his lips. Heedless of the water dribbling down the front of his shirt, Wataru continued to drink and drink.

Catching his breath and looking around, Wataru noticed red fruits resembling tomatoes lying on the ground. They appeared to have fallen from the trees around the well. Most were overripe and squashed by the fall.

Wataru picked one up and sniffed. *Sweet, a little tangy. Seems edible.*

Wataru gazed up at the trees, but the branches were all high off the ground, and the trunks were perfectly smooth. He had never been one for climbing trees much anyway.

He thought for a while and then began gathering a few palm-size rocks. Taking one in his right hand, he threw it up at the branches, trying to knock down some of the fruit that had yet to fall. Wataru had played enough catchball that he had a pretty good aim.

His efforts soon met with success. Picking up one of the fallen fruits and brushing off the dirt, he carefully took a bite. *Tastes like a tomato too.* But it was a far richer, juicier fruit than any tomato Wataru had seen at the supermarket. Wataru was starting to wonder if all the fruit in Vision tasted so delicious.

Even better, if he gathered enough of these, he wouldn't be thirsty—or hungry—on his journey. Wataru continued picking up the fruit. He was so absorbed in aiming and throwing rocks, that when a dusty wind blew through the wood along with the sound of hooves it took him entirely by surprise.

"Oy! Ooooy! You there!"

Someone riding on a drawn carriage was approaching the woods, waving his arm in Wataru's direction. The voice was loud and carried well in the dry air. Wataru ran to the edge of the woods, and shielding his eyes from the glare of the sun with one hand, he looked out over the glimmering green grassland. The dust line he had seen before must have originated from this carriage, he realized. *Odd that so much dust would come up from this grassland.*

Then Wataru noticed the road. *Maybe it's the road to Gasara!*

The carriage-like thing had slowed down, no longer kicking up dust. As it came closer, Wataru noticed something quite odd. The covered carriage was the same as anything you might see in an old Western movie, but what was pulling it wasn't exactly a horse. It was—*what is that thing?*

The creature pulling the carriage looked like a cow, but its neck was far too long. Two horns grew from its forehead. It was large, with silken gray fur, and enormous hooves that spread out at the bottom like a pair of bell-bottom jeans.

"Oy! You there! Don't eat too many o' those *baquas* now, y'hear?"

The person riding on the carriage drew in the reins, and the vehicle came to a stop nearby. "Darbabas love 'em, I know. Ah, they're sweet as can be. But not for people folk. Eat too many o' those and yer stomach'll tie itself into all sorts of knots."

Wataru dropped the half-eaten fruit in his hand. The driver laughed out loud and stepped out of his carriage. "Still, that's no reason to waste what you've got already. They're not poisonous, mind you. And they *are* delicious, eh? Maybe I'll help meself to one o' them 'fore I let my darbaba at 'em. Hrmm…"

Wataru stood with his mouth open, shaking.

It's a lizard!

The man driving the carriage pulled by the long-necked cow was a lizard. He stood about six feet tall, and his skin was covered in dun scales. Fishing up one of the fruits from the ground, he wiped it off and began to munch at it noisily. Sharp teeth glinted in his mouth. He looked exactly like one of the monsters in the *Saga* series—the Lizard-Men—so much so that were he holding a sword, Wataru wouldn't have been able to tell the difference.

"What is it, boy? Something on my face?"

The lizard-man walked over, smiling broadly. Wataru took a step back. The driver tilted his neck and scratched thoughtfully at his cheek with his hooked claws. "Hrm, what's wrong, scared of something? You sure are a small one, aren't you? Alone, eh? Your pa around?"

Wataru thought to answer, but his tongue caught in his mouth.

"Where did you come from, little one?" The lizard-man asked kindly, munching one of the red fruits as he spoke. "Wouldn't expect to see refugees from the Empire out in a backwater like this...you're an ankha, right? First time meeting a waterkin, is it?"

Wataru swallowed noisily, and managed to say in a strained voice, "Y-y-you're a *waterkin*?"

"In the flesh!" the lizard-man replied. As he talked, he gathered up more of the fruit in his big hands and fed them to the long-necked cow. The cattle-thing made a mooing sound and worked its massive jaw. It seemed happy.

"A-and I'm an...ankha?" Wataru asked, pointing at himself.

"Of course you are. First race made by the Goddess. That's why you look so much like her. Didn't they teach you that in school?" the lizard-man said, baring his teeth. *That must be a grin,* Wataru hoped.

Wataru thought. These "ankha" the lizard-man was talking about must be the name for the race that look like humans in this world. That meant that Wayfinder Lau was an ankha too. So there were other races in Vision.

"Th-that animal..."

"My darbaba? What, first time seeing one of them too? Don't be frightened, they're gentle as can be. He loves it when you rub him behind the ears."

The darbaba was happily munching away, baqua juice dripping from the corner of its mouth, getting an ear-rub from the driver. He adjusted the short leather kilt around his waist, and peered again at Wataru.

"If you've not seen a darbaba before, boy, then you *must* be from the Empire. I hear they don't use livestock to pull carriages there. Why, once a traveling merchant bought five head off o' me, said he'd bring 'em up to the city and charge people just to look at 'em. Course I heard he went bankrupt a few months later, but still."

Wataru wondered about this Empire the lizard-man was talking about. *So there's more than one country in Vision.*

"If we're not in the Empire here," Wataru began, "where are we? Does this place have a…"

He was going to ask if it had a name, but he stopped halfway. Wataru gaped. He couldn't believe what he was hearing.

What are these words coming out of my mouth? It's not Japanese. It's not even English. I've never heard this language before in my life.

Yet he spoke without difficulty and seemed quite fluent. He had no difficulty understanding the lizard-man's speech, either.

"Somebody must've switched my head on me when I wasn't looking," Wataru muttered to himself. "I've become one of them, one of the people of Vision. Like someone cast a spell on me."

The darbaba mooed plaintively for more baqua, and the lizard-man obliged with what seemed to be a bemused expression on his face. Although, to be honest, Wataru wasn't exactly sure what kind of expression was on his face. The lizard-man's eyes were set on either side of his nose and his mouth was hanging half open. His sharp teeth glistened brightly in the sun.

As Wataru stood frozen, trying to think of something to say, a long tongue slipped out of the lizard-man's mouth. It looped around in a wide arc and licked the very top of the lizard-man's head. Wataru stiffened, but, not wanting to appear rude, stopped himself from stepping back.

"Well, this is a surprise," the lizard-man hissed through large, sharp teeth. "Don't often see ignorance on this scale in a—wait, you wouldn't happen to be a Traveler now, would you?"

Wataru nodded slowly.

"You are! You are?!"

The lizard-man lifted his scaly arms and clapped his massive hands together. Then, with a surprisingly fast motion he strode over to Wataru and embraced him.

"Whoa! What're you doing?"

Wataru's feet dangled almost three feet off the ground. The lizard-man had muscles befitting his size. Lifting Wataru seemed to require no effort at all. It was like getting a hug from a pro wrestler.

The lizard-man seemed overjoyed. With squinting eyes he lifted Wataru high into the air, and began to jump around like he was doing a little dance.

"Happy, happy! When I woke up this morning, I knew something good would come of the day, but little did I know! To meet a Traveler, this is a joy beyond joys! What a lucky fellow am I!"

Tossed about like a rag doll, Wataru felt like his eyes might spin out of his head. "Uh, er, excuse me," he gasped. "My stomach—I think it's going to fly out of my mouth."

"Very sorry, boy," said the lizard-man, bringing Wataru back to earth. "Well, Mr. Traveler, tell me, when did you come to Vision? You're headed for the Goddess's tower, no? Or perhaps you have some other destination in mind?"

Wataru rubbed his temples with his fingers. He was pleased to see that his head hadn't been entirely warped by the shaking. "I've only just arrived yesterday. This morning I left the Wayfinder's village, and I've been walking in these grasslands ever since. I came here looking for water…"

"I see, yes, I see. A new Traveler, are you now? That explains why you know so little. Where were you headed?"

"I thought I would head to the town of Gasara—where the Wayfinder told me to go. He said if I didn't get lost, I'd get there just after noon."

"Gasara? Then I'm afraid you have gotten lost. It's not far, true, but you're well off the path. On your legs, I don't think you'd make it there before sunset."

Wataru frowned. He had walked toward the sun, just as he was told. Where could he have gone wrong?

The lizard-man grinned, baring his fangs. "It's okay, don't worry. I'll take you to Gasara. Ride in my carriage, and we'll be there while the sun is still high in the sky. That darbaba you see over there, he's the surest and swiftest-footed of my lot. Name's Turbo."

Swiftest?? To Wataru, the creature looked like he was sleeping on his feet. Oh well, a free ride would be welcome—no matter how fast or slow the pace. On cue, Turbo made another friendly mooing noise.

"My name's Wataru."

"Wataru? My name's Keema, but, well, you see it's a rather popular name among us waterkin, so most add on my middle name too, so as not to confuse me with someone else."

"So, what should I call you?"

"Kee Keema," he replied, enunciating carefully. "The first syllable, you pronounce that about a half tone higher than the second part. Else it sounds like a girl's name, see?"

Kee Keema. Wataru tried saying it, practicing the pronunciation several times. It wasn't a particularly difficult thing to say, which somehow made it hard to mimic exactly. At about the twentieth try, Kee Keema scratched his head. "On second thought," he said, "let's not worry about my name, eh? We've got better things to do, places to go!"

"Sorry…"

"Don't let it bother you. That seventeenth time, just then, that was headed in the right direction."

Kee Keema rose lightly to his feet and prepared to set off. Wataru hesitated. "But, Kee Keema, I'd feel bad just riding along with you. Don't you have work? I wouldn't want to get in the way…"

Kee Keema waved his hands, hooked claws and all. "Who cares about work! Once I tell my boss I met a Traveler, why he wouldn't be mad at me over a little detour."

"What's so great about meeting a Traveler?"

"Why, it's the best, most happiest thing that could ever happen to a fellow!" Kee Keema shouted, swinging his arms wildly. He began dancing again. "Frankly, I can't quite believe my own fortune! When I was a wee one, they used to tell me that Grandpa came across a Traveler once on the outskirts of Takio Town, and right after that he had himself a windfall trading mining stocks. Why, my own Pop went out looking for Travelers once, spent months searching and couldn't find a thing. So here I come along, thinking to wet Turbo's throat at the well here, and who do I meet but you!"

So people from Wataru's world were like omens of good luck. That made sense, considering Travelers could come only once every ten years. Meeting one would be a rare thing indeed.

Kee Keema helped Wataru scramble up into the darbaba carriage. He sat by the waterkin's side. The bench had been fashioned from a single plank of hard wood, and couldn't exactly be called comfortable. But compared to walking across the endless grasslands, it felt like a seat in paradise.

"Now you'll want to tie your waist to the baggage cart with that leather strap there," Kee Keema cautioned. "I'm used to it so I'm fine, but when Turbo really gets going, the carriage, she rocks a bit."

Then with a loud and crisp *hyah!* and a quick snap of Kee Keema's whip, they were off. Turbo gave a low bellow and steam arose from his nostrils, reminding Wataru of his mother's favorite pressure cooker.

"That's right, Turbo's feeling it now!"

Half of Kee Keema's words fell short of Wataru's ears as Turbo launched into motion and the hard seat below Wataru's rear suddenly transformed into a trampoline. If he hadn't been holding on so tightly, he would have been bumped up and out and deposited on the ground right then.

"Hang on!" Kee Keema shouted, grabbing Wataru by the collar and pulling him back to the seat. "Don't be jumping around like that. Stick out your legs, put little a strength in yer gut."

"I'm tr-trying," Wataru stuttered, barely able to catch his breath for all the jostling. He was being tossed about like a lottery ping-pong ball, afraid to talk for fear he would bite off his tongue. Every time he tried to grab something to hold on to he clutched empty air. It wasn't just bouncing up and down either. They lurched to the right, then the left, and sometimes curved through the high grasses at an angle so steep Wataru feared they might tip.

"Can't you slow down a little?"

Suddenly, Wataru found himself in the air, his arms and legs flailing uselessly. Then he was landing on Kee Keema's shoulders, until he was riding the lizard-man piggyback.

"Ha ha!" Kee Keema laughed with his mouth wide open. "You're welcome to sit up there if you like, Traveler Wataru!"

"N-n-no I c-couldn't! R-really, I-I'll get off. I'm t-too heavy…"

"Nonsense! Yer light as a feather."

"But, but, but…" But he couldn't get off even if he wanted to. The waterkin's skin looked just like a lizard's, but it wasn't slippery at all. Rather it was a dry and sturdy, and his neck was just the right size for grasping onto for dear life.

Wataru found himself wondering how many years it had been since he last rode on his father's shoulders. His father wasn't a big sturdy man like Kee Keema, but riding up there, Wataru always felt secure. He would bounce and his father would get angry at him, saying he was too heavy—but Wataru knew he didn't really mean it. *Or did he? Was I too heavy all those years?*

Wataru looked up. Now that he didn't have to be so worried about falling off at any moment, he could enjoy the scenery a little. As far as he could see everything was grass, glowing like a green saucer catching the sun's light. The thing like a road Wataru had seen in the distance now seemed to be more of the path worn by the passing of darbaba carriages. It narrowed and widened, at times twisting like a snake, at times lying straight like a white line across the grass, shooting toward the horizon.

The air was a little gritty, but the feel of the wind on his face and in his hair was exhilarating. Wataru breathed deep and felt like shouting at the top of his lungs for no reason at all.

"Fast, isn't he?" Kee Keema shouted, turning his head so his voice wouldn't be entirely lost in the wind.

"Amazing!"

"Raised this one from a baby, I did. Best runner in Nacht, or me name's not Kee Keema!"

Are we in Nacht now? Is that a country?

"Kee Keema, do you think you could tell me some things about Vision?"

"Sure. But, you should know I dropped out of school kinda early, so I might not be able to teach you very good."

"You were talking about an empire before, right?" Wataru asked. "That's in a different place from here?"

"That it is. And a good thing too."

Kee Keema explained that, back before time flowed in an orderly fashion, the land of Vision was born from a swirling rainbow sea. It was the Goddess who first reached down and drew the new land from the waters.

"And this goddess is the same one that Travelers go to see in the tower? The Goddess of Fate?"

"Think so. But no one knows the truth of it. No one's met the Goddess, you see—we don't even know quite where she is. We only know there's a place called the Tower of Destiny, somewhere, and that's her home. It's a legend."

"A legend…"

It seemed odd to Wataru to find that this land that was something like legends and myths and a fantasy world all jumbled into one would have legends of its own.

"Does this goddess have a name?"

"That, I don't know. Most of the races consider calling her by name a taboo. They don't teach it in school, and I'm sure no scholar would dare try to research it. But, we waterkin have an old word for the Goddess, it's *Upa de shalba*. Means "the one who is beautiful like the light," he said.

One as beautiful as the light. An image of Venus, the goddess of beauty, rose in Wataru's mind. Whatever she really looked like, she was certainly kind. She would have to be if she really sat in the tower waiting for Travelers to arrive and then honored them with any wish they desired.

"There are two great lands, continents, in Vision," Kee Keema began to explain. Turbo had slowed somewhat, until he was trotting amiably along.

"One in the north, and one in the south. They're about the same size, but that's where the similarities end. Down in the southern lands, we've got mountains aplenty, and the seasons bring all sorts of weather. It's warm though, so there's lots of animals and greenery. They say the northern continent is covered in ice and snow for near half the year."

The two continents, he explained, were separated by a vast sea. And this sea, he said, was shrouded in a thick, nearly impenetrable mist.

"It's hard to see much in that mist, so not a whole lot is known about the open sea. The sailors say there's a cluster of tiny islands right between the northern continent and the south, but no ships sent out to find 'em have ever returned. Now, some say that right where those islands are, that's where you'll find the Tower of Destiny, but if you ask me they've got it all wrong. Those islands are where the monsters and villains and enemies of the Goddess are bound in chains. A prison colony, it is."

Wataru just hoped the Tower of Destiny wasn't in such a hard-to-get-to place. "But you *can* travel between the two continents, right?"

"Of course you can. There are several known trade routes between the two lands, and merchant sailships ride them pretty often. Sailships ride the waves by the power of the wind, you see. Of course, when there is no wind to be had, they don't move. That's why it's so important to know just how much wind you need for how many days to cross by a certain route, and knowing when that wind's going to blow, well, that's the most important thing of all."

Kee Keema explained that the ones in charge of foretelling the winds were called "starseers."

"They can tell which way and how hard the winds can blow just by reading the stars, see—thus the name. And knowing about the wind isn't their only job. Why, they know all sorts of things about the world. They're virtual treasure houses of information. Should you need anything on your travels, you might try asking one of them a question. The largest towns'll have at least one set up in a fancy old Seerhall. You'll find it in no time."

"So we're on the southern continent? It must be, with grass like this."

"Exactly!" Kee Keema said brightly. "Nacht is one of the United Southern Nations, you see."

There were four of these smaller countries on the southern continent, Wataru soon learned: Nacht, Bog, Sasaya, and Arikita, along with a place with the rather convoluted—to Wataru's ear—name of the "Special Administrative State of Dela Rubesi." All of them together formed a sort of Republic. Lacking a notebook, Wataru repeated the words inside his head. *Nacht, Bog, Sasaya, Arikita.* He couldn't remember ever being this interested in social studies class.

"Speaking generally, Nacht is a country of agriculture and livestock. Most of it is flat plains in the southernmost part of the southern continent. On the opposite side, next to the ocean, is Bog, land of merchants. Sasaya, then, is a haven for scholars. Just about every starseer goes there once in his lifetime to study. Arikita is the most industrious of the southern nations. Lots of mines there too."

"What about this Special Administrative State of Dela Rubesi place?"

Kee Keema tilted his head. Instead of an answer, he asked a question. "What sort of gods do you pray to, Wataru?"

"Gods? Um..." Wataru hesitated. He hadn't ever really thought about God, or gods, before. "I'm not really sure. Maybe my mom could tell you."

"What, is she a priest?"

Wataru laughed. "No, but, my grandpa in Chiba's grave is at a temple that belongs to some sect or other. I'm really not sure..."

"Hrm? A sect you say? What's that?"

Kee Keema let go of the reins with his right hand and scratched at his lip with a crooked nail. It was the exact same gesture Katchan would make when the teacher asked him a question at school and he didn't know the answer.

Wataru wondered how old Kee Keema was. His body was quite large, but it occurred to him he might be younger than he looked.

Who knows? The waterkin may age differently than us—than the ankha, I mean.

"There are many different peoples living in the southern lands, you see, but they all pray to the Goddess of the Tower."

When Kee Keema spoke about the Goddess, his tone became very serious. "Why, she was the one who made this world. She started it all. In a way, the Goddess is like our mother."

But, he went on to explain, there were some in Vision who thought differently.

"Some people say that she didn't make the world at all—that some other god made the world, and she's just watching it for 'im."

"Watching the world?"

I don't suppose a world is the kind of thing you can just throw in a coin locker and forget about.

"So somewhere there's a god that's even more powerful than the Goddess?"

"More powerful…or just older. That's why they call him the Old God."

He explained that the Special Administrative State of Dela Rubesi was formed of people who believed in the Old God as Creator. In some ways, it was more of a church than a nation.

"Right in the middle of the southern continent is a high plateau, the Undoor Highland, and that's where you'll find Dela Rubesi. The people who live there don't mingle much with us low-landers. They grow all their own food—or so we have to assume, since they never trade for it. Truth be told, no one knows much about them. They don't let in outsiders, you see."

"So what do these people who worship the Old God think of the Goddess?"

"What do they think? Not much, frankly. To them, the Old God is much more important. When the apocalypse comes to our world, and the end is near, they say the Old God will come again and bring order to the world."

"What does everybody else think about this? What would you think, Kee Keema?"

"Hrm…well, I don't know much about history," Kee Keema said, avoiding the subject. "But I know about the Old God, because they tell you all about him when you're a child. They say he's a god from way way back. We waterkin call the Old God *Il-da Yamyamro,* which means the One Who Brings Order to Chaos."

"The One Who Brings Order to Chaos." *Cool name.*

"'Course, since the Empire came together 'bout three hundred years back, no one just believes in the Old God anymore. You're either a true believer in 'im, or a follower of the Goddess, and never the twain shall meet."

He explained that the northern continent used to be made up of tiny city-states, like the southern continent, with many different races mingling together.

"My grandpa used to talk about how it was so cold up there, and the land was bare, and the mines were stripped—that's why they spent so long fighting each other."

The northern continent had starseers too, but they had been too distracted by the war that their knowledge hadn't advanced to the point of their southern fellows. Without the skill to read the winds, they were unable to cross the waters easily—sparing the rich lands of the southern continent from invasion.

"Until about a hundred years after unification, when our sailships first started making the passage north, we had no idea what it was like up there. That's what I heard from my Grandpa, and he heard it from his parents when he was just a wee one.

"When at last there was the signing of a trade agreement between the United Southern Nations and the Northern Empire, the South had to agree to an odd sort of promise: we would teach only the history of the North beginning with the Empire's creation. That's why, to this day, in the schools of the South, world history begins only three hundred years ago."

"That's ridiculous!" Wataru said, a bit too loudly, and he threw up his arms, forgetting his precarious position on top of Kee Keema's shoulders. He toppled off and was caught only at the last moment by a quick grab by Kee Keema's strong fingers.

"Watch it, there," Kee Keema growled, dragging Wataru back up to his shoulders. "Wouldn't want me good luck charm to get run over by me darba-ba. That'd curse me to the end of my days for sure."

Far across the grassland, Wataru spotted another clump of trees. "We're 'bout halfway there," Kee Keema said, pulling on the reins. "How's about we take a rest at that oasis, hrm?"

Instead of a well, this stand of trees had a small spring surrounded by stones, from which clear water bubbled and burbled in an ever-flowing stream.

Wataru cupped some in his hands and tasted it. It was sweet.

"I'm famished! Aren't you? Let's eat."

Wataru sat down by the spring and spread the package he had received from the Wayfinder on his knees. Meanwhile, Kee Keema brushed down Turbo, then went back to his carriage. Thrusting his hands beneath the cover, he pulled out something that looked like a slab of some dried meat.

"What's that?" Wataru asked, craning his neck to see, when he saw with horror that the thing in Kee Keema's hands had two eyes shining a violent shade of red. Kee Keema's jerky had a face.

"This? Dried n'bara. Best thing on the road," the waterkin said, licking his lips and taking a big bite out of the thing's side.

Wataru swallowed the bile he felt rising in his throat, and steadied himself. Though it was hard to tell from its current desiccated state, he figured the n'bara was a small animal that looked something like an extremely ugly raccoon.

So the waterkin are carnivores.

Wataru noted this new fact in his head, and quietly ate his bread. Kee Keema finished the n'bara jerky in three bites, and began picking fruit from the trees around the spring. Crunching one between his teeth, he offered another to Wataru. "Mako berries! They're a little on the sour side, but they won't mess with your stomach like baquas. Careful not to get any of the juice on yer shirt, 'cause you won't be able to get it out later."

Wataru was reminded again of the importance of knowing what you could and couldn't eat around here. He would have to learn a lot if he was going to be able to travel in this place alone. He was incredibly fortunate to have met someone like Kee Keema so soon after beginning his journey. Wataru was determined to learn as much as he could before they parted ways.

First things first, though. Back to the history lesson. Wataru begged Kee Keema to continue. The waterkin gave a satisfied belch, and raised an eyebrow. "What were we talking about again?" His long tongue lashed out and licked the top of his head. "Oh right, the northern continent, unification thereof. Well before unification, the Empire was just another small country in the North, a land of ankha."

Three hundred years before, this small country had tenaciously clung to victory through a long series of wars, and proceeded to slowly unify the entire continent.

"That's when the first emperor, Gama Agrilius I, arrived on the scene, saying his family was directly descended from the old God. And the Goddess who said she received the world from the old God—the Goddess that we pray to—they said she was of a lower rank than even their own ancestors. She wasn't even qualified to rule our world, they claimed, but she had deceived the old God and tried to steal the world away from its rightful owners: House Agrilius. Can you believe it?"

And that wasn't all.

"When I first picked you up, remember I told you that the ankha were the first race created by the Goddess, and that's why they look so much like her? Well Gama Agrilius I, he said that was a pack of lies. The ankha don't look like her, he said, they look like the Old God. After all, according to them, he's the one who made the world."

This new emperor went on to claim that the true form of the Goddess wasn't anything like the ankha at all, but was a crude, aged thing too horrible to bear looking at.

"That's why she doesn't tell us her name, and that's why she hides in the Tower where none can see her. Because, if we could see her, then we'd know the truth. That's what they say, anyhow."

Wataru folded up his lunch while Kee Keema continued with his story. The lizard-man's face was drawn tight.

"Like I said, the lands to the north knew war for years, and the people there lived on the brink of starvation. Oh, they had to struggle terribly just to stay alive. Gama Agrilius I, he said the endless wars, and the lack of food, were all the fault of the Goddess. See, she visited plague and hardship on the ankha because she resented them. She'd rather have ugly, twisted things, like her, to take their place. The long and the short of it was, the Goddess was trying to exterminate the ankha, and it was up to them to fight back."

Kee Keema tilted his head and blinked slowly, deep in thought. "What happened next I can hardly believe. The ankha living in the northern lands—not only the emperor's family, but them that lived in the other smaller countries as well—they all ate it up, every last word! Oh, they clapped and shouted and cheered him for saying it."

There were many different races living in the northern lands, Wataru learned, but of them the ankha were by far the most numerous.

"They joined together and started exterminating the other races, and they were strong, real strong. If you lived in the northern lands and you weren't an ankha, your house and fields'd be taken away, you'd be killed, or thrown in a camp and made a slave. The number of non-ankha dropped by the day. And then, the ankha had their glorious empire."

It was clear to Wataru now why Kee Keema had said he was glad to have been born in the south.

"Now, three hundred years since unification, they say there's hardly anything but ankha living in the north. If there are any other kinds left, why, you can bet theirs ain't an easy lot. It's enough to make you cry."

It didn't take much imagination to conclude that the Empire would like nothing better than to invade the southern continent with the excuse of strengthening ties with their kinfolk in Dela Rubesi. Then they would proceed to make an empire of the south as they had in the north, Kee Keema said glumly. "But, these three hundred years, not a single high priest of Dela Rubesi has made the slightest motion toward joining House Agrilius's empire. They seem content to live in seclusion up in the mountains, with no ties to the world below. Us nonbelievers here don't even know what the high priest looks like."

The Northern Empire couldn't make ties with Dela Rubesi if the latter had no contact with the outside world.

"We in the United Southern Nations are careful how we deal with Dela Rubesi and the believers, though. Wouldn't want to rile 'em up and give 'em cause to look for *friends* to the north, if you get my meaning. That's why we agreed to their odd demands in the trade agreements, so as not to provoke them and give them reason to come storming into our territory. Aye, dealing with Dela Rubesi's a bit like having a snake in your bed. You don't want to kick it out or try to trap it because it might bite you. You just leave it alone."

Wataru nodded slowly. The whole story sounded vaguely familiar—like maybe something of the sort had happened in his world—but whatever it was, they hadn't learned it yet in social studies.

"When I came here," Wataru said, "I was told that Vision was created by the imaginations of people—humans—living in my world. Maybe that's why events here seem kind of familiar?"

Kee Keema scratched at his upper lip. "What're *hoomans*?"

Wataru grinned. "Don't worry about it. Thanks for telling me so much."

"Right, then, let's be off," Kee Keema said with a smile. "The long and the short of it is, stay in the south and you'll do fine. We know peace, here."

chapter 5
Gasara, Merchant Town

Once again they took off, rocking and swaying across the grasslands. By now Wataru had grown used to Turbo's gait and was able to sit on the wooden seat without the constant risk of falling off. Wataru asked his helpful guide question after question: what was safe to eat, what dangers lurked in the wilds of Vision. Kee Keema was happy to oblige with answers.

After they had gone some distance, Wataru spotted a thick, verdant forest far ahead of them, a hundred times larger than the small wooded oasis they had previously seen. A building like a tower with a triangular roof stood among the trees.

"The town of Gasara," Kee Keema announced, pointing ahead. "A merchant town. Lots of folks come here: darbaba teamsters like myself, sailship merchants, even starseers on their travels from town to town in search of new knowledge. It's a lively place, Gasara."

The air was bone dry here, and the sun was hot. Wataru wiped the sweat off his brow, and squinted as he looked over the town of Gasara. He noticed something glinting to the left of the woods surrounding the town—riders on darbaba, heading out over the grassland.

"Who are they?"

Kee Keema looked out over the grass. "Oh, them? Them's probably the Knights of Stengel—the ones in charge of keeping the peace here in the United Nations. That's quite a few of them too. That sparklin' you see is the sun on their armor. From their direction, I'd say they're off to fight gimblewolves out in the Fatal Desert."

Ack! Gimblewolves!

"This Fatal Desert...it's close?"

"Aye. Turbo here could make the journey to the gorge that leads into the desert in about a day."

"Why the name?"

"Because it's big, and it's surrounded by rocky crags, so you can't even get a good look at it until you're right in the thick of it. With no maps of the place, and gimblewolves running amok, many are the fools who wander in never to be seen again. No return, see?"

Wataru remembered his run-in with the gimblewolves, and the hair stood up on his neck. "Wait, why do they have to go kill the gimblewolves? The wolves don't come out of the desert, do they? Do they attack people?"

"Sometimes. Those corkscrews'll eat anything, and they never seem to get full. That's why they come over the rocky crags and attack merchant caravans traveling the road on the other side—huh?" Kee Keema looked curiously at Wataru. "You know about the gimblewolves?"

"Unfortunately," Wataru answered. He didn't want to think about it. "I've...heard stories."

"Have you now? Well I'm happy to say stories are as close as I've ever gotten to the things meself. I hear they stink something fierce."

Turbo glided to the left, and the gates to town appeared before them— heavy wooden panels suspended between two thick pillars of stacked brick. Atop one of the pillars sat a man wearing what looked like a straw hat. Kee Keema waved, and the man waved back and shouted something in a loud voice to someone behind the gates.

Turbo approached the gate slowly, stopping a good distance before them. Just then, the gates creaked into motion, opening outward. Turbo was wise. He stopped just far enough away that the gates wouldn't hit them when they opened.

"Kee Keema of Sakawa," Kee Keema announced, pulling something that looked like a card with a long string attached from the folds of his kilt. He waved it at the man atop the pillar. "I carry *mai* and *mamas* to Posura, by request of the Mercaid Merchants of Bog. Here's my writ."

A man strode purposefully out from inside the gate and began inspecting their cargo. His clothes resembled a single burlap sack with a hole cut in it for the head. His pants were short, looking like Wataru's silk pants, but cut off just below the knee. He walked swiftly on woven sandals.

"You may pass."

Turbo walked into town. Once through the gates, Wataru saw many houses like log cabins. As he looked around, Kee Keema hunched toward him and whispered in his ear. "Wataru, I forgot to tell you something very important. Listen up."

Wataru leaned in closer.

"Remember when I first asked if you were a refugee from the north?"

Wataru nodded.

"Now everyone thought the ankha of the Northern Empire had peace of sorts until the refugees started arriving. Most of them risked their lives in handmade sailships to cross the sea, and as many that made it, many more probably died along the way. But some of them, they came across in merchant ships, and brought with them a great deal of gold."

Something about that sounds familiar...

"To hear them tell it, there was fighting among the ankha of the north. Those refugees, they brought with them news, which was good, but they also brought their religion—the faith of the Old God. And it spread."

In addition to being a rejection of the Goddess, the faith in the Old God had one more characteristic, Kee Keema explained. "Those who believe in the Old God think that Travelers like you are, well, evil."

The followers of the Old God had a name for the Travelers who came through the Porta Nectere: "zaza-aku."

"In an old ankhan tongue, it means 'false gods,' or 'those who pretend to be gods,' see?"

To deceive the Old God, the story went, the Goddess sought to remake herself in his image. Yet to perfect the form, she needed to practice, which she did by making false ankha—trial subjects, in other words. When she was done with them, the Goddess discarded them into the Abyss of Chaos at the edge of the land. But one of them lived, and passed from Vision into the other world—Wataru's world.

"They say that the Travelers to Vision are the descendants of that one false ankha." Kee Keema whispered, his teeth gnashing. "Don't seem fair to me. Nobody ever talked such nonsense when I was a wee one. It's a recent rumor about ancient things, it is, and that's just backward."

Kee Keema warned Wataru that among the followers of the Old God there might be some who would seek to do a Traveler harm. These men believed that killing a zaza-aku was one of the greatest demonstrations of faith possible—proof that one was a true warrior of the faith.

"Now normally you don't need to be worried about anything. In other towns, that is. But Gasara is a merchant town, and all sorts gather here. You've a much greater chance of running into one of those Old God believers here than anywhere else. That's why you might want to keep it under your hat that you're a Traveler, 'kay?"

"Okay," Wataru whispered back. "I'll be careful. Thanks."

Kee Keema sat up in his seat, and in a loud voice asked, "Well, Wataru, where shall we go? Lodgings first, I think."

Suddenly, Wataru realized he had a problem. His fortune in finding the darbaba driver had completely distracted him from his situation. He had no money, and he had no idea what to do. He didn't have a single lead as to finding one of the gemstones. He felt a bead of cold sweat trickle down his forehead. Kee Keema frowned. "Something wrong? I said something strange, didn't I?"

It occurred to Wataru that this kindly waterkin had no idea that his lucky charm, Traveler Wataru, was nothing more than a lost boy adrift and alone in a place he did not understand. Wataru was so lost he didn't even know what help to ask for.

"I, um…"

"I know, you're tired, you must be! Of course! Of course! I'm used to the riding, meself, but for you it must have been quite a trip. Let's find lodging and rest up," Kee Keema said, without waiting for affirmation from Wataru. "Ah, but first you must let me stable Turbo. The darbaba post is right over there. That's where darbabas stay, you see. Don't worry, the lodgings for people aren't far."

Turbo walked slowly through the town, making for the darbaba post—a structure much like a walled parking lot in Wataru's world. Other waterkin like Kee Keema were busily scrubbing down their stabled darbabas, feeding and watering them. In the corner, a small circle of waterkin stood, smoking what looked like tobacco on the end of long, slender pipes. One of them smiled broadly and waved to Kee Keema.

Kee Keema tied Turbo up, and then turned to Wataru. "Well, don't you look miserable! If you're too tired to walk, shall I give you a ride on my shoulders again?"

Wataru swallowed. "I...actually, I don't have money for lodging."

"Urk?" Kee Keema blinked.

"I have no money. Not a single cent," Wataru said, talking so fast his words ran together. "Wayfinder Lau gave me a lunch, but he told me everything else was up to me. But I...but I have no idea what to do."

Kee Keema blinked again, six times in fact. The blinks were rapid, but Wataru, staring intently at Kee Keema to gauge his reaction, was able to count each one.

"Wataru," he said. "I'll pay for your lodging."

"You can't do that!" Wataru protested. "You've already given me a ride this far—I can't impose on you anymore."

Kee Keema raised his hands. "Now, now. No need to get agitated." The waterkin's long tongue slithered out between his lips. He smiled. "Then I'll tell you what. I'll loan you the money. It's hot out here, so let's get on inside. We can talk more then."

The inn in Gasara was a long lodge with walls of thick logs. The guest rooms were arranged down the sides of a long central hallway. The cheapest rooms were called "come-alls"—something like group bunk rooms—but Kee Keema asked for a small private room instead. Hearing his banter with the innkeeper, Wataru learned the unit of currency in this world for the first time: the *tem*.

The innkeeper was a little man with a bristly beard, an ankha, and he stared at Kee Keema and Wataru for a long time with his glittering eyes. Kee Keema didn't seem to notice. Bringing Wataru to his room, he laughed and left again, and soon returned carrying two cups.

"Here, drink this," he said, handing one cup to Wataru. "Nothing feels better than a ride across the grass, but the sun beating down'll make a man tired. This is best for what ails you."

The drink was slightly sweet and had a faint medicinal taste.

"Thank you so much," Wataru said. Sitting down in a simple wooden chair, he breathed a sigh of relief.

Kee Keema licked his lips with a whip of his long tongue. It was hard to tell, but he seemed almost shy. "Like I said, don't mention it. You're my lucky star, after all."

Wataru grinned. *A lucky star. Is there anyone in my world that would do so much for a stranger just because they thought they were lucky?* Wataru thought it was quite the opposite.

Mitsuru had said that Vision was created by the imaginative energies of the real world. Wataru wondered: would more visitors from his world change Vision for the worse? He didn't know.

"You're going to the Tower of Destiny to meet the Goddess, right?" Kee Keema asked, sitting on the clean, if a little hard-looking, bed.

"Yes, I think so. I want to change my, I mean my and my family's fate…"

Kee Keema cut him off. "No, don't tell me. We are taught that Travelers who come from your world to Vision are called here by the Goddess. We do not know why she calls them, and it is not good to ask. Why, it is the Goddess's will, and that is enough. So, don't tell me your reasons for coming here."

Wataru nodded.

"And, Wataru, you know you must reach the Tower on your own."

"I do."

"But, there's nothing that says someone can't go with you on the way. So, I was thinking, I might join you for a while. If it's okay with you?"

"Kee Keema!"

"I don't think the Goddess would mind, not if I only went a little ways," Kee Keema hastily added. "I mean, look at you, you're tiny. The Traveler my uncle met, he was already a young man. He could make the trip on his own. But Wataru, you're still a boy. How would you make money for your trip? I couldn't abandon a child and live with myself, no sir. That wouldn't be good at all."

Wataru felt warm and fuzzy all over. "I would—I mean, that would make me really happy. But what about your work? You can't quit, just on my account. That's not good, either."

Kee Keema's eyes glimmered. "True, true. That's why I'm going to deliver my cargo—then I'll head back up to Sakawa, see? I'll talk to the chief. If I go by swift cart, the trip should take me only three to four days. So, I want you to wait here for me. 'Kay?"

"But—you'd do that? For me?"

"Of course! Why, I don't think the chief would think too kindly on me if I just dropped off everything here and went off on my merry way. He'd be right angry, he would. 'When did you become such a mean old waterkin?' he'd ask me." Kee Keema scratched his head. "The chief, he's four hundred and twenty years old now, but he's still strong as an ox. Why, he's been scolding me since I was a wee one, and has given me more than my fair share of swats on the hindquarters. Wouldn't do to make him cross with me, no sir."

Over four hundred years! Wataru's eyes went wide. *Waterkin can live that long?*

"So then, I should…"

"You should take me up on my offer!" Kee Keema said clapping his hands and jumping to his feet. "Time's a-wasting, boy! I'll be heading out. I've paid for a five nights' stay, so you need not worry about a thing. They'll feed you here too. When you've rested up, take a walk around town. There are lots of folks around here; maybe you can talk to them and get a hint about where you want to go next. Just watch out for the believers of the Old God, like I told you."

Kee Keema lumbered out, happily humming to himself. Wataru watched after him. *I wonder how old he is?*

Wataru lay down on the bed and stretched. White plastered walls. A ceiling made of woven reeds. The cool of the air inside the room felt good. Wataru relaxed.

For dinner, a round-faced ankha woman delivered bread, stew, and fruit. She said nothing and did not even look at Wataru. But the food was so delicious it more than made up for the lack of hospitality.

When the sun had completely set, Wataru gazed up at the stars through a small window in his room. It looked as though he could reach out and catch them in his hand. Happy, Wataru walked out of the lodge. At night, the town of Gasara was quiet, the lights sputtering here and there on buildings. From some buildings he assumed were restaurants or bars poured more light, and the sounds of music and people talking. Wataru walked, being careful to note the way he had come, and finding a small rise in the middle of town, he again looked up at the night sky.

Filled with the magic of the night, Wataru eventually returned to the lodge.

When he reached the front doorway, someone pushed him hard from behind. A vile stench filled his nose.

"You're the boy that came in with that waterkin today, aren't you!"

It was a skinny ankha man; spit flew from his mouth as he talked. He reached out in an attempt to grab Wataru's chest, but Wataru knocked his hand away.

"What, you want to fight?" The man spat. His breath was foul. From the slight wobble in his motions, Wataru realized he was drunk. The stench must have been the smell of liquor. *Maybe alcohol here in Vision is stronger than it is in my world.*

"Hanging out with waterkin—you've got that damn smell on you," the man muttered, glaring at Wataru. "Hang out with them too long and you'll sprout scales and get a forked tongue. You know that?"

Wataru stood up silently, feeling the bile rise in his throat. Then he turned his back on the man.

"What? I give you some friendly advice, and you're going to ignore me?"

The man grabbed Wataru by the shoulder, and Wataru whirled around. "Let me go! That waterkin is ten times the man you are!"

"Why you little…" the man swung his fist. Just then something came flying out from the lodge and struck the man in the face. It was a wet towel.

"None of that!" came a loud voice. It was the unfriendly woman from before, standing with her hands on her hips and glaring at the man. "Drunkard! Get back to your room or I'll toss you out into the road!"

The inebriated man suddenly became meek, and walked past Wataru into the lodge.

His room is right next to mine!

"Thank you," Wataru said to the woman. She made no reply, but picked up her towel and tossed it into a nearby wooden bucket filled with murky water.

Wataru had an idea. "Ma'am?"

The woman wrung dirty water out of her towel with thick arms and said nothing.

"Actually, I'm looking for work, to pay for my journey. Is there anything I might do here, like, maybe, cleaning?"

The woman looked at Wataru out of the corner of her eye and spat,

"What are your parents thinking, sending a little boy like you out on the road alone?"

Then she picked up her bucket and walked away. Deflated, Wataru trudged back to his room. *My parents…* As he was falling asleep, Wataru saw his mother drifting across his mind's eye. *That's right, the Mirror of Truth. I have to find it quick—I have to tell Mom I'm okay.*

Wataru slept soundly, with no dreams. It was a peaceful, restful sleep. But he awoke with a jolt.

"Wake up! Wake up, I said!"

Wataru's eyes blinked open. The innkeeper with the bristly beard had him by the neck and was shaking him. It was already light outside, and the morning sun through the window hurt his eyes.

"Huh? What's wrong?"

"As if you didn't know!" the bearded man shouted, dragging Wataru out of bed. "Get up, I say. Sleepy eyes won't fool me, murderer!"

Murderer? The word was like a bucket of ice water dumped over his head. Wataru was wide awake now.

"What do you mean 'murderer'? Did somebody die?"

"Don't play the fool with me! Look at your hands!"

Wataru took a glance at his hands and his breath stopped. They were covered in blood. It wasn't only his hands. His undergarments, too, were caked with dried crimson. *What's going on? What happened?*

"No use feigning innocence this time!" the man shouted. "You cut the throat of the man in the room next door. This blood is proof of it. You killed him and took his money, didn't you? Tell me—where did you hide it? Where's your knife?"

Still in shock, Wataru was tied up with rope and dragged outside in front of the lodge. A crowd of onlookers had already gathered. Some of them began shouting angrily. Any other day, Wataru might have been surprised that the faces in the crowd were those of dogs, cats, bears, even lions, but right now he had more important things to worry about.

"He's just a boy!"

"I always said ankha were precocious!"

"And this is the third he's killed? Monster!"

"I've heard of a boy thief, but he's a murderer too?"

The words came at Wataru in a frightening whirlwind of sound. The faces were drawn, as if gazing upon something horrible. Wataru's spine went cold.

I haven't killed anyone. I haven't even stolen anything. What are they talking about, three people?

"C'mon!" The bearded innkeeper gave Wataru a swift kick in the pants, and yanked on the rope tied around him. "It's off to the branch with you."

The inn's proprietor began dragging his bound prisoner through the streets of the city. He looked as proud as he was angry, and occasionally he would announce in a loud voice that he had caught the young murderer, scourge of Gasara.

People looked from doorways and windows as Wataru stumbled down the street. Some of the lodge patrons even fell in behind them. He heard a child clapping and shouting in a shrill voice, "They caught him! The killer-thief's been caught!"

Up to this point Wataru had been mute with confusion and terror, but when he heard the boy he shouted, "I haven't done anything! This is all a mistake!"

The innkeeper lashed out with his foot again, and Wataru was knocked to the ground. His cheek scraped on the dirt road, and gravel filled his mouth.

Just then, soft hands reached out and picked Wataru up from the ground. He looked and saw that the arms were covered with pure white fur—with stripes the color of milk.

He looked up to see the face of a cat, white with brown stripes, with large blue-gray eyes, staring at Wataru.

"Are you okay?" the cat asked. Tiny silver whiskers grew from its pink nose. Its voice was unmistakably feminine. It moved like a girl too—like one of his classmates back in the real world.

"Stay away from him, you! This boy is a murderer!" the innkeeper barked as he yanked Wataru to his feet. The cat-girl backed away trembling. Her eyes never left Wataru's.

She had the face of a cat, but she was beautiful. She stood like a human, and was wearing something like a short-skirted jumpsuit. *Kitkin, I wonder?* She looked as frightened as Wataru felt, like she might start crying at any time.

She turned around and walked back into the crowd, glancing back at

Wataru as she left. Her slender tail wrapped itself around her waist, and she crisscrossed her arms in front of her chest. Just then, Wataru saw her mouth move. She was saying something, and to Wataru's eyes it looked like "I'm sorry…"

"Look forward! Walk!"

Something slammed Wataru on the head, and he blacked out.

When he came to, he was in a room. It was smaller, but sturdier, than the one he had stayed in at the lodge. He was tied to a thick wooden post with shackles on his hands. The chain was also fastened to his feet.

His cheek stung. His jaw hurt. His spine sagged. One of his eyes seemed to be swollen.

"You're awake," said a woman's voice from directly behind him. The tip of a bright red boot slid under his chin and lifted his face. "Well? Beginning to regret what you've done?"

It was an ankha woman, with short, glossy black hair and fierce eyes. A cigarette dangled from her cruel lips. She was tall, and she was also quite attractive. She wore a shiny black leather vest, short trousers, spiked pads on her knees, and a red leather armband on one arm.

"What's the matter? Hope he didn't hurt you too bad," she said with a guttural laugh. The woman slowly walked around until she was standing in front of Wataru. She was dragging something behind her on the ground that licked at the heel of her boot. Wataru blinked and looked at it again to find it was a whip of black leather.

"Well, well," the woman said, chewing on her cigarette. "I'm Kutz, head of this branch. Of course, you probably already knew that. It takes some nerve to cause trouble in town on Kutz the Rosethorn's watch. I admit, I'm impressed."

In the back of the room, a man laughed. He had the face of a tiger, and he was wearing glasses.

"I haven't done anything," Wataru said. The act of talking made his mouth ache. "I haven't stolen anything, I haven't hurt anyone."

Kutz guffawed. "You hear that, Trone?" She said to the tiger-faced man sitting nearby.

The tiger-man stood and walked over to where he could get a better view of Wataru. He was wearing a short leather kilt like Kee Keema had worn, with a large leather strap crossing over his chest. A sword was in the sheath on his back.

"Better for you to admit to your crimes," the tiger-man said. "You cut the throat of the man next to you at the lodge, and stole his money. We know you were fighting with him the night before, and we know you needed money for your journey. The innkeeper told us everything."

So it was the drunk who had been killed. Wataru grew even more frightened. The reality of the situation pressed in on him.

"It's true, I was looking for work, and I did get mad at that drunk guy. But I didn't kill him. Why doesn't anyone believe me?"

"Well, for one thing, you're covered in blood," Kutz said plainly, tossing her stubby cigarette like a dart across the room. The cigarette disappeared into a bucket in the corner and went out with a fizzle.

"But I don't remember doing anything!" Wataru said, shaking. The shackles binding him rattled in distress. "I only got here, to Gasara, yesterday…"

"One month ago," Kutz said, entirely ignoring him, "a traveling merchant's throat was cut at a certain lodge, his money stolen. The next time was ten days later, at another lodge…"

"It wasn't me! I wasn't even in Vision a month ago, or ten days ago! I'm a Traveler!"

At Wataru's outburst, Kutz and the tiger-man looked at each other. Together they laughed.

"I wondered how you would try to wriggle out of this! A Traveler, are you? Of course!"

"It's the truth! My sword—at the lodge you should be able to find my Brave's Sword! Ask Wayfinder Lau, he gave it to me!"

"Wayfinder Lau? Who's that? Sorry, but we Highlanders don't truck with their sort."

Wataru gaped. *They don't know the Wayfinder? Was the Watcher of the Porta Nectere some kind of hermit, secluded from the larger world of Vision?*

"Then ask Kee Keema. He's a waterkin, a darbaba driver. He left for Satoko, but he'll be back in three days."

"Three days? How unfortunate. He'll miss the big event." Kutz stood before him with her weight on her left foot, her whip thrown over her left shoulder. "You see, you're to be hanged as soon as the gallows are finished. Isn't that right, Trone?"

"Quite," the tiger-man said distractedly, picking up some sort of documents from the desk. "Shouldn't take more than a day to build. Too bad for you, boy."

"I expect every carpenter in Gasara will be hammering away soon. They're building it right out here in the square—you should be able to see it through your window."

"One day?!" Wataru said in a strangled voice. "What about an investigation? What about proof? What about a trial?"

"No need. We have the statement from the innkeeper, and need I mention again the blood on your hands?"

"What if the real murderer put the blood on me while I was asleep! What if I was framed!"

The thought had just occurred to him, but now that he said it, Wataru was sure that was what had happened. But Kutz and Trone merely laughed.

"Nice try, boy," Kutz said, leaning down to eye level. "But we knew it was a child's work from the first killing. Why? Because all three victims were killed in rooms with the door locked."

"Even the drunk next door?"

"Indeed. And the only way into those rooms without having a key is to go through the roof from an adjacent room. But the crawl space between ceiling and roof is too small for an adult. They'd fall through."

"But you can't just accuse me because of that!"

"Please. You're covered in blood. And you didn't have a tem to your name the night before."

Kutz stood and stretched luxuriantly. "I wouldn't worry about it too much. They say hanging is surprisingly painless."

"I've even heard it feels good," said the tiger-man.

"No way!" Wataru yelled. "I have a right to prove my innocence!"

"A right to prove your innocence? Big words," Kutz said, turning her back to Wataru.

"What about the Knights of Stengel? Aren't they the keepers of the law in this place? How can you try me on a whim?"

Kutz whirled around. In a single smooth motion she lashed out, her whip cracking the post an inch away from Wataru's ear. "That's enough of that!"

Wataru froze.

"I suppose this is all part of your act as a 'Traveler'—pretending you don't know things that everyone else knows. But know this: you take the Highlanders lightly at your own risk!"

"But the Knights..." Wataru sputtered through trembling teeth.

"Newcomers!" Kutz said with agitation. "Before they came along with their United Southern Nations, we Highlanders kept the peace in the south."

The tiger-man continued. "And, boy, the Knights of Stengel are too busy fighting monsters to care about keeping the peace. Who knows where their camps are now—or when they'll return?"

"Feh!" Kutz spat. "It suits them just fine to play with those gimblewolves!" she snorted. "Trone, I tire of looking at our little felon here. Take him to the cell."

The tiger-man stood, untied the ropes around the post, and picked him up. He had removed his sword, but his powerful arms and sharp claws were enough to keep Wataru in line. He didn't even look for an opening to escape.

Trone tossed Wataru into a cramped cell, locked the door, and placed the key in a bracelet around his arm. Wataru noticed that he and Kutz wore the same red leather strap.

"Don't even think about trying to escape," Trone said, baring his fangs in a grin. "Try to enjoy your last few meals in this life."

Wataru lay back on the wooden bed. The shock and fear were so great he couldn't even cry. As he lay there in a daze, he heard the sound of hammering drift through the thick bars of his window. He stood up on his tiptoes and looked outside to see men working, as promised, on a platform in the middle of a large square.

A gallows.

Just like in a Western movie, Wataru thought, and then his knees knocked together so fiercely he couldn't stand. *What do I do now? They're really going to hang me.*

Wataru wondered where his Brave's Sword was. In the real world, they would search his belongings, but Wataru didn't think they paid much mind to things like procedure around here. The innkeeper had probably taken it for himself. That little woman was probably using his Brave's Sword to cut bread and vegetables by now.

What happens if I die in Vision? Do I go home? Does my body stay here?

Outside, the rhythmic hammering continued. *Bang bang bang.* The sound of lively conversation. Happy voices. Would he stay here, in the cell, until the gallows were completed? Would he even get a chance to defend himself?

The bars on the window and door were as thick as Wataru's wrist, and shaking them or hitting them only made his hands hurt. Finally, he was able to cry. But no matter how loudly he wept, no one came to check on him.

After the sun had set, an ankha dressed similarly to Trone brought him dinner and a wool blanket. Wataru pleadingly asked him questions, but the large man merely pushed the food through the cell's bars and left without saying a word.

"But I'm innocent!"

Wataru's shout echoed sorrowfully down the hall.

Dinner was watery soup and stale bread. Wataru wasn't hungry at all, so he curled up in a ball on the bed and cried himself to sleep.

But he slept in fits and starts, and had a bizarre dream. His mother was in it, and, for some reason, Kaori Daimatsu. She was trapped behind iron bars, just like Wataru. Her eyes were glistening, and she was staring at him. In his dream, Wataru realized that Kaori was a prisoner too—a prisoner in her own body, broken by some horrible crime. Unlike Wataru, her prison had no key. It didn't even have a door.

—*How do I get you out of there?* he asked, but in the dream she didn't respond, only looking down and shaking her head.

—*Your dad and your brother, they're worried about you.*

Kaori looked up and whispered something. He couldn't hear. *What? What did you say? Talk louder. Louder—louder—*

"Don't make me shout, boy!"

Wataru jerked out of his dream. He was still curled up, trying to hide under his blanket. Kutz stood by the bed, hands on her hips, looking down at him with a sour expression. "Finally, you're up," she growled. "You're a late sleeper, aren't you? Do you know how many times I tried to wake you? I thought I'd go hoarse. Your mother must scold you something fierce."

Wataru got out of bed, still hunched over. Maybe she was here because the gallows was ready. He couldn't hear the hammers anymore.

Kutz's mouth curled and she snorted. "You are free, boy. You're lucky, you get to leave."

He couldn't believe what he was hearing. It made no sense.

"I said you're free! Stop moping. If there're two things I can't stand, it's mopey kids and wimpy men."

Wataru looked up at her face in a daze and said the first thing that came to mind. "Why?"

Her mouth curled even more. "Why? Why? Because you're no longer under suspicion, that's why."

"But why not?"

"Do you always ask so many questions? You're free to go, isn't that enough? If that doesn't make you happy I can just close the door and leave you here, you know."

Wataru dashed past her through the open door into the hallway. Kutz scratched her head and followed him. She kicked the cell door closed behind her.

"While you were in here last night, there was another incident at another lodge—same scenario," she said, not sounding too happy about it. "The victim this time was badly wounded, but not killed. So we have a firsthand witness, you might say. It was two small men, working together, and they sounded awful pleased that you had been caught in their place. They were the ones who put blood on your hands and clothes, it sounds like. We were all taken in. Bastards!" she said, spitting.

"I told you I was innocent. You should've listened to me."

Kutz glared violently at Wataru, and took him back to the office where he had first been brought the day before. Now that he was a little more relaxed, he looked around to see that it was exactly like a sheriff's office in a Western.

"Go back to the lodge where you were staying," Kutz ordered him. "The innkeeper says he's got all your stuff. And he says he'll treat you to dinner as an apology. If that doesn't do it for you, you can hit him a few times if you want. But don't go overboard, or we'll bring you in again on new charges. That's all."

Wataru was walking out the door when Kutz called after him. "You really are a Traveler, aren't you?"

Wataru turned around.

"That pig-sticker of yours," said Kutz, referring to Wataru's Brave's Sword.

"The innkeeper told me he tried to pick it up, but it was too hot to handle. That one's straight from the Goddess, it is. He was a bit taken aback."

So the sword is safe.

"He was a little worried, seeing as how Travelers are sent here by the Goddess. He hoped he hadn't got in your way."

Kutz walked over to the desk and played with her whip that hung over the back of her chair. "So if you meet the Goddess, tell her I'm sorry, would you? And for the innkeeper, as well."

"Fine."

"Still, you'd be well advised to eat quickly and get out of Gasara right away. You're free of suspicion, but we haven't caught the killers. Things could get ugly here if you hang around too long."

Wataru went out without saying anything. The sun was bright in his eyes, and the sky was perfectly clear. He made his way to the lodge, and the innkeeper came running out, apologizing profusely. The little woman herded Wataru into the back kitchen where he saw so much food he couldn't imagine eating even half of it. As he sat down to gorge himself, the innkeeper brought him his sword, wrapped in a thick cloth.

"We're sorry, boy," he said, his shoulders hunched. "Here's your sword. Take a look at her. Nary a scratch, I guarantee it. I thought I could slice some of our meat with it, but I gave up that notion right quick."

Wataru hung the sword at his waist. The innkeeper sat across from Wataru and went to grab a T-bone from the table. The little woman slapped his hand away.

"Still, I have to say I'm impressed," the man said, rubbing his stinging hand. "Such a small kid like you, coming on over to our world. I guess there's no age limit on the Porta Nectere, eh?"

"Have you never been to the other world?" Wataru asked.

The man shuddered. "Madness! Never!"

"Do you know anybody who has?"

"No, no. The other world is no place for we who live in Vision to tread lightly. The Goddess would never allow it, and even if we made it over, we'd be as good as the dead."

The dead. Ghosts?

"It is a scary place, I'll agree to that," Wataru admitted.

"I knew it, I knew it!"

"We have burglaries and murders, and worse."

"Do you now? That is scary. Then again, we've got our own bit of worrisome trouble here in Gasara, don't we? If we don't catch the criminals soon, I fear for business."

"But last night—they didn't actually kill anyone, did they?"

"No, but that poor kitkin's back was ripped up something fierce." The innkeeper said with a shudder. "Never should've let a girl stay alone in a cheap place like that."

"A kitkin girl? The cat-girl!"

"Aye. Pretty thing too, with white fur. Poor girl."

Something clicked inside Wataru. He put down his fork and stood. "Thank you for breakfast. I don't think I can eat any more."

"You sure? We really are sorry. If you're heading out, I'll make a lunch for you to take."

"No, I'll be staying here longer."

The innkeeper looked flustered. "Eh? But didn't Kutz tell you to leave?"

"She told me to leave, yes, but I'm waiting for someone. And, I want to know where the girl is, the one who was hurt last night."

"At the hospital, I should think."

Wataru thanked the innkeeper for the meal, and immediately took off toward the hospital.

The "hospital," overflowing with patients, was little more than a shack. A husky doctor with the face of a St. Bernard and a nurse with floppy ears who looked like a terrier were bustling around in white smocks. Wataru spoke to them briefly, and the nurse pointed toward a small ward in the back. "She's just eaten. I should think she's still up."

Wataru thanked her and headed back to the door. He knocked, but there was no answer. Opening it quietly, he found the cat-girl lying bandaged on a simple wooden bed, facing away from the door. Her long tail hung listlessly over the side of the bed.

Even without seeing her face Wataru knew. She was the girl who tried to help him the day before.

"Hello," Wataru said, and the girl turned, her eyes opened wide. She winced at the pain of moving.

"No, don't move." Wataru walked over and squatted by the bed. The kit-kin looked at Wataru with trembling gray eyes.

"Why?" he heard her ask in a whisper.

"I came to see you. I heard you were hurt," Wataru said. Then he added quietly, "You helped me up the other day, on the road. Thank you."

The girl looked away.

"You said something then. You said 'sorry.'"

The girl trembled, and her eyes looked frightened. Her tail twitched. *But there's no one else in the room.*

Wataru had another realization. "I'm sorry for intruding. I hope you feel better." And with that, he left.

Wataru went straight to Kutz's office. She was sitting at her desk, the whip thrown over her back, writing something in a notepad. "What?" she scowled. "You got your sword back, didn't you?"

"I did. I want to help you look for the criminals."

Kutz's eyes opened wide. "What's that?"

"Let me help you try to find the lodge killers. I think I can."

"You?"

"Yes," Wataru said, looking at Trone and the large ankha sitting at the back of the room. "You don't mind, do you? I just want to prove my innocence beyond all doubt."

"You did yesterday, but now there's no…"

"Yes, but if you haven't caught the real criminals, there's no guarantee I won't come under suspicion again," Wataru said, flashing as competent a smile as he could muster. "Trone, will you take me to the lodge where the previous two killings took place?"

Trone growled. "What gives you the right?"

"I'm Wataru," he said, smiling again. "Didn't you want me to put in a good word with the Goddess?"

The three exchanged glances, and after a tense moment of silence, Kutz sighed. "Fine, *Wataru*. I'll take you."

Wataru visited the two lodges. At both places, the staff stumbled over themselves to help Kutz. But when Wataru started asking questions they merely stared at him, unsure of how to respond. They all hopped to attention the minute Kutz announced—with a bark—that he was her assistant.

Both of the rooms were like the one Wataru had stayed in, with woven rush mats for a roof. They were built that way to let in the air, he was told. He took a look above them and found a narrow crawlspace that seemed quite impossible to get through unless you were a child.

After inspecting the two lodges, they headed to the inn where Wataru was staying. When they got there, he calmly announced that he knew who the criminals were. He told Kutz to assemble the innkeepers.

Kutz went red in the face, and Wataru thought he could see steam coming out of her ears. "What the hell are you talking about?"

Before Wataru could respond, the bearded innkeeper cut in, "Now, now, Kutz. That's no way to talk to our Traveler. He's special, you know. Chosen by the Goddess. Children, they understand things we can't see sometimes. I'm sure that's what's going on here."

Kutz's face grew redder. "Whatever. I saw him crying his eyes out in the cell room just the other day."

Wataru did his best to look unruffled. "Don't worry, sir, we'll catch the criminals tomorrow for sure."

"Very well," the innkeeper replied. "I'll let everyone know, don't you worry about a thing."

"Also, if it's okay, I'd like to spend the night here again. And I need money for my trip. Do you think there's anything I could do to help out? Also, if anyone wants to ask me anything about what's happened, please let me know. I'd be happy to talk about it."

The rumors spread through Gasara like wildfire. While Wataru busied himself around the inn by washing dishes, sweeping floors, and chopping firewood, person after person came by to talk to him. *Have you really found the criminal? Are you really a Traveler? Is the Porta Nectere really open?*

Wataru was swamped with both work and questions. Some people even asked him to beg favors of the Goddess—if or when he met her.

Many children dropped by too. One of them Wataru recognized—the boy who taunted him on the street the other day. Wataru slowly began to realize that people respected, and even feared, Travelers. And they were especially curious about the world from which they came. Kee Keema's warning to not reveal his identity flashed briefly through his mind, but now there didn't seem much point in trying to hide it. He even enjoyed feeling a bit like a celebrity.

As he sat around talking to a crowd of children, he noticed a pair of young ankha boys standing a short distance away. They stared at him shyly. Their cheeks were sunken, their clothes were covered in dirt, and they slouched. When their eyes met, they either glared at him or looked away.

Wataru made sure to memorize their faces. One of them walked like he was carrying something under his vest. *A knife, I'll bet.*

Wataru waited for night to come.

On his second night in the lodge, Wataru came to realize that the concept of time was similar in Vision as it was in his own world. But it seemed to him that an hour here was slightly longer than an hour in his world. With some guidance from the little woman of the inn, he was able to easily read wall clocks. That night he waited until midnight before heading to the hospital again.

He had been careful to pay attention to the building's layout during his first visit, so he knew which window led into the room where the kitkin slept. There was a tavern across the street from the hospital, and Wataru spied several large empty casks out front. These, he figured, would make a convenient place for him to hide.

He lurked behind the liquor casks for a while because the lights were still on at the hospital. When they eventually went out, he heard a sound like the hooting of an owl, and darkness descended upon the street. The only source of light now came from the starry sky above.

A whiskey-like smell drifted from the empty casks in front of the tavern. Wataru was afraid that if he stayed there too long, he might get drunk.

Just then, something moved in the shadows outside the hospital. Wataru held his breath.

It was a small, dark shape—two of them. They cut through the darkness, moving nimbly like monkeys, deftly opening the window to the kitkin girl's room. They darted inside without hesitation.

Wataru quickly counted to ten. Then, walking as quietly as he could, he ran up to the window.

"—didn't, did you?" he heard a young man's voice say.

"You're in trouble too. And you know what will happen if you rat on us, eh?"

"What did you tell that boy? We know he came here today."

He heard the kitkin respond in a voice choked with tears. She was swearing she hadn't said anything.

"Liar!"

"Your tail says you're a liar. Maybe I should cut it off?"

Wataru took a breath, then, drawing his Brave's Sword, he yanked the window open and jumped inside.

"Stop, y-you...huh?!"

Wataru had intended to land on his feet, but his shoe caught on the window frame, and he tumbled into the room. Landing with a thud on the floor next to the bed, he looked up to see one of the boys holding the girl down, and the other holding a knife to the middle of her tail. The white blade glimmered dangerously in the dim light.

"I kn-know you did it!" Wataru said, lifting his sword and struggling to his feet. His jaw throbbed from where it had hit the floor, and it took some effort to speak clearly.

"Who're y—hey! It's that kid!" one of the boys said, pointing at Wataru and holding out his knife. "Let's get 'im!"

The boy howled and leapt for him, but Wataru managed to move aside in the nick of time. The boy made a wild grab and was able to latch onto the sleeve of his shirt. He swung his knife again.

Uh-oh!

"Huh?"

The Brave's Sword had deftly blocked the boy's knife. It was as though his arm—no, the sword itself—had moved of its own accord. Wataru took advantage of the boy's forward thrust and leapt up on his back.

"Put the sword down, or she gets it!" Wataru heard the other boy shout. He saw him standing with a knife pressed close to the kitkin. "Move a muscle, and I cut her throat!"

Wataru hesitated, and in that instant the boy beneath him threw him off. Wataru fell to the floor.

At that moment, something black and slender came through the window from outside, wrapping itself around the hand of the boy holding the knife.

Wataru saw it jerked taut, and the boy was yanked away from the cat-girl.

"Whoa!" the boy shouted, as he flew through the open window and disappeared outside.

The three remaining in the room stood in shock. Again the long black cord lashed through the window, this time wrapping itself around the chest of the boy next to Wataru.

Of course! The whip!

One hand on the window and the other gripping her whip, Kutz leapt inside onto the bed. "I'm a Highlander, and you are under arrest!" she said with authority, jumping down to the floor in front of the boy and giving him three swift kicks with the tip of her leather boot. The boy groaned and slumped to the ground.

"The one outside didn't fare much better than this one," Kutz said, baring her white teeth in a smile. "Are you two okay?" she said to the girl on the bed. "Ah, the wound on your back's opened!"

Then the world began to spin.

"What's wrong, Wataru?" Kutz chided. "Don't worry, you saved her. Of course, you wouldn't have been able to do it on your own. Good thing I was watching your every move."

"I...see...thanks," Wataru said, clinging to the edge of the bed.

"You okay?" the cat-girl asked, twitching one ear.

"The open casks..." Wataru muttered. "I think I'm drunk."

chapter 6
The Highlanders

It took a full day for Wataru's hangover to mend. By the time his headache, dizziness, and nausea subsided and he was able to eat again, Kee Keema returned from his trip to Sakawa.

"Never have I been so surprised in all my days!" the waterkin announced, clapping his hands furiously and literally bouncing in his chair. His loud voice echoed through the lodge. "I made it between Gasara and Sakawa in record time, I did. Yet still, in a few days, you managed to not only tangle with Kutz the Rosethorn but become the hero of Gasara!"

"I didn't do anything so amazing," Wataru said. "Just the sort of thing they're always doing in the TV mysteries my mom watches."

"TV mysteries?" Kee Keema said, cocking his head. "Something from the other world? Anyway, Kutz wanted you to come down to the branch when you were feeling better. So let's get going!"

Down at the branch they found not only Kutz waiting for them but the tiger-man Trone and a wizened man with long whiskers that Wataru hadn't met before. He looked like a goat. *Must be another -kin,* Wataru thought. His eyes were gentle and sparkling with intelligence.

"This is High Chief Gil, responsible for all thirteen Highlander branches in the land of Nacht."

High Chief Gil reacted to Kutz's rigid introduction with a warm smile, as he took Wataru's hands into his own. "Quite impressive to stand up to two violent criminals like that at your young age, my brave Traveler."

"If Kutz hadn't been there, I wouldn't have stood up to much," Wataru admitted. "I was wondering, what happened to the wounded girl, the kitkin?"

It was Kutz who answered. "She needed more stitches after the fracas in her room, so now she's resting. Give her a few weeks and she'll mend up nicely, I think." Then she grinned. "Her name's Meena, by the way."

Wataru's face reddened. "I gathered from what they said that she was helping them…she wasn't going along with their plans willfully, I hope?"

Kutz glanced at the Highlander official. Gil, still sitting, leaned toward Wataru. "Indeed. Those two boys threatened her and made her help them steal. She pretended to be a victim to save you, in fact. How did you know?"

Wataru explained how he had put it all together: the girl whispering "I'm sorry," how she could have used her tail to cut her own back with a knife, and how he realized if he claimed to know who the criminals were, they would suspect Meena had ratted them out and come to get her.

"That's some brain you got, Wataru!" Kee Keema said, clapping his hands. "Why I could be as old and grizzled as the Elder, and I'd never come up with that!"

Wataru didn't bother explaining that co-conspirators pretending to be victims were a pretty common plot twist in the TV shows his mom watched.

"You want to meet them?" Kutz said, standing up and dangling a ring of cell keys in her hand. Wataru quickly followed after her.

"It turns out they're both refugees from the north," Kutz explained as they walked down the hall. "Five years ago, when they were nine and eight years old, they paid a smuggler to take them and their parents on a merchant ship crossing the sea. Sadly, the ship ran into trouble, and their parents died. These two washed up on the shore near Bog and moved to a refugee camp. Apparently they didn't care for life there, so they escaped and began their career as thieves. They've been moving from place to place, stealing and worse, for about a year now."

"I don't get it. They risked their lives to cross over here, only to become thieves? Why?"

"Ask them yourself."

The two were being kept in the same tiny cell that Wataru himself had been thrown in when he was the suspect. One was lying down on the bed, but the other—the older of the two, Wataru thought—was sitting on the floor, and his eyes gleamed when he saw Wataru in the doorway.

"Having fun, boys?" Kutz asked cheerfully. "I brought you a friend. He went through quite a lot on your account. Thought you might want to apologize to him, hmm?"

The sitting boy looked to the side and spat on the floor. The boy on the bed sat up and glared at Wataru. Seeing them in the light of day, Wataru realized he had seen them before that night. During the day, when everyone had been visiting him at the lodge after he claimed to know the identity of the criminals, they had been there, standing apart from the onlookers.

They looked better fed now than they had been then, for sure, but their eyes were still hungry.

Trone appeared at the end of the hallway and began walking toward them when the older of the two leapt suddenly to his feet, grabbed the bars to the cell and began shouting. "Keep that stinking foul beast away from us! I don't want his stench in our room!"

Shocked, Wataru took a step backward. Trone kept walking toward them, grinning broadly. On the other side of the bars, both of the boys were standing up now, spitting and raging.

"See?" Trone said, coming to stand beside Wataru. "They risked their lives to escape from the north, yet inside their hearts, they're still living firmly within the borders of the Empire."

In the Northern Empire, the dominant ankha had decided that other races were inferior and without value, Trone explained. They imprisoned and killed his kind for the slightest offense.

"Oh be quiet, you two," Kutz snapped. "If you don't like it in there, I'm happy to send you back up north."

Kutz's words only agitated them further. "You look like one of us, but you smell like one of them," the older boy growled.

"Death to you all!" his brother joined in.

"I'm afraid the one on its way out is your empire, not us," Kutz said, almost sorrowfully. "By pushing the non-ankha out of the way, you're ignoring so many resources, so much potential."

"Shut up, beast-lover! All of you together don't add up to one of us!" the older brother shouted.

Wataru took a step closer to the bars. "Where did you find Meena? What did you threaten her with?"

The brothers looked at each other for a moment, then pointed their fingers at Wataru and laughed uproariously.

"Stop that!" Wataru shouted.

The older brother's face suddenly went serious. He stepped up to the bars and muttered something in a low, poisonous voice.

"What did you say?" Wataru asked, leaning closer.

The boy spat on his face at point-blank range.

"Ack!"

As Wataru wiped his face, the brothers laughed again. "Just watch. When we ankha have brought the south together, you'll all be sent to the camps. You can lick our boots three times a day for your meals."

"Boots?" The younger brother said, howling with laughter. "You mean butts! They can all live in our latrine and eat whatever drops down!"

Trone put his hand on Wataru's shoulder. "Back to the office."

Wataru nodded. Kutz stood a while longer, looking with weary eyes at the two boys before turning to follow.

"I've heard about conditions up there from refugees, but still..." Kutz frowned as she collapsed in her chair. "Even if it's all true, what makes boys like that tick, I wonder?"

"You're seeing the shallow pool that is us, Kutz," said Gil. "Sadly, we all have it in our natures to be like them."

It was true that the Northern Empire had suffered greatly due to its discriminatory policies against non-ankha peoples. Their workforce had dwindled, and their strength had weakened. Things were so bad, they couldn't even grow enough food to feed their own people, the high chief explained to Wataru. "There are formal trade agreements drawn between the North and the South. Only the agreed-upon amounts of food and supplies may be exchanged. Still, that does not cover their need, nor do the supplies reach all the peoples of the north."

So northern merchants had formed alliances with treaty-breaking smugglers in the south and lined their pockets with black-market trade.

"But of course, this contraband entering the North is far overpriced, again, not reaching the hands of those who need it most. Thus, the refugees come."

"So who exactly lives well in the Northern Empire?" Wataru asked.

"A circle of privileged elites," the Highlander replied slowly. "The family of the current Emperor Agrilius VII, nobles, politicians, officials, and the wealthier merchants."

Gil nodded in the direction of the holding cell. "My bet is that the parents of those two boys belonged to that elite class. That's the only way they would have been able to raise the funds necessary to purchase passage to the south. Not too high-class, of course. Perhaps the father was a petty official of some kind. I would assume some venture of his didn't pan out, and washed up, he found himself unable to stay where he was."

"You'd think they would come here and absorb what was different from the empire in the north. Why can't they let go of their prejudices?"

The official's lip curled in a faint smile. "Not all refugees from the North are like those two brothers, you know."

"Yes, of course, but…"

"Failure and disillusionment are realities, but ideologies are made of dreams. And dreams, it would seem, do not fade easily," the high chief explained. "Those two could not find success in the North with its prejudiced system. Yet still, those ideas were burned into their hearts from a young age. Such things are hard to give up. That is why, even though they may change their location to the south, those same ideas stick with them here. Doubtlessly, they would like to claw their way up to being privileged elites in our land and repeat the same mistakes their parents made."

"Stupid," Wataru spat.

"Stupid, indeed. As foolish as the North's policy of discrimination against non-ankha. Yet, Wataru," the Highlander leaned forward, his voice still calm, "that which is foolish is sometimes far stronger than that which is right, possessing an uncanny power to move men's hearts. And foolish ideas have always found easy purchase on small parts, hearts with holes, hearts like hollow, barren trees waiting to be filled."

In the corner, Trone nodded. "We in the United Southern Nations, we Highlanders do not fear the Northern Empire. But we fear the ideas they bring to our land. Like a plague, they cannot be seen with the eye. But they afflict not those who are weak of body but those who are weak of mind."

Wataru remembered the drunkard at the lodge, how he had said those things about Kee Keema, yet quailed at the slightest word from the little lady.

"By the way, Chief," Kutz said, tapping Gil on the shoulder. "Think it's time to tell Wataru?"

His eyes went wide. "Of course! I had almost forgotten."

Gil looked between Wataru and Kee Keema. "Wataru, as a Traveler you have a great journey ahead of you. You go to meet the Goddess, yes?"

"Yes."

"You will need funds for your journey, then. So, you must find a way to earn them. It just so happens I have an idea." Here, the Highlander official grinned. "I was hoping you would join us. You would perform tasks for the Highlanders, and for that you would be rewarded, even as you travel. You can even use our branches in other lands to help gather information about the tower you seek. It is like two birds with one stone, yes?"

Wataru glanced up at Kee Keema. The waterkin's long tongue went whistling out to lick the top of his head. He looked as surprised as Wataru felt.

"But, he's just a kid," he said. "Isn't he a little young to become a Highlander? I mean, it's quite dangerous…"

"Yet he has already proved himself on one case, has he not? I believe he is qualified. And you will accompany him on his journey, yes?"

Kee Keema broke into a smile. "Of course! I've just received the chief's permission!"

"Really, Kee Keema?" Wataru asked. "You'll come with me?"

"You bet!" Kee Keema shouted, picking up Wataru and placing him on his shoulders as he had when they first met in the grassland. "I'll be with you through thick and thin, as far as the road takes us!"

"Then it is decided," said the Highlander chief.

Once the high chief had left—rather in a hurry—to some meeting of the United Southern Nations, Wataru was officially introduced to the members of the Gasara branch for the first time. Kutz was the head of the branch, with Trone her deputy, and beneath them were three other Highlanders. One was the large ankha that Wataru had seen before. Another was a waterkin, somewhat shorter than Kee Keema, and the third was a leaperkin—a sort of rabbit-like fellow with long ears.

"You sure had a rough introduction to our town, didn't you, shorty," the leaperkin Highlander said. "Kutz is always taking things too far, if you ask me. I mean, it was a good plan to use you as a decoy to catch the real criminals, but building a gallows like that…"

"That's enough out of you," Kutz snapped. Wataru looked at her in surprise.

"I was a decoy? You mean you really weren't going to hang me?"

Kutz frowned. "Please, we do have trials and due process in our world. We're not complete barbarians."

Wataru burst into laughter. Pretty soon everyone in the room was laughing with him.

"Well now, it feels a bit backward telling you this, but you should know a bit about our history. You see, the Highlanders began in the southeast of this continent, in a place called the Ghoza Highlands," Kutz explained. "There is a legend too."

In the distant past, the legend went, when the Goddess created the world out of chaos, she had with her a great firewyrm, to defend her from those creatures of chaos that sought to foil her works. When the creation was complete, she thanked the firewyrm by bestowing upon him the form of a man. Taking the dragon skin he had shed, she made from it armor and a helmet. Bequeathing these to him, she made him a knight, and sent him out upon the land.

"The knight first arrived in the Ghoza Highlands, and there began to live among other people. His descendants were all brave, and given to great virtue, and in the many years that followed they spread across the land until the name 'Highlander' became synonymous with one who is brave and just."

This was the origin of the Highlander name. It was even said that the small militia that first took the title was formed from none other than descendants of the firewyrm knight himself.

"Thus do we all wear the band of the firewyrm," Kutz said, raising her left hand and showing him the red leather strap on her wrist. "It is the sign of membership, and also, a warning."

Should a Highlander forget his calling and fall into disgrace, dirtying his hands with evil, then it was said that the band of the firewyrm would blaze and sear his flesh.

"These are yours," Kutz said, handing out two red wristbands. "Place them on your left wrist, and stand straight. Then put your left hand upon your chest, raise your right, and swear after me."

Everyone formed a circle. Kutz's voice was loud and clear in the silence.

"Goddess Creator, we are those who receive the will of the firewyrm, protectors of the code, hunters of the truth. We who come before you now bow at your feet, Goddess, give to you our souls, and swear a solemn oath. To despise that which is evil, to save that which is weak, to drive back the chaos, and stand true as steel, until our bodies fall to dust, we will walk hand in hand, following always the star of righteousness."

When Wataru and Kee Keema had finished repeating the oath, Kutz smiled. "Welcome to the family!"

For several days after that, Wataru joined Trone on walks around the town of Gasara, learning the duties of the patrol and searching for information about the gemstones and the Mirror of Truth. Kee Keema, hearing about some wounded gimblewolves escaping from the Knights of Stengel, set out on a hunt with the other members.

"I'll see what I can find out from other Highlanders," he promised.

As he walked around town, Wataru was impressed with the sheer number of people who came through the place every day. Yet no matter how many people he asked, he never received any information that seemed relevant to his quest. "No need to be in such a hurry," Trone laughed, consoling him. But Wataru couldn't help but feel that his time was limited. Now that plans were laid for his journey across Vision, he thought even more about his mother. *Is she okay? What did she think when I went missing? Maybe they all think I disappeared like Kenji and his gang did.*

He knew she would be worried. He just hoped she hadn't given up.

Word came that the wounded gimblewolves were roaming together in one large pack, and Kee Keema and the others didn't come back for some time. Kutz, left behind at the branch to continue the interrogation of the brothers, wanted nothing more than to join them on the hunt. She spent her days in a foul mood, muttering about how the Knights of Stengel weren't fit to round up a coop of chickens, let alone a pack of feral gimblewolves.

"Kutz is a dyed-in-the-wool Highlander, you see. She doesn't place much faith in this knightly order the United Southern Nations cooked up." So Trone had told Wataru in a quiet voice that evening while writing the day's patrol report. "You see, the Knights of Stengel are under the direct control of the Senate, and compared to us Highlanders, they're newcomers. Nor are they all warriors as their title would make one think. Some of them are scholars too.

Why, their captains are also senators in the Union."

Sitting back, Trone pushed up his glasses and folded his thick arms in front of his chest. "Of course, they did that on purpose, to ensure the Knights would remain loyal to the Senate…but most senators are decrepit old politicians—certainly not what you'd expect for the captain of a knightly order. In other words, were something big to happen, it's not likely the captain would pick up a sword and go to battle. It's an honorary post, you might say. And Kutz, well, she's a pragmatist. She won't stand for decorative posts and titles without substance, if you know what I mean.

"Within the Knights of Stengel," Trone continued, "there is a special division of peacekeepers, much like us Highlanders, called the Lancers. Each region has two units responsible for it, but because their jurisdiction ranges over the entire southern continent, they often travel quite a bit more than we do. It's a hard task they have, no doubt about it."

"And they're made up of different races, like the Highlanders?"

For some reason, Trone hesitated in his response. "Well, not actually. There are other races within the Knights of Stengel, especially the scholarly types, but the Lancers are all ankha."

"Why?"

Wataru thought that was a shame. Surely the winged karulakin would be ideally suited as a mobile strike force for the Lancers.

"It's politics, really," Trone said, stroking the ridge of his nose with a finger. "See, ankha are the most numerous race in Vision. You could put all the other races together in a group, and the ankha would still outnumber us six to four. They are the majority, and we're the minorities. That sort of thing carries weight in the Senate."

Not that this had anything to do with Wataru, Trone explained. "The real reason Kutz doesn't like the Knights of Stengel is, well, she just can't abide people who think they're so important."

Trone paused, and then added in a whisper, "That, and a long time ago she got dumped by a certain Captain Ronmel of the First Lancers division. Ever since then…"

"What was that, Trone?!" Kutz shouted, shooting him a look sharper than the tip of her whip. Trone jerked back so fast his glasses fell off his nose.

"Uh-oh! Let's be going, Wataru. We need to meet with the doctor down at the hospital."

That morning, the town guard had opened the main gates to find a merchant from Bog lying on the ground outside. It caused quite a commotion. The man himself said it was food poisoning, but the opinion of the doctor was that it could be some sort of plague, so they had him secluded in a hut outside the town walls. At the hospital, the doctor seemed busy as ever, but when Trone and Wataru showed up, he smiled.

"Well, it's not the plague."

"That's good news."

"Yes, but I was wondering if you might talk to the merchant for me?" The doctor continued, speaking quietly so the other patients wouldn't overhear. "He says he grew sick to his stomach after drinking water from a well outside town."

His symptoms, the doctor explained, were not unlike the plague he had feared, but also resembled the effects of drinking a solution used to keep insects off fruit trees.

Trone's whiskers perked up. "Do you think someone might have poisoned the well?"

The doctor put a finger to his lips for silence. "I can't imagine why anyone would do such a thing. But the merchant, that's what he thought. Though he did say the water tasted fine."

"Where is this well?" Wataru asked. For moment, he worried it was the well at the oasis where he had met Kee Keema. "Shouldn't we put a lid on it so no one will drink the water until we get to the bottom of this?"

"Absolutely, let's make haste."

The merchant, still in his isolation hut, looked pale and was in some pain, but he was able to speak. The well from which he had drunk was not the one Wataru had visited, but an ancient, half-buried well at the base of some low rocky hills to the east of town. The merchant claimed he had never drunk water from there before, but with the heat that day, he hadn't had a choice.

"The hills to the east..." Trone muttered, scratching his chin. "That's an odd place for a merchant from Bog to be passing through."

The merchant scratched his head. "To tell the truth, I heard a rumor that a treasure was buried out there. Normally, I just travel the roads between Bog and Sasaya. This is my first time in these parts."

A merchant whom he shared a room with in an inn on the Sasaya border had told him that the ruins of a church could be found at the base of the hills east of Gasara, and all the treasures that the believers had once donated were still lying there, untouched for many years.

Trone made a sour face at the merchant. "Then I'm sorry to say you've been duped. I know the ruins of which you speak, but there's no treasure to be found there. It wasn't the sort of church to ask donations of its believers."

"It just asked for their undying faith?"

"Quite the opposite. It asked for their lives."

The merchant yelped.

"Is that a church of the Old God?" Wataru asked.

"No. Its teachings were not those of the Old God, nor those of our Goddess. Long story short, the whole thing was a lie."

Ten years before, a traveling man by the name of Cactus Vira had briefly visited the town of Gasara and opened up shop, claiming to be a doctor. He was soon revealed to be a sham, and the branch chief at the time apprehended him and tossed him out of town. That's when he dug a foundation at the base of the low hills to the east and built a hut, where he went into business again, claiming he could cure any ailment by the power of holy water given him by the ancient gods.

"Suspicious, to say the least. The branch apprehended him several times, but he always seemed to find a way to escape. As soon as they turned around, he'd be back doing the same old things. Over time he accumulated more victims, or should I say believers, and one day they began building their church."

"So are these ancient gods older than the Old God?"

"Not sure. I believe the story went that they were deities from some other world."

Once the church was built, Cactus Vira was installed as its pastor, and the believers began to worship him. Many of them took up residence in the hills around the church. They cut fields out of the barren soil, and brought their produce into Gasara, where they traded for daily necessities. Yet industrious as they were, they were very poor, and all of them—woman, child, and elder alike—were rail-thin.

"Since most of them had come at the promise of a cure-all, many of them were elderly or sick to start with. It had always been impossible to support the church merely through the efforts of its believers."

Wataru remembered having heard news of something similar happening in the real world. *How had that ended?*

"Still, the believers were a tight group, and it was hard for the Gasara branch to know when the time was good to step in. Then one day, flames were spotted rising from the church. The Highlanders hurried to the scene, but they were too late…"

Hand in hand, the believers stood inside the burning church. Even as the timbers fell about them, they continued to sing the songs of praise to Cactus Vira.

"They did all they could to put out the flames, but the church had been built by amateurs, and it quickly collapsed. The bodies of the faithful were everywhere."

Since all the corpses were badly burned, they were never able to identify the body of Cactus Vira. Even the branch didn't know how many people had been living in the church commune by the end.

"Cactus Vira may have met his maker that day, or he may have escaped. Nobody knows for sure."

It didn't seem like the kind of place one would find a treasure, that was for sure. The merchant stared out into space, frowning. "But the man I talked to, he said that he passed by those hills at night, and he saw something glittering—a gem—giving off a light among the ruins of the church, making everything around it as bright as day."

Trone chuckled. "Sounds like a great yarn to me. It would take a mighty big gem to glitter that bright!"

"He didn't say how large it was, only that it was the most beautiful gemstone he had ever seen."

"Gemstone?!" Wataru said, leaping to his feet.

Trone shook his head. "Don't jump to conclusions. It's just a rumor. And we don't even have the source here to confirm it with."

"Yeah, but we should check it out, all the same. We have to go seal up that well anyway, right? Let's go, now!"

chapter 7
The Abandoned Chapel

After some preparations, they rode out of town on udais. The udai was an animal somewhat smaller than the darbaba—about the size of a pony in the real world—and the preferred mode of transport for the Highlanders on patrols in the grasslands and hilly areas. Their smaller size made them more maneuverable than the darbaba, and able to fit through narrow spaces. They were also quite smart and easily tamed. Wataru was able to ride one on his own with ease after only a half-day's practice with Trone. The udai was covered from head to foot with thick, soft fur, so even riding bareback didn't hurt.

Trone led them unerringly to the base of the rocky hills. The landscape on the eastern edge of the grasslands was not as dramatic as the gullies and rifts where the gimblewolves roamed, but it was barren. Where the grasslands grew green, here, lumpy boulders sat in piles beneath the blue sky. It was as though a giant's children had been stacking rocks when they were suddenly called to dinner, leaving their playthings behind them.

"Not the kind of place you'd expect to find a well, eh?" Trone muttered, frowning. "The grassland wells are all watched closely by the town nearest to them. Their locations are known. Our records show no well here."

"Maybe it was dug by the church members? That would explain why it's half buried now," Wataru suggested. "Let's go find the ruins. Do you know where they are?"

"Fine, fine, we'll go," Trone said with a toothy smile. "But remember, this is your first expedition. You'll do as I say."

"Yes, sir!"

Trone spurred his udai past a small crag and around a pile of rocks, coming to a stop in front of a rise of reddish brown earth. "There it is."

Wataru didn't need to look where he was pointing to find the ruins. In a large section of earth where no grass grew, several posts stood supporting nothing, their sides blackened by flame. It was as if a bundle of evil-looking spears had been dropped down from the sky and stuck haphazardly into the ground. You had to squint and look at them from a distance to see how those black spears formed the outlines of what was once a building, and even then it wasn't easy.

"So the roof burned and fell down?"

"It was still there after the fire, actually. Wind and rain did the rest. It's been ten years, after all."

The two slowly rode the perimeter of the chapel ruins. If they had just been passing by without knowing the history of the place, the burnt skeleton might not have seemed quite so ominous, so threatening. But to Wataru's eyes, every lump of soot on the blackened ground inside those pillars looked like a body, frozen in a final agony. He felt sick to his stomach.

Trone's udai snorted plaintively and took a step backward. Trone patted the beast on its neck. "He's scared."

Wataru's udai also kept its distance from the ruins, stomping its hooves in place.

"Have there been no reports in Gasara about strange things going on here, or strange lights?"

"Not a one. Most of the folks that come to Gasara have no business coming to a place like this."

"And you probably would have to get quite close to see the glow of the gemstone anyway," Wataru muttered.

Trone growled deep in his throat. "We've no proof it's a gemstone, so don't jump to conclusions. Let's dismount and take a look around."

Roping their udais to a protruding rock, they approached the ruins on foot. Trone walked with his hands empty, swinging by his side, but Wataru couldn't relax without his right hand resting on the hilt of his Brave's Sword.

"I don't like the feel of this place," Wataru whispered.

"Nor I."

The two stepped inside the outline of the ruins and began pacing its border.

Every time his foot fell on something that cracked, or he felt a lump in the soot, Wataru was sure he was stepping on someone's bones, and it sent shivers down his spine.

"The bodies of the believers were all carried from here and buried in the town's communal grave site," Trone said as he looked around. "You won't find any corpses left here. So don't worry about stepping on anyone's remains."

"That's a relief," Wataru said, still walking on tiptoe.

"Take a look," Trone said, touching one of the blackened pillars. "It's thin. Your leg could hold more weight than this. When all your builders are women, children, the elderly, and the sick, you can't carry anything much sturdier than this."

The sun had begun to angle down in the sky, but it was still quite light. Still, Wataru felt that here, where the chapel once stood, seemed somehow darker than it had been outside the line marked by the scorched ground.

"Wataru, the well."

Trone called him over, and he hurried to find a small well opening behind the building, half covered by a fallen pillar. The ground around it was littered with rubble, but the well, its rim fashioned of sturdy rock, remained intact. Wataru looked down to find the water level was much higher than he had expected.

"It's full."

"Yes. There's a lot of underground water here."

Trone cupped one hand and lifted some water from the well. Clear droplets fell through his fingers. He brought his hand to his nose, and sniffed.

"Hard to say, but it does smell a bit odd. Like medicine, maybe."

Trone poured some water into the leather skin at his waist and firmly sealed the cork. Then, he and Wataru took the rope they had brought with them and ran it around the edge of the well, attaching a small sign that read "Do Not Use."

"So that traveling merchant came all the way inside the ruins. There's no other way he would have found this well."

"Maybe he wasn't frightened since he didn't know the history of the place."

"If he came here with greed at his side, he might have made it this far even if he was scared."

Trone's comment reminded Wataru suddenly of his mother. He smiled. He remembered asking her how she always managed to carry so much when she went to a bargain sale at the local department store.

—*Oh, I didn't go alone. I had greed to help me.*

"Let's go home," Trone said. "No point in lingering. This place is starting to give me the willies."

After asking the doctor at the hospital to analyze the sample of water they had retrieved from the well, Wataru and Trone returned to the branch. Wataru was relieved to hear that the traveling merchant seemed to have improved greatly during the time they were gone.

In the remaining hours of daylight, Wataru assisted Trone in looking through old records. It seemed that Cactus Vira and the church had given the branch in Gasara quite a deal of trouble. Wataru noticed several handwritten comments on numerous reports detailing these escapades. The church, he discovered, was a constant headache for the authorities.

"In the end, they never did find out who Cactus Vira was," Trone said, removing his spectacles. "And who knows about these ancient gods."

"Did the holy water come from that well?" Wataru wondered out loud. "Maybe it wasn't medicine. Maybe it was poison."

"If they mixed something in the water at all," Trone replied, stretching. "Well, this is about as much as we can do today. Go home, Wataru. You must be starving."

Wataru retired to the lodge and ate his supper. He asked the little lady who brought his food about Cactus Vira and his flock, but she claimed to not know anything about it.

"Have you heard any of the guests here talking about some sort of treasure buried by the church near the hills?"

"Can't say that I have."

When the innkeeper arrived he said much the same thing. But Wataru couldn't let it rest. *That light spilling from within the ruined church...what could it be?*

What if it only glows at night?

He could investigate the ruins later—tonight! Once the thought occurred to him, he couldn't let it rest. Wataru packed a small bag, wrapped the Brave's

Sword around his waist, and left the lodge.

It was almost time for the Gasara town gates to close, and the road was busy with darbaba drivers and merchant trains rushing to get in before they were locked out. Wataru borrowed an udai and made his way through the throng, relying on the ruckus to cover his departure. Soon he was riding across the night grassland.

As he neared his destination, Wataru could see, almost on the horizon, a countless number of lights glimmering like fireflies. They appeared to be moving slowly. Perhaps it was the Knights of Stengel returning. Kee Keema might be with them. If Wataru wasn't home when they arrived, he'd notice for sure. *I'll have to try to get home as soon as possible.*

Black oil smoke rose from the lantern at Wataru's waist. He dismounted at the same place they had stopped earlier that day. The only sound was the faint sizzling of the lantern's wick.

The burnt remains of the chapel looked like a patch of pure black in the darkness. Wataru picked his way carefully through the rubble, recalling the path Trone had walked.

It seemed to him that there was a burnt smell on the night air. *Odd, I didn't notice anything during the day.* Placing his right hand upon the hilt of his sword, Wataru tried to drive all such thoughts out of his mind. *Look for the light. That's what I'm here for.*

When he heard a sound like a strangled squawk come from the rocks above the ruins, he nearly jumped three feet. *Probably some wildfowl having a bad dream*, he thought to himself. *I hope it didn't startle my udai. On second thought, he's probably braver than I am by far...*

It was pitch black. Wataru saw nothing even resembling a light. He started to look around the well, but the only thing shining were the stars in the sky above. Wataru chuckled, half out of relief, half in disappointment. He lowered the lantern, lighting the ground by his feet, and turned around.

Just then, something white moved on the border between the lantern's light and the darkness of the night.

Wataru whirled to see something bobbing in the air, just brushing the edge of his lantern. Wataru looked at it in shock. He felt like he had been punched in the gut.

It was a white arm floating in midair.

The scene was almost too surreal to be frightening. The arm didn't appear to be severed, rather it looked as if it was somehow growing out of the darkness itself. A long slender arm, beginning just below the shoulder. A woman's right arm.

Now it waved from side to side, the index finger pointing straight at Wataru. Then it motioned to him. *It wants me to follow.*

The arm looked like a narrow white fish swimming through the water of night. It slid gracefully through the darkness until it stopped. The arm tilted, pointing down, and quite suddenly, it was sucked into the ground. No sooner had it disappeared than the ground began to glow. The light grew until it lit Wataru's face. Then it was almost too bright to look at.

Wataru ran to the spot. Suddenly, the ground shuddered and he started to wobble. One of his feet sunk into the ground.

There must be a room under here.

During the day, the hole would have been hidden by rubble. Wataru crouched and began to examine the ground. Soon he found a handle that seemed to be attached to a half-open lid. He lifted it, and the light blazed pure white, and then quickly faded. It was as though whatever lit the ground had scampered away.

Wataru looked to see a ladder descending down into the earth. Fixing the lantern to his waist, he began to descend.

As he climbed down, he counted the rungs until he reached forty—and then he gave up. It was a long way down. Wherever this was going, it was deep. He didn't want to think about it too much, lest he start to get frightened. Right now, he needed to focus only on the simple act of climbing.

Wataru began to sweat. He was breathing heavily when at last the hard tip of his leather boot touched something that wasn't a rung. Holding tight to the ladder with both hands, he craned his neck and looked down to see a damp, rocky floor.

It was a cave. From where he stood, he could see a rough winding passage leading off into the darkness. The white light appeared to be coming from far down the tunnel. It had grown much fainter than it had been when he first saw it on the surface.

Moving the lantern to his left hand and holding his sword in his right, Wataru began to walk forward. The color and the feel of the walls around him resembled tombstones. Water seeped through unseen cracks, dripping in the tunnel, and making the walls and floor slick. He reached out a hand to touch it and found it incredibly cold. He lifted a finger to his nose and sniffed, but there was no trace of medicine. Since he had been in a hurry to leave, he had forgotten his gloves. He resolved not to touch things any more than he had to. It wasn't hard to imagine something living in the crevices in the wall, something with poisonous fangs or stingers.

A little further down, the stone tunnel took an abrupt turn to the right. At the corner, Wataru paused and pricked up his ears. Hearing nothing, he quickly turned the corner, sword held ready.

Nothing—just the tunnel hewn from the rock continuing on into the distance. Wataru stuck his tongue out. *See? I'm not scared.*

The tunnel had grown narrower, and the ceiling was low over his head. The width of the passage as he walked was irregular—sometimes widening, sometimes narrowing. He finally reached the end, a solid wall of rock, with a hole at the bottom near the floor just large enough for a person to crawl through. The faint white light was coming from the other side.

I don't like this one bit.

Wataru didn't fancy going anywhere more cramped than the tunnel he was already in. But if he didn't go through the hole, this was the end of the road. He looked around but didn't see any other passageways.

Oh well. Wataru set the lantern down by his feet, and pressing himself to the ground, he peered through the hole. As he expected, the passageway continued on the other side. It seemed to be dimly lit, and he could feel a faint breeze on his cheeks.

Right. Steeling his body, he thrust himself headfirst through the hole. The wall was thin, and he was quickly on the other side.

He took a look around. The place he was standing was significantly different from the previous passageway he came from. A large dome stretched above his head three stories high. The chamber was very wide—about the same size as his schoolyard back home.

Wataru found himself unable to believe that such a large space could exist underground without some visible means of support. He looked around in amazement. On the far end of the chamber, he saw two more tunnels disappearing into the distance. The tunnel on the right seemed larger, and had some long metallic objects lying near it. There was nothing remarkable about the tunnel to the left, except—of course—for that suspicious white light pulsating from its depths.

The sound of a thin trickle of water was coming from somewhere. Wataru felt a sudden thirst in his throat. *One thing's for sure: I'm not drinking any water in this place.*

Wait, my lantern! Crouching down, Wataru reached back through the hole he had just crawled through, when, right before his eyes, his lantern was *taken away*. Something like a long black arm, dried like a mummy's, reached out and snatched the lantern out of sight. It had happened in an instant.

What was that? What thing has an arm like that? Was that even really an arm?

Was it his duty as a Highlander to crawl back through the hole and investigate? What if that strange arm belonged to some kind of monster? It could even be a thief. A mummy thief! *Whatever it is, I have to get that lantern back.*

But then again, he was standing in an area that was plainly lit—though Wataru had no idea how. And there was that same white light shining from the corridor on his left. He at least had someplace to go without the lantern. *I'll just keep moving forward. There, I've made my decision and I'm sticking to it. It's not that I'm scared to meet the owner of that nasty, dried-up arm. Really.*

Holding his Brave's Sword before him, Wataru took a few cautious steps toward the middle of the chamber. From here he could see that the metallic objects piled up in front of the right tunnel appeared to be spears—primitive things made of simple metal poles sharpened at one end. Also, he could also see traces of some large platform having been attached to the wall. Here and there along the rock were marks left by some sort of fastenings. In other places he saw the wall was discolored and scorched black with soot—perhaps where torches had been attached. Wataru looked around carefully, tracing the outlines in the rock, finally reaching the conclusion that whatever had once stood there was not entirely unlike an altar one might see in a church in the real world. Maybe this was where Cactus Vira and his followers had worshipped.

Then what are those spears doing there?

Chapter 8
The Dead

Two voices began arguing inside Wataru's head. One wanted to check out the mysterious, darkened right-hand corridor. The other, a far more persuasive voice, cautioned to let sleeping gods lie, and go down the left, toward the light.

As he stood, pondering his decision, something emerged from the tunnel on the right. It was a person in rags. *Somebody lives here!* Using one of the spears as a walking stick, the figure came forward tentatively—slowly making its way to the altar remains. Wataru stood rooted to the floor, unable to move.

That's no person. Though it might have been once. It was a skeleton. A skeleton, wearing rags wrapped around its bony frame, and walking with a spear. With every step its jaw would rattle.

Relax, I have to relax. I'm not frightened. Wataru closed his eyes for the briefest of moments, repeating those words to himself. *I beat the four statues in the Cave of Trials—they gave me wisdom and bravery. I've even got the protection of the firewyrm! No bag of bones is going to send me running.*

The skeleton, now at the altar, stood clinging to the spear and swaying gently from side to side. Then, with a hollow knocking sound, it collapsed into a formless pile of bones.

Wataru steadied himself and began to walk toward the right-hand tunnel. He noticed right away that the spears by the mouth of the tunnel were baked with grime and rust.

Only the entrance of the tunnel was clearly visible. But when Wataru held up his Brave's Sword in front of him, the blade began to glow with a wan light.

It was almost as if it was catching that white light coming from the other tunnel and somehow augmenting it. It wasn't as bright as his lantern, but it was more than enough to see by. Wataru held his sword high and began to walk.

He had gone about four or five yards when he saw what looked like wooden bunks stacked three high on either side of the tunnel. He stepped closer and saw that they were full. There were people in the bunks.

Not people—skeletons! Bunk beds filled with bones!

There was a clattering noise behind him. Wataru spun around to see one of the skeletons, wrapped in rags, fall out from its bunk. Arms held out, it began walking toward him.

Wataru leapt backward, too startled to shout. He dodged the skeleton's bony embrace, but got nicked in the nose by one of its fingers. The skeleton waved its arms like it was doing the breast stroke, then fell to the ground with a clatter.

Wataru heard a sound like a racing locomotive. It was his own breathing. He wiped his forehead with his hands and looked up.

Skeletons were rising from every bunk. Some clung to the edge of their beds, others held on to the back of the skeleton in front of them. The sound of their bones rubbing together was like the beating of a thousand moth wings.

Their eyes—swimming in empty sockets—were fixed on Wataru. The army of bones made their way toward him. Wataru felt the hair on his nape stand on end.

Suddenly the strength returned to his legs, and he fled. He didn't think he had come that far down the tunnel, but the distance back to the entrance seemed to take forever. The hall of worship was filled with dim light, and it seemed like the tunnel was even brighter. His escape. His road to freedom. Wataru ran like the wind, and found himself going nowhere. It was like he was running in a dream. Skeletal hands reached out, pleading and grasping. They hooked his clothes, they looped through the belt at his waist, and they yanked at his hair.

Wataru realized he was screaming. The skeletons were going to charge him, collapse upon him in an avalanche of bone, burying him under their weight. *I can't let myself fall! I can't fall!*

Wataru was so panicked he couldn't run straight. He felt his speed decreasing. Bony arms reached out from behind and grabbed his shoulder. He brushed them away with such force he lost his balance and nearly fell to one knee, clawing at the air to keep on his feet.

That was when he noticed the bars jutting down from the top of the tunnel. *A portcullis.* If he could get out of the tunnel and drop that behind him, he could lock those skeletons up forever. There had to be a lever somewhere—a trigger he could activate.

He looked around desperately. There, just inside the tunnel mouth, stretched a length of rope hanging from the portcullis above. With a mighty swing he brought the Brave's Sword down on the rope.

There was the slightest bit of resistance, and the rope split cleanly in two. With a great screeching sound, and dust flying everywhere, the steel trap came hurtling down. For an instant, everything went black. *It's falling too fast! I'll be trapped inside with them!*

Another fleshless hand clutched at Wataru's sleeve. Its strength was ferocious. Wataru screwed his eyes shut and dove, headfirst, for the tunnel entrance.

The portcullis nicked the tip of his toes as it crashed down. The metal bars successfully trapped and crushed the skeletal horde.

Face down on the floor, Wataru crawled farther away before he had the courage to turn and look. Behind the sturdy bars, the skeletons lay in a pile of bones. The force of the impact had shattered them into bits and pieces. But he could see various arms and skulls still struggling to extricate themselves from the debris. Hesitantly, Wataru stood and walked closer to take a look.

Things were moving. Bony fingers twitched, searching for his boots, and jawbones rattled, snapping for his toes. Wataru's chest seized up with fear, and he had to take a step back.

"Who are you guys?" he asked in a whisper. The bones made no reply. "Why are you here? Were you the believers? Did Cactus Vira shut you up in here? Or did you shut yourselves up?"

Eventually the movements slowed, then stopped altogether. Soon they were nothing more than brittle bones, lying scattered on the cavern floor.

Wataru took a deep breath and let the tension go out of his shoulders. He then turned toward the tunnel on the left. It sloped slightly downward.

How far down does it go, I wonder?

It was more or less straight down, only snaking to the right and left now and again. The further down he went, the brighter the light seemed to grow. It eventually grew so light he could see writing and painting on the damp stone walls.

Here was a man who looked like he had been crucified. Here was a crowd of people kneeling before an altar. Here was a man cutting the head off an animal that looked very much like a darbaba. Beneath these images was text that Wataru couldn't read, written in ink the color of blood.

Above the praying figures stood a single man—more of a silhouette, really—pitch black, its arms spread wide. On closer examination, it didn't look human at all. Its body was far too massive, and something like horns grew from its head. Behind it a great disk shone like the sun. It was almost as if the darkened figure was trying to block its light from those who knelt before him.

Was the figure with the horns Cactus Vira?

Wataru noticed something else as he continued his descent into the earth. There were many sconces set in the wall, and torch fragments scattered about on the ground. They were all quite old, but they did not appear to have been simply discarded. Rather, they looked like they had been broken on purpose. He passed a broken lantern that clearly had been smashed against the tunnel's wall.

It was obvious that many people had come here before Wataru. And wherever they were going, they weren't allowed to bring light with them. They had to discard their torches and lanterns before they were allowed to proceed any further.

He continued down. The tunnel grew narrower and began to gradually rise and fall until at one point it plummeted in a steep incline. Wataru looked up to see a hole in the rock wall about a foot above his head. The white light was emanating from that hole.

Wataru jumped, catching on to the rim of the window-like hole with his fingers. Straining, he was able to pull himself up and crawl through. The room into which he emerged was so vast, its ceiling so high, that for a moment it was all Wataru could do to stare, gaping in awe.

This chamber was at least twice the size of the hall of worship he had found before. Wataru was standing on top of a small rock jutting out of the floor.

Except he couldn't see the floor. Everything was covered with water—it was an underground lake. The water was clear, beautiful. The pure white light was streaming from its depths.

Whoa.

The underground lake was shaped like a pentagon. Seen from above, the entire room would have looked like a giant gem, breathtaking in its beauty. The more he looked, the more Wataru felt like he would be sucked into its depths.

Finally, he managed to tear his eyes away and look at the walls for some other exit. Here and there he saw protrusions much like the one he was standing upon. If he jumped and picked his way over the rocks just right he thought he could make it to the edge of the water.

He moved carefully, measuring each jump. It took quite a while to finally reach the rocks at the lake's edge. The tension he felt took his breath away. Standing at the edge of the water, the white light was more brilliant than ever, and his ears were filled with the sound of waves lapping at the stony shore. *Odd that there should be waves. There isn't any wind.* Wataru thought there might be a spring of some sort toward the middle of the lake.

Returning his sword to the scabbard at his waist, Wataru got down on his knees and stuck his right hand out to the water's surface. It was quite cold, and felt like silk. He stuck his hand in, and got the strong impression that he was touching something very holy.

The source of the white light was definitely coming from the bottom of the lake. Maybe he could find it if he dove in. But if he went into cold water like that without warming up first, he'd probably cramp up and sink to his watery grave.

As he sat pondering his next move, he realized something. He wasn't just watching the clear, shining water. He was being watched.

By what?

Just beneath the surface of the water, a giant eyeball appeared—the size of a basketball—and it stared at Wataru, unblinking. The pupil was jet black. He could even see red veins running through the white of the eye.

Thus commenced a strange staring contest that went on for several seconds. Wataru was entranced and stood there motionless. Then, suddenly, he came to his senses and pulled his hand from the water.

Too late! Something came rushing out of the water and grabbed his wrist. It was the white arm, the one that had beckoned him into the chapel ruins. Water ran in rivulets down its fingers, and glimmering droplets sprayed as it broke the surface. From this close, Wataru could see that it was indeed a slender feminine arm, yet its strength was incredible. Wataru struggled to free himself from that pale grasp. All the while, the huge single eye continued to stare at him.

"Let me go!" he shouted, but the arm tugged even harder until it felt like his shoulder would pop. Suddenly, something grabbed onto his leg. Wataru twisted and looked down to see a black mummified arm coming out of the water.

The arm that took my lantern! Wataru noticed that this arm was a left arm. White and black, the two arms formed a pair. Together, they held Wataru firmly in place.

"I said let me go!" Wataru yelled. He tried kicking the black arm off his leg, but lost his balance and fell with a thump on his behind. The arms pulled even harder, dragging him into the water directly in view of the giant eye's unblinking gaze.

"Help me!" Wataru's scream echoed off the high vaulted ceiling of the cavern.

Help me...help me...help me. His words mocked him as they echoed off the walls.

As he struggled, Wataru reached for his sword with his left hand. Just as his fingers brushed against the hilt, the black hand yanked his leg with ferocious strength. In the same instant, the white hand released him. Wataru fell on his back and was dragged into the water all the way up to his waist.

Oh no!

The white hand appeared in the air above him. Fluttering above his face like some evil bird, it grabbed his shirt collar and dragged him down, deeper into the water.

His left hand found his sword, and he drew it from its scabbard. He swung without thinking, without bothering to aim. Once again, the sword moved of its own will, cutting an arc through the air with dreadful accuracy, slicing the palm of the white hand as it hung twitching like a spider over Wataru's face.

A horrible scream assaulted Wataru's eardrums. It was so loud he feared he might never hear another sound again.

The cut palm flapped open, revealing pink, bloodless flesh. The wound looked almost like a mouth trying to talk—a mouth with no tongue. Wataru didn't linger on the sight, but turned his sword toward the black arm clutching his ankle.

The surface of the water began to stir. A disturbance deep in the lake sent waves rolling toward the shore. Then the water rose into a column high enough to touch the ceiling.

The water came crashing down on his head like a waterfall, soaking him to the bone. But as a result, his arms and legs were now free. Standing quickly and jumping to the shore, he steadied his grip on his sword. A giant black form emerged from the water, silhouetted against the white light streaming from the center of the lake. It looked like a monk in long flowing robes—save that it was enormous.

It turned until it was facing directly toward Wataru. Then its eye opened, a single giant eye—the very one he had seen beneath the water—shining from the center of its head.

"What are you?" Wataru shouted. "Are those skeletons the remains of the ones you killed?"

The looming black form said nothing as its eye moved from side to side. Then Wataru spotted the two arms, right and left, flying through the air until they were next to the giant creature. Wataru half expected them to attach themselves to its body.

But that didn't happen. First the arms waved in the air, then, together, they formed fists so tight Wataru could see the tendons bulging on the backs of their hands.

What's going on?

Then, suddenly, the hands opened, and like a magician producing a rose out of thin air, something came pouring out of the palms—scores of needle-thin objects. White needles from the white hand, black from the black.

They were coming for him. In the split-second before he turned to run, Wataru saw that those countless needles were actually hands—swarms of tiny hands. They came together like a school of piranha descending upon their prey.

Throwing up his arms to cover his head, Wataru dashed along the water's edge, the tiny hands in hungry pursuit. The noise as they cut through the air was like the thrumming of a thousand insect wings.

Wataru ducked and lashed out with his sword at the mass of hands. If he didn't find a way out of here soon, they would rip him to shreds. They were each only a few inches long, but their fingertips were cruelly sharp. They scratched at Wataru's skin, poked at his eyes, and wormed their way up and under his clothing.

I can't stop running, Wataru thought. And he ran.

A great roar rose up from behind him. The cyclops was standing at the water's edge. Without a doubt, Wataru knew that this was the creature that was staring at him earlier.

The thing didn't even seem to have a mouth, so Wataru had no idea where its voice was coming from. But one thing was clear: it was laughing. *It's having fun!*

The monstrosity was still howling with mirth as it slid to the edge of the chamber. It pulled back the sleeves of its robe to reveal arms that looked like two giant snakes—ending not with fingers but with fins. Then the creature lifted its arms high into the air and brought them down on the surface of the lake at incredible speed.

There was a great splash, and water fell in a torrent around Wataru. He couldn't see. His feet slipped. *If I fall now…*

"Hraaah!"

A yell rang through the room, and an instant later, something long and sharp cut straight through the air of the chamber and impaled itself in the beast's left arm. The monster howled again, this time in pain.

"Wataru! You okay?"

Wataru looked up through the haze of miniature hands. *Kee Keema!* He was standing high on one of the rocky walls. Directly above him was Trone, a bundle of throwing spears over his shoulder, and above him was Kutz, kneeling on a rock shelf.

"Hang in there, we're coming for you!" Kee Keema shouted, bounding down the rocks with surprising agility for his size. The black cyclops pulled the spear out of its arm, and heaved it back toward the waterkin. Kutz reacted quickly and knocked the spear to the ground with a crack of her whip. Trone threw a second spear, which successfully grazed the monster's giant eye.

"Hah! We'll cut you down to size!"

Kee Keema dashed up to Wataru, and covered him with his arms. He then swung his axe like a hammer thrower in the Olympics, and scattered the cloud of tiny attacking hands.

"H-how did you know where I was?" Wataru asked, dizzy with relief and excitement.

"You don't think I can't second-guess what you're up to?" Kutz snapped. She jumped from her rocky perch, and knocking aside one of the creature's giant fins, she did a flip in midair to land by the side of the lake. Without even looking, she sensed the floating white arm lurching through the air for her throat. A flick of her whip, and it was knocked aside.

"What is this thing? Something Cactus Vira was worshiping down here?"

"Or maybe it's what Cactus Vira himself became," Trone said, slowly moving into position, his third throwing spear aimed at the giant eye.

"Who cares? Let's take it down," Kutz spat, wrapping her whip around the black hand this time, flinging it against the wall. The arm made a distinct splat and fell to the ground limp as a discarded rag.

The edge of the lake was now littered with hands—victims of Wataru's sword and Kee Keema's axe. There were so many of them, in fact, that it was hard to walk without stepping on one. Kutz and Trone stood alert, facing the towering black creature by the side of the lake.

The creature's eye, red and bloodshot, rolled back and forth. Then, with great effort, it blinked.

When the eye opened, the water of the lake began to stir. The monster's robes fell from his body and into the water. Wataru and the others could do nothing but stand and stare.

Now totally exposed, the creature looked like something not quite man and not quite fish. Armor-like scales covered its torso, and giant fins protruded from its side.

With its good arm, the one-eyed giant tore the remains of the robe from its head, revealing two long horns. Wataru instantly thought of the image he had seen painted on the wall of the tunnel.

Then the skin beneath that great eye split into a hideous maw. The creature pursed its lips as though to whistle, puffed out its cheeks, and spat a great ball of fire.

"Look out!"

Trone and Kutz dodged to the side. The flaming balls smacked into the wall, sending rocks crumbling to the ground. *That thing exploded like a missile!* Wataru tried to run to help Kutz, but the shockwave knocked him off his feet.

The second fireball flew toward Kee Keema. He dodged just in the nick of time, shouting, "Yowch! That's hot!" despite himself.

"Enough of this!" Trone roared, fixing his aim—when another fireball flew straight at him.

"Gah! What is this thing?"

As they ran, they did their best to avoid all the fireballs and falling rocks. The creature lunged at them, using its sharp fins as weapons. Kee Keema lifted his axe to block one, and the head of his weapon was sliced clean off. It was like fighting a flying guillotine.

Now on the defensive, the small team secured its position, and began fighting back. Robbed of his weapon, Kee Keema picked up chunks of rock and hurled them at the giant's eye.

The creature's weak point was obviously its eye. Wataru's friends had realized this early on. Every one of their attacks had been aimed at that single unblinking sphere. Unfortunately, the creature triumphantly knocked aside every frontal attack they threw at him. Wataru, for his part, tried to distract the monster so his friends could score a decisive blow.

But the creature never looked at him. Its fins continued to lash out, often slicing through the air inches above Wataru's head, but the eye never turned away. Instead, it remained fixed on the rocks at the edge of the lake—right where the Highlanders stood. Never once did it glance back toward the white light from the center of the lake.

Wataru recalled once more the painting he'd seen in the corridor. He also thought about the discarded lanterns and broken torches. Kee Keema, Kutz and Trone were not carrying lanterns. Doubtlessly, the black hand had confiscated whatever lights they brought with them.

Maybe it doesn't like light?

It appeared at first as though the creature were protecting the white light at the bottom of the lake. That's why it stood steadfast at the shoreline.

But what if it's the other way around? Maybe it *couldn't* look at the light, it couldn't stand it.

Right!

Wataru ran to the water's edge and dove in. Lit by the white light, the lake's water was incredibly clear. Despite this, the irregular depressions in the rock floor made it difficult to find just where the bottom was. Wataru kicked with all his strength, and once he had the creature behind him, he resurfaced.

The creature was facing the Highlanders, spitting out ball after ball of flame. Wataru was now directly behind the creature. *This has to be it,* he thought

The light. The rocks near the bottom of the lake were practically glowing with it. Driven by some impulse he didn't understand, he drew his sword. Then, of its own accord, the sword jerked to the right. *Okay, I guess I should swim over there.* Wataru kicked at the water and dove farther down.

He was coming to the end of his breath. Just a little farther…

Just then, the bottom of the lake came into view. There, in the middle of a small flat patch of rock, was a white gem about the size of a baseball. It was shining with an incredible light.

Wataru reached and grasped it with his empty hand. In his other hand, the Brave's Sword shone, almost as if it were happy.

Wataru shot toward the surface. His lungs felt like they were ready to explode. The one-eyed creature roared, shaking the cavern with its thunderous voice. Quickly catching his breath, Wataru dove down again. This time he swam fearlessly to the front of the bellowing monster.

Timing was everything. Staying underwater, he held his breath until he was directly in front of the beast. Then he kicked hard and came to the surface, holding the white gem in both hands.

The gem shone brightly—directly into the creature's eye. That baleful eye opened wide, and a roar of pain rocked the cavern walls. Its two arms rose in a last-minute attempt to shield the eye from the light.

"Now!" Wataru shouted. Trone threw his last spear. It flew true, cutting straight through the air, hitting the eye dead center.

Wrrrrrooooowwwr!

The monster howled and flapped its arms and fins, trying in vain to pull out the spear. Like a punctured balloon, the creature began to deflate.

As it dwindled in size, its scream lessened in volume. Slowly the howl became less bestial, and more like the screaming of a person.

Before long, the creature had shrunk down until it was no larger than one of them. Then ever so slowly, it sank beneath the waves, no longer a threat.

chapter 9
The Escape

Wataru slumped into the water.

"Wataru! Are you okay?" Kee Keema charged in, and yanked him up onto the shore.

When he came to, Wataru was still clutching the glittering gemstone to his breast. The stone glowed with a soft light and seemed warm to the touch.

"What was that thing?" Kutz muttered, glaring at the water. "And all those hands? Anybody ever heard of a monster that's all hands?"

"The old records say that Cactus Vira called the believers who gathered at his feet his *good working hands*," Trone offered.

"Working hands, indeed," Kutz spat. "I guess they didn't need brains. Sad that even in death they were bound to follow the every whim of their one-eyed master."

Just then, on the far side of the lake, another column of water rose. The party jerked to attention, but there was no monster to be seen. Instead, the rock wall of the cavern had began to crumble. Giant chunks of rubble broke free and fell into the water, accompanied by a great overall shaking.

"Run! This place is coming down!" Trone shouted. As if on signal, part of the ceiling gave way with a loud crack, and a boulder the size of a darbaba's head came crashing down. The rocky protrusions they had used to get here began to fall, as though plucked off the wall by unseen hands. Kutz moved quickly, her whip reaching one of the remaining footholds, but no sooner had her whip wrapped around the pointed end of one stone, than the whole thing broke off and fell. It was all she could do to retrieve her whip.

"Damn it!"

"Everyone, this way!" came Kee Keema's cry. He stood holding a slab of rock from falling. "We can take shelter here!"

"The ceiling's coming down!"

Wataru looked up at Kutz's warning cry. A giant, jagged hole had opened above the underground lake. He could see the stars.

"An exit!" Wataru shouted, as he ran to help Kee Keema.

"And just in the nick of time," said Kutz, dodging a chunk of rock. "But how do we get up there?!"

"This wall is solid enough to climb...I think," Trone said, evaluating the situation. They were on the west side of the lake, directly opposite from the way they had entered. There were no large protrusions, but plenty of cracks and crevices that would make suitable handholds.

"I'll climb to the top and lower a rope to you." Trone loosened the rope around his waist and made a loop with it. "You'll have to leave your weapons. Make yourselves as light as possible."

"Wait, I'll go!" Wataru said, snatching the rope from Trone's hand. "I'm lighter than you!"

"Don't be silly..."

"No, if I fall, you can catch me!"

Wataru leapt on top of the flat slab of rock Kee Keema was holding up, and jumped from there to the wall. He had seen a movie where Jackie Chan had climbed a wall like this. He heard that he really did it—no stuntmen. Well, Jackie Chan is human, Wataru figured. *If he can do it, so can I!*

Wataru began to climb. His mind went blank. *No fear. Pure concentration.*

And then he was there, only another two yards to the star-filled hole in the ceiling.

Just then, a particularly large jolt hit the cavern, and Wataru's center of gravity shifted. His hands, then both his feet, detached from the wall. And just like that, he was cast into space. Below him beckoned the underground lake. He was falling, with the rocks, falling down...

Then something soft and slender wrapped around him. Wataru was floating in midair.

"Grab on!" said a girl's voice. An arm covered in silky white fur hooked around his waist.

Meena! She was hanging from the hole in the ceiling with a rope tied around her waist. Both of her arms were gripping Wataru tightly. She carried another coil of rope on her back.

"Up my rope! To the top!"

Wataru grabbed the rope at her waist and pulled himself up hand over hand, clambering toward the hole.

Another shock came just as he reached the edge, but Wataru held on and crawled out through the hole. Looking down, he saw Meena hanging just below the level of the ceiling. She was trying to control her swaying motion while lowering the rope on her back. Wataru quickly looked around. He was on the western edge of the chapel ruins. Everywhere he looked things seemed wrong—tilted. The rocky crags around him were crumbling and sloping dangerously. The rope supporting Meena was attached to a rocky projection some distance away. Wataru turned to the hole and held the rope as firmly as he could to help Meena steady herself.

Meena moved her arms in a graceful motion, lowering the rope to Trone and the others. Afterward, she deftly spun in midair, getting a foothold on the edge of the ceiling hole, and flipping up to stand by Wataru's side.

"Pull! Pull now!"

"Right!"

First Kutz, then Trone came clambering up the rope. By the time they reached the top, it was apparent that the whole place was sinking.

Kee Keema!

"Quickly! Quickly!"

The rope swung over to where Kee Keema stood, and he latched onto it with his powerful arms. He proceeded to dash up the rope. He was the fastest of all of them, but Wataru was still afraid for his safety. *Please don't let him fall!*

"Hraah!"

With a triumphant roar, Kee Keema shot out of the hole. The ground shifted and buckled.

"Let's get out of here!"

Now together, they ran as fast as possible. They didn't have to look behind them to know that the ground just behind their feet was cracking and falling. Wataru ran holding Meena's hand, with Kee Keema tugging on his elbow.

A short distance from the chapel ruins, they reached a small rocky outcrop, about shoulder height to Wataru. "There—that rock!" Trone shouted. "Jump on the other side!"

Meena yanked Wataru's arm hard, and they jumped through the air so fast it startled him. Just before they hit the ground, she led them in a midair flip. They landed on their feet, knees bent. *Touchdown.*

All around, dust rose in a great cloud. But the sounds of rock and earth collapsing had stopped. They were safe behind the outcropping.

"Well now, that was a close one," came Kutz's voice through the dust. A sudden snort sounded in the whirling sand and grit to her side, and two holes appeared, floating in the air. They were Kee Keema's nostrils. He and Kutz were both covered with so much dust they blended in perfectly with the debris behind them.

"You okay, Wataru?"

Wataru nodded. He was sitting on the ground, the strength gone out of his legs. He was still holding Meena's hand.

"Meena?"

"I'm fine," she said brightly. "But, aren't we missing someone?"

"That's right, where is Trone?" Kutz said, looking around. "Trone! Stop messing around and get over here!"

"If you're that concerned about my well-being, you might try getting up," said a muffled voice.

Kutz looked down. Everyone's eyes followed her.

"Oh, my," Kutz exclaimed. "Sorry about that..."

Kutz was sitting on the tiger-man's head. She rolled to the side, and Trone rose, his whiskers twitching.

"I've never been so frightened in all my life."

"Oh, really? There are lots of guys who would love to be sat on by me," Kutz laughed. She stood up, wiped the layer of grit off her face, and put her hands on her hips. "That's quite the sight."

Right in front of them—stretching out for about half a mile—was a gaping sinkhole. The ruins of the chapel clung precariously to the edge, but all of the standing timbers had fallen. What once had been the skeleton of a building was now just a pile of rubble.

"Nice of you to drop in," Kutz said gently, turning to Meena. "You saved our lives."

Meena lowered her eyes, embarrassed. Her tail was quivering down to its very tip.

"You move light on your feet," Trone said, impressed, "and you're skilled with a rope."

"How did you know we were here?" Kee Keema asked.

Meena flinched. "I'm sorry."

"Nothing to apologize about. There was such a commotion when we left, I'm sure you would have heard it all the way from the hospital," Kutz offered. "And besides, who could blame you for wanting to come help rescue Wataru from certain danger."

chapter 10
The First Gemstone

What parts of Meena's face weren't covered with soft white fur were glowing a bright red. Wataru felt his own face redden. He realized he was still holding her hand, and quickly let go.

"Well, aren't you two something," Kutz said, throwing her head back with laughter. "You're both red as beets!"

"Leave me alone!" Wataru retorted, when a sudden bright light filled his eyes, and he staggered back.

"What was that? Wataru, that came from your shirt!"

It was just like Kee Keema said. Wataru looked down to find his chest shining with a white light that radiated from inside his shirt.

Wataru gasped. *The gemstone!* He had tucked it inside his shirt so that it would be safe as he climbed up the cavern wall.

When he pulled it out, the gem glowed in his fingers with a soft, warm light. Then it drifted from Wataru's hand, defying gravity to float up in the air. They all had to lift their gaze to see it.

Shining brighter than before, the light took the form of a woman wearing white robes. Everyone stood, eyes open wide, unable to speak.

She looked like a nun, or a saint. Except she was very young, and smiling ever so faintly. Her eyes moved, looking at Wataru.

Wataru heard a voice in his head. A young girl's voice.

—*You have freed me. Thank you. Thank you from the bottom of my heart.*

It was all Wataru could do to blink.

—*For too long I was held by Cactus Vira's evil strength, locked within that lake. Cactus Vira brought me there, hoping to use my power, but I never let him. Nor did I give my blessing to his deeds. That man thought to rule people, to stand above them, to be worshiped by them, all to fill his empty soul. For this he lied and killed—and worse, he locked the spirits of the dead in his cave, and made them serve him even in the afterlife. By saving me, you released those who could not free themselves, and purified this land at long last.*

Wataru took a step toward the glowing woman. "Who...who are you?"

The phantom woman smiled a benevolent smile.

—I am the white strength, the Spirit of Healing, the manifestation of a portion of the Goddess's power.

"The Spirit of Healing..."

Then the phantom woman put her hands together in front of her face, as though in prayer, and closed her eyes.

—And I am the one who opens the way for the Braves whom the Goddess has summoned.

The white light shone brighter for a moment, then began to coalesce into a single point. It became small, like a tiny star, and drifted down until it was level with Wataru's eyes.

Wataru reached out and cradled the light in his palms. The gemstone, now only as large as a fingernail, shone once more in his hands—then was still.

"The first gemstone," Wataru said quietly.

With the gem resting on the palm of his left hand, Wataru drew his Brave's Sword. The indentation on the topmost point of the sword hilt shone once brightly, and the gemstone responded with a faint pulsating glow. He put stone to the hilt—it fit in the indentation perfectly.

The Brave's Sword glowed from the inside with a gentle light. It was hard to say, but it seemed as if the blade had lengthened at the same time. Yet it felt lighter in his hand, somehow.

—The sword grows with you.

Wayfinder Lau's voice rang in Wataru's ears.

No one said a word. The sky was growing light in the east. The dust had settled, and the light of dawn became a single white glimmering line on the horizon. A new day was beginning.

Meena yelped. This time, something was shining at her breast. It was much smaller than the glow of the gemstone, but it radiated the same warm light from under the pink shirt she was wearing.

She reached down her shirt, and pulled up a small compact-size mirror. It was hanging around her neck on a leather strap.

"What's this?" Meena asked, eyes wide. "Did my lucky mirror just glow?"

"Mirror?" Wataru said, rushing over to her. His Brave's Sword glimmered again, and light spilled from the mirror.

Wait, does this mean...

"Is that the Mirror of Truth?"

Meena nodded, without looking away from the mirror. "Yes. My parents gave this to me. It's a good luck charm that has been in my family for generations."

Kee Keema gave Wataru a slap on the shoulder. "Now you just need to find the star sigil."

Wataru was lucky. He didn't even need to look for the Mirror of Truth. It had found him. Wayfinder Lau was right again. Wataru nodded.

They had just started back down the road to Gasara, when Trone stopped, hands on his hips, looking at the ground. "Looks like you won't need to search long."

They were standing by the ruins of the chapel. There in the sand amongst the rubble was drawn a large five-pointed star.

Just like the one on the Brave's Sword.

chapter 11
The Real World

Wataru stood in the middle of the sigil with Meena's mirror hanging from his neck. The mirror began to shine.

Though no one had ever told him to do so, Wataru drew his sword and held it over his head. He closed his eyes. The tip of the blade shone, and the sigil glimmered in response. First white, then red, and then blue. Eventually it changed back to white. Finally, the lines of the giant star-pattern in the earth glowed with a golden radiance, and disappeared.

Wataru opened his eyes.

Darkness. It was pitch black. He was surrounded by darkness so thick he couldn't even see the ground upon which he stood. Before him, behind him, the Brave's Sword in his hand, even his nose—he could see nothing.

But there was light coming from the mirror on his chest. It was an odd light that stretched forward like a corridor ahead of him, yet cast no light at all on the surrounding area.

Wataru began to walk. He was alone. His feet made no noise. Outside the tunnel of light was only darkness. Maybe this was the Vale of Eternity of which Wayfinder Lau had told him.

Soon, he saw a man some distance ahead of him, down the corridor. It was Wayfinder Lau! Wataru began to run. "Master Lau!"

Wayfinder Lau did not seem to be in the best of spirits. He looked bored. "Certainly kept me waiting, didn't you," he said, yawning. "Didn't think it would take quite so long for you to find the first gemstone."

"Sorry! A lot of stuff was going on."

"No matter, it is done." The Wayfinder finally smiled. "A bit farther down the Corridor of Light you will find an exit. Beyond that, the real world."

Wataru swallowed. His throat was dry with excitement.

"It will lead you to the place with the person whom you most wish to meet. There is no need to fear getting lost. Now, go." Wayfinder Lau gave Wataru a push on the shoulder. "But do not forget. When you hear the bells ring, you must return to the corridor. Your mirror will become more agitated as well. Go back through the tunnel and run, for should it disappear, you will fall into the Vale, never to be seen in either world again."

Wayfinder Lau cocked his jaw to one side. "I'll leave now. I will not wait for your return. Listen to the mirror. Be careful, and listen well."

"I understand."

Wataru began to run forward. Soon he saw something white in the distance. The exit! There was something white there. White…

White sheets. A hospital bed.

Wataru was in a hospital. His mother was sleeping right in front of him. He stood at the head of her bed. There was another bed in the room, but it was empty.

The lights were off. Through the curtain he could see the night sky. He looked out. Streetlights burned on the road below. This was the third floor. *So it's not the same time here and in Vision, then.*

"Mom?" Wataru said. His mother was breathing heavily but quietly.

She looked unchanged from the time when he left for Vision. Maybe, thought Wataru, she looked a little thinner. There was a placard on the headboard with the name of the doctor and the date she had entered the hospital. The doctor was a specialist in internal medicine, it said. The day she had entered the hospital was the day she had left the gas on in the apartment.

It looks like somebody called an ambulance.

That was a relief. Wataru felt his legs wobble a little bit. *Thank you, whoever did that. Thank you…*

I should wake Mom up, tell her what happened. That's why I came here. But Wataru found himself unable to speak, unable even to touch her. He was filled with sadness mingled with relief that his mother was sleeping safe and sound in the hospital. She would be okay.

There was a red flower in an empty milk jug at the head of her bed. A box of tissues. A paper bag at the foot of the bed. He looked inside to see his mother's underclothes and her purse.

In her purse, he found a small pad of paper, an address book, and a ball-point pen. Wataru ripped out a page of paper and wrote a short note.

—*Mom. I'm okay. I'll come home soon. Please wait for me. Wataru.*

Wataru folded the note and slipped it into his mother's hand. Then, just for a moment, he gave her hand a squeeze. She moaned and rolled in bed.

Wataru waited a moment. She didn't wake up, and he heard a sound from somewhere behind him. The ringing of bells.

Was someone coming to visit her? he wondered. *Grandma from Chiba, or Uncle Lou? What about Grandma and Grandpa in Odawara?* They would all be worried.

What about Dad?

When he thought of his father, all the feelings he had forgotten during his adventures in Vision came rushing back to him. His hands balled into fists, and he had to consciously remain calm until the storm in his heart went away.

He heard the bells ring again, faster this time.

Wait for me. Everything will be okay. I'll go to the Tower. I'll make it okay. I promise.

Wataru turned and began to run.

chapter 12
meena

Wataru bent back through the tunnel of light—arriving at the chapel ruins at the symbol on the ground. He thought he had run the whole way, but he wasn't out of breath. He hadn't even broken a sweat.

Nearby, Kee Keema stood atop a rocky outcropping. Alongside him was the slender silhouette of Meena, the two of them framed by the rising morning sun. Their faces were cast in shadows, making their expressions impossible to read.

Wataru silently climbed to the top of the protruding rock formation. Kee Keema and Meena looked at each other. The waterkin shook his head ever so slightly as if to say, "Best not to ask."

"Kutz and Trone have already gone back," Kee Keema said in a cheery but slightly affected manner. "We should go too and get ourselves some breakfast."

The three began to walk along the outcropping. Wataru took care where he placed his feet, keeping his eyes on the ground below. The next time he looked up, the day had fully dawned.

He turned and glanced back at the barren land they had just left—the grasslands, the rocky crags. Vision. The wind whipping across the grass stung his eyes.

That's why I'm crying...it's the wind stinging my eyes. Or maybe it's the beautiful view.

Not because I thought, just for a moment, how much I'd like to show it to Mom. That's not why I'm crying. I'm not a little boy, not anymore.

Yet his cheeks were damp. Kee Keema stopped for a second and looked at him, then resumed his plodding pace forward. He motioned to Meena with his eyes as if to say "Let him cry."

Up to this point, the cat-girl had been walking behind Wataru. Now she hastened her pace to catch up to him. "Did you see your mother?"

Wataru nodded. He wiped his face with his arm.

"I'm glad." Meena gently patted the boy on the back.

"She was asleep, so…we couldn't talk," Wataru said. "I wasn't there long enough to explain anything anyway."

"I'm sure she understands. I'm sure she knows you were there, even if she was asleep."

Wataru lifted his eyes to look at her. Meena shot him an encouraging smile. "That's how mothers are. Even when they are far away, they know how their children are doing. Perk up, Wataru. If you're sad, she'll sense that, right?"

Wataru blinked. A final teardrop fell from his eye. "Right!"

According to the doctor's analysis, the well water by the chapel ruins had been contaminated with a strong insecticide for repelling insects and other pests. When Wataru told him about the skeletons he had met by the altar in the underground chamber, the doctor said he would very much like to examine those bones.

"If they died by insecticide, the bones would bear traces of it. I wonder if they all died from drinking that water? That would clarify at least one aspect of Cactus Vira's curative activities."

"Isn't it a bit late to worry about what happened?" Wataru asked.

"Of course," said the doctor gravely. "No amount of investigation will bring back those who have died. But if we expose the facts about Cactus Vira, about exactly what sort of man he was, then perhaps we can prevent people from being fooled the next time some crazy guy comes along."

Meena's wounds were raw and exposed. The doctor administered more ointment and scolded her for not being careful. She yelped at his brusque treatment—yet, for some reason, sat there with a big smile on her face. It was like looking at a different person than the cat-girl Wataru had seen in the crowd only a few days before.

Where did she come from, I wonder? Why was she with the ankha refugees from the North? Where did she learn to move like she does? How did she come to wear the Mirror of Truth? Wataru had so many questions he wanted to ask that he tagged along with Kee Keema during his hospital visit later in the day.

Meena saw the look on his face when he entered the room and beamed. "You want to know my story, don't you," she said, anticipating his question. "One thing you should know is that originally, there were very few of my kind on the southern continent at all."

Three hundred years ago, when Agrilius the First helped build the Northern Empire, his policies of extreme ankha-centrism drove out all the other races. Back then, in the early years after the bitter civil war, the refugees from the north to the south were even more numerous than today.

"My ancestors, too, came here at that time. More than half of the kitkin in the south are descendants of those early immigrants."

Meena's ancestors had settled in the mercantile country of Bog. Apparently, Meena's great grandfather was something of a financial genius, and he had great success selling produce in bulk. As a result, their clan lived a peaceful and rich life.

"So you come from a proper house, eh?" said Kee Keema, quite impressed. Meena laughed shyly, but her smile soon disappeared. A look of sorrow crept into her eyes as she thought back upon her distant past.

"It happened during the summer when I was seven. We were living in a small house—me, my grandparents, and my parents, just the five of us—by the lake, a short distance from town. One night, we were attacked…"

Meena explained that she was too young to remember the details precisely. She only knew she had been awoken suddenly by her mother in the middle of the night and made to hide under the bed. She was not to move until her mother or father called for her, even should she hear her name. Her mother's face was stern, and, Meena realized, very frightened.

"That's when she gave me this," Meena said, touching the Mirror of Truth at her neck. "She told me to take it with me, and to treasure it always. She said it was my good-luck charm. I begged her to let me stay with her, but she refused and left me alone under the bed."

The young Meena had done as she was told. She heard footsteps, great thudding footsteps, all through the large house. She also heard people shouting, and even a scream. She was so frightened she thought she might cry out loud, but she held back her tears. She made herself as small and invisible as she could.

Wataru remembered how he had curled up under his bed when his mother had attacked that woman—his father's lover—on the balcony. The situation was completely different, of course. Wataru had been running from a fight—there was no threat to his own life. Yet he thought he could imagine something of what Meena must have felt that night.

"Just then I heard three or four people running through the house," Meena continued in a small voice. "It sounded like they were looking for something. They were all men, and they talked to each other in loud voices. I became even more frightened and held my breath, and hid under the bed and did not move."

Unable to find whatever they were looking for, the intruders began breaking things and flipping over furniture. Still, Meena stayed in her hiding spot. She smelled smoke.

"I crept quietly out from under the bed and looked down the hall, when I saw flame. It was all burning…"

She heard a sound from outside the house—in the distance—the ringing of bells. The fire squad!

"I went out on the balcony, where I could see the fire-cart coming toward the house. That was the first time I realized that it was already near dawn. It was bright enough for me to see the dust rising from the cart's wheels."

The house was soon engulfed in flames and it eventually burned to the ground. Meena was saved by the fire team, but the bodies of her grandfather and grandmother were discovered in the smoldering wreckage. Her parents were nowhere to be found.

"They told me that bandits had killed my family, stolen our money, and set fire to the house. They said I was lucky to have been saved."

Unlike everyone else in town, they lived in a house that was far from the nearest neighbor. There were no witnesses, and the authorities were never able to figure out what happened.

"But that didn't explain what had become of my mother and father. I was only a child, but still…it didn't make sense. I had survived, and I knew it was because of the lucky charm my mother had given me. I knew the two were related."

Meena was taken in by a merchant house run by her father's relatives in Lanka, the capital of Bog, but no matter how many years passed, she couldn't forget that horrible day. What had happened that night? What became of her parents? Were they still alive somewhere? She wanted to search for them, to get to the bottom of it all. She was eleven when she ran away from home.

"I was a bit reckless, I guess," Meena said, blushing.

"No kidding," Wataru said, smiling. "Did you have any idea where you were going?"

"Not at all. But it just so happened that around that time a large circus troupe was performing in Lanka. My relatives also ran a restaurant, and many of the circus backers frequented our place. They had invited us to the circus many times. I'd even talked with the troupe leader."

Meena figured that being a member of a circus would be the perfect way to travel the land. She could keep her ears open for information, and meet lots of people. One thing was for certain: she'd never unravel the mysteries of the past by staying in Lanka. Moving from town to town, she might come across a clue that would lead her in the right direction. And hopefully that would lead her toward the truth.

"I barged in on the troupe leader, told him my story, and asked to be allowed to work in the circus."

Luckily for her, the circus leader Bubuho was a kindly sort. After extracting promises that she would work hard and learn to read while she was with the troupe, he granted her request.

"The circus! That's why you move so well," Kee Keema said, clapping his hands and grinning.

Wataru furrowed his brow. "So, were you with the circus the whole time?"

"Yes. The Aeroga Elenora Spectacle Machine, we were called. I swung from swings so high it would make you dizzy. I was part of an acrobatic aerial show—it was quite a spectacle!" Meena looked proud. "I even did a little bit of aerial rope tricks. It was the troupe leader's family secret—a real crowd pleaser."

"So where did you meet those ankha boys? Why were you with them? It sounded like they'd been using you for quite a while."

Meena's smile faded. "That was…I was foolish."

A year before, when the boys had still been in the refugee camp in Bog, the circus had paid a charity visit to the camp. That's where Meena first met them.

"They said that before they left the North, their parents had been officials with the Sub-race Control Board. They had seen things no one else knew about."

The Sub-race Control Board was an organization under the control of the ruling government. In the North, non-ankha were labeled "sub-races," and every aspect of their lives was carefully administered by the Control Board.

"Administered! Bah!" Kee Keema snorted. "They rob them of their fortunes, shove them in camps, and force them to do manual labor! To hear the waterkin refugees tell it, they would be locked in a pen, doing repairs on sailships without proper tools, and no food or drink. Every day ten or more would drop from exhaustion, unable to work, but they didn't get any doctors, and you can forget about medicine. The weak were left to die and thrown into the ocean once they'd breathed their last. I heard someone say they'd seen a whole pile of waterkin dead just lying there!"

Meena lowered her eyes and nodded. "I've heard many such stories."

"So what did those two say they knew?" Wataru asked.

"They said that the Northern Empire was secretly abducting the descendants of non-ankha who escaped to the south, and bringing them back up north." Meena's voice trembled slightly. "They've been doing it for the past twenty years or more. Their parents lived in a special center where the abductees were made to work, that's how they knew."

Wataru and Kee Keema looked at each other.

"When they heard my story, those boys told me that my parents had probably been taken back to the North. That's why their bodies were never found. I thought this was the answer I had been looking for. My parents might be in the Northern Empire. They might still be alive..."

Meena's eyes sparkled.

"But why would the Northern Empire do such a thing?"

"I don't know. They didn't know the particulars either, but they said that one of their parents' superiors had come to the south before them, and if I met him he might tell me. That's why..."

"Hrm," Kee Keema growled. "You believed their story, and helped them escape, is that it? They led you astray with their promises, and made you work with them."

Meena said nothing, but her head hung so low Wataru could no longer see her face. That was answer enough.

"But what about the circus? Aren't they worried about you?" Wataru asked. "You must have snuck away, right?"

"I did. If I had told them, they would have stopped me for sure…"

"I would have stopped you too. You must have come from a good family, to take the word of those two," Kee Keema said, jokingly.

Meena frowned. "But, there were some things I did find out. Those two hadn't made up *everything*, after all."

Apparently, a special unit known as Sigdora was involved with the forceful return of refugees from the North, though the reasons for their activities were unknown.

"Are they military?"

"They don't have anything to do with the Imperial Army, no. The current emperor, Agrilius VII, and the commander of the Imperial Army, General Adja, were friends in their youth, but among the people in the north it's widely known—though never openly discussed—that they don't get along very well these days."

The Northern Empire had its own peacekeeping force like the Knights of Stengel and the Highlanders here, but theirs was directly tied to the military. Unable to bend them to his will, Agrilius VII had gone behind General Adja's back and created his own special forces to do his bidding. Thus was Sigdora born.

Kee Keema's long tongue snaked out and brushed the top of his head.

"What's wrong, Kee Keema?"

"Hrm? Nothing, it's just, I don't much like that name. Sigdora…" Kee Keema cleared his throat. "Sigdora was the name of the monster that the Old God created when he learned of the Goddess's betrayal—according to how they tell it in the north, of course. Three heads it had, and six legs, and a tail split in two with a snake's head at each tip. In the tales we waterkin tell, it's merely one of the horrible nasties living in the depths of Chaos, eating the souls of those who are lost there."

"Three heads…six legs…?" Wataru shivered.

"It's always fiercely hungry, and it will eat anything, and once it finds its mark, it never stops until it's sated. The word Sigdora means 'cursed hound' in the old ankhan tongue, you see."

And Meena's parents had been taken by an organization that named itself after that?

"Wataru, I have a request," Meena said, turning her large eyes to look at him. "Won't you let me come with you on your journey?"

Wataru felt his face redden. "H-huh?" he stammered, "Wh-what? My journey? With me?"

"Please! I know I'll be of help! And with you, I'll be able to travel faster and farther than with the circus. Please!"

Meena begged, leaning closer, so that Wataru leaned back until his chair was in danger of falling.

Kee Keema grabbed Wataru by the back of his neck, and grinned. "Can't refuse such a cute girl her one request, can you now?"

"N-no. I mean yes, you can come," Wataru said, wiping the sweat off his brow. "You did save my life, after all."

"Thank you!" Meena said, jumping to her feet.

"But, before we leave, you need to tell the Spectral Machine folks you're okay. That's my condition," Wataru added.

"It's 'Spectacle Machine,'" Meena said, giggling. "But, you're right. I will."

"How about we all go visit the circus together?" Kee Keema suggested. "You'll be able to see everyone, Meena, and Wataru might get a lead for the next step of his search. How's that for a plan?"

Chapter 13
In Maquiba

They waited a few days for Meena's wounds to mend, and then the three left Gasara. They chose a darbaba with strong legs for the arduous trip, and loaded up supplies in a cart. Kee Keema took the reins, but allowed Wataru to take over during the smooth patches of road.

Seated in back on the cart, Meena enjoyed the passing scenery. Thus inspired, she would occasionally burst out into song. Her voice was surprisingly beautiful. The rhythms and tones reminded Wataru of the music from South America his father used to listen to at home. Sometimes sorrowful, sometimes bright, the songs added their own texture to their days on the road.

It had been almost a year since Meena left the Spectacle Machine troupe, but she figured they would be back around Bog by this time. They were determined to head for the town of Maquiba, the spot nearest to Gasara on the border between Nacht and Bog. Maquiba was a small but rich town due to its vast herds of livestock. Apparently, most of the meat and vegetables that Wataru had eaten in Gasara came from there.

"Bog is the smallest of the four countries, and the circus always creates a buzz. If they're in Bog now, word of their passage will surely have reached Maquiba."

As expected, when they reached the town of Maquiba—little more than a cluster of small, plain buildings built of brick and log—they heard that the circus troupe had pitched their tents just over the mountains to the north.

"That's great!" Meena exclaimed. "I had no idea they'd be so close!"

"Did you see the show?" Kee Keema asked, but the darbaba postmaster shook his head. "Not a soul in Maquiba did, sadly."

Apparently, when the circus was scheduled to perform there had been a great fire in the mountains. The darbaba postmaster gestured with his hand, indicating the wide spread of mountains from the west to the southwest of town. "See the burnt color of the hills in that direction? They should be covered in green this time of year."

Indeed, it was as he said. Three of the smaller hills had been stripped bare of their leafy summer clothes and stood naked and gray.

"That must have been some fire," Wataru said.

The postmaster shook his head. "That was no mere bushfire, and it took some extreme measures to put out. Not a single blade of grass is left on those hills, son."

All the lands around Maquiba were verdant green, with the exception of that corner to the southwest. In the distance, the travelers saw numerous pens and enclosures holding livestock—in fact, it resembled a massive crossword puzzle. Wataru saw some animals that looked remarkably like sheep. Here and there stood farmhouses and silos, their pointed roofs shining in the sun.

"The livestock here are mostly munmas," Kee Keema had told him, indicating one of the white, woolly creatures in a corral they had passed on their way into town.

"Munmas are good eating, and their hides are strong and pliable. These woolly critters are strong 'gainst disease, and pop out babies like there was no tomorrow. Good things all around."

The darbaba postmaster nodded. "Our munma herds are the lifeblood of Maquiba. They feed in the pastures on the hillsides around town. Maquiba's greenery is like gold to our herders, you see."

The fire had broken out near the mountains three days before. A strong southerly wind had been blowing close to the ground that night, and the fire grew and grew, blazing so hot that firemen couldn't even get close. It was all they could do to cut down trees in a circle around the mountain to prevent the fire from spreading any farther. The whole town had come out to help herd the panicked munmas away from the smoke and smell of the fire. But the fire moved quickly, and the blaze burned hotter and hotter.

"We were all worried that by dawn the fire would eat up the hills and make its way farther east. If it did that, the town would be in danger. Worst-case scenario, the whole place would burn. There's certainly fuel enough with all the grass. We moved the elderly and the children out of town, and those who remained did everything they could to control the blaze, but people were falling from the smoke, and there was little they could do. We couldn't even put a dent in that inferno. A wind like the breath of a firewyrm swept down the hills, making it hard to even stand on your feet without holding on to something."

Just as they were preparing to pack up and leave town for good, one of the guests staying at the only lodge in Maquiba announced he was a sorcerer of some skill, and were they to ask him, he could stop the blaze.

"He only warned that, if we did it his way, though the fires be quenched, not even grass'd grow on those mountains for many years."

The postmaster rubbed his nose. Wataru caught a glimpse of a bandage poking out from under his shirt. He noticed burn marks on the man's arm.

"If we left the blaze as it was, the winds would carry it through all the southwest pastures, ruining them all. That alone would take years to recover from. We figured the sorcerer's way didn't sound all that bad, you see?"

The postmaster looked at their faces and grinned. "Of course, nobody in town could make up their mind. Reason being, this sorcerer was a boy."

The darbaba postmaster pointed a stubby finger at Wataru. "In fact, he was about your age. An ankha boy. We were all surprised he hadn't been moved out of town with the other children and the elderly."

Wataru's eyes opened wide. He took a step forward. "This sorcerer, was he wearing a black robe? Did he have a leather band around his waist, and a staff with a glimmering stone on the end?"

The postmaster seemed surprised. "How did you know that? You know this boy sorcerer?"

Kee Keema grabbed Wataru's shoulder from behind and broke in. "What happened in the end? You take this sorcerer up on his offer?"

"Huh? Erm, yes, we did." The darbaba postmaster nodded. "It was so hot even here in town by that point that our hair and clothes were threatening to catch fire. Not that anyone went up to him and specifically asked, you see. While we were all muddling about, trying to make up our minds, that boy sorcerer took control."

Wataru smiled. It had to be Mitsuru. It sounded exactly like the sort of thing he would say.

"What happened then?" Meena asked, leaning forward.

"What happened? We saw sorcery." The postmaster wiped the sweat off his nose. "And what sorcery it was. Makes me dizzy just t'think about it. He held his staff in his right hand, and with his left, he drew letters in the air, like this. Then he started shouting, or more like singing, words none of us could understand."

Then the miracles started. The first to appear was a great cyclone. It formed suddenly in the air over the burning mountains to the southwest, and soon wrapped itself around the entire blaze.

"That cyclone covered the blazing hills peak to foot. Suddenly, the air around us got cool—cold, even. It wasn't hot anymore at all. The wind stopped too."

The sorcerer waved his staff, and the stone at its tip shone a bright blue. The villagers shielded their eyes from the sudden glare, when a great blue dragon appeared out of nowhere.

"I saw the whole thing. That was a seawyrm, it was, straight out of legend. No mistaking it," the darbaba postmaster declared. "From the way it kind of erupted in the air above 'im, I think its power had been trapped in the stone at the tip of the sorcerer's staff."

The blue dragon twisted and writhed, spinning its body around the great cyclone enveloping the blaze. Then the cyclone began to fill with the purest water. Its twisting winds became a spray, the spray became rain, and the entire town of Maquiba and surrounding hills were drenched.

"Then the cyclone began to move."

It left the hills, spun into the air, and went off toward the sea. Only the great ocean could stop such a blaze, and the cyclone was taking the blaze right to it.

"We all stood there staring, like idiots. By the time we realized our lives had been saved, night was breaking. The boy sorcerer was gone. Only those bald hills remained as proof of what had happened."

The townspeople were so excited, said the postmaster. The fire and the sorcerer's trick was all anyone could talk about.

They didn't even have to ask, as they soon discovered. Everyone in Maquiba was eager to tell visitors about what happened, going so far as to stop them in the street to ask if they had heard the news. By the time they reached the lodge, the three travelers knew the story down to the last detail.

Wataru excitedly told the villagers that the sorcerer was his friend—from the other world. But each time he did so, Kee Keema shot him a withering glare. When they reached the lodge he told him, "I just don't think it's a good idea for you to tell people you're a Traveler. There was no helping it in Gasara once the word got out, but here and on the road we'd best avoid any unwanted attention, if you know what I mean."

Wataru agreed to restrain himself. Then he remembered something that Wayfinder Lau had said.

"That's odd. The Wayfinder told me once that the Vision I travel through and Mitsuru's Vision weren't even the same world. That it changed for each person who traveled through it. That's why we couldn't help each other."

Meena cocked her head to one side. "Maybe it's different for you and your friend—Mitsuru, was it?—because you're so small. Maybe you're allowed to work together?"

"I don't know. I think if that were the case, Wayfinder Lau would have told me that from the start."

"Well, maybe he wanted you to figure it out on your own."

Something about Meena's suggestion tugged at Wataru. "If I was with Mitsuru, I bet it would be easy to reach the Tower of Destiny. He's quite the sorcerer, you know."

Meena smiled. "You're not so bad yourself, Wataru. You didn't need magic to catch the two boys that had trapped me."

At the lodge, too, the story of the wildfire and the boy sorcerer was hotter than the fires themselves had been. The townspeople came to the lodge for no other reason than to spread the tale to travelers. From the mingled conversations, Wataru heard something of great interest. Before the fires had even broken out, the boy sorcerer had been asking about the road to a town called Lyris northwest of Bog.

"Is it far to Lyris?"

"It would be, if you aimed to go straight there. There's a great river in the way, the Grandera, so swift-flowing they can't even build bridges over it, and boats can make the crossing only at times when the current's slow. If you're not lucky, you might have to wait weeks or months to cross. The most reliable way to get there is to climb the mountains to the south, and go around to the southwest. There is a road that heads that way too."

If they went into the mountains to the south, they would pass through the place where the Spectacle Machine troupe was said to be performing on the way. Perfect. Wataru knew what the Wayfinder had told him, but he still wanted to follow Mitsuru.

Kee Keema smiled. "Then let's do it. We know where he's gone, and I'm of a mind to meet this Traveler friend of yours and see what stuff he's made of."

Chapter 14
The Spectacle Machine

The sound of cheery music drifted through the green woods. Even the trees swaying in the breeze seemed to move to the echoes of the rhythmical drums.

Friends o' the whirlwind we are, we are.
A dance with the whirlwind we dance.
One of a kind, under the skies.
One of a kind we are.

Aeroga Spectacle Machine!
Come, let us open your eyes!
Aeroga Spectacle Machine!
Turns geezers and grannies to young gals n' guys!
Aeroga Spectacle Machine!
Hearts o' the young we're winning.
Aeroga Spectacle Machine!
The show is just beginning!

Meena's face broke into a smile. "It's the chorus," she said excitedly.

The woods were deep and the trees so tall one had to look up to see the tops. Wataru and Kee Keema followed after the ebullient Meena, when suddenly they came into a clearing. Wataru shouted in surprise at what he saw.

A giant floating stage rested upon a lake that mirrored the blue sky. Brightly painted banners and furls of fabric had been attached to the framework of the stage. On closer inspection, Wataru saw that the pieces of fabric were actually boys, girls, men and women in bright, flowing clothes. They clung to high rafters and stood atop poles. Some hung by their legs from ropes as they moved quickly and deftly, constructing the stage before Wataru's eyes. As they worked, they sung in a beautiful harmony. Wataru couldn't imagine the actual performance being any more fascinating than this already was.

"Look, Wataru. That's the swing I used to use!"

A swing in the shape of a crescent moon made of thin wires hung from the highest part of the stage.

"What a view!" Kee Keema said in a bellowing voice that seemed to ride on the wind across the lake surface. A boy dressed completely in red looked in their direction and called out.

"Hey, it's Meena!"

Meena waved. "Puck!"

"Everyone! It's Meena! She's come home!"

The boy in red clambered nimbly down the scaffolding. The other people stopped working, and all looked in Meena and Wataru's direction. The song halted, and in its place came shouts of *Meena!* and *Welcome home!* and *Where did you go!? We were so worried!* Meena ran toward the edge of the lake, and Wataru and Kee Keema followed her into a reception warmer than any they could have imagined.

"I'm so sorry I left without saying anything, I really am." Meena hung her head, and her eyes were filled with tears.

A large hand, spread like a fan, patted her on the head. "I read the note saying you were gone, but no one could figure out why you left. I'm just glad you're safe."

Bubuho, troupe leader of the Spectacle Machine, was a large man, larger even than Kee Keema. His eyes reminded Wataru of a pig from his world, but he had a dignified look to him and a broad smile that eased all fears. In real-world years, he looked to be about fifty. He wasn't fat, merely massive and muscular. There didn't seem to be a wasted inch of flesh on his body.

Meena and the boy Puck sat next to him on small stools. The boy seemed younger even than Wataru, probably about the same age as a first-grader in his world. His hair was so red it looked like it was on fire, and his face was covered with freckles. Wataru thought he was an ankha at first, but on closer inspection he found the boy had a long gray tail. He looked between Meena and the troupe leader with sparkling eyes, his tail twitching all the while.

"I learned all sorts of new tricks while you were gone, Meena. I was good and practiced all the time," he declared proudly, when he saw that Meena and the troupe leader were done catching up. "I can even do the triple flip! Well, I only did it once, but it was perfect. Bubuho says I'm still too young for it, though," Puck said, pouting.

Meena tousled his hair. "Your singing's really gotten good," she said, smiling. "I could pick out your voice from far away. You're not only an acrobat, you've the makings of a fine singer too!"

"You think?" Puck said, jumping to his feet. "Maybe I can sing on stage!"

The circus had set up its tents along the edge of the lake. They went first to Bubuho's tent, where they sat in a circle, while Puck danced back and forth between them. He stopped only when Bubuho sternly told him to get back to work. Reluctantly, the boy left the tent.

"Finally, a little peace and quiet," the troupe leader said, turning to Wataru and Kee Keema. "It sounds like Meena, and all of us, owe you a great debt. Thank you, kind sirs."

Wataru shook his head and said it was he who had been saved, and proceeded to tell the story of all that had happened. When he was finished, Bubuho once again gave Meena a pat on the head. "I see, I see, you've been through quite a lot. I had no idea you were so determined to get to the bottom of what happened to your parents."

"It's not that…it's just, I didn't know enough not to trust what the boys told me," Meena explained.

"And so, you will join this Traveler in his journey?"

Meena shifted in her seat. "Yes."

Bubuho squinted his tiny eyes and looked at Wataru. "Traveler, you give your permission for Meena to join you?"

"Of course," Wataru said, nodding firmly.

"Then I've no problem with it," said Bubuho smiling. "But, since you've come to us, I demand you spend the night and watch a rehearsal of our show. Opening day is tomorrow, so tonight's rehearsal will be a preview of the real thing. You'll be our audience."

"That's great! Let's stay, please, Wataru? Kee Keema?" Meena said, jumping about so energetically as to give Puck a run for his money. "Say I can help you on stage, Bubuho, please?"

"We saw your rope tricks back in the cavern," Wataru said laughing. "But, if you've time to practice, I'd love to see you do your thing on stage."

"Me too," Kee Keema added enthusiastically.

"Then you'll want to talk to the other swing artists."

Bubuho sent Meena out and showed Wataru and Kee Keema to an empty tent. They settled in, and after a time, an old woman came in, bringing them a fragrant tea.

"Ah, Granny! Many thanks." Bubuho stood and welcomed the old lady. "This tea will ease your fatigue from the journey. Drink up."

The old woman was very short, and her face was wrinkled, like tissue paper crumpled into a ball. Her face was that of an ankha, but she had a bit of the look of a frog about her.

"I just came to see our Traveler here," the woman said, staring into Wataru's eyes so intently that he became embarrassed. "Tell me, how is Wayfinder Lau?"

Wataru was taken aback. "Huh? What? You know him?"

"For nigh well eight hundred years now. That one couldn't call a bolt of lightning to save his life back in the day. I do hope his spellcraft has improved?"

Wataru smiled. "Sorry, I can't say I saw him cast any spells."

"So you've come to see the Goddess, eh?" Granny continued. "But have you thought of what you'll do if you can't see her?"

"Well…" Wataru looked at Kee Keema, who was also squirming uncomfortably. "I guess I never considered the possibility."

It was an honest answer. The old woman snorted. "Then I've nothing else to ask you."

And with that, she left the tent. Wataru blinked, and Bubuho smiled wryly. "My apologies. You'd be a bit cranky too if you were her age." He turned back to Wataru. "I've heard the Traveler's journey is a difficult one. Now, as you know, Meena is a girl with a special past and a unique destiny of her own. Take her along with you, and your journey may become more difficult still.

She told you of Sigdora, yes?"

"Yes, she did."

"And still you will take her?"

"I will," Wataru said, nodding firmly. "I don't know if traveling with me will help Meena find her parents again, but I think we will be able to help each other on our travels, at least."

"Then I have nothing else to say." Bubuho smiled gently. "Please, rest until rehearsal begins. The other members want to meet you, I'm sure. You're free to go about as you wish."

Wataru and Kee Keema took the opportunity to look around and talk to various circus members. In total there were about fifty people in the circus, and they learned several things: that the Elenora in the circus's full name was the troupe leader's deceased wife, and that their show on the lakeshore had been delayed on account of the wildfire.

"The hot winds blew even up here, and the waves on the lake were so bad we could barely go out in a boat, let alone set up our stage."

Kee Keema had already become fast friends with the waterkin in the circus, and he spent his time practicing their staff-tricks. While they ran about hooting and hollering, waving wooden swords shaped like spears, Wataru continued walking through the camp, asking if anyone had seen, by the lake or in the woods, a little sorcerer in black robes. No one had noticed a thing.

The sun had set when rehearsals finally began. The stage was lit and stars were twinkling in the sky. Music started and dancers appeared, singing the song heard earlier in the day. Wataru was enchanted. It was a show just for two, and he loved every moment of it.

Though she must have been out of practice, Meena was the headliner of the show. In bright-colored clothes she leapt from swing to swing, high above the stage, flitting with light grace, twisting in midair, catching herself just when you thought she was going to fall, and striking a pose for the crowd. Wataru's palms were sweating as he watched the performance. But when Meena landed safely in the spotlight, he clapped until his hands were sore.

Wataru began to wonder if Meena wouldn't really be more happy here with the circus than traveling with him.

Still, her past must drive her to find out the truth. Wataru wondered how he would feel in her position. He turned the question over in his mind as he lay down in his tent, still excited from the show. Finally, with stars watching over him, Wataru fell asleep.

About that time, Bubuho returned to his tent to find Granny waiting for him. "Something the matter?" he asked.

The old woman stood staring up at the night sky. Then she raised her arm, and pointed. "See that, Bubuho?"

Bubuho looked up. The starry sky was beautiful, like fragments of jewels scattered on lacquer-black silk.

"Which star do you mean, Granny?"

She looked up again and sighed. "So you can't see it."

Bubuho walked over and stood next to her.

"Then it's the Fellstar of the North, for sure. I can see it. It's not a trick of my aging eyes." She sounded somehow sad. "That Traveler is the Half. The Fellstar has come to tell us this."

"Ah," Bubuho said quietly. "Then I hope no harm will come to Meena."

Granny made no reply. She merely stood, staring up at the northern sky.

Chapter 15
The Camp

The road to Lyris wove its way through thick woods, across mountain passes, and over jumbled rocky ravines. It seemed that every hour brought them into new terrain. The Vision landscape was beautiful, severe, and a bit unfriendly to travelers, Wataru thought. *Just like it is in my world.*

Often they would come upon small villages that didn't provide lodging. On those nights they were forced to pitch a tent and camp outdoors. Kee Keema taught Wataru how to do everything: pick a campsite, make a fire, fish for food in the rivers and ponds, and gather edible berries and mushrooms from the forest. Tagging along, Meena was also curious about learning these things. But when it came time to cook, the kitkin didn't need any schooling. She was a hundred times better at preparing meals than Kee Keema.

In his travels across the southern continent, Kee Keema had walked many lands, and knew many of the towns and villages they came to. But Wataru was surprised to hear that he had not yet made the trip to Lyris.

"Lyris has a shipping guild of its own, so they have little business with us darbaba drivers. They need specially made carts and containers for importing and exporting goods and services. Plus, they have their own specific way of doing things. I've passed by the area many a time, but never had a chance to visit."

It was, he learned, a village of craftsmen. They trafficked in metal, stone, wood, and leather to make all sorts of things. The design and quality of their craftsmanship was legend—and all of it made not by magic but by hardworking hands.

Their wares were known even in the north thanks to sailship merchants. In faraway lands, the necklaces and rings they made fetched ten times the local price. For the past several years, the most coveted of these items were a series of baubles called Heaven, made by a master craftsman known as Toni Fanlon.

"Seems it's sparked a bit of a craze up north. A sailship merchant friend of mine asked me to drop in on Fanlon's workshop should I ever go near the place. Apparently, he crafts 'em all by hand, so that means there's only ten or so made a year. You have to be very lucky to get your hands on one of those."

"Can't you reserve one in advance?" Meena asked, gently swaying back and forth in the cart behind them. She seemed quite interested in them herself.

"Out of the question. Apparently, this Fanlon fellow's not much for customer service."

He sold his works only to people he had met, and liked, Kee Keema explained. "You can bring all the money you want, and if he doesn't like you, he won't sell you a thing. Of course, if he gets along with you well, he'll charge you only the cost of materials. They say he even sometimes gives stuff away for free."

"Odd fellow," Meena said, sniffing.

While the two talked, Wataru was thinking. If Lyris traded in beautiful crafts, they would need lots of rare metals and jewels. Maybe someone there would know something of the second gemstone Wataru needed to find. It made even more sense, when he considered that Mitsuru was said to have gone to Lyris ahead of him.

Was Mitsuru on a quest to find the gemstones too? But didn't he already have a gem—the one on the end of his black staff—with enough power to quench the wildfire in Maquiba?

When they were no more than a day's journey distant from Lyris, they encountered their first accident on the road. A large cart drawn by two darbabas had tipped over, spilling a great load of rock salt. The mess would have to be removed by hand, then the cart would have to be moved out of the way before anyone could pass. The men there couldn't say how long it would take, and until it was done, no one could go farther.

A short distance ahead was the border for both Sasaya and Bog. At the checkpoint gate, officials observed travelers as they passed from one land to the other. The United Southern Nations valued the independence of each of its lands, but times were peaceful, and there was little hassle involved with passing between any of the four countries. This policy was what made it possible for drivers and merchants like Kee Keema to travel all through the south. The gates' only duties were to record the number of people who passed, and make sure that the contents of each cart matched the writ the driver carried.

They decided that rather than wander aimlessly around while they waited for the road to clear, they might as well help with the cleanup. As such, they were all working and sweating in the noontime sun, when two officials flew down from the gate. They set up a desk in a small teahouse to the side of the road, and announced that they would proceed with the gate-passing formalities to help expedite congestion after the road was clear. It was such a reasonable suggestion that Wataru was rather surprised.

"I can't imagine any official in the real world being this thoughtful."

The officials had actually *flown* down. They were both karulakin. Wataru immediately remembered being saved by a kindly karulakin during his first visit to Vision.

"What? What are you looking at?" asked the karulakin who was wearing eyeglasses.

"Oh, I'm sorry. I didn't mean to stare. I met one of your kind before—that is, one of your people saved me once."

"Well now, that's fine, just fine."

"Ah! Quite good, quite good."

The two gate officials flapped their wings enthusiastically. They looked pleased. "We always seek to serve the public good, you see. Tell me, what was the nature of your predicament?"

"Ah, um, well, I was attacked by these gimblewolves…"

"Aaah!" the officials shouted. "Gimblewolves!"

"I've not had one of those in a long time!"

"Can barely remember the taste!"

"Ach, we should go home more often!"

"No, no, it's our duty to serve the people!"

"Then we should at least write home and have them send us some gimblewolf jerky." The karulakin smacked his lips.

When they walked away from the desk, Kee Keema put a hand to his chest and made a faint gagging noise. "I'd heard the karulakin liked that foul-smelling flesh, but I never imagined it was really true. Makes me ill just to think about it."

"So the homeland of the karulakin is near the desert where the gimble-wolves live?"

"Aye. Up on a rise, at the top of a cliff over the gulch. But many, like these two, leave to become officials. Bird-men have good heads for figures."

"Say," Wataru asked. "If I ask you something, would you promise not to get angry?"

"What's that?"

"What would happen if these karulakin took up transportation, like your kind? Wouldn't they be pretty stiff competition? I mean, they could *fly* things anywhere!"

Kee Keema threw back his head and laughed. "Not a worry there. Not even a little. They haven't the strength to lift much more than a crate. It would take one the whole day to load a cart."

Kee Keema put a hand to his jaw and struck a pose of exaggerated thought. "The day our livelihood is threatened will be the day a creature shows up that's faster than a darbaba, doesn't need care and feeding, and can go just where you tell it to go without you yanking on the reins the whole time. But I'm not worried. The Goddess looks out for her own. She wouldn't leave us waterkin out in the sun to dry and shrivel up. Everything exists according to her plan. She didn't make a creature so convenient as that, and I don't see why she would in the future."

Wataru nodded and said he was probably right, not voicing the doubt that flashed briefly through his mind.

—But, Kee Keema, there's something in my world that's just like the creature you imagined. Except it's not living. It's called a machine. Not just machines, but power in general. That was what made Wataru's world move.

—I wonder what would happen if someone invented machines here in Vision? Or brought them back from my world? The thought didn't sit well with Wataru for some reason. He shook his head and went back to clearing rock salt off the road.

By evening, a small campground had sprung up by the teahouse. Wataru's group pitched their tent and traded supplies with their neighbors. They all sat around a common fire, ate, and talked merrily.

The night was growing deep, and just as Wataru began thinking about lying down in his tent, he saw lights from several torches coming down the mountain road from Maquiba toward their makeshift camp.

"Look…" Meena said, stifling a yawn. Everyone turned and peered out into the night. "It's the Knights of Stengel."

Pretty soon everyone in the campground joined her in craning their necks, trying to get a better look at the approaching lights. Soon they saw not only the lights, but silvery reflections in breastplates and helms.

"What're they doing all the way out here?" a merchant next to Wataru muttered. "Looks like their great captain is leading them, no less."

"What? Captain Ronmel? Here?" said one of the gate officials coming out of the teahouse, flapping his wings. "We must greet him properly!"

"If you're going to greet anyone properly, shouldn't you call the master of the teahouse?" the merchant said leisurely, hands in his pockets. "Those bird eyes of yours don't see well enough to make tea in the dark."

"Indeed, just as you say!"

There were five Knights in all, one riding up ahead of the others. Their helms covered their faces, but the darbaba upon which they rode wore cloth banners hanging over their foreheads, with five-petal flower designs upon them. Trone had taught him that mark back in Gasara—these were indeed the Knights of Stengel.

The master of the teahouse came running out so fast it appeared he might stumble and roll out into the road. Composing himself, he went to greet the Knights while they were still some distance from the campground. They spoke briefly, and the Knight in the lead and the one sitting directly to his rear left got off their darbabas and approached the camp with the master.

"That one in front, is he Captain Ronmel?" Wataru asked the merchant.

"Aye, that's right."

"How can you tell if you can't see his face?"

"The shape of his helm says enough. Take a closer look. You see how it is formed like a dragon's head? That's the helm worn only by the warriors of

House Ronmel."

"You know your stuff."

The merchant snorted. "I may be a down-on-my-luck merchant now, but a long time ago, I was studying to become a starseer. I even studied in Sasaya for a while, I did. You have to learn your history to study the future, you know."

Before they came in range of the campfire, the two Knights had taken off their helms. They were both quite tall, each standing at least two heads above the stocky teahouse master.

"We're the first Lancer Company of the Knights of Stengel," the one walking in front announced in a loud, clear voice. "I am Captain Ronmel, and this is my lieutenant, Vais. This evening, while we were stopped at the Grandera River crossing house, we heard of the darbaba cart accident here, and how passage along the road was stopped. We came to survey the damage. I know you must all be tired from your day's work, but we ask a moment of your time to assist in our investigation. We will erect a tent for this purpose—but if there are any injured, tell us now."

Wataru had expected a stern, authoritative proclamation, but the man was rather polite. Wataru wasn't the only one surprised. Many of the others around him seemed startled as well. Ordinary people didn't often have the opportunity to meet a Knight of Stengel, Wataru realized.

Everyone was quick to comply with the request. When the investigation began, the Knights removed not only their helms, but all their armor. This gave them a much more casual look, but they still maintained their stiff posture and spoke with utmost formality.

Wataru's tent was right next to the tent set up by the Knights. But for some reason, he wasn't summoned immediately. Those who were interviewed first said they hadn't been asked anything really difficult. Yet, at the same time, they seemed relieved as they walked back to their own tents.

"Don't see why Captain Ronmel has to come all the way out here over a darbaba cart flipping," Kee Keema wondered aloud. Half of his mind was not on the Knights at all but on their team of darbabas. He looked like he was ready to drool as he talked about their fine manes, and wondered how far they could run or whether they were good on the rocks. He would have gone over to examine their hooves if he hadn't thought it inappropriate.

While they waited, the night slowly passed. Meena was having trouble staying awake and started leaning against Wataru. She looked so comfortable that Wataru soon found himself drifting off too. Suddenly a voice called out, "You three! You're next."

It was Lieutenant Vais. Wataru leapt to his feet, but Meena actually leapt through the air, almost reaching the doorway. The lieutenant quickly stepped back, raising his hands.

"I'm so sorry, sir," Meena hurriedly apologized, blushing. "I didn't mean to startle you!"

The three obediently followed the lieutenant. They noticed his shoulders shaking slightly, as though he were trying with all his might to keep from laughing.

The Knights' tent was a small affair, with a folding table set directly in the center. Captain Ronmel was patiently waiting for them. Next to him sat the shortest of the five Knights, holding a pen poised over a large booklet bound on one side. The open page was covered with writing.

"Having a laugh, Vais?" Captain Ronmel asked as the three sat across the table from him. "What sort of spell did you weave to achieve this?" he asked them. "It's not anyone who can make old stoneheart here crack a smile."

Meena blushed even deeper—maybe it was more than embarrassment from having overreacted back in the tent. Maybe it was because Captain Ronmel was a strikingly handsome man. His nose cut a sharp line in the center of his face. Even the wrinkles at the corner of his eyes were charming. Wataru guessed he was about the same age as Uncle Lou.

"So, you're Highlanders." The captain's blue eyes hadn't failed to miss the firewyrm armlet Wataru wore. "I heard that quite recently in Gasara there was a young boy who helped apprehend the criminals behind a string of killings. He was invited to join the Highlanders. Might that be you?"

Wataru faced the captain directly and nodded. "Yes."

"Then you are a Traveler from the real world, then? Is this true?"

Wataru could see no reason to hide the truth from him. He responded yes again. The captain's expression did not change, nor did the wrinkles at the corners of his eyes move. The Knight taking notes, on the other hand, seemed to hold his breath, even scooting back noticeably in his chair. A single drop of ink fell from the tip of his pen. Kee Keema was flustered so much by this—though there was really no reason for him to be worried at all—that his tongue whipped out and licked the top of his head.

"Excuse me," the young Knight and Kee Keema said at the same time. The Knight's face blushed deep crimson. Meena giggled and slapped a hand over her mouth, growing even redder. The young Knight began to fidget in his chair.

At last, Captain Ronmel laughed out loud. "You'll have to excuse us. It's been a long journey, and with all the serious investigations to be done, we haven't had a break in a while. And it's late, we're all tired."

I guess people get giddy when they stay up late here in Vision too.

At last everyone was sitting comfortably in their chairs, and the questions proceeded quickly. Wataru's group hadn't witnessed the accident directly, but they had seen the aftermath.

It was a stroke of luck that there hadn't been any serious injuries, Captain Ronmel concluded. "We've had a number of accidents involving darbaba carts turning over on roads all over the country lately. We investigate them seriously because some of them seem to have happened on purpose in order to obstruct traffic."

That's why they came to investigate in the middle of the night.

"Everyone was quite surprised that you came here yourself, Captain," Kee Keema said.

Captain Ronmel looked at Wataru. "I thought it might be a good chance to meet this Traveler that Kutz was talking about. I counted the days since you left Gasara and determined he would be around here by now."

"Kutz told you about me?"

"'For all his crying like a baby, he's a brazenly clever little one,'" The captain said, doing a passable imitation of Kutz. His eyes were smiling. Wataru laughed.

"That sounds just like her!"

"We've known each other for a while. You might say we're rivals."

Because you dumped her?

"By the way, there was another thing I wanted to ask. You stopped at Maquiba, did you not?"

Wataru nodded.

"Then you were there at the time of the fire?"

"No. When we arrived, it had already gone out."

Captain Ronmel's eyes glinted. "Then you heard the story of the traveling sorcerer—the one who put out the wildfire?"

Wataru related the tale as he had heard it in Maquiba. The captain listened intently to every word, and the young Knight recorder sitting next to him scribbled furiously in his book.

"The power of the seawyrm—a water incantation, then," the captain muttered. "And the sorcerer was a boy as well…"

"That's what they said."

"Could he be another Traveler, such as yourself?"

"I believe he is. I think he's my friend. He came here before me."

For some reason a shadow moved across Captain Ronmel's eyes. Wataru had noticed nothing of the sort when he told the captain he was a Traveler. Why should this news of another Traveler concern him?

"Have you met this friend of yours here?"

"No. I thought I might like to though, so I've been following him. That's why we're going to Lyris."

The captain nodded slowly and rubbed his jaw with one hand. His brow furrowed ever so slightly. "You, or rather, Wayfinder Lau…" He glanced at the recorder. "On second thought, don't write that. It has nothing to do with the matter at hand. I'm sorry to have taken so much of your time," he said, turning back to Wataru.

He told them they would examine the overturned cart once dawn broke and then they would head back to Maquiba. They were going to investigate the cause of the wildfire. When Wataru commented how busy they were, the captain shook his head. "We've been running ourselves ragged dealing with monsters of late—there always seems to be more, and they grow fiercer every year. Most local peacekeeping and investigations we've had to leave to the Highlanders. And of course, that won't do."

"It reminds me of something that Puck was saying," Meena said. "In the towns they passed through, they always heard one or two stories of people being attacked by monsters. They had never heard such stories before now."

"Same here," Kee Keema nodded. "That's all people talk about nowadays in the darbaba huts. Stories of mountain-rats, usually quite tame, forming great masses and attacking udai and the like. And then there was that roaming gimblewolf near Gasara."

"That's right. We had to send the Highlanders out with one of our patrols, we were spread so thin," Captain Ronmel said with a wry smile. "Kutz had a field day with that one. That's right, you were one of the ones that rode out. Thank you for your help. We couldn't have done it without you."

Wataru and the others went back to their tent. Kee Keema and Meena fell asleep right away, but Wataru couldn't get his eyes to shut. He kept thinking about that suspicious shadow he saw briefly across Captain Ronmel's face. He couldn't help but think that somewhere hidden in that shadow was the real reason why the Knights had come all the way up into these mountains.

Maybe I'm thinking too much about it. But then again…

Wataru was restless, so he got up and quietly slipped outside. *Maybe a look at the stars will calm me down.*

Wataru wasn't the only one out and about. He found Captain Ronmel standing alone a short distance from the campground. His profile toward Wataru, he stood gazing up at the northern sky.

The captain noticed Wataru right away. "Couldn't sleep?"

"No. I'm not sure why…"

"You saw a big accident today. Let the starlight wash it from your eyes."

What was the captain doing out here all alone? Why did he look so forlorn? What was he thinking?

Wataru couldn't think of the right words to say to him. And he felt like asking questions might be a mistake. This man was one of the most important people in the southern continent. Who was to say he couldn't look moody now and again when he was alone? Still…

The two stood there silently side by side. After a short time, they both returned to their tents. Wataru had a bad taste in his mouth, but even if he were asked, he wouldn't have been able to say why.

chapter 16
Lyris

when they first looked down upon Lyris from a nearby hill, Wataru had the distinct impression that this was not his first time seeing it—that he had been here before, somehow. Everything looked familiar: the brightly colored peaked roofs on each of the houses, the cathedral with the bell tower, the brick-lined streets, the green trees, the loose, comfortable clothing people wore, the bright smiles on the faces.

That's right! It looks just like Wizdom, the town where the Academy of Magic is in the second Eldritch Stone Saga!

"What a lovely place," Meena said breathlessly, standing next to him. "No wonder they make such beautiful things here. They need only take a quick look around for inspiration!"

Their first destination was the Lyris branch of the Highlanders. If they ended up staying awhile, they would need to find some employment.

"You're Highlanders? That's a surprise. I suppose you live long enough, you see all sorts of things," said the branch chief, an older ankha man with a polished bald spot on his head. He introduced himself as Pam.

"To tell the truth, my first name's Tat, but my last name's Pamskarovmael-tostralasky…Everyone just calls me Pam."

There were four Highlanders working for the local branch, all of them ankha. According to Pam, more than eighty percent of Lyris was ankha, with only a smattering of the other races living in town.

"It's the ankha who work at crafts. Our fingers and hands are built for that work, you see. And little kitkin ladies and big old waterkin can't stand the heat by the furnaces for long."

Chief Pam was easygoing and a big talker, and he asked them for any news they might've heard on the road. It was his first time hearing of the wildfire in Maquiba and the overturned darbaba cart accident, and he listened with eyes wide in surprise. Wataru was amazed by how laid-back he seemed. *Like night and day from Kutz.*

"Lyris is a peaceful place, as you can see. The only incidents we have are little things: a child who got lost while picking berries, an explosion at a workshop near the town offices."

An explosion seemed like a big thing to Wataru.

"Just a mishap while making fireworks. There were no injuries, and since it happened at night, it was rather a nice show."

There were a number of empty rooms at the branch offices, so they were told to stay there in lieu of lodgings. While they stayed, they could help with town patrols, and there was a regular watch. While they listened to Pam's explanation, a pretty girl with long black hair brought tea to them.

"Ah, my daughter, Elza. She helps with the busy work around the branch."

"Hello," the girl said with a smile that made dimples in her cheeks. "You've had quite the journey!" Wataru guessed she must be about fifteen or sixteen years old. In real-world terms, she would be a high school student. The color of her skin made Wataru think of the white bowls he often saw at expensive Chinese restaurants—as delicate as flower petals. She was almost too pretty to be believed.

Suddenly, Wataru found himself thinking of Kaori Daimatsu. Their faces were completely different. But the graceful air to them, like a fairy's, was quite similar. Theirs was an unearthly beauty.

I wonder how Kaori is doing?

A sharp elbow jab in the ribs snapped Wataru out of his reverie. Meena coughed. "Shouldn't you ask him about Mitsuru?"

Oh, right. Through sheer force of will, Wataru tore his gaze away from the girl's face.

"A sorcerer about your age? Hmm..." Pam scratched his round, bald head. "This isn't like Gasara, where we check everyone at the town gate. It's hard to say who's visiting the town at any given time. You might ask around at the lodges."

Too bad. He hadn't expected finding Mitsuru to be that easy, but still, it was a disappointment.

"Of course, a boy sorcerer would stand out, and if he's still staying in Lyris, it shouldn't take long to track him down—not for us Highlanders." The chief suggested that they take a walk around and familiarize themselves with the town. There was still time before the scheduled patrols began.

Kee Keema leaned forward. "Actually, I was hoping we could visit Toni Fanlon's workshop. Could you tell me where it is?"

The chief's eyes suddenly became sinister-looking slits. "Eh? Fanlon?"

Elza, carrying tea to some of the other Highlanders, let a cup slip from her fingers. It fell on the floor and smashed. "I'm sorry," she said, hurriedly picking up the pieces. The chief shot a quick glance at her. When he turned back to Kee Keema, the same pleasant smile from before had returned to his face. "If you're looking for his workshop, it's off to the north end of the marketplace. You won't have any trouble finding it."

Roughly speaking, the town of Lyris was shaped like an apple. The core was home to the branch and town offices, hospital, school, and the mayor's private residence. Four large roads ran from the core out to the edges of town, one in each of the cardinal directions. Each of these roads had a name, and the marketplace took up much of Bricklayer Street that led to the north, running along it in a narrow succession of shops and stalls. At the very end of the north road, right where the stem of the apple would be, stood the cathedral with a large bell tower.

The tower stood high over the cathedral, casting a shadow across the rooftops in the afternoon sun. Completely captured in that shadow, on a small street corner, they found the Fanlon workshop. Here there were several houses crammed tightly together. Each seemed to be leaning in its own direction without any regard for its neighbors. There was no sign of any sort, nor any wares on display. It was a two-story house of old brick that had dried and cracked in the sun over the years. Wind and rain had leached the color from its walls, and the door was a simple, single panel of worn wood.

The people on the street were very kind, and everyone was happy to show them the way to the workshop. Someone even offered to take them there—it was easy to get lost in the marketplace crowds. When they finally came to the house they couldn't believe their eyes. How could the most famed jeweler of Lyris, known even in the lands of the Empire to the north, live in such a humble house?

"Well, nothing left to do but knock, I suppose," Kee Keema said, making a fist with his massive hand and stepping toward the front entryway. Just then, the door swung out and smacked him directly on the nose.

"Ouch!"

Bouncing off Kee Keema's leathery snout, the door slammed shut into whoever had opened it.

"Ack!" came a yelp from inside.

"Ah, many apologies," Kee Keema said, bowing. A young man stepped out from behind the door, holding his bruised nose with one hand.

"Hmm? Who might you be?" the youth asked, favoring them with a suspicious glare. He was an ankha, and very tall for his age. He wore a black shirt, black trousers, and a white workman's apron that reached down to his knees. His glossy black hair was tied in a knot behind his head, and this made him look like a rock star—or maybe somebody from a kung fu movie.

"Toni Fanlon?" Meena asked cheerfully. "We came here from Gasara hoping we could take a look at some of your crafts."

"Customers, are you?" the young man said, rubbing his nose and sounding relieved. "Then come on in. I'm not making anything very special at the moment, but you're welcome to have a look."

He opened the door for Wataru and the others, and then took a step back. "But I must head out on an errand shortly. I'm afraid I can't welcome you for long…"

The young man's eyes narrowed. He was staring at Wataru. Rather, he was staring at the firewyrm armband Wataru wore on his left wrist. "You're Highlanders?"

His voice sounded entirely different from a moment before. "You are, aren't you? That's the mark of a Highlander, isn't it?"

Wataru became suddenly nervous. "Yes. Yes it is."

Toni shook his head, his ponytail waving back and forth, and stood in Kee Keema's path just as he was about to step inside.

"Then I'm afraid I have to ask you to leave," he said quickly, his face going pale. His face was ashen and seething with anger.

"But, but why?"

"We came all this way…" Meena cut in. "Is there something wrong with Highlanders? Don't you like them?"

Lightning flashed across Toni Fanlon's eyes like two black jewels. "Hah. I take it you've not met Chief Pam yet?"

"We met him, sure," Kee Keema answered. "We asked him where we could find your workshop."

"And he told you?" the man asked, his every word clipped. "You lie!"

"It's not a lie. I mean, he only said you were off to the side of the market, he didn't tell us the exact location. We had to ask a few people on the way."

"It's true. We want to see your work. I didn't think we'd be able to buy anything, of course, they must be very expensive…"

Toni bit his lip and shook his head. "I wouldn't sell one of my works to a Highlander, or any friend of a Highlander, no matter what the price. No selling, no showing. Now leave."

The door shut with a slam.

The three stood with their mouths open, uncertain how to process this rapid turn of events. Faces peeked out of nearby windows and doors, then quickly withdrew. This must be a common sight, Wataru thought. He heard stifled laughter from somewhere above his head. It seemed like even the cries and pithy market noises drifting from Bricklayer Street mocked them.

Kee Keema closed his mouth with a snap. "Step aside, please," he said to Wataru and Meena. They each took a step back.

"Many thanks," Kee Keema said with a toothy grin. Then he clenched both hands into fists and stepped back across the narrow road saying "One step, two steps, three steps," in a loud voice as he paced backward.

"What are you doing?" Meena asked frantically. The waterkin charged toward the door, answering as he flew past, "I could break through five of these doors!"

"Wait! No!"

"Kee Keema!"

Wataru and Meena tried to tackle him. He growled like a hunting dog and shook them off in two steps. "What?"

"No violence!"

"You saw how rude he was? What's with that attitude? And he calls himself a merchant. Bah! When you meet someone like that, you give them a good whack on the chin, that's what you do. The Goddess herself don't stand for that kind of attitude."

"Please, wait!" came a girl's voice from down the street. They turned to see Elza picking up her skirts as she ran toward them, her long hair flowing behind her.

Breathing heavily, her hand on her chest, she said, "Y-you…Toni, he…"

"He turned us away at the door," Kee Keema said, gnashing his sharp teeth. Wataru knew the waterkin was a gentle soul and would never do a girl like Elza any harm, but seeing him there baring his teeth would have given anyone a fright. Elza caught her breath and pleaded with them. She looked on the verge of tears. "I'm sorry, I should've come with you…"

And then she collapsed.

"I must have given you quite a scare."

Elza was sitting on a hard cot in the corner of Fanlon's workshop. She had regained consciousness, but her face was whiter than the sheets on the bed.

Wataru's earlier shout of surprise had brought Toni running out into the street. With no hesitation he picked her up off the ground and carried her inside. Wataru and his friends took advantage of the situation and shuffled into the workshop. Until she opened her eyes, Toni hovered protectively by Elza's side, and wouldn't let anyone approach the bed.

"I bet they're lovers," Meena whispered to Wataru. "And Elza's the branch chief's only daughter—that's drama just waiting to happen."

Elza sat up, and when she saw Wataru and the others, she immediately began introducing them to Toni.

He shook his head. "Who cares about them? How do you feel? Are you all right?" Toni asked worriedly, trying to keep her from sitting up. "Your heart is weak. How many times have I told you—you shouldn't be running."

Elza smiled weakly. "I'm sorry, you're right. I guess I'm still just a child at heart."

"You came chasing after us. Thank you. Are you okay?" Wataru asked from behind Toni. The craftsman whirled sharply around.

"It's your fault," he said coldly.

"Please, Toni. Don't be that way to them," Elza said, taking his hands into her own. "They've come from Gasara searching for one of their friends. Yes, they're Highlanders, but they just arrived here and only spoke to my father briefly."

Toni Fanlon rubbed his forehead. His mouth was still curved into a jagged frown. "All Highlanders are the same."

"That's not true. I've not been to Gasara, but I hear it is quite lively. There're all sorts of people there, all races and classes, living together, no?" Elza looked each of the three in the face as she asked them. They all nodded in agreement. She then grabbed Toni's hands and looked into his eyes. "Please…things are different in other towns. Don't judge them based on the Highlanders here."

"Erm…" Kee Keema began hesitantly, scratching at his cheek with a long hooked claw. "Sorry to interrupt, but could somebody explain what's going on here?"

"Yes, of course," Elza said, catching her breath and blushing. Then, leaning on Toni's arm for support, she sat up.

"I'm guessing there's a difference of opinion between your father—the branch chief—and Mr. Fanlon, here?"

"Opinion!" Toni said, his anger rising again. "That racist has no right to an opinion."

"Can you please not get angry like that, just once?" Elza said with a laugh. Wataru and Meena smiled too. Toni's scowl only darkened.

"He's my father, so perhaps it's not my place to say this…" Elza began, looking down at the floor. "But my father, he thinks that ankha are superior to the other races."

"But isn't Pam the branch chief? How can he do a fair job of keeping the peace if he's prejudiced?"

"Who says it's fair?" Toni said bitterly. "The non-ankha in town can't go to the Highlanders for protection. No matter what happens—theft, burglary, arson—if the victim isn't an ankha, the Lyris branch won't budge. More than that, if the criminal in question happens to be an ankha, they erase all record of the incident off the books, and let them go free."

"That's terrible!" Kee Keema exclaimed.

"Worse, should a non-ankha commit a crime against an ankha, or even

injure them or damage property by mistake, they are arrested without question. Sometimes they're killed on the spot without a trial, or brought back
to the branch cells where they are tortured to death." Toni clenched his fists.
"And things have gotten worse lately. When something happens to an ankha,
there's no investigation, they just assume it was a non-ankha who did it. They
pick a likely suspect from the houses near the victim, say poverty was the mo-
tive, and take them into detention. We all know what happens next."

It sounded like South Africa during apartheid. "Are there other kinds of
discrimination in daily life here? Like separate facilities for different races?"
Wataru asked.

Toni's eyes opened wide. "There sure is. How did you know?"

"I know of a similar situation in another place," Wataru replied. *I saw it
in a movie once.*

Toni folded his arms across his chest. He walked over to the workshop
window and looked outside. "The main avenue around here is Bricklayer
Street. That's where the workers who first built Lyris lived. They used to bake
bricks in their houses. The noise and dust was fierce, and it was always hot
from the furnaces. That's why, when the pace of construction in town slowed,
the old bricklayers all left, and this became a place for the poor to live." Toni
turned back around to Wataru. "Didn't you notice outside? The people you
see in the windows here are all non-ankha."

Now that he mentioned it, Wataru realized it was true.

"I'm the only ankha living on this road, in fact," Toni spat. "The non-
ankha make up less than a quarter of Lyris's total population. There were
more in the past, but they got angry at their unfair treatment here, and left.
Of course, that was only the young, or those with a place to go, or artisans
with talent. There are many more that couldn't leave. Those who have stayed
behind have assembled here along Bricklayer Street in the narrow slums—
packed in like livestock. Go for a walk on the other roads and you'll notice the
difference right away. There are great mansions and roomy stores, all owned
by ankha. Every morning the non-ankha leave their cramped, inconvenient,
dusty shacks for their dreary jobs. Of course, nobody can get any decent work
around here. There are no permanent positions for anyone but ankha in Lyris.
So of course the non-ankha are all poor."

"It's a vicious cycle," Elza said, bitterly.

"Does this prejudice against non-ankha have anything to do with faith in the Old God?" Wataru asked. Elza and Toni looked at each other.

"What do you know about the Old God?" They all looked at him.

"Um...Kee Keema told me about him."

All eyes turned to the waterkin who quickly repeated the explanation he had given Wataru.

"So there's some even in Gasara then."

"Yes, but nothing is all that clear in Gasara. Everyone is wary of the Old God believers. We don't trust anything that has something to do with the Northern Empire."

Elza nodded. "Sometimes I fear that we've become like the Empire, detaining non-ankha just because of their race, and even killing them. Of course, it's on a smaller scale, but the things that are happening are the same..."

"I can't discount the influence of this belief in the Old God, but Lyris has never provided a warm welcome for non-ankha. I can't figure out what the cause might have been. The first settlers came here one hundred and fifty years ago, and just like settlers elsewhere, they were of mixed races," Toni told them. "Things only changed when the mines were discovered in the mountains around the city. To reach the mines, you have to dig deep into the ground. The beastkin, with their strong bodies and constitutions, were perfect for the job. At the same time, the nimble-fingered ankha were the best at crafting the stones they unearthed. That's how the division of labor came about."

"And Lyris became a crafting town," Meena said. "What happened to the mines? Are there non-ankha—beastkin—working there still?"

Toni shook his head. "The veins were depleted about eighty years after their discovery, and the mines closed. They weren't that large to begin with, really. Now and again somebody will find a fragment of precious metal, or gem, but nothing in salable amounts. Most of the jewels that are fashioned in Lyris now are imported from Arikita."

Of Lyris's past, only the ankha rule remained.

"So these jewels from Arikita...the shipping guild brings them in?" Kee Keema asked.

"That's right. Of course, the guild is just as prejudiced as the rest of town. They would never let a waterkin darbaba driver set foot in our borders."

"It's not just us waterkin you know, there are some ankha drivers as well…" Kee Keema said, then snorted. "I see how it is, anyway. I always thought the guild monopoly on shipping to Lyris was a little odd."

"Not many people from the outside know what it's like here in Lyris," Elza said, sadly hanging her head. Her long black hair flowed down one shoulder. "Only ankha are interested in learning our craft. And, frankly, there's really no other reason to come here. Very few people come and go."

"But, what I don't get is," Kee Keema said, "if Branch Chief Pam is so prejudiced, why didn't he frown when he saw me and Meena walk in?"

Meena's tail twitched side to side, echoing Kee Keema's question.

"That's because you're Highlanders from outside. If he was too open about it, the Gasara branch might get angry."

It did sound like the sort of thing that would get Kutz's whip cracking.

"Well, I don't know if such a deep-rooted thing can be fixed, but surely it's a problem if we have Highlanders supporting this kind of activity. Has anyone thought of speaking to the high chief of the Bog branches?"

Toni turned to Wataru, fixing him with the same cold stare he had when they first met. "You think we didn't try?"

"We did. Many times," Elza continued. "But High Chief Suluka said he didn't want to get involved. I think he wants to pretend it isn't happening."

"No—he is as prejudiced as the rest of them," Toni spat. "When the United Government formed the Knights of Stengel, there was a big debate about whether to make them mixed like the Highlanders, or to separate companies by race. In the end, they voted on it, and during the referendum, the only Highlander chief who showed support for separating races was Suluka."

"And the Knights of Stengel are all ankha too, aren't they," Wataru said, half to himself. "I don't see what the point is, separating companies by race."

"Oh, they think up all manner of reasons. Different-size gear making equipment difficult to manage, or the value of grouping people with similar customs together." It was clear from how he spoke that Toni's rage hadn't cooled down in the slightest. "Whatever the reason, once you separate people by race, you end up giving them different duties. In fact, when the Knights of Stengel were first formed, some non-ankha rode with them. Now they wander without armor or helms, helping repair towns hit by disaster, or building roads through the mountains. When people say the Knights of Stengel, they only think about the ankha riding in their silvery armor. All the *other* Knights are forgotten."

"Well, I'll say one thing," Kee Keema snorted. "I don't feel like lingering here longer than we have to. You know what I mean, Meena?"

Meena sat deep in thought, her tail twitching.

"Haven't you ever thought to leave town, Mr. Fanlon?" Wataru asked. Toni and Elza looked at each other again.

"How could he leave Elza behind?" Meena answered for them.

"But, well, they could always elope?" Wataru suggested.

Elza looked at him with tear-filled eyes. "I would go with Toni. But I cannot leave my father. I want to help them, if I can. To change him—he wasn't like this when he was younger, I'm sure of it."

"What changed him?"

"I think it was something that happened seven or eight years ago. My mother died of illness…" said Elza. "That's when he became passionately involved with the church—I think because he was lonely. You know, the cathedral with the great bell tower."

"But isn't that a church to the Goddess?"

"It is, but—well, it's a long story. Nothing is quite that simple in Lyris. There are some who say the cathedral was built to worship the spirits that created the beautiful jewels and gemstones we use in our craft."

It occurred to Wataru that there hadn't been a cathedral of any kind in Gasara, save Cactus Vira's cursed ruins.

"The teachings of the Goddess are very simple," Elza said, sitting upright, her voice like a song. "You who fill the land with your life, be compassionate, help one another, flourish, and gather to the light."

"What, that's it?"

"That's it. Those are the basics, anyway. There are a few precepts that go with the teachings, though. Like you're not supposed to create an image of the Goddess, nor build grand places of worship to her. Those two things are strictly forbidden. That's why, no matter which town you go to, you'll find many books written about the Goddess's teachings, and you'll hear people singing songs to her praise in the town squares, and you may even see a procession of the faithful. There are gathering places for these times, of course, but no chapels, no cathedrals. Only in Lyris."

That made it sound like the cathedral with the great bell tower wasn't built in honor of the Goddess but in defiance of her. It struck Wataru as extremely odd.

"I think my father began going to the cathedral, and he met someone there who put those ideas into his head."

Wataru knew where he had to go next.

chapter 17
The Town and the Cathedral

They returned to the branch to find Pam waiting for them. It was time for the regular patrol.

"So, did you meet Mr. Fanlon? He's an odd bird, isn't he?"

It was difficult to take his question at face value after all they had heard. Wataru's confusion showed on his face.

"What, you didn't meet him?" the chief asked with searching eyes. "My Elza didn't…go with you, did she?"

"She showed us the way," Meena said crisply, speaking in place of the fidgeting Wataru. "She is as kind as she is beautiful. You should be quite proud.

"But," she added, "she didn't visit the workshop with us. As it turned out he wasn't even there, so the trip was wasted."

"I see, I see," the chief said, his gaze softening. "Perhaps you can drop by there again on your patrol. You should have enough time."

The chief opened a map on top of his desk, and began explaining the division of patrol routes, and which route he thought best for Wataru and the others to walk. The route didn't take them along Bricklayer Street. Nor close to the cathedral.

"Thanks, Chief. Understood," Wataru said. "Though I was hoping to visit the cathedral at some point. That's quite an impressive belltower. I've not seen its like in any other town. Would it be possible to see inside sometime?"

The chief smiled. "Maybe not on patrol. Why don't you visit tomorrow?"

Wataru pushed again, but the chief wasn't to be budged.

"Only believers are allowed inside the cathedral, really."

"But isn't this a cathedral to the Goddess? If so, we'd all qualify as believers, then."

"Well," the chief responded slowly, "the cathedral in Lyris is a bit different. I'm sure you learned in school that it's forbidden to erect places of worship to the Goddess."

"So then who…"

"That cathedral was erected to Cistina, Spirit of Beauty. Cistina appears before only the most skilled of craftsmen, taking the form of a beautiful young ankha boy or girl."

"So is this Cistina more important than the Goddess in Lyris?"

"More important than the Goddess? Of course not. But I'm sure you understand the need for craftspeople to give thanks to the source of the technique and talent necessary to create beauty. That's why we built the cathedral."

Having no more time for chitchat, the chief led the three out on patrol. They first walked to the center of town, and around the branch and town offices. Then they went down one of the main boulevards leading directly away from Bricklayer Street. The buildings here were made of stacked white stone. Clean laundry hung in the windows, and they could hear the sounds of children playing. In the spaces between the buildings, or in the little squares here and there, were planted trees and flowers, woven in between the cobblestone streets. It was a beautiful town.

"The buildings around here are all communal households," Pam said, looking around with a smile. "Young families who work in Lyris and elderly couples who have already raised their children can live here cheaply. Clean and pleasant, don't you think? Lyris is rich on account of her crafts, so we can afford to spend money on keeping our town nice."

It wasn't a lie. This part of town was very nice. Wataru could even imagine himself living here and enjoying it. But the residents here were all ankha. When he thought of that, and remembered the cramped, unsanitary conditions of Bricklayer Street, he could barely restrain himself from bursting out. It was even worse when he noticed that the young couples walking down the street and children playing in the squares would flinch when they saw Kee Keema and Meena walk by. Some would point, and even hide behind their friends. Each raised eyebrow and whispered comment drove a spike through Wataru's heart.

"Most of the single-family houses are a block farther to the south from here," Pam explained. As they walked, residents would stop and say hello, or wave. "There are quite a few mansions there. Craftsmen and merchants who've made their fortunes enjoy living in this part of town. A lot of them have second homes in Lanka too. Quite fancy, though. You'll be impressed, I'm sure."

They were indeed impressive. Wataru was reminded of the residences of prime ministers and presidents he had seen in the real world (all on television, of course).

"Magnificent, aren't they?" Pam asked, as proud as if they had been his own. "The streets are safe too. That's why I'll have you patrolling this area until you're more familiar with the town."

"You sure it's okay to have me and Meena walking here?" Kee Keema asked innocently. "Looks like only ankha live here."

Wataru and Meena exchanged glances, but the chief didn't seem to notice. He put his hands on his hips and laughed out loud. *A little too loud,* Wataru thought.

"Nothing to be worried about! You're Highlanders. And there are other races in this part of town." Pam smiled broadly, and then reluctantly added, "Mostly servants," through his teeth. "Shall we trace your route back, now? Once you've gone both ways you're sure to remember it."

They were walking back through the communal dwellings when Kee Keema, in the rear, gave a sharp yelp. "Yowch!"

Something fell from the side of his head to the ground by his feet. The chief made to pick it up, but Meena was quicker. Her tail snaked out and around the object.

"What's this? It's sharp!" Meena said, transferring the object from her tail to her fingers. "A chunk of rock?"

It was a semi-translucent, pointy rock about the size of a large coin. It must have been thrown hard to get a yelp out of the thick-skinned waterkin. If its target had been Meena or Wataru, they might've been seriously wounded.

"Grrr...who did that?" Kee Keema's shoulders were tensed as he looked around at the windows of the nearby communal dwellings. "That's a nasty prank throwing rocks down at people...and if it's a fight they want, they sure are cowards!"

Wataru grew suddenly worried. He couldn't see anyone in the nearby windows. But what if whoever threw that was hiding, waiting for another chance? What if the next rock hit Meena?

"Kee Keema, let's go."

"Right. We've taken our time. We should hurry up," Pam said, his leisurely tone at odds with his words. He almost sounded amused. "Don't worry about it—probably just some kids having a prank."

Kee Keema, hands on his hips, looked down at the chief. Seeing them stand together, Wataru realized he towered over the short, balding man. "Maybe it was meant as a prank, but that rock could've seriously hurt someone! I don't think you can just let something like this slide, chief."

"On second thought, maybe you shouldn't patrol this area," the chief said, his expression perfectly still. "You and the girl here are a rare sort in these parts, I'll admit. You draw attention—especially from children. I'm sure they don't mean ill by it, but kids will be kids, and you can't catch them all. I know, I'll assign you two to Bricklayer Street. There are plenty of non-ankha down there."

After breakfast the next morning at the branch, Pam took Wataru out for morning patrol.

The night before, Wataru, Kee Keema, and Meena had decided to play along with the chief for the moment. Determined to talk to the people on Bricklayer Street, Meena was hoping to hear actual incidents where Chief Pam had placed the blame on someone or refused to take up a case because the victim had been a non-ankha.

"Be careful, though," Kee Keema had warned her. "We don't have many friends in this town. Wouldn't want to get into trouble."

"Don't worry about me," Meena had confidently replied. "I'll be fine."

For his part, Wataru decided to follow Pam's schedule as closely as possible, all the while looking for opportunities to get a glimpse of the hidden Lyris beneath its polished veneer of happy prosperity.

As they walked, Pam asked Wataru about himself. He was keeping the fact that he was a Traveler secret, so many of the questions were difficult to answer. *I was born in Nacht. My parents ran a lodge in Gasara, but they died of illness soon after I was born. I was taken in by the branch and raised by the branch chief.* Wataru had heard about Kutz taking in lost children and orphans at the branch in the past. Now he was one of them.

"That's how you've become such an accomplished Highlander at such a young age," Chief Pam said, smiling. "Ankha children sure are outstanding, I've always thought. Smart, and brave."

"I don't know," said Wataru, "I've never felt particularly brave."

The chief laughed. "If that were the case, you'd never have made the trip from Gasara to here. Particularly not with that *baggage* of yours slowing you down."

Wataru didn't realize that when the chief said "baggage," he was talking about Kee Keema and Meena. Momentarily confused, Wataru smiled vaguely. Then the meaning of the chief's words sunk in, and the smile froze on his face.

Pam was watching him out of the corner of his eye. His mouth was smiling beneath eyes cold as ice. "You're a smart kid. The kind who knows when to take the advice of his elders," he said, waving to a shopkeeper along the side of the road. He spoke low, without moving his mouth, so that only Wataru could hear. "I can't say I approve of such an outstanding ankha Highlander being too friendly with waterkin, kitkin, and their sort. Though I suppose with all the folks going in and out of Gasara such an arrangement wouldn't stand out so much."

"It stands out here?"

"Aye. You remember the rock that hit that waterkin yesterday?"

"The one you said was a prank?"

The chief opened his eyes exaggeratedly wide. "Oh, it was a prank, to be sure. A child's prank. Children, you see, are honest…straight. They can tell the good from the bad better than we can sometimes."

Pam smiled smugly, as if to say, *You know what I mean*. Wataru felt the bile rise in his throat.

"I was wondering if we could visit the cathedral?" he said, stifling his rising anger. "I would like to see the statue of this spirit of beauty, Cistina."

"Of course, of course!"

The chief didn't take Bricklayer Street to the cathedral. After returning to the town center, they took a wide detour through parts of the city Wataru hadn't seen yet. Their alternate route served only to reinforce what Wataru already knew: that conditions on Bricklayer Street were far worse than on other streets. And that the cathedral stood like a giant, arrogant overlord, looking down on the slums.

Seen from the front, the cathedral reminded Wataru of the churches in the *Saga* games, with its stone walls and round columns. Stained glass in the windows depicted a barefoot maiden with long hair and flowing robes—Cistina, Wataru reasoned. She was shown running across a grassy field, or playing a lute, or cooling her feet in a spring, or holding up a burning torch before kneeling believers.

The churches in the games he had played didn't have a particular religion, but there was always a kindly priest who, at various points in the game, would teach the players valuable holy magic—he was even kind enough to heal the entire party! Wataru wondered how the cathedral in Lyris would measure up.

Seen from this close, its beauty was certainly impressive. It looked like the epitome of what a cathedral should be. If a hundred children had been asked to describe a cathedral, this is the kind of building they would describe. It was perfect.

"Lovely, isn't it?" Branch Chief Pam asked, breathing out through his nose. "Officially, it's called the Cistina Trabados Cathedral. Trabados is an old name for this area, you see. The fairy Cistina was said to have been born from a spring coming out of the ground near here. When she carried a handful of water from that spring to the Goddess, the Goddess was so pleased she asked her to join her and stand at her side.

"It really is beautiful," Wataru said. "But don't you think the Goddess would be jealous of such a magnificent cathedral being built for Cistina alone?"

"I think not. Why, the Tower of Destiny where the Goddess lives is surely a hundred, or even a thousand times more magnificent than this," the chief replied. "The Goddess probably forbade the building of cathedrals to her because she didn't think the many races she made capable of building anything sufficiently grand enough in the first place."

The way he said it made it sound like he didn't think much of the Goddess and her creations. At least not all of them.

"Shall we have a look inside? Get ready to be even more surprised!"

When they pushed open the great doors and walked inside the cathedral, it was like stepping into a sea of multicolored light. Sunlight coming in through the stained glass windows filled the cathedral, washing over Wataru.

On either side of the central aisle were set rows of pews for the faithful to sit while they prayed. At the end of the aisle sat an altar beneath a window of particularly brilliant stained glass. Before the altar stood a stone carving of Cistina. Fresh-cut flowers were heaped in a pile at the statue's feet.

Here and there, young people sat with heads bowed. A few elderly sat in the pews, quietly reading from books. Walking softly so as not to make noise, Wataru walked up to the altar and examined the statue.

She was a maiden with long hair and a perfect face, wearing a robe with long sleeves and skirts. In her right hand was a scepter set with a gemstone. Her left hand gripped the handle of a mirror held upward toward the sky. The sleeve of her robe fell down almost to her elbow.

"That mirror reflects that which is beautiful and that which is ugly in every man's heart," the chief explained. "The scepter in her right hand serves to smite down those who would destroy beauty."

Wataru took another step forward, his eyes going over the statue from head to toe—when he noticed something about her feet. Though it was hard to see through all the flowers, Cistina was definitely not standing upon the ground. Her surprisingly heavy-duty sandals were standing on something, or someone.

Wataru knelt and moved aside the flower stems. Looking up at him was the face of a waterkin. *That looks just like Kee Keema!* His expression was twisted in pain. Just behind him, a beastkin reminding Wataru of Trone lay in repose, his head tilted back, his mouth an agonized grimace.

The stone Cistina was treading on their faces, crushing their chests. Wataru abruptly stood. Pam put a hand on his shoulder from behind. "Isn't she beautiful?"

Almost at the same time, another voice from the right of the altar said, "Branch Chief Pam! So good to see you here." An elderly man in white robes carrying a silver scepter much like the one the statue held stepped toward them.

"I was remiss in not saying hello sooner," the chief said. "This is Father Diamon. He's the most important man in the cathedral."

Father Diamon smiled brightly and returned the bow. He stood straight as a rail, his wide shoulders and clear eyes sparkling beneath bushy white eyebrows. His perfectly round head was smooth and hairless. Wataru felt over-whelmed. No matter how old this man looked, he certainly wasn't old inside. Wataru sensed something in him—a fierce spirit. It was almost savage.

"Important? No, not at all. I merely do my best to humbly serve our Lady Cistina."

"Of course, of course," Pam said with a smile.

"I see we have a visitor," Father Diamon said, looking at Wataru. His gaze was cool, calculating, just like the look Pam had given Wataru before.

When the chief introduced Wataru, the priest seemed quite surprised. "To become a Highlander at so young an age, that's impressive indeed! I thought surely you'd come for an apprenticeship with one of our craftsmen."

"Wataru is searching for a friend of his. He did say he wanted to visit Toni Fanlon's workshop, of course, but I'd feel embarrassed for the town if he went away thinking we were all like that strange fellow."

"Ah yes, Mr. Fanlon..." Father Diamon held the tip of his scepter to his forehead and shook his head. "Few craftsmen are so loved by our Lady Cistina. Fewer still reject her blessings so vehemently as he does."

Words bubbled up in Wataru's throat. *Come on, say it. Say it!* Wataru swallowed and looked back up at the statue of Cistina. "Her face looks a bit like Ms. Elza."

Pam dissolved into laughter. "Well, that's sacrilegious of you to say, but I can't say I'm not pleased."

"Elza is a rare beauty," Father Diamon added. "I would not be surprised if she turned out to be Cistina reborn."

"I don't know about that," Wataru continued. "Elza is very kind—not only to me, but to Kee Keema and Meena too. Not like Cistina here at all."

Wataru let the words stream out. A moment too late, he shut his mouth. The chief and priest were giving him looks that made him feel as if the temperature had dropped by about twenty degrees. But the two were still smiling.

"I should be leaving," Wataru said with a crisp bow.

As he walked out through the front doors of the cathedral, the bell in the great tower began to toll. Each deep ring reverberated in his stomach, like someone high above was casting the sounds down at him, trying to crush him with their weight. Wataru put his hands over his ears, and left without once looking back.

Chapter 18
Mitsuru's whereabouts

"We should move out," suggested Wataru to his friends. He had told them about the Cistina statue he had seen at the cathedral. Beyond that, he had decided to keep his mouth shut.

"But what about finding Mitsuru?" Meena asked, concerned. "We're okay staying here a little longer if it means finding him, aren't we?"

"Sure. No problem," said Kee Keema. "I've only just started talking to the people on Bricklayer Street. You won't believe the stories I've heard. They really have a bad deal down there. Wouldn't feel right just leaving them."

"Of course I don't mean for us to abandon them. But don't you think it's a bit more than the three of us can handle? We should talk to Kutz at least. And if High Chief Suluka in Bog won't help, we should talk to Gil in Nacht. We'll get a lot farther a lot faster that way for sure."

Kee Keema gave Wataru a doubtful look. "It's not like you to back down so easily."

"It's just…I have a bad feeling about all of this," Wataru said. "We should leave this place as soon as we can. We'll just have to tell Mr. Fanlon and Elza that we plan to come back as soon as we can and hope they understand."

After dinner, the three were quietly talking in a room at the town branch. When they heard the chief's booming voice outside their door, Meena jumped in surprise—much higher than the other night.

"Sorry to bother you while you're resting…"

The chief strode into the room, casting sharp looks at Kee Keema and Meena where they sat on soft cushions on the floor. "Wataru, someone who sounds like that friend of yours is apparently staying just outside Lyris."

Wataru stood. "Really? Where?"

The chief had brought a map with him. He spread it on the floor, and pointed. "North of town, there is a forest of sula trees we call the Spiritwood."

"Sula trees?"

"Aye, a fragrant wood loved above all others by Cistina. Her scepter is carved of sula. In fact, all of the devotional objects in the cathedral are made of sula and silver alone."

The Spiritwood was also the location of the Triankha Hospital, oldest in the Lyris area.

"An outstanding place, that is. There is something in the fragrance of the sula trees that quickens mending."

"And that's where Mitsuru is?" Wataru asked, suddenly concerned. *What if he's injured?*

"I haven't heard a name, but they say he's a sorcerer about your age, wearing a black robe. Couldn't think of who else it might be. Don't worry, he's not wounded or ill. He apparently came upon the hospital while lost on the road. He's staying there, resting awhile. He's been asking people for news about the road—unusual for a traveling sorcerer."

Chief Pam smiled. "It's good fortune for you we heard something so quickly. You should leave first thing in the morning. If it turns out he's not this Mitsuru fellow, well, you won't be so far from Lyris that you can't come back."

And now they had their excuse to leave. Wataru was thrilled. He'd never been so uncomfortable in a place before—then he remembered how he had felt when his mother and Rikako Tanaka had fought on the balcony. He had been scared then too, sad and powerless. He'd been so miserable hiding under his bed, he thought he might die.

"What luck, Wataru," Meena said, giving him a hug. Wataru snapped out of his reverie to see Chief Pam's cold eyes drilling holes through them.

The next morning, they left the branch as early as possible so they wouldn't have to see the chief again. A spearman stood guard alone. He smiled and said goodbye to them with a wave. As they left, he walked into the room they had been using and closed the door.

The three got into their darbaba cart and rolled away from the branch. Wataru looked back furtively so his friends wouldn't notice. The spearman was in their room, tossing the bedding and cushions Kee Keema and Meena had been using out the window. Wataru bit his lip, and regretted looking back.

After a short time, the Spiritwood suddenly appeared before them. The area was hidden behind the hills so well that they had to check the map several times to make sure they were going the right way.

"Sula trees, eh?" Kee Keema said, craning his neck. "If they're good enough for a fairy's scepter, they might have a little magic in them."

Despite Wataru's rising joy at the possibility of meeting Mitsuru, he started to feel a nagging doubt in the pit of his stomach.

chapter 19
The Magic Hospital

The sula trees were fragrant as described. They had a perfume-like smell, heavy and cloying. Their trunks and branches were slender and intertwined like dancers on a stage. No flowers appeared to be blooming beneath the thick canopy of pointed leaves, so Wataru assumed that it must be the trunks themselves that smelled so strongly.

Their darbaba cart had only just entered the forest when Meena complained her nose hurt. "This smell—it's too strong."

"Yeah?" Kee Keema said, flaring his nostrils. "I don't smell much."

"We kitkin are blessed with a sense of smell a hundred times keener than yours or Wataru's," Meena explained. "It's making me dizzy."

"Dizzy? Well, you're in luck, we *are* headed to a hospital."

Just then they caught sight of a gray, square building through a gap in the branches that tangled above them like the outstretched fingers of a hundred ballerinas.

"Is that it?" Wataru asked, leaning forward.

"Hmm?" Kee Keema lifted his whip and pushed aside some low-hanging branches that threatened to snag the darbaba's fur. "Ah, must be!"

It was a building of whitish gray rock, a perfect cube, standing about three stories tall. There were several windows, each lit from the inside. It being morning, this seemed odd, but then it occurred to Wataru that ever since they had entered the sula wood, the light had grown decidedly dim.

Looking up from the darbaba cart, he was startled to discover that he couldn't see the sun at all. *How is that possible?* It had been a perfectly clear day. But here, the patches of blue sky were hazy, as though a white veil had been drawn over the heavens.

"Strange, there isn't a fog," Kee Keema muttered, gripping the reins. His darbaba shivered and snorted, stomping its hooves. With a little bit of coaxing, the steed took a few more steps forward before completely stopping. "Oy, oy...what're you so scared of, then?"

Kee Keema rubbed the darbaba behind its ears. Now it wasn't just stomping, it began stepping backward.

Meena, sitting hunched over in the cart with both hands on her nose, suddenly shot to her feet, her ears standing straight up. "Something comes!"

Wataru felt it too. *Where? Here—and there, and there.* He felt like they were being swiftly surrounded. The air moved. In front of them. Behind them. The sula trees rustled, and the thick scent assaulted them anew.

Fzzing!

Something cut through the air. The next moment, Meena fell from the cart with a shriek.

"Meena!"

The darbaba cart creaked to a halt, and Wataru jumped down onto the ground. Meena was lying next to the front wheel, face down, out cold. Her cheek was stained red with blood.

"Yowch!" Kee Keema shouted from atop the cart. "Wataru, get down!"

Wataru glanced around and saw an arrow stuck deep into the waterkin's right shoulder. The arrow was fletched with venomously red feathers.

"They're firing from the trees! Hide underneath the cart!" Kee Keema barked, crawling off the driver's platform. He seemed to be moving clumsily, in slow motion. *It looks like he's drunk—like he's swimming through water.*

"This is bad. This..."

Several sharp noises came all at once, and Wataru saw a whole quiver's worth of arrows thwunk into the cart frame right above his head. One even came close enough to graze the tip of his nose.

"Paralytic..." Kee Keema gasped, falling to the ground like a sandbag. Unthinking, Wataru ran to him. His eyes were closed, and his long tongue hung limp through his teeth.

"No, Kee Keema! Wake up!"

Wataru felt a fiery sting in his right leg. He looked down to see an arrow protruding from his calf. For a moment he stared at it dumbly, unable to comprehend what had just happened.

Blood immediately began to seep from the wound. Wataru reached down and pulled out the arrow. To his chagrin, the flow of blood increased. His pants were soon stained a dark crimson.

The world around him began to spin. Up became down, down became up. The thick scent of the sula trees assaulted his nostrils. His tongue felt numb. He tried to move his hands, but they seemed frozen. He felt his knees begin to knock...

Then he collapsed to the forest floor, flopping over forward, like a student falling asleep on his desk after an all-night cram session. He fell across Kee Keema, feeling his own body rise with Kee Keema's breathing.

At least he's still alive.

Two feet in leather sandals appeared in his field of vision, just before his eyes closed. Sturdy sandals. Strong legs. "We only need the boy," he heard a cold voice say. "Toss the other two. They'll never be able to survive in the woods."

Then Wataru plunged into darkness.

A low, whispering sound coming from somewhere.
Where?
Where am I?

I'm asleep. I'm lying on the floor in my living room. Mom would get so mad. "If you're going to nap, do it on the sofa! Don't roll about like a dog. You've got a dust allergy, you know! Do you want to be sneezing the whole day?"

But I like it here—the feel of the hardwood flooring on my cheek. Cool in the summer, and right where the heater fan blows out warm air in the winter. I can stretch here, I don't sink in, the ceiling is so far away...

But something hurts. And what's that noise? I wish it would go away. Sounds like moths flying through an open window. They're hovering around my face. I have to brush them away—lift my hand—brush them away...

"Wataru. Wataru, wake up!" came a clear voice from above him. It was a sweet voice. He remembered having heard it somewhere before. A girl's voice.

"I said get up, Wataru, up! You have to escape! Please! You don't know how much trouble you're in!"

The voice made his ears throb. Wataru closed his eyes. *Escape? Why? I'm just lying on the floor in my living room...*

My body hurts. This floor—this isn't the wood floor in our apartment. My leg hurts. My right calf. An iron claw, stuck in my calf. What is that?

Something was moving by Wataru's head. *Rustle...rustle.* He tensed, and the sleepiness faded from him in an instant. He tried to jump to his feet, and the pain in his leg flared. He looked down to see a filthy rag wrapped around his pant leg. It was stained the color of dried blood.

Suddenly it all came rushing back to him. The attack on the darbaba cart, Meena and Kee Keema, the two sandaled feet he had seen just before he passed out, the cold voice giving orders.

He was in a square room. The floor, walls, and ceiling were all that same whitish rock as the hospital he had seen in the distance. *That's why it's so hard and cold.* Wataru saw a single door in the room. *Looks heavy. Locked, of course.* On the opposite wall was a single small window, just high enough so that Wataru could touch it with his fingertips when he stood on his toes. Thick metal bars prevented exit.

The strange rustling sound was coming from a large amount of dried leaves spread evenly through the room. They looked like sula leaves. That peculiar scent remained, though it was somewhat stale.

"Whew, you're awake. How do you feel? Can you walk?" The sweet voice was coming from the window. Someone was outside the bars. "It's me, Wataru. Remember?"

The fairy! No, he corrected himself, *the voice I* assumed *was a fairy.*

"Are you really there this time? Where am I? Are Kee Keema and Meena all right? What's going on?"

"I asked if you remembered me, Wataru," the sweet voice said, sulking.

Wataru crawled up to the window, and lifting himself up on the wall, he raised his voice. "I'm sorry. I just—wait, have you come to save me?"

"I would if I could," the voice said simply. "But there's really nothing I can do."

Wataru's mouth opened and shut a few times, then he finally managed, "Well, at least tell me what's going on. I was shot by this arrow and carried here...I know that, but that's all."

"Well, you're right so far."

"What about the other two?"

"How should I know?" the sweet voice said with a sigh. "So the girl with a tail, she's your type, is she? That's a disappointment."

"I'm not even talking about that!" Wataru said, gritting his teeth. "Where is this place? Am I inside the hospital?"

"Yes. In the middle of the sula forest."

"Are you captured here too?"

"No, actually."

Wataru leaned against the wall. "Then, can't you do anything? Maybe there's a key to the door…"

"Like I said, there's nothing I can do," the sweet voice said quickly. "I just came to cheer you on. I crawled all the way up here just to talk to you before it was too late. You should thank me."

"Thank you…" Wataru glared at the window. *What did she mean "crawled up here"?*

"Wataru, you should really try to stop breathing so heavily in there. Breathe by the window."

"Why?"

"The smell of the sula isn't good for your head."

Wataru leaned flat against the wall, staring at the heaps of leaves rustling in the faint breeze from the window.

"Not good for my head?"

"They cloud your mind," the sweet voice said. "They're used, sometimes…for torture."

Wataru was about to protest how ridiculous that sounded, when he heard a clattering noise against the heavy door.

The door was thrust open, and a large man holding a bowgun quickly entered the room. He was wearing workman's clothes, heavy boots, and had a bristly beard.

The arrow set in the bowgun was pointed straight at Wataru's head. Without a word, the bearded man moved to the side of the door, and a second person entered. His companion was smaller, and thinner, and he wore a long-sleeved robe—much like the one worn by Father Diamon at the Cistina Trabados Cathedral. Not only that, but in his right hand he held a scepter, and in his left, a small hand mirror, just like the statue of Cistina.

"You have awoken," the robed man said in an oddly high-pitched voice. "Do you know where you are?"

Wataru worked his numb tongue into motion. "Triankha...Hospital."

"I see. Then your memory is intact." The robed man smiled faintly. On closer inspection, he seemed little more than a boy, a pretty, naïve boy—wait, or was he a girl?

"I—I came looking for a friend," Wataru said, his voice trembling. "Branch Chief Pam in Lyris said that a boy of his description had been seen at Triankha Hospital..."

The robed man, still smiling, approached Wataru. As he walked, the sula leaves on the floor of the cell swirled to the side, making a path. "We, too, received word from Chief Pam. He said that a daemon—a servant of the Goddess— with a terrible madness in his eyes, and evil plans in his heart, had set foot on our holy ground."

"Pam said what?" Wataru gaped. "But he was the one who told us about Triankha Hospital!"

That was when he finally realized what had happened. They had been drawn here on purpose. The chief had lied. He didn't know where Mitsuru was. He had sent them off into the sula wood so that they could be captured. *He lied to me!*

"It was a trap..." Wataru muttered, unable to control his trembling. The robed man stepped even closer, still smiling. He knelt, and brought his face so close Wataru could feel his breath. "You're a Traveler, yes?"

Wataru didn't answer. Chief Pam didn't know that. And he thought it best not to tell these people.

"You need not say a thing, you still cannot hide the truth from us," the robed man continued. "We know what you did in Gasara. We hear many things. Chief Pam only feigned innocence. He knew it all from the very beginning."

So that's how it was. Wataru now totally regretted telling people his secret. He should have listened to Kee Keema.

"So what if I am a Traveler?" Wataru said, forcing himself to breathe calmly. "What do you care? Is that wrong?"

"Travelers are our eternal enemies," the robed man answered quietly. "To go against the teachings of the Old God would be a sin."

Wataru didn't like the sound of that one bit.

"You're believers of the Old God?"

The robed man nodded curtly. "It is so."

"And I bet you're behind the rise in discrimination in Lyris. And the cathedral—that's for your purposes, isn't it. It's really a church to the Old God."

The robed man did not answer, but the glimmer in his eyes was enough for Wataru to know he was right. "You're proselytizing for the Old God at the Cistina Trabados! And the chief is one of your converts!"

"He seems a bright lad. Pity," the small man said. The bearded man made no reply—he just continued to point his bowgun at Wataru's head.

Just then, the robed man moved his hands quickly. Thinking the scepter would hit him, Wataru flung up his arms, covering his head. But the blow never came. The robed man was holding out his small hand mirror, sticking it in Wataru's face. "Look! This is absolute proof! Evil daemon of the Goddess, know that the Mirror of Truth reveals only pure souls. You are as nothing to me!"

Indeed, there was nothing in the mirror. Even when it was pressed up so close it nearly touched his nose, all Wataru could see reflected was the white rock wall behind his head.

"Your destiny ends here, servant of the Goddess. By our hands shall you be reduced to the filth and sinful dust whence you came."

The robed man shouted so loud his cheeks flushed red. Jumping in the air, he thrust the scepter and mirror above his head. Seizing his chance, Wataru mustered all his strength and pushed as hard as he could against the man. With a great cry, he fell on top of the bearded man behind him. Both tumbled to the floor, the bearded man flipping onto his back with a heavy thud. Wataru leapt up and shot for the door.

"There is no escape!" the robed man shouted, climbing to his feet behind Wataru. He swung his scepter, and a whirlwind rose in the room, lifting the dried leaves from the floor. As Wataru watched, they fluttered into two piles at either side of the room, but he didn't stop to see what happened next. Grabbing the handle and yanking the door open, Wataru dashed out into the hall.

Along the side of the smooth rock wall that ran down the hallway, Wataru saw several doors just like the one he had come through. The wall on the other side of the corridor was smooth, without a single window. He looked right and left, but both ways faded quickly into darkness, and it was impossible to tell how far they went.

Wataru ran to the right. His leg was on fire. The white hallway was perfectly straight and featured an endless string of heavy metal doors. No matter how far he went, it was exactly the same.

Suddenly, a door about fifteen feet ahead of him opened wide, swinging so fast it bounced off the wall and started to close again. Then, from the other side of the door, a large lump of dried leaves appeared. It looked as though the leaves had gathered to form the shape of...

It's a man. The leaf-man was twice as tall as Wataru, with an oversize head, and it walked with two bristling arms extended, like a mummy in an old horror movie. It stood before Wataru, blocking the passage.

Wataru screeched to a halt and whipped around so fast it hurt his neck. One by one, the doors behind him were opening. From each stepped a leaf-man. He was surrounded.

The long corridor filled with the pungent odor of leaves. Wataru felt his legs shake beneath him. He felt dizzy. His vision dimmed.

"*Edoro wara sabtalongi sigur!*" a high voice was chanting. It was the robed man, standing at the side of the corridor, scepter and mirror crossed on his chest. "Come forth, o spirit of the woods, destroyer of the evil Goddess's schemes, your voice shall join ours and bring righteous victory!"

As one, the leaf-men opened their mouths and howled. A sound like a giant cloth ripping filled the air. Then they charged.

When Wataru came to, all around him was darkness.

The wound in his right leg continued to throb. He was lying on his side. The floor beneath him was hard. He couldn't move his hands. *Am I tied up?* He couldn't move his feet. He couldn't stand.

When he tried to roll over, there was a metallic clinking sound. The sound of chains jostling against one another. *Why is it so dark?*

He heard low singing—not one but many voices. They weren't that far away, but Wataru couldn't decide which direction the sound was coming from. *Right? Left? In front? Behind?*

He heard a footstep and sensed someone's presence. A hand grabbed him from behind by the collar and dragged him violently upward. He felt the hand unfastening something by the nape of his neck. Suddenly, the darkness broke. Whatever had been covering his head was taken off.

He was outside. It was night. He could see the Triankha Hospital, the sula forest.

A great crowd surrounded Wataru. They were wearing clothes that looked like large grain sacks. They held candles in their hands, and they wore white hoods. He couldn't see their faces, but Wataru instinctively knew they were all ankha. This must be them, the believers in the Old God, the flock of Triankha Hospital and the cathedral back in town.

The chanting voices belonged to the men. They had formed a large circle with Wataru at its very center. His hands and feet were chained.

The stench of sula leaves stuck in his nostrils. He felt lightheaded.

"Stand," said a voice from someone at his side. He looked to see a believer standing next to him. Large hands emerged from beneath his grain-sack clothes.

"Stand."

The giant hands stretched out, grabbed Wataru by the collar, and dragged him to his feet. The hands were covered with thick black hair on both sides. If he hadn't seen the hair, he might have thought the hands belonged to a statue, they were so hard and cold.

"Walk."

The hands moved, pushing Wataru toward the edge of the circle. Wataru stumbled and fell, only to be dragged once again to his feet.

"No stalling," the giant grunted. "Stand. Walk."

Wataru began to walk on unsteady feet. His Brave's Sword was still at his waist, though his chains were too short for him to grab it. There was nothing he could do. He could hardly even think straight. He staggered forward, and the singing of the believers grew louder, turning into a great chorus. Part of the circle broke, giving Wataru a view of what lay beyond.

He couldn't believe his eyes. Even after blinking several times and shaking his head, the scene before him didn't change.

It was a guillotine. He'd never seen one before, but he was familiar with them from video games and comic books: a simple stand, with an angled blade for cutting off the heads of criminals.

The young man in the robe, holding only the scepter in one hand, still smiling, walked up to stand next to the horrible device. He wore a wine-red sash over his robe. Directly behind him, a great bonfire blazed, making him look as though he were surrounded by a golden aura of light.

Wataru found he couldn't take another step forward. His knees shuddered, and he froze in place. "*Your destiny ends here, daemon, servant of the Goddess,*" the robed man's voice sounded in his ears.

Wataru looked up. The blade of the guillotine shone as though with evil intent in the reflected light of the bonfire. He felt like it was smiling at him, teeth bared, ready for the kill.

This is ridiculous. That was all he could think. *How could this happen to me? What have I done?*

"And so we see that evil, too, knows fear," the robed man said in a gentle voice. "But do not worry. Only by destroying your body, puppet of the Goddess, will your soul be purified. By the benevolence of the great Old God, your purified being will be reborn again in Vision, in whatever form you desire…"

"I'll pass, thanks," Wataru spat. "You have no right to kill me! I don't believe in your Old God. I'm a Traveler, from the real world. I came here to change my destiny, not die!"

The robed men smiled even more broadly. "We have no words for those enslaved to the false beliefs."

"Whatever! You don't know what you're talking about!" Wataru yelled. He turned to the other believers gathered there. "You know what you're doing? Do you even know? Why…"

Just then, Wataru noticed someone standing beyond the guillotine. He wore the same robe as the rest of them, and he was holding an axe. Wataru's words froze in his mouth. That's the axe that will cut the rope that holds the blade…

"Enough of your foul words, polluted daemon."

Wataru was pushed hard from behind onto the forest floor. The believers swayed, rapturous with joy and anticipation.

Heavy hands dragged Wataru to his feet, pulling him toward the guillotine. He stuck out his legs and jabbed to the side with his elbows, trying to resist, but the man holding him was incredibly strong. He only succeeded in kicking up dust, and further amusing the believers. He felt dizzy and nauseated. *I'm only wasting my strength. I won't be able to escape this way. But how, then...how?*

The hands yanked on his chains, and he took a few more wobbly steps toward the platform. *No, I don't want to die this way! This is insane!*

The more he shouted, the louder the song of the believers rang in his ears.

"I will give you one chance," the robed man said, walking toward Wataru. "To truly purify your soul, and ease your rebirth into Vision, you must confess before your execution. Now, tell me, where is the other Traveler?"

Wataru's hair stood on end. *He's asking about Mitsuru! They want to capture him too!*

"I don't know!"

"So you will be difficult."

"I wouldn't tell you even if I did know!" Wataru shouted, his voice hoarse. He spat at the robed man, surprising even himself. *Didn't know I could do that. No one ever taught me to do that.*

His aim was good. His wad of spit scored a direct hit. The robed man slowly wiped his cheek, and smiled broadly. "You are pitiful, you who are to be sacrificed. The Goddess has consumed you, and destroyed your soul. Our voice, no matter how righteous, cannot hope to reach you as you are now."

"Righteous? Says who?"

"We serve the Old God," the robed man said solemnly, as though that in itself were proof enough.

"I don't care!" Wataru yelled, summoning all his strength. "What? Are you from the Northern Empire? Let me guess. You don't give a whit about the Old God. You just want to spread your system of prejudice to keep yourself on top!"

At last, the smile faded from the robed man's face. His mouth formed a straight line. "Speak," he said in a low voice. "Where's the other Traveler?"

"Never!"

"If you do not tell us, we will search for him by our own means. And we will find him. But I fear much blood will be spilled along the way. Many will look into the flames and scream for mercy before our work is done." The man laughed. "Those deaths will be on your conscience."

Wataru stood dumbfounded. *What did he mean, the flames?* "That fire near Maquiba—did you do that?"

The robed man did not answer, but instead asked again. "Tell me. Where is the other?"

"Here," came a clear voice from the dark sky above their heads.

chapter 20
Mitsuru

Wataru looked up, his mouth still hanging open. *Where did that voice come from?*—there, on top of the hospital building, at the highest spot overlooking the courtyard where the guillotine sat.

A small figure stood on top of the high rock wall. His black robes stood out even against the dark sky. The gem atop his staff shone with a clear blue light. And illuminated by it was…

Mitsuru.

The robed man looked up. "You!" he shouted out in surprise. The man holding the axe by the guillotine and the man grabbing Wataru by the neck stood frozen in place.

"Servant of evil, what business have you on our holy ground!" the robed man shrieked in a high voice. "Come down! Come down here! Do you know what penalty your trespass carries?"

The circle of believers wavered, losing its shape, and the candles began to flicker. Some went out in the commotion.

Mitsuru didn't move an inch. His face was drawn in his usual condescending smile. Even though he stood quite a distance away, his expression was clear. Somehow, the sight of those slightly crooked lips made Wataru incredibly homesick. *No time for that now*, he thought. *They're going to capture Mitsuru!*

"Mitsuru, run!" Wataru shouted as loud as he could. "Get away from here! Quickly! Run, and call for help!"

Mitsuru turned, looking at Wataru. Then he sighed—another familiar gesture. "Exactly who would I call for help?" he asked, shaking his head. "While

I was traipsing through the woods looking for someone, you'd be here losing your head."

"Go or they'll get both of us!"

"I think not." Mitsuru sighed again. "I never took you for the self-sacrificing sort. Such a good kid."

"What're you saying, Mitsuru? Quickly, we don't have…"

"Time, I know," Mitsuru finished the sentence for him. With his free hand, Mitsuru pointed directly at the robed man. "The one who inscribed the magic circle on this rooftop—is that you?"

Though he had only pointed his finger, the man reeled as though struck with an arrow, his face twisting into a grimace. "Watch your tone, young whelp! Just who do you think you are talking to?"

"You."

Mitsuru's voice contained not a grain of hesitation, but instead rang with all the confidence of a teacher scolding a naughty pupil. "I have no idea what you were trying to summon up here, but you got it all wrong," Mitsuru said, chuckling. "Your orientation is off, and the lines are the wrong length. Where did you study? Did you even graduate?"

"Y-you!!" The man ran up to the building. It looked as though he might claw his way up the side in his rage, but he merely stamped his feet, powerless. "You mock me!"

"I'm only asking you a question. But you're a little far away—I couldn't quite hear you. Why don't you come up here? Just cast an air ladder. Simple, no?"

The robed man's face went pale. The circle of believers had completely dissolved, making a ragged semi-circle, not centered on the robed man, but on Mitsuru.

"What, you can't even chant up an air ladder?" Mitsuru asked with mock surprise. "Well, then you're quite hopeless. Isn't the Old God a sorcerer?" Mitsuru put his hand to his chin and frowned. "Are you sure you haven't been taken in by some creature claiming to be the Old God?"

"You blaspheme!" the robed man hissed, raising his scepter in the air. Just then, Mitsuru extended his finger above his head and uttered a brief incantation. In the next instant, a single bolt of lightning cut across the sky.

"Augh!" screamed the man in robes. The blinding light flashed, and the lightning bolt disappeared into the ground, leaving behind a hole—a sharp, jagged hole, as though a giant spear had pierced the earth.

"I won't miss next time," Mitsuru said. "If you don't want to be blackened to a crisp, I suggest you remove those chains from Wataru."

The robed man fell upon the ground, his mouth flapping uncontrollably. Mitsuru's gaze turned from him toward Wataru—and then to the giant standing by him. "Hey, you. Yeah, you—the big guy!"

Wataru heard the giant suck down a mouthful of air.

"Release those chains!" The giant followed Mitsuru's instructions with hardly a moment's hesitation. His large fingers were clumsy and trembled terribly, making the simple task of inserting a key into a keyhole a difficult feat.

"Look, I'll do it," Wataru said, and took the key from his hand. He unlocked the chains himself. Mitsuru watched until Wataru was free. He then pointed up toward the sky again and swung his hand back down at the guillotine. A lance of light shot through the killing machine's rope, and disappeared into the top of the platform. In the brief flash, Wataru saw the guillotine blade drop, biting into the platform. Behind it, the man with the axe fell to the ground.

"Never liked those things," Mitsuru muttered almost to himself, then changed his position slightly. Turning toward Wataru, he said, "You may not realize it, but we're inside a circle here."

"A circle?" Wataru shouted up to him.

"Yes, a magical barrier. Quite primitive, really, but I think the sula trees help make it more effective."

"I'm not sure I get you."

The believers followed the exchange between them, looking back and forth like a crowd of onlookers at a tennis match. Hands holding candles were lowered to the ground.

"There's no such thing as the Triankha Hospital," Mitsuru continued. "Oh, there used to be, long time ago. But now the only thing remaining is the ruins. They drew their barrier around this place, to use it as their fortress."

One hand at his waist, Mitsuru snorted. "The only annoying thing is the sula wood. The raw essence of magic fills the place. It will take more than a weak-willed sorcerer—such as the one trembling in his boots over there—to break this. You understand what I'm saying?" Mitsuru said, now to the robed man. "You made this barrier, sure, but you drew in too much magic from the sula trees."

"Nonsense," the robed man said. Though he was hunched over, looking anything but dignified, a bit of his earlier strength had returned to his voice. "This is blasphemy most foul. You shall be punished!"

Crawling to his feet, the man began to chant a spell. On the roof, Mitsuru leaned on his staff and looked down at him, an expression of deep interest on his face.

As Wataru watched, the dried leaves of the sula trees began to swirl together into two figures—leaf-men like the ones who had attacked him before. Just looking at them made the bile rise in his throat. Wataru took a step back. The giant who had been standing by his side had long since run back to the circle of believers.

"Faithful servants! Destroy the evil blasphemer before us!" the robed man shouted, pointing at Mitsuru.

The leaf-men strode to the outer wall of the hospital, and began to climb like great apes. Mitsuru watched from the top of the roof with great interest. Then, when they were close to the top, he swung his staff and began another incantation. "Arrow of my inner will be upon you!" he shouted, and the two monsters of dried leaves stopped cold. Then they began to descend just as fast as they had gone up.

"What? What's happening?" The robed man gaped. He staggered back, stepping on the hem of his robe and falling to the forest floor with a thud. His scream cut through the darkness as the leaf-men approached.

"I banish you!" rang out Mitsuru's sharp voice, and the two leaf-men—their hands around the robed man's throat—lost their form, and collapsed into piles of dried leaves.

"And that's that," Mitsuru said, throwing his staff over one shoulder. "Call up as many of those as you want, you'll wear yourself out."

The group of believers wavered and dropped their candles. Expecting the worst, Wataru braced himself. But when he saw what happened next, he could only laugh.

All at once, the believers began prostrating themselves on the ground. Some held their heads in their hands, begging that their lives be spared, while others bowed over and over again—and not to the robed man. They were bowing to Mitsuru where he stood atop the roof of the hospital.

Wataru, still smiling, looked up at Mitsuru. "I think we're okay! Thanks."

Mitsuru wasn't smiling. In fact, he looked almost frightened. He let his staff down from his shoulder and stood with his feet wide apart.

"You sicken me," he said looking at the believers and spitting. "Following the strong. You're happy as long as you're doing what everyone else is doing, is that it?"

"Mitsuru? Come down!"

Mitsuru turned his cold gaze toward Wataru. "The show is over, but there's still a barrier to be broken."

"Huh?"

"I'm only standing up here because I didn't want to get too close to the sula trees and their magic—it's too thick, and troublesome to fight against. But with so many people on our side now…"

Wataru took a step toward the building. "What are you talking about? What are you going to do?"

"It takes focused willpower to break a magical barrier. I need to gather enough magic to cut down the forest and scatter every leaf to the four winds."

"Mitsuru…"

"Sorry," Mitsuru said with a grin, glancing at Wataru. "I've no idea where we will be blown to. That's up to the wind. Curl up and cover your head as best you can. I'll pray that you don't get hurt too much."

"What are you talking about?!"

"This."

Mitsuru spread his arms and looked up toward the sky. Then he began to chant in a loud and clear voice:

"Great spirit of the winds, with your power filling all the heavens, I who walk the paths of magic summon you. In your benevolence, sweep away all the magic that binds us, send it to the very depths of the chaotic abyss. *Aero lar stenigel…*"

The gem on the end of Mitsuru's staff shone brightly. A part of the night sky suddenly became brighter. The clouds split.

Then the wind came.

He's calling the wind down from above the clouds.

That was the last coherent thought that passed through Wataru's mind. The next instant, he was tossed like a rag doll to the ground. Finding nothing to grab on to, he hugged his knees and rolled until he bumped into the hospital building. There, he latched on to a standing column, and somehow managed to regain his feet.

He could barely comprehend what he saw next.

From out of the blackness of night, a great cyclone, shimmering with a faint silvery light, whirled into view. Its movement was slow and curving, almost graceful as it whipped from side to side.

It was nearing the ground. One by one, the vortex sucked up the believers. Wataru could see them flailing, and he knew they must be crying, shouting, and praying, but the roar of the winds swallowed them all. He also saw the guillotine snap in two and disappear into the center of the cyclone. The axeman and his axe were also sucked up into the swirling torrent—disappearing forever.

Wataru saw something like a discarded washcloth whipping through the sky. From its folds a hand emerged, then a foot. Finally, he saw a head. It was the robed man, his mouth caught in a soundless scream.

Wataru felt the column shift in his grip. It suddenly became nothing more than a pile of dried leaves. Dismantled by the wind, they scattered in all directions.

And then Wataru too was pulled up into the air.

chapter 21
The Swamp of Grief

Wataru shot across the sky, wrapped in winds, flying so high it made his head spin.

He saw stars through a gap in the clouds below. But they were not stars; they were the lights of various towns. It was strangely quiet here in the eye of the cyclone. A constant, gentle updraft cradled him like a baby in its mother's arms, ensuring he would not fall.

He descended gradually, at last breaking through the clouds. He had no way of knowing how far the storm had carried him—everything below was shrouded in darkness. He could see no signs of where he might be—no roofs of houses, or pastures, or mountain ridges. It seemed to him as though it wasn't the cyclone that was descending, but rather that he was slowly moving toward the bottom of the funnel. It was like he was going down an elevator in the sky.

He touched ground. Released from the cyclone's embrace, his right calf suddenly throbbed with pain, and he fell to the ground. The soil beneath him was wet, sodden, like a sea of mud.

He looked back around to see the silvery tail of the cyclone disappearing up through the clouds. The sky was still dark, and studded with stars.

Mitsuru had warned him that the cyclone wasn't quite under his control. But the storm, ultimately, had been quite kind. Wherever he was now, it was certainly better than where he had been moments before. When he had seen that guillotine, it was like death had been staring him in the face. It had even been worse than the night he spent in that Gasara cell.

His life had been saved two times along the way.

The mud where he lay was cold but soft. Chilly air wrapped around him. Realizing he couldn't sit there forever, he tried to stand, but the ground was so slippery even that proved difficult. He looked around for something to hold on to, but the only thing nearby was a patch of thin reeds, and they provided little in the way of support.

By the time he was standing on two feet again, Wataru was covered in mud. The bandage around the arrow wound on his calf was black and filthy. He knew he had to change it soon. *What was that horrible disease Mom was always saying I'd get? Tetanus or something?*

Wataru parted the stand of reeds with his hands and saw a flat black expanse of ground ahead. *A clearing*, he thought. But when he approached, he found it was less of a clearing and more of a muddy lake. The water rippled faintly in the night breeze, reflecting the starlight. He stood at the quiet shore, and the cold night air enveloped him.

Wataru sneezed. He began to shiver.

Where am I now? It's so dark here, so cold. I'm practically freezing.

He examined his surroundings by the starlight. The muddy lake was so large that much of it faded into the dark distance and he could not see the far shoreline. Behind him a wide expanse of reeds and other swamp grass extended to the edge of his vision as well. There was one irregularity: up ahead and to the right he could see a larger lump of darkness, like a small forest. A faint light came from its center. Wataru stared at it a long time but couldn't tell what it was.

Wataru hugged himself, trying to stay warm, and began to walk. *May as well go and see what I find. Better than staying here and dying of pneumonia. Walking will keep me warm, and maybe dawn will come soon.*

The closer he got to the forest, the better he could see the object that caught his eye. It was a lantern, or maybe even a torch.

The cool, muddy flats seemed completely devoid of life. The silent night was punctuated by the soft cooing of wild birds. He could make out a small, triangular roof among the trees. It was a hut, somewhat smaller than the one where he had first met Wayfinder Lau. Even though it was partially obscured by trees, Wataru could tell the light he'd seen in the distance was emanating from its window.

He knocked on the door and called out, "Hello? Is anybody home?"

There was no answer. He knocked at the door again, announcing him-self as a traveler on the road who had lost his way. There was the sound of faint footsteps, and the door opened inward. A small robed individual peered out—the robe's hood completely masked the person's identity.

"Sorry to call so late at night," Wataru said, bowing his head. "I've lost my way, and I saw your light so I thought—if it's not too much trouble, might I rest here a moment? Perhaps you could help me find my way?"

The voice that came from under the hood was surprisingly soft. "You're wounded."

It's a woman.

Wataru looked at the fingers holding open the door. They were white and slender.

"Please, come in. That wound of yours needs tending to."

The woman stepped to the side and let Wataru into the small room be-yond. A fire was burning brightly in the fireplace. A lamp sat in the window. There was a small rocking chair—still rocking slightly—next to the fireplace where the woman had most likely been sitting a moment before.

She motioned for Wataru to sit on a small wooden stool. She immediately began to tend his injury. A while later, she brought him a mug of something hot and warm.

"Thank you. Thank you so much."

The woman nodded, her face still hidden in the shadow of her hood.

"You should change. I'm afraid I don't have clothes your size, though."

"It's okay."

"Perhaps just a shirt, then. I believe I have one large enough."

Wataru was glad for her charity. Grabbing his muddy shirt and the blood-soaked bandages, the woman stepped outside.

The inside of the hut was sparsely furnished. A small basket sat next to the rocking chair with balls of wool dyed jet black. A half-knit garment was nearby. Comfortable now, and growing more curious, Wataru looked inside the basket. The clothes were tiny—like something a child might wear. He no-ticed a pair of socks, also small. *Maybe she has a child?*

Still, that seemed odd. The half-knitted garments in the basket, and the socks, were all black. *Who gives their child black clothes to wear?* Of course, her clothes were all black too.

"Excuse me," Wataru asked when the woman returned. "Would you, by any chance, happen to be a sorcerer?"

The woman stopped. She seemed to be staring at Wataru.

"It's just that, you're wearing that hood. Maybe, perhaps, you're a star-seer? Are you doing research out here?"

The hood tilted, as though the woman was looking down at the floor. Then she slowly walked over to the rocking chair, sat, and said in a small voice, "It is perhaps best that you do not know much of me." Her voice sounded sad, somehow. "It will soon be dawn. Already, the sky in the east grows light. Go to the far side of this woods and you will find a small road that will take you to the town of Tearsheaven. Speak to the mayor there. He shows kindness to travelers upon the road such as yourself."

"Very well," Wataru said, bowing his head slightly. "Thank you for everything. I'm sorry to have pried. But, really, I was in quite a fix, so thank you again. I just feel odd not even knowing your name or what you look like, and..."

Quizzically, the woman tilted her head slightly to the side. Then she lifted her white hands and drew back her hood.

Deep inside his heart, Wataru screamed.

Rikako Tanaka!

His father's lover. The reason his father abandoned Wataru and his mother. The woman who came to their house and said it was all his mother's fault. The similarity was uncanny. She was ghastly thin.

"Is that better?"

The woman's voice was soft, gentle. She had not a trace of a smile on her face, and none of Rikako's arrogance and aggression. But still, the voice sounded so much like hers. It was even possible to imagine that this was what Rikako's voice sounded like, were she ever to speak softly.

"So long have I worn my clothes of grief, I had forgotten I was even wearing a hood."

Wataru couldn't speak. This, he thought, was a good thing. He had no confidence he would be able to say anything useful at the moment.

"Is something wrong? You seem quite startled," the woman said, taking a half step toward him. Wataru took a step backward.

"My..." the woman put a hand to her cheek. "Have I frightened you, somehow? If that is so, I apologize. But please tell me, why?"

I apologize... Those were words he could never imagine Rikako Tanaka ever saying as long as she lived. *This is Vision. This isn't the real world. She can't be here.*

"I-I'm sorry," Wataru said, shaking his head. "You look so much like someone I knew, it startled me."

"I see." The woman nodded but did not smile, not even a little. It occurred to Wataru that he was looking at a person very deep in grief.

"You said clothes of grief...are you sad?"

The woman quietly walked over to the window and put out the lamp. Then she nodded. "These wetlands, and this lake...are called the Swamp of Grief."

Even with the lamp out, a dim light came through the window. It was nearly dawn. Wataru walked over to stand by her and look out on the black surface of the muddy lake.

"Only those in the deepest grief are permitted to live here on the shore. When our grief is gone, so too must we leave the swamp. While here, we must wear only clothes of black. When we leave, we throw these clothes into the lake."

"And you're not allowed to smile, I take it?"

"That's right. While we remain."

"Who decided all this?"

"It is the law in Tearsheaven."

The woman looked down and rubbed her belly with one hand. "I used to live in town. Perhaps someday I shall return..."

Looking at her hand, something clicked. *I don't believe it.* "Are you... pregnant?"

The woman nodded deeper. "Yes..."

Another thing she has in common with Rikako Tanaka. Is this a coincidence? Is there some sort of weird synchronization between Vision and the real world?

"What is it?" the woman asked, looking into Wataru's eyes. "You're sweating. I hope you've not caught a cold walking along the lake."

Hearing the concern in her voice, Wataru tried to rein in his wildly roaming thoughts. *This isn't her. She's too kind. She must've lived an entirely differ-*

Something else didn't fit, though. A baby should be the happiest thing in the world. Yet here she was, sunken in grief. *I know,* Wataru thought, *I'll bet the father of this child died. That's why she's here. That has to be it.*

"I'm sure you'll be better soon," Wataru said, though he had no reason to believe she would. Still it gave him confidence to find that he could be gentle with this woman. *She's not her.*

The woman looked down at Wataru. Just then, the rising sun lit her face, casting a golden light on Rikako's features. Wataru saw the reflected gleam in her eyes, and again the anger rose inside him, and again he forced it back down. *No. No! It's not her!*

"You're kind to say that. Thank you." The woman rubbed Wataru's shoulder gently, then pushed him toward the door. "But, you should leave. And please, do not tell the people in Tearsheaven of the kind words you gave me."

She closed the door without even saying goodbye.

Wataru walked around the hut, finding a small path leading out of the woods on the other side. The path wasn't as wet as it had been on the shore of the muddy lake, and so Wataru walked, listening to the good-morning calls of little birds in the trees around him. Out of the woods, the road became wider, a path with ruts left from the weight of darbaba carts. Wataru came up on a sign.

Nearing Tearsheaven

Just below the neatly printed block letters announcing the town, someone had scrawled graffiti:

Happy? Stay away!

Chapter 22
Tearsheaven

Nearing was an understatement.

The town sat in the middle of a large, even field, encircled by a pretty white stone fence. On the side facing the road was a gate much smaller than the one at Gasara. A heavily built watchman sat atop a small platform by the gate, smoking a cigarette.

Something seemed different to Wataru about this town from the other places he had visited in Vision, but he couldn't quite put his finger on it. As he was thinking about it, the watchman called out in a booming voice. "You over there, boy! Have you business in Tearsheaven?"

Rubbing his hurting leg, Wataru thought. The graffiti he had seen on the sign was fresh in his mind. *Am I happy?*

In the end, he replied simply, "I'm not sure." It was the truth. "I got lost and—I'm not even really sure where this is. Am I still in the country of Bog?"

The watchman stuck his cigarette in his mouth and leapt down to the ground. He walked toward Wataru. "Not even close," he said. "This here's Arikita—though we're a sight closer to the border with Bog than we are to the capital. Where did you come from again?"

"From outside Lyris."

The watchman's mouth gaped open, and his cigarette fell to the ground. He was a beastkin, with clear blue eyes. "That's quite a journey! Don't tell me you walked all that way on that leg? Looks like you got yourself into a bit of a scrape."

When Wataru explained that a cyclone had picked him up and deposited him in the Swamp of Grief, the watchman's mouth gaped even wider.

But it didn't seem to be the story of the cyclone that was the source of his amazement.

"The Swamp of Grief, eh?" he said in a low growl, whiskers twitching. "Did you run into anyone by the lakeside there, boy?"

Wataru mentioned how the woman dressed in black had helped him. He had only made it halfway through his story when the watchman practically howled with astonishment. "A hut? You're telling me he's built her a hut? Who'd have thought Yacom had it in him!" The beastkin looked at Wataru. "Boy, welcome to Tearsheaven. The mayor would like to meet you, I'm sure."

The watchman took one look at Wataru's limp and offered him a piggyback ride, which Wataru gladly accepted. Upon entering the town, the reasons for its novelty became readily apparent. The buildings were flat. The roofs were perfectly level, with wide troughs running along their edges. In addition, they were all built extremely close together.

"Interesting construction you have here," Wataru said from the watchman's back.

"I suppose it would seem that way to someone who knew nothing of this place," the watchman said, smiling. "These are built to catch every last drop of rain that falls. We filter it, and filter it again to make our tears."

"Tears?"

"The purest water in the world. Used for the finest medicines and the most expensive perfumes."

The mayor's residence was in the very middle of a cluster of cube-like buildings. To get there, they had to actually open the doors to many of the surrounding houses and walk through them. Each time they went in a door, Wataru expected to be walking into someone's living room.

"Certain houses are designated for public passage, on account of the town being built this way," the watchman explained. That explained the lack of significant furniture in the houses they walked through. Still, when they reached the office of the mayor, it too was rather bare—hardly different from the public passage houses they had come through. The only furniture was a simple wooden desk and chair, and a small table.

"Greetings!" said a waterkin with a large red fin sticking out from the top of his head. "I am Mag, the mayor of Tearsheaven."

As it was clear that the important posts in this town were taken not by ankha but by other species, Wataru felt secure in relating his encounter with the followers of the Old God at Triankha Hospital. He related everything up to his meeting with the woman in black in the swamp. But he did not mention the kind words he had given her, as she had requested.

"A surprising tale, indeed," Mayor Mag said, knocking himself on the head with large webbed hands. "And you, a Highlander at your young age. Impressive, most impressive. But you must be worried for your friends."

Continuing, he said, "Head west from here, and just over the border to Bog you will find the town of Sakawa. The waterkin there do more than transport goods, they also trade in information. Ask around, and you'll be sure to find your missing friends."

"Thank you so much. I'll go there as soon as I can."

"No," the mayor said, "I think you'd best stay and mend your leg first. We have the best medicines and poultices here, you know. Medicine brewed using our tears is better than any you can buy in other parts."

Wataru wondered if all mayors were like this: part politician, part salesman.

"Mayor," said the watchman suddenly, "perhaps I should fetch Yacom's wife?"

"Wataru here might be a fine Highlander," said the major, "but he's still a boy. I would not involve him in this affair."

"It's just, not a soul has gone to see that woman since we sent her out. If Wataru were to tell his story…"

"Sent her out?" Wataru asked. "Was she exiled from the village for some reason?" He remembered her saying that she used to be a resident of Tearsheaven.

The mayor hung his head sorrowfully a moment, then said, "Very well, Wataru, I'd like you to come with me. Don't worry. It's not far."

The watchman went back to his post, and the mayor took Wataru by his hand. They passed through one house, and when they opened the next door, the mayor called out in a bright voice, "Morning, ladies, how does the day find you?"

They appeared to be in a hospital. Six simple beds were lined up in a bright, warm room, five of which were occupied. The occupants were all women of different races.

"Ah, Sara—here to see your mother?"

In the nearest bed lay an ankha woman. Her face was pale and she was horribly thin. Watching over her was a girl with dark eyes—young enough to be in kindergarten. The mayor gave the girl a hug. "Sara, you've grown into quite the beauty, haven't you!" he said, rubbing her cheek. "I'd sure like to see you happier though. The sun is up. You should be outside, playing."

The girl was very cute. Their eyes met, and Wataru smiled, but the girl's eyes were cold.

"I'm sorry, Mag," the woman in the bed said in a fragile voice. Her head never left the pillow. "I have gotten much better, but still…"

"Never you mind about that. The last thing you want to do is trouble yourself, Satami. The only medicine in this world better than one made from our tears is time itself."

The mayor sat Sara on the bed and patted her on the head. "Well now," the mayor continued with a smile, "I'm off to show our little guest here around. Listen to what the doctor says, and rest up well. Agreed?"

Wataru followed the mayor back to his offices. When he sat down he noticed that the mayor's eyes were as dark as the little girl Sara's had been.

"Now, Wataru," the mayor began. "The woman you met on the shore of the lake in the Swamp of Grief is named Lili Yannu. Three months ago, for various reasons, I cast her out of this village. She may not return until I, and the rest of the residents, permit it. Nor may she go elsewhere. There is no other town that would take in a castaway from Tearsheaven."

"What crime did she commit to have this happen to her?"

Mayor Mag sighed. The fin on top of his head wobbled to the side. "Before I tell you that, I should tell you a bit about the history of Tearsheaven."

As it turned out, Tearsheaven was known as the Town of Sorrow long before the formation of the United Southern Nations.

"There is little different in our lives here from that of other places. What *is* different is that all of the residents here once lived elsewhere. They only came here because, at some point in their life, they knew such sadness that they wished to die. You see, here, they have a chance to heal. This town serves as a sort of hospital for the heart, you might say. Those who live here stay only until their illness is cured. That is why our houses and furnishings are so simple."

Once their sorrow was cured, residents could leave anytime. "And we never see them again," the mayor explained. "The reasons for our residents' sorrows are many. Some lost those whom they loved, or were betrayed by those whom they trusted. We do not inquire too deeply about these matters. We only live together, help each other, and wait until time heals our wounds. Some leave after only half a year, others after ten. The depth of each sorrow is different."

The start of the local industry, making tears out of rainwater, was a relatively recent event.

"We began producing tears in earnest only thirty years ago. The mayor before myself, a bright fellow, was the one who noticed the purity of the local rainfall, and he realized also the value of simple labor that still requires constant attention in the mending of sorrows."

Once the production of tears became the local industry, the town's buildings were remodeled to look the way they did now. In Arikita, the tears sold for an incredible price, and so the town grew quite well off as a result.

"No one knows exactly why the water that falls here is so pure, though the great starseers in Sasaya claim that winds sweep the white mist enshrouding the Undoor Highlands far to the south all the way here, where it falls as rain."

Undoor Highlands: home to the mysterious Special Administrative State of Dela Rubesi. Bastion of belief in the Old God.

"No matter how pure the rainwater, you must distill it to make the tears. Through this purification process, the water becomes even clearer, and that which is impure is left behind. These impurities we take to a place not far from our village, a dark swamp where neither fish nor bird choose to live: the Swamp of Grief."

So that lake was like their trashcan. Wataru remembered the cold feel of the mud, the utterly still water. He shivered.

"And that's our town," Mayor Mag continued. "All our residents are, in a way, visitors. We know our population down to the single person. And we have one rule that is more important than any other. Since everyone is here to mend themselves of some sadness, we must look out for one another, encourage one another, and give one another space to heal. We cannot, under any circumstances, allow strife in Tearsheaven, for that would generate only more sadness. Lili Yannu was the first to openly break that law in the long, long history of this town."

She had stolen another woman's husband, the mayor explained. "That woman you saw in the hospital, Satami—her husband, a merchant named Yacom, fell in love with Lili, and she became pregnant. Together, they planned to elope."

Suddenly, Wataru's world went red. He heard a sound like a tidal wave crashing against his inner ears, and for moment he was deaf to everything. He could only watch Mayor Mag's sad face and moving, soundless lips…

She is Rikako Tanaka.

She did the same thing as Rikako Tanaka.

She's an invader, just like Rikako Tanaka.

A parasite feeding on the happiness of others.

"When we discovered the truth, I banished Lili Yannu at once," the Mayor was saying. "Satami forgave her husband, and he returned to her. I was hoping that they could put the past behind them no matter how long it took. But Yacom's heart was captive. Claiming business, he fled town, and went back to Lili. He lives elsewhere now, and I believe, still visits her."

The mayor explained that it was Yacom who built the hut in which Lili Yannu lived. "Poor, poor Sara," the mayor said, wiping his eyes.

"What sadness brought Satami and her family to this town in the first place?" Wataru asked, finally regaining his voice.

"They hail from Bog. There was a plague there, and Satami lost both her parents, and a child—younger than Sara. They came here only a year ago."

"And the woman Lili Yannu?"

"I heard she lost her betrothed to illness. Her father is a starseer in Sasaya, a very important man. The one whom she was to marry was also a starseer in training."

Wataru broke out in a cold sweat. The back of his shirt felt damp. His heart was racing as though he had been running at full speed.

Sara's dark eyes floated in his mind. *Those eyes—they're mine. When Rikako Tanaka was saying those things to Mom, when she told her she was pregnant, when she said she would take me away, when I hid under the bed. I had those eyes too. If Lili Yannu is Rikako Tanaka, then Sara is me. And Satami, lying pale and worn on the bed, is Mom.*

"How could she?" Wataru said quietly. He hadn't thought to say it—it was as though his mouth had formed the words of its own accord.

Mayor Mag tilted his head and looked at Wataru. "What was that?"

Wataru wiped his face with a hand. "How can Yacom be convinced he's done wrong?"

The mayor looked at him with wide eyes. "How, indeed."

"If Yacom is still visiting Lili Yannu at her hut, then it might be possible to meet him, to talk to him directly."

"It might, but we who live in Tearsheaven are not permitted to go near the Swamp of Grief. The pollution there would cling to us."

"Then I'll go," Wataru said crisply. "I don't live here, I'll be fine."

Mayor Mag seemed flustered. "But you're just a child…"

"And a Highlander."

"That is true, but…"

"Mayor, I have much in common with Sara. My father left my mother for another woman. He made up all sorts of reasons, pretending that what he was doing was somehow right. I know what it's like to be abandoned. Please, let me try to bring Yacom back. For Sara's sake!"

Mayor Mag's mouth opened and closed, his red fin wobbled from side to side, he clasped his hands and shook them, and for a while was unable to speak. Finally, he gave a short sigh. "Very well. This is not something I would be able to do myself in any case. To you who understands Sara's sorrow, I entrust this task."

chapter 23
Dark Water

Mayor Mag insisted that Wataru stay clear of the Swamp of Grief until his wounds healed. He was assured that the curative properties of Tearsheaven would have him back on the road in ten days or less.

While he recuperated, Wataru walked around town and toured the facilities where they made the tears. He even learned a bit of the craft himself. It rained in Tearsheaven every day—for about an hour in the mornings and evenings. This kept the town reservoirs full, and there was always more water than they could distill in any given day.

The lustrous, silky white cloth used in the refining process was also spun locally. It was woven from threads made from the fiber of a peculiar grass called huhulune, and was quite valuable. Everyone who worked on the tears had to wear clothes made entirely of this indigenous grass. Clothes made from huhulane were very expensive—one outfit, for example, would cost an entire year's salary in a place like Nacht.

When she had been working, Satami was a weaver in one of the workshops. Weaving the fibrous turf was a taxing chore, requiring great focus of mind. More than half of the weavers were women. These days, when Sara was not by her mother's bed, she would be in the workshop, where some of her mother's friends took care of her. Wataru would wave and say hello whenever he saw her, but she would shyly run away, or hide behind a nearby adult. She never warmed up to him no matter how much he tried.

There were few children in Tearsheaven. Most of the residents had come alone, and many of them went for weeks without having contact with the outside world.

"It makes sense, if you think about it," Bhuto had said. "The people here…their family and friends couldn't cure what ailed them. Or, even worse, they're here because they lost family and friends in the first place. They come to us with two burdens: sadness and loneliness."

Bhuto had been born in Nacht. A drifter by profession, he was a hired hand in the direct employ of Mayor Mag.

"It was about five years ago, I guess. Ran into somebody at a gatehouse wanting to go to Tearsheaven, and too afraid to make the journey alone. So I helped him along the way." He had ended up staying in the town. "There are lots of women here, so most of the men are busy doing strong-work, like carrying water. They needed more people for guard duty. The mayor asked me to stay."

He seemed like a nice enough person, but Wataru had no doubt that when push came to shove, Bhuto could shove pretty hard.

"I've been a drifter since as long as I can remember, so it doesn't bother me too much being alone. Funny, isn't it? Loneliness isn't such a bad thing, but mix in a little anger and sadness, and it can become the worst punishment in the world."

It was a little after noon. Bhuto was puffing on a cigarette, while Wataru dangled his feet from atop a town gate.

"Not that being a watchman is all that demanding a job. If you see someone on the road, you ask if they're a visitor to Tearsheaven. If they are, you open the gate. If they're not, you wave them along. That's about it. It's just an excuse to sit out in the sun."

Shortly, an individual riding an udai approached the gate.

"Ooy!" Bhuto called out. "Have you business in Tearsheaven?"

The rider took one hand off the reins and waved, calling out, "I'm a traveling merchant! Have you business with me?"

"You got tobacco?"

"All kinds, my friend. All kinds."

The traveling merchant was an ankha man, and his goods included cakes and toys as well as cigarettes. A carved wooden figurine caught Wataru's eye. It was a simple doll, but he thought the smiling face was cute.

"Can I buy this?" he asked. "For Sara," he explained to Bhuto.

Bhuto smiled. "You'd make a good brother!"

The traveling merchant dismounted. Between cigarette puffs, he proceeded to make small talk. There had been a strange occurrence over in the woods north of Lyris, he said. Apparently, a curious silvery cyclone had appeared out of nowhere and took a good chunk of forest with it.

Bhuto listened to the story intently, his face blank, but never once betraying the fact that he had heard of the cyclone before—and that it had carried the boy sitting next to him all the way to Tearsheaven. The watchman of the town of sorrows knew the value of tight lips.

"By the by," the traveler said, finishing his cigarette and mounting his udai. "Have you heard the rumors of folks selling counterfeit tears?"

Bhuto leaned forward, his expression suddenly intense. "What?"

"Just something I heard in Arikita, haven't seen it myself. Someone out there is selling tears made in a place that's not Tearsheaven, and for a fine price. Of course, any price would be too high—I hear that these false tears have claimed a few lives already."

"Something's got to be done about that," Bhuto said severely.

"Someone is out there selling counterfeit tears…" Wataru said, thinking aloud. "Is there any way of distinguishing them from the real thing?"

As far as he knew, tears looked just like water. Put them in a bottle with a convincing label, and no one would be able to tell the difference.

"Of course there is," Bhuto answered. "It's simple. Fish can't live in real tears. A guppy in a bowl of tears would die by the time you counted to ten. Not that it's poison, mind you. It's too pure for them, you see. Our buyers always use the fish test to prove what they're getting is the real deal."

"Then these counterfeit tears are even worse!" Wataru exclaimed, standing up. "They must be adding something to kill fish."

"Yet that's not the case," the traveling merchant said, shaking his head. "The Highlanders in Arikita are a tough bunch, and not ones to be easily taken in. The moment they heard that a patient had died in an unusual manner, they confiscated the remaining tears, and had a look. They found no poison in it at all. The only thing they discovered was a bit of medicine used for their brew."

Bhuto snorted in response. "If the branch in Arikita is on the move, then this is no passing affair."

They rushed to tell Mayor Mag. He greeted the news with wide, rolling eyes, burbling, "If this is all true, then the future of the whole town is at stake!"

Wataru left the mayor's office with a heavy heart. Out on the street, he caught sight of Sara. She was running as fast as her legs would carry her from the workshop toward the town gate.

"What's wrong?" Wataru called out, running after her. The little girl didn't look around, but continued straight for the gate.

"Oy there, Sara! What's the matter?" Bhuto called down from his perch.

"Where's the udai?" she asked, breathlessly. "I heard an udai came to the gate."

"Ah, that was a traveling merchant, my girl. He's left already."

Sara's head drooped. She looked so forlorn that Wataru merely stopped and looked at her, lacking the right words to say.

Bhuto leaned out from atop the gate and called down to her gently. "Don't worry, if your father's udai came back, I would shout the news so loud you'd be able to hear me no matter where you were."

So she was hoping it was her father... Wataru felt an ache in his chest.

"Now, Sara," Bhuto said, pointing to Wataru. "This gentleman here has something for you. I wonder what it is?"

Wataru hurriedly fished the wooden doll out of his pocket. Kneeling so his eyes were on a level with Sara's, he handed it to her. "Here."

For a while Sara stood, arms behind her back, staring at the tiny doll. "That's for me?" she said, looking at Wataru's face at last.

"Yep."

"Why?"

"Its face reminded me of yours."

Hesitantly, the little girl reached out her fingers and touched the doll. Wataru gently pressed it into her palm.

"Thank you," she said in a small voice. "What's his name?"

Wataru blinked. "Uh...I don't know."

"He wants you to give the doll a name," Bhuto suggested to Sara.

"Tochee," Sara said, patting the doll on her head with a finger.

"Tochee? That's a nice name."

"It's my sister's."

Sara's younger sister. The one who died of the plague.

"Mom says that Tochee became a star, and she's never coming home. But Dad will come home. He will, won't he?"

"Just you stay happy and healthy, and I'm sure he will," Bhuto assured her. Wataru stood with his hands clenched into fists, watching the little girl run back to the workshop.

It was two days later that the word came: Yacom had been spotted near the Swamp of Grief.

Wataru prepared to leave for the swamp immediately. His leg was almost healed, and Mayor Mag lent him a swift udai. He also gave him a set of what looked like paddles. The udai could wear them on its hooves like snowshoes for crossing wet terrain.

"Put these on, and your udai will never get snared in the swamp."

Wataru had no script for what he would say when he met Yacom. He only knew how much Sara missed her father, and how much pain she felt. If he could only get that across, things would work out. They had to.

As he passed through the woods and approached Lili Yannu's hut, he noticed that the windows were boarded and no smoke came from the chimney. Wataru knocked on the door and the windows, but he got no response.

Maybe they had left together? He tried waiting around, but no one came. Wataru mounted his udai again, and set off toward the lake. He couldn't imagine anyone going there voluntarily, but who knows? If you make your living in the swamp, perhaps a trip to the lake is a requirement.

The swamp water was jet black, even under the midday sun. Not a single ripple marred its dull matte surface. Knowing that all the impurities from the town's rainwater had been dumped here, Wataru couldn't help but feel something horribly unclean lurked beneath the surface. It was as if the water itself was a giant living thing, like an amoeba, silently waiting. If anyone approached, thought Wataru, the creature would lash out with a giant tentacle like a pseudopod. Once it had devoured its prey, it would settle back, perfectly still, pretending to be a great black lake once again.

Even evil and filth needs to sustain itself with energy from somewhere.

Wataru chided himself. *Why do I make these things up? Is it just to scare myself?* He gave himself a rap on the head with his knuckles, and urged his steed to hurry forward toward the deserted shore.

Just then he heard a faint sound coming from the underbrush at the edge of the lake.

—*Kee...*

Wataru stopped his udai and listened. Had he been hearing things? Had it been a bird or an animal of some kind? But nothing lived here in this swamp.

—*Kee keee, kuh kuh kuh.*

It was definitely some sort of animal. It sounded weak. Wataru looked around. Then he heard it again, close.

A clump of reeds just ahead of him rustled suspiciously. For the briefest of moments he caught a glimpse of something that looked like a red wing.

Wataru got off his udai, and drawing his Brave's Sword, he slowly approached the clump. Brushing aside the reeds with his empty hand, he found the red wing immediately. To his surprise, it wasn't a bird. Instead of down and feathers, he saw scales—deep crimson scales. And at the tip of the wing, there was a claw as big as Wataru's own hand.

It's a dragon.

Wataru was so startled he forgot to breathe. A dragon was lying on its side, half submerged in the water of the Swamp of Grief. Its wings and forelimbs moved weakly. It seemed to be in pain.

The dragon's dark eyes blinked, and its long mouth snapped open. Fangs glowed white like pearls in its maw.

"Oh? A man-child!" the dragon said, raising its voice. "Yer a good man-child, aren'tcha? Help a dragon out?"

Wataru was stunned. Here was this magnificent, fantastical beast—albeit lying on its side half submerged in mud—and it spoke in a voice that was plain, almost childish.

"What's the matter?" Wataru asked, stepping closer to the dragon, careful not to step in any puddles. The dragon lashed out a long, forked tongue and made a short barking sound. Wataru froze.

"Touch the water and you'll regret it!" the dragon warned.

"It's fine, I'm wearing boots. As long as I don't lose my footing..."

The dragon assessed the youngster in front of him. "I see. Good manchild, you'll put that sword away won't you? Promise not to bite."

Wataru sheathed his sword and took another step closer. Gingerly, he reached out a hand, and touched the dragon near the neck. The scales were dry and warm to the touch. *A bit like Kee Keema's shoulder.*

"Are you wounded?"

The dragon lowered its eyes mournfully. "I was doin' a few loop-de-loops and kinda got carried away, see. Lost my balance...and ended up like this."

Now that's funny. So dragons make mistakes too.

"So you fell? Well, you're lucky that the ground you landed on was so soft..."

"Lucky?!" the dragon cut him off. "This swamp water is like some kind of numbing potion! As soon as I landed in it, I felt my body freeze up. And now I can't move, 'cept for the front half of my body. My neck, these two hands—the smallest ones I've got. And this mud is too wet for me to dig in my claws! See?" he said, groping futilely at the mud. "What's a dragon to do?"

It became obvious to Wataru that this dragon was young—just a kid. Still, he was over six feet long. How was he going to drag this creature out of the water? Then he had an idea.

"If you could somehow get a foothold, do you think you could drag your-self out of the water?"

"Sure," the dragon said, nodding. "And if I can dry my wings, I'd be able to fly out."

"Wait a second, okay?" Wataru said, dashing back to his udai. He pulled two paddles from the animal's hooves and brought them back to the prone dragon. "Here, put these on your hands. They should allow you to grab onto the mud."

The dragon did what he was told, and though his progress was slow, he began to inch out of the water. "Yerrrsh!" he said with great effort. Wataru imagined his face would have turned beet red, if it wasn't red already.

Finally, his wings emerged from the water. The parts that had been sub-merged hung limp, as if anesthetized. The sight sent a shiver down Wataru's spine.

"Just a little farther!" Wataru put a hand on his back and pushed. Finally, most of the dragon was out of the water, leaving only his tail dangling in the murky blackness.

"Just a bit more!"

"Yoik?" The dragon's eyes opened wide. "Gah! It's a kalon!"

"Huh? What?"

The dragon twisted and turned, trying to shake his tail. "A kalon! A kalon's eating my tail!"

Wataru looked to the lake to see the stillness of the water disturbed by a thrashing where the dragon's tail disappeared beneath the surface.

"What's a kalon?!"

"The only fish mean enough to live in this lake! Oh, they're fierce eaters!" The dragon scraped at the mud with both arms. "Ack! It's pulling me in! It'll eat me alive!"

Wataru saw that it was true. Even as he struggled, the dragon's body was slowly sliding back into the lake. The paddles on his forelimbs left skid marks on the mud. The waves on the water's surface were growing larger by the moment.

"I'll deal with that fish!" Wataru said, drawing his Brave's Sword.

The dragon shook his head, pushing Wataru away from the water with his wing. "No, no! That little sticker of yours won't dent the kalon's skin. You'll have to cut off my tail!"

Wataru looked back and forth between the dragon's panicked face, and his tail, drawn taut as a fishing line.

"Cut...your tail?"

"What did I just say? Look, I'll tug real hard to pull it out as far as I can. Then you cut it—as close to the water's edge as you can get. Got it? As close as you can! Cut off too much and it'll hurt something fierce and I'm no big fan of that. When I give the signal, you cut as swiftly as you can. And make it a clean cut—I want that sword all the way through the first time, got it? The first time!"

"Wait!"

"Wait?! Wait and the kalon'll eat me alive! You got your sword ready? Get a good footing, now. Ready? I'm going! One, two, three!"

Then the dragon yanked on his tail with every ounce of his strength. In a daze, Wataru lifted his sword and aimed for the tail right where it emerged from the water, a trembling taut cord of energy.

Snick!

Wataru felt the blade connect. The dragon howled. The lake water erupted with waves, and through the spray, Wataru saw something like a great round saw blade arc above the surface, before disappearing into the dark depths.

"That hurt!!!" The dragon thrashed with its forelimbs on the mud. Great tears fell from its eyes. "I said as close to the water as possible! You cut practically half the thing off!"

Wataru sighed, unsure what to say. "What was that thing?" he said at last.

"What was—I told you! A kalon!"

"I mean that thing like a round saw blade. Was that its mouth?"

"Nah, just the back fin. Its teeth are much, much longer than all that. Believe me, I know," he added, glancing back at his tail.

The severed section was about as thick as a large carrot. Red blood seeped from the wound. Wataru was worried at first, but before his eyes, the wound slowly began to close, and the blood stopped quicker than the dragon's tears.

"It's cold," the dragon muttered, shaking. When he shivered, the grass around him shivered as well. "Think you might give me some room?"

Wataru took a step back.

"A bit more room than that. Say, back by that udai of yours."

Wataru did as he was asked, and from a distance, he watched as the dragon took a deep breath, and, angling his neck back toward the lake, he breathed.

Wrrrooooooooarrr!

Wataru's mouth gaped open. A great jet of flame came from the dragon's maw, like a giant-sized flamethrower. The heat wave washed over the dragon, pushing its way up the slope to Wataru. He felt it on his skin like a dry wind—a moment of heat, followed by a faint singed smell.

That's my hair burning.

"Dry at last, dry at last," the dragon said gleefully, and gave his wings a mighty flap. His eyes were dry too. "You okay up there? Thanks a bunch. Your sword wielding could use a little work, but the long and the short of it is, you saved my life. And I thank you for that."

"I d-don't know about that," Wataru stammered, his knees knocking together. The dragon moved lightly up the slope toward him.

"Where'd you come from, anyway? Where're you headed to? You've got an udai. You a traveling merchant?"

"Uh, yeah, something like that."

"Hrm. Then I'll give you something you're sure to appreciate in return for helping me out."

The dragon lifted a claw—small in comparison to his large body—and plucked a bright red scale from the back of his neck.

"Here, take this."

Wataru took the scale. It looked like it was cut from a precious gem.

"Bring that to Lyris, find yourself a good craftsman, and have him make you a flute. A wyrmflute! Blow upon it once, and no matter where you are, I'll hear it. I'll come flying and give you a ride on my back. We can go wherever you like."

But there was a catch.

"Wyrmflutes are fragile things. You'll only get one use of out it, so use it wisely, eh?"

"Thank you."

"My pleasure! And with that…"

The dragon waved goodbye, and began to slowly beat his wings. Gradually his speed increased as he went from an idle to full throttle.

The dragon's thick hind legs were just lifting off the swampy ground when Wataru shouted, "Hey! What's your name? I'm Wataru!"

"And I'm Jozo!" the dragon yelled back, his wings beating ever faster. "Descendant of the great firewyrm!"

Jozo took off. Wataru lifted his arms to shield himself from the mighty swirl of wind. The dragon was little more than a speck of red against the blue sky by the time the wind calmed down.

Wow! A real dragon! The only time Wataru had heard mention of a dragon in Vision was when Kutz had told him the story of the firewyrm. He hadn't even suspected that dragons were things that spoke, flapped their wings, and fell out of the sky. Amazing.

He was so absorbed in thinking about the dragon that he didn't bat an eye when he saw the small udai cart stopped at the edge of the lake. The flat bed of the cart was filled with small bottles. The rider had walked away, down to the edge of the Swamp of Grief. His hands were moving, doing something.

His hands are in the water!

Wataru shouted out, "You there! Stop! Don't touch the water!"

His warning rang out like a bell across the lifeless lake. The man at the water's edge shot upright and whirled around to look in Wataru's direction.

Wataru galloped his udai out toward the water. As he approached, he saw the man snap to attention. He was wearing a hood that concealed his face.

Even as Wataru drew nearer, the man didn't retreat. Wataru could feel his eyes observing him through the slit in his hood.

"Are you lost?" Wataru asked, dismounting. "If you're thirsty, I have drinking water. Believe me, you don't want to touch the swamp here."

The man was wearing sturdy leather boots, a tight-fitting, long-sleeved shirt and pants, and a leather jacket with many pockets—typical traveling merchant garb. Wataru looked closer, and saw that the man was wearing sturdy gloves. In one hand he held a bottle much like the ones stacked in his cart. The rim of the bottle was damp.

"The water in the swamp is like an anesthetic..." Wataru began. Then suddenly a little spark ignited deep down inside of him.

The bottles on the cart. The hooded man. The lake water.

—There are counterfeit tears about.

—People have died.

What Wataru knew and what he was seeing suddenly came together. His eyes opened wide. The next moment, the hooded man was hurling the bottle at him.

Wataru moved aside in the nick of time. The man turned to run, heading back toward his udai cart.

"Wait!" Wataru shouted, drawing his Brave's Sword almost by reflex. When the man heard the sword being drawn, his boots came to a sudden halt on the wet ground. He turned. "Brazen lad, you think you can wave your sword about and threaten me?"

The voice was clearly a man's, and by his tone, it was clear he wouldn't hesitate to harm Wataru.

"More than that, I'm taking you in." Wataru yanked up his shirt sleeve, revealing his armband. "By the authority of the Highlanders!"

The hooded man laughed. "Now this is a surprise! What has the branch fallen to, giving a firewyrm band to the likes of you. Tell me, boy, do you take the band off when your mama sings you to sleep at night? Come now, admit it. You're lying. That's no real armband. You're playing at being a Highlander!"

Wataru didn't budge. "And you're gathering water from the swamp and selling it as tears! Well, your medicine is killing people. Do you know exactly what you've done?"

The man clapped his hands together and laughed out loud. "I think it's you that needs to consider your position here, boy."

Swiftly reaching under his jacket, he pulled something out and pointed it at Wataru.

It was—a gun. It had more curvy parts than any real-world guns Wataru had seen, but its purpose and function were clear.

Wataru took a step back, and the hooded man came a step closer. "Ah, you know what this is? Impressive! Not many people know a magegun by sight. The latest from Arikita. Far better than a sword in any fight. The moment you lifted your blade, I would take you down with the merest twitch of my finger."

"I know guns," Wataru replied quietly. It was hard to keep his voice calm with his heart racing wildly.

"Then you've saved me a lot of tiresome explanation. Boy, if you value your life, you'll be quiet and do as you're told. I'm leaving here now. When I leave, you'll forget you ever saw me, and you'll tell no one. You wouldn't want to waste your life at such a young age and make your mama cry, would you?"

Wataru took a half step to the right. The barrel of the magegun followed him precisely.

"Don't think you can just turn around and flee. It's not the kind of thing you can run away from. Look, I'm giving you a chance because you're just a kid. A stupid one, it seems."

"I'm no kid, I told you, I'm a Highlander. I have a responsibility to the people of Tearsheaven, and a responsibility to the people whose lives will be taken by your fake tears."

"Bah!" the hooded man spat. "What's the point protecting a town like that? The biggest collection of crybabies in history."

"You don't know what they've been through! You know nothing!"

"You're wrong there. I know plenty about Tearsheaven. See, I was stuck in that accursed place until just recently."

The hooded man put a hand on the saddle of his udai. "Sorry, but I've got no more time to waste chatting with you." He then pulled on the reins and made to jump into the saddle. Wataru charged.

Eyes wide, the man brought the magegun around until it was pointed straight at Wataru. He fired.

Bang!

Before Wataru had time to duck, a brilliant flash of light filled his eyes. There was smoke and the zing of metal against metal. Wataru stood unharmed.

"Huh?"

It was just like before. The Brave's Sword in his hand had moved on its own, slicing from left to right in front of him, knocking the bullet from the magegun out of the air.

Startled, the hooded man glanced down at the revolver in his hand, then lifted the barrel again. "I don't know what kind of trick you pulled, but that's your last chance!"

The gun fired again. *Stay calm.* Wataru let the sword do its work. The blade leapt in his hand again, knocking aside the bullet. The shot whizzed through the air and into the lake—a cold splash of water landed on his cheek.

"How many bullets do you have in that gun?" Wataru asked, slowly closing the distance between him and the hooded man. "Want to try firing them all and see what happens?"

The man growled and nimbly leapt astride his udai. Then, pointing the barrel of his gun at the rope attaching the harness on the udai to the cart, he fired.

Wataru watched the man move—everything seemed to be in slow motion, and there was a voice ringing in his head.

Wataru, use the Brave's Sword.

It seemed like the voice was somehow coming from the sword—from the gemstone fixed to its hilt. The voice ran up Wataru's fingers, up his arm, and echoed in his head.

Use the sword. Not only guns may fire bullets.

Without hesitating, Wataru lifted his Brave's Sword and aimed for the man's arm.

The sword moved again on its own. Swiftly the tip cut a cross in the air, then returned to the center of the cross. As the blade moved, Wataru recited the words he heard in his mind.

"Great Goddess, send the power of your holy spirit into the void!"

The gem on the hilt of the sword glowed. A white light shot from the tip of the blade, straight toward the man. The bullet of light impacted the man's right shoulder. He screamed and fell to the ground.

The startled udai galloped off, nearly trampling the fallen rider in its haste. Wataru ran to the man. His cheeks burned with excitement and exertion. *Who knew the Brave's Sword could do this! Who knew it had such power!*

The man lay on the ground, groaning, hand clapped over his wounded shoulder. His hood had slipped off in the fall, revealing his nose and unshaven chin.

"A Highlander with a mageblade...?" the man grunted, his voice tinged with bewilderment. "And a child! Who...who are you?!"

Wataru knelt by the man, hardly hearing his words. That chin. His nose. He had seen them before. They seem so familiar they looked like, like...

Impossible.

Wataru's logical mind pushed away his instinctual understanding of what was going on, but it couldn't stop the racing of his heart. His left hand slowly reached out toward the man's hood. *No, don't take it off. You don't want to see. You'll regret it,* said a little voice inside him. But he didn't stop.

Wataru ripped off the hood.

The face was his father's—the living image of Akira Mitani, right before his eyes. Those eyes, always cool and collected, sometimes seeming devoid of any feeling at all.

No way!

The man was glaring at Wataru with hatred in his eyes. His teeth were clenched as a result of the pain of his wound.

"Who are you?!" Wataru managed to ask. His tongue was numb in his mouth.

"What's it matter who I am?" The man said, gritting his teeth. "I'm just a man. I don't expect a kid like you to understand, but I'm not a bad man. I'm just someone doing what he can in search of happiness."

"No. I know you who you are. You're Yacom!"

For the first time, a shadow of fear passed over the man's features. He turned his eyes away from Wataru.

"You're Yacom! You abandoned your wife and Sara and ran off—or tried to run off—with Lili Yannu, now banished to the Swamp of Grief..." Wataru figured it out. "You've been selling those counterfeit tears to support her, haven't you? That's how you made the money to build her a house, isn't it?"

Yacom's eyes narrowed dangerously. "How do you know about me and Lili? Who told you those stories?"

"No one told me stories. I've met Lili myself, and I've met your wife Satami. I know Sara too. I know how much she misses her father. That's all."

Yacom, covered with mud, sat up, holding a hand over his wounded shoulder. Something Wataru had said turned the man's eyes as dark as the water of the swamp.

"Who are you to say that? You're just a kid," he muttered, the fight gone from his voice. "Don't tell me. I know what I'm doing, I know I'm being selfish. I know that."

"Then why..."

Yacom faced him, looking so much like Akira Mitani it sent a stab of pain through Wataru's chest.

"What you don't know, boy, is that people have feelings that don't obey logic. Satami's not a bad woman. She's a good worker, and a gentle soul. But when I met Lili I fell in love. I knew I could never go back. Once you know true love, how could you settle for anything less?"

"How do you know that your love with Satami is false, and your love with Lili is true?" Wataru asked, his voice tense.

Yacom's mouth curled in a faint smile. "You'll understand when you become a man."

"I don't want to understand!" Wataru shouted so loud it surprised him. His heart leapt in his chest, threatening to burst out of his mouth.

This isn't my father. This is Yacom—Yacom the traveling merchant. Not Akira Mitani. He's a different person. Even if they look the same, even if he's doing the same thing, hurting the same people, he's not Dad. He's not, he's not.

"Love is the most important thing a person can know," Yacom said, his tone like that of a preacher giving a sermon. "If you should win love once, you'll know it is harder than death to let go. Of course, I can guarantee you'll never meet your true love."

Wataru let his gaze drop to the mud beneath his feet. "What about how Satami feels? What about the love she feels for you? Isn't that real? If what you said is true, then won't it be harder than death itself for Satami to give up her love?"

Yacom shook his head. "Satami doesn't love me. She was only clinging to me for a livelihood."

"How can you just decide that?!"

"You seem to be making a lot of decisions about other people's affairs yourself, boy."

Wataru didn't back down. "What about Sara, then? What about the love she has for her father?"

"That's different. That's the love between a parent and a child."

"You're a coward. You're making up logic just to suit your own whims. Did you know that every time an udai passes by Tearsheaven, Sara runs out as fast as her little legs will carry her. She thinks it's you coming home. Tell me you can look her in the eye and say what you just told me."

For a moment, Yacom fell silent. Then, suddenly, his uninjured right hand moved swiftly, scooping up a clump of mud from the ground and flinging it at Wataru. The young boy ducked to the side, but the wet mud left a trail across his cheek. "Are you crazy?!"

Yacom's eyes were blazing. Hatred shone from them, just as it had when he first drew his magegun.

"Kids...kids...kids!" Yacom shouted. "What's so special about kids! She wouldn't even be alive if it weren't for me! Just being someone's kid doesn't give you the right to latch on to them for your whole life! Bah!" Yacom was raging now. "A life that depends on someone else is not even worth living. I'll kill her myself, with my own hands if I have to. Satami too! If she can't live without me, then I'll spare her the trouble!"

Wataru felt his breath catch in his throat. His cheeks were burning. *He looks just like Dad. No, he is Dad. That voice in my ears isn't Yacom's, it's his. This is Akira Mitani talking to me, saying these things.*

—*I'll never abandon you, Wataru.*

—*If I didn't exist, you never would have been born.*

—*I'll just pretend you weren't born. It never happened. I wasn't there.*

—*I won't abandon you. I'll erase you.*

That's what you want, isn't it Wataru?

Wataru felt dizzy. His legs buckled beneath him. The anger in his heart seethed like magma, yet at the same time, it felt impossibly distant, like his mind and his heart were at opposite ends of the galaxy.

I'm going to fall.

Wataru stuck out his hands, searching for something to hold on to. There was nothing. He wobbled and lurched to one side.

"What's wrong with you, boy?" he heard Yacom asking. His voice sounded muted, like he was hearing him from the other side of a window. It wasn't just Yacom. Everything seemed turned down: the chill of the Swamp of Grief, the gloomy breeze; it was as though a translucent wall separated him from his surroundings. Like he was inside a fishbowl looking out at the world outside.

"You should go home," Yacom said, a slight smile playing across his lips. "Go home and ask your dad. Ask him which one of us is right—you or me. He'll say I'm wrong, of course. But, boy, he is lying. It's not the truth. It's not what he really thinks. If he had to make a decision that would affect his entire life, the only life he gets, he'd come to the same conclusion as I have. You'd be abandoned. And what of it? He gave you your life. You should be grateful for that. And if he wants to throw you out, well, you'll just have to live with it, won't you?"

Everything went black.

chapter 24
A Vision of Death

Falling. Pulled backward. Crashing into the ground straight as a board, looking up at the sky. *Standing at the edge of the water, feeling the sand underneath your feet being washed away by the waves—that's what it feels like.* Falling, falling, falling…

But Wataru didn't fall.

He watched himself split into two.

A translucent Wataru stepped out of his body, like a soul leaving its earthly shell. The soul-Wataru stepped out on the muddy lake, turned and looked back, and smiled knowingly.

Wataru didn't move. He couldn't move. He couldn't speak. He was paralyzed, unable to move a single finger.

It was the mud.

The mud that splashed against his cheek—*its poison has begun to work on me. That's why I'm paralyzed. And the Wataru standing in front of me, that's an illusion, a phantom. The poison is making me see things.*

The phantom took a step toward Yacom. Then, smoothly, it drew the Brave's Sword.

Yacom was sitting in the mud, face twisted with fear. He was shouting something at it.

The ghostly Wataru raised his sword. Yacom covered his face with his own wounded arm. He began screaming for his life.

—*No. I wouldn't do that.*

The sword shone in the phantom's hands, its edge gleaming.

I don't want to kill Yacom I don't want to kill Dad I don't hate Dad this isn't my dad this isn't me—

Then the Brave's Sword swung down.

One stroke, two. Yacom screamed, crawling away on all fours. The blade stuck into his back. In vain, he tried to wrest the sword away from the Wataru apparition. The sharp edge cut into his palm.

Yacom was covered in mud, his face streaked with his own blood. He trembled in fear and could barely move—yet still he tried to escape. The phantom grabbed him by the collar, and put the sword to his neck.

No!

The Brave's Sword broke flesh and blood shot out like a fountain, splashing on the phantom's shirt. Yacom groped desperately for some salvation, but none came. His arm dropped back down to the ground and did not move again.

The specter drew the sword from Yacom's body. He gave it an expert flick, and blood sprayed from the blade. Casually, the sword was resheathed, and Wataru's supernatural twin gave the corpse a swift kick in the side.

With another kick, Yacom's body rolled deeper into the shallows. The lake water seeped into Yacom's clothes, and finally, the weight dragged him down toward the bottom of the swamp.

The dorsal fin of a kalon broke the water's surface. Wataru stood paralyzed as before, frozen to his core with fear. The kalon traced a wide arc around the spot where the corpse sank. A tailfin like a great scythe lifted from the water and slapped at the surface of the lake. The great fish disappeared into the watery depths, leaving an evil silvery afterimage on Wataru's retinas.

The boy's phantom was observing him, a kind smile on his face. Wataru wanted to shake his head, but he couldn't move. He wanted to shout, *What have you done?* but he had no voice.

Still smiling, the apparition turned his back and began to walk away. Wataru found himself following. Even though his legs couldn't move, even though he couldn't walk, he was following. It was almost as if Wataru were the ghost, immaterial, floating through the air.

Where are we going? Wataru's doppelgänger walked steadily forward. His feet squished down in the muck of the swamp, and his head bowed.

Eventually, Lili Yannu's hut came into view. The phantom Wataru walked toward it. He opened the door without knocking or hesitating. Then he stepped inside.

The woman dressed in black was sitting silently in her chair. She held her hands over her face, beneath a large cowl.

Wataru stood next to her, and Lili looked up. Tears streaked her face.

"Ah," she gasped. "You have killed him."

The avenging specter drew his Brave's Sword and smiled.

"I helped you, yet you killed the man I love," Lili said, reaching out and clinging to the hem of his robe. "Why? Why did you kill my Yacom? What evil did he—did we do? We were only in love. We had finally found our true love. Why did you cut him down a like a common criminal? Why did you sink him in the lake, and leave him for the kalon to eat?"

Wataru's phantom image readied his sword. "You are evil," he said. Still smiling, he drove his sword through Lili Yannu's chest. She slumped from the chair without a word onto the floor—a lifeless pile of black cloth.

Sheathing his sword, the apparition stepped closer to Wataru. Suddenly, his head snapped upright, as though waking from a daydream, and his entire body tensed with the shock of suddenly being whole again.

He found himself standing outside Lili Yannu's hut. The door was shut tightly. Wataru was out of breath, as if he had been running at full speed. He was drenched in sweat.

It was all a nightmare.

I was seeing things. None of this really happened. If I just reach out my hand and open the door, Lili Yannu will be sitting there in that chair, knitting baby clothes out of black wool. She's not dead. She's not dead because I didn't kill her.

It was the easiest thing in the world to check. All he had to do was knock on the door. *Hello, is anyone home?* She would open the door, and he would smile.

Well, what are you waiting for? Do it.

—I can't.

Though he didn't consciously think to do so, Wataru's legs moved him away from the door.

I can't do it. I can't.

Back to the lakeshore. There, where I helped Jozo out of the water, my udai will still be standing, waiting for me. I'll mount up, and go back to Tearsheaven.

I'll have the doctor take a look at me. The lake water hit my cheek. I need an antidote. Then I'll change into a dry shirt, and go see how Sara is doing.

The door to Lili Yannu's hut suddenly opened. Through a gap of maybe four inches came a tiny hand. Followed by an arm, then a face.

It was an infant. It was naked, with chubby round arms and legs. Its face looked like a cherub from some painting, except that its eyes were closed.

Something about it was wrong. Something was strange. This wasn't an ordinary child. Its skin…

Its skin was gray. The color of stone. *A child made of stone.*

The stone-baby stepped clear of the door and turned to Wataru, its eyes still tightly shut. Wataru realized with a start that the child was blind. Then the baby opened its mouth and spoke, not with the voice of a child, but with the heavy, gravelly voice of an old man.

"Killer," it said. "Killer without blood. Killer without tears."

Wataru's hair stood on end. His legs began to shake.

"When you took their lives, you took mine as well. Never will my eyes know the light of day, never will my mouth know my mother's breast, never will my ears know her soft lullaby, never will my feet know the feel of the earth beneath them."

Wataru stepped back, slowly shaking his head. "It wasn't me." His voice came in trembling fits and starts. "I didn't kill them."

"Your excuses are empty," said the baby, pointing a chubby finger in accusation. "What will become of your tainted soul? What will become of my sorrow? My body is stone, my tears are dry."

Wataru screamed. "I didn't kill them!"

The baby's mouth twisted into a hideous scowl. "I will take your sword, stab your body, and carve your soul from it. Your flesh will rot, your bones left bare to the wind upon the frozen ground, singing hollow curses for a hundred nights and a hundred dawns. You will never know the peace of death, and your soul will wander, forever burning in the hellfires of sin, deep within the chaotic abyss!"

Then the baby came at Wataru with unbelievable speed, crawling on its arms and legs. Wataru turned and ran.

No matter how far or how fast he ran, when he looked over his shoulder, there the stone-baby was, speeding after him. Wataru tripped and clawed his way back to his feet. And when he looked back over his shoulder again, for an instant he saw people in the air above the child's face. Yacom, Lili Yannu, Satami were there. So was his father, and his mother. And Rikako, and countless others. Everyone who had ever hated or cursed someone was there. Everyone who had ever wounded another, or kicked another when he was down...

And there, in the crowd, he saw his own face.

Wataru ran. He ran past his udai, standing stiffly by the water's edge. He ran past Yacom's cart, filled with glass jars of swamp water. He ran and ran, and as he ran, he noticed the dorsal fin of a kalon cutting through the surface of the lake, keeping pace with him.

It knows there's prey to be had. It's waiting for the stone-baby to catch me, knock me to the ground, and throw me in the water. Wataru ran and ran on, tears of fright streaming down his face, his breath harsh and ragged in his throat.

Before long, a white mist began to creep through the swamp around him. The ground under his feet, the black water of the swamp—all were soon covered in a gauzy white veil. Wataru ran, swimming through the thickening mist. He looked over his shoulder and could no longer see the baby behind him.

I can't stop now. I have to run.

Yet his feet were slowing. His knees bent, and buckled down to the ground. He couldn't stand.

No. No! I have to run.

Wataru felt his soul inside him, quivering with fright, screaming for help. It was the last thing he heard before blacking out. Darkness crept under the blanket of the white mist. Soon blankness filled everything, and Wataru lay there, face down, utterly drained. He was asleep.

Croak... Croak...

From somewhere came the sound of a frog.

Crrrrroak. Wataru... Crrrrroak...

What's a frog doing in a place like this?

Crrrroak. Wataru? Can you hear me?

The voice was sweet. He had heard it many times before. *I know who that is.*

Crrrroak. Don't worry. You saw what happened. You did the right thing. You did what you had to do.

Sometimes ending a life is the right thing to do. The people you killed were evil, Wataru. You were right...

"No!" Wataru shouted. "I didn't kill them!"

He cupped a hand over his mouth, gasping for breath. He was shaking uncontrollably. *Where am I? What is this place? Where's that stone-baby?*

"You okay?" came a voice from right beside him. Wataru shouted again. He tried to run but only fell, rolling off something and onto a hard floor.

"Oy, oy, calm down there. You've had quite the nightmare. But you are awake now. You're safe."

Wataru opened his eyes to see a pair of concerned dark eyes staring back at him.

chapter 25
The Blood Star

The man leaning over Wataru was young and wore a gray robe like the one donned by the priest in Lyris. But the sleeves were longer, and the hem was shorter, making it look somewhat more practical.

"Well now, how's your fever?" he said, reaching out a hand to touch Wataru's forehead. His face broke into a smile. "Very well, it seems to have gone down! Glad I had my analgesics with me. I was worried there for a bit."

They were in a small room with one door. Wataru lay upon a simple bed, with a thin blanket and a hard pillow. He was also quite grateful for a fluffy, warm comforter.

"Where am I? Who are you?"

The young man smiled and lowered his head. "My name is Shin Suxin. I am a researcher at the National Observatory in Sasaya."

"Nice to meet you," Wataru managed. "You saved me, didn't you? I owe you my thanks."

"Not at all. Hungry? I don't have much, but some warm soup should do you good."

The man took a few steps to a small stove in the corner of the room. The only other furniture in the room was a small desk piled with books and a simple chair. The walls were covered with shelves; these too were crammed with books. Some of the books had drifted off the shelves into a pile on the floor, leaving only a narrow corridor between the bed and the stove.

Wataru guessed he was in another hut. The roof was high, and there was a sort of loft halfway up. A ladder next to the desk provided access.

The National Observatory in Sasaya? Wataru thought back to all that Kee

Keema had told him about Vision during their journey to Gasara.

"Are you by any chance a starseer, Mr. Suxin?"

The man nodded. "Yep. In training, that is. And please, call me Shin. Here you go, drink up."

A bowl filled with deliciously fragrant soup sat upon the tray Shin carried from the stove. "My instructor, Dr. Baksan, always says that a starseer should not be locked up in his observatory. He should travel, get to know the land, its seasons, and its crops. Only then may he look to the stars for guidance. That is the true path to knowledge."

This was the reason, he explained, most students spent a good portion of the year scattered across the southern continent. "Some choose a particular region for their observations. Others have their fate determined by Dr. Baksan. He's a tough nut, our instructor. If there's anything fishy with your observations, he'll flunk you in a heartbeat," Shin said, seeming perfectly happy regardless. For a moment, Wataru saw the face of Yutaro Miyahara, star student from his class back in the real world transposed over the face of the young researcher standing over him. *He's like Yutaro. He's not some bookworm driven to study. He actually likes it...*

A great sense of nostalgia, combined with homesickness, and a desire to see his friends again filled Wataru. Even though he knew this was hardly the time, the feelings—and the questions—were impossible to stop. *What am I doing here? What's the whole point of this anyway?*

"Ah, sorry there," Shin said, looking concerned. "Here I go running off at the mouth and you've only just awoken after three days asleep. I've been here alone for more than a year now, and the only conversation I get is from darbaba drivers. I'm a bit starved for chitchat, you might say. Now, drink your soup 'fore it gets cold."

"No, no, it's fine." Wataru shook his head, trying to hold back the tears. *I can't cry in front of him. He's worried enough as it is.* "Was I really asleep for three days?" Wataru asked, cradling the bowl of soup in his hands.

"You sure were. You had a heavy dose of swamp poison running through you. I thought you'd had it."

"Um...where am I?"

Shin waved a finger and answered his question with another question. "You don't remember at all?"

To his regret, he remembered everything that happened in the Swamp of Grief. Yet, it all felt unreal, like a passing dream, and many of the details were blurry. But still, he remembered what he had done. That was burned into his heart.

"You know the town of Tearsheaven?"

Wataru nodded.

"Well, I found you by the marsh on the opposite side of Tearshaven from the Swamp of Grief. This observation hut we're in now is on the edge of that marsh."

Wataru noticed for the first time that the light streaming through the simple striped curtains was a shade of pink. It was evening.

"About three days ago, right around this time, I came upon an udai wandering lost a little ways behind my hut. He was wearing a saddle, and paddles for walking in the marshes, so I started thinking someone had gotten lost out there. I went out, and found you lying near the path to the swamp."

Though it made his stomach ache with fear, Wataru asked, "Did you find anyone else? Maybe an udai with a cart?"

Shin shook his head. "Nothing of the sort. Were you with someone?"

"No..."

"Right. Oh, by the way, that lost udai I found, I passed it off to a darbaba driver who came through here the other day. I've no food to feed such an animal, you see. He's since gone to Sonn—that's the village nearest to here. There are handlers there who will know how to take care of the thing. They'll be expecting you to come pick it back up when you're well."

Wataru slowly sipped his soup. From the smell he thought it had to be delicious, but it tasted like sand in his mouth.

Where had Yacom's udai gone if it wasn't in the swamp? *Maybe he's alive. Maybe he rode off somewhere with his bottles filled with swamp water.* Maybe the horrible images burned into Wataru's mind were mere illusion, a nightmare shown him by the swamp poison. That would mean Lili Yannu was still alive, and the horrible stone-baby never existed.

That had to be it. He wanted it to be. *There wasn't a bone in my body that had wanted to kill Yacom. I may have been angry at him, and frightened. He was so like Dad.* And more. He had been brutally honest, saying things Wataru could never imagine his father saying, even though he feared they might be true. *But I never wanted to kill him. I can't do that sort of thing. I'm not that kind of person.*

But then, when he thought about it, it occurred to him that he had done many things he never would have believed possible since coming to Vision. He had done battle with monsters—tests that took him to the limits of his strength and wit. Twice he had almost been executed, and twice he hadn't shed a tear, or uttered a single cry for mercy. All the while, the Brave's Sword hung at his side…

Maybe he had become a different person—ever since he had passed the test at the Cave of Trials. From that point on, he wasn't Wataru. He was a Traveler; stronger, braver, and smarter than Wataru.

If I had to, couldn't I kill someone, really? Isn't this the brave Wataru I always wanted to become? Isn't that why I'm wielding a Brave's Sword?

Yacom was a bad person, an evil person. The depth of Lili's evil might have been lesser than his, but still she had hurt others by acting out of pure self-interest. *What if it wasn't an illusion? What if it were true? Would I really have to blame myself?*

"You're a Highlander, aren't you?" Shin asked. Wataru looked at the firewyrm band on his arm. "Which branch are you from?"

"Gasara."

"I see. You've come quite a long way, then."

"You don't think it's strange to have a child like me be a Highlander?"

"Not at all. In the village where I grew up, the grown-ups would always go elsewhere for work. We children and the elderly were left to defend our town against bandits and monsters alike. The branch chief in our town was an old man with a bad back, and all the Highlanders under him were quite young. They did good work, though." Shin blushed and scratched his head. "I was always a bit on the cowardly side. Can't say I was much of a help to them."

The sun had set, and it had become quite dark inside the hut. Shin stood and lit the lamp on his cluttered desk. A soft golden light filled the room, along with the faintly medicinal smell of lamp oil.

"I think it takes bravery to do research here all alone like you are, though."

"Well, that has less to do with bravery, and more to do with me wanting to keep my job." Then he fell suddenly silent, though it seemed as though he still had more to say.

He's shy. Wataru thought it best not to pry too deeply into his private affairs.

Wataru touched the red leather of his firewyrm band. He remembered what Kutz had said. If a Highlander's hands should ever be stained with unjust deeds, the firewyrm's flame would blaze out of the band and burn him alive. Those very flames he had seen firsthand when he met Jozo in the Swamp of Grief.

But there was his band, still on his arm. Did that mean he hadn't done anything wrong?

It must've been a dream. Or, even if it really happened, then it was the right thing to do. The more he thought about it, the more confused he became. Dreams, dreams, and more dreams. That's what it had to have been. How could it be right to murder someone? How could someone who was truly brave run a blade through a defenseless woman?

"I don't mean to pry," Shin asked, "but where were you headed?"

Wataru looked up.

"Were you doing something in the Swamp of Grief?"

"Well, no, not really," Wataru lied. "I got separated from some friends…"

Wataru briefly explained what had happened outside Lyris. As he listened, Shin's clever eyes opened wide, then fell dark. "Lyris, eh?" He sat with his arms folded across his chest, shoulders slumped. "It's hard to say whether the people you encountered were true followers of the Old God, but it's clear the movement is gaining a foothold." Dr. Baksan had warned them all of this, he muttered.

"Do you think it's coming from the north?"

"Oh, I have no doubt that's a factor—but more than that, we have the times to consider."

"The times?"

Shin nodded, his eyes still dark. "This isn't something we're allowed to say publicly, but I only give it two weeks or so before word gets out, and trouble starts. And, anyway, you're a Highlander, so you should know first. I'm afraid you'll have busy times ahead."

Every thousand years, a great danger visits itself upon Vision, he explained.

"This world in which we live exists at the depth of a vast chaos. In the past, all matter, once formed, would eventually return to this chaos, and nothing could last for long…"

It was the Great Barrier of Light that protected them from the chaos. "When the Goddess created our world, she made a pact with the Lord of the Underworld who presides over the chaos. Once every thousand years, an Age of Making comes when Vision must make a human sacrifice to the Lord of the Underworld. He then uses the life energy of that sacrifice to create the Great Barrier of Light. So is Vision able to exist."

Wataru's eyes went wide. "So, when you said the times before…"

"Yes. The time of the sacrifice is nearing. It will soon be time to create a new barrier."

"How do you know?"

"In the north sky," Sheehan said, pointing to a section of the ceiling in the little hut. "A star—the Blood Star—appears, telling us that the time has come. In fact, the society of starseers began with the express purpose of finding and identifying that star as early as possible."

"And you can see this Blood Star?"

Shin nodded. "I can now, though I wasn't able to find it on my own. More than two months ago, another student, far more advanced than me, released the first report of a sighting from the observatory in Arikita."

Shin's instructor, Dr. Baksan, had consulted the ancient tomes. He was able to find observational reports linked to the Blood Star. All of the star charts had been perfectly recorded. "That place was close by, so he sent me out here to make observations."

That had been more than a year ago.

"That long ago?"

"Yes, but it was only ten days ago that I first saw what I thought might be the signs. Dr. Baksan wasn't too pleased with me, I tell you," Shin admitted, wilting like a flower.

"Isn't human sacrifice a little harsh? I mean, the person dies, right?"

"No, they do not. Yet their fate is worse than death, for they must live for eternity in loneliness."

Until the next Age of Making came, they were bound to serve the Lord of the Underworld, and look upon everything that lived in Vision, ensuring that nothing was corrupted by the chaos…

"It would not be such a mean task if one only had to observe love, friendship, helpfulness, smiles, and songs. But there is hatred and betrayal and jealousy in this world, stealing and killing. Living beings are sadly capable of all these things."

It was a fact of which Wataru was painfully aware. For a moment, he felt a chill, as he recalled the faces of Yacom and Lili.

"I'd imagine it's hard, seeing people driven by greed—never knowing happiness or joy. But endure it they must. They must take in everything, and let it be as it is. If they do not, the Great Barrier of Light would break, and all Vision would be destroyed. This is the burden the sacrificed must bear."

Wataru thought. As Shin said, it would be hard protecting people who merely fought with one another. He could see how it would even seem ridiculous at times. But wouldn't it be harder defending their happiness? Being a sacrifice for their smiles? Enduring such terrible loneliness, while the people below merely laughed? Wouldn't he wonder why it happened to him, and why it couldn't have been someone else? Wasn't that terribly unfair? Wataru imagined that holding that kind of grief inside for one thousand years would be the hardest thing of all.

"How is the sacrifice chosen?"

Shin shook his head. "That I do not know. There is no record in the ancient tomes. It all depends on the will of the Goddess, I suppose. Sometimes a very young person is chosen, other times a very ancient one."

"So it's a matter of chance?"

"Pretty much."

When the Blood Star first appeared in the northern sky, it would be like a beacon, shining with a bright white light. But once the Goddess began selecting the sacrifice, it would glow blood red until the Lord of the Underworld carried the chosen one into the abyss. When the making of the barrier was complete, the star would again glow white, and then fade by the next dawn, not to reappear for another thousand years.

"We call the time that the Blood Star glows Red Halnera—it means the 'time of sacrifice' in the ancient ankha tongue."

"Halnera," Wataru repeated. *When the Goddess chooses her sacrifice.* "But if the Goddess was the one who started this whole thing, why did she have to make it work that way? It seems unnecessarily cruel."

If she were powerful enough to create all of Vision, it seemed to Wataru she should be able to protect her creation from the chaos herself without having to sacrifice a person to do the job.

"You think so?" Shin said, blinking sadly.

"Of course!"

"Yes. It is a question that has plagued the starseers for many long years. What does the Goddess want of us? Why must she test us in this way? Is she not torturing us, forcing us to endure hardship at her whim?"

A Goddess playing whimsically with her creations. It wasn't so hard to imagine.

"This is also one of the tenets of the belief in the Old God. They claim that the Goddess does not love the people of Vision, that if she did love us she would never require this horrible sacrifice, not even once in a thousand years."

She did not love the people of Vision, they claimed, because she did not create Vision. She merely stole what the Old God created.

"Thus, whenever Halnera comes, there is a surge of support for the belief in the Old God. The followers come together and they pray. They pray that the Old God will hear them, and come down once again to Vision, and drive away the evil Goddess once and for all. This is the great rectification of which they dream."

When Shin put it that way, Wataru found himself becoming confused. So the ankha extremists had at least one good reason for their denial of the Goddess. Wataru saw how it would make sense that people would turn to the Old God. "Shin, is what you've told me a well-known fact in Vision? Or is it knowledge held only by the starseers?"

Shin Suxin rubbed his weary eyes. "It was known only in a few circles until recently."

"Until recently?"

"When it came time for the Blood Star to appear again, the starseers held many conventions at the National Observatory in Sasaya. Then there was a debate with the United Southern Nations government. They've only just now come to a decision—I received my copy from a darbaba driver yesterday."

Shin stood from his chair and opened the topmost drawer of his desk. He pulled out a tightly rolled scroll. "This is their promulgation. They decided that knowledge of Halnera should be told to all people in the south."

The Highlanders would be busy indeed.

"There are many millions of people living in Vision," Shin said quietly, standing at the window, looking up at the night sky. "Only one of them will be chosen as the sacrifice. Many think that there will be little reaction when people hear of Halnera. The chances of any one person being chosen are quite low, you see."

"But if you got chosen, it would be you, and only you!" Wataru said, a little louder than he had intended. "There's no odds anymore once you're it. What if you were the one chosen, Shin? Think about that!"

"Indeed..."

From the window came the soft hooting of a night bird. The night was otherwise quiet. But somewhere, high in that silent sky, the Blood Star was waiting.

"Do you think it would have been better not to teach people about Halnera? If they did not know, there would be no need to fear. One day, in some city or town, a person would simply disappear—their family and friends would worry. Perhaps they would search for a very long time, but on the grand scale of things, this is a trifling matter. Do you think this way is better?"

Wataru didn't have an answer.

"Dr. Baksan says that no matter how difficult it is to bear, or how evil the news, everyone in Vision has a right to know. There were two schools of thought at the debate in the National Observatory in Sasaya: those who sided with Dr. Baksan, and those who claimed that ignorance is bliss. They argued for days and days. Some of those opposed to spreading word of Halnera wanted to take it a step further. They felt that all reseach should be banned. If we do not know about it, they claimed, then it is as if it didn't exist at all."

Shin, still standing by the window, cradling his head in his arms. "I am frightened," he said. "I did not want to know of this. The more I learn about Halnera, the less I want to know. I regret that Dr. Baksan told me. I even regret having become a starseer."

It was more than loneliness that prompted Shin to tell Wataru all this. It was his fear. If Wataru had not been a Highlander, perhaps he would have held it back.

"I'm not worried only for myself, of course. I'm worried for my parents, my brothers, my fiancée, my new colleagues at school, everyone that I know and love. What would I do if someone I knew was chosen? I think about this at night and I cannot sleep."

Who wouldn't go crazy thinking about it, Wataru thought. Then he realized that Yacom wouldn't. What if Satami were chosen as the sacrifice? Wouldn't he be pleased? People only worried about the well-being of those they knew when they also happened to like them.

Wataru was the same. He certainly didn't want to be sacrificed, but what if it were Kenji Ishioka instead? He could see himself living with that. Thinking back, he hadn't been all that concerned when the school delinquent was consumed by that Vision creature.

"I'm sorry, I have spoken overmuch," Shin said, rubbing his eyes. "I did tell you I was a coward."

"I don't think you're a coward, Shin. We're all like you inside."

"You should rest now. You must be tired. I'm sorry to talk so much."

"It's okay. Actually, I was wondering—is your observation equipment in the loft up there?"

Shin nodded.

"And you are using it to watch the Blood Star? Might I see it too? Or would I need some special knowledge?"

"I'm not sure. We could certainly give it a try. The Blood Star rises after midnight. Go to sleep now, and I will wake you when it is time."

As promised, when the night had grown deep, Shin Suxin nudged Wataru awake, and he let him peer through his telescope. It was a very powerful telescope, and the night sky was like luxurious velvet, studded by countless stars. Still, even with Shin's careful instruction, Wataru was unable to pick out the Blood Star from among them.

chapter 26
To Sakawa

The next morning, after eating a simple but delicious breakfast, Wataru was ready to leave.

"You're welcome to rest longer if you'd like. Are you sure you'll be okay?"

"I feel much better, thanks."

Kee Keema and Meena weighed heavily on Wataru's mind. What had happened to them? He hadn't seen them captive at Triankha Hospital, so they must have escaped, but to where? Now that he knew Halnera was coming, he wanted to see them again more than ever.

"If one of your friends is a waterkin darbaba driver, they might have gone to the town of Sakawa," Shin suggested. "That's the darbaba drivers' base of operations for much of the shipping that goes on in the south. Even if he's not there, someone might know where he is."

Both Sakawa and Gasara were equally distant. "You might try going to Sonn and speaking with the karulakin there. They're quite proud, and if it was a Highlander asking, they very well might lend a helping hand. A karulah could get you to Sakawa in, oh, two days or so. You are pretty light, after all."

Now that he had thought of it, Shin Suxin agreed Wataru should make all due haste. "The United Nations will soon be summoning the karulakin to carry word of Halnera across the land. Make your journey before then, or you may be forced to wait."

The path to Sonn wound through marsh and thicket, but it had been well trodden by Shin on his trips for supplies, and was relatively easy to follow.

Sonn was by far the smallest of all the towns and villages Wataru had seen during his time in Vision. A grand total of ten simple houses with thatched roofs sat huddled together in a small clearing cut out of a copse of trees. But it was adjacent to a vast pasture on the sloping side of a hill, many times larger than the town itself. The pasture was divided by several fences. These separate enclosures held darbabas, udais, and other strange livestock Wataru had never seen before. The beasts bleated and bellowed, locked horns, chewed grass, and slept.

The town master was a beastkin who looked like a long-eared dog, with warm eyes peeking out from beneath bushy eyebrows. Wataru's udai had been taken special care of, and its coat shone with a recent brushing.

"Why, we've some karulakin in town right now."

The karulah, it turned out, came to Sonn to trade their decorative feathers for furry creatures called mols. Mols were smaller than mice, and famous for their voracious appetite. They especially liked the tiny insects that were fond of living on the underside of karulakins' wings.

"You're young, yes, but a Highlander is a Highlander," said the karulakin to whom the town master introduced Wataru. With his red feathers, gaudy headdress, and stately way of speaking, the karulah reminded Wataru much of the one who had saved him from the gimblewolves in the Fatal Desert. So striking was the similarity that Wataru started to wonder if even the karulah had trouble telling each other apart.

"And if we were to turn down a Highlander's request, why, that'd be to the shame of all karulakin everywhere, wouldn't it, town master?"

"Yes, quite," the long-eared town master replied, smiling. "This here's Togoto of the Kakkuu. He's the swiftest-winged of the Kakkuu, I hear. You'll be in Sakawa in no time."

"You speak imprecisely, town master," Togoto said with a frown. "I am not only the fastest of the Kakkuu, but the fastest of the Rakka as well. Even still, the trip to Sakawa will not take 'no time,' as our dear town master suggests. Why I think you should have time enough to, say, hear me recite the History of the Karulah from the birth of the first ancestors up to, well, about the reign of the Second King and the Battle of the Breaking of Gara Pass if you so desired!"

While Togoto prepared for departure, the town master spoke in a hushed voice to Wataru. "Stick a ball of rolled up mol-fur in each ear, and you'd be able to sleep like a baby at the foot of a roaring dragon. Here's two of them for the trip. Togoto may be fast, but his pontifications are anything but."

"Understood," said Wataru, smiling.

"And don't worry too much about having to say anything yourself. Just go 'Oh, right' and 'Ah, yes' and throw in a 'My, that's quite remarkable' every once in a while and you'll do fine."

Wataru had imagined Togoto would carry him in his claws, as it had been with the karulakin in the gimblewolf desert, but when he was told they were ready to depart, he found a chair like a wicker basket waiting for him. It hung by means of a cleverly designed harness from Togoto's torso.

"I'm sorry you have to do all the work."

"A Highlander should not be so eager to apologize. When an apology is called for, it should be for a suitable crime, and only after all proper documentation has been submitted. Why, at the Accord of the Battle of Taro, the ancestors of the karulakin…"

And so the lecture started even before takeoff. With most of the village folk waving goodbye, Wataru sped up into the air.

They passed so close over the thatched roofs of Sonn, Wataru could've stretched out his toes and touched them. A child waved, and Wataru waved back. They were blessed with perfect weather. The sky was a solid sheet of blue, without a trace of any clouds. Togoto ascended rapidly, so fast that Wataru felt himself wanting to shout, like he was on a jet coaster at the fair.

Beneath Wataru's feet the nature of Vision spread out in all its glory: mountains, hills, plains, streams, and forests as far as the eye could see. When he figured out which direction they were heading, he looked back around to the left to see the black glimmer of the Swamp of Grief fading into the distance. A veil of fog hung over the marshes. And beyond the swamp, he caught a glimpse of Tearsheaven.

Wataru was grateful for the cotton vest the town master had lent him for the trip. Their elevation and the cutting winds made it a chilly ride. They flew past foothills to mountains Wataru had never seen, over a village, and then a river. The town master had warned him that Togoto would take his charge quite seriously. It was likely they would fly on without more than a brief rest now and then. "Watch that you don't nap and fall from your chair."

Wataru looked down at the incredible view and wondered how anyone could fall asleep. The first place they rested was at the gatehouse on the border between Arikita and Bog. There was a teahouse there where traveling merchants gathered and baqua trees grew thick along the roadside. While they waited for their papers to be processed, Wataru selected one of the fruits and ate it.

"Have you a map in your head yet? Do you know where we are flying now?" Togoto asked while resting his wings.

"Not a clue," Wataru replied honestly. "But I'm having the time of my life!"

"A Highlander should not allow himself to be satisfied with such trivialities as sightseeing," Togato chided. "We have ridden the wind due west from Sonn. As we make for Sakawa, we must head north from here, for Sakawa is on the Bog coast. Understood?"

Wataru nodded.

"Incidentally, before heading north, we need to find a rising current, and that will take us to our highest elevation yet. It won't be for long, but you should be able to catch a glimpse of the Undoor Highland. It is a foreboding plateau shrouded in mist and cloud all year round, with not a single road or footpath for travelers."

Togoto looked up at the sky, beaming proudly. "I would think that, as a Highlander, you might value this rare opportunity! Blessed be the all-powerful Goddess for her gift to the karulakin of mighty wings!"

The Undoor Highland. Home to the Special Administrative State of Dela Rubesi. Secret haven to the followers of the Old God.

"Looking forward to it!" Wataru said. Togoto also seemed to be in high spirits, and they left as soon as their papers were ready.

Togoto was not only a speaker of some eloquence, but some reliability as well. Their ascent was breathtaking as promised. Wataru feared he might be knocked out of his basket, so swiftly did they climb up through the shifting air currents.

After a brief but very fast ascent, they began to climb more gradually, tracing a slow upward spiral. Even with his earplugs, Wataru could feel the beat of Togoto's crimson wings as they cut through the air. They climbed, and climbed, passing through white mists and clouds. When Wataru felt his basket-seat lift up into the air briefly then settle, he knew they had arrived at their planned elevation.

The view was hardly any different than the one from an airplane window. The buildings of the gatehouse looked like matchboxes, the dense forest like a broccoli patch. Wataru was entranced by the panorama beneath him—a vast mottled blanket of greens and browns. He could see towns and villages scattered in the distance, small lakes mirroring the sky, and rivers winding through it all like silken threads.

Togoto was saying something. Wataru took out the plugs. "Highlander! There is Undoor!" he shouted, jabbing southward with his beak. "Look! The clouds have broken! See the snow on the uppermost reaches!"

Wataru looked. In the middle of a massive tower of white clouds, he could see a great, gray plateau. The countless streaks of glimmering white draped down its sides must be glaciers, he realized.

The highest reaches of the plateau were covered in white. It was hard to get a good view, because the break in the clouds was very narrow, and constantly shifting. No sooner had he realized what he was looking at than the upper reaches of the plateau were once again concealed behind a wall of white. Yet in that brief moment, Wataru saw something like a shining tower. Not one tower, but several, catching the sun through the gap in the clouds.

Are they glass? Or crystal? Or even towers of ice? They glimmered like rainbows, like they were made of the stuff of clouds, crystallized and given form. *Is there really an entire country up there?*

"Now on to the northerly current! Hold on tight!" Togoto called, and gave his wings a large flap. The scene beneath Wataru's feet shifted. Lifted on a powerful gust of air, Togoto shot like a bullet through the sky.

The Undoor Highland and its towers of cloud faded farther and farther away. Wataru twisted in his chair and looked back for as long as he was able. Even when the wind blew frightfully cold, and his cheeks burned, he did not look away.

It's like...like....

Like a place where the gods live.

The thought surprised Wataru, even though it had been his own.

What if one of those towers was the Tower of Destiny? What if the Goddess was there, after all? So few seemed to be able to enter the Undoor Highlands, wouldn't it make sense if the tower that none had seen was there as well? What if the people of the Special Administrative State of Dela Rubesi did not communicate with others in Vision not because they followed the Old God, but because they were sworn to protect the domicile of the Goddess in all its secrecy?

Maybe I just saw it—my final destination.

Wataru sat in silence. Even without earplugs, the sound of blood rushing through his veins and the beating of his heart drowned out everything else.

They took a few brief rest breaks, but Togoto never seemed to weary, and they made good progress northward. The sun grew low in the sky and it was nearing twilight when he first caught a glimpse of the sea far ahead of them.

There were flying at a much lower elevation now. Wataru was able to talk to Togoto without having to shout. "Is that the sea that surrounds the southern continent?"

"The very one!"

"So beyond that is the northern continent? Have you ever flown there, Togoto?"

"Flown there? Never!" Togoto said, shaking so much that Wataru's basket began to swing from side to side. Wataru hurriedly grabbed on so he wouldn't fall.

"Do you not know, Highlander? In the middle of the sea which separates north from south looms the Stinging Mist!"

"The Stinging Mist?"

"Indeed. It's a sight different from the mist and clouds you saw surrounding the Undoor Highland earlier today, different from any mist we know—a fearful, baleful storm of death!"

According to Togoto, each droplet of that mist was sharp and pointed like a blade, and all foolish enough to fly through it were pierced until they bled to death.

"No matter how strong the wings of the karulakin, none may fly when torn to rags! Only the great dragon warriors covered with hardened scale armor might hope to penetrate such a mist. It is said that the few remaining dragonkin in this world live upon a small island in the sea in the midst of this mist. Thus, we see them only when they choose to venture out, and then only rarely."

Wataru thrust his hand into his trousers pocket, and felt the red scale Jozo had given him. So it was an unusual thing to meet a dragon, even in this world. A chance encounter.

"The merchant sailships catch the winds sent by the Goddess to ply their way from north to south and back, but even then sometimes the Stinging Mist sweeps low across the sea and blocks their passage. When the mist drops, all hands must leave the sails and oars and hide below deck, lest they be ripped painfully and bloodily apart!"

Night fell before long, and stars twinkled into existence above Wataru's head. A blanket of darkness covered the land. Wataru shivered in the night wind and lifted the collar on his cotton jacket.

From there on, he slumped in his seat, unsure of how far and how fast they flew. But it was not too long before he saw a cluster of lights below. Wataru blinked.

"Lanka, capital city of Bog!" Togoto announced.

That's where Meena lived.

"Sakawa is close, a little way to the northwest. We should see it soon. The merchant city of Lanka knows no darkness, even in the depths of night, but the waterkin of Sakawa can see in the dark, and shun wasteful use of lamp oil. It will be more difficult to see from the sky."

With the lights of Lanka on their left, Togoto swept his wings to the east and descended even farther. The wind brushing against Wataru's cheek was salty with the taste of sea brine.

"There, Highlander! The town of Sakawa!"

Wataru leaned forward in his basket, but at first all he could see was more darkness. Soon, they passed over a narrow beach. Even in the darkness he could see the white ridges of the waves as they crashed against the shore. Togoto went out over the sea, then slowly curved back, his speed dropping as they descended.

And there was the town. Wataru saw thatched roofs and the outlines of buildings. Here and there hung what looked like signs. And in corrals throughout town were more darbabas than he had ever seen before.

chapter 27
The Reunion

In the dark streets beneath him, Wataru saw waterkin on the roads and in corrals taking care of darbabas. Clusters of houses stood open to the air, screens made of long rushes hanging from the roofs in place of walls. Waterkin lifted the screens and looked out. There were similar houses along the shore, with verandas sticking out over the waves, where waterkin sat around tables talking and drinking.

"Oy! A karulakin! A karulakin's come!"

"He's got a passenger!"

Waterkin shuffled out into the center of town, waving toward Togoto.

"Settle down on the dunes to the west!"

"Aye!" Togoto replied as they flew out over the spray where white waves crashed against the rocks. They alit on a beach of white sand. The waves were gentler here.

"Highlander!" Togoto cried from above him. "As soon as your feet touch ground, leave your chair! Tarry too long, and I'll land on top of you!"

The sea spray wetted Wataru's face. His foot touched to the sand for an instant. Then both feet connected softly, and Wataru leapt, rolling off to one side. Behind him, Togoto came to an expert landing.

Shhhhh Shhhhh Shhhhh…

The waves of the night sea rolled soothingly in, sounding like a gentle lullaby.

"We made great time!" Togoto chortled, folding his wings behind him. "A good trip, a very good trip."

"It was. Thank you!"

Several waterkin were coming in along the shore. One among them was particularly large, and he jumped and waved both hands. "Oy! Ooooy!"

Wataru knew who it was even before his voice reached them. He began to run across the sand, stumbling a bit until he had run off the numbness in his legs from the journey. "Kee Keema!"

"Wataru! It *is* you!"

Wataru jumped into the beaming waterkin's arms. Kee Keema snatched him effortlessly out of the air, lifting him up over his head and spinning him around. "My lucky Traveler! You made it! I knew you'd make it!"

Then, from Kee Keema's shoulder, Wataru saw another familiar face in the crowd rushing toward them. "Meena!"

There was so much he wanted to say and so much he wanted to ask.

Kee Keema lived in a small house near the shore, a simple affair with a roof fashioned from the giant leaves of some indigenous tree. The leaves resembled giant palm fronds, and, as Wataru soon discovered, were used for flooring, roofing, and even some tableware. The leaves also doubled as fans for relief on hot and sticky days.

The three sat in the small house, listening to the sound of the waves. They talked about everything that had happened since they were separated at the Triankha Hospital. As they chatted, Kee Keema's neighbors and friends dropped by with stewed fruits, giant roast slabs of meat, savory roasted fish, and sweet water in vessels made of carved wood.

Slowly, they pieced together the puzzle of what had happened at the hospital. Kee Keema and Meena had regained consciousness not long after Wataru was taken away.

"One of those arrows wasn't enough to keep a big fellow like myself down for too long," Kee Keema boasted.

"Luckily, one only grazed me," Meena added.

"Anyway, when we regained consciousness, you were gone. Oh, Meena cried something fierce," Kee Keema said, chuckling.

"Don't exaggerate," Meena snapped.

"Hrm? It's the truth."

"I was just worried."

"It's okay, I was worried too," Wataru said with a smile.

"We ended up getting lost in the sula woods. I think it was on account of the trees, but no matter how far we walked, we always seemed to end up in the same place. And weirder still, whenever we caught a glimpse of the hospital we'd try to make for it but couldn't seem to get any closer."

"That forest was bad news," said Meena, frowning. "I got so dizzy, I was seeing two Kee Keemas, and believe me, one is enough!" Meena chuckled, but her mirth didn't last long. "And there was that sound, like singing…"

"I remember looking at Meena and seeing her face go all twisty, like this!" Kee Keema said, taking his hands and squashing his face like a pancake. Wataru laughed out loud, but inside, he shivered, remembering what the man who fired arrows on them had said.

—*Toss the other two. They'll never be able to survive the woods.*

"We were in a bit of a fix, no two ways about it. If we'd stayed out there, that sula forest would have gotten the better of us both. I figure we would have walked ourselves to death."

Yet while they walked, stumbling through the magic woods, a great cyclone had suddenly appeared, and changed their situation considerably.

"That cyclone swept up the entire forest down to the last tree. I thought it was heaven come to punish that evil place. I didn't care to get blown away with those trees, though, so I dug us a hole and we hid." Kee Keema flourished his long-clawed hands with pride. "Before we knew it, the trees were all bent over or gone entirely, the leaves were scattered, and the mist was gone from the starry sky. With all the trees cleared out, we could see the hospital quite clearly—except it didn't look anything like it looked before. Where that big block of a building had stood was only an old ruin."

The cyclone, of course, had been Mitsuru's work. The illusion of the hospital had been the work of the cultists.

"Meena and I rushed to the hospital, but everything was a wreck, and there were wounded folk everywhere. When they saw us, some of them tried to run—like they were scared something fierce. I caught one of them, though, a fellow wearing an awfully fine-looking robe."

"You should've seen it," said Meena, smiling, "Kee Keema snatched him up by his collar, like a baby kitkin!"

She continued: "'Who are you?' he asked the man. 'Were you the ones who fired poison arrows on us? Where did you take that boy?'"

The man had told him everything, which is how they learned Wataru had been inside the hospital. They also learned that the cultists there were radical followers of the Old God.

"When I asked him what had happened to the boy, he told me that the cyclone had picked you up and tossed you into the air—and as far as he knew, you'd never come back down."

The two had gone back to Sakawa to enlist the aid of the other waterkin in their search for Wataru. "I wasn't sure how we'd find you," said Kee Keema, "but I knew you'd turn up eventually. After all, you're a Traveler under the protection of the Goddess herself. I figured no wind storm would do you in that easy."

"Your friend must be quite the sorcerer, Wataru," Meena said, her tail twitching. "To conjure a cyclone like that—that's wind magic of the highest degree. None but the greatest of mages can wield such power."

"What can I tell you? He's a Traveler," Kee Keema said proudly. "Strength and courage just like our boy here." Wataru smiled, but the memory of a particular incident flashed across his mind, and his smile froze.

He hadn't told them what happened in the Swamp of Grief. How was he supposed to tell them? *I killed someone. No, I killed two people. And the stone-baby pointed at me and called me a killer without blood or tears, and all I could do was run.*

No, it was an illusion. I had a nightmare brought on by the the swamp water. None of it really happened. If I went back to Tearsheaven now, I would see Lili Yannu knitting clothes by the edge of the lake. Satami would still be sad, Sara would still be waiting for her father to return, and Yacom would still be driving his cart and selling the black water.

"Somethin' wrong, Wataru?"

"Huh? Oh, nothing."

"Well, we got a bit sidetracked, you might say, but now that the three of us are back together, it's time to get looking for that second gemstone. I don't think we need to rush right out though. We should relax a bit and enjoy the sea. This is a busy place, with lots of folks coming and going. We might hear something."

"The traveling waterkin will be our ears and eyes," Meena said with a smile.

"You know it! So, how do you like Sakawa, Wataru? Nice place, eh?"

"It's beautiful—and the food is great. And the people seem really nice and friendly. I guess I can't complain."

"Sure can't! The beauty of Sakawa and the bounty of the sea are both gifts from the Goddess herself. That's why we work hard every day to repay her. None are harder working in the south than us waterkin, after all," Kee Keema said, puffing out his chest.

"I have to admit I've grown a little tired of hearing Kee Keema boast about his home," Meena said, "but I can now see where it's coming from."

Wataru watched the two smiling, yet he couldn't feel at ease. He knew terrible news would be arriving soon—something that would wipe smiles off faces even here in carefree Sakawa.

Had the United Southern Nations sent their karulakin messenger here yet? Was the word already spreading, carried on red wings to every part of the land? When would it reach them?

When Wataru had first heard the story of the barrier and the sacrifices from Shin Suxin, it had frightened him, and seemed cruelly unfair. But now, sitting here with his friends, he felt something more than fear: he felt anger. *What if Kee Keema or Meena were chosen?* Wataru couldn't stand by and let one of his friends be dragged away. Even if the one chosen said they would go willingly, Wataru couldn't let it be.

Still, he didn't want to be the one to have to tell them. They would find out soon enough. He kept his mouth shut and listened to the sound of the waves rolling onto the shore.

There was only one path to take. *I have to get to the Tower of Destiny as soon as possible. I'll meet the Goddess and ask her to stop the sacrifices. Who cares about some treaty with the Lord of the Underworld? Treaties are made to be broken. They can be rewritten and amended. She can say that it was wrong.* If he begged, if he asked from the bottom of his heart, he was sure she would hear his plea. What kind of benevolent Goddess wouldn't?

That evening, all the waterkin in Sakawa gathered at the Elder's pagoda. A great feast was planned in Wataru's honor. Plates of food and jugs of wine were piled on the table. The dining hall was overflowing with villagers and many more were squeezed outside. Kee Keema had warned Wataru away from the wine—waterkin liquor was powerful stuff—though the older waterkin insisted there was no harm in a cup or two.

The Elder of Sakawa was more than four hundred years old by Kee Keema's account, but it was difficult to tell his age from his thick lizard-like scales and smooth skin. But his face did look quite dignified. It was the face of a leader.

Everyone was full of questions for Wataru: about his journey, about the trials he had faced when he first arrived in Vision, about the real world. All the while, the Elder sat silently with a smile on his face. Wataru felt something in that warm, genteel gaze—like he was being tested or judged. He had the distinct impression that the Elder had a question for him too, but not the sort of question one asked at these types of affairs.

Kee Keema also weathered an onslaught of inquiries about their adventures in the cave outside Gasara and the state of affairs in Lyris. He retold the story of their capture in the sula woods with much prancing about and exaggerated gesturing.

Even Meena got into the act. Egged on by the crowd, she started to sing, and the level of excitement escalated even further. There was a thunderous storm of applause when she finished, and cries for one more song. She was happy to oblige.

A great crowd formed a circle around her. There ensued much clapping of hands, stamping of feet, and dancing. Wataru was swept up with the crowd—grabbing on to hands and shoulders as the waterkin jumped in the air. It wasn't long before the waterkin wine took effect. He started to swoon and thought he'd collapse on the floor before the song was finished.

"You okay?"

"Maybe not," Wataru said. "I think I'll go for a walk along the beach. Some fresh air will do me good."

Walking down the outside steps, Wataru had to step over clumps of waterkin drinking and laughing. Alone at last, he let himself relax and flopped down onto the sand.

A soft sea wind brushed his cheeks. The night was anything but dark. Twinkling stars shone like silver sand spread on the deep navy blue cloth of the sky. Wataru enjoyed the feel of the sand beneath his fingertips and let the rhythm of the waves wash over him.

Vision was beautiful. Lying back like this, the night sky seemed even closer than when he had been sitting up. He felt like he could reach out and touch the heavens. The lilting sound of Meena singing reached his ears.

It was a ballad—a beautiful thing, with a shifting melody. Her sweet voice trembled sorrowfully, matching the rhythm of the waves.

So far away, the one I love.
What sky are you under tonight?
What wind will my song ride...
To carry my voice to you?
Tell me, winds,
Where he may be.
Tell me, winds,
What star he looks upon.
My ears are like two white seashells,
Listening for dawn to come.

It was a song about long-distance lovers. Or maybe it was a one-sided love. He closed his eyes and let his heart fill with happiness.

"Wataru, you're not sleeping, are you?"

"Huh?!" he said jumping to his feet. "I haven't heard from you since the hospital,"

"No, no, we talked after that too. Have you forgotten? Remember when that meek little starseer saved you by the Swamp of Grief? I spoke to you in your dream, while you slept. Don't you remember?"

Wataru racked his foggy head, trying to remember. His memories were vague. He remembered Shin Suxin's concerned look when his eyes first opened...

"Tsk. I'm disappointed. But no matter. We've met again, after all," the sweet voice said cheerfully.

"I'm sorry, the poison from the swamp was making me hallucinate."

"Oh? You weren't seeing things. Everything really happened."

Wataru froze. *What? It wasn't an illusion—a nightmare?*

"You..." he began.

"It's okay, what you did. Really. Forget that now. What you need to focus on is what you're *about* to do."

"What I'm about to do?"

"You plan to go to the Goddess and ask her to stop the sacrifices, no? Do you really think you can do that?"

Wataru rubbed his eyes, and sat down on the sand. "How do you know that?"

"Your thoughts are easy enough to read," she said with a chuckle. "I'm worried, though. I don't think you know what it is you're trying to do. I don't think you're fully aware."

"Aware?"

"Oh, to be sure, it's your choice if you want to go meet the Goddess and ask her to stop the sacrifices. She grants a wish to every Traveler who reaches the Tower of Destiny on his own. That is how it has been for ages. But I think you're forgetting something. The Goddess may grant each Traveler only one wish. You don't get two or three. If you ask her to stop the sacrifices, what will happen to your own destiny? Isn't that why you came to Vision in the first place, to change your own fate?"

The sea breeze that blew gently through his hair suddenly turned cold. He could practically hear his body temperature drop.

The Goddess grants only one wish.

"I think you've remembered," the sweet voice said, sounding satisfied. "You are too nice for your own good, Wataru. Who cares about the people here in Vision? You have to go back to the real world someday, and once you do you'll never meet the people here again. What does it matter to you who's chosen for the sacrifice?"

Wataru wrapped his arms around his shoulders. *It's true. I forgot. I was having so much fun here in Vision, I forgot why I came in the first place.*

I forgot about my mother.

"But, but I..." Wataru began, his voice choked. "How can I let the sacrifices continue if I have a choice?"

"Even if it has nothing to do with you?"

"It does have something to do with me!" he said, suddenly shouting. "I've been through a lot since I came here. I've seen a lot. Some things have been scary, and some cruel, but I've also met lots of kind, gentle people. They're my friends! What goes on here in Vision does have something to do with me!"

"More than your mother does?" the voice said, her words like tiny needles on Wataru's skin. "You have a choice, but you can choose only one. What will you do? Can you just tell your mother sorry, you can't help? Can you tell her to just accept her fate?"

"I..."

"Would you sacrifice your mother's happiness for people you'll never meet again in a world you'll never visit twice? Would that make you happy? Would that make your mother happy? Would she be proud to have you as a son?"

Wataru clapped his hands over his ears. "Stop! Don't say those things."

"But you have to hear them," the syrupy voice echoed in his mind just as loud as before. She sounded almost happy at the consternation she was causing Wataru. "You either choose Vision, or you choose your mother. Choose Vision, and you must go back home and apologize to your mother. I think I know what she'll say. She'll say she's happy she raised you to be so kind, that you would help others before you help yourself. Of course, she'd be lying. You know how she really feels..."

"Shut up!"

The sweet voice continued: "Inside, she'll be torn to pieces. All that time I spent raising you, oh, what a cold, cold son, she'll say. Never thinking of his mother's happiness, always wanting to please the crowd, and secretly never reaching out to the one who needs his help most—when it was so easy. He had a chance!"

"I said shut up! My mom's not like that! You're wrong!"

"Oh? Are you so sure? Your father just betrayed you, didn't he? You didn't think he was capable of doing that, and yet he did. Just. Like. That. You were discarded, Wataru. Tossed aside—baggage, unwanted litter. That's how people are and your mother's no different."

Wataru could no longer hear the whispering of the waves. That horrible sweet voice echoed in his ears, lodging itself in his head.

"Think about it. You're the same too," the voice said. Wataru swore he could hear her grinning.

"I'm the same?"

"Yes. You came here to change your destiny, no? You wanted your father to abandon his lover, abandon the child she would bear for him, to come back to you and your mother."

That's true. What he had done was wrong. Wataru just wanted to set it straight again.

"But what about his lover then? Have you thought about her? Or the child? If you had your way, they'd be the ones abandoned. Or would you try to change things earlier, so she'd never met your father in the first place, perhaps? That still wouldn't change how he felt. It wouldn't fill that hole in his heart that cried out because he'd never met the one he truly loved. Would you ask him to make that sacrifice just so you and your mother could be happy? Would that be true happiness?"

Wataru felt his strength—his will—draining into the sand on the beach. He couldn't stand. He couldn't even lift his head. It was all he could do to slouch there, pummeled by the sweet voice's words over and over again.

"You're just as selfish as he is," she said crisply.

"So...what are you telling me to do then?" Wataru asked, his voice weak.

"Ah hah! I've been waiting for you to ask me that. Destroy the Goddess. Then you can become Lord of Vision. I don't know what foolishness Way-finder Lau told you, but I know the truth. The real world and Vision are like two sides of the same coin. How else could the Goddess affect the destinies of people in your world, Wataru?"

Two sides of the same coin.

"You could go to the Goddess on bended knee and beg to change your little meaningless destiny...or you could grasp all of Vision and your world in your hands. All would bow to you, and do exactly as you say. If you told your father not to carry emptiness in his heart, he would not. He could not. If you told your mother to love you she would, dutifully. And if you told your father's lover she wasn't needed in the world, she would simply cease to be. If you said that her baby never existed, it never did. The whole world would change as you see fit, and you wouldn't feel a shred of guilt. You will be enlightened."

The world would exist for you alone.

"What happiness, what joy! What a beautiful way for the world to be. Don't you think so, Wataru?"

For a moment there was silence—an utter absence of sound.

Wataru slowly shook his head. "I won't do it," he whispered. "I won't." The trembling faded from his voice.

I like Kee Keema and Meena because of who they are. Their kindness, their gentleness touches me—that's why we're friends.

And Togoto—he carried me through the sky not because I willed him to do it but because he respected the station of a Highlander. And Kutz, when she followed me into Meena's hospital room, she did it out of a sense of duty.

Their actions have meaning because they act of their own free will. What would be the point if everything happened as I wished it? I don't think that would be beautiful at all.

"You're wrong," he said quietly. "What are you, really? Why are you telling me these things?"

The whispering of the waves. More silence.

"You really disappoint me, you know that?" the sweet voice answered in a low tone. "But, fine. Do whatever you like, my little goody-two-shoes Brave. You still have time to reconsider. I have a feeling you'll end up following my advice."

"Never!"

"Now you're shouting. Here, let me tell you something. You've been duped, right from the very start.

"That young starseer doesn't know all there is to know about the Great Barrier of Light, or the sacrifice necessary to maintain it. In fact, he was unaware of the most important part. Not only him, but most of the people here in Vision don't know."

"Don't know what?!"

"Not only one person is sacrificed," the sweet voice said slowly. "To rebuild the Great Barrier requires two sacrifices: one from Vision, and another, a Traveler from the real world. Each of these...is called the Half."

Wataru had trouble understanding what he was hearing.

"It's like I said. Vision and the real world are two sides of the same coin. How could something as great and powerful as the Barrier be built from only one side? A sacrifice from the real world is necessary too."

Once every ten years, the Porta Nectere opens, and a lone Traveler comes from the real world burning with a passion to change their destiny.

"The Porta lets in a Traveler and delivers them to the Goddess—a sort of sharing of blood between Vision and your world. But, once in a thousand years, when it comes time for the Mending, things are different. Two Travelers come to Vision and one of them, the Half, must give himself up as a sacrifice.

If he does not, both the real world and Vision will be plunged into chaos forever."

Duped. Tricked.

"And Wayfinder Lau saw fit to tell you nothing of this, did he? What was your friend's name—Mitsuru? You are the two Travelers. One of you has been chosen to be the Half already…and that old coot didn't tell you a thing, did he? Be sure of it, he knows the truth. He just didn't want you to become frightened and try to go back to the real world. Of course, Mitsuru doesn't know what's going to happen, either. Though, he's much, much smarter than you are. I should think he's gotten an inkling of the truth by now."

Wataru heard bubbling laughter in his ears. Who could be laughing?

"I'm sorry, I'm sorry," the voice apologized. "It's just, you looked so cute there, staring at the sea, frightened out of your wits. You don't have to be so worried. We don't know that you are the Half yet. But be warned: Mitsuru is a stronger Traveler than you, and he did come here first. Perhaps he will beat you to the Tower of Destiny, have his wish, and go home to the real world. Two minus one is one, Wataru. That would leave only you here in Vision to become the Half. So sorry."

Lies! All of it, lies! The words rose in Wataru's throat, but there they stopped. *She's mocking me.*

"You don't believe me?"

How does she know what I'm thinking all the time?!

"It's okay, you don't have to believe me if you don't want to. Soon you won't be left with any choice but to accept the truth of what I've told you. Of course, by then, it will already be too late," the voice giggled. "I think I'll be leaving now. See you soon."

Oh, and don't forget…

"Destroy the Goddess. No matter which way you turn, there's no other path for you to take."

chapter 28
The Elder of Sakawa

Wataru went back to Kee Keema's place and tried to get some rest. Sleep, unfortunately, proved elusive. Wide awake, he stared up at the ceiling all night.

With the dawn, the sky grew light, and the sound of the waves grew louder. It was as though the sea had been asleep too, and now was waking for the day. Wataru lay still, hoping beyond hope that the soft sounds from the shore would somehow wash away all memory of what happened on the beach the night before.

Somebody was shuffling across the sand outside their hut.

"Oy, a messenger!"

Someone else was waking another person up in a hushed voice. There was talking.

"Look, in the sky to the east. Why, it's another karulakin!"

"You're right. That golden banner—isn't that the mark of an official emissary from the government?"

So it had come already. Wataru sat up on the broad, soft leaf that covered his bed. Walking to the wooden frame that marked the door, he lifted the screen to see a crowd of waterkin gathered, pointing toward the eastern sky. Some had even climbed atop the roofs of their houses.

Something red was glimmering like a bright star. Wataru squinted to see flapping wings and a long, flowing golden banner stretched across the sky. He turned and gave Kee Keema a light push.

"Hrm? Urk? Up already, Wataru?"

Wataru looked into his friend's sleepy eyes. He was going to tell him to get up and get washed, but the words caught in his mouth. Kee Keema frowned and, finally, sat up.

"Oy, what's the matter there? I know, your head hurts! I never should've let them make you drink that stuff. Heh. Sorry about that!"

Wataru shook his head. Then he asked a question that surprised even himself. "Kee Keema, where are your parents?"

"Huh?" he said rubbed his eyes.

"We didn't meet your parents yesterday, did we?"

"That's true. I guess I was too busy talking and partying for all that. My Ma and Pa have been in Arikita for three months now. They're building a big hospital in the town of Parth, and my folks are helping carry up the materials. Sorry you couldn't meet them."

"Do they live with you, normally?"

"Nope. This here's my place, and mine alone. Ma and Pa live in a big two-story affair near the Elder's pagoda. Why do you ask?"

"It's...nothing."

Kee Keema grunted and scratched his chin. "Maybe you saw your parents in a dream, eh? That it? Feeling a bit homesick?"

No, that's not it. I just can't...

Just then, a sound like someone banging on a metal washbasin drifted in from outside.

"Oy, oy! A messenger! A messenger's come! Everybody! A messenger from the government! All to the Elder's pagoda! Messenger, messenger!"

Kee Keema's mouth opened. "This is something! I wonder what's up?" The giant waterkin stood, cradling his throbbing head in his hands, and rushed out, saying something about taking a quick dip in the sea first. Wataru stepped outside. The karulakin was no longer visible in the eastern sky.

That means he's already landed.

Wataru sat at the top of the steps leading up to the entrance to the house. The town crier came by, banging on what looked less like a washbasin than it did a large stew pot. Wataru heard similar noises coming from around town. The criers were out in force.

"Good morning, Wataru."

Meena's face peered out from beneath the rolling shade next to him. A white patch of hair behind her ear was ruffled from sleep. "I wonder what that's all about?" she asked with a worried glance at the crier.

"Do they often send out messengers like this?"

"No. I've seen them only once before, myself. I think it was when somebody important in the government died. Quite a rare event, in any case."

A large crowd had gathered around the pagoda. Everyone was quiet, and someone—perhaps an adviser—was standing next to the chief, speaking with him in hushed tones. He was the first to tell the crowd about the message the karulakin had brought. Then, like an interpreter, he relayed the Elder's comments as the Elder muttered softly in his ear. Meena explained it was because the Elder's voice had faded with age.

Wataru and Meena stood behind the large crowd of waterkin and observed the gathering. The crowd didn't seem too surprised by what they heard.

Said the adviser: "The Elder speaks! He says that this world, and our lives, were given to us by the Goddess. This is a certain and known truth. Our daily livelihood, our strong arms and backs, and the sea which gives birth to us and receives us in our final days—all were made by the Goddess."

"It is so!" the crowd chanted.

"If the Goddess were to demand of us a sacrifice, it would be our pleasure to provide such. Do not fear, my friends. For the finger of the Goddess points always unerringly toward the truth."

"It is so!"

"The one who is chosen is the embodiment of all our hope. If the finger of the Goddess should point at you, you would rise as a hero! It is so!"

"We shall not fear!" all the waterkin gathered there cried as one.

When the crowd quieted down, the Elder began speaking to his adviser once again.

"We waterkin honor the ancient teachings of the Goddess," continued the adviser. "As such, we are distinguished among all the races in Vision. We have much knowledge. Many of us already know of the Barrier of Light, and of the sacrifice, as it has been told from generation to generation among our people."

Many heads in the crowd nodded. "My," said Meena, looking startled. "I don't think many other people know about it. It was sure news to me."

"It is because of this that our Elder weeps not a tear for our village. He believes in you all."

A great cheer rose up. The adviser lifted his massive arms and silenced the crowd. "But Vision is vast. There are some races and peoples who do not share our unerring faith in the Creator. And these tidings are sure to bring them much fear. I ask that none of you be swayed by the disturbances to come. We waterkin have lived since antiquity under the Goddess's wing and so shall we for all time!"

"For all time!" The crowd hooted and hollered, pumping their fists in the air. Then the adviser turned and pointed toward the northern sky. "The starseers of Sasaya predict that Halnera shall begin this very evening. The Blood Star will appear upon the horizon—a glowing red sign of the age. But, I ask you, let us pass these days of Halnera in peace. On the honorable soul of our people let us swear our loyalty to the goddess here. We will wait with reverence the renewal of the contract between our goddess and the Lord of the Underworld!"

As one, the waterkin rose and gave a great cheer. Wataru spotted Kee Keema in the crowd, cheering along with the rest. Then, the waterkin joined their voices in harmony in a song of praise to the Goddess.

"According to the karulah who brought us this message, there are already some disturbances in parts of Arikita and Bog. When we lose our faith, we become weak. As we drive our darbabas across this land, we may encounter some of those who have lost sight of their faith, but I ask you to remain stead-fast and continue to aid one another. To our leaders, I ask you to give guidance to those whom you can reach."

And the gathering was over. The darbaba drivers— over half of the town, as it turned out— were directed to go to a separate meeting later. The waterkin shuffled slowly off.

"Are you okay, Meena?" Wataru asked.

Meena smiled. "I'm fine. It's quite a surprise, but still, it's only one person in all of Vision. I doubt I would be chosen for such a task."

Meena pulled Wataru away from the crowd so as not to get in the way, and pranced over to sit on some nearby wooden crates.

"I wonder where everyone in the Spectacle Machine Troupe was when they heard the news. I hope the children aren't too frightened. Then again, with Bubuho in charge, I'm sure he'll keep them all in line."

Wataru looked down at the ground.

"How about you? You look pale," Meena said, still holding his hand. "You're worried for us, aren't you?" She smiled. "Well, don't be. We kitkin may not be as fervent as these waterkin here in our faith for the Goddess, but we are devout in our own way. Starting tonight, I will pray to the star in the north. I will ask the Goddess. If she must take a sacrifice, I would ask that she do it with kindness, that there not be more sorrow."

"Is that enough?" Wataru asked sharply. "Don't you think it's cruel of the Goddess to demand something like that in the first place? Shouldn't we try to change it somehow? I mean, it just doesn't seem right. Even if it's only once in a thousand years, why should they need a sacrifice to defend the world?"

"Well, it is the Goddess's world after all. We didn't make it. I don't think there's anything we can do about it."

"Could you say that, even if you are the one chosen as the sacrifice?"

Meena withdrew her hand from Wataru's and put it on her cheek. "Why, I—I don't know."

"You do know! You wouldn't like it one bit!"

"I suppose. But maybe being chosen would free me from that. Maybe the people left behind wouldn't be sad either. I'm sure the Goddess would arrange things that way." Meena shook her head. "It's like what the messenger said. The sacrifice, the Great Barrier of Light, and Halnera have all existed for as long as we know. They were only kept hidden until now, save in places like this, where knowledge was passed down the generations by stories."

"That's the way it's been in the past. It should stay there. It shouldn't have to happen now, still. Isn't the fact that the United Southern Nations decided to make the knowledge public proof enough that times have changed? I was relieved to hear that there were disturbances in Arikita and Nacht, to be honest. It would be weird if everybody just took it smiling like these waterkin here."

"Wataru…" Meena said, her voice choking, "do you know what you're saying? Didn't those fanatics almost kill you back at that hospital? Have you forgotten that? What you're saying is no different than what those believers in the Old God say."

No, it is different. But Wataru couldn't bring himself to say it. *It's not about faith in the Goddess…*

I'm just frightened. I was scared when I heard the sacrifice would be chosen from the people in Vision. I was scared when I thought it might be you or

Kee Keema.

And now it's worse. I'm a Traveler. That gives me a fifty percent chance of being chosen. It's either Mitsuru or me. One of us has to go. Of course I'm scared.

But Wataru didn't know what to do. Should he try to get to the Tower of Destiny before Mitsuru, have his prayers answered, and escape to the real world? Would that make him happy?

Or would he ask the Goddess directly? *No, don't change my destiny. I only ask that you abandon the practice of taking a sacrifice. Then I can go home in peace.*

But what would happen then? He would be alone with his mother, hurt, without hope. His father would never look back, that was clear. Even if Wataru tried to chase them, he'd just have to face that woman again, Rikako Tanaka.

It's not fair, it's not right, it's cruel. No matter which way I go, it's a dead end. And if I sit here feeling sorry for myself, Mitsuru will reach the Tower of Destiny before me, and I'll be left alone. The sacrificial Traveler.

"Traveler!" a loud voice called out.

Wataru looked up. The Elder's adviser from the gathering was standing at the foot of their stack of crates, looking up at him.

From this close, Wataru could see that around his eyes and on his bared shoulders were written countless letters in fine ink. Tattoos. The adviser smiled, and the words by his eyes twisted upward. "The Elder wishes to speak with you. Might I?" the second half of the question was directed at Meena. She nodded.

"Then come with me," said the adviser, reaching out a hand to Wataru. "And you, kitkin girl, you might be interested to know that the karulakin messenger from the United Southern Nations is resting in the hut by the town gate. I believe he will leave soon, but if you wish to entrust with him a letter for your home or family, you should ask now."

The Elder was sitting where he had been that morning. He seemed more relaxed now, leaning up against the wall, with one leg bent.

"You may sit here," the adviser said, indicating a round woven mat in front of the Elder. When Wataru sat, they were only a few feet apart.

"Our Elder is quite old, and as such he can hardly hear," the adviser said, taking up a position at the Elder's side. "Still, he hears with his heart, and he heard the voice of your heart from the very beginning. He knows your pain and that is why he has called you here."

"The voice of my heart?" even before Wataru finished asking his question, the Elder slid forward with surprising speed and placed his clawed hands on Wataru's head. Wataru jerked backward reflexively.

"Do not move!" the adviser said harshly. "Be still a moment."

Wataru crouched and was still. It only lasted ten seconds or so. The Elder released him and slowly sat back down. Then he whispered in the adviser's ear.

The adviser nodded slowly and looked back at Wataru. "You have been bewitched by a demon."

"A demon?"

"Yes. But not a demon as you might imagine one to be. This demon is not of venom and darkness, but of sweetness and light. It lingers near you—it is near you even now. This is what the Elder says."

That voice that talked to him on the beach the night before—the voice that had been with him since that night in his room, in the real world. Was that whom he meant?

The Elder nodded and said something else to the adviser.

"It seems you have been aware of this."

Wataru put his head in his hands. "But I..."

"Do not be frightened," the adviser said. "The demon feeds on your fear. Look up, look into the Elder's eyes."

After being prompted a few more times, Wataru finally looked up.

The Elder, sitting there in a heap, seemed unfit even to stand on his own two feet, let alone support the hopes of an entire village. Yet his eyes—blue like the sea—burned with a light brighter than that of a man in his prime. The Elder spoke and the adviser relayed his words. "Traveler, we ancients know that Halnera is more than a trial for our people. It is a test for the two Travelers, as well."

"You know that? You know that I might be the sacrifice?"

"I know it all. Since ancient times, whenever it has come time to renew the Great Barrier of Light, the Goddess has made things this way."

Wataru leaned forward. "Then, how can you let it happen? It's cruel to sacrifice people like that!"

The Elder seemed unfazed. "Vision has its own ways. You were summoned here by the Goddess, a visitor to our world…It is not your place to meddle."

"But why don't you do anything about it?"

"The doubt you hold in your heart—you will not be able to ease it on your own."

Wataru's doubt. Wataru's dead end.

"All that you consider now—your fears of being chosen as a sacrifice, of leaving your friend behind, of abandoning your quest. All these fears you have created, and given shape, but none of these fears will disappear on their own."

He really did know everything. Wataru sat back down weakly. He hadn't said a word, and yet the old waterkin had seen it all.

"Traveler, you are summoned here by the Goddess, yet even still your faith in her wavers. You are losing the objective of your journey. The demon seeks to lead you from your path and into the darkness."

The Elder continued talking and the adviser dutifully relayed his words. "These things that trouble you, they are like a mirage in the desert. You fear what does not exist, and seek to escape what cannot chase you. You are merely wasting your time. Go, meet the Goddess. The world rests within her heart."

"But Mitsuru will get there before me…"

"It is not always the Traveler who runs fastest who will reach the Tower of Destiny."

Huh?

"The Tower of Destiny appears only before the Traveler who has walked the true path. Young Traveler, let go of your doubts, make for the Tower of Destiny. There you will find the truth. Only when you ask the Goddess will you receive your answer."

The Elder smiled faintly. "And only when you reach the tower and stand before the Goddess will you know the question you must ask."

He then instructed Wataru to make for Sasaya. "Now is the time to borrow the knowledge of the great scholars. They have studied the history of Vision, and wish to know of its making. The Tower of Destiny, where sits the Goddess, is distant indeed. Yet the true path goes there directly. You must find it. Only the starseers who possess the power and knowledge of the ancients know the whereabouts of the gemstone that lights the way to that path."

With that, the Elder leaned back against the wall and closed his eyes. The adviser stood and placed a small blanket over the old waterkin's knees.

"He is weary now," the adviser said. "Do not forget what he has said. My hopes go with you as well, Traveler."

Wataru hesitated and then nodded. "I will go to Sasaya as you have requested."

"Good," the adviser replied. "The National Observatory is there. It is a great gathering place for starseers. You will find the Observatory in the town of Lourdes. Take a darbaba. You should reach your destination in five days."

Without thinking, Wataru grasped the adviser's hand. "I-I don't even know if I want to change my destiny anymore. I'm not even sure what that means."

"Do not fret. All Travelers who come to Vision know this doubt at one time. Some are able to free themselves from it, and others are not, and fall off the path."

"What happens if you fall off the path?"

The adviser shook his head. "That is something not known to us who live in Vision. It is something for the Goddess to decide and know."

"That's what I don't get," Wataru blurted. "How can you all just trust the Goddess to do everything, without even bothering to question it? Isn't the weakening faith throughout Vision a sign of something? Aren't the disturbances in Arikita and Bog a sign of unhappiness?"

Wataru had no doubt that the people upset with the news of the sacrifice and Halnera would understand how he felt. They might even go along with that suggestion—destroy the Goddess, she had said. *What if that was the correct way? What if that was the true path?*

Wataru heard the gravelly voice of the Elder. The adviser quickly moved to his side, put his ear to the Elder's lips, and returned to Wataru. "Now go, Traveler."

The adviser put his hand on Wataru's back and gave him a gentle push. "If your path is true, you will not see us again. In parting, let me tell you what the Elder has just said, his final words for you."

How can you defeat a god in whom you do not believe?

chapter 21
The National Observatory of Lourdes

The journey across Sasaya to the town of Lourdes was more depressing than Wataru could have imagined.

For one thing, he was still thinking about his discussion with Meena by the pagoda in Sakawa. For another, he couldn't easily forget the advice he received from the Elder. He needed to put aside all his distractions and find the Goddess. But that was easier said than done...

He also wondered how Mitsuru was faring. He thought about it all the time. Where *could he be?* Wherever he was, Wataru was sure that he wasn't wavering from the path. Undoubtedly he was using the powerful sorcery he had acquired in Vision and making a beeline straight toward the Tower of Destiny.

He's not as weak as I am.

Now that he thought about it, he realized it had always been that way. Mitsuru was totally amazing when he saved Wataru's life at the Triankha Hospital. The wind storm he conjured destroyed the barrier around the hospital and reduced the sula woods to a barren field of stumps.

Looking back, that was probably the best way to deal with the situation at the time. *But what about what Kee Keema said?* The cyclone had left many wounded in its wake. *Of course. There would have been injuries with that many Old God followers milling about.* There were a hundred people or more, all snatched up by the cyclone. *The injured were probably the lucky ones.* How many people had died that night, Wataru wondered.

Who cares? You reap what you sow, don't you? They attacked us first, anyway. They caught me, locked me up, were going to execute me.

But would I have been able to do the same thing? Without any hesitation? Would I have used all my strength like he did?

—I've no idea where we will be blown to. That's up to the wind.

Could I have cast that spell, trusting my own life to fate like that?

Speaking of which...

Wataru remembered the incident that started it all—in the Taimatsu building, with Mitsuru surrounded by Kenji and his gang. Mitsuru had summoned a demon, and the situation had flipped dramatically. That thing, Balbylone, had devoured Kenji and his two goons—Kenji head first—and swallowed their souls.

What had Mitsuru intended to do with them, really? Did he know what Balbylone would do when he called her to attack? Did he know and do it all the same?

There hadn't been a shred of hesitation in his face. They struck him so he struck back, that was all the rationale he required. Mitsuru was always like that—unwavering. No matter what difficulties awaited him on the way to the Tower of Destiny, he wouldn't blanch or falter.

And then there was Wataru: weak and insecure. And he knew that when it came to competitions, the strong always won. The Elder in Sakawa had told him that it is not always the one who runs fastest who finds the tower first. But Mitsuru wasn't just fast, he was determined. Wataru hadn't had a chance from the very beginning.

Just thinking about it made him swoon so much he had to grab on to the side of the cart to keep from falling off. Even faking a smile for the sake of his friends was out of the question.

The scenery on their trip didn't do much to raise their spirits, either. It was fine when they left Sakawa and camped their first night in a field by the sea. But when they reached the high road, things changed. There were more people traveling on the road now. Some had loaded furniture into crude carts, and others walked with large bundles on their backs. Some were elderly, and others carried children in their arms. Darbaba carts passed by now and again, carrying those too sick or old to walk.

In the beginning, Wataru had no idea what sort of people they might be, nor where they were headed. But on their second night out, when they were nearer to the border between Bog and Sasaya, the number of people on the road had greatly increased. And soon, they all began to trade food and share stories. That was when he found out who they were.

They were refugees—hiding themselves until Halnera had finished.

"I wouldn't go against the Goddess, not me, but what if she took my husband? It would mean the death of me and our children," a beastkin mother leading six small children behind her explained. They had brought a tent with them but had no idea how to set it up. Kee Keema and Wataru lent them a hand.

"Where are you headed to, then?"

"I was born in a woodcutters' village in the mountains on the border. I've no home there and my parents are long gone, but we still have the original hut. We'll live there while the Blood Star hangs red in the sky."

Her husband, a large beastkin man walking next to her, watched this exchange with a frightful frown. Later Wataru heard him scolding her. "What if they want to come along with us? We've a place to hide, but not all are so fortunate. You keep our plans to yourself, woman!"

Indeed, there were many among the refugees that had no particular destination. They merely wanted to go someplace where they could blend in and drop out of sight. Some asked Wataru where he was going, noticing his Highlander armband. When Wataru told them Lourdes, one replied, "Ah, with the observatory. The starseers there might know how to avoid being chosen. You might learn something, eh? Be sure to pass it along now, son."

In the end, some decided they'd go to Lourdes themselves, and it was the same with others they passed along the way.

At the end of all these conversations, Wataru would force a smile and say, "But only one person is chosen as a sacrifice. And there's so many people here, it's not like you, or anyone you know, would be the one chosen. I can't see why everybody's so worried."

People would agree, nodding their heads and muttering about how true it was. Some would even smile back. But then someone would frown, and a cloud would pass over their face, and they would say, "But what if the odds went against us? If I've any chance of getting out of it entirely, I'll take it."

"The rich, the merchants, and the officials have it easy," someone complained. "They hold prayer meetings to the Goddess every day, and make places of worship, and give her flowers. None of them will be chosen, for sure."

Indeed, the refugees on the road were mostly poor, with hardly enough money to feed themselves. What could they give to the Goddess?

"And you think that makes you more likely to be sacrificed?" Wataru asked them.

"Sure. Why, our bodies are the only things of value we have left."

The more refugees Wataru saw on the road, the more certain of it he became. The ones leaving their homes in fear of Halnera were almost entirely poor.

It wasn't just the refugees—they saw other things along their journey to make it even more miserable. In one town just beyond the border, from a small chapel where they would expect to hear songs of praise to the Goddess, they heard shouting and crying—followed rather unexpectedly by something that sounded like many voices chanting a spell. They approached to find a chapel in flames, and before it, a young man in a black robe standing on top of a wooden box. He was shouting a sermon, his fist raised into the air. Villagers gathered around him and watched, entranced. Bathed in their attention, the man's eyes sparkled like sunshine on shallow pools of water. *What if he's the next Cactus Vira? Will he lead his new flock astray in the same way?* Wataru grew more and more worried.

On the afternoon of their second day in Sasaya, they came to a fork in the road. A sign announced that the right headed to the sea and the capital of Sasaya. The left led into the mountains, toward Lourdes. The road to the left had less refugee traffic but was crowded with starseers commanding darbaba carts and udai. Some were headed from Lourdes to the capital, others in the opposite direction.

The starseers were of many ages and races, but all of them wore coats with tubed sleeves like Shin Suxin's, making them easy to spot. There appeared to be different ranks among them, as well, each with its own costume. By far the most elaborate of the garments Wataru saw among the starseers was worn by an ankha woman about his mother's age. She had on a rich purple coat with golden embroidery on the sleeves and hem. Her odd, conical hat was adorned with the same five-star pattern as that on the hilt of the Brave's Sword.

They had been traveling along the mountain road through mixed forest for half a day when they saw it.

"Look, there!" Kee Keema leaned forward in his seat, pointing ahead of them. "See that rounded roof? That's the National Observatory!"

It was already evening. The dome sparkled majestically against a pink-tinged sky. It looked exactly like a planetarium from Wataru's world. There was a half-transparent dome, with a large window cut out from it—probably, for some sort of telescope. Judging from the size, it must have been ten or twenty times larger than the one he had used in Shin Suxin's house.

They finally left the forest and arrived at a place where they could see the National Observatory and all the town spread around it. The town looked as though it had been carved from the side of the mountain. A brick wall surrounded the whole of it. More than half the buildings were fashioned of the same indigenous material. Everything looked old. Some of the houses had broken windows and crumbling bricks. It was clear where the focus in the town lay: most of their money had gone to building the majestic observatory.

"The starseers come here to study and live. All of the buildings on the outside of town are their apartments."

Men and women in those same tube-sleeved shirts were walking around everywhere. A darbaba cart, burdened with a mound of packages, was stopped by the town gate, and one of the gatemen was helping the driver unload his goods—all heavy-looking wooden crates. "Most likely books," Kee Keema ventured. "Starseers spend the nights taking observations, so they tend to sleep during the day. That's why the apartments in town are made with more floors beneath the ground than above it."

Indeed, the buildings along the inside of the town wall were barely taller than the wall itself—only a single story high. Surprisingly enough, many of the roofs and the top of the wall were crowded with Highlanders on patrol. Wataru could see the bright crimson of their firewyrm bands clearly from the road.

"I wonder what they're up to?" Meena wondered out loud. "Has there been trouble here?"

After the darbaba cart had been driven away, Wataru and the others approached the small guardhouse by the gate. The doors to the gate were made of thick iron bars, with a sturdy-looking bar drawn across them. The gateman was a beastkin with long, pointy ears.

"Oh? Highlanders, are you? Here to relieve some of the watch, perhaps?"

The gateman wore a breastplate of boiled leather, and a short sword hung from his waist. When he spoke it was with the crisp, no-nonsense tone of a soldier.

"Actually, we've come to speak with Dr. Baksan at the observatory. We were sent by the starseer, Shin Suxin."

Wataru felt guilty using Shin Suxin's name like that, but he didn't see any other way of getting in to meet with the—no doubt very busy—Dr. Baksan.

"Ah, right. I'll write you up a writ of passage. One moment."

One of the Highlanders was watching them from atop the wall. She was of a race Wataru hadn't seen before. Shape-wise she looked exactly like an ankha, except her skin was a shade of vibrant green that reminded him of new leaves in the spring. In her right hand was a bow, and on her back was slung a quiver full of arrows. She wore simple leather pads on her chest and shoulders, but her arms and legs were otherwise bare. She didn't seem to have a hair on her body, and her head was gleaming and smooth. Wataru thought she was beautiful.

Their eyes met, and she began walking slowly toward the gate. She smiled, revealing pure white teeth. "Where you from?"

"Gasara."

"You've come a long way then!"

"They're here to see Dr. Baksan," the gateman explained. "Here, your writ."

The writ was a piece of paper about the size of a postcard. A map had been drawn on the back.

"Dr. Baksan's study is on the top floor of the observatory."

"Thanks."

"You might have an easy time talking to Dr. Baksan, little one," the woman said, chuckling.

"Huh? Why is that?"

"Go see him and you'll understand."

"I was wondering," Meena said suddenly, "why all the security?"

"Can't you see?" the green-skinned Highlander said, pointing down the road behind them. A large crowd of people had gathered. Behind them, they saw more people streaming out of the forest.

"It's been like this ever since the messengers came. They all want to know who will be chosen as a sacrifice, and how to avoid being chosen. They think the starseers will tell them something. As if we knew something they didn't."

"We don't like them loitering outside the walls, so we've told them to keep their distance," the gateman said. "Go around to the back, you'll see their campgrounds. It wouldn't be a problem if they kept to themselves, but some of them get a little hot under the collar, demanding to be let into the observatory and meet with a high starseer. We've had some vandalism too. Thus the security."

"I'm afraid their kind will only increase as the Blood Star waxes in the sky," the green-skinned highlander said, looking down at the crowd. "This place, along with all government buildings, has been designated for level one security until Halnera ends. So they sent us out here..."

The woman stopped right in the middle of her sentence and burst into motion, swift as a gazelle, running down the top of the wall.

"Look!" Meena pointed.

A terribly emaciated man was climbing the wall, his hands clinging to the cracks between the bricks. The green-skinned Highlander ran until she was in firing range, then she stopped and lifted her bow. "You there! Stop! Off the wall! Comply or I'll shoot!"

Another Highlander on patrol came running from the opposite side. He was carrying a spear. Meekly, the man jumped down from the wall and stepped back.

No wonder you need security," Kee Keema grumbled.

"I just want to get inside!" the skinny man shouted up at the Highlanders. "I don't mean anyone any harm."

"No one without permission may enter the observatory."

"So where do I get permission then?"

"This is a government facility. The public isn't allowed inside."

"That's not fair!" the man said, scowling. "I see how it works. You government folks are sitting pretty up there. What do you care about us? You won't get chosen for the sacrifice. Put yourself in our shoes! This is life and death for us down here. You can't blame me for wanting to talk to the starseers and find out how I can avoid getting chosen, can you?"

A small crowd had gathered around the man, murmuring their approval.

"Even the high starseers cannot know the Goddess's intent before it is made plain to all of us. Go home. Pray and wait," one of the Highlanders called down to them.

"Go home and wait to die, you mean."

"You'd best enter while the getting is good," the gateman whispered to Wataru, unlocking the gate. "I need to close this up quick."

The three went through, and the gate swung closed behind them with a clang. The crowd heard the sound and pressed closer. Pushing aside the gateman, they clung to the iron bars and stuck their faces through.

"Let us in too!"

"Why do they get special treatment? It's not fair!"

Wedged between the iron bars, the faces of the crowd looked even sadder, more helpless, more pitiful. Wataru wondered how he looked from the other side. The whole situation was depressing.

"Let's hurry up and get to this Baksan fellow's place," Kee Keema said, urging them on. He looked gloomy—a rare state for the usually jovial waterkin. "Seeing people who have lost their faith like this makes me ill."

Meena was silent. Wataru, too, held his tongue, as they began to walk and follow the map.

Inside the building, the corridors were like a maze. There were tiny rooms everywhere, and even some places where they had to go through rooms to get to the next hall. They knew they had to go up, but they couldn't find the stairs.

There was a surprising number of people in the building. Most of them were starseers, with those familiar tube-sleeved shirts, but there were many other younger people dressed in regular workmen's clothes. Wataru had imagined they would find the starseers gathered in rooms, hotly debating esoteric facts about the universe. Instead, he found most of them sitting at desks making speculations, or examining thick books, or copying down passages from scrolls. In the hall, he ran into one particular starseer with his hands full of books. No sooner had Wataru apologized and picked up the books, than he ran into another. To make matters worse, most of the starseers seemed to have their heads in the clouds, and try as they might, they couldn't get a straight answer as to where the stairs to the top floor were located.

"I have a feeling this place wasn't quite so tall to begin with," Kee Keema said, breaking a sweat. "It looks like they built on top of a pre-existing building, and then did it again. There's probably no one stair that goes all the way up."

They found one staircase and then began their search for another one. Still, they were making progress. After ascending a few staircases, Wataru could look out a random window and see how high they were from the ground. After a while, they could see the campground in the forest behind the town.

"According to our map, this should be the floor," Wataru said, catching his breath. They had come up ten or eleven flights of stairs. There were fewer people and the hallway was empty. It was quiet.

"I think it's here, at the end of this hall," he said, pointing, when the door in front of them opened. A female starseer wearing a red shirt came hurrying out. Her arms, of course, were filled with books.

"Is Dr. Baksan in?" Wataru asked loudly. The woman shuffled past them, mumbling some formula to herself, and went down the stairs without even looking in his direction.

"Guess we'll have to go see for ourselves," Wataru said, stepping up to the door and knocking.

"Unnecessary!" a loud voice called from inside. It was a man's voice, filled with a strange high-pitched tension. The three looked at each other.

"Maybe he's saying that it's okay to go in without knocking?" Meena suggested.

Wataru slowly thrust his head into the room to see a veritable mountain of books and scrolls. And not just one mountain—he counted at least five separate stacks. Two walls of the room were actually large windows. The room was filled with sunlight, so bright Wataru had to squint.

"Is Dr. Baksan in?"

A cloud of dust rose from between two of the piles of books toward the back of the room.

"Unnecessary!" the voice said again.

"Um, we've come here to see Dr. Baksan."

More dust rose. "Then come over here! I'm not there, that's for sure."

So it was Dr. Baksan. Wataru stepped inside the room. "Excuse me, but where are you, sir?"

"Here!" came the voice, accompanied by another cloud of dust, this time in a slightly different place than before. The three split up and began moving between the piles of books, looking for the source of the voice.

He seemed to be nowhere. Kee Keema craned his neck. "I don't see him."

✳

"Excuse me, but where are you, sir?"

"I said I'm here!" shouted a voice from Wataru's feet. He sounded angry.

"Here?"

Someone was tugging on the laces of Wataru's boot. Wataru glanced down and yelped. By reflex, he jumped back, colliding with a nearby stack of books.

"Oy! Watch out!"

The sound of the books tipping over was followed immediately by a scream from Kee Keema. He was quickly buried beneath a mound of books.

Chapter 30
The Lecture

"Such rudeness!" Dr. Baksan scowled, raising a tiny fist and driving it against Wataru's shin. "You could take all the gold, all the crystals, all the jewels the Goddess ever made and you still wouldn't be able to buy the books in this room! Do you understand? Watch where you're stepping!"

Wataru moved quickly to an empty spot on the floor, and knelt. Only when he had done this was he finally at eye level with Dr. Baksan.

Baksan, he discovered, was a very, very short person. He only came up to Wataru's waist. He was wearing a tube-sleeved shirt of rich purple cloth, inlaid with many strands of gold thread, and the cylindrical hat on his head was embroidered with that familiar star pattern.

He was also very, very old. Bushy white hair reached down to his shoulders and his eyebrows were so long and wispy the ends reached down to his chest. The whiskers on his chin curled downward, reaching to the tips of his fingers. Indeed, apart from the pink nose jutting out from the center of his face, everything else was covered in white hair.

"Dr. Baksan?" Wataru asked.

The tiny scholar raised his fist again, his face beet red. "The only one with that title in this room, I daresay! You waste my time with your questions—no, you waste the very air itself!" This last comment was punctuated with a sharp jab to Wataru's leg.

"What are you doing down there, Wataru?" Kee Keema asked from behind him. He had just finished extricating himself from a mound of books.

"You there! Big waterkin!" Dr. Baksan cried, leaping into the air. "Don't touch that pile of books, or so help me..."

At last, Kee Keema and Meena could see who Wataru was talking to.

"Dr. Baksan is a pankin!" Meena gasped.

"First time meeting one of them."

"What's a pankin?"

"A very small, and very smart, race. Long ago, they lived in harmony with the ankha," Meena began.

"And then there was a war between pankin and ankha," Kee Keema continued. "The pankin couldn't hope to prevail against the ankha—giants from their perspective—and so they fled. After that they wandered the land and…" Kee Keema peered at Dr. Baksan, an unusually thoughtful expression on his face. "I thought they were all gone."

"Well, my apologies for defying your expectations!" Dr. Baksan said, lashing out with a foot this time. He was wearing tiny woven leather boots. "Sasaya is a haven for quite a few races that don't deign to live among the barbarians in Nacht, or the self-serving wretches of Arikita."

"I'm sorry! We had no idea," Wataru apologized, holding out his hands to ward off Dr. Baksan's attack. "We've come here to ask you something. Shin Suxin sent me."

Dr. Baksan's fist stopped in mid-swing. "Eh? Shin Suxin, you say?"

"Yes. He's your apprentice, right?"

"Apprentice? No. He's my student," the ancient scholar said, tugging on his whiskers. "It surprises me to hear that he would have any business with Highlanders. He was such a good-for-nothing punk."

Wataru's firewyrm band had not escaped Dr. Baksan's notice, apparently.

"Shin isn't a good-for-nothing at all, sir. When I met him he was carrying on his observations quite dutifully by the Swamp of Grief. I had gotten lost, and if it weren't for him, I might never have gotten out of there alive."

"Yes, yes, I see. Quite impressive, to be sure. Though one can't help but wonder at a Highlander who gets lost in the first place."

Wataru heard a snort of laughter from behind him. *Meena!*

"I don't know why you've come, but as you can see, I'm quite busy."

"We know, but if you could just spare us…"

"No, no sparing, not today. I'm busy. The door is right over there. Farewell!"

As nimble as a kitten, the scholar tried to slip between two mounds of books. Bracing himself against the onslaught that was sure to come, Wataru reached out and grabbed the pankin by the collar. Then he yanked him back by the nape of his neck, making the poor guy look even more like a kitten.

"Ack! What are you doing? How rude!"

"I'm sorry, but there's something we really need to know, and I'm afraid you're the only one who can tell us. You see, I need to know how to get to the path that leads to the Tower of Destiny."

"The Tower of Destiny?" asked Dr. Baksan, spinning around in midair to look at Wataru.

"Yes, I'm a Traveler."

Dr. Baksan's eyebrows lifted and his eyes opened wide. It was actually the first time Wataru could see his eyes under those bushy brows. They gleamed with a fire that was anything but old. For some reason, Wataru found himself recalling Mitsuru's eyes.

"If he's supposed to know so much," whispered Kee Keema to Meena, "why does he look so surprised to meet a Traveler?"

"I see," Dr. Baksan said, his voice suddenly quiet. "Perhaps I might enlist your aid, then, in searching for my boots?"

"Your boots?" Wataru asked, frowning. "Aren't they on your feet?"

"No, no, not these shoes. My boots. They're around here somewhere. Behind the big waterkin, perhaps."

The boots turned out to be something like platform shoes made out of wood. Once on his feet, the pankin could easily look Wataru in the eye.

"And this waterkin and the kitkin miss, they are your friends?" the scholar asked Wataru.

"They are."

"Then they need to step out. You are aware of the situation downstairs? Ever since the messenger came, the ignorant and unwashed masses have been disturbing our studies, making these halls of research as noisy as a city bazaar. Perhaps your friends could go help with security, eh?"

The two gave Dr. Baksan suspicious looks, but Wataru nodded, so they left the room in silence.

"Close the door now," Dr. Baksan said to Wataru. "When you're done, come back here to me."

Wataru returned, and the scholar lifted his bushy eyebrows to get a good look at the boy before him. He thrust out his little hands and took a hold of Wataru. "Welcome, Traveler," he said with gravity. "From the set of your face and your clouded eyes, I surmise you've come here because you know exactly what Halnera entails. Is this so?"

"I know that I may be chosen as one of two sacrifices."

"Hrm, yes." Dr. Baksan let go of Wataru's hand and wound his fingers together in front of him, as though in prayer. "And your two friends, they do not know what you know. Is this so?"

"Yes. I haven't told them yet."

"So. What is it you have come here for?"

Finding the answer to that question was the reason he had come. Wataru paused a moment, then said, "It's a long story."

"Good, I like a long story," the scholar said, smiling.

Wataru started from the beginning—from when Mitsuru saved his life, when he became a Traveler, up to his discussion with the Elder in Sakawa.

Perched motionless atop his wooden platform boots, Dr. Baksan listened intently to every word.

Finally he said, "We starseers compare the movement of the heavens with events here in Vision to divine the principles and workings of this world." His voice rang with weight and authority. "Yet, it is my deepest regret to inform you that the Elder of Sakawa overestimates us. No one in my school knows of the location of this gemstone that will reveal the path to the Tower of Destiny. Nor is there any record of such a thing in the ancient tomes. In fact, this is only my first time ever meeting a Traveler such as yourself." The scholar gave Wataru a curt bow.

"Oh..." said Wataru with obvious disappointment. But at the same time he was relieved. Even if a miracle should occur, and he suddenly came into possession of all the gemstones, he lacked the confidence in his ability to face the trials on the path to the tower.

"The Elder said that when I stood before the Goddess, I would know what to ask of her."

"Yet you do not believe his words. Am I right?"

"No, I don't."

"That's because you do not believe in yourself," the scholar replied quietly.

"What should I do?"

Dr. Baksan's whiskers twitched. He seemed to be smiling. "Were I to tell you, would you do it?"

Wataru couldn't answer.

Dr. Baksan assumed a lecturing pose, his arms crossed at his chest. "As I said before, we have spent many ages attempting to divine the principles that move our world. It goes without saying that the road ahead of us is still long, and there is more that we do not know than we do. Were you to compare our knowledge now to a spoonful of sugar, that which we do not know would be a field of sugar cane stretching as far as the eye can see."

"I was expecting you to say a mountain of sugar."

"No, because it is not enough to add to what we know. To obtain knowledge from that field, we must cut it and refine it. We must learn the most effective ways of harvesting and the methods of removing impurities. All this we must obtain as well as simply the knowledge we seek. That is what it means to study and learn."

Wataru had never heard this in school.

"If there were a grain I could give you from the spoonful in my hand now, it would be…"

Dr. Baksan swiveled on top of his boots, turning his back to Wataru. "Vision reflects the heart of the Traveler, and changes accordingly. That is what you must know."

Wataru recalled having heard those exact words before. *That's right, Wayfinder Lau. That's what he told me before I set off for the Cave of Trials.*

—*Vision changes for each person who comes to it.*

That's why the Vision he saw and the Vision Mitsuru saw were different. But something was wrong, because he and Mitsuru were definitely in the same place.

"It is very rare for two Travelers in Vision to be friends in the real world," Dr. Baksan continued. "This is why, in the two Visions that you both see, there are many similarities, and these similarities overlap. Because you each think of each other, this happens all the more frequently. That is why you will sometimes encounter each other—rub shoulders as it were. Do not think that Wayfinder Lau was trying to lead you astray."

Wataru nodded, but he wasn't completely satisfied. "Dr. Baksan, there's something I don't get. I would never wish for something as cruel as a human sacrifice. If Vision really is a reflection of my own heart, how could such a harsh tradition exist?"

"Oh, I think you know why!" Dr. Baksan cut Wataru off in a loud voice. Then, arms still crossed at his chest, he turned back around—a little too fast for his wooden boots.

"Ack!" the scholar yelped, falling backward onto the floor.

"Dr. Baksan! Are you okay?" Wataru shouted, peering beyond the platform boots. At that moment, the door to the study flew open.

A roar sounded through the room. "Where's Dr. Baksan? Come out! I said come out!"

Wataru slipped between the piles of books and turned toward the door. He peeked out from between two weighty tomes.

"Stay back! Nobody come close! Do what I say, or she gets it!"

Wataru gulped and ducked down behind the stack. When he took another look, he saw a giant man—the beastkin—standing at the door. He wasn't alone. The woman starseer they had passed earlier was with him. He was holding her pinned. Her arms were behind her back, and one of his sharp claws was at her throat.

"I know you're here, Dr. Baksan! Come out! You want your student to die?"

"I am here!" the scholar said in a loud voice. "I'm here, but I'm afraid I cannot get up by myself!"

Wataru looked behind him to see Dr. Baksan lying on the floor, pinned underneath one of his tall wooden boots. Wataru must've knocked it over with his knee when the door slammed open. Hurriedly, he rushed over and began helping the diminutive starseer up.

"I am here!" he shouted again as soon as he was on his feet, and began to run for the door. Wataru grabbed him by his collar a second time and held him back. "Don't run out there. He has a hostage!"

"What?"

"Sir?" It was the woman starseer. She was sobbing. "I'm sorry, I know you're busy. But I think he's going to kill me!"

"Eh? Romy? Is that you?"

This time the scholar bolted for the door faster than Wataru could grab him. Wataru crept along the floor to the opposite side of the stack of books. He wanted to get a better look at the beastkin.

"Ach, Romy! What's the meaning of this!" Dr. Baksan said, running to the door.

The beastkin man lashed out with a powerful kick. "I said stay back! Back! Where's Dr. Baksan?"

The scholar dodged the kick at the last moment, sprawling on the floor. He stood up, coughing and waving his arms. His nose was bright red. He was furious. "I'm Dr. Baksan! You told me to come out, so here I've come. Now let go of my student!"

"Be careful, sir," the woman named Romy said. "He's serious!"

"And I'm not?!" Dr. Baksan roared, hopping to his feet. "Fool! I don't know why you've come here, but this violence is utterly unacceptable! If you've something to say, I'd have you say it without threatening my students!"

The request was reasonable enough, but Wataru wasn't sure the beastkin holding Romy would react in a reasonable fashion. His overall appearance reminded Wataru of the Highlander Trone in Gasara, but he was almost twice Trone's size. He wore simple cloth garments that were dirty and torn. His eyes were bloodshot with excitement, and there was foam at the corners of his mouth. His breathing was ragged, and his breath was hot. Even the nails on his feet were sticking straight out.

Blood was dripping onto the floor. For a moment, Wataru was afraid that it was Romy's, but then he saw an arrow sticking into the beastkin's left calf. One of the Highlanders on watch must have shot him.

"You, little old man! Are you really Dr. Baksan?"

"That's what I've been trying to tell you!" the scholar raged, stomping his feet. The beastkin frothed at the mouth and pinned Romy's arms behind her back even tighter. She gave a little yelp.

"You look like a man of knowledge. So tell me. How do I make sure I don't get chosen?"

Dr. Baksan stood absolutely still and stared at the beastkin. "Oh, is that it?" he asked at last.

"Of course it is! I know you know too! That's what you've been studying here all these years, isn't it? And you've been selling your secrets to the politicians and the rich to make your fortune! Well, now it's my turn!"

"I'm sorry, but I've done nothing of the sort," the scholar said, his voice noticeably quieter. "I can understand why you would be tempted to believe such delusions. I understand, but it is entirely without basis in fact. No one in our world knows how to avoid being chosen, if indeed there is a way at all."

"Lies! You can't trick me, little man!" the beastkin roared. His bloodshot eyes were opened wide and spit flew from his mouth. "It's her blood on your hands if you don't tell me! I'm serious!"

The beastkin tightened his grasp on Romy's throat. The slender woman appeared to be in considerable pain.

Wataru began to move between the stacks of books, trying to position himself at the beastkin's side.

"I know you're serious. And indeed, none of us shall rest easy until Halnera is done," Dr. Baksan said consolingly. "For all I know, it may be me who is chosen. This affects us all. We must cling to the thread of hope that only one person will be chosen. That, and faith, are the only two ways we can master our fear."

Wataru circled around to the beastkin's left. From his hiding place, he had the beastkin on his right, and a window on his left. If he fired a shot from his blade, he might be able to get him to release his grip on the woman. Then he could dash forward, getting himself between them.

There was another thing to consider: from a few moments before, he had been hearing voices from outside the entrance to the study—probably the Highlanders coming up the hallway. The moment they knew Romy was free, they would be inside in a flash.

It's all in the timing. Wataru slowly drew his Brave's Sword, and steadied his grip on the hilt. *Come on, just turn a little more to the left—just a little more. I don't want to hit Romy. Just a few inches more and I've got you.*

Just then, with a heavy clang of armor, a knight appeared in the entrance to the study. "That's enough," he said with calm authority. "Dr. Baksan has told you the truth. No matter what you do here, no one can help you. The only thing you'll earn is a trip back to prison."

Blinking, Wataru lowered his sword. *It's Captain Ronmel of the Knights of Stengel!*

Sheathed in platinum armor, the captain looked like he was made of solid steel. But on closer inspection, Wataru saw that his chest plate and greaves were covered with countless nicks and scratches. The captain's helm was off, his hair was tussled, and his cheeks looked more sunken than they had when Wataru had first met him.

Sword still at his waist, and gauntleted fists hanging loosely by his side, the captain walked toward the beastkin.

"Halnera is ordained by the will of the Goddess alone. All we can do is humbly wait until she makes that will known to us. Now, release your hostage, and come here."

The beastkin froze, drawing his breath in ragged gasps, still holding on to Romy. For a moment, it looked as though he might follow the captain's instructions. His arms pinning his captive's hands behind her back relaxed ever so slightly.

But in the next instant, something like a violent storm surged up from inside the beastkin, and he began to tremble uncontrollably. "You're one of the Knights of Stengel," the beastkin growled between clenched teeth. "I don't listen to murderers!"

Both Wataru and Dr. Baksan were taken aback. *The Knights of Stengel, protectors of the peace in the south, murderers?*

Captain Ronmel made no reaction. Then, slowly, he reached out his left hand, pointing at the beastkin. "If you are Gyu Titus, peasant of Nacht—and I think you are—then that title is better directed at yourself."

"More lies!" the beastkin howled. "I'm no murderer!"

"You were involved in a theft in Ghoza. You took down two Highlanders on the scene and escaped. The Highlanders asked for our help, and I sent men—who you also killed," the captain said, calmly. "You were caught for that crime, tried in Gasara, and sent to Golgog Prison to be executed. Three days ago, when you escaped, you attacked two of your warders, killing one. Wherever you go, blood is spilled, and lives are trampled. It is not I, nor the Knights of Stengel, who have done this. It is you."

"Lies, lies, lies!" the beast-man howled, slashing the air with his sharp claws. "Who drove us out of our village home? Who tightened the screws on us until we had to steal and rob to survive? It's you and your United Southern Nations! You tried to wipe us out! And now you want to take me, the lone survivor of my tribe, and make me the sacrifice! I know what you're about, I know! The United Southern Nations aren't going to wait for the Goddess to choose her own sacrifice, they're going to catch some poor unlucky bastard! A prisoner! You're going to take a prisoner like me and sacrifice him!"

Captain Ronmel was perfectly still, moving not so much as an eyelash. His eyes, the darkest blue possible, burned with a cold flame.

"More delusions."

"Lies!" the beastkin shrieked. "I won't be caught! I won't go in again!"

Howling, and still desperately clutching his hostage, the beastkin charged toward the window by Wataru. Apparently in his madness, he had forgotten they were on the uppermost floor. Wataru stood stunned for a second, watching Romy, eyes wide with fear, struggle futilely against the powerful clutch of the beastkin. The vibrations of the beastkin's pounding feet as he charged sent books tumbling. Captain Ronmel, who had leaped for the beastkin as soon as he saw him move, was buried beneath a collapsing stack of leather-bound volumes.

"Woorrrrh!"

The beastkin's shoulder collided with the window and shattered glass flew everywhere. A moment later he hung suspended in space, many stories off the ground. For a nanosecond, it seemed as though they were stopped there, the beastkin and Romy, hovering in space.

There was a scream.

It was the beastkin. The impact with the window had brought him to his senses, and now he remembered where they were. His ears stood straight up.

And then he began to fall, dragging Romy down with him.

Wataru leaped. Glass crunched beneath his shoes. Flinging aside his sword, arms outstretched, he ran, his abdomen colliding with the bottom of the window frame. Reaching…

The beastkin fell straight toward the ground, but Wataru's fingers touched something soft. The sleeve of Romy's shirt fluttered in the air. Wataru grabbed, clutching for her wrist.

Even though she was small, the effect of gravity was unforgiving. Holding the sleeve of her shirt with one hand, the waist of her shirt with the other, Wataru felt his own legs sliding over the frame of the window. *I'm being pulled down. She's pulling me through the window. I'm going to fall…*

She had gone through the window and was now looking up at Wataru. Her glasses had flown off her face. *She's next. Then it's my turn.*

What happened next was pure coincidence. Wataru's toes had been pointing up when he slipped through the window, and now they caught on the frame. He found himself hanging precariously by his feet upside down. Basic physical laws predicted that Romy would swing back and collide with the side of the building—and this is exactly what happened.

We haven't fallen yet. My foot, my toes—they can't hold for long. Just a little. My ankle will give. Then we'll be following, upside down…

He could hear shouting and a tremendous commotion coming from inside the building. Someone was yelling about books and he could hear banging and sliding noises coming closer to the window.

"N-no!" squeaked Romy. "I'm falling! You'll fall too!"

Wataru couldn't answer. If he put so much as an ounce of energy into opening his mouth, he knew his ankles would give. His fingers would slip.

Just thinking about it made his grip loosen ever so slightly. His hand slipped from her shirt and she dropped slightly.

"H-hang on to me!" Wataru said through clenched teeth. "Grab my arm!"

Somebody help! Captain Ronmel! Get over here!

"I-I can't. I'm going to fall!"

Wataru tried pulling her up with his one hand. *Bad idea.* The slippery cloth slid underneath his fingers. *Get another grip—quick—she's slipping…*

Then, miraculously, something small and hard slid into his fingers just as he was about to run out of sleeve. Romy's legs dangled. The movement threatened to rip her out of his grasp entirely. Her boots touched the wall, skidding downward.

"Let go!" she gasped. "Let me go or you'll fall too!"

That small, hard thing turned out to be the button of her sleeve. It had slid right into the cleft between two of his fingers. *I can grab onto this. I can pull her up.*

There was a light popping noise, and the button came loose in his hand. The thread had snapped.

Romy's hair billowed in slow motion. She began to fall. In shock they looked at each other, one above, one below. Wataru's feet began to straighten. His ankles were giving. Still upside down, he began to slide down the wall of the building.

Suddenly, he felt strong arms around his waist, pulling him upward. From the corner of his eye, he caught sight of something red, shooting like an arrow. The shooting red Star.

"Romy!"

As Wataru slid now in reverse, he saw a karulakin, wings tucked tight to its body, plummeting down after the falling student starseer, catching her just before she hit the ground. Then he was up and through the window.

The floor was covered with books. Wataru landed with the spine of a particularly thick volume digging into his back.

"He made it!" Captain Ronmel shouted, leaning out the window. Wataru could hear people cheering and whistling from below.

As he got up from the floor, the captain turned and smiled at him. "We meet again."

"Y-yes," Wataru stammered, his voice still weak from his brush with death. "You...were the one who pulled me in?"

There were several people in the room now, weaving through the heaps of books scattered across the floor. Some of them wore the armor of the Knights of Stengel.

"You saved yourself. I'm surprised you managed to hang on so long."

"You caught me in the nick of time."

"Yes, well, it took me a while to get to the window. This place was like an avalanche of paper. I had to claw my way out."

"What is everybody doing on the floor?"

"Searching for Dr. Baksan."

Shortly, they heard a voice from somewhere beneath the books. "Over here! I said over here!"

Wherever he was, the starseer sounded unharmed, if a bit grumpy.

"Wataru!"

Wataru looked up to see Meena running through the door—until she was stopped by one of the Knights. "Careful," he warned her. "You might step on Dr. Baksan."

"No problem!" Meena said. She leaped into the air, bounced off one of the walls, and landed on a patch of bare floor right next to Wataru's side. "I was watching you from below. I thought you were done for!"

"So did I."

"Are you okay?"

Researchers finally managed to excavate Dr. Baksan. One of the Knights picked him up and cradled him in his arms like a child.

"Ooh, Traveler, you made it!"

"Yes, and Romy as well."

"Excellent, excellent!" the starseer walked toward him, slipping on books as he came, and took Wataru's hand. "My son, you've saved Romy's life!"

"That beastkin man…"

The starseer looked up at Captain Ronmel. "You came here in pursuit of the beastkin, Gyu Titus?"

Captain Ronmel straightened himself and gave a curt bow. "Indeed. I apologize that you had to be involved in this affair."

"And this Gyu Titus…was a prisoner?"

"Yes."

"I had heard of a rumor—particularly vile—circulating through our facilities of detention, that prisoners would be offered up as the first for sacrifice. Little did I dream that it would go so far as to spur a prison-break!"

"We were lax in our security." The captain's eyes showed the strain of being responsible for the safety of the people in a land gripped by chaos. *That's why he looks so haggard.*

"We didn't run into any major disturbances on our way here—but I gather it's worse in some parts?" Wataru asked.

Captain Ronmel nodded. "I fear you Highlanders will be summoned to an emergency meeting shortly. Perhaps that is what brought that karulakin here today. Lucky for the student."

Meena gave Wataru a worried look, but Wataru's attention was elsewhere—he was looking at his right hand.

A golden light was spilling out from between his fingers.

"What's that?" Meena asked, eyes wide.

Wataru slowly opened his hand. In his palm, the round button from Romy's shirt sleeve was glowing.

chapter 31
The Second Gemstone

The button lifted into the air, floating up from Wataru's palm until it was at eye level. There it hovered. It grew brighter, sending a lance of light straight as a sword into his eyes.

"The second gemstone."

Almost in response to Wataru's whispered words, another light spilled out from underneath a pile of books. It was exactly the same type of light emanating from the gemstone in the air before him.

"My Brave's Sword!"

Wataru recalled throwing it aside when he leaped to save Romy. He now walked over to the light and reached out to recover the sword. Whether Wataru grabbed the weapon or whether the weapon jumped into his hand—nobody could say for sure.

He gave the sword a swing, and the gold light began to spread from the second gemstone until it enveloped Wataru and half the room.

Wataru could hear shouts of surprise, but he kept his eyes focused on the gem.

Ding. The gemstone winked. And then, in a flash, a boy appeared. His body, hair, eyes, and skin all seemed to be fashioned from scintillating golden rays. A pair of golden wings beat slowly upon his back. In his right hand he held a sword. In his left, a shield.

—*We meet at last, Traveler.*

The golden boy called to Wataru, his face filled with pride.

—*I am the spirit of bravery, who gives honor to those with wills strong as steel.*

His voice sounded like the notes of an exquisitely crafted instrument, yet his tone was serious.

—*I am the one who opens the way for those Braves whom the Goddess has summoned.*

Wataru nodded.

—*Listen well, Brave. I appear before all those who desire me. Yet, when I leave upon these wings, it will be without sound, and swifter than time itself. Bravery is not difficult to summon or to create, but it is very difficult to keep. Be wary. There are few doors to me, and many windows out of which I may be lost.*

"I understand," Wataru said, a slight tremble in his voice.

The Spirit of Bravery's mouth was a flat, unmoving line, but his eyes smiled.

—*Blessings of the Goddess be with you.*

Then the spirit disappeared, and immediately the circle of light began to dwindle until it was sucked entirely within the second gemstone. Wataru reached out his right hand and the stone settled into his palm.

Until Wataru placed the second gemstone into its spot on the hilt of the Brave's Sword and sheathed the sword at his side, the room was completely silent.

It was Captain Ronmel who first spoke. "So this is the power of the Traveler."

Someone began chanting a prayer to the Goddess. It was Romy.

Her voice was beautiful as she prayed, eyes closed, hands clasped before her breast. The Knights, the Highlanders, the starseers, Dr. Baksan, and even Meena joined in.

When the words of her prayer were finished, Romy looked at Wataru. Her eyes sparkled.

"That button—no, actually it's not a button, in my house we called it the starseer's stone. It's a family heirloom."

As it turned out, the Romy family had been starseers for generations. Her father, his father, and his father before that—all of them had been scholars of the heavens.

"When he learned that I would come to study at the observatory, my father took the stone off his own sleeve and gave it to me. He told me to wear it always, and keep it safe. It is a gift from the stars, and from the past."

A long time ago, so the story went, one of Romy's ancestors (also a star-seer) had been out one night, when he witnessed a golden shooting star. He ran in the direction in which it had fallen, and found a brilliantly glowing stone upon the ground.

"Every scholar in my family has worn the stone during their time of study. My father gave it to me so I would remember my heritage. He hoped it would keep my mind on the task at hand. But I had no idea it contained a spirit of such deep importance."

Behind her, Dr. Baksan cleared his throat. While they had been talking, he had managed to once again climb to the top of his wooden platform boots, putting him more at a level with the crowd.

"It takes great bravery to search for knowledge and continue one's studies," he began. "Not all new knowledge is beautiful, or even to be desired. Yet there comes a time when, no matter how hard it is to accept what we see, no matter how much we do not want to believe it, our studies will cease and we will learn no more. Though the world may point and criticize, if the truth has been found, sometimes you must shout it from the rooftops in the face of all opposition. The pursuit of knowledge requires an iron will that always looks forward and never falters. Thus, I find it quite appropriate that a spirit of bravery should have found a home in the family of a starseer."

Romy nodded and smiled. "Thank you for saving me, Wataru."

"Well, Knights of Stengel," Dr. Baksan began, addressing the crowd, "other places await your arrival in these troublesome times, I'm sure. I'm afraid their number grows by the day. Please, be on your way. Highlanders, I fear that the events of the day will have struck more fear into the hearts of the uninformed. Console them, and put them at ease. And, to my students..."

Dr. Baksan clapped his hands and coughed smugly. "Get this room cleaned up right away!"

Chapter 32
Wataru

"It may be my first time meeting a Traveler, though I have some knowledge of the related phenomena," Dr. Baksan said, trudging up the stairs ahead of Wataru. "You can use that gemstone to peer into the real world, is that not so?"

"Yes, I've done it once before."

"And for this you need a sigil, similar to the one engraved on the hilt of your sword? It just so happens that we have one here. It's in the room with our observational equipment. Follow me."

They ascended a gently curving staircase and quickly reached the observation room. The walls and floor were made of a lustrous shining white rock, polished so well that Wataru could see his reflection. The room was circular, with a giant telescope sitting in the very middle. It was at least ten times larger than the one Wataru had used at Shin Suxin's home. The barrel of the telescope was pointed up at the translucent ceiling like a cannon.

"When the sun goes down, the roof becomes transparent," Dr. Baksan explained, waving his hand in the direction of the ceiling. "It's made from a special kind of stone that becomes cloudy white under sunlight, yet perfectly transparent when it's dark. Yes, a curious stone. Only a single vein of it has been found in a mine in Arikita."

The starseer stopped beneath the barrel of the telescope. "See?" he said, pointing down at his feet. "The sigil is here. But it is not visible now. The sigil is made out of the same stone as the ceiling. While the sun is up, it blends in with the floor. When the sun sets, it will rise from the stone."

Turning to Wataru, the starseer continued, "But before that, I would have a word with you. First, let me thank you again for saving my student. I have seen with my own eyes the extent of your courage and kindness, and the rightness of your heart."

He's praising me, Wataru realized belatedly. *Then...why is he staring at me like that?*

"Because of this, I shall tell you something. Know that I tell you this only because I am assured by your actions that you will understand my meaning."

Subconsciously, Wataru straightened his posture.

"Remember I told you that Vision is a reflection of your own heart? Wayfinder Lau told you the very same thing. Think on this a moment. If the events that occur in Vision are a reflection of what lies inside you, then why is there prejudice? Why does the Goddess demand a sacrifice?"

That's what I want to know! That's why I came here...

"Why does such backwardness and cruelty exist here in your Vision?" he asked again. After a pause, he resumed, speaking slowly. "There is one answer, and it's simple. It is because there is backwardness in your heart. There's a part of you that hates what is unlike you and avoids those who think differently, that curses, hates, and wants to live better than others. It envies what others possess, and schemes and plots to take what is theirs for your own happiness, and their despair. Vision reveals this part of you only in such a manner that you cannot look away from it."

"Wait a second..." Wataru began, startled by the sudden criticism. "I don't think those things..."

"Oh, I know, I know," Dr. Baksan said, holding up his hands. "You are brave. You are kind. You think well of others, and your friends. You have a good heart. But within you there is also hatred, jealousy, and the will for destruction. This is a fact you must learn to accept. You cannot turn your back to it and hope to run away."

Wataru stood there dumbfounded, when a memory emerged that made his jaw tighten and snapped his eyes wide open.

How could he forget the events he had seen in the Swamp of Grief? He remembered his ghostly twin, the one who killed the image of his father. And, later, how he witnessed the senseless slaughter of Lili Yannu, and how he ran from the stone-baby who accused him of murder.

Was that part of my truth too? Maybe it hadn't been an illusion after all.

Maybe it was a part of himself he hadn't noticed until now.

"It is not only you. All people are like this. There are no exceptions. No one can have a perfectly good heart. If someone did, he would doubtlessly be capable of doing more harm than evil itself. If there were a Vision made by a heart such as that, you wouldn't find me going there anytime soon."

"Dr. Baksan…" Wataru began. The strength went out of his legs. "Are you saying that the hate, and the rage, the prejudice, and the desire for sacrifice in my own heart are causing pain to the people of Vision? If I left, if I went away, would the bad things go too?"

"Not at all, not at all."

"So then what do I do? How do I fix it?"

Dr. Baksan took a step toward Wataru and took his hand into his own. "It is all within you. Vision exists as a reflection of the entire being that is you. Go on, knowing this fact. Let yourself and your heart wander in your search for the way to the Tower of Destiny. In your doubt lies the true path."

"That doesn't make any sense!" Wataru cried, trying to free himself from Dr. Baksan's hands, but the tiny scholar merely tightened his grip.

"If prejudice and destruction and hate are you, then friendship and kindness and bravery are you as well. If the one who does not wish to be sacrificed is you, then so is the one who feels anger at a Goddess who demands that sacrifice. If the fellow who disdains other races and wishes to pin the injustices of the world on them is you, then so, too, is the one who would give his own life to save that of a friend. Your life has been in danger many times since you have come to Vision. Yes, there are those here who would kill you. Yet, at the same time, there are those who seek to aid you, and save you, without a thought for their own personal gain."

The followers of the Old God. The guillotine. The ankha boys who dreamed of a day when they would rule the south.

Meena's song. Kee Keema's smile.

It all came from me.

"Look at yourself. Hatred and anger, kindness and bravery. They are all yours, and rightly so. Accept this, face it straight on, then ask yourself what it means to change your destiny. When you have your answer, the way to the Tower of Destiny will be open to you. By the time that path opens, you will know what you must ask of the Goddess. You see, you will not find your answer from the Goddess. It is the path to the Goddess that is itself your answer."

Wataru shook his head. "But what about the sacrifice? I can't accept it. I can't imagine it happening to someone else, and I sure wouldn't want it to happen to me! If I could, I would go to the Tower of Destiny right now and ask the Goddess to stop it once and for all."

"And then you would return to the real world," Dr. Baksan said quietly. "You would go back to the real world, your destiny, and yourself, unchanged. The desire that brought you to Vision in the first place would be unrequited."

"And if I said I was fine with that?"

"Perhaps you are fine with that now. Perhaps you would be fine for a year. Perhaps even five."

But what about the future?

"I believe you would reach a point in your life when you would regret your decision. You would regret having given up your only chance to change your destiny because you lost to your fear of being chosen as the sacrifice, you lost to your anger at the cruelty of the tradition. You will feel responsible, and you will hold your friends responsible as well. You gave up your chance to save them from being chosen. If no one had been kind to you while you were in Vision, perhaps you wouldn't have cared who was chosen to be the sacrifice. This is what you will think. You would think that, instead of letting yourself be chosen as a sacrifice, you should have overtaken the other Traveler, changed your destiny and gone home before he had the chance. Yes, you will grind your teeth and spit curses in your regret. All the unhappiness and ill luck that befalls you in the real world will be due to that one decision you made here in Vision. And then the ultimate irony: your wounded, hating heart will create another Vision, filled with horrors more terrible than any prejudice."

I won't—I won't ever be like that, Wataru thought, but he couldn't say it out loud.

"You see? You have not yet found the true path," Dr. Baksan said, his voice becoming gentle. "That is why the decisions you make now betray your future. Make no mistake, you would betray yourself. The Elder of Sakawa was right. Take his words at face value. It is no riddle. Find the path, and meet the Goddess. I will give you the same advice. It is the only advice I can give."

Dr. Baksan let go of Wataru's hand and looked up at the domed ceiling.

"When the sun sets, you will walk the pattern beneath the stars and go home to the real world for a short time. I will not ask whom you will meet, or whom you will speak with. Nor will I ask you anything upon your return. Follow your heart, Traveler. Should you decide to abandon your journey, and only then, come to my study. I will send a letter to Wayfinder Lau and arrange for your passage back through the Porta Nectere."

"Have there been Travelers in the past who have just given up like that?"

"Of course. It is not unusual for a Traveler to end his journey before it is finished. The ancient books tell of this. Some returned to the real world, and others, though there are few, remain here in Vision. I suppose one could find a certain sort of peace living in a world that reflects the inner workings of one's own heart."

Wataru hung his head. *I can't do it. I can't run away to the real world, not now.*

"I'm going to see Mom," Wataru said, lifting his head.

He passed through the Corridor of Light to find himself, once again, in a hospital room. This time it wasn't night, but evening. His mother was sitting up in bed, enveloped by the pale pinkish light of the setting sun. She was staring out the window.

Wataru popped out of the corridor and came down by the side of her bed. Kuniko didn't seem to notice. She was very thin. She looked much older, but she was still his mother. His throat choked up with a combination of home-sickness and guilt.

"Mom?" Wataru called out softly. He was surprised at how weak his own voice sounded. He wanted to talk to her, and at the same time he didn't want to see her looking so sad. For a moment he thought it would be better if he just left and came back when it was all over. What good would it do to talk to her now while everything was still unclear? Wouldn't it make her worry more?

He was on the verge of turning around when Kuniko lifted a hand and wiped at her eyes. She was crying. Tears made a line down her cheek in the fading light.

The realization shook Wataru even further. *I can't leave her here to cry. That's worse than making her worry more. If I leave her now, she won't make it until I get back. Her body will wither away. Her heart will crumble to dust.*

Wataru's journey was no longer for him alone. What Wataru needed in Vision was also what his mom needed, waiting here in the real world.

Hope.

"Mom?" This time he made sure his voice was loud and firm.

Kuniko's eyes opened wide in surprise. "Wataru!" she exclaimed. With both hands she yanked off her comforter and jumped out of bed. Wataru ran to her with his arms outstretched and hugged her tight. It had been a long time—years even—since he had hugged her like this. He noticed immediately how thin and sickly she was.

"Wataru! It's you, isn't it?" she said, rocking back and forth, tears streaming down her smiling face. Then she let go and held her son's face in her hands. She looked into his eyes and said, "You came home! Where did you go? Why did you leave?" She was sobbing loudly.

"I'm sorry, Mom," Wataru said. He was crying too. It felt like his heart had swollen to fill his entire body. A strange mixture of tears and joy filled every part of his body.

"I'm sorry. I'm sorry I left you alone. I never stopped thinking about you."

"Where have you been? Did someone take you? Did you run away? Were you scared?"

Wataru wiped his eyes with his sleeve, and, holding his mother's hand, stood up straight. "Mom, I've started on a journey—a journey to change my destiny."

His mother blinked, uncomprehending. "What's that? What are you talking about? I don't understand. You're going on a trip by yourself?"

Then she spread his arms and looked him over from head to toe. "What are these clothes? Why are you wearing this costume? Is that a sword at your waist? What are you doing with such a dangerous thing? Where did you get that?"

The Corridor of Light won't be open for long. I have to hurry. Wataru stilled his racing heart and said, "First, tell me, how are you? Have you been in the hospital this whole time? What does the doctor say?"

"I'm fine, don't worry about me!"

"You're not fine, Mom. And look, I'm not hurt. I'm healthy. Okay? You inhaled a lot more gas than I did, after all."

Kuniko's skin went even paler. "I-I'm sorry, Wataru. That was foolish of me. What if I'd hurt you? I…"

"It's okay, Mom. I'm not angry. You were tired, and unhappy. It happens. But I'm fine. I have friends helping me. Mitsuru Ashikawa's there. He's the one who took me to Vision…"

"Vision?"

It was difficult to explain quickly. Wataru realized he was probably talking in non sequiturs. The more he said, the more his mother looked confused, and the tighter her grip on him became. It was like she was trying to pull him back and save him from some danger.

"I wanted to change my destiny. I wanted to make it so Dad never met Rikako Tanaka, so he never left us. I wanted to change all this, to get back our old life. That's why I'm going to the Tower of Destiny."

But then I forgot why I was there.

Suddenly, a realization crept over him. "Even if I change destiny, I wouldn't be changing myself," he heard himself saying. "And if I can't change myself, then no matter how I change what happens, I will never get rid of the sadness, or the hate. Vision's shown me that—it's shown me what's inside myself."

That was it. He hadn't understood fully until just that moment. He finally felt the advice of Dr. Baksan, the Elder in Sakawa, and Wayfinder Lau becoming a part of him, their words running through his veins.

"At first, I thought I could make the past just go away. I thought that would make us happy. But it doesn't work that way. I'd still be the same old Wataru. Changing your destiny doesn't mean getting rid of everything you don't like. Even if you made everything go away, you still couldn't take it out of your heart."

He knew now that even if he went to the Goddess and demanded that she abandon the sacrifices, it still wouldn't change the fact that deep in his heart, he feared being the one chosen. If he used the Goddess's power to abolish prejudice in Vision, it still wouldn't change the part of him that wanted to blame others for his own hardships. It was all the same. *Vision is a reflection of my own heart. That's what they meant.*

"Wataru…"

Though her cheek was still wet, Kuniko was no longer crying. A mix of confusion and surprise still played on her face, but somewhere in her eyes a new fire burned. It was small, but it was there all the same.

—*What is he talking about? It's like he's dreaming, or hallucinating with a fever. Like he's gone too far into one of his games, and can't get out. But still, something's different.*

Then, she knew what it was.

—*He's stronger now.*

Though his words didn't make any sense, it was clear that he had grown.

"Sometimes I'm scared," Wataru was saying. "Other times I'm sad. And most of the time, I have no idea what I'm supposed to do. I have a feeling there's more of the same to come. But, Mom, I have to continue this journey. I have to find the true path to the Tower of Destiny. I know that what I'm searching for awaits me there. Maybe it's not what I wanted at the beginning, but it's what I need. So wait for me, okay? I promise I'll come home when my journey is done."

The strength in Wataru's words caught Kuniko by surprise. For a moment, she let go of his shoulder and clasped her hands in front of her. She looked just like Romy praying in Dr. Baksan's study.

"You promise to come home?"

"Promise!"

"Are you...are you alone?"

Wataru shook his head firmly. "No, I have friends."

"This journey..." Kuniko stopped, searching for the words. "You're not the only one who's gone missing. That Ashikawa boy..."

"I know. He's in Vision too. But I'll find him and bring him home with me. We'll come home together. I promise."

Though Wataru's words made little sense to her, the strength behind them was beginning to have an effect on Kuniko. "What should I do then?"

"Believe in me, and wait," Wataru said, smiling.

Then Kuniko did something she hadn't done in a long time. She smiled back. "Are you sure? That's all?"

"Yep!"

From somewhere behind him, Wataru heard the ringing of the bell that signaled the Corridor of Light was beginning to close.

I'm running out of time.

Wataru gave his mom another hug and said, "Get better soon. And tell Grandma and Uncle Lou I'm okay."

Kuniko hugged him back.

"I have to go," Wataru said, stepping back from the bed. At that moment there was a knock at the door.

"You up, Kuniko?" came a voice from outside. The door opened. It was Uncle Lou. Wataru stopped, one foot already in the corridor.

"Uncle Lou!"

His uncle took a step inside the room and froze in his tracks. His eyes and mouth went wide open, and he dropped the paper bag he was holding onto the floor.

"Wa-Wa-Wa…" he babbled, shaking his head. "Wataru?!"

Uncle Lou ran toward him, but Wataru's ears were filled with the ringing of the bell. It was ringing faster, more insistently now. The entire entrance to the Corridor of Light was flickering—blinking like an emergency cone.

"I'm fine!" said Wataru from the entrance of the corridor. "Take care of Mom for me, okay? I'll come home, I promise! Wait for me!"

Wataru dashed into the corridor. Uncle Lou's outstretched arm caught only air.

"I'm sorry!" Wataru called back over his shoulder, his feet racing along the corridor that threatened to disappear under him. "I'll be back soon!"

As he ran, fresh tears welled in Wataru's eyes. He ran on without bothering to wipe them away. He could feel the corridor fading, crumbling just behind his pounding feet.

Up ahead he saw the exit to Vision. Dashing forward, he threw off the encroaching chaos with flailing arms, and dove through the exit headfirst…

…and collided with something very solid. "Oof!" It said, catching him in midair. "Urk? Wataru? Wataru!"

It was Kee Keema. He was huddling with Meena, Dr. Baksan, Captain Ronmel, and Romy.

"You made it!" Meena said, running up. "We were worried—the corridor was about to disappear."

Kee Keema gave Wataru a massive hug. His powerful chest and strong arms reminded Wataru of his uncle. The warmth in Meena's gentle voice reminded him of his mother's.

That's right. Of course. The real world and Vision have the same heart: me.

"Are you well?" Dr. Baksan asked, his eyes showing that he knew better than anyone what was happening inside Wataru.

"I'm fine, thank you."

"There's been an emergency summons," Meena said, a serious look in her eyes. "The Highlanders have new orders to help rein in the disturbances that are spreading through the south."

Wataru nodded. His eyes met with Captain Ronmel's.

"Right. Let's go!"

Chapter 33
The Fugitive

The Highlanders had gathered outside the gates to the National Observatory. Wataru's group hurriedly arrived to find that there were far more assembled than before. The faces of the Highlanders still on duty looked serious and drawn.

"Your attention, please," said a hefty voice from the center of the gathering. A giant waterkin was addressing the crowd using a wooden crate as a podium. He wore a round shield on his back and a curved sword at his waist. Though his body was covered with armor-like scales, he was wearing a boiled-leather breastplate.

"My name is Boré Kim Nan, chief of the branch here in Lourdes," he said in a voice strong and clear. "First, I would like to thank you for coming here to help us with the protection of our town—now designated a first-priority security zone by the USN government. Thankfully, the worst has yet to befall us here in town and in the Observatory. Save one small incident a short while ago, disaster has been averted. This is thanks to your vigilance."

Most of the Highlanders were tall and Wataru found himself surrounded by an impenetrable wall of bodies. Thankfully, Kee Keema was there. He grabbed both Wataru and Meena and hoisted them atop his shoulders. Now that they could see, Wataru spotted Captain Ronmel coming down from the front entrance to the observatory. He was wearing his armor, and held his helm cradled under one arm. Wataru watched him walk down the front observatory steps and cut across the courtyard to stand a short distance away from the gathering of Highlanders.

As soon as he stopped, five or six Knights in armor came around the side of the observatory, a train of udais trailing behind them. Once they were acknowledged by their captain, they saluted, after which they stood at ease.

One of the udais had a heavy-looking hempen bag slung over its saddle. *That's no ordinary baggage.* Wataru could clearly see the shape of a shoulder and a head wrapped up in the bag. It was the body of the beastkin who fell from the tower, Gyu Titus. They were probably going to deliver him to the branch office here in Lourdes.

"In this time of emergency, the branches have received an urgent request," Boré Kim Nan announced, taking a folded document from beneath his breastplate. "This comes not from the USN but directly from our branch chiefs. It is an order to chase down and capture a fugitive criminal. This criminal has stolen sensitive materials that could affect the fate of the entire United Southern Nations. Our latest information is that he has passed over the border from Nacht into Arikita. We think it a good possibility that he could turn up here in Lourdes."

Murmurs ran through the crowd, and one voice piped up, "Is he alone?"

"To the best of our knowledge, yes," Boré Kim Nan replied. "His name and age are both unknown, but we do know he is an ankha."

"Where's he from?"

"That too is uncertain. We have a drawing of his face that I'll hand out to you all shortly."

"Even if he's here in Arikita, this is a big place. Don't we have any other leads?" Others in the crowd murmured their agreement.

Boré Kim Nan nodded gravely. "The fugitive seeks passage to the empire in the north."

This latest revelation drew shouts of surprise from the crowd.

"Then he'll be heading for a port town."

"Hataya or Dakla—maybe even Sonn."

"We'll have to close the roads soon, or he'll slip through."

Just then, a woman's shrill voice shot like an arrow through the crowd. "Is he a spy for the emperor?"

"We do not know for certain, though it seems likely."

The murmuring grew even louder. Wataru saw fists clench and firewyrm bands sway, making the crowd look for a moment like a field of red flowers caught by a sudden wind.

"All of you, listen," said Boré Kim Nan. The crowd fell silent, quelled less by his authoritative voice than the grave expression on his face. "As I said before, this order comes not from the USN but from our branch chiefs, on their sole authority. You know how rare an occurrence this is."

Wataru looked over at Meena. He felt flustered, or excited—he couldn't tell which.

"As one might expect, the government has not given us its blessing. In fact, the senators have gone so far as to say that they regret our decision to release the order without proper authority. Word has it that the Senate meets on this even now, though we will have to wait for the results of their deliberations."

"The senators? Useless bunch of bureaucrats," a woman nearby swore under her breath. She spat out the word *senators* as though it were a particularly bitter morsel.

"The Senate's in Zakrheim, the capital of Arikita," Kee Keema whispered to Wataru in a low voice. "Zakrheim is landlocked—so there's no port. There are no factories or mines there either. It basically exists just for the politicians. Representatives from each country live there, and the Senate itself operates for about half of the year."

Wataru was wondering what they did for the other half of the year, when Boré Kim Nan's voice caught his attention.

"Of course, our branch chiefs have reason enough for their decision." He looked around at the crowd. "Friends, last night, the Goddess came down to our branch chiefs while they slept. She was the one who told them of this threat to the peace in the south. That is why they moved so quickly, without worrying about possible retribution from the government."

Wataru could feel Kee Keema inhale deeply. His eyes were glistening. "This is truly a miracle…" he muttered. "For the Goddess to appear…"

He was about to prostrate himself on the ground, when Meena gave him a sharp kick in the back. "Stop. Stop, Kee Keema! We'll fall off!"

A stir went through the other Highlanders. Around them, the wall of people crumbled. Some of them knelt, others bowed their heads to the ground. Without exception, they seemed to all be as moved as Kee Keema.

"We are warriors in the service of the Goddess Creator. The time has come for us to make good on our promise, and act in such a way as to bring honor to the descendants of the firewyrm."

At those words, a great cheer rose from the crowd. Wataru could feel the enthusiasm rise in a storm around him.

At Boré Kim Nan's direction, the Highlanders broke into teams to divide up the work that needed doing. Everyone was excited and talking quickly. Some teams mounted straightaway and rode out on the high road.

"What should we do? Maybe join one of the road patrols? Or we can help with the search here in Lourdes," Kee Keema said, anxious to get started. He paced back and forth, still carrying Wataru and Meena on his shoulders.

"I wonder why they think there's a chance the fugitive will come to Lourdes?" Meena said, her arms around Kee Keema's neck for support. "If all he wants to do is go north, then there's no reason for him to come through here. He should go straight for Arikita. I wonder where he's coming from, anyway?"

"He said in his announcement they didn't know," Wataru noted. "But it makes you wonder. Maybe it has something to do with whatever it is he's stolen?"

"That's right. Maybe he needs the help of a starseer here to read them or something?"

If that were the case, their first priority would be protecting Dr. Baksan, Romy, and the other scholars.

"Let's stay here in Lourdes and help with security," Wataru was saying, when Captain Ronmel approached, his men behind him. Wataru and Meena slid from Kee Keema's shoulders to the ground.

"Captain..."

Captain Ronmel nodded toward Wataru. The captain was a tall man, but still he came up only to Kee Keema's chest. "It seems like big trouble is afoot. Keep an eye on your young Highlanders."

Kee Keema bared his teeth, suddenly angry. "Wataru's tough. You don't need to worry about him, Captain."

Wataru tugged at Kee Keema's leather belt, worried at the sudden harsh tone in his voice. Meena was looking at him too, her blue-gray eyes open wide.

"We'll be heading toward the mining town of Arikita," the captain said. "A group of miners there have gone on strike, and riots have started. We fear there could be injuries or even deaths if we were to stand by and let them run their course."

"The strike...is because of Halnera?"

"Indeed. Take care should your hunt for the fugitive bring you to Arikita. It is the largest of the four countries, with the most people. It is a rich land, but that has made the poor even more desperate. I'm afraid the fear of Halnera is creating more hysteria than in places like Sasaya and Nacht." The captain made to leave, but after taking a half-step, he turned around and placed a hand on Wataru's shoulder. His silver gauntlet shone in the sunlight.

"You are a Traveler," he said, staring deep into the young Highlander's eyes. "You must reach the Goddess. Take care that you are not distracted by trivial matters, or placed needlessly in harm's way. Leave the defense of Vision to those of us who live here."

Wataru stood, stunned for a moment by the gleaming light in the captain's blue eyes. It reminded him of the light of the gemstones, the source of the Brave's Sword's power.

"I heard what the branch chief was saying," the captain said in a low voice. His eyes did not leave Wataru's for a moment. "If the branch chief truly intends for the Highlanders to act without the government's approval, and the Senate is displeased with this, then it is not inconceivable that we who are the arm of the government will find ourselves at opposite ends of a sword."

Suddenly, Kee Keema's animosity toward the captain made sense.

"Even should such a thing occur, I urge you not to get involved. You are a Traveler. You must follow your own course. Do not forget that."

Then, the captain's worn and weatherbeaten face broke into a smile. "I'm sure that Kutz the Rosethorn would say the same. She is your leader, and I would have you follow my advice as though it were hers."

This time, the captain turned and did not look back. Springing lightly into the saddle of his udai, he gave a command to his men, sharp like a whip crack, and galloped off.

Wataru watched his dust trail disappear into the distance. When he could no longer see the captain, Wataru turned, feeling someone's eyes on his back. Most of the Highlanders had dispersed, but there were still several milling around by the gate. They were looking at Wataru with cold eyes.

"We're not friends of the Knights or anything," Kee Keema said in a loud voice to no one in particular.

A vague unease had begun to spread in Wataru's chest like a thick fog. Would they all really make it through Halnera? Would Vision descend into chaos?

He was glad for Captain Ronmel's concern, but Wataru was also worried about the fate of Vision—as worried as he was that he might be the Half, chosen by the Goddess as a sacrifice.

"Oh!" Next to him, Meena gave a sudden gasp of surprise. "What's that? Wataru! Look!"

Chapter 34
S.O.S.

Meena held her arms at her side, and leaned toward Wataru. Her tail was dancing behind her.

"Look, the Mirror of Truth! It's glowing!"

Indeed, a white light was spilling from beneath the collar of Meena's short vest. With one hand, she grabbed the leather strap around her neck and fished out the mirror. "It's showing something! I wonder what it is?"

The three of them looked into the mirror. It was indeed showing something. Or, rather, it was showing someone. He was wearing a white robe and carrying a staff in one hand. Was he a sorcerer? He was making some motions with his hands like he was trying to tell them something, but the image was too foggy to see anything clearly.

"It's too bright out. Maybe if we went to the shade…"

"Wait, weren't the starseers saying something about a break room in the basement of the observatory?"

Meena grabbed Wataru by the hand, and the three returned to the observatory. Once inside, they asked for directions.

The break room was simply furnished, with a round table, four chairs, and a single lamp. Kee Keema blew out the lamp. Now in total darkness, the Mirror of Truth seemed to glow even brighter.

The light opened, forming a circle like a lotus leaf in the air above the mirror. In the middle of that circle, a picture formed. It was the man from before, now in focus.

"Ah, Traveler!" He was looking directly at Wataru.

He's talking to me.

The figure had on a long robe of pure white that reached down to the floor. He also wore a simple silver crown upon his head. The object he carried in his hand wasn't a staff but something like a silver hammer with a long, slender handle. For a moment, Wataru found himself thinking of the statue of Cistina inside the chapel in Lyris.

"My voice has reached you at last, Traveler. What's this? You too are a child, I see."

The figure was a man, probably about thirty years old, maybe older. Whether it was the light streaming from his robe or the light generated by the image itself, Wataru couldn't say, but the man's face looked very pale, and it was hard to make out his expression. Oddly, though his voice sounded young, the hair above his crown was pure white. Even his eyebrows were white.

"Who are you?" Wataru asked, trying to hide the surprise in his voice. Was this some kind of spirit that lived inside the mirror?

The man in the white robe did not answer his question but instead transferred the hammer to his left hand, and placed his right over his heart. "Hear now the voice of our heart, Traveler. Please, you must help us. What little hope remains rests upon your shoulders."

"Oy, oy, what's this all about?" Kee Keema snorted.

"Our strength has weakened, and our remaining time slips through our fingers. Please, Traveler, you must save us."

Wataru took a step forward, leaning closer to the image. The light from the mirror stretched from floor to ceiling, but walking near didn't make it seem any brighter.

"What can I do? You want me to help you, tell me how."

"Come to us. Come, and listen to our request. For the safety and peace of all Vision, come, please."

The peace of all Vision.

He now had Wataru's full attention.

"I cannot say much. My words dance empty and meaningless through the air. We are waiting for you here, Traveler. Come to us upon your wings."

Then, the white-robed man disappeared. In his place, they saw another image.

Wataru's eyes opened wide. *Wait, that's…*

Shining spires between towering clouds of pure white. A bridge of rainbow light. A gray land in the heights, shrouded in glaciers.

The Undoor Highland! It was that same land he had seen for a moment while traveling with Togoto.

The image faded. The Mirror of Truth ceased its glowing, and the room returned to quiet darkness.

Stunned, the three stood there in the dark, gaping. From a nearby room, they heard the light snoring of a starseer taking a break from his studies.

Kee Keema lit the lamp.

"What was that?" Meena asked, holding up the mirror. She was staring at it as though she expected it to answer her question.

"The Special Administrative State of Dela Rubesi," Wataru said. Meena and Kee Keema both jumped.

"Really?"

"How do you know that, Wataru?"

Wataru told them about his flight from Sonn to Sakawa. "At the highest point of the flight, I caught a glimpse of it. Togoto told me what it was."

"Dela Rubesi…"

"So the man in the white robe lives there, you think?"

"It seems that way." Wataru looked at his friends. "We have to go."

Meena slid the mirror back under her vest. "I agree, but how?"

"W-wait a second now," Kee Keema said, putting a big hand on Wataru's and Meena's shoulders. "Let's think about this a moment. I don't know if you should just believe what that guy said, Wataru."

"Why not?"

"Why not…" Kee Keema hesitated. His long tongue whipped out and licked the top of his head. "Well, if that's really Dela Rubesi we were seeing, that place is a haven for followers of the Old God. They've got connections to the Northern Empire! Surely you haven't forgotten them!"

"No—though that is just a rumor."

"Sure, it's a rumor, but it's dangerous," Kee Keema muttered. "What if this is some kind of trap?"

"A trap?" Wataru was surprised.

"You remember those guys at the Triankha Hospital! They were going to kill you! If this fellow in white is one of them…"

Wataru certainly hadn't forgotten the events outside Lyris. He'd never been so frightened in all his life.

"But it was the Mirror of Truth that brought the message. Do you really think the Mirror of Truth could lie?"

"Hrm…" Kee Keema's heavy eyelids blinked. "I don't know. But you've got to figure that the mirror is just a tool. Maybe it's magic, but it's a tool all the same. It doesn't have a will of its own. And like any tool, someone might use it for evil."

"You just don't want to help anyone who believes in the Old God!" said Meena sharply.

Kee Keema winced, his long tongue licking the top of his head twice in rapid succession. "Whoa, hold on a second…"

The kitkin girl was mad. Sparks flew from her blue-gray eyes. "Isn't that right? You talk about danger and traps, but that's how you really feel. They could be in a whole world of trouble, and you'd leave them to die just because they don't believe in the Goddess. That's why you don't want to go!" Meena stomped her foot down on the floor. "If Wataru says we go, I'm going with him. You can do what you want!"

Kee Keema wobbled backward away from the furious kitkin. Wataru stepped between them. "Meena, don't be so angry. He's just thinking of our safety. Please?"

"Th-that's right. I'll admit, I don't much care for going to Dela Rubesi. But if Wataru says we go, then let's go. I said I would be his companion, so I go where he goes. The decision is up to him."

"Then you're forgiven," Meena said, suddenly breaking into a grin. "There's no time to lose. Let's get going!"

"But how do we get there?"

"Why, we'll ask the karulakin to take us, of course. They wouldn't turn down a Highlander."

With all the recent commotion throughout Vision, the karulah, uniquely suited to deliver urgent messages and information, were understandably very busy. Communications between the starseers at the National Observatory and the USN Senate were a priority. That meant that many karulakin could be present in town at any given time. Meena was certain they could find some of them who would help.

"Then I'll go ask where we can find some carrier karulakin," Kee Keema said, charging up the stairs. Now that they had decided to go, he seemed overly eager to help. Meena watched him go with a smile.

"Maybe I was a little hard on him. I'll give him a backrub later."

Wataru barely heard what she said. In his head, he was replaying the events surrounding his close shave at the Triankha Hospital. And that reminded him of his dashing savior, Mitsuru.

He remembered something the man in the white robe said.

—*You too are a child, I see.*

It was a strange choice of words. Did that mean that somehow he knew the other Traveler to Vision? Had Mitsuru already answered the white-robed man's call, and gone to Dela Rubesi?

If that were the case, then it meant Mitsuru hadn't been able to help them. Is that why they were calling on Wataru now?

"What is it, Wataru?" Meena asked, looking into his eyes.

"Nothing," he replied as he hurried up the stairs. There was no point thinking too much about it. They wouldn't know what was going on until they were standing in Dela Rubesi.

The headquarters for the karulakin carriers was a terrace on the third floor. When they got there, three karulakin were resting their wings beneath a large white banner shielding them from the sun. The terrace was suffused with an overpowering stench. "Pardon me, I've just finished eating," said one, picking at his teeth.

Lunch was, of course, gimblewolf meat. Wataru heard the soft sounds of Kee Keema quietly gagging behind him.

It fell to Wataru to voice their request, which he did, leaving out as many details as possible. The three karulakin listened attentively, craning their necks, until he was finished. "We understand," one replied. "But we are not, at present, able to honor your request."

"Is your need to go to Dela Rubesi perhaps related to the emergency summons from your branch chiefs?" another asked. "If so, there is nothing to hide. After all, we were the ones who carried that summons to all corners of the land."

Wataru mumbled a vague answer in response. It was hard to claim that this request had anything to do with the fugitive at all. It probably wouldn't even classify as official Highlander business, for that matter.

"In any case, even if we wanted to help you, we could not. Our wings cannot take you to Dela Rubesi now."

The other karulakin nodded in agreement, their heads bobbing up and down.

"You will recall that when Togoto carried you to where you could see Dela Rubesi, it was to catch a rising current that crosses over all of the south."

"Yes, that's what he said."

"But," the karulakin continued, "for several days now, there has been odd weather near the Undoor Highland. That strong current you rode is no longer there. It has stopped."

"That is not all, that is not all," said one of the other karulakin, flapping its wings. "The clouds around the Highlands have swelled in size, and the temperature in the air above has dropped precipitously. No matter how strong our wings, in such weather we could muster only half our strength at best. In the worst-case scenario, we might freeze even as we flew."

"This is no normal shifting of the air currents. We believe something is happening on the ground in the Undoor Highland that has caused this to happen," another one said thoughtfully.

"At any rate, we cannot carry you. I apologize, but we must ask you to find other means."

Wataru sighed. If even the karulakin—ever proud of their aerial prowess—said it was impossible, it probably was.

Unease began to seep back into Wataru's consciousness. Something terrible was going on in Dela Rubesi, he was sure. That must be why the white-robed man was seeking his help.

"I understand. Thank you for your time."

"I am only sorry we could not be of help."

Wataru waved to Meena and Kee Keema, then turned. As he began to walk away, for no particular reason he thrust his hand in his trousers pocket. His fingers touched something hard and smooth.

What's that? What did I put in my pocket? He fished it out and looked at it. It was shiny and crimson, glowing like a ruby—it was a scale.

The firewyrm scale! Wataru had completely forgotten his encounter with the dragon Jozo in the Swamp of Grief—and the scale he had received in return for saving the dragon's life.

Wataru smacked himself on the forehead. He had never done that before, but he had always seen people doing it on TV. It seemed like the right thing to do.

"My! What's wrong, Wataru?" Meena said, looking into his eyes.

"Karulakin sirs!" Wataru said, running back out onto the terrace. "You think a dragon would be able to fly to Dela Rubesi?"

The three karulakin looked at one another. "I would think a dragon's wings could carry you there, even without a current. And cold is nothing to a dragon. Yes, I believe one could get you there without much difficulty at all."

"If they can fly through the Stinging Mist, then they can certainly fly to the Undoor Highland," another agreed.

Then the third spotted the crimson scale in Wataru's hand. "My, my, my, what's this?"

Wataru told the story of the scale. The karulakin watched him as he spoke, their beady eyes open wide.

"Then it is clear what you must do! You must make a wyrmflute out of that scale! Like us, a dragon is a proud-winged soul, strong in virtue and bravery. He will keep his promise to you, you can be sure."

Kee Keema gave a big clap with his hands. "Then let's get started making that flute!"

"How do I make it? Jozo said I needed to seek out a master craftsman..."

"We'll go to Lyris!" Meena said, her face brightening. "You could ask Toni Fanlon! I'm sure his skill would be a match for that scale!"

The largest of the karulakin took a step forward with one long-clawed foot. "If you go to Lyris, it is on the way to my next destination. Were it just you, young Highlander, I could certainly carry you that far."

"Excellent!" Kee Keema shouted. "Wataru, you fly to Lyris first. Meena and I will follow by darbaba. Shouldn't take us more than three or four days to get there—and by that time Fanlon should have the flute ready! We'll find a suitable place, call us a dragon, and wing it to Dela Rubesi together!"

Kee Keema was all ready to get their luggage for the trip, but another of the karulakin stopped him, a dark look upon his face. "Waterkin, and you, kitkin girl. You would do best to not go too close to Lyris. By order of the branch chief, Lyris has been closed off to all traffic, both in and out. You see, they have a problem between the ankha and the non-ankha in that town…"

"We know all about it," said Wataru, clenching his hands into fists.

"Ah. Then you can guess how word of Halnera has pitched the community into strife. We've heard reports of rioting and arson—most directed at the non-ankha, it seems. I've heard that many of the other races living in town have been incarcerated."

"Sounds like Branch Chief Pam's style, all right," Wataru said with a grimace. Apparently, Halnera had brought the ugly tension beneath the surface of Lyris out into the open.

"Young Highlander, you may be allowed inside, being an ankha, but your friends…I believe it would be best for you to arrange your rendezvous at a location outside of town."

At the karulakin's advice, the three decided upon the Great Marker Tree as their meeting place. The tree was a famous landmark for aerial navigation.

"You'll have no problem finding it by darbaba, either. And it's in the woods, so there'll be plenty of places to hide if there's any trouble."

Wataru and the others began to prepare for the trip with great haste. As he packed, Wataru could feel the anxiety in him growing.

I hope Toni Fanlon is weathering the storm in Lyris.

And what about Elza?

chapter 35
The Tragedy of Lyris

The karulakin that gave Wataru a ride was most cautious. When they arrived at Lyris, he circled briefly before setting him down.

"Did you see those tents down there, young master?"

Still airborne, Wataru had to shout to be heard over the roar of the wind. "The white ones? Yes!"

There were several pentagonal tents below—one particularly large one in the very center—with flags streaming from their pointed roofs. If Wataru's memory could be counted on, the building nearest to them was none other than the Lyris branch.

"Those are field tents of the Knights of Stengel," the karulakin told him. "Town hall is flying one of their flags as well. Judging from the size of those tents, that's more than a patrol. Looks like a whole division is stationed there in town. I'm afraid matters are unfolding on a somewhat larger scale than even we had imagined."

The karulakin slid through the air and flapped its wings—this time directly over the field tents. Wataru could see Knights standing around in silver polished armor.

"When Branch Chief Pam called for martial law, he must have requested help from the Knights," said the karulakin, making another pass over the encampment. "Those flags bear the mark of Zaidek Company. If I recall correctly, Captain Zaidek was born here in Lyris. A friend of the chief."

Wataru felt fear wrapping itself around his heart. "So, those Knights of Stengel down there are working with the branch chief."

"It is most likely. Look."

The karulakin flew over Bricklayer Street. Too high to see much detail, Wataru still couldn't miss the devastation below. Buildings were demolished, and the entire area was scarred by fire. The street itself was empty and devoid of people. Here and there, broken furniture and mounds of clothes lay mixed in with the ash and mud. It was hard to tell the location of Fanlon's workshop from here. Wataru feared it, too, was little more than a smoldering pile of rubble.

It looked as though something giant and terrible and full of violence had passed down the street. That was exactly it. Something named Hate: formless yet full of strength, it had chewed its way through the buildings and left detritus in its wake—a ravenous child with bad table manners.

And Hate, Wataru thought, *is always hungry.*

"Looks like there was quite a riot. No wonder the Lyris branch was unable to contain the situation."

Wataru had nothing to say.

I wonder where everyone went who lived on Bricklayer Street? He hoped they had escaped, but he feared that many had been arrested and imprisoned.

And the Knights of Stengel helped him do it.

Wataru remembered what Fanlon had told him about High Chief Suluka in Bog sharing some of Branch Chief Pam's feelings about non-ankha. *Suluka was the one who decided the Knights should be all ankha too.*

Above all the destruction, the Cistina Trabados Cathedral still towered, its great bell sparkling in the sun. Somehow, seeing it from the air made it seem all the more threatening. The shadow it cast upon the town dominated more than ever before. The cathedral basked in the sun, while Bricklayer Street was cast in darkness. Wataru knew it was impossible, but it seemed like the church's shadow was trying to swallow the entire town.

For anyone who didn't see eye to eye with the cathedral and the followers of the Old God, Lyris would be a very dangerous place to live. Even for a Highlander.

Lyris did not have a town gate like the one in Gasara. But checkpoints had been set up by both Highlanders and the Knights of Stengel. At the entrance where Wataru had first entered Lyris, a large blockade of logs had been erected. This handily blocked anyone from coming in or out of the town.

"What will you do, my young Highlander?" the karulakin asked.

"Let me down in a forest outside town. I'll find a way to sneak in."

"Very well. Be cautious."

The karulakin flew away from town, setting course for the nearby woods. After making sure no spies were lurking about, Wataru was delivered safely to the ground. The whole time, Wataru thought about how he was going to get inside Lyris.

Maybe I can pretend to be an ankha kid who lives there. I'll say I'm coming back from some errand. Wataru discarded the idea immediately. *They'd suspect me in an instant.* None of the well-to-do ankha living here would send their kids out on an errand with martial law in effect. *Maybe I could pretend I was lost, that I didn't know my way home. Excuse me, Mr. Knight sir, could you help me find my home?*

Wataru stood, chewing his lip, pondering his options (none of which sounded particularly appealing), when he felt a strange warmth at his waist. He looked down to see the Brave's Sword shining. Wataru quickly drew the blade from its sheath.

—*Wataru, Wataru.*

It was the voice of the spirit in the second gemstone.

—*You remember using this sword as a mageblade in the Swamp of Grief?*

—*Now that we are two, there is another use for this sword.*

—*Raise it, lift the sword!*

Startled, Wataru brought the sword to eye level. Of its own accord, the tip of the blade moved, tracing a pattern in the air. Right and left, then up and down forming a cross. All the while, the shining blade reflected Wataru's own face.

Suddenly, he felt lighter. *What's going on? Is this the new power?* If it was, it was nothing like the magebullet he had fired in the swamp.

Then, Wataru realized he could no longer see the sword. In fact, he couldn't see his own hand gripping the sword, although he still felt the hilt firm within his grasp.

I'm invisible!

The Spirit spoke.

—*Wataru, this is the sword's new power. As long as the cross is bound, your form cannot be seen. The sword has created a sacred barrier, hiding you from all eyes.*

—*Yet you must listen, for this barrier draws its energy from your own body. Do not maintain it for very long. Unform the cross as soon as you find a place to hide yourself. Hold it too long, and your strength will falter, and you will fall.*

"Understood!" Wataru felt himself fill with courage.

It was time to find Elza.

The branch in Lyris was overrun with people, both Knights and Highlanders. Branch Chief Pam could be seen sitting in a back room across the table from a Knight of Stengel, his helm resting on his knee. The two were engaged in a heated debate. From the armor and crest he wore, and the attitude of the Knights around him, it was clear this was Captain Zaidek.

Elza was nowhere to be seen. *Maybe she's at home.* Wataru stepped behind a potted plant and took a break from invisibility. After a brief moment, he raised the barrier again and went in search of Pam's private residence. As the spirit had warned him, keeping himself hidden with the barrier was exhausting—like climbing a mountain—and he found himself running out of breath and having to rest frequently. His pulse seemed to be racing faster than usual, another side effect of the barrier sucking its energy from his body.

Everyone Wataru saw on the streets of Lyris, including the Highlanders and the Knights, were all ankha. Most of the shops were closed, and some even had their windows and doors boarded up. But compared to the devastation on Bricklayer Street, the center of town was quite peaceful. The shops that were open had long lines out in front. Walking by one, Wataru overheard conversations about where each place was getting its goods. The supply routes into the city, he learned, had been shut down.

"I suppose we'll just have to make do until they finish rounding up the undesirables," he heard one ankha woman grumble. Wataru felt a chill run down his spine. *Undesirables. They've closed off the town, and now they're hunting down all the non-ankha. Hunting them down...and then what?*

By the time he reached Pam's residence, Wataru was gasping like a fish out of water. As he got closer to the house, he was able to spot Elza directly in front of a second-story window. There was no one on the first floor when he slipped inside the front door.

Quickly releasing the barrier, he found a nearby chair and flopped down. His shoulders heaved with each pained breath. A sudden wave of dizziness came over him, and he had to hang onto the back of the chair to keep from slipping onto the floor. The chair creaked.

He heard soft footfalls from the floor above.

"Who's there?"

It was Elza. She was coming down the stairs. Wataru looked around, still clinging to the back of his chair.

"My, it's…it's you!"

Her beautiful black eyes were just as he remembered them. But her slender frame was even more sticklike. She seemed practically emaciated now.

"Where…is Mr. Fanlon?" Wataru managed to say, before tumbling off the chair. He fell to the floor, and it was all he could do just to breathe.

Elza hid Wataru up in her room and brought him some cold water. After a while he regained his composure and explained the wyrmflute to her.

"Yes, yes," she nodded. "I'm sure Toni could make that for you. In fact, he's probably the only one who could do it."

Wataru noticed her eyes filled with tears. "But he can't help you now…he was arrested," she said. "When my father deployed a unit of Highlanders to Bricklayer Street, he was taken prisoner."

"Do you know where he was taken?"

"The Cistina Cathedral."

"There? Not some detention facility?"

What, were they cramming people into the cathedral and trying to force them to believe in the Old God?

"There's a large dungeon beneath the church," Elza explained. "My father worked it out with the pastor there. They said the power of Cistina was the best thing for holding heretics."

The pastor would be Father Diamon, whom Wataru had met earlier. He remembered his shiny bald head and those eyes like thorns.

"So all I have to do is get into the dungeons beneath the cathedral?"

"Yes…but how will you get down there? I don't know the way. I've been there many times, but I've never seen any stairs going down."

Wataru took a deep breath. He would have to go and see for himself. He felt a strange fluttering in his chest, like his heart was beating slightly out of step. His legs, too, were a little weak.

"Have another drink of water. You look pale. And you should probably eat something too."

He shook his head. "Thanks, water's enough. I don't have much time." Still, he was deeply grateful when she brought him more water and a damp towel to wipe the sweat off his face. "How are you doing, Elza? I've seen the town—things arc rcally bad, aren't they?"

In response, Elza turned her tear-streaked cheeks toward the window. Walking over, she drew the curtain. "It's all because of the news about Halnera, about how a sacrifice is needed to remake the Great Barrier of Light."

Wataru had guessed as much. "There've been disturbances in other towns for the same reason. Prisoners and poor people seem the most worried. They're afraid they're more likely to be chosen. Some of the prisoners think that the USN government wants to sacrifice them to the Goddess before somebody important can be chosen."

"Yes, it is the same here."

"I think some people are taking advantage of the chaos for their own selfish agenda…"

Still gripping the curtains in her hands, Elza turned and frowned. "Yesterday, my father said there was some trouble in the mines at Arikita."

"That's right. The Knights of Stengel were sent there."

"Oh," Elza sighed, slumping.

"It looks like the distubance here had a lot to do with the ankha taking advantage of the non-ankha…more openly than usual, even."

Elza buried her face in the curtains.

"I just don't understand how things got this bad," Wataru said, half to himself.

Elza responded, her voice thin. "Only one person in the whole world will be chosen as the sacrifice. There's no cause for this much alarm. And it certainly doesn't have anything to do with race relations."

Wataru was silent. He thought there was plenty enough reason to be worried, even if there really was going to be only one sacrifice. For him, the chances were fifty-fifty.

"But it was worse than Toni and I had feared," Elza said, looking around.

"Even my dad and Father Diamon were surprised just how deeply the teachings of the Old God had spread through the ankha in town. You know about the teachings?"

Wataru nodded. "Enough to know they believe that the Goddess made the non-ankha races in her own image to fight against the Old God. They also believe that the Old God would one day destroy them all and make a paradise for ankha here in Vision."

A tear fell from Elza's eyes as she continued. "According to the teachings, the need for a sacrifice every one thousand years to rebuild the Great Barrier is another of the Goddess's schemes to persecute ankha. So, of course, an ankha would be chosen. Even if it is only one, every ankha is sacred and valuable in his duty to uphold the revival of the Old God, yet the Goddess chooses one of them. It's all a part of her strategy to weaken them, they say."

Wataru snorted. "Sounds ridiculous."

"I wonder," Elza said, looking at Wataru with sad eyes. "You are a Highlander, but I'm afraid you're still a child. No matter how ridiculous it may sound, for those who believe, it's the truth. To the followers of the Old God, the one whom the Goddess will choose is destined to be the savior of the ankha. That is why they must stop the sacrifice by any means possible."

Father Diamon had gathered a large crowd of believers at the Cistina Cathedral, explained Elza, and he had given a great sermon. That was when he explained to them that Halnera was not the time of the Great Barrier's remaking—that was a fabrication of the Goddess. To those believers in the Old God who knew the truth, Halnera was the time when the Old God appeared through the Blood Star in the north. At that time, the Goddess and all her followers would be destroyed.

"They say it's a sign of the coming of a holy war, when the followers of the Old God finally destroy the Goddess, and take back Vision for their own."

Elza's words reached Wataru, brushing against his cheek like a cold breath. He shivered. "The National Observatory in Lourdes didn't say anything like that."

"Of course they didn't. But people in Lyris believe Father Diamon, so it doesn't matter what the observatory said." Elza shook her head so vigorously the braid in her black hair came undone and her hair streamed over her shoulders. "That's why Toni was arrested. But he couldn't stand against them alone.

There was nothing he could do. They burned his workshop..."

Defeat pressed on Wataru's shoulders, and he felt like he was sinking into his chair. *Even if I did save Mr. Fanlon, he'd have no workshop to make the flute.*

Still, he wasn't about to leave Toni Fanlon to his fate. Wataru placed his empty glass down by his feet, and stood.

"What will you do?" Elza asked quietly.

"I'm going to Cistina Cathedral."

"By yourself? What will you be able to accomplish?"

"I don't know. But I have to find out the truth. If there are that many people down there held without investigation or trial, I can't let that stand. I'll expose the truth, get branches in other towns involved. Maybe there is something we all could do then."

Elza clung to the curtain, barely able to stand. The words left her trembling lips. "Toni might already be dead. My father told me. He said I'd never see Toni's face again..."

Wataru looked up at her. "It's too early to give up."

A tear ran down Elza's face. He touched her cheek with his hand.

"If you give up, they'll be no one left waiting for Mr. Fanlon. Don't give up hope."

"But..."

"And besides, I need that wyrmflute, and he's the only one who can make it. I'll save him, I promise."

"But you're just a boy. What can you do?"

Wataru drew his Brave's Sword and made the cross in the air. Before Elza's eyes he vanished.

When he released the barrier and reappeared, Elza's dark eyes were opened wide, and her face was so ashen he feared she might collapse on the spot. "Wh-what was that?"

"A little magic. It will help me."

Elza staggered, and Wataru jumped to keep her from falling. She was trembling and her shoulders were heaving with every breath, much as Wataru's had moments before. When she stood, she held his arms. "W-wait, just a second. Don't leave."

Elza walked over to a small drawer next to her bed, retrieved a small wooden box, and clutched it to her breast. It was small enough to be held in one hand.

"Take this with you."

Wataru took the box and looked it over. There was a small cloth belt attached to it. There was also a lock keeping the lid closed.

"Open it."

Obeying her wishes, he lifted the lid and discovered a bundle of neatly arranged craftman's tools.

"Toni's toolbox. He used it for all of his delicate work. He carried it around with him always, but before they set fire to his house, he gave it to me. He said that even if his workshop on Bricklayer Street was destroyed, he could use these tools to work anywhere. They're as important as my soul, he said."

"Are you sure?"

Elza nodded. Her eyes were still moist with tears, but her gaze was firm. "I believe you. Save him, and he will make your wyrmflute. Tell him that I will be waiting for him. Please."

"Understood," Wataru said, fastening the toolbox around his waist. "I'll give this to Mr. Fanlon when I see him. Soon."

Chapter 36
The Cathedral Cages

As it happened, Wataru arrived just in time for afternoon worship at the Cistina Trabados Cathedral. Believers sat on long pews arranged on either side of the center aisle. Standing at the altar, Father Diamon wore a heavy-looking embroidered silk shawl over his white vestments, and in his hand he held a leather-bound prayer book. He was reading in a loud, clear voice.

With his sword, Wataru formed an invisible barrier around himself. Once inside the cathedral, he stood at the far back of the room behind a row of burning candles. The long, slender tapers provided a blue smoke screen for him to hide behind. He released the barrier and took a deep breath. The air smelled of wax.

Wataru estimated there were about a hundred people praying. He had expected to find only ankha, but much to his surprise, there were several beastkin praying, as well. Their heads were lowered piously as they listened. The prayers themselves were palatable enough—Father Diamon urged his flock to give thanks to the Creator, and prayed for the swift recovery of those who had been harmed in the riots. But when Wataru thought about the real purpose of the cathedral here, he couldn't understand why beastkin would willingly participate in any worship.

Could it be that they don't know?

The reading of prayers ended, and Father Diamon began to give a sermon in a voice that echoed through the room. This too focused on the recent troubles in Lyris, and urged the people of the town to join hands and persevere through these hard times. It all sounded empty to Wataru. Still, the believers hung on every word, muttering their approval. All at once they stood and burst into song.

When the prayer service had finished, the congregation shuffled out of the cathedral. Father Diamon closed the front doors and lowered a bar to lock them. The hem of his vestments swept across the polished floor, making a soft rustling sound. The pastor inspected the candles around the altar, and seeing that all was in order, he disappeared through a small door in the back.

Good thing he didn't come to inspect the candles back here.

Wataru took a step out beyond the cover of smoke, brushed the dust off his sleeves, and looked around.

Just what is going on here?

The large doors in front served as the only exit and entrance to the building. It was the door behind the altar, the one Father Diamon had disappeared through, that interested Wataru. That led to another part of the cathedral for sure. *That's my way in.* But once he went through, his chance of running into Father Diamon or someone else grew exponentially, and he might have to maintain the barrier for quite some time. Wataru wasn't sure if his body could take the strain.

Surely a building this size has some other exit. Wataru considered going out again and examining the place from the outside.

Then, Wataru had the distinct impression he was being watched. He blinked.

No one was there. The cathedral was as empty as it had been a moment before. No one could be watching him.

I'm nervous. It's just my mind playing tricks on me.

Walking as quietly as he could, Wataru cut behind the pews, heading for the large central doors. He placed a hand on the bar...

Someone is watching me. Wataru could feel eyes following his every move.

Resting his hand on the hilt of his sword, Wataru slowly looked around. Where were they hiding, whoever they were?

Wataru's gaze went to the colorful stained glass on the walls. He could see the images of Cistina traced over and over again. Here she was appearing before a crowd of bowing craftsmen. There she was vanquishing foul beasts with the gem-tipped scepter in her hand.

She was drawn quite beautifully, with utmost attention paid to every detail. But the artwork was inanimate. There was no life in any of the images. Surely, they couldn't be the source of the eyes watching Wataru. Or was he wrong?

He grabbed the bar again, and this time heard a rustling sound behind him. Wataru tensed and whirled around.

What was that?

Wataru's nerves were so taut he could hear them giving off electric sparks. But that wasn't the noise he heard. No, this sounded like something moving...

The smell of freshly cut flowers tickled his nose. As it had been the last time he came here, a pile of flowers lay at the feet of the statue of Cistina. Wataru assumed they were arranged in that specific manner to hide the awful truth—that Cistina represented hate for beastkin.

False flowers.

Wataru allowed himself to catch his breath. Standing near the large doors he could see from here that a few of the white flowers had fallen from the statue pedestal onto the stone floor. That was the source of the sound he'd heard. They had probably been piled too high and fallen naturally of their own accord.

There was no time to lose. Carefully, so as not to make a sound, he removed the bar and began to push on the door. Five or six more flowers fell off the pedestal, revealing one of the statue's feet.

For a moment, Wataru shivered. It looked as if the flowers had fallen because the statue of Cistina had *moved*.

It's just a statue, silly.

He held his breath and watched. Just then, a rattling sound came from the door through which Father Diamon had disappeared. The door began to open. Wataru dove behind the nearest pew. The door opened, and someone stepped through. There was the sound of robes sliding across the floor.

Father Diamon? Uh-oh. If he comes straight down the center aisle, he'll see me!

Wataru hurriedly made a cross with the sword again, hiding himself behind the magical veil.

The sound of robes against the floor came closer. Wataru peeked over the pew to see that it was, indeed, Father Diamon. He had taken off his elaborate shawl and wore only his white robes. In his hand, he carried his scepter with the gemstone at its tip, just like the one the statue of Cistina carried.

His face seemed fuller, somehow, then when Wataru had met him the last time. He looked preternaturally lively, as though years had been taken off him within the span of a few days. Sweat gleamed on his shiny head, reminding Wataru for a moment of the view of the cathedral from the air. The cathedral had seemed to tower over the town of Lyris, blanketing it in shadow. Had the building somehow grown stronger, and Father Diamon with it?

The pastor walked by the pew Wataru was hiding behind. He went two rows farther, then stopped in mid-stride.

"I smell magic."

When he spoke, it was with that same gentle but powerful voice he used when reading prayers or giving a sermon. Wataru hunched down, and for a second he forget he was hidden behind the barrier. His heart thumped in his chest.

Father Diamon slowly looked around. A thin smile played on his lips.

I'm fine. The barrier is up—he can't see me. Wataru felt his breathing getting ragged, so he focused on slowing down, taking deep breaths. *I have to conserve strength.*

"Meddling wretch," Father Diamon said, turning his whole body around this time. "Where are you hiding, I wonder?" he muttered gleefully, his back to Wataru.

Just then he whirled around, and the scepter in his hand pointed directly at Wataru. "There!"

Before Wataru could react, the gemstone flared brilliantly, and a bolt of lightning shot from the scepter's tip. There was no time to dodge. Wataru took a direct hit from the bolt, holding his arms up to shield himself as best he could.

Numbness, like from an electrical shock, spread from the palms of his hands down his arms. Wataru was thrown into the air.

He was too surprised to feel pain. Wataru was scrambling to get to his feet when he realized the barrier of invisibility was gone. The bolt of lightning had caused it to dissipate. And there was Father Diamon looking at him with a broad smile on his face. His eyes shone with a dark fluorescence.

"H-how…"

Father Diamon took a step toward Wataru. "Did you seriously think your juvenile cantrips would deceive my eyes? I've known you were here for quite some time now."

So he knew, but he chose to wait and let me struggle.

Wataru got up on one knee, then stood, placing his hand on the hilt of his sword. Father Diamon's smile grew wider. "Who *are* you?" he asked, eyes glinting. He took a step closer. Wataru took a step back. "Juvenile though it was, not every child can work barrier magic of that caliber. When you came here before, you claimed to be a Highlander?"

"I *am* a Highlander," Wataru said, prouding lifting his chin. "Sworn to right injustice and defend Vision from evil."

Father Diamon gave a short, cruel laugh—like a dog barking. "Oh, very nice. You must be very proud."

Wataru felt the pastor's eyes looking him over, sizing him up. He began to tremble.

"That sword…" Father Diamon said, pointing at the Brave's Sword at Wataru's waist. His eyes narrowed. "That look in your eyes, and the scent of your magic…" Once again, the pastor's face broke into a leering smile. "Of course! You're a Traveler, aren't you?"

Wataru didn't answer. His body was tensed, ready to launch an attack at any moment.

"That's it. You *are* a Traveler." The pastor seemed very pleased with his discovery. "A cursed zaza-aku! A false god! Lowly servant, born from the primordial muck your false goddess stirred up in her vanity. Why have you set foot in this holy place? Do you think that your base existence can comprehend the radiance of this cathedral?"

"Where're the people from Bricklayer Street!" Wataru snapped back.

Father Diamon lifted his long, elegant eyebrows, gray with a dusting of white. "What's that?"

"Where's Toni Fanlon? The dungeons under this cathedral—where are they?"

"Oh, so *that's* why you've come. Let me guess: you intend to rescue them?"

"Tell me where they are!"

"Search for them, if you must, my little zaza-aku." Father Diamon held up his scepter in both hands, lifting the gemstone until it was at eye level. "Yet I fear you'll find it quite difficult to rescue the unclean dregs of this town...when you're dead!"

Father Diamon pressed the gemstone to his forehead and began to chant in a loud, resonant voice. "By the immortal cry of our God, bound in antiquity, by the power of his spirit, chained for eternity. Come now, honor those who are faithful to you. Bring destruction upon our foes!"

At once, all the stained glass in the cathedral shone brilliantly. It was as though lightning had struck each one of them at the same instant. Wataru lifted a hand to shield his eyes against the dazzling light. A shockwave passed through the floor beneath his feet, and he had to grab onto the back of the nearest pew just to stay standing.

"Lord above us, bring your judgment down upon those who would sully thy name!"

Father Diamon spread his arms, his voice a wild screech that echoed off the vaulted arches of the ceiling. In response, the stained glass shone again. In the glare of light, Wataru saw that each of the images of Cistina in the stained glass had turned. They were...

They're looking at me!

As one, they held their scepters high in their right hands. The mirrors in their left hands reflected Wataru's own image.

—*Here, our enemy is come among us.*

—*Look, our enemy is here in our grasp.*

As one, the eyes of all the Cistinas flared.

Crack!

Behind him, Wataru heard a clump of flowers dropping to the ground. Quick as a whip, he whirled around, then froze.

Not again.

Before his eyes, the statue of Cistina was stepping down from its pedestal, knocking aside the flowers that covered its feet. Dropping down, it sounded like stone grinding against stone. Its hand holding the scepter was thrust out to the side like a great wing.

"Observe!" Father Diamon howled with laughter toward the ceiling. "See our glorious Lady's wrath at the false god's defilement of her holy ground!"

The pupil-less eyes of the stone Cistina turned toward Wataru. He could feel rage and hatred boiling from those smooth gray stone orbs, rooting him to the spot.

The stone idol walked across the floor, mirror now held over her head. She swung the scepter up behind her, like a tennis player making a backhand shot. A great blast-wave burst from the tip and shot down the length of the cathedral. A wind smelling of poison and thorns buffeted him. The back of the pew directly in front of him was cut clean in two, like some stage magician's trick. Fragments of wood rained down on Wataru.

Without a word, he turned and ran.

"Yes, run, run, unclean wretch! Do you fear the judgment of God? Does it frighten you? There is no place in this cathedral where you may hide!"

As he shouted, a second blast-wave shot across the room. Wataru dove headfirst to avoid it. The sleeve of his shirt ripped, and he saw two or three rows of pews tossed up into the air.

Fthunk. Fthunk.

With each step of the stone Cistina, the cathedral floor quaked. She was only three rows away from Wataru now. Behind her, Father Diamon withdrew, holding his scepter aloft, and resumed his prayers.

Another blast-wave struck. Wataru dodged in the nick of time, but it ripped his left ear lobe as it shot past his head, sending a fine spray of blood across his cheek.

If I slip and fall, I'm done for.

The eyes of Cistina were fixed on him. The scepter swung again. Wataru drew his sword, and, using it like he had in the Swamp of Grief, he fired a magebullet at the onrushing blast-wave.

The blast-wave came straight for him, kicking up fragments of wood in its wake. Thankfully, Wataru's magebullet deflected the attack and sent it ricocheting back at Cistina. The collision between the blast-wave and magebullet formed a stunning white crescent-shaped barrier for the briefest moment. Absorbing the blow, the stone god wavered for a second before resuming her stride.

The statue isn't moving by itself. Father Diamon is controlling it with his chanting. Wataru thought hard. *It's Father Diamon I have to stop. I have to break the spell!*

Another blast-wave came and he deflected it. This time, the leftover energy from the blast careened at an angle and toppled a row of candles to the floor.

No, that wasn't exactly right. It had actually cut the candles clean in half. The severed tops fell onto the floor, their fires flickering pitifully on the stone.

These blast-waves...that's it!

The tip of Cistina's scepter pointed again at Wataru.

I have to direct the blast at Father Diamon!

This reminded him of something. *Softball. I played softball with Katchan. I couldn't swing the bat very fast, but Mr. Komura always said I had a great sense of timing. "That Wataru can hit any ball—not very far, but he can hit it! He's got good instincts. Why, Ichiro Suzuki ain't got nothing on him!"*

It was all about the timing. Wataru steadied his breathing. The stone Cistina was winding up again. *Here it comes.*

The blast-wave shot at Wataru. He could see it cut through the air, howling. It was coming straight for his neck.

Wataru swung his Brave's Sword and let fly another magebullet. But he had flinched when he saw the blast-wave coming, and his swing came a second too late. The barrier of light spread right in front of his nose, and the impact of the blast-wave sent Wataru sprawling. Three candelabras off to the side had their stands cut from underneath them. In the wake of the blast-wave there remained an eerie silence.

"What's wrong? Is it all you can do to avoid getting hit? I'm afraid you can't hold on much longer, boy!" Father Diamon's cackling laughter echoed off the walls of the cathedral.

Cistina's stone face was close now. It smiled, anticipating the final blow. The scepter cut an arc through the air. Wataru heard the keening disharmony of a blast-wave fired at point-blank range.

—*"Ichiro Suzuki ain't got nothing on him!"*

Wataru swung his sword just like a baseball bat. This time, the magebullet fired slightly to the side, catching the blast-wave at an angle. The part of the blast-wave that wasn't blocked by the barrier grazed Wataru's left elbow. It stung like a razor blade cutting into his skin. His shirt sleeve ripped, and the blood splattered on his side.

"Waah!"

Far behind the statue Father Diamon toppled over backward, knocking over a pew as he fell. His white robes fluttered out like a sail, and a whole section of his sleeve ripped off and fell fluttering through the air. For a moment,

Father Diamon cowered, and the statue halted its advance.

Now's my chance!

Wataru ducked underneath Cistina's right hand holding the scepter, and charged straight for Father Diamon.

"Wretched boy!" Father Diamon howled. He was attempting to stand, but his flowing robes got in the way. Wataru crossed the distance to the pastor in three giant leaps, and successfully pinned him to the floor.

He then grabbed Father Diamon by the collar and yanked him up. He turned, so the pastor was between him and the stone Cistina, like a shield.

"Try your spells now! Make her attack, and she'll take you down with me!"

"Cowardly cretin!"

"That's a funny thing for a guy who hides behind statues to say!"

The stone Cistina wobbled, its mirror and scepter held high above its head.

"Let go of me with your filthy hands. Let go!"

"No way!"

Roaring, Father Diamon tried to escape, struggling against Wataru's grasp. The collar of his robes tore. The pastor kicked with his feet and swung his scepter as best he could. "Unhand me, thing of evil!"

Hey, good idea.

Wataru let go with both his hands at once. The pastor, struggling with all his strength to get away, suddenly found himself unexpectedly free, and his momentum sent him crashing to the floor. His bald head hit the stone with a cracking sound.

With a soft moan, the pastor curled into a ball. Wataru reached out his hand and took the scepter from the pastor's loose fingers.

"That's enough of this thing!" Gripping the handle of the scepter, Wataru smashed it against the ground as hard as he could. The gemstone shattered into a thousand pieces, giving off a smell like blood as the fragments scattered. The Cistina statue stopped, its hands still raised above its head. Then, the fingers of its right hand loosened, and its scepter fell to the ground with a thunk. Wataru blinked. Where the scepter had been only a moment before was a small pile of sand.

"My Lady!" Father Diamon's forehead was cut, and blood streamed down over his face. The blood had gone into one of his eyes, forming a pool that looked comically like an eyepatch.

He's no pastor. He's a wicked old pirate captain.

"Boy! The Lady Cistina will never forgive this!"

In response to Father Diamon's voice, the stained glass again flashed like lightning. The mirror in the stone Cistina's left hand responded with its own flash. Then a new light shone from the surface of the round mirror, forming a beam that shot straight at Wataru. Wataru dodged to the side. He rolled and jumped to his feet. Where he stood before was a scary black scorch mark.

Okay, now she's shooting lasers from her mirror at me. Wataru couldn't decide whether to scream or laugh out loud. His heart threatened to beat out of his chest in panicked excitement.

Just then, the firewyrm band on his left wrist blazed red. A burning sensation passed up his arm, clearing his mind. He remembered the oath of the Highlanders—those who received the will of the firewyrm, protectors of the code, hunters of the truth.

Wataru stood. He pressed the blazing red firewyrm band to his chest for an instant, then, lifting his sword, he flew into motion.

Beams shot from the mirror in the stone Cistina's hand in rapid succession, following Wataru as he ran, leaving a succesion of black scorch marks on the floor and walls behind him. Splintered chunks of the pews smoldered and burned.

I'm not after the statue. I'm after the source of the mirror's power—the stained glass!

Wataru ran, dodging to the right, leaping to the left, and tumbling forward through the cathedral. He fired a magebullet at one of the stained glass windows.

Colored shards of glass tinkled to the floor.

We come before you now and bow at your feet.

Glass rained from the next window.

To despise what is evil, to save what is weak.

Another window broke, then another. Wataru thought he could hear a woman's scream mingled with the sound of breaking glass.

Until our bodies fall to dust.

The last window remaining was the stained glass next to the altar itself.

The Cistina pictured on it glared at Wataru, her eyes flashing with wrath. She seemed ready to leap from the window and fly at him. But a well-aimed shot from Wataru transformed the image into countless fragments.

Following always the star of righteousness!

Out of breath, his eyes stinging with the dust, Wataru turned back toward the statue of Cistina. She stood there facing him from across a veritable mountain of broken pews and mangled flowers.

"Take this!"

Wataru fired. The magebullet flew true, striking the stone Cistina square in the middle of her chest. The bullet shattered into fragments and disappeared, but the stone Cistina still stood.

Nothing?!

The strength went out of Wataru's legs, and he fell to his knees, still staring at the statue. Then the statue's right hand loosened, the fingers coming apart, and the mirror dropped to the floor. Just like the scepter, this too transformed into a small pile of dust.

"Oh, my Lady…" Face caked with blood, Father Diamon crawled to the statue's feet. Clinging to her leg, he cried, "What have you done! Wretched boy, do you know what you have done here?"

Before Wataru could say anything, the statue abruptly lurched to one side. It was, he saw, just a statue now. Broken, and off its pedestal, the Lady Cistina had become nothing more than a heavy, unstable lump of stone. Before Father Diamon realized what was happening, the statue slowly toppled over, crushing the screaming pastor beneath it.

Silence came abruptly. The only things moving within the cathedral were the swirling eddies of dust and tiny wicks of flame licking at the broken pews. That was all. The raw light streaming in through the broken stained-glass windows made the inside of the cathedral seem unnaturally bright.

I did it. I won.

Wataru sat down. He was gasping for breath as though he had been underwater for far too long and only just now broken to the surface.

The small door to the side of the altar opened outward, and a few robed men peered out into the room. They stood stunned. When Wataru turned to face them, they screamed and ran off into the room beyond the door, leaving it swinging behind them.

There's no time to waste. Those men were probably the pastor's underlings. If they tell the Knights of Stengel or Branch Chief Pam, they'll come running here in a flash. There's no way I'll be able to fight all of them at once.

Time to run. Wataru stood at last, turning toward the main entrance, when he heard somebody shouting in a loud voice.

"Someone, help! Help! There's been an attack on the cathedral! Tell the branch at once! We need help!"

Uh-oh.

The main entrance was looking less and less like a viable escape route. Wataru lifted his sword to make another barrier, but he was too tired. Just beginning to form the cross with the tip of his sword made him so dizzy he nearly toppled over.

They'll catch me...

"What happened here?!"

Wataru looked up. There, from the flower-covered pedestal where the statue of Cistina had stood, a man's face had emerged, his eyes wide.

The pedestal! The pedestal where Cistina stood crushing the beastkin under her feet was the entrance to the dungeons. *How like Branch Chief Pam and Father Diamon.*

Before the man had time to duck out of sight, Wataru summoned the last of his strength and fired another magebullet. The man shrieked and disappeared, making a *bonk bonk bonk* sound that faded into the distance as he fell.

Downward.

Wataru dragged his feet into reluctant motion, running over to the pedestal. As expected, the pedestal slid easily off to one side, revealing a ladder stretching into dim light below. Wataru peered down and saw the man from before lying unconscious at the foot of the ladder.

With trembling hands, Wataru grabbed the ladder and began to descend. At the bottom, he found himself in a narrow corridor with stone walls, lit here and there by shaded lanterns. Directly to his right was a small room with a chair and a desk, covered with piles of documents. *That must be the guard room.*

There was no mistaking it—he had found the dungeons. Directly in front of him was a gate, and Wataru saw bars running down the sides of the corridor beyond it. The people trapped inside scampered in their cages to see who had arrived.

Apparently, the man Wataru had knocked out was the dungeon master because he had a keyring at his waist. Wataru grabbed it, and pressing himself against the gates to the corridor, he called out, "Is everybody okay? Are the people from Bricklayer Street here?"

A great commotion answered his call, and a thousand questions came at him so fast he couldn't hear them all. "Who are you?" "Have you come to save us?" "What happened upstairs? The ceiling was shaking!"

"I'm a Highlander! I've come to get you out of here!" Wataru shouted, then he returned to the base of the ladder, climbed it, and closed the pedestal door. Using a coiled rope he found hanging on the guard room wall, he tied up the unconscious man and pushed him beneath the desk.

There were so many keys hanging from the ring that it took Wataru a while to find the one that opened the gate to the corridor. Meanwhile, the shouts of joy and frustration coming from the people trapped in the cells filled the narrow hall with a cacophony of noise.

Finally, he got the gate open. Everyone was shouting so loudly, that even when he put his hands to his mouth and bellowed back, no one could hear him. Wataru drew his sword and banged it against the bars of the gate.

"Quiet! Everybody quiet!"

When the prisoners had finally quieted down, Wataru called out, "Is Mr. Fanlon down here?" He heard Toni's excited reply from a cage a little ways down the corridor. Wataru ran up to the bars.

Toni Fanlon was as emaciated as Elza. His long days of incarceration had left him pale as a ghost, and the bones of his cheek jutted out from his face. Even his long black hair, bound into a ponytail, seemed thinner than when they had met before. But his eyes were open, and when he saw Wataru, they gleamed with a lively light. "You're the Highlander from Gasara." Toni grabbed the bars of his cage with both hands. "Did you come here alone? Do you have friends?"

"Sorry, it's just me," Wataru said, grabbing the bars himself to stay on his feet. "I meant to sneak in, but things kind of got out of hand. We can't go back up there. I'm afraid that by now, Branch Chief Pam and his men and the Knights of Stengel are out there surrounding the cathedral."

Another chorus of cries, this time cursing him, went up from the beastkin and waterkin in the cages. Only Toni was smiling. "So then, you haven't come to save us. You come to join us."

"I'm afraid so. Sorry."

"What did you plan to do?"

"Is there another way out of here, besides that ladder?"

"Of course not," Toni said, laughing out loud, then he turned to the beastkin and waterkin sharing his cell. Together, they howled with laughter. "Of course there isn't, which is why we made one. In secret, of course."

The man applauded, then began removing simple boards from a section of the floor, revealing a large hole beneath.

"This tunnel goes all the way outside the village!" the beastkin next to Toni roared, brandishing his long, pointed claws with pride. "We could have left anytime we wanted—but we were worried about the men in the other cells. You came at just the right time, my little Highlander! Now get to opening those cages!"

Wataru was so stunned he almost collapsed on the spot. Toni reached through the bars in the nick of time and caught him by the arm, holding him up. "Stay with us. You look hurt. If you're going to pass out, do it later. We need to get to safety first."

"Right."

Toni grabbed his hand holding the keys and pulled him toward the bars. His black eyes were wide. "That's my toolbox!"

Wataru looked down at the belt around his waist. Miraculously, the box hadn't come loose in the struggle upstairs.

"You've seen Elza?"

"Yes. She's fine. She's worried about you, but unharmed."

"That is good news," Toni said quietly.

"She gave me this for you. I want you to make me a wyrmflute. That's why I came to Lyris, to find you."

Toni's haggard face filled with raw determination. "Understood. I don't know exactly what you're talking about, but whatever it is, I'll make it. For now, let's just get out of here!"

chapter 37
Jozo's Wings

Once they were through the long tunnel and into the mountains outside Lyris, the escapees parted ways.

"Tell the branches in other towns. When they hear of the situation in Lyris, they're sure to come to our aid."

Wataru looked at the crowd of mostly women and children and worried about their future. But despite the situation, the former residents of Bricklayer Street seemed to be euphoric.

"We know the lay of the land around here," one beastkin who looked like a rabbit assured him. "They won't catch us. You can be sure of that."

Toni Fanlon at his side, Wataru made his way through the forest, crossing over a hill, toward the Great Marker Tree. Kee Keema's darbaba cart, its wheels caked with mud from the long journey, was waiting for them as promised. Meena had climbed onto one of the branches of the tree, so she was the first to spot Wataru and Toni approaching. She nearly fell to the ground when she saw Wataru's bedraggled condition.

"I guess even acrobats slip sometimes," laughed Wataru. "I know it looks bad, but it's just a lot of scrapes. Nothing too serious."

"You lie. You look terrible. What happened?"

There would be time enough for talk later. The party piled onto the darbaba cart.

"We need to get out from under the eyes of the Lyris branch first, find some place where Toni can work on the flute. It's a bit of a rocky ride, but hang in there. Taclou's a bit farther up in the mountains. They're pretty much cut off from the rest of the world, so we should be safe from Lyris—and the branch. That's where we'll head."

Kee Keema gave his darbaba a hearty crack of the whip, and they took off, sending up dust in their wake.

The little village of Taclou wasn't much to look at. A long, long time ago it had seen a rush when gold was found in the surrounding hills. But as soon as the veins were mined out, the town's golden age came to an end. Now only a few lived here, most of them elderly, and they spent their days working quietly in fields cut from the mountainsides.

"The goldcraft of Taclou is famous among antiques dealers," Toni said, looking over the collection of thatched-roof huts that made up the town. "I've handled them once or twice, to make repairs. Never imagined I'd see the place where they were made."

When the darbaba cart pulled up to the entrance to town, a few wizened faces appeared at windows. Moments later, villagers were streaming around them, greeting Kee Keema warmly. Wataru was surprised. "It's almost like they know you!"

"Oh, I've been here several times, though not really for work. Some of the older folks here can't make it down into the larger towns, so we darbaba drivers buy supplies and other things and bring them up to the village."

Most of the residents were beastkin who, in their youth, had worked in the mines. They were all very kind, and seemed overjoyed to see Kee Keema again. When he explained the situation, they were given a small hut to use, and someone brought them food and a little water to drink.

The town master was a beastkin with white hair all over his body—there were even tufts poking out of his ears. To Wataru, he looked like an extremely old but vigorous Siberian husky.

After a night's rest, Toni began his work on the wyrmflute. His excitement when he first laid eyes upon Jozo's scale was palpable. "This will be the greatest work of my life," he said, his cheeks flushed. "Not even the master craftsmen who taught me ever worked with a dragon scale. And here I am. I cannot afford a mistake. We have only one scale."

Toni asked for three days to make the flute. "I'm confident I can do it," he said as he shut himself inside the hut.

"Did you see his eyes when he looked at that thing? That's a craftsman for you, a real artist..." Kee Keema said, grinning. "It's hard to imagine that he was locked up in a cage for days. Look at him now—like a little boy!"

"He just wants to lose himself in his work," Meena suggested. "That way he doesn't have to think about Elza back in Lyris."

Wataru had been worried about Elza too. The escape of Toni and the others would surely cause a stir among the ankha in Lyris. Security would be tighter than ever. But still, even though she was on their side, Elza was Branch Chief Pam's daughter. It was doubtful she would come in harm's way. That's what Wataru told himself.

At least he was back with his friends, and they were safe. As soon as he was lying on a flat surface he fell deep into sleep. As he slept, his temperature rose until he was feverish, causing Meena no end of worry. One of the village men brewed him some tea from a medicinal herb said to be efficacious in easing fevers from injuries. It was so bitter that Wataru had great difficulty choking it down. And so it was that Toni Fanlon was absorbed in his work, and Wataru was resting, when a group of Highlanders and Knights of Stengel paid a visit. Contrary to Kee Keema's assumptions, the tiny village of Taclou had been included in the search for the escaped prisoners.

But the searchers didn't stay long, and quickly became frustrated with the slow-talking, long-eared residents.

"The people here are made of stauncher stuff than you might think," Meena whispered, sticking out her tongue and smiling. "They can hear much better than they let on—they just pretend to be deaf because they know it infuriates those Highlanders."

Wataru was able to recover in peace and quiet. Slowly, and in bits and pieces, he told Meena what happened inside the Cistina Cathedral.

"I'm amazed you made it out of there alive," Meena said, her gray eyes shimmering.

"It's thanks to the sword, really," Wataru said. "I just…I still can't believe I killed Father Diamon."

"He only got what he deserved. And if he'd been able to kill you, you know he would have. Then you wouldn't have been able to save anyone—least of all yourself."

Wataru knew it was true, but the guilt lingered in the corner of his mind. Lying there, looking up at the simple wooden rafters, listening to the wind rustling through the thatched roof, smelling the stew warming on the stove and freshly baked bread, it seemed like it all had been a bad dream. But, every time he stirred in his sleep or woke from a nap, he felt like he was back in the Cathedral, witnessing it all happen again. He saw the Cistina statue slowly toppling, crushing Father Diamon. Blood streamed from the wound on his forehead. He was screaming.

Whenever Wataru cried out in the middle of a dream, whether it was day or night, Meena would be there at his bedside. Sometimes he would look at her, and think that her profile looked much like his mother's. Similar, but not the same. Maybe her face belonged to someone else—perhaps a girl Wataru might meet in the future. Whoever she was, she was gentle and kind, and Wataru wanted to meet her very much.

When he was at last able to get up and walk around, albeit still wrapped in bandages, Toni Fanlon emerged from his hut. In his hand he grasped a tiny, shining red flute.

"It is done," he said, exhausted. He had gone for three days with no sleep or rest, and barely a drink of water.

Wataru picked up the flute. Though the scale was gone, its ruby-like brilliance lived on in the new form. The long, slender masterpiece looked less like a flute and more like the beak of a bird yet unknown to man. Wataru found himself wondering what sort of sound it made.

"This spot should do nicely."

The village master of Taclou led Wataru and the others to a clearing in the forest a short distance from town. The grass was soft, sprinkled with small white flowers. In the village's more prosperous days, the clearing had been used for festivals and town gatherings.

"Dragons are a large sort, I'm sure, but he should have plenty of room here. Footing's good too."

Wataru took a deep breath and looked up. Not a single cloud marred the blue sky above him. A gentle wind blew through the clearing.

"What are you waiting for? Give it a blow, Wataru."

Meena and Kee Keema held their breath. The town master and a curious group of villagers stood nearby. For most of them, it would be their first time seeing a dragon. Even though they were old, their faces shone like kids at a birthday party.

"Right."

Wataru found himself getting nervous. Gripping the flute firmly between his fingers so that he wouldn't drop it, he brought it to his lips. The crimson flute was slightly warm to his touch as he blew softly into the mouthpiece.

Sound came flowing out of the flute in a rich flood. It was as though a translucent veil had been wrapped around them, making everything seem at once sharper and yet more unreal. The forest leaves, dull just a moment before, became a radiant green, and the tiny white flowers in the grass beneath their feet sparkled.

The wyrmflute wasn't changing its tone with Wataru's breath. Rather, it felt like it was touching his very soul. It sang its own song and called out to the farthest reaches of the sky. The sound rode the wind, rising above the clouds, soaking in the light of the sun, and whispering sweetly to everything upon the ground as it rose, higher and higher.

"It's beautiful," Meena whispered, looking up at the sky. It was almost as if she could see the waves of sound rolling through the heavens. Wataru saw it too. It was like a pure wind of terrific energy, cutting across the clear sky of Vision, circling around the clearing in which they stood.

The illusion remained briefly, even after Wataru took his lips from the flute. The instrument glimmered once—a bright crimson light between Wataru's fingers—before falling into a satisfied silence.

No one there was really sure how long they waited. They had all lost sense of the passing of time. As one, they looked up at the blue sky, excitement filling their hearts. At length, a single small crimson speck appeared far away in the blue sky. It was as though another wyrmflute had winked into existence high above their heads. But this crimson star shining in the middle of the day was clearly moving. It was coming closer, answering the flute's call, flying straight across the cloudless blue.

As they watched, the crimson speck grew larger until they could see the wings. Each powerful beat sent air swirling behind it, giving it a rainbow trail as it flew, closer and closer now.

Wataru, unthinking, lifted a hand. Everyone began waving. The crimson wings were distinct against the sky now. There was no mistake—it was a dragon. The dragon spread its wings, circling once over the crowd, then stopping in midair. The villagers scattered, opening a space in the center of the clearing. With an artful twist of his wings, Jozo slowly descended, his clawed legs extended. The underbrush in the forest swayed in the wind with every beat of his wings. Wataru's hair, Meena's ears, and the loose-fitting clothes of the villagers were whipped about. Everyone smiled and laughed and waved their hands like crazy.

Jozo's feet touched the ground. The giant firewyrm landed carefully, so as not to knock anyone over with his massive wings. His large, round eyes scanned the crowd searching for Wataru.

"Jozo!" Wataru ran out, his arms spread wide. The firewyrm folded his wings and greeted Wataru with a sound like a soft bark.

"Ah! It's been a while, hasn't it?" Jozo said. He had grown considerably since they had met in the Swamp of Grief. His wings were strong, his fangs gleamed, and every inch of his body was covered in hard, crimson scales. Still, his cheery voice was no different. "It sure took you a while to call me. I was starting to get worried."

"Sorry. A lot has happened since then. I'm surprised you remember me."

"How could I forget?" Jozo said, blinking. "You did save my life."

Wataru looked at Jozo's tail and saw that it was still severed where he had cut it with his sword to save the dragon from the ravenous kalon in the swamp.

"Your tail didn't grow back?"

Jozo swung the stump of his tail against the grass and laughed. This sent a smattering of Taclou folk scampering in every direction.

"I may be a dragon, but some things are beyond me. Ach, the wyrmking was right furious. Said that's what comes of my inordinate fondness for aerial acrobatics. Still, it's good to have a few battle scars. Makes you look more experienced, if you know what I mean."

Jozo craned his neck to look at the crowd. "Friends of yours, Wataru?"

"Yes, they are."

"Why are their eyes and mouths so big?"

Wataru laughed out loud. "They're startled to see you. I think it's their first time seeing a dragon."

"Is that so? Well, good day, everyone."

Shouts of surprise went up from the villagers at the dragon's friendly greeting. Some of the older among them fell straightaway onto the ground.

Even the town master was wiping beads of sweat from his forehead. "This is, this is…it's real. It's a real firewyrm!"

"In the flesh," Jozo said proudly.

Meena took a tentative step forward. "Wa-Wataru…"

"Jozo, these are my traveling companions, Meena and Kee Keema."

"Nice to meet you, Miss Kitkin. And big Mister Waterkin!"

"N-not so big compared to you," Kee Keema said.

"True enough, true enough. But you might be three times my age. Never can tell with waterkin."

Never can tell with dragons, Wataru was thinking. Jozo was a perfect example: his body was huge, but he was still clearly a child of his species.

"So, Wataru, where is it you want to go? I can fly a whole lot faster and higher than the first time we met. I'll take you wherever it is you need to be."

Wataru explained the situation. Jozo listened, casually taking it all in. "Dela Rubesi, you say? Indeed, the air around the Undoor Highland has been a trifle odd of late. Probably would be dangerous for the karulakin to fly."

"You knew about that?"

"Of course I did. Vision's skies are my home. You ready to leave?"

"You bet!"

Wataru and his friends had already prepared for their departure. Jozo stuck out his neck, and Kee Keema climbed on first. He then pulled up Meena and Wataru. The entire village had come out to see them off.

"Thank you for all your help, we are in your debt," Wataru said to the town master.

"Not at all, not at all. Glad to do it."

"Please look after Mr. Fanlon for us too."

"You leave that to us. When he's well again, we'll take him on a pass we know through the mountains. Don't worry, we'll make sure he reaches Gasara safely."

Wataru had given a letter to Toni that detailed the recent events in Lyris. He asked him to take it directly to Kutz in Gasara.

"Just the three of you? Okay, sit tight, and hold onto something!" Jozo said, twisting his neck to make sure everyone was in place. "Well then, we're off! Things'll be a bit bumpy at first, so be warned. Off we go!"

Jozo gave a powerful beat of his wings, and Wataru could feel the current sweeping underneath them. The air rushed past Wataru's cheek, and he felt his spirits rise in anticipation.

"Safe travels to you!" the town master called out to them. Then, light as a feather, Jozo lifted off the ground. Moments later the forest was falling away beneath them. Wataru waved as he heard shouts of farewell and good luck from the villagers far below.

They were in open air. After one last farewell circle above the clearing, they climbed again, heading for Dela Rubesi. Back in the clearing, the villagers of Taclou watched as Jozo once again became a red dot in the sky. Together, they stood there until he disappeared.

The town master smiled. "Makes the last fifty years all worth it, doesn't it?"

Chapter 38
The Icy Capital

Even for Wataru, who had ridden on a karulakin twice, Jozo's speed was exhilarating. For Meena and Kee Keema, both newcomers to air travel, it was quite a shock. Meena quickly forgot her fears and spent her time looking at the ground far below. She laughed and squealed every time they took a dip. Kee Keema, on the other hand, spent his time hunched over the dragon's back. His gray, mottled skin seemed even paler than usual as the blood drained from his face.

"Y'know, I don't think I'm too good at this flying thing," the waterkin said through clenched teeth. He was clinging to Jozo for dear life.

"So much for the great wanderer of the south," Meena joked. But not even that could get a rise from Kee Keema.

"I'll go above the clouds," Jozo called back to them. "The air is a bit thinner, but you won't be able to see the ground anymore. That should make things easier for our friend the waterkin."

After a few moments in the mist they broke through the clouds. As the dragon had promised, the sea of white below them did look fluffy and comfortable (provided you could forget how high up you were) and made the ride slightly less thrilling.

Clinging to Jozo's back, Wataru and Meena asked a million questions. Do dragons always fly this high? Is it true there is an island in the Stinging Mist that hangs over the sea between the north and south?

"That there is," the dragon told them. "I was born in the Stinging Mist. The island where we wyrmkin live is shaped just like the scale I gave you."

In the distant past, the wyrmkin had been much more numerous than they were now, and many lived in both the north and the south, he explained. "But, in the end, it was difficult for us to live with your kind."

"Why's that, Jozo?"

"We're just too darn big. And too strong. Oh, and we breathe fire."

Meena's eyes went wide. "What happened? Did we, did the other races— the ankha and the beastkin—drive the dragons off?"

"Well, not exactly," Jozo said hesitantly. "I've heard only what my folks and the wyrmking have said, so I don't know all the particulars myself."

For some reason, Wataru was surprised to hear that Jozo had parents. Of course it made sense, it just seemed odd to think about it.

"Well, if they did, I think it's a shame," Meena said, frowning with her ears pressed back against her head. "We all owe the firewyrm a great debt for helping the Goddess create Vision. To think that we pushed his descendants away..."

"Well, we weren't exactly pushed," Jozo hurriedly added. "See, the wyrmking says that Vision is like a living thing. That's why it changes over time. It grows. He said big things like us have to dwindle, and at some point, disappear entirely. That's just the way it works." Despite his words, Jozo didn't seem concerned in the least.

"Doesn't that make you sad?" Wataru asked.

"Sad?"

"I mean, that your race is destined to die out?"

"I dunno. It all seems kind of unreal anyway. I sure feel fine. And I've got plenty of friends back on the Isle of Dragon."

Still, he told them, few of the adult dragons ever left their homes these days. Most of them chose to live peacefully on their island. The only ones who ventured over the wide vistas of Vision were the young dragons bursting with curiosity. So it had been exceptional luck for Wataru to run into Jozo that day in the swamp.

"I think the Goddess might have had a hand in it, personally," Jozo said, squinting as they cut through a cloud bank.

The three had dressed warmly, guessing correctly that their flight through the skies would be rather cold. But even still, when they neared Undoor Highland, the clouds grew steadily thicker, and the temperature dropped drastically.

"Shall I make a fire to warm things up?"

"Fire?! No! No thanks. Not for me," Kee Keema shouted, waving his hands so furiously he nearly fell off. Wataru and Meena laughed.

"There's really no need to suffer," Jozo looked around at the clouds looming before them. "Hmm. There is something odd about these clouds though. We should be catching glimpses of Undoor Highland by this point, but I can't see a thing."

As they flew, the clouds that had formed a steady carpet beneath them slowly started to swallow them up. Jozo rose higher, but they were still firmly within the cloud bank.

"Do you feel something? These clouds taste funny."

"Taste funny?"

Wataru and Meena stuck out their tongues, licking the cloud-puff as it rushed past. This is more difficult than it sounds. It wasn't exactly solid, like cotton candy.

"It tastes like…tears. Perhaps the Goddess is sad," Jozo said solemnly.

Still he flew on, his wings beating through the clouds in a steady rhythm. Before long, they saw something glimmer to the right. It was only for an instant.

"We should be right over Undoor Highland by now. I'm going to dive down and see what I can find."

Jozo began his descent. It was like riding on an invisible jet coaster. Wataru felt his stomach rise in his chest. Next to him Kee Keema moaned.

"There!" Jozo said. "Why, we're already right over it."

The clouds streamed by, tossed by the strong currents generated by Jozo's wings. Suddenly a city appeared around them. Wataru swallowed.

The city sat on top of Undoor Highland. It was bound by glaciers and shielded in a layer of snow. Two massive walls of stone formed concentric ovals around the city. Spires towered like trees, linked together by circular patterns and ramps that spun through the city like a spider's web. Here and there, stone buildings sat with the stairs and terraces jutting out over empty space. The entirety of the frozen city shone like a cold labyrinth.

At first, Wataru thought the buildings were made out of pure crystal. But when he squinted his eyes, he saw that wasn't the case at all. They were frozen. Every inch of stone was covered with ice. Wataru found himself thinking about a glass museum he had visited once with his parents. There had been a castle in the museum too, made entirely out of crystal. Even the flag flying from the highest tower had been made out of delicate glass.

"Look at the forest. Even the trees are frozen."

Below them, vines stretched between frost-covered branches. The foliage was laden with strange fruit that sparkled coldly in the sunlight.

"It's all covered with ice," Meena breathed. "What kind of person lives in such a cold place?"

"Maybe no one," Wataru said quietly. Everywhere they looked—the roads, the walkways, the towers—not a soul was to be seen.

Wataru's ears felt numb in the cold. "Jozo," he said, "are there any paths down from Undoor Highland that can be walked?"

"Not that I've seen."

"It's been covered with glaciers forever, I hear," Kee Keema said.

"That's true—but when I came here last time, the buildings in the forest weren't frozen, I'm sure of it. I saw flowers blooming, and I even saw people walking around."

Near the northeast section of the city stood a hall with a wide, flat roof. Jozo picked this as his landing spot. "Ooh! That's frigid!" he snorted as he touched down and folded his wings. "I'm about ready to start sneezing myself. What will you do, Wataru? Try going inside?"

"I guess so," Wataru said, sliding from Jozo's back onto the roof. "Can you stay here? You won't freeze, will you?"

"I can breathe every now and then to warm myself up, no problem. Still, I wouldn't want to stay here any longer than I have to. Can't imagine it would be all that good for you, either."

"Right. We'll come back as soon as we can."

Getting from the roof of the hall to the ground proved an arduous task, and searching the city proved to be exhausting. The ground was so slick with ice it was difficult to walk straight. Still, they made slow progress, each taking turns slipping on the ice, catching each other, then falling themselves, over and over. In other circumstances, it might have been comical, but no one was laughing.

Everything was quiet and cold. Wataru found himself wondering whether anything could truly live in a place like this—it felt as though his very heart might freeze in his chest. Maybe during the time it'd taken for them to get here, the man who had asked for help through the mirror had already frozen to death.

"Is anyone there?"

"Oy! We've come to help!"

The city was silent, swallowing their voices whole. Or maybe it was that their words were freezing in the air as soon as they left their lips.

Several years before, Wataru's mother had taken him to a children's play based on Greek mythology. The main character was the son of Pegasus. The play itself hadn't been terribly interesting to Wataru at the time, but he remembered being enchanted by the beautiful stage design. There had been a great temple of marble surrounded by a deep forest made of painted papier mâché.

The city of Dela Rubesi reminded Wataru of that set. Some of the buildings had gently sloping stairs that led up to tall doors carved with images of flowers, birds, and angelic figures. Great windows were hung with carved roses, and pillars stood by doors, topped with glaring guard dogs of stone.

Everywhere the scale was epic. Every house was a mansion, with large flat roofs and angled eaves, each carved with fantastic designs. There were sages and heroes, sorcerers and knights, and beautiful women standing in stone. There was even an amphitheater opened to the air with a half-dome arcing above it.

It was like a city from some Greek myth. A city of the gods.

Though it looked like a model reproduction of some fantasy city, it didn't seem strange to Wataru at all. Was this the ideal city according to followers of the Old God? Wataru thought back on the towns and villages he had visited in Vision so far, where the Goddess reigned, and he realized that, for the most part, their buildings and layout were determined by the daily work of the people who lived there. That sense of daily life was completely lacking here. Maybe that was why it reminded him of a set for a play.

I wonder what that amphitheater is for? Who were the statues made to honor? Who wanted to build a city like this in the first place?

Wataru found himself wondering what the people here labored for, what made them laugh, what made them sad. Even if every surface in the city hadn't been covered with ice, Wataru thought it would still feel cold and lifeless.

"Say, Kee Keema," Wataru asked. "Have you ever seen another city like this in Vision?"

Kee Keema shivered in the cold. "Not me. I doubt any place is as cold as this."

"I don't mean the cold, I mean how the city is built. It seems like every building is some great temple or shrine."

"Nothing I've seen comes close," Meena said. "It's strange—and more than just because it's all frozen. I don't see any stores or lodges or anything that suggests people might live here at all."

The three arrived at a small park in the center of town. Immediately they noted a pedestal surrounded by planters filled with flowers. Atop the pedestal was an abstract sculpture shaped like a globe. Wataru thought it might represent a planet or the heavens, but when he approached he saw that its surface was smooth. It looked so cold Wataru didn't dare touch it for fear that his finger might stick. On closer inspection, Wataru saw that there was a crack running through the center of the sphere. He decided that this must be a sculpture of a gemstone—it was, in fact, shaped exactly like the ones on his sword.

But that was odd. The gemstones were there to guide Travelers, and weren't Travelers despised and hated by believers in the Old God? It didn't make any sense.

"What should we do, Wataru? I can't just keep walking around aimlessly like this much longer," Meena said, hugging her arms to her chest and rubbing her shoulders. "I'm afraid Kee Keema is going to freeze solid. Waterkin aren't very good in the cold, you know."

Come to think of it, lizards were cold-blooded. Put them in a cold place, and their body temperature drops. They slow down. The two turned to see Kee Keema squatting near the entrance to the park, eyes closed. He wasn't moving.

The two ran back to him as fast as they could. Wataru slipped, barreling into his friend, and Kee Keema's eyes blinked open.

"You okay?"

"Sorry," Kee Keema said, his eyes turning slowly. Wataru looked and saw frost forming in the spaces between his fingers. "I just got so sleepy all of a sudden."

"Oh no! He'll freeze to death!"

"Let's go back to Jozo. Kee Keema, can you stand?"

"I'll be fine," he said, his tongue moving sluggishly in his mouth. His entire body seemed incredibly heavy. Wataru and Meena each grabbed one of his arms and began walking him back.

"I'm fine...really..." Kee Keema said, practically talking in his sleep.

Everything around them was glazed frosty blue with ice. They left no footprints as they walked across ground slick enough to skate on. The roads were laid out like squares on a checkerboard, so Wataru thought it would be easy to retrace their steps. But that was not the case. Everything looked so similar the threesome soon found they were lost. Even Jozo, the crimson firewyrm, was nowhere to be seen.

Suddenly, Meena let go of Kee Keema's arm and stopped. Wataru took two or three steps before he realized. "What's wrong, Meena?" He looked back to see her eyes opened wide and her mouth hanging open. "What is it?"

"Look at that!"

To the left of where they had been walking was a small courtyard surrounded by low hedges. Everything was glazed over with a layer of white. It was like a schoolyard the day after a big snowfall.

"Look at what?"

"Don't you see it?"

Wataru squinted. The cold wind made his eyes tear. "I don't see anything..." Wataru began. And then he saw it. There, in the middle of the courtyard, was a pattern formed from interlacing lines of eyes.

It's the pattern—the one that opens the Corridor of Light!

"I wonder if that means you can use the Mirror of Truth here?"

If that was the case, then Wataru was even more confused. All of this, the sculpture, the mirror, the pattern, was connected to the Travelers. They shouldn't have anything to do with the Old God at all, yet here was irrefutable proof that they did.

"Let's go take a closer look," Kee Keema said slowly. "Might find some clues."

"But..."

"It's okay, I won't freeze on you yet."

The three cut across the frozen courtyard, nearing the pattern. On closer inspection, it was definitely the pattern they had seen twice before. Wataru stood in the center, kneeling down to trace the lines of ice with his finger.

"This part here is higher than the rest."

"You're right."

Meena walked over to Wataru and squatted. They both touched the ice with their fingers. It made a cracking sound as they scraped at it.

"What could it be…" Wataru began to ask, when out of the corner of his eye he saw a gleam coming from Meena's chest. She reached beneath her vest and pulled out the Mirror of Truth. Suddenly, the ground beneath them shuddered, and the three slipped and fell down at the same time.

"Whoa! What was that?!"

The hard frozen ground beneath them was vibrating. A crack formed around the edge of the pattern. Then, the crack widened, sending up a spray of fine ice particles. The sheet of ice covering the courtyard broke, and for a moment it seemed like the entire courtyard around the pattern lurched upward. No—it was the pattern that was sinking down, leaving the rest of the city behind it. Like a giant elevator it dropped beneath them, carrying the three down into the frozen earth.

chapter 39
The Precept-King

When the pattern-elevator had gone down as far as it was going to go, it stopped, forming the floor of another pattern-shaped chamber.

It was just as cold down here as it had been outside. A fine dusting of ice particles blew through the air. But the walls here were the first ones they had seen in the city that weren't frozen. A single corridor cut from stone opened in the wall before them.

"Down we go."

With Kee Keema sandwiched in the middle, the three began to walk. There were no torches or candles in the corridor, yet all was suffused with a dim light. The light came from the slick stones making up the floor, ceiling, and walls, Wataru realized. They gave off a wan radiance like moonlight.

The corridor turned to the right, then to the left, continuing on for some time. In places, heavy-looking doors had been set into the walls on the right and left sides. Without exception, all of the doors were frozen shut, and no matter how hard they pushed and pulled, none would budge.

Here, too, there was no sign of life.

Wataru walked in silence, half from nerves and half from the cold. The corridor seemed to stretch on forever until an arch shaped like a candle flame came into view ahead of them.

The three passed through the arch onto a broad terrace that overlooked a larger, circular room. The ceiling here was very high, at least a hundred feet above them. Stairs curved up along the walls. Wataru stepped out on the terrace, moving over to the railing that ran along the terrace's edge. The railing was elegant, exquisitely carved in the shape of a flowing vine. He looked over the edge and gasped.

In the center of the room was a large, round mirror—as wide across as Wataru was tall. He recognized it at a glance. *A—or maybe even the—Mirror of Truth*. Next to it a white-robed man sat slumped in a single chair, like a night watchman dozing off on the job. It was the man who had talked to them through the mirror. The hammer he had been holding lay on the ground by his feet.

Wataru ran down the staircase leading from the terrace to the floor below. Not knowing what to say, he ran up to the man and grabbed him by the arm. Wataru shook him, and the silver crown slipped from the man's forehead. His hair was as white as it had looked in the mirror. Yet he seemed much younger than Wataru had thought. *He's not even thirty years old. Is he dead?*

The man's head listed to one side, and his eyes opened. They peered into Wataru's face, filling with a look of relief. "Ah, it is you! You heard my call!" The man blinked his sleepy eyes and attempted to sit up in his chair. A barely audible moan escaped from his lips.

"You are the Traveler."

In person, his voice, too, sounded quite young. His eyes were clear, his skin smooth and free of wrinkles. *So why the white hair?*

Wataru nodded. "My name's Wataru."

Behind him, Kee Keema and Meena finally reached the bottom of the stairs from the terrace. The man watched them as they approached.

"These are my traveling companions. They came here with me. I'm sorry it took us so long."

"How…did you reach this place?"

"We rode here on a dragon."

The man's eyes opened, and he smiled. "Magnificent. So, you have met a dragon? I…never did. They are rare creatures, even in Vision."

Everything about the man, from the words he chose to the way his face lit up when he spoke made him seem so much younger than he had before. It was uncanny.

"We need to get you out of here. Your face is pale. This cold will give you pneumonia if you stay here too long," Wataru said, putting his hand on the man's forehead. Where he thought to feel the warmth of a fever, it was cold to the touch. The man's skin was the color of lead.

"Are there any others here? We should get them too. We need to go someplace warm."

The man slowly shook his head. "No one is left. All have died. Only I remain." More than sad, the man sounded deeply ashamed to have lived. "You may call me the Precept-King. That is what everyone called me. I was their leader—in name at least."

The Precept-King. Precepts were religious teachings or laws. If the Special Administrative State of Dela Rubesi was indeed a bastion of belief in the Old God, it seemed a fitting title for their leader.

Still, there was so much that made no sense.

"What happened here?" Meena said, kneeling by the man. "Was it a plague? Did everyone die of illness? Was it always this cold here?"

"Time enough to talk later. Let's get out of here," Kee Keema growled. "Meena, would you mind giving my back a quick rub. That should get me moving again. And I need to carry this guy."

The white-robed man reached out and placed his hand over Wataru's. "No. I may not leave this place. This city will die soon, and I plan to die with it. I cannot escape. The Goddess would not allow it."

The Goddess? Wataru's eyes opened wide. He pointed at the room around them. "What do you mean? I thought this was—aren't you believers in the Old God?"

"No, it is not so." The man gave a weak smile, the expressionless mask falling from his face like a shard of ice. "This too was part of the agreement with the Goddess. It was the best way to ensure that we did not trouble the lowlands. That is why we kept our promise—for so long, we kept it. Yet promises were made to be broken, and our time finally came. Surely, the Goddess knew it would. Men are crafty, and their hearts are weak. Someday, one among us would go against our promise held for eternity—and all of us would be punished for his trespass." The man muttered softly to himself, half singing. Wataru had trouble following the meaning of his words.

"What are you talking about?"

Then the white-haired, youthful Precept-King looked Wataru straight in the eyes. "I was once a Traveler, like yourself."

He's from the real world too?

"Including myself, there were eleven of us from the real world in this place, all of them Travelers. All thought to change their own destiny, and so passed through the Porta Nectere to Vision." His eyes looked back in time as he spoke. "But we were never able to realize our dreams. We failed on the difficult journey through Vision and chose to abandon our path. Yet, at the same time, none of us wished to trudge back to the real world in defeat, having been unable to change our destinies."

Wataru silently watched the man's sharply cut jaw move. Oddly, the look in his eyes was less one of fatigue and more of boredom. There was something else too. He looked familiar—like someone Wataru had met before.

"So you stayed in Vision?" Meena asked quietly, her breath a wisp in the air.

"Yes," the Precept-King nodded. "The Goddess made this city for us, the failed Travelers. Here, we were commanded to live our lives apart from the rest of the world. That was the condition of our stay in Vision."

Meena looked up at the high ceiling. "You were all trapped in here? Unable to even step out into the world outside?" It was clear from her expression that Meena couldn't imagine ever being so confined to one place.

"Didn't you ever get tired of it, or bored?" Wataru asked. "Did you have some sort of work you were meant to perform here?"

The Precept-King lifted his eyes and looked at the large Mirror of Truth to his side. "Our task was to protect this."

"The mirror?"

Kee Keema took a step toward the mirror, reaching out his hand as if to touch it. Then, thinking better of it, he stepped away.

The Precept-King nodded. "All Travelers find the Mirror of Truth at some point during their journey through Vision. Each of them, in their own way, will find it. Yet, when their journey is done, they must return it to the Goddess. They're not allowed to return it to the world of Vision. It is too dangerous."

"Dangerous?"

"Yes. The Mirror of Truth may be used to go between this place and the real world, you see."

Wataru looked at Meena. A spark of understanding lit in her eyes. "I was always told I should never let my mirror leave my possession—though I had no idea what it could do. I don't think my parents knew either."

"That knowledge is forbidden," the Precept-King said, smiling gently at Meena. "But now, you know its secret, don't you?"

Meena nodded hesitantly. "Not that I would ever dream of doing anything with it myself."

"Ah, if only everyone in Vision was as honest as you."

The Precept-King cast his eyes downward, spotting the hammer lying at his feet. He slowly reached down to pick it up, and placed it on his lap. It was as though he hadn't even realized it had dropped out of his limp hands until now.

"This Mirror of Truth is actually a collection of twelve mirrors once held by the Travelers who lived here. Each mirror has a soul, you see. Those souls have fused, and here they have a form. That is what we were protecting. We sought to keep anyone with schemes to travel between this world and the real world away."

Wataru felt his heart beat faster in his chest. "Twelve? You've added one more to your number."

The Precept-King looked at Wataru and smiled. "Indeed. You see, one of us escaped quite recently. Even now, he is still at large. He is the fugitive, the breaker of the oath with the Goddess, the traitor. He is the rebel that appeared from among us. That is why we must be punished."

"And that punishment..." the words caught in Wataru's throat. "This frozen city? Did the Goddess do this?"

The Precept-King nodded. He lowered his chin to his chest and closed his eyes.

"Isn't that a bit harsh?" Kee Keema spoke. His speech was still slurred, numbed by the cold. "The Goddess we know is benevolent. I can't believe she would punish everyone for just one broken promise. There must be some mistake?"

"Gods are ever strict," the Precept-King said, his eyes still closed. "And men ever weak. Their eyes filled with greed, they scheme foolishly against the heavens. The Goddess knows this all too well. After all, it has happened many times before."

One of the twelve, escaped. Still at large. And the Goddess is furious. Wataru's heart beat even faster. "An emergency call went out to the Highlanders in the lowlands. They're looking for a fugitive!"

Meena's eyes opened wide. "That's right! They said he he stole vital national secrets and was heading to the north. Maybe he's the one…"

The Precept-King's jaw tightened. "Is this so? Then, yes, it probably is him. So the Goddess has acted on her own, has she?"

That solves the mystery of the fugitive's origins.

"As it turns out, we happen to be Highlanders," Kee Keema said proudly, his eyes brightening with interest for the first time since arriving in the cold city. "If this fugitive was one of yours, maybe you have some clue as to his whereabouts, where he might've gone? It's our duty to find him."

Gripping the back of his chair, the Precept-King tried to stand, but his legs were unresponsive. Giving up, he sat back down. "Then you understand our predicament better than I thought. The reason I summoned you—the reason I asked you to come all this way—was to capture that fugitive. I do have a clue as to his whereabouts. I can tell you exactly where he is now."

"How?"

"The mirror will show us. Please, give me your hand."

Wataru and Meena grabbed the Precept-King's arms, and managed to help him stand. Slowly, he hobbled over to the Mirror of Truth, and standing before it, he raised his hands along its curved edge. His reflected image in the mirror blurred and faded. Wataru blinked, and the next instant, he could see a city pictured in the mirror's depths.

A port city. He caught glimpses of a blue sea between buildings that looked like stacked warehouses. The warehouse walls, made of simple boards and pilings, had been painted with a design in yellow: a clenched fist. It must be a marker of some sort.

"That…that's Sono," Kee Keema said, warily squinting his eyes. "No mistaking it. Look at how old those buildings are, how they're practically falling down. Sono used to be the busiest fishing port in Arikita, but when industry took off there, the sea became too polluted for fishing, and the town went to rust. They tried changing it to an industrial port, but the harbor had always been small, and they never were as successful as places like Hataya and Dakla."

"Do any of the sailships go north from there?"

"No large ships use the port. But there are several medium-size vessels that might be able to make the passage."

"So the fugitive is hiding here?" Wataru asked.

The Precept-King clutched the Mirror of Truth, his shoulders heaving with every breath. "He is waiting for a favorable wind. As you have probably heard, the sailships passing to the north must wait for the starseers' word that the winds will move with them before they set out."

"How often do these winds blow? "

Kee Keema scratched his thick neck and shrugged. "I don't know for certain, of course—I'm no starseer. But this is certainly the season when most sailships make the journey. There are only about three or four times a year when that happens."

"Then we have to hurry!" Meena said, her tail bobbing in the air. "We have to let everyone know: we're looking for a shipping company with this mark of the fist."

"So the mirror tells us. The fugitive seeks passage by boat. Perhaps it is the captain who hides him until the time is right?"

Kee Keema and Meena looked ready to run off instantly, but Wataru stood still. He was staring directly at the Precept-King's black eyes, half hidden beneath his bushy white eyebrows. "What are these national secrets the fugitive is carrying? You must know."

"We'll just ask once we've caught him," Kee Keema said impatiently.

The Precept-King slouched, falling over the arm of his chair. The motion revealed a horribly emaciated body under his white robes.

"The fugitive—that man used the Mirror of Truth to return to the real world, and brought back with him plans for a powered ship and a motor. He was going to take them to the north."

Meena looked understandably confused. It was clear that not a word the man had said made any sense to her. Kee Keema too stood scratching his head.

Only Wataru seemed to get it. "He was going to sell that to the Northern Empire?" With a fleet of powered vessels at their command, the North would no longer have to brave the Stinging Mist or wait for the winds to turn in their favor. They could invade the South whenever they wanted.

"What does it mean, Wataru? Sell what? Why do you look so frightened?"

Wataru turned to Meena, and as simply as he could, told her briefly about engines and what a powered ship would mean in Vision. The impact of his words was clear. Rage burned deep in Meena's eyes. "That's insane! Why would a Traveler want to help the North like that? Why? Does he hate the South? Why would he want to destroy the peace in Vision?"

When the Precept-King answered, he spoke to Wataru, not Meena.

"He said it would bring about Vision's industrial revolution."

Meena stared blankly at the white-haired man.

"It's something that happened in the real world," Wataru explained, gritting his teeth.

Power. Mechanical power that didn't rely on the strength of men. Wataru had thought of it many times since arriving here. More than half of the things that were done by physical strength here were done with motors in the real world. Wataru had been astonished by the difference it made on many occasions.

"I spoke with him many times on these matters," said the Precept-King, half to himself. "I wasn't shy about giving him my opinion. Most assuredly, Vision will have its own industrial revolution…but in its own time. That it has not already arrived is a sign that Vision is not ready for it. Yet he thought that would take too long,"

The Precept-King continued, "What was wrong, he asked me, with bringing things that already existed in the real world here, to Vision? He thought he could make Vision richer, add to its prosperity overnight."

"Would these motors give us prosperity?" Meena asked innocently. Wataru didn't have a good answer. It depended on what one meant by prosperity. And it was unclear that the kind of prosperity that mechanical power promised would really bring happiness to Vision.

"Of course, he had other motives."

"Like what?"

The Precept-King turned to Meena. "With that information he carried, the Northern Empire would welcome him with open arms. He would be a most valued citizen there. My dear kitkin, it is as you fear. With powered ships, the North would defeat the South in the blink of an eye. Vision would be unified under one leadership, whether it wished it or not. That would make our fugitive a grand contributor to the new order. He would stand at the top of Vision along with the Imperial Family of the North."

The light in Meena's eyes dimmed. "That's it? That's what he wants?"

"Indeed. That is why he brought knowledge from the real world here to Vision—to satisfy his own greed. That is why the Goddess is angry."

Wataru glanced at the Mirror of Truth. Its smooth surface once again reflected the three of them, standing around the robed man.

"Do you really think the fugitive can secure passage to the Northern Empire so easily? I wonder if anyone would really believe him when he told them about the boat."

"Oh, they would believe," the Precept-King said, his eyes filling with sorrow. "As I have heard, the empire in the north has been trying for some time now to obtain a Mirror of Truth for themselves. It appears that someone in the Imperial Family knows of its workings. If they could open passage to the real world, they know what power it would place in their hands. There was a time when they tried any number of despicable ways to create a mirror such as the one we have here."

Wataru looked at Meena. All expression had drained from her little face. Her thoughts were racing backward through time.

When Sigdora—the special unit of the Northern Imperial Army—attacked Meena's home, they had been after her family's Mirror of Truth. Her parents were merely casualties. That was why they were after fugitives to the south as well. It was all for the mirrors.

The Precept-King furrowed his brow as he gazed at the mirror beside them. "Do you know what the Mirror of Truth is?" he suddenly asked Wataru.

"I'm not sure what you mean. It opens a corridor between this world and the real world, right?"

"Yes, this is one of its vital functions. But that is not why the mirror exists in the first place."

The mirror presides, as its name might suggest, over truth in Vision, the Precept-King explained. "It is composed of the very elements that make Vision what it is the seeds of the world. A gathering of parts that create the world—perhaps this is the best way to describe it," he said, running his finger along the edge of the mirror.

The seeds of the world? Wataru shook his head.

"It is not surprising that you do not understand. You are still a child, after all," The Precept-King said with an ironic smile. "Vision is but a void, yet it has form. It is here, yet it is not. It exists, yet it may not exist."

Oh, that clears it up. Wataru began to feel like he was listening to a lecture at school.

"You do not know the story of Vision's creation, do you?"

Wataru frowned. "Actually, I do. Vision is created by the imaginations of people living in the real world."

"Yes…I suppose one might say that."

"Isn't that right?"

"Vision exists in the space between two mirrors. These two mirrors are the seeds of our world."

Meena, finally recovered from her shock, blinked slowly and looked up.

"One of these mirrors, of course, is the Mirror of Truth. The other is called the Mirror of Eternal Shadow."

"The Mirror of Eternal Shadow?"

"If the Mirror of Truth is the accumulation of all that is good, then the opposing mirror, is, perhaps, the accumulation of all that is evil. I say perhaps, because I have not seen it for myself. But, the Mirror of Eternal Shadow does exist. Of this you can be certain."

Kee Keema glanced at Wataru and then back at the Precept-King. He was having a hard time following their conversation.

"The Mirror of Truth—the accumulation of truth that determines the very form of Vision—was broken into countless fragments and spread throughout our world. Every time a Traveler comes, these mirrors guide their path. So then, where is the Mirror of Eternal Shadow?" the Precept-King asked before answering his own question. "Certainly, without a doubt, it is in the north. Thus are North and South opposed."

"But that doesn't make sense," Meena said, raising her voice. "My mirror came from my parents, and they're from the north, originally. That would mean there are fragments of the Mirror of Truth on both continents. It would make more sense if the Mirror of Eternal Shadow were also broken up into many fragments and scattered everywhere too."

Wataru's eyes widened. He had never heard Meena talk in this way. She seemed older, somehow.

The Precept-King smiled at her like a pastor about to deliver knowledge to an ignorant believer. "Yes, truth has been broken into many fragments, too numerous to count, and spread among many people, but Eternal Shadow—

which is evil—this exists in one place. Can you not see that this is Vision as she stands today?"

Kee Keema shook his head, not following the train of discussion. His face looked even more pale than before.

"That is why Vision knows happiness still," the Precept-King said mysteriously. "Yet the question is, is this a good thing? Is it good for evil to be so bound in one place? I do not know the answer."

Kee Keema's head jerked up. His voice was loud, despite the fact that his lips didn't want to move in the cold. "You don't mean that everything that's going on in the North—all the prejudice and the killing—is because that other mirror is up there?"

The Precept-King slowly turned his back to Wataru. "I do not know. Yet it is certain that the Mirror of Eternal Shadow is in the north. And I would think that the Northern Empire considers it quite a burden. That is why the emperor will stoop to any means to obtain our mirror here, for only a whole mirror can hope to contain the threat that is Eternal Shadow. Or perhaps he merely wishes to use our mirror to obtain knowledge from the real world. It is hard to say…"

Wataru stood, his mouth closed. He hadn't said anything in a while, and now it felt like his lips were sealed together. The cold seemed to seep into every fiber of his being.

"Didn't the Goddess tell you anything about it?"

The Precept-King shook his head. "It is not knowledge I would be privileged to know in the first place. Not I, a weak Traveler who ended his journey halfway toward completion.

"In any case, you see the situation at hand. Should the fugitive cross to the north, things would progress rapidly. This fugitive came to Vision when the Porta Nectere opened ten years before. He is a Traveler. His knowledge of affairs in the real world was much more current than mine. It is possible that he had begun to plan all of this—his betrayal—from the very moment he abandoned his journey."

Meena put her hands to her mouth and knelt on the floor. Kee Keema, looking concerned, patted her on the back. It was a noble gesture—by all accounts, he was the one out of all of them who was suffering the most.

"Please," the Precept-King said, his hands brushing Wataru's arm. It was almost as if he wanted to grab on tight and plead but lacked the strength to do so. The freezing cold and hunger had mixed with despair, robbing him of his strength and willpower. "Please, you must stop the fugitive before he crosses to the north. Save our souls."

It was the first time anyone older than Wataru had pleaded with him like this, and he found the experience oddly frightening.

"Since the fugitive left, I have called out to Travelers through this mirror. I know that the Porta Nectere is open now, and new Travelers have come to Vision. How many times I wished my cries would reach them."

"When you called me, I remember you saying something about me being a boy too..." Wataru began. "Does that mean that another Traveler answered your call, before I did? A boy?"

The Precept-King nodded quietly.

"Was his name Mitsuru? He's not a warrior in training like I am—he's a great sorcerer."

"Ah," the Precept-King said, his eyes opening wide. "You know him?"

"Yes. He's my friend."

"Your...friend? This is a surprise."

Mitsuru had answered the call, the Precept-King explained, and only a few hours after had used a great wind magic to come to Dela Rubesi.

"Yes...he's much more powerful than I am," Wataru admitted.

"Perhaps, but he did not listen to my request. He said he had come to Vision to meet with the Goddess, and as such had no interest in the affairs of Vision, or the enmity between the North and the South. It did not concern him."

Wataru had to admit that sounded a lot like the Mitsuru he knew. It made sense when he thought of his objective as a Traveler. For some reason, Wataru felt embarrassed on Mitsuru's behalf. Half of him wanted to defend Mitsuru's actions, and the other half was irritated with his selfishness.

"He told me then that there was another Traveler come to Vision. He said this other Traveler was too kind for his own good. From the way he spoke, I did not imagine that you two might be friends."

Wataru's face grew red with embarrassment.

"Sounds like Mitsuru wanted to sidetrack you so he could get to the Tower of Destiny before you, doesn't it," Kee Keema said, snorting. His anger and his tongue, numb with cold, made him sound like a belligerent drunk.

"I don't think he'd do that."

"I wouldn't be so sure!"

"Anyway, now we know what's going on. Let's get out of here quickly and go to the port in Sono."

"Right. If we leave him waiting much longer, even Jozo will freeze," Meena said, springing to her feet. *She's a real fighter,* Wataru thought, impressed.

"We're leaving now. Here, take my hand. Can you walk?" Wataru stretched out his hand, but the Precept-King pushed it away. "What's wrong?"

"I cannot leave. Did I not tell you?"

"But you asked me to come here and help you!"

"I asked you to save our souls. I do not hope to escape death."

Holding onto the chair for support, the frail man leaned over and picked up the hammer from his seat. He was unable to lift it, and so it hung down by his knees. "We allowed the fugitive to escape, and, through the breaking of our oath, won the Goddess's wrath. That is why we must be punished. My companions have already died. As their leader, it would not do for me to live any longer. The Goddess would never allow it."

"That's no fair!"

The Precept-King shook his head. "Capture the fugitive, undo his plans, and our sin may yet be forgiven. Only then will our souls be purified, and ourselves reborn into the next world. Fail, and not only my soul, but those of all my companions, will be laden with sin, fated to wander the Eternal Vale for all time. That is why you must go. Now."

This wasn't the deal! "Don't you want to live? You're still young. How can you just give up on yourself like this?" Wataru asked, the words coming out of his mouth in a flood. The Precept-King whirled around with far more speed than Wataru would have thought possible. His face was twisted. "Give up on myself? Me?"

"Yes, that's what I said."

The Precept-King chuckled. "I'm not giving up on anything. No, I want to protect myself. As, I'm sure, did my fallen companions. I do not wish to go to the underworld. Nor would I go to Vision or the real world. Our paradise was here and here alone."

The Precept-King spread his arms, pointing around them, spinning as he looked up at the ceiling in a strange dance. "If I am to lose this, what need have I of life? It is far more desirable that I be reborn, a purer soul, to search for paradise again in the next life."

Shivering, Meena stepped over to Wataru.

"In the real world..." the Precept-King took his hand holding the hammer and pressed it to his chest. "In the real world, nothing ever happened as I wished it. All my efforts came to nothing, all my dreams were crushed. No one understood me, and no place accepted me. My life did not love me, there can be no doubt of that. It gave me nothing. That is why I left it and came to Vision."

The Precept-King's feet stomped on the stone floor. "Yet even here, in Vision, my dreams were not fulfilled. Reach the Tower of Destiny?—I could not even make it from one town to the next! Here, as in the real world, nothing went as I hoped. That is why I abandoned my journey. I chose instead to align myself with the Goddess. From that moment on, I lived here."

He chose to live here? This barren city of the gods? This beautiful, empty temple?

"The Goddess knew us for who we were. This city is concealed beneath the hem of her robes. We were the chosen ones, living above the clouds, given the high calling of defending her mirror. At last, we'd found the world in which we wished to live. We had no dealings with the lowlands, with their filth and corruption. Dela Rubesi was our paradise."

Yet one among them didn't understand that—he couldn't give up the mean greed that ruled in the lowlands, and so he betrayed the oath.

The Precept-King put a bony fist to his forehead. "We lived like gods here. From this place, we looked down on the lands of Vision. We lived our days in solitude and grace. This is what I truly desired, you see. That is why they called me the Precept-King—I held in my heart a purer essence, a belief that separated me from the ignorant world's inability to understand. Do you see?"

Wataru didn't see. What precepts did he teach exactly? And to whom? And if he was a king, where was his kingdom?

"If you had all these great precepts," Kee Keema said, slowly forming the words with numb lips, "and you were king of these people here, how come one of them betrayed you and ran away?"

The Precept-King made no reply, and instead stared off into space as though he had not heard the question. It was as if the question had never been asked at all. Then he sighed quietly. "Those who could not understand us were not our companions. The traitor, he did not qualify to be among us in the first place."

"Had you noticed this before? Before he ran away?" Meena asked. "Did you see he was somehow not qualified? If so, why didn't you do something about it earlier?"

The Precept-King frowned slightly. "I do not believe you have the right to accuse me of wrongdoing here. All of this is his fault, you see. You do not know what it is like to be betrayed and wounded like I have been."

"Still..."

"No! That is no way to speak to a chosen one of the Goddess."

Meena looked at Wataru. She didn't know what to say, and she was rapidly running out of the desire to say anything. Suddenly, it occurred to Wataru that he knew why this man had abandoned his journey through Vision. He had always been like this. The only thing he held dear was his own excuses. The only things he saw were what he wanted to see. The only things he desired were those things he wanted for himself. The only one ever hurt was him. He had abandoned everything that didn't go the way he wanted it to go, cut away everything that didn't please him, ignoring things that didn't make sense.

Of course he had never found a place where he belonged. No kindness could ever reach him. He would be the last to see the signs of a coming betrayal. And here, in this land of peace that he had finally found, he clung to his oath with the Goddess.

The Precept-King called himself chosen. What did that mean? Chosen for what, and for what reason? Had this place been his reward for failure?

He's no Precept-King. He's a Void-King. The high King of nothing. And the Goddess knew it. That's why she made him this fake city of the gods.

Wataru's body felt like ice, yet the thought still sent chills down his spine. Suddenly, he realized who the Precept-King's face had reminded him of. It was that man—the young man that stepped on his hand without so much as a word of apology, back when he'd gone out shopping with Uncle Lou.

His uncle had been furious, Wataru remembered, and the man had been mad too. Yet the man's anger was simply indignant rage at being yelled at, with no understanding of why.

To him, Wataru hadn't even existed. In his world, there was no boy lying there on the ground. Wataru was just an obstacle in his path. That's why, when he stepped on Wataru's hand, he kept going. It was like he had tripped on an empty can, or stomped on a plastic shopping bag in the street. If he had ever visited Vision, Wataru thought, he would make a great Precept-King. And he would be satisfied, down to the very bottom of his heart.

Wataru shook his head. *I'm thinking too much.*

"Your hair…" Wataru said quietly. "What made it white? Was it fear at the Goddess's punishment of your city?"

The Precept-King's face had returned to the expression it held when Wataru first saw him: he looked bored to death. His mouth opened slowly. "I wished it to be this way. I did not need youth. Youth, and the immaturity that comes with it, were not fitting for one chosen."

Wataru had nothing else left to ask.

Kee Keema and Meena looked frozen solid. Wataru stood, his eyes still on the Precept-King's face. "Let's go."

"But, Wataru…"

"No, he wants to stay here. We don't have the right to tell him otherwise."

"Yes, go," the Precept-King said, smiling slowly. Then, with great gravitas, he lifted his hammer over his shoulder and turned toward the Mirror of Truth. "My last task lies before me. I must break this mirror. All of the fragments we brought here will return again to fragments. And they will spread throughout Vision. There, they will wait until they can find new Travelers. This is as the Goddess desires it to be."

The Precept-King closed his eyes as if in prayer. "When this is done, the Goddess will mete out her final punishment. You had best hurry, lest it find you too." Then his eyes turned toward Wataru one last time. "Go. Finish your journey. Do what we could not."

For that one brief moment, Wataru thought he could see the mask drop, revealing the man's true face. It was a lonely face—the face of a man who had resolved to change his fate, who had come all this way…for this. A lonely Traveler.

Wataru felt tears rise in his eyes. *I can't leave you here, after all. Don't make me do it.*

But the Precept-King saw what he was thinking. "Go," he commanded before Wataru could protest again. "And be wary of evil." Then he fell silent and turned to the task at hand, mustering all the strength he had left in his thin arms to lift his hammer.

Wataru slowly shuffled backward. Unconciously, Meena tugged on his arm. Then it was like a thread snapped. Wataru began to run. Together, the three of them dashed up the stairs and out of the hall, turning only once at the arched entrance to catch a final glimpse of the Precept-King. It was an image which would be forever burned in Wataru's memory. The face of the Precept-King blended for moment with that of the young man in Tokyo. *Maybe they don't look so alike after all. Maybe it's just me throwing them together in my head.*

Their pace quickened the farther away they got from the mirror room. Even if the destruction of the city hadn't been imminent, they would have run just as fast. They felt like if they didn't run, if they didn't get away, then the weight of what they had left behind would draw them in, like a sinking ship, and they would drown in this place.

"There you are!" Jozo was jumping up and down. "I was getting worried. You do what you came to do?"

"Y-yeah," said Wataru. While they had been under the surface, it seemed that the city had grown even colder. His lips were frozen shut.

"I was afraid you weren't going to make it in time! We're flying now— hang on!"

"Make it in time? What's wrong, Jozo?"

With his crimson wingtip, Jozo pointed toward a corner of the sky. "Look up there. It's coming straight for us."

There, among the clouds that shrouded Dela Rubesi, a single star shone in the sunlit sky with a hard, diamond-like radiance. On closer inspection, it was moving.

Either my eyes are playing tricks on me, or whatever that is has wings.

"That's a servant of the Goddess, that is. Bringing a wind of punishment down on this place, I should imagine," Jozo said with a shiver. "And where that wind blows, I don't want to be! Let's fly!"

The three clung tight to his scales, and Jozo lifted into the air. As soon as they were in a cloud bank, he began beating his powerful wings, taking them as far away from Dela Rubesi as he could go.

Through the swirling clouds, Wataru watched the approaching star. It did have wings, after all, wings of frost—as though countless shards of ice had come together to form a giant bird. It was even larger than Jozo. Each beat of its wings sent a frigid gale down to the earth below. The great ice-bird was headed straight for Dela Rubesi.

"Jozo?"

"What?"

"Do you think you could circle around here, just a moment? I kind of want to see what happens."

"It'll just give you nightmares. I don't recommend it."

"Please. I...I have to see this through."

Jozo snorted, then, reluctantly, turned his nose back toward Dela Rubesi. He began tracing a wide circle around the frozen city.

The ice-bird alighted on the innermost of the two walls surrounding Dela Rubesi, and rested a moment before it extended its wings to the side and began to thrash them furiously.

With the first beat of its wings, a blizzard rose. With the second beat of its wings, the very air stiffened around it. With a third beat, every spire, street, and wall in the city froze and began to crumble into scattered shards of ice.

The sculptures holding up the domed roof of the amphitheater froze and shattered. Corridors cracked, sending plumes of ice-dust into the air. Like a sand castle swept away by the waves, the temples and shrines began to lose their form, crumbling at the edges. The city walls collapsed, first the outer wall, then the inner. Then the ice-bird took flight, blasting the city from the air with waves of frigid cold.

"Look!" Meena said, pointing. "The pattern is crumbling!"

The pattern on the elevator rose for moment, becoming more distinct, then let off an icy sigh before sinking. At first, its descent was level, but soon it tilted to one side. One of the edges crumbled away, and then the lines of the pattern began to shatter. Soon it was nothing but a countless pile of ice shards, thundering down into the earth like an avalanche.

"The Goddess is angry," Jozo said. Even though he had no idea what had happened beneath the surface, his eyes held a knowing glint. "I can taste the sadness in the air. She laments. What horrible sin did these people of Dela Rubesi commit to earn this?"

Clinging to Jozo's neck, Wataru watched the final moments of Dela Rubesi.

What is empty returns to emptiness, what is nothing returns to nothing.

Moments later there was nothing on Undoor Highland but a thick layer of snow and ice.

As it had come, the great ice-bird flew up without a sound and disappeared into the clouds. Wataru did not watch it go, and Jozo, for his part, flew as fast as he could in the opposite direction. The sky was silent. Little by little, their view widened. The time of punishment was over.

"Let's get someplace warm," Kee Keema said in a raspy voice. "I've had just about all I can take." Wataru was about to agree when Kee Keema's fingers clumsily grabbed his sleeve.

"What?"

"Wh-what's that? I see something shining!"

Kee Keema was pointing back toward Dela Rubesi. There, on the snowy field where the city had stood, something was shining with a brilliant red light.

"Jozo, you didn't drop a scale back there?"

"Absolutely not. What a waste that would be."

"Then what is that?"

Wataru felt his heart stir in his chest. For the first time in hours, he felt hope.

"Kee Keema, you think you can hang in there for another five minutes?"

"S-sure."

"Jozo, would you take us back?"

Jozo rolled his big round eyes at Wataru. "You serious?"

"I am. Sorry."

Sighing and snorting, Jozo did a U-turn and began to descend. The frozen snow that covered Undoor Highland was fine, like flour, and the wind blew it up in great drifts. On Jozo's back they were safe, but Wataru feared that, down on the ground, he would be lost in the snow an instant.

"Stay here, I'll be right back."

Wataru grew increasingly sure that he was right. Brushing aside the snow that made his face and arms numb, he forged his way across the snowy plain, heading for the red glimmer. Meena was right behind him.

"Wataru, you think that's…?"

"Yeah."

The pedestal was gone without a trace. The planters, too, had frozen and shattered, returning to the snow. But the sculpture was still there. It had shrunk to only a quarter of its former size, yet it was still shaped like a sphere. It sat upon a cushion of snow, the red light winking from its very center.

Wataru approached and stuck out his hand, and the glimmering red sphere floated up into the air. There was no mistaking it now.

The third gemstone. Wataru drew his Brave's Sword and held it up in his right hand.

The gemstone winked. The light it gave off was like an aurora, a tiny version of the northern lights, floating above the snow. There, wrapped in a crimson shroud of light, the image of a girl appeared, wearing a breastplate of platinum. A single strand of her braided hair was loose, falling down her forehead.

—*I was waiting, Traveler.*

Wataru knelt.

—*I am she who protects the hope of this world and the future of men. Too long I was held in the hands of those who belittled me, who feared me, who did not need me. I thank you.*

An image of the Precept King rose in Wataru's mind. He had abandoned hope, forgotten the future, and now his peace was shattered and gone without a trace.

—*Turn around, Brave.*

Wataru looked behind him and saw his footprints and Meena's stretching across the snow.

—*I exist only for those whose past does not waver or halt. For those who have stopped walking, their path is ended, and there I cannot dwell. Go forward, Brave, with hope held to your breast, looking toward the future, head held high. Do this, and I will always be at your side. And remember that the path you have left behind can be a marker, showing you the way you must go.*

Then the Spirit of Future Hope smiled and disappeared. The third gemstone glimmered brilliantly, and then was sucked into the hilt of his sword. Wataru felt its energy joining the other gems. It was exhilarating.

He closed his eyes and stood on the snowy plain with his head held high. He raised his sword to the heavens. And, as though it had been waiting just for him, a golden ray cut through the thick layer of clouds. Wataru was bathed with joyous light.

Only two gemstones to go.

chapter 40
Parting

The port town of Sono.

In a lonely corner of the wharf, a warehouse with a discolored tin roof stood silently. Rain pipes rusted by the relentless sea breeze dangled from the eaves. With each gust of wind, the pipes knocked together in a mournful rattle. The sea looked dead, the color of an old bruise. The smell of brine swept through the mostly deserted streets. Even though Sono was a port town, there was no hustle and bustle there. The people who walked the winding streets did so with a sluggish gait.

Sono couldn't keep up with the changing times. Too late did it think to attract the sea merchants that prospered with the development of the sailship. Too late did it establish itself as a dependable land route for merchants. Once a fishing town, Sono also lacked the know-how to process goods the northern and southern continents wanted. Those who tried to trade soon realized that the same warehouses they used for holding fish couldn't be used for cloth and furniture. The antiques sold to sailship merchants required delicate handling, but the thick-fingered fishermen of Sono simply lacked the skill needed to ensure safe handling. In desperation, they looked for ways they could accept goods at their port and then ship them to other towns for restoration and resale—they held meetings and formed committees that bickered into the late hours of night. Unfortunately for Sono, sailship merchants have a keen nose for incompetence, and they soon took their business to brighter ports.

The working men of Sono were not true seafarers, after all. They were merely fishermen. When industry clouded the waters and they saw they could no longer make their living off the sea, they cut their lines and left town. Those who remained clung to their ever-thinning purses as the economy of Sono sputtered and stalled.

Yet, as time passed, and the industrial and shipping ports of Hataya and Dakla saw their fortunes peak, the USN government began to regulate and control the shipping business in the busier towns. Ironically, fortune smiled upon the little port of Sono. In the wake of regulation, there were many sail-ship merchants without the wherewithal to get official permits for trade. These were men of little means and even less influence with the government. With courage and eagerness, these businessmen brought their own special kind of industry to Sono.

Smuggling.

Within a few years, the black market became a vital source of income for the town. Officially, no one knew about it, yet those looking for alternate, non-government-regulated sea routes found friends in Sono. Smuggling was the only means left for the people of Sono to keep their town alive. The business carried the promise of added value too: here there were thrills one couldn't find in other towns by other means.

The warehouses that stood shoulder to shoulder facing the sea looked like itinerant workers trawling for employment. One of these warehouses bore a clenched-fist icon—the trademark of a small shipping company. The office on the second floor was drenched with the stench of sea and mold, and the warped window frames gave it a rather shabby look. But not a single employee cared a whit about the appearance of their office space. The old ankha man who ran the company lived on a ship moored in the harbor. This saved him the money it would take to buy or rent other lodgings. Plus, he could maintain the ship himself, thus saving even more money.

No employees or customers ever came to the office. It was simply a holding tank for anyone who desired secret passage to the northern continent. Since newcomers to Sono attracted a lot of attention, the captain had to accept the fact that it was safer to keep his clients locked away and out of sight. He didn't want Highlanders sniffing around his business.

It wasn't such a burden, in any case. Ships could make the passage northward only three or four times a year. It was not as though he had to hide someone year-round. Usually, the time between when clients arrived and when they left was only a few nights—four or five at the most. As soon as the starseers gave word that weather was favorable, he would cram his clients into the bottom of his sailship, and head out. After that, he would never have to see them again.

But this latest customer proved a bit more trouble.

He was a young man, and he was in an incredible hurry. He kept saying he wanted to go to the north, the tone of his voice almost threatening. He wanted to leave that very night, even though he had arrived several days before any ship could hope to make the crossing. In the end, the captain had lost his temper with the man.

The ships can't go if the winds don't blow, he shouted. Even when the time was right, they had to go out in such a way as to not catch the attention of the watchful branch. If those conditions weren't satisfactory, said the captain, the man was welcome to go elsewhere. At that, the man flew into a rage and kicked a chair against the wall. When he tried to leave the warehouse, he fell down the stairs. It wasn't that his foot slipped—he had simply collapsed. In his excitement, he seemed to have gotten dizzy and then simply passed out.

The captain was at a loss. He could kick the man out on the street, but if word of suspicious behavior reached the local branch, they would surely come sniffing around. The smugglers had long since learned the art of buying the law's favor. But there were some among the Highlanders who could not be bought, and, on occasion, the branch in Sono had to make some arrests to please the high chief in Arikita. One could never tell when a crackdown was coming. Caution was mandatory.

There was nothing to be done about it. The captain dragged the unconscious young man back into his office and put him on the thread-bare couch. The man had been carrying very few possessions. The only thing he clutched was a bundle of paper that he held in his arms like it was more important than life itself. He was terribly thin, and the clothes he wore were in rags. The sole of his one shoe was missing, and his foot was covered with blisters. There were cuts on his hands too, like a rope burns, making the captain wonder if he had been climbing some mountain somewhere.

Stranger still was that even before the young man had regained consciousness, another person came asking after him—this one a boy. He looked like an ankha starseer, or perhaps he was actually a sorcerer. He wore a long black robe that went down to his ankles, and he carried a staff topped with a heavy-looking gem. Yet he was only eleven or twelve years old at the most. He, too, wanted to go north.

"You with him?" The captain asked.

The boy glanced at the pale face of the young man lying on the floor. "No, not with him. I merely knew that he was going north, and that if I followed him, I could go there as well."

From the utter lack of concern in the boy's voice, the captain concluded that he actually didn't know the other man. When he had looked at him he hadn't raised so much as an eyebrow. Pretty cold for such a young one, the captain thought.

But the boy who looked like a sorcerer said he had money. The captain, not being in the business of taking people at their word, took a down payment. He was about to ask how the boy had made the money when he thought better of it. *On second thought, I don't really want to know.*

The youngster helped himself to the paper bundle the unconscious man had held so dearly. He nodded and smiled as he examined its contents.

"What's that, then?" the captain asked.

"None of your business."

"Hmph, you sure are a brazen lad, aren't you."

"I'm a customer."

The contents of the package appeared to be some sort of diagram, but of what, the captain couldn't say.

When, at last, the young man regained consciousness, he began speaking earnestly and in a hushed tone with the boy. The captain brought food and water up to the office and caught snatches of their conversation. It was mostly the boy who was speaking.

"I heard about you from the Precept-King…"

"The mirror will be broken for sure…"

"I don't care what it is you want…"

No matter what he said, the boy always seemed aloof and uncaring—though the words he said made little sense. The young man seemed utterly cowed and unable to put up much of a defense. Before long he was bowing his head and begging the boy to join him on his journey northward. It turned out that the young man's down payment to the captain had been the whole of his funds. *He was going to take passage and leave me short half my income for the month.*

Because of the unusual circumstances, the captain took great pains to keep his clients in the office and out of sight. Thankfully, the boy and the young man did not seem interested in venturing outside at all. This worked well for the captain, who didn't fancy spending any more time with them than he had to. Whenever he did have to say something, the boy favored him with a look cold enough to freeze a man solid.

The oddness of the situation grew daily. As it happened, the boy seemed quite well-heeled for his age, and his staff surely had value. The captain, for his part, began having thoughts about stealing the staff and selling it for some extra money.

Of course, the captain kept his thoughts to himself. There could be no way the boy suspected anything. But once when he was bringing his clients their meal, the captain's eyes drifted over to the staff leaning against the wall. Quite suddenly, one of the crude desks that sat in the office leaped from where it was standing, slid across the uneven floorboards, and slammed into the wall between the captain and the staff. No one had pushed it; it moved by itself. The captain was shocked.

Chuckling to himself, the boy sat on the tattered sofa, dangling his feet over one of the armrests. "Don't get any ideas," he said. Then, just as suddenly, the desk jumped back to where it had been before. A jar of ink and an old pen stand clattered to the floor.

The gemstone on top of the staff glowed: first red, then a light green, then blue, and finally amber.

Furiously mumbling a prayer to the Goddess under his breath, the captain fled the room. *He really is a sorcerer. That really was magic. Oh, what have I gotten myself into?*

Already it had been five days since these two strange clients had arrived.

Opening the door to the warehouse and going inside, the captain drew the security bar firmly shut behind him. This was his custom whenever he had clients. He began the climb up to the second-floor office.

Word had come at last. They would leave after sunset that night. To be honest, the captain was relieved. He wanted to get these two out of his office as soon as possible. On the other hand, the thought of spending two weeks at sea with the young sorcerer gave the captain indigestion. *It may be high time for me to start looking for another profession.*

He had made it to the first landing on the stairs when he heard someone yelp in pain. The captain froze. *What was that? Whose voice was that? What is that little sorcerer up to now?*

For a moment, he didn't know what to do. Should he run upstairs to see what the problem was? Or should he run downstairs to safety? In that instant of indecision, he heard another sound, this time more like a sobbing sigh. Then there was a shout, and the tinted glass window of his office shattered. A moment later, the door itself swung outward, slamming into the wall. Shards of glass fell down the stairs, coming to rest at the captain's feet.

The captain looked stunned. If a cold wind—impossibly cold—hadn't blown down from the top of the staircase, he might have stood there forever. As it was, the brisk sting of the wind on his face brought him back to his senses. He began crawling up the stairs on all fours, brushing shards of glass off his face, out of his hair and whiskers.

"Wh-what in the name of chaos was that?!" he shouted, fearfully sticking his head through the office door. Then, he sneezed. A wind cold as ice was blasting against his face. It felt like his ears would freeze off.

The boy was standing against the wall. Something was curled up at his feet.

A lump of ice.

It was shaped like a person. The body was twisted, and the expression on his face was one of abject fear.

"What...is that?"

The boy shrugged. "Your customer."

"Th-th-that young man?"

"Did you have another?"

Still on the floor, the captain crawled like an infant over to where the boy was standing. "What happened? Why did he freeze? Why is it so cold in here?" The captain looked up at the sorcerer, his eyes wide. "Did you do this? Y-you cast a spell on him, didn't you?"

"Not I." The boy sorcerer shook his head. "If I had to guess, I'd say it was judgment."

"Judgment?"

"Yes, you know, the wrath of the heavens and all that. Looks like the

Goddess finally passed judgment on Dela Rubesi and this one here tried to escape. Quite clearly, he failed." The boy sorcerer turned with a whirl of his black cloak and picked up the bundle of papers from beside the frozen man's pillow.

"You can't take that…"

"Why not? It's certainly not doing him any good now. But I may have some use for it."

"Yeah, but that doesn't belong to you, boy," the captain said, deciding that perhaps this boy was just a boy after all, and in need of a scolding.

The black-haired sorcerer raised an eyebrow. "Nor to him," he said, pointing the rolled bundle of papers at the block of ice on the floor. "He stole it from someone else. He didn't write it himself, that's for sure." He shrugged. "So, when do we leave?"

For a second, the captain had no idea what he was talking about. "Leave? Ah, this evening. Leaving at night would be better, but there'll be no moon in the sky, and it's too dangerous to sail out in the dark. We'll wait until the branch guards have finished their rounds, and set sail."

"I see. More waiting. Great."

The captain shivered, half from the cold, half from fear. "What do we do about this…ice?"

"Leave it. Ice melts."

Melt? The captain recalled the young man's face. He had last seen him that morning. "Won't it, er, bleed?"

"I don't think I'd worry about that, but if it bothers you, I can easily clean this up."

The captain swallowed. His mouth was suddenly very dry. "What if the branch…finds out?"

"The branch? Oh, right, those Highlanders or some such rabble," the boy sorcerer said, sounding not at all concerned.

"Yes, them. If they decide to search us, we won't be able to leave. Get on their bad side, and things won't be easy for either of us."

"Don't worry, I won't leave a trace of my work," the boy said with a grin that sent another chill down the captain's spine. He gritted his teeth, regretting for what must have been the hundredth time taking on such a client.

Just then, something banged on the door downstairs hard enough that the captain feared the bar might fly off the latch. Someone was shouting from the street outside. "Captain! You up there? Open up! Branch chief wants to ask you some questions."

The captain looked at his client. He could feel his stomach rise into his throat, but the boy seemed calm as ever. "It seems we have some visitors," the boy said, standing. "Could your ship leave this moment if it had to?"

"A-aye, she's ready for sea."

"Then let's leave."

"But we won't make it out of harbor with the branch following us."

"You just worry about getting us to your ship. I'll get us out to sea." The boy sorcerer picked up his staff, and the gem on its tip flared brightly.

Wataru, Meena, and Kee Keema parted ways with Jozo in the forest along the border gate between Arikita and Bog. Jozo offered to take them all the way to Sono, and he even flew over the border once, but after they passed a few villages, they noticed they were causing quite a commotion on the ground. Dragons were rare creatures, but in industrialized Arikita, they had been largely relegated to the stuff of fairy tales. Jozo told them that the air in Arikita was the dirtiest of any place in the southern continent. Dragons tended to steer clear of the area, thus the general surprise at their passage.

With people already astir, the last thing they wanted was to cause any further trouble. Nor did Wataru want to involve Jozo in problems not his own. So they turned back, allowed Jozo to return to the Isle of Dragon, and made their way to the border on foot. Once at the border's gatehouse, they decided not to share their experiences at Dela Rubesi. Instead, they talked about the warehouse in Sono. A karulakin messenger was dispatched to the branch office. Wataru, Meena, and Kee Keema set off after him.

When they arrived at the branch in Sono, everyone had already left for the warehouse. The only ones left behind were a director and a communications officer. The sailship company bearing the mark of the yellow fist was a small operation run by an old ankha sea captain, who apparently had been involved in several smuggling operations. Wataru was relieved to hear they were on the right track, but he caught Kee Keema scowling out of the corner of his eye.

"What's wrong?" he asked quietly.

"I've got a feeling that the branch here has been letting this smuggling stuff slide for while," the waterkin whispered back.

Wataru had heard of similar things happening in the real world. Sometimes it made more sense for the police to cooperate with crime than try to stamp it out. "Still," he assured Kee Keema, "they're doing everything they can to stop it now—high chief's orders and all."

"I suppose you're right."

It wasn't long before one of the Highlanders who had gone to the warehouse came running back. The captain wasn't there, he reported. Still, there were signs that people had been living in the second-floor office, and something else...

"It's a little hard to believe, but there's someone up there, frozen. Or rather, it's like a lump of ice in the shape of a person."

The three exchanged glances. Meena gasped. "The fugitive..."

So he hadn't been able to escape the punishment of Dela Rubesi. The Goddess's wrath had found him all the way here in Sono. *But if she could do that, why would she go to the trouble of appearing before the chiefs to tell them to capture the fugitive?*

Wataru frowned. "Was anything unusual found in the office? Something like a blueprint—it might be a bundle of papers, or a tube."

"Well, it was kind of messy up there. Most of the Highlanders went down to the harbor. We don't know where the captain is, so we needed to check out his sailship."

"Then we'll go to the warehouse and check it out. Is that okay?" Wataru asked, turning to the chief.

"It's fine by me."

Before the chief could finish, the entire branch building shook. The building itself was a simple structure of wooden planks topped by a tin roof and was quite old. The first jolt made the rafters squeak. The second and third rattled the windows out of their frames and sent shock waves through the floorboards, making it difficult to stand.

"What's going on?!"

Wataru thought it was an earthquake. But Meena corrected him. "Tornado!" she screamed as she looked out the window.

Everyone ran outside. Meena was right. It was a tornado, and not just one; several twisting columns of air, one hundred feet high, rose all around the town. And they were moving in the same direction. Coming together. The simple, decrepit buildings in their path were shattered and smashed, scattered far and wide. The tornadoes pressed on. Toward the sea.

"That way's the harbor, right?" Wataru shouted over the roar of the wind, pointing in the direction they were headed.

"Yeah," the branch chief shouted back. "Those twisters'll rip our sailships apart!"

In Wataru's mind he replayed the scene at Triankha Hospital. The cyclone there had snatched up all those believers, leveled the thick-growing sula woods, and whisked Wataru all the way off to the Swamp of Grief on the far side of the continent. Mitsuru had done that with his wind magic.

Mitsuru's at the harbor.

"I have to go!" Wataru shouted. Behind him, the branch building collapsed in a pile of rubble.

Running down the twisting streets of Sono toward the harbor, Wataru watched roofs ripped off warehouse homes and wooden pilings tossed and splintered. Windows broke, and rain gutters were twisted and ripped away. Things were falling and breaking everywhere. People ran out of their homes, hands over their heads, trying to escape. An old lady watched, astonished as her laundry was torn out of her hands, clothesline and all. Wataru saw her mouthing the words "My apron," over and over. Dogs and cats were whipped into the air. Trees too. Wataru saw an oven slide up into one of the whirling vortexes.

Still the tornadoes advanced, and Wataru, Kee Keema, and Meena ran after them. Wherever the tornadoes had passed, people stood in shock and silence. As the three drew nearer to the tornadoes, the twirling winds buffeted them. Undaunted, Kee Keema forged onward, picking up a wooden door that had blown from somewhere along the way. He used it as a shield to block flying objects.

"Hang on to me!" Kee Keema shouted over the wind. Wataru hunched down, clinging to Kee Keema's waist with both hands and putting his head against the waterkin's broad back. Meena did the same, wrapping her tail around Wataru's torso for good measure.

They were only a street away from the harbor now. They could see the quays from the road.

And then the wind stopped. Everything that had been lifted into the air suddenly came plummeting down. Wataru and his friends looked up into the sky over the harbor.

The tornadoes—ten in all—were floating over the sea. They were gathered near a single sailship, tied to one of the wharfs. They were no longer exactly tornadoes, either. Each of them had become like a round ball of wind, bobbing in the air, slowly rising and falling.

The harbor was perfectly calm. The sailship surrounded by the wind-spheres was an old craft with a leaning mast. The mark of the yellow fist on its side was almost completely worn away. Practically everything on the ship was rusted. Its sails were down, and only the mainmast stood, like a sickly tree stripped of all its leaves. Still, the ancient-looking craft sat calmly on the water, rocking gently with the slow movement of the waves. The other ships in the water sailed nearby with their sails hanging limp from the masts, as though nothing had happened.

Wataru and Meena started running toward the ships. A second later, Kee Keema tossed aside his wooden door and joined them.

The wooden quay was ancient, with yawning gaps between the boards. Wataru caught glimpses of the water below. Sticking his foot through a rotted plank, he came to an abrupt stop.

"Mitsuru!" he shouted, wringing the last ounce of strength out of his body.

The back door of the captain's cabin opened, and a small male figure walked out toward the stern. He was wearing a sorcerer's black robe.

Mitsuru.

In one hand he held his staff. His other hand gripped the gunwale. His expression showed half surprise and half amusement. "Oh, it's you."

Wataru could hear the waves lapping against the quay. Seabirds that had flown away from the tornadoes in fright were slowly beginning to circle back to shore.

"What are you doing here?"

"That's my line!" Wataru shouted back. He caught a glimpse of someone moving behind Mitsuru in the cabin. *That must be the old captain.*

"I'm crossing the sea in this sailship. We're about to set sail," Mitsuru said, his voice ringing clear over the water, even though he didn't seem to be shouting.

"What, to the Northern Empire?"

Mitsuru didn't answer. He was inspecting the balls of air floating above his head as one would examine a piece of machinery. The twisters that had so violently smashed their way through town just moments before were now tamed, floating in their translucent spheres, spinning in silence.

"Is there some other place I might go?" Mitsuru asked.

Wataru began to walk toward the sailship. One step, then another. Meena and Kee Keema started to follow him, but he waved them back. "Why are you going to the north?"

"Isn't it obvious? That's where my next gemstone is."

In response, the gemstone atop the staff in Mitsuru's hand begin to glimmer: first red, then green, blue, and finally, amber.

Four colors. *He already has four colors.*

Wataru realized all at once that his Brave's Sword and Mitsuru's staff collected gemstones quite differently. His sword added gemstones into the fixtures on its hilt. But Mitsuru's staff seemed to absorb energy and power from the collected gemstones.

"Just one more," Mitsuru said, looking at his staff. "And that's in the north. That's why I have to go."

"And you were too busy to listen to what the Precept-King in Dela Rubesi had to say?"

Mitsuru's dark eyes opened wide. "Oh, so you went to Dela Rubesi, then?"

"We did."

"You're too nice for your own good. I figured even you wouldn't waste your time there."

Wataru ignored the chiding tone in Mitsuru's voice and stared back at him. "Dela Rubesi is gone. The Precept-King is dead."

Mitsuru said nothing.

"The fugitive is dead too, frozen solid even while he lived. You know, don't you?"

Mitsuru continued to remain silent, his hair blowing freely in the breeze. Wataru noticed that his hair was longer now than it had been when they met at the hospital.

"You were with the fugitive, weren't you? You knew he was going north, so you used him to find passage, didn't you?"

"He was a source of information," Mitsuru said, simply. "And he did beg me. You know, he didn't even have enough money to pay his own fare."

"Where are the diagrams the fugitive was carrying?" Wataru asked, his eyes never leaving Mitsuru's face.

Mitsuru laughed, his eyes narrowing. That was answer enough. Wataru faced the stern of the sailship and stretched out his hand. "Give them to me. Now."

"Why?" Mitsuru shot back.

"If the Northern Empire gets its hands on those, all of the south will be in grave danger."

Mitsuru's smile widened. "You sure are funny sometimes."

"I don't see what's funny about it."

"What's so dangerous about plans for a powered boat?"

Wataru was getting impatient. "What? You don't know? You don't understand? I have trouble believing that."

"Sorry, I'm not really up on my current events." Mitsuru yawned. "I hardly know anything about the south. I know even less about the north, save that's where I have to go." Mitsuru turned his eyes back toward the town of Sono—or what was left of it after his sorcery had reduced half the houses to rubble. "I didn't come here to sightsee, Wataru. And I don't have time to care what happens to the place. I've got my hands full trying to finish my journey." He smiled. "But you—you sure have been taking a few detours. What's with that wristband of yours? I noticed it the last time we met. That's the mark of a Highlander, or something, isn't it? Defenders of safety and peace in Vision? You sure have a lot of time on your hands."

Mitsuru's words stung far more than he had intended, and far more than Wataru had expected they might. He thought he knew why he was here, what he was doing. And yet the words still hurt.

"What do I care about the north or the south? Nothing. Think about it, Wataru. Take Arikita, for instance…" Mitsuru spread his arms on the stern of the boat like an orator giving a speech. "A town of mines and industry. Everything is done by manpower, quite primitive, if you ask me. But eventually, someone will discover mechanical power, I'm sure. It's just a matter of time. Vision must advance, as our own world did. Why are you so scared of something that would help it along its way?"

"Because those blueprints aren't from here. They aren't of this world," Wataru replied without hesitation. "I'm sure you're right, Mitsuru. I'm sure they'll invent those things in time, but that time hasn't come yet. Those blueprints are from the real world. It's not right."

"What's not right about it? Wait, on second thought, I don't really care. Let's just say I need these blueprints. So, I can't give them to you."

"What could you possibly need them for?" Wataru said, his voice sounding whiny in his own ears.

"I'm going to offer a trade to the emperor, Gama Agrilius VII," Mitsuru replied coolly. "You see, the last gemstone that I need just happens to be set in the Imperial Crown of the Northern Empire."

Wataru felt the blood drain from his body. If he looked down, he fully expected to see his blood leaking through the rotting boards of the quay to mingle with the sea water below.

"An Imperial Crown! He won't just give it to me if I ask nicely. That's why I need something he'll want so much that he's willing to deal. To tell the truth, I had no idea what I'd do until the Precept-King in Dela Rubesi gave me a call. Too bad I won't be able to return the favor."

The friendship Wataru felt toward Mitsuru evaporated in a flash. In its place now burned a fierce anger. "Something he'll want so much?"

"That's right. The North is trying to invade the South. I know that much at least."

"So to get your fifth gemstone, you'll just sell the entire southern continent to the Empire? Do you even realize what you're doing?!"

The chiding look melted from Mitsuru's face, replaced by concern. "Mitani, are you okay?"

He's really worried. Wataru had no idea why. *What is he saying?*

"You're babbling, Wataru. Hallucinating."

"I'm not."

"You are. Have you forgotten why you came through the Porta Nectere? Was it to become a Highlander? Was it to make lots of friends and live here in Vision forever? I don't think so."

Wataru fell silent. His head swirled with things he wanted to say, but he couldn't find the words for any of them.

"You came here to change your fate in the real world, Wataru. Vision isn't for us. If we can't change our fate and go home, then we've come all this way for nothing. You've forgotten the most important thing."

Wataru was speechless.

Wataru remembered being scolded by his father once. He hadn't agreed with something he said, and his father took the time to methodically destroy each of his arguments. *You're wrong, Wataru. You're so wrong, you can't even see it. You'll just have to accept it.*

"I haven't forgotten what I'm here for," he finally managed to say in a quiet voice. Mitsuru heard him. Or rather, he knew that was what Wataru was going to say.

"No, you have forgotten. You need to clear your head and give this some thought," Mitsuru said with a sigh. Then he picked up his staff in his left hand. "Sorry, but I'm in a bit of a hurry. I can't sit here waiting for you. Once the designs are delivered to the North, it will only be a matter of time before the invasion begins. Things are bad here now, but they're going to get much worse before this is all over. Say, how many gemstones do you have? If riots—or war—come to the south, finding them won't be so easy. You might want to get going."

"It doesn't matter. If you get to the Tower of Destiny before I do, it won't matter if I've found the gemstones or not. The one left behind becomes the Half."

Mitsuru had begun to walk away from the stern, but now he turned back, surprised. "The Half? What's that?"

So there were some things Mitsuru didn't know. Wataru was surprised, and at the same time pleased. "A sacrifice from the real world is required to remake the Great Barrier of Light," Wataru said simply. He hadn't bothered to go into all the detail, but it seemed that Mitsuru understood.

"I see," he said curtly, nodding. His eyes were wide open.

For the space of a breath, there was silence. Seabirds cried in the distance.

Then Mitsuru continued, as calmly as before, "Then I must hurry all the more. It's apparent that our best interests lie contrary to each other. Now it seems that there will be a winner and a loser in our little contest. We can't both win, Wataru. That's a stroke of bad luck, eh?"

Wataru wasn't sure what reaction he had expected. No matter how hard he tried, he couldn't picture Mitsuru looking alarmed, let alone frightened. In the end, his reaction was quintessentially Mitsuru. Mitsuru had come to Vision and become stronger.

Wataru blinked back tears. He told himself he wasn't sad. *It's the sea breeze. It's the dust stirred up by the twisters.*

"Wataru."

Meena stood standing by his side. Kee Keema was there too.

"What you just said…is it true?" Meena asked, her voice trembling. Wataru nodded quietly.

"That's ridiculous," Kee Keema growled. His voice seemed tiny in comparison to his giant frame. "I don't believe it. Not a word. I don't believe the Goddess would ever choose you as a sacrifice!"

Wataru looked up into Kee Keema's big face. He found comfort in those round, kind eyes.

"But you believe that someone from Vision must be sacrificed, don't you? It's the same thing."

"It's not the same!"

"It is. The only difference is that, in Vision, one is chosen from many, and from the real world, well, it's just me and Mitsuru to choose from."

Wataru grabbed Kee Keema's arm. "The Elder in Sakawa, he knew this. He told me I shouldn't stray from my course."

Suddenly, it seemed like Kee Keema had shrunk a full size. "The Elder…" the big waterkin fell silent.

I'm sorry, Kee Keema.

"When did you know this? Why didn't you tell us sooner? We're your friends!"

"I know."

"If we knew earlier, then me and Meena, well, we would have moved quicker, so you could meet the Goddess sooner…we want to help you."

Kee Keema's eyes were watering. Wataru felt his own eyes begin to tear up. He jerked his head back toward the sailship. "Mitsuru!"

"What is it now?"

"What would you do if I…" Even as he asked the question, Wataru knew the answer. *Why do I do this to myself?* "What if I said that I don't care about peace in the south? What if I told you that I came here to get those blueprints just to stop you from getting your final gemstone? What then?"

"What then?"

"What would you do?"

Mitsuru replied without a moment's hesitation, his voice clear and strong. "Then I would've faced you." *In battle.* Mitsuru stared directly into Wataru's eyes. "And I would've won. I'm stronger. We both know that."

The strength was sapped from Wataru's body. Meena, unable to restrain herself any longer, ran to his side for support. Addressing Mitsuru, she shouted, "You call yourself a friend? Do you even have a heart?"

Mitsuru stood smiling, both hands on his staff. He didn't even look in Meena's direction.

He lifted the gemstone-tipped staff above his head and began to chant. His voice was too low to be heard from where they stood, but the effect of his words soon became clear.

This spheres of wind hovering above the sea began to stir. They broke apart for a second before coming together as one. Soon they had transformed into a great cloak of wind, wrapping itself around the sailship. Gently, Mitsuru's sailship rose from the surface of the sea. Riding on a platform of wind, it lifted into the air.

Wataru looked up and made eye contact with Mitsuru. "Goodbye," he heard him say.

The cloak of wind around the ship undulated, then extended, becoming a tube that stretched out over the endless sea. The sailship carrying Mitsuru slid along it, disappearing into the distance.

Wataru watched it recede, becoming smaller, and finally disappearing where the sky and the sea became one.

He's gone.

"They're already out to sea," Kee Keema said, stunned. "If they can ride like that, there's no way we'll catch them by sailship. Once they're out on the open water, even if his magic runs out, they'll have the wind in their sails to take them to the north."

Meena grasped Wataru's arm with a trembling hand.

—*Goodbye.*

Wataru had seen a light flash deep in Mitsuru's eyes. It was a spark, he thought, that reflected an ongoing internal conflict. Despite what he said, Mitsuru was still grappling with a difficult moral dilemma. Would he do the right thing or continue pursuing his personal agenda?

Or maybe there wasn't a light in his eyes at all. Maybe the conflict was in me—between the half of me that's given up already, and the other half of me that wants to win. Who's right? Me or Mitsuru?

So, Wataru thought, *which is it?*

chapter 41
Night in Gasara

Twilight wrapped itself in a curtain around the town of Gasara.

The large gate at its entrance was closed. Here and there on the giant wall circling the town, torches burned and sputtered, shooting sparks into the sky. There seemed to be more torches now than when Wataru had last been here. *There's a need for more security, I guess.*

Still, even in the midst of all the Halnera turmoil, there had been little rioting in Gasara. More or less, it was business as usual for everyone.

Initially, there had been some fear that Gasara would be susceptible to infiltrators from the North. Because the town was a popular destination point for traders, many believed outsiders would attempt to spread the tenets of the Old God. Yet that was not the case. People who knew the real conditions in the North were less susceptible to rumors. The ankha in Gasara knew first-hand that simple faith in the Old God wouldn't save them from Halnera.

Most significantly, Gasara had Kutz the Rosethorn, widely regarded as the toughest branch chief in the land. That alone was a huge difference from Lyris. The truth about Halnera didn't faze her, nor did she let it concern the people in her town. If the Goddess must choose someone to protect Vision, what business was it of theirs to protest? The one chosen by the Goddess was given a great and important task. They should be proud, not quivering with fear.

When people came to her, frightened and worried, she would laugh them away. "Don't be so obsessed with yourself. The Goddess sees all. I hardly think she would rely on a sniveling coward who's afraid to die for such a vital task. Sorry, chap, but you were never in the running to be the sacrifice."

Wataru stood on the watchtower, looking down on the town. The top level was about six stories high. The guard had warned him when he started climbing the ladder.

"If you must climb to the top, boy, I won't stop you. Just remember, once you start climbing, don't look down until you're all the way to the top."

"Sure thing."

"You can still turn back, you know."

"I like heights."

"Suit yourself."

Following the guard's advice, Wataru didn't look down as he climbed. When he reached the top platform, he stretched his arms and legs, feeling the evening breeze against his cheek. When he looked down he felt himself swoon. Thankfully there was a railing to hold on to.

The guard behind him wore a rope around his waist, carried a megaphone made of copper over his shoulder, and stood with his arms crossed. Every five minutes, he turned to look east, west, south, and north. Three guards per day took turns watching over the town.

Lamps flared in the countless windows of Gasara. Already the lively sounds of customers talking and laughing spilled out of taverns and lodgings. Steam rose from various windows, and the hearty smell of stew drifted through the air. At their post, darbaba stood freshly washed and fed, the dirt of their long journey cleaned away. Next to them, a group of waterkin sat around talking and smoking. From somewhere came the sound of a stringed instrument being plucked.

Wataru turned his eyes beyond the town walls to look out on the vast grasslands surrounding Gasara. Here and there, he could see outcroppings of rock in between darker patches where copses stood. Everything was dyed a dark pink by the setting sun, still and silent at the ending of the day. A flock of birds like dark specks shot across the sky, disappearing toward the forest in the distance.

Wataru took a deep breath, resting his elbows on the railing, and looked up at the night sky.

The Blood Star.

It shone a brilliant crimson. Yet, perhaps on account of the twilight, it did not look so ominous tonight. If Wataru reached out and plucked it from the night sky, it would make a nice pendant for Meena.

Wataru stared at it for a long time, trying not to blink. The Blood Star winked first. Wataru felt like it was smiling at him. *What are you so worried about, boy?*

Wataru, Kee Keema, and Meena had come back to Gasara after their confrontation with Mitsuru in Sono. Once it became clear that Wataru would become one of the sacrifices, there was nothing to do but wait. And if that was to be his fate, Wataru wanted to wait here, in the first town he had come to in Vision, where he had met his friends, where he had taken the Highlander's oath.

Meena had cried a lot on the road from Sono. Kee Keema had been silent for the most part, and it seemed like his darbaba, too, was grumpier than usual.

Wataru asked Meena to sing for him. She had always sung earlier on in their trip, swinging back and forth on the darbaba cart. Meena nodded and began to sing in her beautiful voice. But before she could finish her first song, her voice choked, and she veered off key.

Then Wataru tried to sing. He would attempt one of Meena's songs, or sometimes, he would sing a song he remembered from the real world.

Back in Gasara, Kee Keema reunited with the other darbaba drivers and went out on patrol with the Highlanders. Meena worked with the dog-eared doctor at the small hospital in town. Wataru once again started working for Kutz, going on patrols like Kee Keema or helping Trone with his paperwork.

"Been busy of late. Haven't had much time to sift through all these files," Trone explained, though it was clear he just didn't like doing paperwork. But he did enjoy making others do his paperwork for him.

After their return, Wataru told Kutz everything. He wasn't expecting any sympathy. He just wanted her to know the details, so that she would be prepared when word got out that he was to be chosen.

As expected, Kutz didn't seem particularly concerned. "Understood," she said simply. "Living in a lodge isn't very comfortable, I'd imagine. Why don't you move in here. There's a storeroom on the second floor; you can clean it up and stay there if you like. If you need anything else, just tell Trone, and he'll get it for you."

And that was all.

When the time comes. Kutz said it as though she were talking about going shopping for groceries or making an appointment. After that, she made not a mention of Halnera or the sacrifice—which Wataru took to be her way of showing that she cared.

Wataru had climbed the watchtower because he wanted to see the Blood Star from as close as possible. *I'm not scared*—which was a lie, but he had made his peace with what was to come. He wanted to let the Blood Star know. *Maybe it is a lie. Maybe I really am frightened.* He wasn't sure himself. That's why he felt he had to say it. If he stood up there, looked the Blood Star in the eye, and was able to say it, it would become true. A least, he hoped it would.

It had already been eight days since their encounter with Mitsuru in Sono. He was probably already in the north by now. Try as he might, there was no way Wataru could hope to catch up. Two minus one was one. That's all he could think about. In fact, he made himself think about it. There was nothing else for him to do.

Above his head, the Blood Star winked and sparkled. Its rhythm seemed steady, no alteration in the pattern. When would Halnera end? *It sure is taking her a long time to choose her other sacrifice.*

"Oh?" The tower guard grunted suddenly, walking over to put a hand on the top of the ladder. "To what do we owe this unexpected honor?"

It was Kutz. She had three steps left to climb on the ladder, but instead of taking the guard's outstretched hand, she jumped up, springing over the railing to land on top of the platform. The black leather whip hanging at her waist shone with a lustrous gleam in the twilight. For those who didn't know the considerable skill with which she wielded it, the weapon might have looked like nothing more than a curious fashion statement, so well did it match her leather attire.

"I came to watch the sunset. I get romantic sometimes too, you know."

Kutz had changed the style of her hair while Wataru was away from Gasara. Previously cut short, her hair now came down over her neck. She looked good. Her right shinguard and the firewyrm band on her left wrist served as crimson accents to her otherwise black leather garb.

"What's with you? You look shocked," Kutz chided, with her hand at her waist and her head tilted. "Stunned by my beauty, is that it? I should think you'd be used to it by now."

Wataru blushed. He had been stunned, it was true. Kutz was beautiful, there was no denying it. If he hadn't come to Vision, Wataru was sure he never would have met a woman as gorgeous, and as capable, as she was.

She turned to the guard who stood chuckling at the edge of the platform. "I'd like to have a few words with the boy here. Can I borrow your post awhile?"

"Of course," the guard nodded. Picking up his copper megaphone, he passed it to Wataru. "Then I'll let you hold on to this while you're here."

"Right. I'll let you know if I see anything."

"That'll do just fine," the guard said, disappearing down the ladder.

Kutz walked over and leaned her elbows on the railing. She looked out over the grasslands in the fading light. "This your first time up here?"

"Yes."

"Great view, isn't it? I think this is my favorite spot in town."

"I like it too."

"You should see the sunrise. Even when it's raining, or there's a mist, the view from here never disappoints."

Kutz shook her head, brushing the hair out of her eyes, and looked up at the night sky. "I was born in a small frontier town in the mountains. Nothing but fields cut into the mountainside and a few simple huts in the middle of a little forest. I remember when I first came out to Gasara and saw the grasslands. What a shock that was. I never imagined the world could be so vast."

This was the first time Kutz had ever spoken of her home. Wataru wondered if she had left by herself. How old had she been? Did she have some reason for leaving?

Kutz didn't say anything else. She and Wataru stood side by side in comfortable silence. After some time had passed, Kutz suddenly spoke. "Got a lot of nerve, don't you."

Wataru spun around. "What?"

"Not you. That," she said, pointing a finger at the Blood Star hanging in the northern sky. "Shining all pretty up there like a jewel. Too high up for anyone to grab and put in its place."

Wataru smiled. "I bet your whip might just be able to reach it."

"I've got half a mind to try," Kutz said, her hand going down to the hilt of the whip quelled at her belt. Then she grinned and looked at Wataru.

Her eyes weren't smiling. They were frighteningly serious. The smile faded from Wataru's face.

"Are you sure you're ready for this?" she said, making it sound like less of a question and more of a confirmation. *I know how you'll answer, I'm just making sure.*

"Yeah...I think."

"You give up easy."

Wataru shrugged. "I guess I feel like there's nothing I can do, so why bother?" Wataru hunched his shoulders, thrusting his hands in his pockets. His fingers brushed the edge of the wyrmflute. "On the road back to Gasara I was tempted a few times to call Jozo and try my chances at following after Mitsuru. I could get to the north if I was riding on a dragon. But even if I did catch up with Mitsuru, I don't think I could beat him. His magic is too powerful."

And Wataru was one gemstone behind.

"In any case, I'm too late. I have to accept my fate—and not worry about it so much."

Kutz stood with her arms folded in front of her. Her leather vest bulged out above her arms. Wataru stared, then blushed, and hurriedly continued, "I'm not one of many, like whoever the sacrifice from Vision is to be. I'm only one of two. I guess that makes it easier to accept."

Kutz said nothing. Pulling a cigarette from her vest pocket, she lit it with a match, puffing in the twilight.

"Also...I don't think I've told anyone this before, but the whole reason I came here to Vision in the first place was thanks to my friend—the other Traveler, Mitsuru. That's not all. If he hadn't come to save me, I would've died. Twice—once in the real world and once in Vision. He saved my life."

When Mom turned the gas on in the apartment and when I was being dragged to the guillotine at Triankha Hospital. "I owe him a debt. Maybe this is how I can repay that debt."

Kutz took a drag on her cigarette and blew out a long plume of smoke. Then she stabbed it out on the railing, twirling the butt between her fingers. "You know," she said, her tone suddenly changing. She was staring out over the grasslands. "I don't care to hear your excuses."

It's not excuses, that's how I really feel. Wataru was going to protest, but something in Kutz's voice made him hold back.

"I won't ask if you're scared of being sacrificed. I don't care if you're fine leaving Kee Keema and Meena to mourn, or if you're happy not meeting the Goddess. You came here to Vision to change your fate. If you become the sacrifice, you won't be able to do that. I won't stand here and ask you if you're okay with that."

Her words were strong and she spoke with no hesitation. "You left your mother in the real world when you came here. You won't ever be able to see her again. Right now, she's worried to death, and she'll never know what happened to you. She'll wait for you and waste the rest of her life in loneliness. But I won't ask how you can stand to do such a thing to your mother."

You are asking. Pain stabbed at Wataru's heart.

"You're a smart kid. Brave too." Kutz praised him in angry tones. "That's why I'm sure you'll have a suitable answer no matter what I ask. I'm sure your answers will be satisfactory. After all, you've had plenty of time to convince yourself. You've had lots of practice."

Wataru was silent. He felt like she was expecting him to say something, but he couldn't find anything worth saying.

Darkness slid over dusk, and the brightness in the sky gave way to the deepening violet of night. Whereas moments before the only light in the sky had been the Blood Star, now other stars appeared around it.

Her back to the starry sky, Kutz faced Wataru and looked him straight in the eye. "There is one question I would have your answer to."

Wataru swallowed and took a step back.

"Are you just going to let Mitsuru go?"

"Let him go?"

"Are you just going to let him get away with this?"

Wataru blinked, uncomprehending. "What do you mean? What is he getting away with?"

"What isn't he getting away with!" Kutz slapped the railing with the palm of one hand. "Think about it. What has he done? What is he doing? At Triankha Hospital, in Sono, he used his magic to kill dozens, maybe hundreds of people. The port town of Sono lies in shambles because of him. What do you think about that?"

Wataru was flustered. It felt like the carefully laid pieces of armor he had put over his heart were coming undone. "B-but…"

"But what?"

"At Triankha—he had to do that. He was up against those fanatics. If he hadn't struck back, they would've killed him, and neither of us would've been able to get out of the magic barrier they created." *And… and…* Wataru's mind raced, looking for more excuses. "He's done good things too. Like in Maquiba. He used his magic to put out a wildfire there. If the fire had been left to burn, the whole town would have been ruined."

But then Wataru remembered how Mitsuru had turned down the Precept-King of Dela Rubesi's request. He simply didn't have time, he said. Yet he did find the fugitive—not to capture him but to use him to cross to the north.

"If he's such a powerful magician, then I'm sure he could have found more subtle means to achieve his ends. If he wanted to, I'm sure he could have found a way without hurting and killing people from Vision and destroying our towns. Why didn't he?"

Wataru took a step back. Kutz pressed on. "Let me answer for you. It's because this Mitsuru kid doesn't care a lick about Vision. As long as he reaches the Tower of Destiny and meets the Goddess, he's happy to leave and never look back. I doubt he'd ever set foot in our world again. That's why he thinks it doesn't matter whom he hurts or what trouble he causes. Even if he should leave a mountain of corpses in his wake—as he has—who cares? Advancing toward his goal by the fastest possible means is paramount to all other concerns."

Kutz reached out, grabbing Wataru by the shoulder. "And you're okay with this? Do you think what he's doing is right?"

Is it right? Is it wrong? I don't think…

"Mitsuru is my friend," Wataru said in a small voice. No matter how deep he reached, that was the only answer he could come up with.

"I didn't ask you that. I asked whether you agreed with the methods he's chosen."

Kutz pushed Wataru and turned away from him. Wataru staggered back and grabbed the railing for support.

"After he's gone to the north, I'm sure he'll keep doing what he does, you know. If something stands in his way, he'll rip it up from its roots and toss it aside. Even if he has to walk over a mountain of rubble and dead bodies, he'll keep walking without a moment's regret."

"B-but Mitsuru…" Wataru spoke haltingly. "I think he has to do what he does…that's how much he wants to change his fate! His lot in life was so bad, he'll do anything…He's much more determined…much more determined than I am."

Kutz whirled around so fast her hair spun up behind her. "And that justifies any means? You'd forgive him what he's done? If it's to get back something you've lost, to make amends for something bad that happened to you, does it not matter what you do to anyone else? Think of what you're saying! I'll ask you again. Do you think he's right? Can you forgive him?"

Wataru didn't have an answer. Not an ounce of pride remained in his heart.

"The Northern Empire is a serious threat to us, yes. But there are many people living up there, same as here. Not all of them agree with the policies of their emperor. Some of them have been beaten down; they're suffering. You said Mitsuru did what he did at Triankha because he had no other choice, because he was dealing with those fanatics? So, by your reasoning, he's free to do whatever he likes to the people of the north? They are mostly believers in the Old God too, you know."

The darkness around them grew deeper. Stars now filled the night sky, but the brightest lights came from Kutz — her eyes flared with rage. "You said the emperor has the last gemstone Mitsuru is looking for, correct? I'm sure he'll go through with his plan of giving the designs for the powered boat to the emperor. That would make both Mitsuru and the emperor of the north very happy, to be sure. Good for them. But what happens next? The North builds their powered boats. There is a war. Thousands of people die. Do you think that's right? Can you forgive that? Do you just stand here, mouth shut, head in your hands, pretending not to see?"

At last, Wataru looked up at Kutz. "What are you saying I should do? What can I do?"

"You're asking me? You should be asking yourself."

Myself. The answer's in me…

Hands back on the railing, eyes peering out into the darkness, Kutz spoke. "You say Mitsuru is your friend. But, Wataru, even if they're friends, even if they're relatives, even if they're lovers, when someone does something that isn't right, it isn't right. If you feel in your heart that they are wrong, you need to follow those feelings."

Kutz's slender fingers gripped the railing tightly. "I once had an argument with a man I loved, a long time ago."

Wataru looked up at her intently.

"It was more than ten years ago now. There was a man, a killer. He murdered many to satisfy his greed. And he was very clever, terribly clever. He spun lies to deceive those around him, never letting us glimpse the truth.

"But one day we took a chance and set a trap for him. It was a chance like none other we'd ever had or would never have again. I can't tell you how happy I was."

The trap backfired, said Kutz. The criminal was eventually released.

"We argued for days. But in the end, the killer was set free. It's true, we baited him. That was the only way we could bring him to justice. And we were told we were wrong. We were indicted. The killer walked away and laughed at us."

Within two weeks, the killer entered a merchant's house to rob him and murdered the entire family. But his luck had run out, and he was caught at the scene of the crime.

"What happened next? He was hanged. But, if we'd never let him go in the first place, he wouldn't have been able to rob and kill that one last time. Even if it was illegal, what we had done was clearly the right thing to do. I believe that even to this day."

A spark of understanding went off in Wataru's head. "Wait…the one who indicted you…"

"Boris Ronmel. At the time, he was a Highlander like myself. Now he's Captain of the Knights of Stengel, of course. You've met him, haven't you?"

Trone had told Wataru that, a long time ago, Kutz had been dumped by Captain Ronmel.

"Boris upheld the law above all else. He supported the Senate too. And the branch chiefs, they listened to his opinions. But I thought people's lives were more important than all that. Yes, I went against the law. But I don't regret it for a moment. That's why I could never forgive him for indicting us. Nor was he able to forgive me."

And so they had parted ways.

"You were in love with Captain Ronmel, weren't you?"

Kutz looked at Wataru, a faint smile on her lips. "We were. But even still there are things one can't forgive—that one shouldn't forgive. In my mind, he's responsible for the deaths of that unlucky merchant and his family. And I'm sure that Boris still thinks I was wrong. Oh, we're both right in our own fashion, of course. It all depends on which side you choose to take. I wouldn't give an inch, nor would he. I knew him better than anyone else in the world. And he knew to expect the same from me. That's why he didn't hesitate for one moment to indict us. That was the only way he knew to stop me."

Wataru remembered Captain Ronmel, his clear blue eyes filled with incredible calm and wisdom, which looked as though they could see straight through to the back of his head. He shivered, imagining a face-off between Kutz and the captain.

Kutz moved silently over to Wataru's side, stooping to put her hands on his shoulders. "Mitsuru is your friend. But if you feel what he does is wrong, you must act. You can't stand silently by and let evil happen. Maybe you'll never see eye to eye, but that doesn't mean you can give up. If he's wrong, you must tell him." Kutz stood up from the railing.

While they were talking, the curtain of night had fallen over the grasslands. In town, torches blazed, and in the sky stars became countless scattered fragments of light.

"I..." Wataru began after a long pause. "I don't want Mitsuru to do what he's been doing. I don't want him to keep hurting the people of Vision just to get to the Tower of Destiny. It's...it's wrong." An image of the wreckage in Sono flashed across his mind. "But I felt like it was cowardly of me to say so. Like I was looking for some excuse to stop Mitsuru, just because I didn't want to lose."

"That's where you're wrong," Kutz said softly. "That's just an excuse you tell yourself so you can give up. If you don't want Mitsuru to do what he's doing, if you think what he's doing is wrong, then you must stop him no matter what—even if he says you're a coward."

"Because he's my friend?"

"No, that's not it," Kutz said with a sharp shake of her head. "You're forgetting something very important."

Wataru raised an eyebrow.

She grabbed on to Wataru's left hand and lifted it above his head. "You've forgotten that you're a Highlander."

She gave his hand two shakes. "You swore an oath. To defend peace in Vision, to protect the word of the law. How can you just stand by and let someone destroy that peace? If you're going to stand here and pretend you just don't see, you're not qualified to wear the firewyrm band."

The red bracelet on his wrist glowed softly in the starlight. Wataru thought he could feel a warmth in it, like when he had fought for his life against Father Diamon in the Cistina Cathedral.

"It doesn't matter that you're a Traveler, that you might be chosen to be the sacrifice, or that you're now in direct competition with Mitsuru. You're a Highlander. That's why, until the very moment you're called by the Goddess, until the very last breath of your life, you must follow Mitsuru. You must yell until your voice is hoarse, calling him back from the chaos. You must plead with him and show him the wrong that he does—the value of those things he crushes and destroys to reach his goals. You must tell him that he is wrong, that you think he is wrong. You must stop him."

Suddenly Wataru remembered his parting with Captain Ronmel at the observatory at Lourdes. Just as Kutz did now, he had put his hand on Wataru's shoulder and looked him straight in the eye.

—*You are a Traveler. You must follow your own course. Never forget that.*

—*I'm sure that Kutz the Rosethorn would say the same. She is your leader, and I would have you follow my advice as though it were hers.*

He was wrong. Kutz didn't feel the same way. She didn't want Wataru to follow his mission to the end, she wanted him to be a Highlander.

Once again, Kutz and Ronmel were a step out of sync, yet both of them were right. And the look in their eyes when they spoke to him was exactly the same. It was funny, and at the same time, a little sad. Wataru felt his eyes sting.

The question before him now was this: Which truth do I follow? Where will I stand? Wataru looked up at Kutz and nodded slowly. She smiled and nodded back. "Then come—come with us to the north."

"You've been planning this?"

"We need your help, Wataru."

Chapter 42
A Conversation at Night

The trees that surrounded the huts of the Watchers glistened with dampness in the rainy night. Large droplets fell from the sky, smacking into the broad leaves, waking them from fitful sleep. *Have to stay up. Can't go to sleep yet. For Wayfinder Lau is still awake in his little home.* The leaves of the forest rustled and shook, and waited.

Wayfinder Lau had spread several thick books out on the desk in front of him, and with a long-stemmed pen in his hand, he wrote furiously. He had pulled a lamp right next to his head and wore small, round glasses balanced on the tip of his nose.

The sound of the pen tip sliding across the paper was loud in the quiet little hut. Oil smoke rose from the burning lamp. Quite suddenly, Wayfinder Lau's hand stopped, as though someone had called out to him. He looked up from his work. It was a small room, but the lamp was even smaller. Someone was standing at the very edge of the tiny circle of light cast on the floor.

Wayfinder Lau took off his glasses and squinted. "M'lady?"

The someone standing in the room shook with laughter and took a half-step away from the circle of light. "Don't look so surprised!" said a girl's sweet voice. The voice that had made Wataru think of fairies.

"Your appearance..." Wayfinder Lau began, setting down his pen and standing.

"You don't think it suits me? I occasionally wish to appear as a person, you know."

Still hidden in the dim light at the corner of the room, the one Wayfinder Lau had called "m'lady" walked in a little circle. The hem of her skirt fluttered as she twirled.

She appeared as a young girl, incredibly slender, with a fragile beauty. From her clothes, she was not someone of Vision. "I don't look so horrible all the time because I want to, you know. Sometimes, well, it's good to get out."

"And where did you borrow that little girl?"

"She was in the Tower of Destiny."

"Then she is from the real world?"

"Yes, in fact. Must be one of his friends," she answered, raising her borrowed right hand and placing it upon her borrowed right cheek. "I wonder if she's his girlfriend? In any case, his mind has been tuned to her for some time now."

Wayfinder Lau maintained his silence, unsure of where she was heading with this.

"Don't you think if I appear to Wataru like this he might grow to like me—and her—all the more?"

"Not your best plan ever," Wayfinder Lau said gently.

"Oh? But I merely want to make him happy."

Make him happy so he'll take your side? People are not quite so simple as all that. Perhaps she does not yet realize this.

"Besides, I'm rather fond of this look," the little girl said, twirling around once more. Despite her childlike bounce, Wayfinder Lau's keen eyes could see the weight that lay upon her heart.

The two were silent, listening to the sound of the rain on the forest leaves outside.

"He's going to the north," she said suddenly.

Wayfinder Lau knew this without being told. All the birds throughout Vision had been keeping tabs on the Travelers, informing him of their every move.

"He's gotten quite far. One more step to the tower. Things are racing toward a finale."

Wayfinder Lau replied slowly. "Then the path ahead of him, as you know, is his true test."

She didn't seem to be listening—instead, she seemed preoccupied with the circle of light on the floor. "It sure rains a lot around here. I don't like the rain."

Sitting in the warm lamplight, staring at her profile, Wayfinder Lau felt a sadness—a kind of pity—swell in his heart.

"Whose side are you on? Mitsuru's? Or Wataru's? Which do you want to win, Wayfinder Lau?"

"What I think is irrelevant."

"But one of them must be chosen for the sacrifice, to become the Lord of the Underworld."

"That is up to the Goddess to decide."

"Why does she get to decide all these important things anyway?" The girl pouted, resting her borrowed hand upon the window frame. "Not that I care who wins. Even if Wataru should lose, my feelings will remain the same. If he is to become the Lord of the Underworld, then I'll become the Goddess. Then we can rule Vision together. If he is to go back to the real world, then I'll follow him like I am now."

The girl sighed. "I've grown quite tired of Vision anyway. You know, I think we should just let the chaos win this time. The people in the real world have active enough imaginations—they'll just make a new Vision. I'm sure there are plenty of little future Visions out there somewhere. One of them will grow, and bloom, and we'll have a whole new world. How beautiful."

"Are you jesting with me?"

"Oh no, I'm quite serious."

Wayfinder Lau sat back down, slowly shaking his head. He reached his hand out toward the lamp.

"Stop!" came a sharp command from across the room. "Leave the light as it is. Please."

"I thought you were fond of how you looked?"

"Oh, I am. I just don't want to see myself right now."

For that would make the transition back all the more painful. Wayfinder Lau took his hand off the lamp and put it back upon his knee.

"I'm going to fight, and this time, I'm going to win." Beyond the circle of light, the girl's eyes sparkled.

"This is why you come to me tonight? To tell me this?"

"Yes."

"All that way?"

"I wanted to let you know that this time, no matter what you do, you won't be able to stop me."

"Oh?"

"Not in the slightest. I'll be working with Wataru, you see. I'll show you."

"Not with Mitsuru?" Wayfinder Lau asked, though he knew her answer. He saw her flutter in the corner. "Mitsuru was too tough a nut to crack, is that it?"

She sighed. "He's useless," she said with a pained expression on her face.

Wayfinder Lau lowered his eyes. It was a simple thing to imagine how things must have gone. Mitsuru was quite talented, and his eyes were sharp. "You beckoned to him, and he saw through your disguise and pushed you away. Is this not what happened?"

The girl did not answer. Wayfinder Lau could see her slender shoulders hunch over tightly. "Wataru is nicer," she said in a little voice. "That's why I want to help him. That, and his determination is unlike that of any Traveler I've ever seen. Oh, I'm sure he'll go far."

Wayfinder Lau brushed his robes, shivering. *When did it get so cold?* "Wataru is not the only one with a will of stone. Mitsuru is the same. I wonder why you cannot see this?"

Continuing, he said, "It is because they are young, m'lady. For the very young to rail against their own bitter fate, they must draw upon all their strength and spirit. That is why they are so steadfast."

And that steadfastness is why you will not succeed. No matter how gentle Wataru may be—so Wayfinder Lau thought.

"Remarkable, simply remarkable," the girl said, with a voice that sounded like grinding teeth.

Outside, the relentless patter of the rain marked the passing of time.

"I'm sure that even if Wataru knew my true form, he wouldn't push me away. That's why it's going to work. I'm sure of it."

Wayfinder Lau turned back to his desk and picked up his pen. He began to write. Before he had even finished a sentence, the girl standing by the window disappeared. Wayfinder Lau did not bother to look up. Even though she was gone, he still felt a presence—something low to the floor, weighty and vile, slinking away from the light of the lamp.

When he could no longer feel the presence, Wayfinder Lau stood up from his chair, walked over to the window, and opened the heavy shutters. A fine mist of rain brushed against his face, dampening the white hairs of his brows and whiskers. The trees in the forest swayed. They were shaking their heads, scratching their branches together, all of them wide awake.

"Sorry about that," the Wayfinder said to them in a little voice. "To bed with you now. There's nothing to worry about. Nothing will happen to our Vision. Sleep, and I'll see you in the morning."

The rain continued to fall quietly. The trees of the forest clung together, half frightened and half wary. They continued their sentry of the Village of the Watchers—the rain falling like silver from the sky.

chapter 43
The Plan

In the morning, Wataru lay on his simple wooden bed and rubbed his eyes with the palms of his hands. Bright sunlight streamed through the window. His late-night chat with Kutz seemed more like a dream than anything else.

I'm awake. A new day is starting. It wasn't a dream.

Last night, Kutz had revealed her plan to Wataru. A select team of Highlanders was to sneak into the Northern Empire and assassinate Emperor Gama Agrilius VII. She wanted Wataru to be part of that team.

"We've been planning the assassination itself for a long time. Still, our means were limited. We thought we might wait for trade season to begin and sneak aboard a merchant sailship. But the danger involved is rather high. You and your wyrmflute changed the situation considerably. If we ride on a dragon, we can get to the north by air. Not only that, but we can make a beeline for the emperor's palace."

So it's not me they need, it's my dragon. The truth had tasted a little bitter in Wataru's mouth. *But what Kutz said last night on the watchtower was right. I have to chase Mitsuru down.*

Wataru quickly got dressed, pulled the wyrmflute out from beneath his pillow, and hid it in a pocket. He was lucky it hadn't broken the first time he used it. He figured he would get only one more chance.

"Be ready to leave at any time," Kutz had warned him. "Ever since our fugitive got away, the four high chiefs in the south have been in secret deliberations. If they give the word to go ahead with the assassination, High Chief Gil will come here with the orders."

It could be today, it could be tomorrow, but in any case, it wouldn't be long. And then they would leave.

"Who are the other members?"

"Right now, there are me and three others—all volunteers—so one of us from each of the four countries: Nacht, Bog, Arikita, and Sasaya."

"So I'm like an extra?"

"Quite a powerful extra! The other three will be coming with High Chief Gil. They're a skilled team. Something to look forward to."

So they would be five. A small team of elites. It sounded good.

"Incidentally, I'll be the leader," Kutz said with a winning smile. "It was my idea in the first place, after all. I'll have direction and responsibility. Are we clear?"

"Clear. And, well, I understand we can't talk about this mission, but…"

"Trone knows about it. He is deputy here. I couldn't hide it from him. He knows that I'll be taking you as well. And I'm sure you'll want to tell Kee Keema and Meena. But I don't want anyone else hearing about it. Got it?"

Wataru nodded. He got it.

As far as preparing for the journey, Wataru had little in the way of belongings. All he needed was the Brave's Sword at his side. Wataru left his room, fastening the sword belt tightly around his waist.

He went in to the branch office to find Trone casually looking over some official-looking documents. The beastkin looked up. "Awake at last, eh? You like your sleep. Go get some breakfast," he said, casual as ever, showing no trace of knowing about Wataru's secret mission.

Wataru ate a late breakfast at a nearby inn, and thought. The food tasted dry on his tongue. How to explain what he was about to do to Meena and Kee Keema?

I can't take them with me, it's too dangerous. Kee Keema's strong and Meena is quick, but we aren't going to fight a pack of gimblewolves. Wataru didn't want to involve them in any more trouble than he had already. If he told them the truth, he was sure they would want to come with him. They wouldn't back down. *So, I have to lie. But what do I say? I don't need their help anymore? I don't like them anymore, so could they please leave? Can't really do that.*

"If you can't tell them, I could always tell them for you," Kutz had offered. "As branch chief I can order the two of them to stay here. There will still be trouble enough with Halnera going on. Gasara seems to have avoided the brunt of it, but branches in other towns are at their wit's end. They'll have plenty of work to do here."

Even if Kutz did tell them for him, there would still be one problem. No matter what the outcome of this mission, once he went to the north, it was unlikely Wataru would ever come back.

Wataru had no idea what lay in store for him. Would Mitsuru reach the Tower of Destiny first? Or would he somehow beat Mitsuru to the Tower, get the Goddess to change his fate, and go home? Their strategy might even fail. Wataru could die alone somewhere.

No matter what happened, the only certain thing was that he wouldn't be seeing his two friends again. That meant, no matter how he did it, he had to say goodbye to them himself. He had to tell them how much their friendship meant, how much he'd grown to trust and rely on them. How much he didn't want to leave them behind.

Wataru had no idea what to say.

He was sitting, absentmindedly chewing on a piece of bread, when the innkeeper called out to him from the kitchen. "Not eating well today, are you? Like another bowl of soup?" There were few other diners at the tables. She had wondered out loud why Wataru was late to breakfast that morning.

"I'm sorry."

"Nothing to apologize for. Everybody sleeps in sometimes."

Here in Gasara, the commotion surrounding Halnera seemed like a very distant thing. The plot to assassinate the emperor of the north to protect the peace of the United Southern Nations, too, seemed like a wild fantasy, compared to eating a hot meal at a clean table here in the inn.

Lively voices engaged in conversation outside the window, and darbaba carts rolled past. A newspaper boy with a bell around his neck walked down the street. Newspapers, an everyday thing in the real world, were a recent invention here. The first newspaper was started by someone who heard news about Halnera and wanted to know more about the phenomenon. This started a boom, and in the space of a few weeks, several newspapers were already in regular circulation. The articles weren't all about Halnera anymore. Some talked about travel conditions along the high roads. There were even advertisements for lodgings and taverns.

Maybe that's how newspapers started in the real world too, Wataru thought. He wondered if, eventually, they might start featuring serialized stories, or cartoon strips. If the assassination succeeded, he was sure that would find its way into an article too. That was headline news, for sure.

Wataru wondered how things in the real world were these days. What kind of news was in the papers? Though his body sat in the warm dining hall, his mind wandered. *Mom. Uncle Lou. I hope you're doing okay. I'm so far away, and I'm going to go even farther. I promised I would come home, but maybe I won't be able to keep that promise...*

"Wataru? There you are! Good morning!" Meena's bright voice snapped Wataru back to reality. "What, just eating now? Sleepy head!"

Meena leaped to the seat next to Wataru and turned her bright eyes toward him. How many times had he been cheered just by the sight of those eyes? She stuck her face forward until their noses nearly touched. Wataru quickly looked down at the table, cramming the remnants of a crust of bread into his mouth.

"You shouldn't eat so fast—you'll choke!" Meena laughed out loud.

"Yeah, I know. What's with you, Meena? You're in a good mood."

"You could tell?" Meena stood up and did a little dance on her stool. "I've got good news. Bubuho and the whole troupe are coming to Gasara!"

Which meant that Meena's old circus, the Aeroga Elenora Spectacle Machine, was coming to town.

"A darbaba driver who came this morning had a letter for me from Bubuho. They'll be here by day's end!"

A wave of relief washed over Wataru. If her old circus friends were here in town, it would be much easier to leave Meena behind. Even if she insisted on coming with him, he was sure that Bubuho would be able to talk her out of it. It would make things that much simpler.

"But that's not the *best* news," Meena said, sitting down next Wataru and lowering her voice. "Remember when you met Bubuho the first time, he was talking to Granny?"

The old ankha woman they called Granny had asked Wataru what he would do if he couldn't meet the Goddess. He had replied that he hadn't thought about it. Then I have nothing more to ask you, she had said.

"I remember her."

"Well, you should know that Granny is a diviner. She has the sight. She can see the future—nothing too far off, mind you, but she can see it. In fact, when she first met you, she was already able to see the Blood Star shining in the north, and she knew that Halnera was coming!"

That would explain her question. Maybe she knew that the arrival of Halnera meant Wataru might be chosen as the sacrifice.

"So...so what?"

Wataru couldn't bring himself to share Meena's joy. But she grabbed both his hands in hers tightly and pulled him toward her. "Listen, I wrote her a letter after what happened in Sono. I asked her to read your future. And I asked her to tell me if there was any way to change that future. Well, the letter got to her, and she looked. She used a great crystal she uses for her divinations, and she says she saw you, walking up the steps to the Tower of Destiny!"

Wataru drew back and stared at Meena's face. "What do you mean?"

"It means that's your future!" Meena was exuberant. "You'll make it to the tower! You won't have to be the sacrifice! You'll get to meet the Goddess and complete your journey!"

Bubuho had written the letter in great haste, telling Meena the good news. They had planned this trip to Gasara so that Granny could tell him in person.

"Isn't that great? I'm so happy! I always thought it would be a horrible shame for Mitsuru to win. It should be you, Wataru. It has to be! Granny has never been wrong before!"

Kee Keema, too, had insisted that it wasn't over yet. *You need only two more gemstones and you're home free!* Wataru would simply smile and shake his head in defeat. After a while, the waterkin stopped talking about it.

But Meena was different. She was persistent. She was all smiles and hope when she spoke to Wataru. Even when Wataru tried to steer the conversation in another direction, Meena kept things on track.

"Well, you sure look out of it," Meena said, waving her hand in front of Wataru's face. "Did you understand what I just said? I mean, isn't it great news? She said she saw many other things in the crystal too. I'll bet they're clues for you to find the next two gemstones! Let's talk to Granny and get the details, and leave as soon as we can. I'm sure we'll find them. You're going to the Tower of Destiny after all!"

In her enthusiasm, Meena jumped back up on her stool and cheered, thrusting her little fists into the air.

The innkeeper came rushing out of the kitchen. "Whatever is the matter?"

"Oh, it's nothing. Sorry."

Wataru hurriedly pulled Meena down from her stool, holding her firmly so she wouldn't be able to get up and dance again. "Meena... thank you, Meena." Wataru wasn't sure where to begin. He decided to just let the words fall out from his mouth as they would. "Thank you for worrying so much about me. I'm really grateful."

"What are you talking about? We're friends! And, I decided, like I said in Lourdes, I'll be with you no matter where you go."

Meena tensed with such excitement Wataru was afraid she was going to lift him up and dance around in circles.

"You have to calm down. There's something I need to tell you. Okay?"

Meena's dancing eyes stopped, though they still glimmered with joyous expectation. She tilted her head and placed her hand on Wataru's shoulder. "What's wrong? Aren't you happy?"

"I am happy," Wataru said, choosing his words carefully. "I still have a chance, I see that."

"That's right!"

"But, Meena," Wataru took a deep breath and continued, "I can't go searching for the remaining gemstones now. There's something else I have to do."

Meena's eyes froze. "Something else? What are you talking about?"

"I'm going north. To the Empire."

Wataru looked around the eating hall. There was nobody else around. The innkeeper was tucked away inside her kitchen.

"I've been given a mission, which, as a Highlander, I can't refuse. I'm going north with the help of Jozo. Kutz is going too—she'll be leading a team. If we achieve our objective we can come back. But it's going to be very difficult, so I can't say what will happen...still, I have to do it. I've decided."

Wataru took three deep breaths. The two stared at each other in silence, their stares turning to glares in the uncomfortable silence. The rich smell of food from the kitchen seemed strangely out of place.

"You're going north?" Meena asked quietly.

"Yes."

"As a Highlander?"

"That's right. We're going to assassinate Gama Agrilius VII, that's why…"

Meena laughed in his face. "That's silly! Why would anyone want to do that? Is the South going to bring war to the North? That's impossible! They already have the designs for the powered boats. We'll lose."

"This will buy us time," Wataru explained. "If the emperor is assassinated, there will be some degree of confusion and chaos in the Empire. The Empire is a dictatorship—if they lose their dictator, it will be like a ship without a rudder. Gama Agrilius VII is only forty years old, so his successor is bound to be quite young. Even if he takes the throne, he won't be able to exert his power to the fullest. If the Empire falls into chaos it will be a while before they can organize an attack across the sea. During that time, the South can bolster their defenses and get ready to repel the invasion. There may even be a diplomatic solution—some kind of trade we can make. There may even be a chance for peace. Either way, what we need is more time."

That was the basis of the plan as Kutz had explained it, and Wataru agreed fully. "I just heard about the plan last night. Kutz said they needed my help. I think so too. I'm the only one who can call Jozo. And if he's involved, then I feel compelled to tag along."

All expression drained from Meena's face. She looked like a newly minted doll. It was all so sudden. She wasn't sure how to respond.

Her face still a blank, Meena sighed. "Then I'll go too." With those words, the life returned to her face and her eyes blazed red hot. "I'm going north with you, Wataru. I'll help."

She smiled, and her grip on Wataru's hand tightened. "I said I'd follow you anywhere and I meant it—even to the Northern Empire. Why, I'm sure this was all in Granny's vision. You'll go after Mitsuru, collect the remaining gemstones before he does, and make it to the tower. It has to be…"

As words came streaming out of Meena's mouth, Wataru was shaking his head. But Meena didn't seem to notice. When she finally ran out of things to say, she looked up to see Wataru still shaking his head. "Huh?"

"No, you're not," he said firmly, surprising even himself. There wasn't a trace of hesitation in his voice. He sounded almost like an adult. "You can't come with me. You have to stay here, in the south."

After one single heartbeat, Meena threw herself at Wataru. "Why? What do you mean? Why can't I go with you? Why are you being so stubborn?"

"I'm not being stubborn."

"You are!" Meena gave Wataru a shove. He would have fallen off his stool entirely if she hadn't caught him.

"I get it! Kutz ordered this, didn't she? She told you to leave me here. Fine, I'll just go to the source. I'll make her let me go!"

"No, Meena. It was my decision."

Meena's hand on Wataru's collar was trembling. "I…"

"I'm sorry. I can't put you and Kee Keema in any more danger than I already have. That's why I can't take you with me."

"Danger…but I…I'm not afraid!"

"It's me who's afraid," Wataru said. That was the honest truth. "If I brought you and Kee Keema with me, you might die. That's what I'm afraid of. It scares me more than anything else. If it was me, I could come to terms with it. But you're my friends. I don't want you to die on my account."

"Who says we're going to die anyway?" Meena muttered.

"You're right, but I have to be prepared for the worst."

Wataru did his best to steady his breathing. He was more afraid than he had ever been in his life, but he needed to stay calm.

"If everything goes well and the emperor dies, then maybe I will be able to beat Mitsuru to the tower."

"Yes, you will."

"But if I did that, and you or Kee Keema died along the way, I would regret it for the rest of my life. Even if I meet the Goddess and she changes my fate, I don't think I would be happy. Not ever."

Even though he knew it was a mean trick to play, he had no other means to convince her. "Please stay here. You're my friend, and I care so much about you. Be safe, for me. Please."

Meena buried her face in her hands and began to cry. "I don't know when I'll be leaving," said Wataru. "We'll take off as soon as High Chief Gil arrives in Gasara. That's why I wanted to say my farewells now. Thank you. Thank you for everything. I'm so grateful, I can't put it into words. Really."

"And Kee Keema?" Meena whispered between gentle sobs.

"I'm going to tell him now." Wataru quietly stood up from his stool. "Thank you, Meena. I want you to be safe here, and happy. You should rejoin the Spectacle Machine and bring smiles to the faces throughout the south—no, throughout all of Vision. Okay? Promise?"

Meena made no reply.

chapter 44
Escape from Gasara

Wataru couldn't summon up the strength to meet with Kee Keema right after talking to Meena. *I'll do it later,* he thought. Thankfully, there were other things to keep him busy.

In the area around Gasara, there were several smaller towns that helped facilitate local trade. Refugees from these places were arriving daily at the town's gates. Wataru, along with his fellow Highlanders, had his hands full with all the incoming traffic.

"If all this confusion continues much longer, then I'd gladly give myself up as the Halnera sacrifice just to get back a little peace and quiet," one of the refugees said with a sideways glance at his exhausted wife. He led a small child by the hand. The simple lodgings that had been set up for refugees had only the barest necessities, yet still, many were glad to be able to bathe and eat a proper meal after four days on the road.

"You don't have much longer to wait. Halnera will soon be over," Wataru told them.

The man nodded slowly. "I hope so..." he said with a sigh. "You get to wondering if they really need a sacrifice. I'd think the Goddess in all her power would be able to make a Great Barrier of Light by herself. I started thinking that maybe the Goddess's intent with this whole Halnera thing lies elsewhere."

"Elsewhere?"

"Yep. Look how we struggle and tremble just hearing that one of us is to be chosen as a sacrifice. We're so weak. And in the end, all we care about is our own hides. That's why there's all this chaos. And of course, some people have tried to make a profit off it. Some have even used the confusion as a cover to do away with people they don't like. It's all greed, and it runs deep. Ugly stuff. That's why the Goddess has to shake us up a little bit every now and then. She wants to remind us of our weakness, and our ugliness. She wants to make sure that we don't fall any more in love with ourselves than we already are. That's why she started this whole Halnera thing—at least that's what I think."

The thought hadn't occurred to Wataru.

"Wouldn't that make the Goddess a little harsh toward her own people?"

"Harsh? You bet. But, I figure she has to be strict. If she was nice all the time, nothing would ever get fixed. Words are empty. You can pass the greatest teachings of the sages down, but if all they see is prosperity day in and day out, they'll forget what the words mean. People are forgetful creatures, you see. That's why at least once every thousand years the Goddess has to come down and give us a jolt—something to remind us of what the teachings really mean."

They spent so much time talking that it was late into the afternoon by the time Wataru could take a break from the refugee camps. The man's heavy questions weighted down his already laden heart, and his feet trudged across the ground as he walked back toward the branch office.

Then he noticed something odd. People were gathered out in front of their houses and talking in hushed voices. *What's going on?*

Just then Wataru turned a corner and ran into the doctor from the hospital. His medicine bag was tucked under one arm, and he was speaking with some of the townspeople. Wataru called out to him, but the man was so engrossed in his conversation he didn't even notice.

"Hello there! Has something happened?"

"Oh, it's you!" the doctor said, blinking eyes half-buried under thick brows. "You mean you don't know?"

"I see people standing around…"

Everyone, including the doctor, looked at him in surprise. "You're a Highlander, aren't you? How can you say you don't know! Gasara has been surrounded by a company of the Knights of Stengel for the past hour!"

Wataru gaped. "Surrounded—what's this all about? Didn't the guards do anything?"

"What was there to do? They saw a company of the Knights of Stengel approaching from across the grasslands, and they thought maybe they were coming for supplies or just to visit. The next thing you know, they had us all surrounded."

"The town gate is closed," the doctor said. "No one is getting out or coming in."

"I've been with the refugees this whole time."

"Aye," said one of the townspeople, "and the Knights of Stengel move fast—faster than the wind. That group is quiet as a snake ready to strike."

"I need to get back to the branch!" Wataru made to run off, when the doctor grabbed his collar from behind. "Wait. You might want to see how things develop first."

"What do you mean?"

"Captain Ronmel came in with some of his men. They went into the branch office. Whatever business they have is in there."

Wataru's eyes opened wide. "You mean they're chasing a criminal or something?"

The doctor shook his head. "Remember when the four high branch chiefs sent out orders to the Highlanders without the approval of the Senate? Word is that Captain Ronmel's business here has something to do with that."

With a start, Wataru remembered the dangerous tension that had passed between Captain Ronmel's troops and the Highlanders in front of the Lourdes observatory. And Captain Ronmel's words: if the branch chiefs and the Highlanders get on the bad side of the Senate, then one day the Knights of Stengel and the Highlanders might stand on opposite ends of the sword.

So what Captain Ronmel feared had come to pass.

"Apparently, the captain has come for none other than Kutz herself," the doctor said. "Someone in the Senate wants her detained and sent to the capital. Not sure what the matter could be…"

Wataru knew. The assassination plot. Word must have leaked from somewhere, and someone in the Senate caught wind of it. There would be those in the Senate who didn't favor the idea of the emperor in the north suffering a sudden demise.

Kutz said it had been her plan. That made her the ringleader. If she's arrested, she'll be tried for sure. Where was High Chief Gil in all this? And the three who were supposed to go north with her?

"I don't care what they say she's done. They can't come in here and take the chief away," one of the townspeople said, snorting loudly. "Those Knights of Stengel are just the Senate's lapdogs. Who can trust them? And they're all ankha too. You can bet they don't think too highly of us beastkin."

Several others standing around agreed. One waved his fist. "If anyone is going to put those Knights in their place, it's got to be us!"

The doctor's ears flattened against his head. "I'm sure the government and the Knights know how you all feel. That's why they have us surrounded. It we strike back unthinkingly, I fear something terrible may happen."

"Then you'd just have us stand here and watch them take Kutz off without a fight?"

"That's not what I'm saying."

"Well then?!"

Wataru slipped away before the argument grew even more heated.

He ran until he reached the front gate. It was closed and barred, as the doctor had said. Knights were stationed outside, and a notice of some kind had been posted in plain sight. *Probably a warrant for Kutz's arrest.* A local beastkin was loudly arguing with one of the Knights. Across the street, a small child was crying as he clung to his mother's skirt hem.

A darbaba cart was parked off the road by the gate—perhaps stalled by the arrival of the Knights. The waterkin driver was upset with the situation and was locked in a debate with another of the guards. Wataru hid behind the large wheels of the cart and listened to their exchange.

"Like I said, I have nothing against the Knights at all. But you have to understand I've got a shipment of the best shulshu here. You ever eaten one? Freshly killed, they make one of most delectable meals to be had, but freshness is everything. Every minute I stand here waiting the value of my cargo drops."

"We'll open the gates as soon as we're done, you have my word. We don't mean to hinder business in Gasara any longer than we have to. Please, be patient."

"That's all fine and well, but my shulshu are rotting here."

"If you have a problem with it, talk to your branch. We're following government orders here, that's all. If your branch chief goes along with us, we'll be out of here in no time."

So they were after Kutz. Where is she? I'll have to sneak into the branch and take a look for myself. Wataru's hand went to the hilt of his sword.

A double circle of onlookers stood in front of the branch. The outer ring seemed to be mostly residents. The inner ring consisted of five Knights of Stengel, standing in a formation in front of the door.

Trone must be inside. Wataru thought a moment, then went around to the back of the building. All the windows were firmly shut. The window to Wataru's room on the second floor, which he had left open that morning, was closed too. Even the shutters had been locked.

Wataru returned to the front of the branch. He mingled with the crowd, waiting for an opportunity to enter the building. Everyone was talking and shouting and demanding answers. It was noisy.

All at once, the Knights moved to the side and the door to the branch opened. A voice was heard from inside. One of the guards nodded in acknowledgment.

Wataru made sure no one was looking and drew his sword. Quickly he made the sign to create the invisible barrier. Once obscured, he slipped through the crowd and past the Knights.

"Hrm?" A Knight grunted. "What was that?" He looked down at his feet, but Wataru had already made his way inside.

Trone was sitting calmly at Kutz's desk in the center of the room. There were two Knights by his side. Directly in front of the desk stood Captain Ronmel.

It appeared the other Highlanders had managed to duck out of sight in the nick of time. Wataru could see no one else. *Either that, or they've already been taken away.*

"I'll ask you one more time," Captain Ronmel was saying to Trone. Wataru had heard the Captain's voice many times before, but never had it sounded so ominous, so full of threat.

Trone, on the other hand, seemed unconcerned. He leaned back in his chair, fixing his glasses on his nose, looking perfectly relaxed.

"Where is Branch Chief Kutz? We know she hasn't left the town."

"I'm sure she's around somewhere. Wish I knew. I'm not her bodyguard, you know."

"Even if you don't tell us, you won't be doing her any good. We'll find her sooner or later and take her in."

"Then I suggest you get busy! Sorry I can't tell you what I don't know."

"If we start searching the town, it will upset the residents more than they already are. I would think you'd want to avoid that from happening. Cooperate." Captain Ronmel's eyes burned with a cold blue intensity. Like Trone, he seemed at ease—like he was ready to wait for days to get the answer he wanted. Still, Wataru thought he detected a hint of weariness in his demeanor. There were shadows under his eyes.

"We know you are the sub-chief at the branch here, responsible for keeping order when Kutz is away. I wouldn't think Kutz would wish to create any needless commotion here in Gasara."

"Oh, I think I know exactly what the chief would wish—and I certainly don't need you to tell me." Trone's words were sharp and to the point. Though he was still leaning back in his chair, his eyes flashed. "I'm still not sure I understand why exactly the chief has to be brought in to the Senate. It sounds like a case of unwarranted arrest to me."

The young Knight standing to Trone's right suddenly beat his fist on the desk. Documents scattered and a pen clattered noisily to the floor. "We have a warrant right here!" The Knight's eyes burned through the gap between his helmet and breastplate. Captain Ronmel lifted his hand to stay the Knight, his eyes never leaving Trone's face.

"I've lived a few years myself, and I've never seen an arrest warrant from the USN before…" Trone began picking his nose. A long nail extended from one round furry finger and began deftly probing one of his nostrils. "Nor had I ever heard of anything like this treason law it talks about. How can I be sure this warrant is the real deal? Could have been faked."

Captain Ronmel's eyes took on a dangerous gleam. "Very interesting. So you claim our warrant is a forgery?"

"I'm just saying it wouldn't surprise me, coming from the likes of you," Trone said, revealing the fangs on one side of his mouth as he chuckled. "I'm sure your keepers in the Senate feed you well. A well-trained dog will do anything his master says. Why, you'd walk through a sea of nightsoil to get a bone if your master said fetch."

Trone would've continued if the young Knight standing by the desk didn't suddenly lash out at him with his fist. *At least he didn't draw his sword,* Wataru thought. The other Knight standing guard quickly moved to stop him, and another ran in from outside. Immediately a great brawl started, rowdy enough to shake the building. Wataru slid across the floor past Trone's feet and hid under the desk.

Wataru was breathing hard with the effort required to keep the barrier up. He let it fade. Clasping his mouth with both hands, trying not to make a sound, he breathed with both shoulders heaving.

When the shouting and yelling and punching had died down, Wataru saw Trone's feet lifting off the floor. There was a heavy slam above his head. They must have pushed him onto the desk.

"You're welcome to your ridiculous delusions…" he heard Captain Ronmel talking, his voice calm, as if nothing had happened. "But we have sworn our allegiance to the Senate, and we act with their full authority."

"Oh? I wonder about that," came Trone's reply, undaunted, even if his face was pressed to the desk.

"Not only did the four high branch chiefs not heed the Senate's admonition and send their Highlanders out without authority, but we know they planned terrorist activities against the Northern Empire. High Chief Gil is already in our custody. We are currently interrogating the Highlanders who were with him about this plot to assassinate Gama Agrilius VII. You've been caught red-handed, Trone."

Captain Ronmel's voice cracked with emotion for the first time. Wataru hunched down beneath the desk. *So High Chief Gil had been arrested.*

It was over. At least Kutz was still free. *Hopefully we can keep her that way.*

"You've known Kutz a long time," Captain Ronmel said. "So you must know her past. You know that I was also once a Highlander, one of her trusted partners. An incident drew us apart, but I always had the highest respect for her work, and I do not wish to see her unfairly treated. More than anything, if she plans these acts against our country's best interest, I will have her stopped."

Trone was silent. Wataru could hear his ragged breathing.

"Tell me, where is she? I want to help her. If she does not surrender herself now, she will be marked as a traitor. She'll be hounded wherever she goes in Vision. Do you really want to put her in that position?"

Miyuki Miyabe

Kutz and Captain Ronmel. Lovers forever, but always a step apart. Wataru felt a stab of pain in his chest, though his breathing had finally become more regular.

Trone sighed softly. "I'm pretty sure Kutz doesn't want your help, not anymore."

Wataru heard the clatter of Captain Ronmel's armor.

"I don't know how it was in the past, but you and Kutz see different things from different places now. Your hopes, your ideals—everything you hold important, you hold alone. Kutz knows this. It looks like you don't."

Trone muttered something about men being like that, before continuing, "Looks like the cowards down at the Senate are clucking and fretting about these powered boat designs reaching the North. They want to form some sort of peace treaty before the North can attack, is that it? You know the Senate is filled with sympathizers, even I can see what it is they'd do. So, what exactly are they planning to offer the North in exchange for peace? You can't say you don't know what the emperor is doing up there. It's bloodshed—worse, genocide. Beastkin are made to work like slaves, ripped away from their homes in the light of day. And you're happy with all this?"

"We are trying..." Captain Ronmel began, but Trone cut him off. "Then again, I suppose you wouldn't care so much. No matter what the beastkin in the south have to face, it won't affect the Knights of Stengel, will it? You're not here to protect the south. You're here to protect yourselves, the ankha."

"You are wrong!"

"Am I? Look at Lyris! Your buddy Captain Zaidek is rolling out his own brand of empire in that town under the auspices of keeping the peace—all in your precious government's name."

There was a brief pause, and Captain Ronmel said, surprisingly calm, "I am not Zaidek."

"Oh? A lapdog is a lapdog from where I sit."

"No. I'm no sympathizer with the causes of the Northern Empire. Nor would I care to raise my sword in defense of their ideals. If our Senate truly intends to allow the ideologies of the North to creep into our lands in exchange for peace, I would not accept it. I would resist it with every fiber of my being. Sometimes, even dogs turn against their masters. We do have a will of our own, you see."

Trone was silent. It appeared that Captain Ronmel was waiting for his answer. The tension in the air was palpable, even under the desk where Wataru was hiding.

When Trone spoke next his voice was hoarse. "Even if we got our peace from the North and had to give nothing in exchange, I wouldn't fancy being their allies. They have enslaved my people and tossed their corpses away like garbage. If peace means friendship with their sort, I choose war. I choose to fight, and fight until there is no one left. That's something more important to me than my own life. Something more important to all us Highlanders. I wonder if you Knights have it?"

"So you mean to say that, for this thing which you hold dearer than life, you planned to assassinate the emperor? Was that your true objective? To me, it looks like you are engaged in nothing more than base revenge."

Trone growled but did not reply.

"Arrest this man," Captain Ronmel ordered his men. "Throw him in the cell here. We'll let him cool off a little bit."

"What about Kutz?" one of the men asked.

"We'll split into three and search the town. If any of the residents get in our way, arrest them for hampering a public official. Our reinforcements should be arriving soon. We'll use this branch office as our temporary headquarters. We must find Kutz by nightfall and take her to the capital."

His man shouted a reply and dragged Trone out of the office. Now Wataru knew everything there was to know, except for where Kutz was hiding. Still, even though he was no longer keeping up the barrier around him, everything he had heard left him depleted. Northern sympathizers in the government...the strife between the dominant ankha and the minority beastkin. The Knights of Stengel, defenders of the United Southern Nations, and most of them ankha, at odds with the homegrown Highlanders organization.

Wataru began to have doubts, until his mind was racing, and he shivered. *I can't let them arrest Kutz. We have to go north together.* Wataru didn't know who was right anymore, Kutz or Captain Ronmel. It seemed like deciding between the two of them had such great consequences it was too much to bear. That was why he needed to see the truth for himself. He had to go north.

Knights were busily entering and leaving the office. Wataru drew the barrier of invisibility around himself once again, crept out from beneath the desk, and walking sideways along the wall, headed for the main entrance.

Captain Ronmel stood directly to the side of the desk. He had spread out a map of the town and was giving directions to a man. His eyes were on the map alone. Wataru could see deep lines etched in the side of his face.

Only a few more steps to the door. *No one can see me.* Wataru nearly stepped into a Knight who came running in through the door. *He missed me. I'm okay.*

"Captain! Word from the reinforcements!"

The Knight handed a communication to the captain. Captain Ronmel took it and looked up.

His blue eyes fixed on Wataru. Their eyes met. *How? How can he see me?*

The next instant, the captain had moved across the room in a few steps and held the tip of his sword pointed against Wataru's throat. The way he moved was like magic. Only a soft breeze blew against Wataru's face—he didn't even hear the captain's armor clink.

"I thought I sensed something strange before. Now I see what it was." He wasn't smiling.

Wataru looked down at his own body. In his surprise, the barrier had come undone.

"C-Captain…"

"When did you learn enveiling magic? Is this another of the Traveler's powers?"

"This is called enveiling magic? I had no idea." Wataru tried a timid smile. "Could you see me? Or could you somehow sense me, even though you couldn't see me? That's amazing."

The captain did not smile. The tip of the sword was still held at Wataru's throat. "You work for Kutz. Where is she?"

"I don't know. I didn't even know all this was going on."

"Then you're an idiot."

"I know."

Captain Ronmel called over his shoulder to one of his men. "This boy is a Highlander. He needs to be interrogated. Throw him in with the other one."

"Yes, sir," one of the Knights said, his steel boots clanging on the floor as he approached. *Now I'm under arrest. So much for my plans.*

Then, Wataru thought he heard a voice calling from somewhere—*it's coming from inside my head.*

—Wataru.

—You have three gemstones. You have a new power.

—Say the words. Azlo, lom, lom. Spirit of the wind, blow through time, carry me faster than light itself.

"Than light itself..." Wataru echoed.

"What?" The Knight stopped.

"Carry me faster than light itself!"

Captain Ronmel, a short distance away, turned to look.

—Get ready!

"Fly!" At the moment he said the word, Wataru felt his body disappear. Suddenly, the world around him filled with light.

He was flying. Dancing up into the air. He left the surprised shouts of the Knights far below and rose up through the light. He gripped the sword hilt tightly in his hands. Climbing, climbing, up to the sky.

Then, the next instant, he shot across the blue sky as though fired from a cannon.

"Waaaah!"

His body floated, then suddenly stopped. He could see his surroundings once more. He was flying, in the air above Gasara. No, he was floating. *Wait, I'm falling...*

"Aaaaah!"

He hadn't been that high, after all. He hit something hard, landing on his behind. Sparks shot through his skull. "Where am I?"

He was on top of the roof of a store on the eastern edge of town that he'd visited many times. He was lying on the red tiled roof. One of the tiles was cracked in two where he had landed.

The people walking on the street below gaped and looked at Wataru. Some were even pointing. The owner of the store came barreling out into the street. "What was that?"

So the third power of the sword was something like teleportation. It felt a bit like he imagined what going warp speed felt like. But he hadn't gone that far, and it seemed pretty dangerous to boot.

—Sorry, Wataru.

It was the voice from the gemstone.

—*You're not strong enough to control it yet, it seems.*

"No, this is fine, this is great, I got out of there!"

Wataru stood on the roof. Several Knights of Stengel had noticed Wataru and were approaching him. *What do I do now?*

"Oy, Wataru! Oy! Oy!" It was Kee Keema. He was running toward Wataru from behind the Knights. "What are you doing up there? Have you heard what's happened?"

"I know!" Wataru said, cupping his hands to his mouth to shout over the crowd. "Look out, Kee Keema! They'll catch you!"

"Huh? What are these guys doing here?" Kee Keema ran on, bowling through a cluster of Knights, knocking two of them off to the side into the wall of a nearby building.

"H-hey! That's hindering a public official!"

"What do you mean? I'm a Highlander!"

"Then you're even more guilty! You're under arrest!"

"Run!" Wataru drew the wyrmflute from his pocket. Looking up into the sky he blew it as hard as he could. *Jozo! Jozo, come quick!*

A red speck winked into existence in the sky far above. Wataru faced it, waving his hands, jumping up and down on the roof, shouting at the top of his lungs. "Kutz! Kutz! Come out! We're getting out of here! We'll ride out on my dragon! Where are you?"

Kee Keema clambered up to the top of the roof. Several Knights came running from the nearby crossroads. At the head of a large group rounding the corner was Captain Ronmel. "Apprehend that boy!"

Suddenly Wataru was cast in shadow. Jozo was directly overhead. "You called, Wataru?"

"I did! Get me out of here!"

The gale from Jozo's wings was almost enough to knock him off the roof entirely. Kee Keema held Wataru up, and both of them climbed onto the dragon's back.

The great gust of wind shot down the streets, swirling around the Knights. The townspeople were cradling their heads and screaming. It was chaos.

"Kutz!" Wataru shouted out into the city streets. "Jozo, fly low over the city! We have to find Kutz!"

"Right. What's with all the people, anyway? Is it some kind of festival?"

"Yeah, you might say that!"

Jozo spread his wings and began to glide over the rooftops of Gasara. They could still hear the screams from the townspeople, but now some of them sounded more like shouts of excitement.

"Look, a dragon!" A small boy leaned out of the window of one house, waving his hand. "Mom! Look, look! It's a dragon, a real dragon, just like in the books!"

Jozo flapped his wings in greeting and sent another blast of wind, knocking over several Knights in pursuit. A stack of barrels sitting by the side of the road collapsed, taking the rest of the Knights with them.

"Kutz, where are you?!"

They flew past a darbaba, its eyes wide with surprise. The driver fell off his cart.

"Wataru!"

It was Kutz, leaning out of the second-story window of a house across the street. Wataru looked over and she nodded, and began climbing up to the roof.

"It's Kutz! There she is!"

The Knights were getting closer. The nearest group was already inside the house—sticking their heads out of the windows, following after Kutz.

"Persistent, aren't you!" Kutz had one hand on the roof, and hanging from the edge, she drew her whip with her other hand. There was a black glimmer and a crack. One of the Knights screamed and fell from the window down to the ground below.

"Jozo, let's pick her up!"

With one flap of his wings, the dragon was over the house. Kutz hoisted herself onto the roof and ran toward them. Several Knights sprang to the roof behind her, fighting against the gale force winds coming from Jozo. Kutz lashed out with her whip, but the air currents were so strong, she could barely aim it.

"Jozo, breathe on them!"

"You sure?!"

"I'm sure! I give you special permission!"

Jozo took a deep breath, then spat a ball of flame across the roof. The

Knights scattered like leaves. Kutz took her chance and leapt astride Jozo's back. "You singed my hair!" She was laughing.

"Let's go!"

Jozo lifted straight into the air and faced upward. Wataru clung to his neck as tightly as he could.

"Wataru, wait! Take me too!"

It was Meena. Wataru looked to see the lithe kitkin unbelievably springing from rooftop to rooftop, coming toward them.

"How dare you try to leave me behind!" She shouted, making a large jump from two roofs away. She flipped in midair, landing right on the edge of their roof. Suddenly, a Knight's hand reached up from the window below, grabbing her ankle.

"Eek! Didn't anyone ever teach you it's rude to grab a lady's leg?" Meena pulled something from her pocket, throwing it down at the top of the roof.

There was a loud series of cracks and the smell of gunpowder. Fireworks went off all around her. *Since when did she have those?* The Knight caught one of the blasts in the face. He immediately let go of her foot and covered his face with his hands.

"Sorry to keep you waiting!" Meena shouted, jumping up to sit by Wataru's side. "Fly, Jozo! Fly as high as you can go!"

Jozo whirled up into the air. The town of Gasara, with its people screaming with exhilaration, and Knights standing dumbfounded, dropped away beneath them. Even as they took higher to the sky, Wataru still thought he could feel Captain Ronmel's eyes on him.

"Didn't I say I'd go anywhere with you, Wataru?" Meena grinned, wiping ash from the fireworks off her nose. "Still, you shouldn't have tried to leave without me."

"I..."

"You may say you're worried about us, but we're worried about you too. What would we do if you went off to some unknown place to die all by yourself? How would we feel? We can't just stand around while you go off and brave dangers. That's why we're going with you, no matter what lies ahead."

Wataru looked silently at Meena, then up into Kee Keema's broad face. The waterkin nodded. "I don't know what you two've been talking about, but I agree with what the little missus says."

"Everything all patched up?" Kutz asked. "Then let's go. You came at just the right time—I couldn't stand hiding in that cellar a second longer. I was just about to come storming out of there. Did you see the look on Boris's face? Priceless!"

Wataru smiled. *Meena and Kutz—two incredible women.* He hunched over, clinging to Jozo's wings as the cool wind whipped over them and they rose higher into the skies over Gasara.

chapter 45
The Imperial Capital of Solebria

Mitsuru looked up at the sky.

The Crystal Palace, seat of the Northern Empire's power, was in the very center of the Imperial Capital of Solebria. Over a span of two hundred years, the city had grown out along boulevards radiating like the spokes of a wheel from the palace, swelling to become home to more than one million people.

The towering central keep of the Crystal Palace, made of a milky-white stone resembling marble, had guest rooms near the residence of the emperor himself. Mitsuru now stood on the terrace near the top floor, looking down on the city. It was, in a way, like looking at the very history of the Northern Empire. The construction of the city of Solebria reflected with uncanny accuracy the class structure that ordered the daily lives of people in the north. In the center, surrounding the palace, stood the looming offices of the government. Beyond them lay the lavish arcade teeming with shoppers that formed the merchant district. Even further out were the homes of the citydwellers, all standing in their approved plots, gaily decorated with the requisite markers of wealth and individual taste.

But the farther one strayed from the center of town, the shabbier things became. There was a deep moat between the city center and the outer ring of town, forming a rift, a natural line of separation that was clear to see from Mitsuru's vantage point.

The capital city of Solebria was, in essence, a castle town. The city walls, much expanded and strengthened over the years, were always a remarkable sight to the merchants who visited from the southern continent. But beyond these walls and the single gate that led to the bustling Merchants Corridor, visitors never saw anything else of the city. That even here, within the city, there existed not one but two Solebrias, was hidden from their eyes. One of these Solebrias belonged to the rich, the other to the poor. The oppressors and the oppressed. Those who were served and those who served.

Farther still from the Crystal Palace, to the northeast, lay the prison where outlaws and criminals were held. This was an area abhorred by the geomancers of the north, their divinations honed by years of coping with the harsh climate of the northern continent.

Behind the prison edifice stood another gate that led outside the city walls. Many people considered this the gate of no return. The road leading to the northeast from this gate was referred to as the Captives Road, and the location of the forced labor camp at its end wasn't marked on any official maps of the Empire. No one knew exactly how large it was, or how many souls it held.

Those who survived the camp knew they were guilty of only one crime: they were beastkin. They knew this, but they could not speak it out loud. The only power they had was the power to forget. The blank spot on the map was one way. If one could forget something that had existed, it never did.

Still, truth has a way of finding the chinks in even the strongest armor. Even if people are silent, buildings speak. The land speaks—and there are some who write down what they hear. On this, his tenth day in the Imperial Capital, Mitsuru already had an excellent grasp of the Empire's history and the true conditions of life here. Much of his understanding came from the documents he found in the archives of the Crystal Palace itself.

Mitsuru had been welcomed as the emperor's personal guest, and enjoyed considerable freedom in the palace. He spent many hours in the archives, and the researchers welcomed his curiosity and helped him in any way they could. Mitsuru, for his part, knew that the history they fed him had been cosmetically altered to suit their needs. Consequently, he took what he could use and ignored the rest. Many of the older books were locked up with a variety of magical locks, but these were easy enough for a sorcerer of his caliber to undo.

In this way did Mitsuru glean intelligence that even spies from the south had not been able to gather after years of searching. Yet the information he truly sought lay maddeningly beyond his reach. All he had gained from his research was a vague idea of how he might acquire that knowledge...

Which is why, these days, he spent his time looking up into the sky, casting his thoughts against the clouds.

The sky in the north seemed somewhat paler than in the south—frozen, drained of color. Even though this season was supposedly the mildest of the year, the cold wind whipped around him and slipped down his collar and out the sleeves of his robe.

The harsh climate had given rise to a harsh society. It was a vicious cycle— the thought brought an almost childlike frown to Mitsuru's face. The ankha in the north had gained their dominance by stomping out the other races. Yet even with a unified populace, peace had not come to the Empire. Now different factions among the ankha vied for power. The dual structure of the capital city stood as a testament to that. The ankha of the north, their history stained with the blood of beastkin, had become addicted to the oppression of others—it was their way of life. And so it continued as a matter of fact, and nobody caught in the cycle was any the wiser.

I've never seen a greater gathering of self-deluded idiots.

Mitsuru had no sympathy for the people of the north. He couldn't even pity them. He wasn't angry, nor did he want to censure them. In this, he was just being impartial. It would make little difference to Mitsuru if the people in the north were the most enlightened in the land.

Everything in Vision is just that—an illusion, a mirage. A fleeting dream that would disappear the moment he returned to the real world.

The very moment he became a Traveler, Mitsuru abandoned the boy he had been in the real world. He had been freed.

It was even possible that Mitsuru was now not wholly human. A Traveler was all he was. And to a Traveler there is only the objective. Nothing extraneous such as feelings of empathy, affection, friendship, or loyalty remained to hinder his progress toward his goal.

The problem before him now was how to deal with this capital city of Solebria. He would have to make plans, concrete plans. Squinting against the chilling breeze, Mitsuru schemed. He would not wait much longer.

He had been lucky. Few obstacles had lain in his path until now. It took him only three days to cross the sea separating the northern and southern continents. After wresting the sea charts from the old captain of the sailship, he had little need for the man. Once he was out on the open sea, and had a feel for direction and distance, he did not need to depend on such unreliable physical means of transport as the sailship. Magic was far more efficient. The sailship merely served as a convenient place to keep his feet dry during the crossing.

When he arrived on the northern continent, he sank the ship along with the captain in the shallow waters near the coast.

On firm land once again, he hid himself in a convenient port town to rest up, then made straight for the Imperial Capital. Along the way, fortune smiled on him again. He encountered a tax collector's party returning to the capital from their rounds in the provinces. This saved him the effort of asking directions and gained him more valuable resources. The remains of the tax collector and his entourage were easily disposed of with a little wind magic that neatly covered his tracks. Some official might be waiting at the tax bureau in the capital for his delayed collector, but that was hardly Mitsuru's concern.

Once in the capital, he used enveiling magic to slip inside the Crystal Palace. He took stock of the layout and let himself into the imperial quarters. After that, it was simple. He waited for nightfall and made his way directly to the bedside of Gama Agrilius VII. Waking up the emperor, he calmly announced his business.

The emperor had been quite startled, of course, and—still in his night-clothes—prostrated himself in abject fear at Mitsuru's feet. It was a better reaction than even he could've hoped for.

In the south, Mitsuru had few occasions to announce his status as Traveler to anyone, nor did his easy progress require him to do so at any point. Now, standing before the emperor, Mitsuru realized exactly what it meant to be a Traveler in Vision.

"We are quite enamored of the real world," the emperor told him. "To us, it is a sacred land. A land of the gods. It is my most sincere wish to fashion my empire to be as much like the real world as I can make it."

This revelation brought a smile to Mitsuru's lips. Considering the wars and slaughter that had taken place in the real world, and comparing those to what he knew of the north, it seemed like the emperor had already been quite successful in his mission, whether he knew it or not. Still, something struck him as odd. Though he had learned it only in passing, Mitsuru was sure that the Northern Empire embraced the beliefs of the Old God rather than the

Goddess. Travelers, everyone knew, were the servants of the Goddess—yet the emperor seemed quite pleased to make his acquaintance.

He asked about this, and the emperor hesitantly replied.

"Of course, as a Traveler you are well informed. I'm impressed to hear you know of our country's religion. Indeed, our empire is, on the surface, a bastion of faith in the Old God. But this is merely a convenient means to an end. It became necessary to spread this religion to unite our people against the nations of the south where the Goddess is worshiped. That is all."

"So, do you mean to say that you, in fact, worship the Goddess as Creator?"

The emperor laughed at the question. "No, no! Of course, the Tower of Destiny does exist somewhere here in Vision, and a Goddess surely lives there who controls the fates of those in the real world. But she is no god of Vision. The Goddess who sits in the Tower of Destiny is a goddess only to those from the real world. She has nothing to do with any of us who live here in Vision."

The true creator of Vision is none other than the real world itself, the emperor explained. "Do you know how Vision was formed? Vision is a world created by the imaginative energies of people living in your world—the real world. It follows that the gods of Vision, if we must name them, are actually the people of the real world. Is this not so?"

It certainly did make logical sense. "Then why support a religion that teaches people to mistrust Travelers? That completely goes against what you just told me."

The emperor waved away Mitsuru's objection. "Master Mitsuru, we know that the Porta Nectere opens once every ten years. But we do not know what kind of person will visit us. If they are talented and wise, this is a good thing. But sometimes, they may be evil or weak. It falls to us to create a difficult environment to separate the good from the bad. If they are truly emissaries from the holy land, they will gain our admiration and worship."

Mitsuru was stunned. Then he remembered something Wayfinder Lau had mentioned earlier. Many Travelers, he said, abandoned their journey, unable to stand the hardships along the way. They lost their lives somewhere in Vision, or disappeared, never to return to the real world.

"Yet you, Master Mitsuru, have reached our palace. All by yourself, you have penetrated its most heavily defended chamber." The emperor bowed deeply. "You have proven your worth beyond all doubt. I'm honored to greet you as a guest in our world. You will be accorded all the respect an emissary of the gods deserves, and I welcome you as a trusted ally. But first, you must rest, for I fear your journey has been quite long."

And so, Mitsuru became a guest at the Crystal Palace.

Mitsuru later asked how many Travelers like him had visited the palace before.

Only one, the emperor told him. Once during the peak of the war to unify the north. "The records say that this Traveler, too, was a man of great power. It was he who first proposed the idea that land should be governed by a single race. He taught us that peace, prosperity, wealth, and power come only to those unified by blood. This became the basis for our empire, and brought us victory in the war of unification."

Mitsuru wasn't sure whether to be astonished or bemused. So the source of the oppression of non-ankha, and the genocide that had occurred in the north, had all been another Traveler's idea. Not to mention the fact that the emperor seemed to think this Traveler was a true emissary of the gods.

Mitsuru was surprised at his own shock. He had decided a long time ago that after what he had been through in the real world, nothing could surprise him.

Still, his bewilderment lasted only a moment. *I've got more important things to do,* he told himself. *Events in Vision have nothing to do with me. I need only to reach the Tower of Destiny and do what I came here to do. Then I'll go home. And I'll use whatever means I have at my disposal.*

The next day, when he awoke in the luxurious guest chambers, his life as an honored guest of the palace had already begun. He was brought before the beaming emperor, his family, and the retainers at the Crystal Palace, and informed that an elaborate welcoming ceremony was in the works. He was shown around the palace and told about its making, and he began to learn the history of the Empire.

But, of course, Mitsuru wanted none of this. Feeling unusually pressed for time, he sought another private meeting with the emperor.

This was when he revealed the reason he came to the north. He told the emperor that the last gemstone he sought was none other than the one adorning the Imperial Crown. If he only had this, the way to the Tower of Destiny would open to him. And he needed it as soon as possible.

He also explained how he had learned of a need for haste in his journey. By this, of course, he was referring to Halnera.

Mitsuru did not care to lose to Wataru in the race to reach the tower. Not that he was worried. But now that there was a danger of one of them being chosen as the sacrifice, it behooved him to achieve his goals and make it back to the real world as swiftly as possible.

But the emperor's only response to Mitsuru's urgent request was to laugh. "We know nothing of this Halnera in our empire. Nor do any of our scholars acknowledge such a thing. It wouldn't surprise me if this was all a legend cooked up by the United Southern Nations government. I'm afraid you've been hoodwinked, Master Mitsuru."

This was a possibility. But the reverse was also true. *Maybe you're just ignorant.* Mitsuru gritted his teeth in silence, and it took a great deal of effort to not let his frustrations show.

"Then, are you saying that I am not to worry about Halnera?"

"Why concern yourself with something that does not exist, my dear Master Mitsuru?"

"Yet, even if Halnera is merely some scheme dreamed up by the south, I would like to reach the Tower of Destiny and finish my journey as soon as possible."

To this the emperor frowned and lifted his heavily bejeweled person from the throne, "I understand how you feel, but I must ask you to wait," he said in a harsh voice.

"Whatever for?"

"This jeweled crown you claim to seek—this is most surely the prized treasure of my family for generations: the Crown of the Seal."

"The Crown of the Seal?"

"Indeed. It would be most difficult for me to give you this treasure now, you see. For, were I to move the Crown of the Seal from its current resting place, a great calamity would visit our empire. It would rock the very foundation of Vision. The gemstone you seek currently protects Vision from that calamity. Thus is the crown that bears it called the Crown of the Seal—it seals the portal behind which the doom of Vision waits."

For a good while, Mitsuru found himself in the unfamiliar position of being at a loss for words. At length, he spoke. "Then, what would you have me do? If the gemstone I need must protect Vision from some calamity, how might I ever hope to claim it?"

"No, there is hope. I merely said that it would be difficult to give you the gem now. In fact, there are other ways of preventing this calamity from visiting itself upon us. Or rather, there is one other way. Yet, sadly, the Northern Empire lacks the power to achieve this other method. We require certain materials from the south."

What's he babbling about now?

"Only a short while ago..." The emperor sat back down on his throne, a tone of sadness in his voice. "Our empire and the lands of the south were locked in a stalemate, and gathering the necessary materials was nigh well impossible. Oh, to be sure, we tried all means at our disposal, but I was not optimistic about our prospects. But the situation has changed somewhat of late. I do not know every detail, but certain sympathizers with our cause in the south have reported that there are traces showing that something has passed from the south to our lands that will radically change the balance of power in Vision. If I am able to identify and locate this something, we would be able to begin our invasion of the south immediately. With victory assured, it would be easy to acquire the materials we need.

"Perhaps Master Mitsuru knows something of this..."

Mitsuru looked up. *The old coot must know what it is he's looking for. You're playing dumb, trying to get information out of me, aren't you?*

Mitsuru produced the powered-boat designs. "Perhaps you mean this?"

This wasn't how the exchange was supposed to work.

He handed the blueprints over. The emperor's joy was evident. "Emissary from the holy land, servant of the gods, I thank you! With these designs our victory is already certain. I would share this victory with you. Please, until that day comes, treat my palace as your home."

And so Mitsuru had been forced to wait. And he would have to wait until the Empire had crushed the opposition in the south.

I've failed. Mitsuru dug his teeth into his bottom lip. *My plan was faulty. I did this to myself. But it won't happen again. Dear emperor, if you think I'm going to sit around here and wait until you can have your fun with the southern continent, you're sorely mistaken.* Standing on the terrace, Mitsuru clenched his hands into tight fists.

If he wasn't given the crown immediately, there wouldn't be time for any calamity—he'd burn this precious capital of theirs to the ground right now. Once the emperor knew what he was capable of he would tremble in fear like he was supposed to. *What did it matter what calamity the Crown of the Seal held in check—it has nothing to do with me. If they want to stop it, fine, they're on their own.*

Yet, there was certain vital information he lacked…

"Master Mitsuru?"

Mitsuru looked around, his hands gripping the terrace railing.

Opening the double doors to the guest room and bowing stiffly was Adju Lupa. He was one of the officers here in the Crystal Palace, under direct orders from the emperor to look after Mitsuru during his stay. He looked to be in his late forties. Mitsuru had instantly been wary of the man's gentle, scholarly demeanor. This was no mere administrator.

Mitsuru had heard of the special task force operating directly under the guidance of the emperor—Sigdora—when he was still in the south. He had been staying at a small village inn where he had heard stories about a Sigdora attack that had burned down half the houses in town, and claimed the lives of more than half of the residents.

Not knowing anything of the Crown of the Seal at the time, Mitsuru had wondered why the North had sent troops into the South. Now it all made sense. They were doubtlessly searching for whatever these materials were that the emperor needed.

"The Northern Empire uses Sigdora to reclaim refugees who've escaped south, or just to kill them," the innkeeper had said in a hushed voice. "No one knows why. They want something…or maybe the refugees know something and they don't want them to talk."

The story had piqued Mitsuru's interest, and he fully intended to get to the bottom of this Sigdora thing when he traveled north.

Adju Lupa was a card-carrying member of Sigdora, Mitsuru was certain. And he was no mere operative but one of its leaders. Yes, the emperor had welcomed Mitsuru to his city, most likely an honest gesture, but that did not mean he was not wary of his guest. Especially now that the emperor had him waiting. It made perfect sense to deploy a skilled and trusted man to shadow him during his stay.

"The lady requests your presence in the gazebo of the Garden of Victory for some afternoon tea, should it please you," Adju Lupa announced politely.

The lady of whom he spoke was the eldest daughter of the emperor. Should nothing unfortunate occur, once the current emperor passed away, she would ascend to the throne as Gama Agrilius VIII, the first female emperor in the north.

But Mitsuru knew that her path to the throne would not be an easy one. The residents of the Crystal Palace were nothing if not talkative. Rumors and whispered secrets were as common as mice in a manger. And the worst of the gossips were easily manipulated—few seemed to realize that the locks on their mouths were loose, nor how important the treasures they let slip between the lips actually were.

"Thank you. I shall gladly accept her ladyship's offer," Mitsuru replied. He put on a long woven robe that reached to his ankles and made his way across the Crystal Palace grounds.

The Crystal Palace was surrounded by several lush green gardens. Each of them had been arranged in a different fashion, and each had its own name. The majority of them were built to commemorate the births of important members of the Imperial Family over the years, these being given names of unclear provenance, such as the Garden of Origins, or Garden of the Spring of Service.

The Garden of Victory had been built three hundred years before when Gama Agrilius I established his unified empire after a protracted political struggle that spanned the entire northern continent. The garden was built on top of a platform that once supported heavyweight artillery. Wood and bricks from a historic fort had been used to build a memorial gazebo. This structure stood in the garden but still maintained its fierce, martial appearance.

Despite its wartime history and severe architecture, Lady Zophie was fond of this garden above all others. This was no less than the fourth time he had received an invitation to tea at this gazebo.

Most of the greenery in the Garden of Victory was shrubbery resistant to the wind and cold typical of the north. Like the other gardens in the Crystal Palace, it was rather drab. There were some high points, such as the former empress's personal gardens, and the rose garden known as the Garden of Revelations. Yet, for some reason, Lady Zophie appeared to favor this desolate corner. Mitsuru remained baffled as to why.

Furthermore, the Garden of Victory was in perhaps the farthest spot from the Crystal Palace one could go without leaving the grounds. Mitsuru rode out on an animal called a paho, which was similar to a pony in the real world. The lady's preferred mode of transport, on the other hand, was a contraption that looked much like a rickshaw. It occurred to Mitsuru that perhaps Zophie's fondness for this garden was not actually for the garden itself but for her rickshaw—arranging meetings out here was little more than an excuse to go for a ride.

Or perhaps it's that she has a fondness for the fellow who pulls the rickshaw?

The servant in question was a ruddy-faced lad without rank or title—he wasn't even a soldier, let alone an Imperial Guard. He was not allowed to wear arms or armor of any sort, only a simple tunic that bore the crest of the sun, the symbol of the Empire. After delivering his lady to the Garden of Victory, he would wait patiently beneath a large shrub cut in the shape of a shield until she was finished with her tea. To Mitsuru's knowledge, he'd never once called Zophie by her name. In fact, he never said a single thing.

But Mitsuru had noticed something in Lady Zophie's eyes whenever she would glance at her servant.

When he'd first met the servant, Mitsuru had assumed he too was a member of Sigdora. Even on the palace grounds, the daughter of the emperor would certainly have a bodyguard assigned to her. It would make sense that the bodyguard would be a member of the emperor's trusted elites.

However, Mitsuru had grown less sure of this with every passing day. His sorcerer's staff was quite powerful, the gem at its tip having absorbed the power of no less than four gemstones. One of its many powers was subtle, yet very effective. By merely tilting it at objects, one could see them with absolute clarity. For instance, if he swung the staff in Adju Lupa's direction, he could see all the weapons the mild-mannered man carried on his person. Not only that, but he could sense the skill with which he used them. Skill at swordplay appeared as an aura around his body. By the coloration and the brilliance of that aura, Mitsuru could determine just how good a swordsman the man was.

But no matter how many times he raised his staff in the direction of the lady's servant, he found no weapons or any trace of martial skill. It was possible, of course, that he was looking at a man who had been highly trained in the art of concealing his identity. Or equally possible that he was simply a harmless rickshaw puller.

When Mitsuru arrived, he found the servant in his usual place, crouched in the shade under his favorite shrub. When he spied Mitsuru approaching, he swiftly stood, took the paho's reins in his hand, and helped Mitsuru dismount.

Lady Zophie smiled pleasantly from a high-backed chair in the gazebo. The seating here wasn't too comfortable, and the lady routinely brought a large cushion with her. An intricately embroidered cloth had been draped over a circular table. A silver teapot gleamed in the sunlight.

Whenever the lady came to have tea here, a full entourage of ten female servants would appear bearing teapots, teacups, and cakes. While they drank, the servants would pour tea, and those with nothing to do would hover by the lady and her guest, waiting with bated breath, ready to fill any request directed toward them. The first time he'd come, it had been rather difficult to enjoy his cup of tea with such excessively attentive service. The lady's calm acceptance had seemed bizarre to say the least. This, Mitsuru thought, is what it means to be royalty. If there was always a crowd of people waiting to please you from the moment you were born, he supposed anyone could grow used to it.

Personally, Mitsuru thought the whole thing was an unneccessary extravagance. To have ten people serving one person seemed an egregious waste of resources. He knew things had been much the same in the real world once upon a time. In a way, visiting Vision was like getting in a time machine to visit the past of his own world.

"It's quite cold today, isn't it? Perhaps not the best day for having tea in a garden," the emperor's daughter said, rising from her chair to greet him. Over by a shrub, her servant bowed on his knees, placing his fists upon the ground in greeting. Mitsuru took his seat opposite the lady.

"Yet I find the sky a remarkable blue. It is so beautiful, I fear it might purify my soul just to gaze at it."

"Such modesty! Did you know, perhaps, that my name Zophie means the color blue in an ancient tongue of our people?"

The emperor's daughter happily gave instructions to her lady servants, and soon the table was covered with fragrant tea and a selection of cakes. All the while she talked in a pleasant, lilting voice. She began by telling him how splendid she had felt upon waking that morning, going on to complain about how difficult her history lectures had been, and how much time it had taken her to stitch the pattern for her new ball gown, and how she'd heard of a new play that was garnering much praise in the capital...

Zophie was all of fifteen years old. She was the daughter of the emperor, yet in many ways she was still just a little girl. She was as giddy and talkative as any girl one might meet in the town. Mitsuru, in general, spoke little, taking in all that she said while making the occasional requisite comment or murmur of approval.

On occasion he would smile or nod, be surprised or impressed. She seemed to revel in Mitsuru's every gesture, and seem quite pleased that she'd found this clever fellow to enjoy conversation with—even if he was a shade on the young side. Mitsuru, for his part, enjoyed these times for his own private reason, which he could never tell her.

When he first went to meet with the emperor's daughter, he'd been so surprised his breath was taken away. Her face looked like someone he knew. They were almost identical.

The woman was his aunt—his father's youngest sister.

After Mitsuru's father, enraged at his wife's infidelity, had killed Mitsuru's mother and his little sister, then taken his own life, Mitsuru had been shuttled around between various relatives, eventually ending up with his young aunt. In truth, he'd been pressed on her. Here was a young woman, just graduated from college, who doubtlessly sympathized with Mitsuru, yet certainly lacked the means and wherewithal to raise a young boy. She tried being nice to him and that failed, and when she tried to control him, she lost control of herself and ended up crying and screaming.

She was not, in general, a happy person. Her eyes always had a sad, forlorn look to them.

Mitsuru grew to hate his father. Had he not committed suicide, Mitsuru would have killed him with his own bare hands. That all-consuming rage opened the Porta Nectere. It provided Mitsuru the chance to enter Vision.

Everything about the emperor's daughter reminded him of his aunt. Her little affectations. The shifts in her expression. The timbre of her voice. Everything. He thought his aunt must have been like this when she was a high school student, beautiful and unafraid of what lay ahead.

The Watcher of the gate, Wayfinder Lau, told Mitsuru he would encounter people in Vision who closely resembled those he knew in the real world.

—*Even though they may look like two peas in a pod, the people you meet here are not who they are in the real world. They may have not a single thing in common. It is merely your own energy that causes them to appear the way they do.*

Mitsuru had taken Wayfinder Lau's words to heart, and, for better or for worse, he hadn't yet met anyone resembling someone from the real world in his travels until now. Lady Zophie was the first.

And now, staring at her face from such a close distance, he began to wonder if Vision wasn't really more than just something created by the surplus imaginative energies of people in the real world. Perhaps the real world and Vision were like two sides of a coin, each complementing the other. Making the other whole.

What had been discarded in the real world, what had never seen form, those dreams that never came true, these were what made Vision. That was why Halnera required a sacrifice from both worlds.

If this were the case, then Zophie's easy smile and unfettered happiness belonged by all rights to his aunt back in the real world. Mitsuru would reach the Tower of Destiny and straighten out his twisted fate. On the morning he returned to the real world, all the happiness that had been Zophie's would be returned to his aunt. This he promised himself.

It made the task before Mitsuru quite simple. The relationship between his aunt and Zophie was a perfect example. He would merely apply the same principle to his mother, his little sister, and himself.

Perhaps this is why, before he claimed the final gemstone, he had been confronted with this challenge and forced to do a little self-reflection. The Tower of Destiny had given him this encounter with Lady Zophie to prepare him.

That is why, in Zophie's mindless prattle, he felt the weight of his mission. The enormity of what he stood to gain made his heart race.

"Master Mitsuru?"

Mitsuru snapped back into focus. Zophie was looking directly at him. He was afraid his attention had wandered in the middle of their discussion. "My apologies! My mind began to drift off into the clouds."

Zophie smiled brightly. Her hairpin—an elaborate affair covered with stones of many colors and bound with a silver chain—swayed elegantly. "Do not worry on my behalf, for I know what it is that concerns you and causes your mind to wander. I know the source of this concern is my father..."

Mitsuru's face tightened.

Zophie turned to her servants standing ready. "I must speak on a very important matter with Master Mitsuru. I will call for you when I need you," she ordered.

The servants shuffled quietly off, leaving them alone in the Garden of Victory.

"Sending your servants away?" Mitsuru asked. "Are you sure?"

"Yes. Of course, sending them away does not ensure that one of Adju Lupa's men does not hear our every word, but I care not. For it was none other than Adju Lupa himself who suggested I speak to you on this matter, Master Mitsuru."

Mitsuru was not surprised to hear that they might be observed. He had assumed that Sigdora's eyes gleamed in every dark corner. But he was startled to hear the revelation that followed. "What is it that Lord Lupa said?"

Zophie bit her lip lightly, glancing in the direction of the shrub where her manservant waited. "Before I speak of that, may I ask you, Master Mitsuru, if you have divined the true nature of the man who pulls my rickshaw?"

Chapter 46
The Mirror of Eternal Shadow

The change of subject was so abrupt that for a moment Mitsuru merely stared at Lady Zophie.

"Adju Lupa told me," she continued, amused by the shock in Mitsuru's eyes. "He said Master Mitsuru possesses strange powers as a Traveler, and he is able to see people's true forms. Perhaps you use your staff for this, no?" Her gaze went to the staff leaning against the armrest of Mitsuru's brick chair.

"Truth be told, I've seen you use your staff on my servant here several times. Each time, you have the most curious look on your face."

So she's sharper than she lets on. Mitsuru returned her smile. "It is as you say. You are quite clever, m'lady."

Zophie did not seem pleased. "Tell me, what did you see? I'm betting you didn't see a thing. That is why you look at him so suspiciously. Am I right?"

Mitsuru nodded, wondering where she was going with this.

"Of course you saw nothing—for there is nothing there to see. Though my servant has the shape of a man, he is not a man at all. He is what we call a *shell*—a form without a soul. Though he follows his master's orders faithfully, he has no will of his own. He feels no emotion, or pain. Yes, he can fall ill, and if you kill him he will die, so he has life. Yet it cannot be said that he lives." *A pity,* she added under her breath.

"This is the first time I ever heard this word, *shell*, used in this way," Mitsuru said. "I never heard of this sort of thing in the south."

"No, of course you did not. Shells are found only in the north."

"Is it some disease?"

Zophie shook her head vigorously. "No!"

Mitsuru squinted. "Then a drug perhaps, or magic? Or is this the effect of some external device?"

For the first time a look of fear came across Zophie's expression. "Such frightful things you say!"

"It was only conjecture."

The emperor's daughter straightened herself in her seat, fixed her hair, and regained her composure. "When a man gazes into the Mirror of Eternal Shadow, he becomes a shell. There are some who think that the mirror itself sucks his soul away. Others believe that what he sees in the mirror is so fearful as to scare his soul straight out of his body. None, I daresay, know the truth. Still, no matter how strong or how wise a man may be, if he should so much as gaze upon the Mirror of Eternal Shadow, he will never speak again."

Mitsuru's mind raced furiously. As far as he could tell, Zophie was telling him the very thing that her father had kept secret. The secret of the Imperial Family, unrecorded in any of the many documents Mitsuru had scoured. Yet this information was coming to him courtesy of Adju Lupa. Somewhere inside Mitsuru's mind a scale was tipping as questions formed. Did Zophie understand the meaning of what she was telling him? What was Adju Lupa's game?

"This Mirror of Eternal Shadow—this is the first I've heard of such a thing." Mitsuru shook his head. "It sounds frightful. This is here, in the north?" Mitsuru spoke calmly, as though he was merely making conversation. Zophie on the other hand was as wary and nervous as a hare who has heard the soft footfalls of an approaching predator. Scare her even a little, and she would jump into her hole, never to poke her head out again. *I must tread carefully.*

As expected, Zophie slowly looked up, gauging Mitsuru's expression carefully before continuing. "My father—he did not tell you about the Mirror of Eternal Shadow? It is about as wide as I am tall, silver in color. It is quite beautiful to behold."

"Nope. I've never heard of it."

"Truly?"

Mitsuru smiled. "Really. It must be a deep, dark secret to make you so fearful."

Zophie sighed and put a hand to her throat. It was a more theatrical gesture than was called for, but her dismay seemed genuine. "Master Mitsuru, you journey toward the Tower of Destiny, where the Goddess resides, yes?"

"That is my mission as a Traveler."

"And you need one final gemstone. And this gemstone rests upon the crown of the Imperial Family."

"Yes, the Crown of the Seal."

"Ah, you know of this?" Zophie's long eyelashes swept down, her eyes closing in thought.

"I was told it was a very important crown, that it might not be moved without proper precaution."

"This is true. Thus my father makes you wait in this way, Master Mitsuru. Tell me, how did my father explain the need for your wait?"

Mitsuru sat up straight and recounted the details of his exchange with the emperor. Just talking about it made rage rise in him. He could feel it churning beneath his skin. He wanted to tell Zophie, right to her pretty face. *I can no longer bear to wait on your father's whim.* What a relief it would be to admit how, only an hour before, he had stood on the terrace, plotting the destruction of her precious capital.

Yet Mitsuru's anger was so great he knew he had to keep it inside. Zophie stared at his face, calm and composed. When Mitsuru was done telling her all he knew, he paused, taking a sip of cold tea.

"And this arrangement—doesn't it strike you as odd?"

"In what way?"

"My father has not told you how important the Crown of the Seal is, or what calamity will visit us should it be moved, has he?"

"He has not," Mitsuru said, carefully choosing his words. "I did ask, but he told me nothing more than I have related to you just now."

Zophie suddenly leaned forward, reaching out her hand and placing it upon Mitsuru's. "Please forgive him. I do not intend to make excuses for my father, but I believe he did not tell you because he did not wish to burden you with problems that are not yours. You see, the conditions surrounding the Crown of the Seal are, for the most part, taboo to speak of. It is…unclean. I'm sure my father felt that these were things unfit for your ears, coming from the real world as an emissary of the gods, as you do."

"I understand," Mitsuru replied, his hand resting under hers. "Yet, m'lady, if I'm not totally mistaken, you are now going to tell me these things about the crown?"

Zophie nodded, her eyes never leaving his. Then, with a start, she lifted her hand and stood from the table.

"I thank you deeply," Mitsuru said, lowering his head. "But I worry. Won't the emperor be upset?"

Zophie smiled the sort of smile one uses for a close friend who has told a valuable secret. Hurriedly, she picked up the teapot and made a motion to pour him some more tea. This was a service she was apparently unaccustomed to performing, as she spilled tea all over the table. Mitsuru quickly wiped it up with a napkin.

"Adju Lupa told me," Zophie said, her voice little more than a whisper. "He said that when you are alone sometimes, Master Mitsuru, you look very sad."

The rotten spy. In one corner of his mind, Mitsuru cursed the man and his prying eyes.

"I think this must be when you remember the real world you have left behind. When you recalled the faces of your friends, and those you loved. It must make one very lonely to be so far from home."

Mitsuru did not reply, which Zophie took to be an affirmation. "Lupa said you must want to get to the Tower of Destiny as soon as possible. I think he is right. It is only natural."

She paused. "Still, still—my father has good reason to make you wait, Master Mitsuru. Adju Lupa suggested that perhaps, with only the explanation my father gave you, you would not understand why. That is why he asked me to speak with you on this matter."

Everything was on account of the Mirror of Eternal Shadow, she told him. "The thing that the Crown of the Seal holds at bay is the mirror. Only the noble gemstone set upon that crown has the power to resist the mirror's horrible strength. This gemstone you seek, it is the stone we call the Gem of Darkness."

The Gem of Darkness. Something inside Mitsuru's chest stirred.

"This gem was brought from the Dark to Vision. That is why it is able to stop the Mirror of Eternal Shadow."

Mitsuru couldn't hold back his curiosity any longer. "What exactly is this Mirror of Eternal Shadow? And this 'Dark'? Is this another world, like the real world or Vision?"

A shadow came over Zophie's lively features, and she seemed reluctant to speak. "It seems odd for me to be explaining this to you, Master Mitsuru, you being the Traveler, but please bear with me. The real world and Vision exist as a pair of opposites. But Vision exists only because the real world exists. Without the real world's energies, Vision would cease to be. Between the two stands the Great Barrier of Light. And around them yawns the Abyss of Chaos."

Mitsuru nodded and she continued. "To be more precise, we might say that the real world and Vision float in the abyss. We are but an ephemeral bubble drifting on the surface of an endless void. Yet I can think of no bubble more beautiful.

"A moment before, I said that the real world and Vision were a pair. This is true, yet their relationship is not equal. You see, while there is only one real world, there are many Visions. In addition to the Vision in which we live, there are many other Visions marking time beyond our knowledge."

Wayfinder Lau hadn't said anything of the sort, but Mitsuru wasn't particularly surprised by this revelation. It made sense, considering that the imaginations of the real world created this one. There were many people living in the real world. With all that energy—all those thoughts and dreams and emotions—it made sense that there would be multiple Visions floating around.

"Parallel worlds, then?" Mitsuru asked, recalling something he had read in a science fiction novel once.

"Parallel?"

"No. Pay me no mind. Please, go on."

Zophie looked to the side, as though she had lost her train of thought. This, too, seemed like a new experience for her. "In most cases, these Visions are peaceful worlds," she continued, thinking while she spoke. "Much like the one that we live in here."

"It is peaceful, now."

"Yes," she continued, choosing to ignore his comment, "but some of these Visions are filled with darkness and fear. They are dark worlds, casting shadows, knowing only animosity and destruction."

"And these worlds are the Dark you mentioned?"

Zophie nodded. "I learned in my history lessons that the Dark are worlds that were meant to become Vision, yet failed. That is why they resent Vision, and would destroy it if they could. The darkness that swirls in those worlds yearns to infiltrate worlds like ours. It is waiting and watching always for that chance.

"Near the bottom of the Abyss of Chaos lie many seeds, as yet undifferentiated, yet each with the potential to become a new Vision," she explained. "If they should rise and form a healthy Vision, then all is well, but if something goes wrong, and they become twisted and bent, then they fall into the Dark."

Zophie trembled with fear as she spoke, yet Mitsuru was utterly calm. To him, it seemed odd that more worlds weren't part of the Dark, given the people who had imagined them into being. In fact, he began to wonder if Visions like this one were not the irregularities. Mitsuru knew far too much about the evil and greed men were capable of to believe otherwise.

"Yet, if you look at their origins, both Vision and the Dark are born of the same stuff," Zophie was saying. "That is why all Visions bear some similarities to the Dark. Perhaps you might call them connections to the Dark. It is thus impossible to have a world completely free of animosity, hate, and foolishness."

"A very accurate observation, I'm sure," Mitsuru said, taking the reins of the conversation back from Zophie. "So, in the case of this Vision in which we now live, this connection with the Dark is the Mirror of Eternal Shadow?"

"It is so."

"So, if my understanding is correct, you need this Crown of the Seal to prevent an invasion from the Dark, right? If that were the case, then it would indeed make good sense that the Crown of the Seal not be moved."

Zophie smiled, looking very much relieved.

"This is merely conjecture on my part, but might it be that the Imperial Family has, from the beginning of time, held the noble role of bearing this Mirror of Eternal Shadow, and preventing attack from the Dark?"

Zophie's face lit up with joyful surprise. "Indeed, it is! It is exactly as you say. That is why my family wishes above all other things to unite Vision and rule it in peace. No, it is more than a desire, it is our mission. Our clan was, in the beginning of time, given responsibility for the Mirror of Eternal Shadow from the Goddess herself—we were chosen."

"Quite a weighty responsibility," Mitsuru said solemnly. "Hearing your story has cleared up another of my questions too."

"Which question is this?"

"In the south, they say that the religion of the Old God followed in the north is a denial of the Goddess Creator. That is why, when I first met the emperor, I asked him first about your religion. Why, if he believed in the Old God, did he not see me, a Traveler, as a false god, and something to be abhorred?"

"I'm sorry," Zophie said quietly.

"No, the emperor was very honest with me. He told me that this religion of the Old God is nothing more then a device to encourage opposition with the south, where the Goddess is revered above all others. In truth, you worship not the Goddess but the real world as your creator."

"Yes, we do!"

"Yet, this does not have to be a denial of the Goddess. The Goddess does exist, and she does live in the Tower of Destiny. But she is the Goddess only of the fates of people from the real world, and she does not preside over those who live in Vision. So the emperor told me. Yet I was somewhat confused until I heard what you told me just now. Now I know that the Imperial Family is, in effect, the caretakers of Vision, ordained by the Goddess. The Goddess does not rule Vision, she has given that charge to the Imperial Family, and retired to her Tower of Destiny, knowing that the fate of her own world is in good hands."

Zophie crossed her hands over her chest, and her face filled with light. "Master Mitsuru, you understood all this from my simple tale? This is truly magnificent. You are wiser than I dared hope."

"No, it is all on account of m'lady's considerate explanations."

Zophie arched her neck in that way only girls of her age can do, and pouted ever so slightly. "If the Goddess truly governed everyone in Vision as those fools in the south believe, then it would be a simple thing for her to fend off the Dark from the Mirror of Eternal Shadow. Yet this she cannot do. That is why it is difficult for us to think of her as a true god."

"I understand."

"But the people of the south know nothing of these truths," she said with such a look of cold disdain that Mitsuru was caught off-guard.

Didn't know she had that in her.

"Still, none of this helps my cause," Mitsuru said, putting a hand to his forehead. "If the Crown of the Seal performs such a vital function, then how can a mere Traveler such as myself ever hope to claim it?"

"Yes, you see…" Zophie leaned forward in her chair. "There's something very important I haven't said yet. There is another way in which the Mirror of Eternal Shadow might be sealed. Master Mitsuru, did you know of the Mirror of Truth?"

This was, of course, familiar territory. Wayfinder Lau had told him all about the mirror. He knew that on his journey he would meet people bearing these mirrors, that they were vital signposts to a Traveler, and that the mirror-bearers would be his friends on his journey, and aid him. He knew also that when he combined the gemstones he found with these mirrors, he could return to the real world—though only for a short period of time.

Just as Wayfinder Lau had said, as soon as he left the Village of the Watchers, Mitsuru had met someone carrying a Mirror of Truth.

The man was a beastkin, and as soon as he learned that Mitsuru was a Traveler, and that he needed the mirror, he asked Mitsuru to hire him. Apparently, the man made his money as a bodyguard. But Mitsuru had no intention of dragging the man along on his journey. Nor was he in need of any friends. And how could he trust someone he had to pay money to protect him?

So Mitsuru had killed him and stolen the mirror. Mitsuru wore it still.

"Yes, I know of it, or rather, them. Unlike the Mirror of Eternal Shadow of which you speak, the Mirror of Truth is not whole but has been broken into many fragments."

"Yes, this is so. The Mirror of Truth was first broken by the hand of the Goddess herself, its fragments spread across Vision. Over time, the fragments fell into the hands of people who did not know their true worth."

"But, if one could gather all the fragments and reconstruct a whole mirror?" Mitsuru asked.

"Yes. With its power, one could stop the Mirror of Eternal Shadow forever!" Zophie said, her voice swelling. "The Mirror of Eternal Shadow opens a path to the Dark, and the Mirror of Truth opens a path to the real world. Put them together, and they will destroy each other."

This, she explained, is why several generations of emperors had made it their mission to gather all the fragments of the Mirror of Truth. "Sometimes they used rather violent means to do this. Yet Vision is vast, and it was difficult to cross the sea and search faraway lands with any thoroughness."

But now the situation was changing. With powered boats, the unified north could create a unified Vision. This would make searching for the fragments and ultimately the reconstruction of the Mirror of Truth a simple task.

"If we use the power of the Mirror of Truth to stop the Mirror of Eternal Shadow, then we will no longer have a need for the Crown of the Seal. Then you will have your gemstone as you desire, Master Mitsuru. That is why my father asks you to wait. I hope you understand the depth of the reasons he has for doing this now."

Mitsuru stood from his chair and bowed humbly. "I do understand. And I thank you for your generosity and consideration in telling me all of these things, m'lady."

For a moment, Zophie was overcome with emotion, grabbing his hand, then clutching her own hands to her breast, and laughing. All the while, Mitsuru was thinking, coldly plotting his next move.

I wonder if this little girl or even the emperor realizes that when they reconstruct the Mirror of Truth and do away with the Mirror of Eternal Shadow forever, they will lose what right they had to special privileges as the chosen guardians of the Goddess. Or perhaps, they don't care—as long as they unify Vision first, with them as its leaders.

Or perhaps they have grown tired, weary of their role as defenders of Vision. Being guardians of the world sounded good, yet he imagined the burden would be great. Not that any of this mattered much to Mitsuru.

"Might I ask one more question—purely to satisfy my curiosity as a Traveler from the real world?"

Zophie was refilling their cups with an unsteady hand. She nodded, her eyes bright.

Mitsuru reached out, grasping her hand. "Allow me to pour. We've covered some difficult territory here. Perhaps you should rest."

"Yes, of course."

"I was wondering, just how dangerous is this Dark? How strong are its powers? Do your scholars know anything of this?"

Zophie's mouth tightened. "Once, and only once in the past...nearing the end of the War of Unification, for a brief moment only, the seal was broken, and the power of the Dark came into our world."

"However did this happen?"

"It was, the histories tell us, done on purpose to defeat a formidable adversary of the Empire. They were nomads, actually, living on the wide plains. Barbarians, they had no central government, yet wherever our troops went, they nibbled at their heels, disrupting our supply lines. Consequently, the emperor at the time decided to draw upon the power of the Dark." The demon army that came through the portal when the Mirror of Eternal Shadow was used demolished the barbarians in the blink of an eye.

"Frightful...yet, were there not injuries to the Imperial Army as well?"

"The barbarians were lured to a particular place, and the mirror was moved nearby. All care was taken in the planning of the attack, and, luckily, our losses were few. As soon as the barbarians were defeated, the seal was replaced, of course. It was open for perhaps all of an hour."

The seal replaced, the demons that had fallen upon Vision became nothing more than dust.

"What form do these demons take?"

"I do not know. If one were to read the ancient chronicles of the war, one might find a drawing, I'd imagine..."

Mitsuru had read every account of the war in existence and found no such drawing. Perhaps whatever they did look like was too fearful to be recorded.

"The field where the demons set upon the barbarian tribes is, even today, a barren wasteland where not a single blade of grass will grow. I have never been there, though, for it is far away from this city."

Then Zophie changed the subject with another question. "Master Mitsuru, do you know why this castle is called the Crystal Palace, though it be built of stone?"

Mitsuru looked up at the towering castle behind him and shook his head. "That I do not. Now that you mention it, it does seem quite odd."

"It has been three hundred years since the War of Unification ended, yet it was a hundred years after that when the capital was moved here. They built a castle, setting the Mirror of Eternal Shadow in a safe place within, and that instant, the castle filled with translucent light as though it were made of crystal. The castle was called the Crystal Palace in memory of that moment. I hear that during the battle when the barbarians were defeated, when the seal on the mirror was lifted and then replaced, a similar light filled the land. I must therefore conclude that this light comes from the mirror itself. Perhaps it is the mind of the mirror revealed."

The mind of the mirror? What exactly would a mirror think or feel, Mitsuru wondered. Was it the joy of release when its seal was lifted? Or perhaps it was merely showing satisfaction at being feared and respected.

Regardless, the discussion had taken a sudden and unexpected turn in Mitsuru's favor.

"So the Mirror of Eternal Shadow is here in the Crystal Palace?"

"Yes," Zophie said, nodding lightly, blanching slightly under Mitsuru's hawklike gaze, as though knowing it would do no good to hide this truth from someone of his powers. "Yet, not even I know exactly where it is. Only my father and the high priest know that."

"But there is a room of some sort, a place where the mirror is held safe? Perhaps a chapel? If one were to look at the blueprints for the castle..."

"No, its location is concealed behind a barrier—a magical veil. The barrier prevents anyone from knowing where the room is. They simply cannot see it," Zophie replied lightly, but the words made a great impact on Mitsuru. It was enough to make him lean momentarily against the back of his chair for support.

A magical barrier—of course. That's why I was unable to find the exact location of the final gemstone all this time.

Finding the four gemstones on his journey so far had been rather a simple thing. His magic staff had shown him the location where the first gemstone lay sleeping. After he'd found that, the second gemstone told him where the third lay, and so on until he had all four. All he had to do was listen to the gemstones' voices and he would know. It was, in fact, the gemstones that had told him the final stone he sought lay in the north. *Go north, meet with the emperor. The emperor knows all,* they had said.

Yet, now that he was here, the staff was strangely silent. It wouldn't even tell him if the gemstone was in the capital city. If he only knew where it was, Mitsuru could take appropriate action and have the stone in no time. Now he knew why. For the first time in days, he felt the tension in his chest melt away. The Mirror of Eternal Shadow had been guarded for generations by the Imperial Family. A barrier erected to hide such a vital room must have been created with very strong magic indeed. It was no surprise that his sorcerer's staff, even with the power of four gemstones aiding it, had not been able to divine its location.

"I hear the barrier was created by placing magical stones at various locations throughout the capital," Zophie said, elegantly tipping her cup to her lips. "That is to say, this city was designed for the express purpose of generating the barrier that conceals the place wherein the Mirror of Eternal Shadow lies. It would serve to reason that these magic stones are used in the foundations of all the great buildings of the capital."

Mitsuru had to exert himself to not burst out laughing. To think she would tell him such a vital fact without him even having to ask. She was a talkative, dimwitted girl, when it came down to it. And how grateful Mitsuru was for that. The emperor's daughter was turning out to be his greatest benefactor on his journey yet.

If the capital city itself is the barrier—Mitsuru mastered his rising elation, taking deep, steady breaths—*then destroy the capital and you destroy the barrier along with it.*

He wouldn't have to destroy the capital as a mere threat to the emperor—its destruction was the very means for achieving his goal!

All the while, the emperor's daughter was staring at him with those innocent eyes. *How kind, how gentle you are. You do not doubt for a moment what the person to whom you speak might be thinking in his heart of hearts. Nor do you wonder at the true intent of the man who suggested this course of action to you—Adju Lupa.*

It was only natural that the Imperial Family, after maintaining a vicelike grip on the wealth of the north for three hundred years would have many branches. In the course of time some of these relations, with no true claim to the throne themselves, would come to resent the emperor and aspire to depose him. It was for this precise reason that any path Zophie might take to the throne would be a difficult one.

Sigdora were the faithful hounds of the emperor, but even hounds have a will of their own, Mitsuru knew. And they were ever ready to switch to a new master—a stronger one, who promised sweeter rewards. Was Adju Lupa not one of these? By whispering to the emperor's daughter he hoped to spur Mitsuru into motion, stir things up, perhaps frame whatever commotion resulted as the failing of the current emperor. And, of course, there would be someone behind him whispering in his ear, dangling some treat before his nose...

Who cares, as long as it serves my ends?

I know what you're up to, Lupa. And I thank you for it.

Adju Lupa was as clueless as the emperor's daughter. When Mitsuru really took action, it wouldn't be on the level of a failing of Gama Agrilius VII. It wouldn't even be close. *They've sorely underestimated me—a miscalculation that will cost them everything.*

"Let us call back your servants. The wind's picking up," Mitsuru said cheerily. "I would not be able to sleep at night if I knew you had caught a cold on my account."

Zophie patted her blushing cheek, smiling. She reached out to pick up the silver bell to summon her servants when Mitsuru stopped her. "Tell me one last thing. If the Mirror of Eternal Shadow is so strongly protected, how can there be accidents such as the one that befell your servant, making shells out of men?"

In an instant, Zophie looked more troubled and haunted than he had ever seen her. The blush in her cheeks faded. "Well, that's…"

"A form of punishment?"

She leaped from her chair, clinging to his hand. "Yes, that's it. Most of them are, at least. Terrible criminals, or traitors to the Empire, those who cannot be reformed…"

"So you break the seal for a moment and show them the Mirror of Eternal Shadow on purpose?"

"Yes," she said, wilting visibly. "It is…quite cruel, I know. But it can't be helped."

"I understand, I do."

"The fact is that it is often more convenient for those who serve our family to be shells—convenient, and safe. Those who do the small work at the castle, they are not, well…they are not great warriors or scholars, you see. They are lower folk." As she spoke, she closed her eyes as if to say she pitied them.

What a piece of work she is.

"But it's not as if it happens all the time. To undo the barrier and approach the Mirror of Eternal Shadow, my father and the high priest must both be present, and there is a ceremony. It takes a great deal of effort. That, and the high priest is often away from the capital checking on his churches in other parts of the Empire. You have not met him yet, have you, Master Mitsuru?

He's a busier man than even my father."

Mitsuru nodded, and his mind wandered. He imagined a scene where captives in shackles were led in a great line, like a string of beads, their every move watched by Imperial Guards. Down they were brought, down before the Mirror of Eternal Shadow. One by one, they were pushed toward the mirror.

This empire is even more twisted than I had imagined.

"So this means that many of the people who serve at the Crystal Palace are shells—and I have just not noticed."

"Yes...but, I'd think your time wouldn't be well spent looking for them, Master Mitsuru."

"The thought hadn't crossed my mind," Mitsuru said with a winning smile. "As I said, I merely asked out of my curiosity as a Traveler."

Zophie summoned her servants, and they began clearing the table. Mitsuru watched them, armed with his new knowledge. If he could learn to identify the shells among the people working at the Crystal Palace...

It would save him the trouble of leaving the capital to find the resources he needed.

After waving goodbye to Zophie, Mitsuru stood awhile in the Garden of Victory, the wind rustling his long hair and robes. His hands hung by his side, clenched into tight fists.

In those fists, he now held something beautiful: determination.

The fate of the Imperial Capital of Solebria was decided.

chapter 47
The Isle of Dragon

When the northern shore appeared on the horizon, the temperature seemed to drop a few degrees. Already they could smell the sea.

"That's Batista—the fishing port of Bog," Meena told them, pointing to at a cluster of houses in the distance.

Wataru's first impression was that this port didn't look anything like Sono. White dunes rolled and twisted along the long, flat shoreline. Small fishing boats floated here and there, none far from shore. Women walked across the sand doing what they could to help the fishermen. Children busied themselves searching for shells.

Jozo wasn't flying as high as he had been when they visited Dela Rubesi. Wataru could see people on the shore reacting to the sight of the dragon. Some children waved. Wataru waved back, half to assure them that this dragon suddenly appearing in the sky meant them no harm.

"You firewyrms sure are popular," Kee Keema shouted.

"They're creatures of legend, after all!" Meena said.

"They never talked about how cold it was up here in the legends."

"Shall I fly lower?" Jozo asked. A giant eyeball as big as Wataru's fist turned slowly toward them, and blinked. "Say, Wataru…"

"What is it?"

"We'll be heading out over the sea soon…I just wanted to ask—are you sure about this? You really want to go north?"

"We are sure. Is something wrong?"

Kutz, sitting toward the back, picked up her ears. Wataru glanced back over his shoulder at the branch chief and lowered his voice. "If something's wrong, tell us now, please."

"Well..." Jozo blinked several times. "I feel bad, after promising to take you anywhere..."

"You can't go to the north? Is it too far?"

"No, not at all. Fly straight, and we'd be there in two nights' time."

The dragon's tongue flicked out between his sharp fangs. "Only, remember when I went with you to Dela Rubesi? After that, I went back to our island. I told the wyrmking about what we saw in Dela Rubesi—the Goddess's wrath."

The wyrmking had become greatly concerned and gathered all the dragons on the island, and asked them, for the time being, to avoid long trips. They were to stay near the island so that they could gather at any time in case of an emergency.

"This never happens. We children are expected to fly all sorts of places, see lots of things. Of course, we're not supposed to make too many friends on the ground. Like Meena says, we're mostly legends in many parts of the land, and because we're quite strong, if we chose to get involved in land-dwellers' conflicts, well..."

"I'm sorry—if I had known what was going on—I hope that using the flute wasn't a bad idea."

"No, no, it's fine." Jozo shook his head violently. The motion made his back lurch, and Kee Keema nearly fell off, clinging to the notches where one of Jozo's wings met his body. Meena giggled, but Kutz's eyes were fixed on Wataru and the dragon.

"You saved my life, after all. The wyrmking always says, if we are in debt to someone on the ground, we must repay them in full. You're a special case."

"I'm grateful for that, but it worries me what the wyrmking said."

"Me too, that's why I was kind of hoping that we could go to our island before going north. It won't take too long. It's on the way. I'd like to make a formal request to the wyrmking before heading any further. You think that'd be okay?"

It wasn't a question Wataru could answer. He looked around at Kutz, who stood up on the dragon's back, and hunching over, crawled up to him. "What's going on?"

Wataru explained. Kutz frowned a moment, then inched up closer to Jozo's head and patted him on the neck, getting his attention. "Sorry for getting you involved in all this, dragon. We really need to go to the north—it's imperative."

"You're the leader of this crew, right?" Jozo asked. "Can I ask why you're going? I can't help but feel like you're heading into some kind of danger."

Wataru wondered how much Kutz was ready to tell him. He glanced at her face, but before she could say anything, Jozo asked Wataru to take out his wyrmflute. Wataru reached into his pocket. When he brought the wyrmflute out, he found it had snapped clean in two. "See, you can't use it again. It won't make any noise."

"I know…"

"If you're going to the north to do something dangerous, that worries me. I can drop you off and leave, but if something happens, I won't be able to hear you, no matter how loud you yell. On the other hand, if I were to hang around and wait for you, I'd stick out like a, well, like a dragon. Can't imagine that would aid your mission much. Am I right, Ms. Leader?"

Kutz smiled grimly. Her black hair swirled in the wind from the dragon's wings, brushing against her cheek. "You've a keen eye, Mr. Dragon."

"Name's Jozo, ma'am."

"I'm Kutz. Sorry for not introducing myself earlier. I'm branch chief back in Gasara. We have deep and profound respect for your ancestor."

"I could tell by the armband."

"Thank you, Jozo, for telling us this. We will go to the Isle of Dragon. Still, I wonder if it's really okay to bring land dwellers such as ourselves to the home of the dragons? I wouldn't want to get you in any more trouble than we already have."

"It's no problem," Jozo replied. "You're Highlanders, after all. Besides, I'm sure the wyrmking had a good reason for making his request—and I wouldn't be surprised if he wants to pass that knowledge on to the Highlanders."

"You think so?"

"Yeah. My parents said pretty much the same thing. They said the time might come again when we have to leave our island and join forces with the people who live on the land."

Again? Wataru and Kutz exchanged glances.

"Did that happen sometime in the past?"

"It was before I was born, about three hundred years ago. Something happened in the north and the dragons left their island to fight."

"Three hundred years ago? That would be around the end of the War of Unification," Kutz muttered. "Do you mean to say that dragons fought in that war?"

"Not in the war, no, no. Dragons never get involved in land-dweller conflicts, or take sides. Especially not something like the War of Unification."

"Then what did you fight?"

"Demonkin," Jozo replied immediately.

From the way Kutz's eyes looked, Wataru guessed it was her first time hearing the word too.

"What's that?"

"I'm not so sure myself. We're not supposed to talk about the demonkin—it's taboo. Still, they sound like incredibly dangerous, terrible foes. If we dragons hadn't flown from our island, all Vision might've been destroyed, they say."

"There is much we do not know about the history of the north," Kutz admitted. "We'll have to ask this wyrmking."

"Do you think he'd just tell us?"

"Never know, unless we ask," Kutz said. The idea of chatting with a king of dragons didn't seem to faze her.

"Then that's it. I'll introduce you to my parents! My dad's amazing! He's at least three times as strong as I am." Jozo grinned with pride.

Wataru wondered if Jozo's parents worried about him when he ventured far away. *And here I am dragging him across Vision on my errands.*

"We're heading out over the open sea pretty soon. We'll be in the Stinging Mist before long. Everybody, keep your heads low and stay between my wings. Don't sit up, whatever you do. The mist will run you through like a thousand tiny swords."

As he spoke, Jozo gave a powerful beat of his wings, and their speed increased.

The island looked like a dragon sleeping quietly in a corner of the mist-shrouded sea. It was actually shaped like a dragon's head and neck. It even had two horns. Its large eyes were closed. Two round nostrils—probably mountains—looked up toward the sky. It had a massive, protruding jaw, and sharp fangs where rugged fjords formed a small bay. This scene would've looked perfectly at home in a museum with a label like "Dragon Taking a Leisurely Bath," if only it weren't so cold, and the sea wasn't the color of pale blue ice.

"Hardly needs introduction," Kee Keema whispered, peering out from beneath Jozo's wing. "But I'm guessing that's the Isle of Dragon!"

"That's right! Home!"

A thick mist veiled the sea from the air, but they could tell that around the island there was nothing but open water. No small outlying islands or even rocks were visible. In all things, the dragonkin stood alone.

"Whoa! Whoa! Stay down, you all!" Jozo called back frantically. "We're still in the Stinging Mist!"

"You're right," Meena said, putting a hand to her face. "I felt a sting!" A small drop of blood formed below her right eye.

"Me too," said Kutz, holding down her hair to keep it from blowing up in the wind. Two lines of blood trickled down her forehead.

Wataru shivered. *Mitsuru passed through this. He must've used his magic to create a barrier to protect himself...*

Seeing the mist firsthand, it now made sense that sailships had to plan their departures from the south carefully. Clear, too, was the value of the starseers' ability to predict when the winds would blow just right so a ship might make the crossing while avoiding the mist. But what struck Wataru the most was the realization that powered ships—without sails or oars—could be easily piloted from inside a cockpit. The army that had those would rule Vision.

Jozo's scales sure are tough.

"Don't your eyes hurt, Jozo?"

"Not a bit. I'm just a little cold—but it will be warm when we reach the island."

Jozo had told him that the dragon island was volcanic. Wataru craned his neck, looking for cones among the mountains on the island below. Just then, as though it had been planned, a puff of white steam from the two hills that were the dragon's nose rose up into the air.

The closer they got, the more impressed they became with the sheer size of the island. It made sense, when you considered how large Jozo was, and that he was only a child. There would be a limit to how many adult dragons you could cram onto a smaller island.

The ground itself was barren, like a giant rock had been carved into the shape of the dragon's head and left to steep in the water. Wataru couldn't see a single blade of grass.

Jozo seemed to be heading for a spot between the dragon's horns, where the various rocks and boulders had been cleared away to form a kind of landing strip.

Jozo descended in a slow spiral, making for the clearing. When the mist finally cleared around them, Wataru spotted two dragons sitting by the edge of the clearing, looking up at them. Compared to Jozo's ruby-like coloring, these firewyrms were a more subdued, darker shade of red.

"My parents!" Jozo said. Then he called down to the dragons on the ground below them. "Father! Mother! I've brought Wataru!"

Wataru was half expecting to see a family scene with Jozo getting scolded for bringing people to the island. Jozo's parents were at least twice his size—even their fangs were as thick as Wataru's wrists.

Jozo touched down, and Wataru and the others hesitantly clambered down onto the rocky ground. Thankfully, Wataru's fears were misplaced, for, while the gust of wind from Jozo's parent's nostrils was steamy, and their voices boomed, the words they greeted them with were as gentle as a spring day.

"Welcome home, Jozo. And welcome, Traveler. Has Jozo been an aid to you?"

It was first suggested that they warm their chilled bodies in the hot springs.

"You have hot springs?"

"The island *is* a volcano."

Kee Keema, sluggish with the cold, and Meena were both ecstatic.

"I've never been in a hot spring!" Meena exclaimed. Kutz alone seemed impatient to get on with the mission. But it turned out that a wait was in order regardless.

"The wyrmking is resting, and it will take some time to arrange the Council of Fang and Wing. Go to the hot springs, and I believe we shall be ready when you are done," Jozo's mother told them.

"What is the Council of Fang and Wing?"

"This is what we call a meeting of all dragons," Jozo's father answered. "Our daily affairs are decided by the wyrmking and the seven pillars—one chief dragon from each clan—yet when important things are to be decided, all dragons on the isle come together to speak."

The dragons on the island were all descendants of the great firewyrm, yet still, there were slight physical differences between them in the shape of their wings or the count of their fangs. They had been divided into seven types by these characteristics. Each of these types formed clans, and each of these clans had a chieftain, called the pillar. Thus, the seven pillars, Jozo's father told them.

Apparently, the wyrmking—who was only slightly younger than Vision itself—spent the greater part of the day napping, and a bit of time was required to wake him. All things considered, even Kutz eventually agreed the hot springs was a good idea.

The interior of the dragon island was made up of a labyrinthine network of caverns. Several side passages led off of the twisting, splitting passageways, and here the dragons made their homes. It appeared they were roughly separated by clan, but the dragons were friendly, and many of the nests housed more than one family, making the network of caves crowded and lively.

While the exterior of the island was all rocks, the inside of the caverns was lush with greenery. There were even small forests here and there. Flowers grew from the walls, and there were fruit trees in small gardens created in nooks in the caves. Wataru had been told that the dragons subsisted mainly on fish caught from the sea, but he couldn't detect any fishy smell in the caverns. On the contrary, the whole place smelled of fresh leaves, tinged by a hint of salty sea air.

The hot springs were open to the sky, being near the upper levels of the caverns. The hot water felt great in the cold air. Shrubs had grown up in the rugged rocks around the springs, and Wataru could see them swaying gently through the steam.

"Ah, nirvana!" Wataru said, repeating something he had heard an old man saying once at a hot spring near Tokyo.

Kee Keema laughed. "What's nirvana?"

"Well, it's kind of like paradise. That's one of the words we have in the real world for talking about the place where God lives."

"So it's like the Tower of Destiny?" Kee Keema asked, then seemed to regret it. He didn't want to remind Wataru.

Wataru pretended not to notice. "A little different. People go there when they die."

"So everybody just goes there when their time comes?"

"Well, not exactly. Only good people go. The bad ones go to a place called Hell."

It occurred to Wataru to wonder for the first time where people from Vision went when they died. He had never even thought to ask.

Kee Keema sunk into the water up to his chin, his eyes half closed. "When we die, we become light," he told Wataru.

"Light?"

"Aye, we become the light of the sun and shine upon the land. And then, when it's our turn, we are born again. But, if you are bad in life, you don't become light—no, you sink into the Abyss of Chaos. Don't think you even get to be reborn from down there."

That reminded Wataru that the Precept-King of Dela Rubesi had said much the same thing. If he died having broken his oath with the Goddess then his soul would be impure, and he would be unable to be born into the next life.

"You don't think people in Vision are reborn as people in the real world, do you?" Wataru muttered, half to himself.

But, after a short while, Kee Keema answered, "I hope that would be true. Then I could meet you in the real world and become friends there too."

Wataru laughed. He could picture Kee Keema in the real world being a deliveryman for one of those express package companies. He'd certainly make the biggest, strongest, nicest, and most popular deliveryman Wataru could imagine.

Kutz and Meena were relaxing in another part of the hot springs. The water felt exquisite, but the heat had opened the wounds they suffered from the Stinging Mist.

"It really stings," Kutz said with a frown. "Jozo's mother was saying something about an ointment—maybe I'll have to get me some of that later. That cut beneath your eye is swelling."

The salty water of the springs stung.

"Say, Kutz..."

"Yeah?"

"I was wondering about what Jozo was saying about the seven pillars."

Kutz raised an eyebrow.

"Isn't it strange to call them pillars? I mean, you usually think of pillars as being intended to support something. I got to thinking — maybe it's got something to do with the Great Barrier of Light."

Kutz was silent for a while before responding. "The dragons were deeply involved with the making of Vision, so it wouldn't surprise me if there was a connection. But I wouldn't think about it too much."

Meena smiled and nodded. Something about being relaxed after so much danger and the chill of the flight made tears come to her eyes. She hurriedly dipped her face in the water.

When they left the hot springs, Jozo was waiting for them. "We're ready for the council. I'll show you to the cavern where it's held."

The place he took them next was the largest cavern they had seen so far. It looked as big as a hangar you might find for one of those jumbo jets at an airport. The torches burning here and there struggled to light the place, and the high ceiling was lost in darkness. Holes for ventilation in the walls let in cool blasts of air, making the cavern chilly after the warmth of the springs.

Between the walls and the rocky protrusions on the ground sat dozens and dozens of dragons. They were of all different colors and sizes, some with long tails, others with barbs running down the length of their wings. Every giant black dragon eye in the room was turned toward Wataru. Their breathing rasped loud in the cavern.

The wyrmking sat upon a particularly high outcropping of rock at one end of the cavern. Sitting—or possibly sleeping. His wings were folded, his legs pulled underneath his body, and his tail hung limply down the side of the rock. When Wataru and the others were brought into a small open area in the middle of the room, he lifted his head slowly and with great solemnity. But his eyelids were only half open.

The wyrmking was roughly the same size as Jozo's parents. His scales had lost their luster and most of their red color, becoming a faded violet. Where the scales met at his neck and joints, Wataru could see wrinkle after wrinkle of tough dragonhide. He was wearing a shining crown upon his head, directly between his two horns.

Seven dragons sat to the right and left of the wyrmking's seat. These must have been the leaders known as the seven pillars. Their scales were a dark blackish-red, and they each wore necklaces of a different color.

"Welcome, guests." One dragon stood, looking down at Wataru and his friends, then turned to look at the other dragons gathered there. "As decreed by our customs, and before the wyrmking, the Council of Fang and Wing shall now convene."

As one, the dragons lowered their heads to the rocky floor. Wataru saw young dragons, smaller even than Jozo, mimicking their parents.

Jozo, flanked by his parents, took a step forward and introduced the guests. He also explained that he was the one who brought them to the island.

When he was finished, Wataru took a step forward. "I thank you for greeting us and making us feel welcome on such short notice. My thanks to the wyrmking, and all the dragons of the Isle of Dragon."

The chamber was perfectly silent. Wataru could hear his heart beating in his chest. "With a scale from Jozo, I made a wyrmflute, and since then he has saved me twice from danger. Now I have called on Jozo's strength to carry me this far…"

The wyrmking lifted his head and called out to Wataru. "Traveler!"

"Y-yes?"

"Can you show us your proof that you are a Traveler, so that all may see."

Wataru drew his Brave's Sword from the scabbard at his waist and held it aloft. One of the seven pillars closest to Wataru took it from him and held it before the wyrmking.

The wyrmking's eyelids were still half-closed, yet he viewed the blade with great interest. It was soon returned to Wataru's hand.

"Is the Watcher Wayfinder Lau well?"

The wyrmking's sudden switch in tone from the stiff formality of a moment before caught Wataru off-guard. He couldn't be sure, but it seemed like the ancient dragon was smiling.

"Yes! He's doing fine!"

"When you came to Vision, did the Wayfinder not give you a pendant?"

Wataru had completely forgotten about the pendant after wearing it so long. It occurred to him now that this was the proof of his status as Traveler, more than the sword. Wataru hastily pulled up the pendant. But when he attempted to take it off, the wyrmking motioned for him to stop.

"No, no, that will do. I have seen your proof."

"Thank you," Wataru said, standing up straight. He was so nervous he had almost lost his balance. Some of the younger dragons made a snuffling noise with their noses that sounded suspiciously like chuckling.

"Traveler and Highlanders." The wyrmking's voice rang solemnly in the cavern. Kutz jerked to attention. "We firewyrms have drawn breath since the time of creation. Now, we pass our days in this corner of the great sea, living in peace and tranquility," he continued, addressing the other dragons as well as Wataru and his friends. Yet, our role as protectors of Vision has not ended. We remain and will ever be the Goddess's sword and shield in Vision's time of need."

As one, the dragons in the room nodded. The seven pillars looked out on the room with sharp gazes.

"Traveler! You need not tell me your path, for I know. I know you go to the north, I know why you go there, and I know your purpose has its roots in the conflicts of men."

While Wataru was wondering how the wyrmking knew what they were up to, Kutz's clear voice rang out from beside him. "Your Highness! If I may, my reason for going to the north is to *end* this conflict."

The wyrmking's mouth twisted again in a smile. "Bold. Your will is good. But no land dweller can hope to end such a thing. It is impossible."

"No, I..."

Speaking quietly, the wyrmking cut her off. "Hatred summons hatred, sadness echoes sadness, and death leads the way to more death. Hatred's roots go deep into the soil, sadness is more vast than the sea, and death never wants for company. This is the hard truth."

Next to Wataru, Kutz bit her lip and kept her silence.

"In normal times, we dragons are not permitted to intervene in the conflicts of the land-dwellers. Yet, Traveler, Highlanders, we knew you would visit our island. And we knew that when you did, we would aid you on your passage to the north."

Wataru looked up. "Jozo told me that you had sensed a change in Vision from a while ago. He said a time might come when the dragons had to leave their island and lend aid to the people."

The wyrmking nodded twice slowly.

"What is this change he was talking about? Is it something we can stop? Is that why you say you will help us?"

The ancient dragon nodded once more. "Traveler. In this Vision there exists a mirror, the Mirror of Eternal Shadow, opposite to the Mirror of Truth. This mirror is in the hands of the emperor of the north. I sense that the seal that lies upon that mirror will soon be broken. I know this because it is our sacred role to watch for signs of this and prevent it from happening."

And so did Wataru finally learn of the Mirror of Eternal Shadow, the Dark, and the Crown of the Seal that held the terrible power of the mirror at bay—and about the final gemstone.

When the wyrmking had finished speaking, Wataru's hands and feet, so recently warmed by the hot spring, were frozen cold with fear. He knew who was trying to break the seal.

Mitsuru. He wants that last gemstone. That's all he'll think about.

Kutz glanced at Wataru, who was clenching his fists. What she had said was right: Mitsuru didn't care a whit about what happened to Vision or its people.

"The emperor of the north broke the seal once three hundred years ago— he sought to use the mirror against his enemies," the wyrmking sighed. "We dragons flew to the north and fought alongside the land-dwellers against the demons that were released from the Dark. At the time, the Northern Empire sought to use the demons' power, but it was ignorant of the danger. They thought they could simply break the seal, repairing it after the demons had laid waste their foes. Their foolishness was such that one could tilt the very sea on its side and still not wash it all away."

If the dragons had not sensed the breaking of the seal early on, Vision would not exist today, the wyrmking told them. At his side the seven pillars nodded in agreement.

"Even so, when the Mirror of Eternal Shadow was unsealed three hundred years ago, it was for only the briefest of moments. This time, I fear this will not be the case. The seal will be broken wide open, sundered beyond all means of repair. Even should we gather forces from all over Vision, we would not be able to drive back the demons."

"We have to stop them!" Meena cried shrilly.

Wataru stood. "I know who is trying to open the seal. He's my friend, a Traveler like myself. I won't let him do it. I'll stop him!"

The wyrmking's head slowly swung to the side, turning his gaze toward the seven pillars. They were all standing at full height.

"Traveler. Go with the seven pillars. They will aid you in this fight. Though there may be limits to the world of men, there are no such limits in Vision. It would be a shame for all Vision to be destroyed by those who are limited in sight and and strength."

"I will!"

"What about me?" Jozo's young voice rang out. "Wyrmking, may I go with him?"

Wataru hurriedly put his hand on Jozo's neck. "No Jozo. You should stay."

"Why? If you're going, I want to go too."

"Your parents will be worried."

Indeed, Jozo's parents were giving them a sorrowful look. Jozo looked back, and Wataru thought he saw the glimmer of tears forming in the young dragon's eyes. Still, he gave his tail a firm shake. "But I'm going. I'm carrying you, Wataru. Please?" he said, turning to his parents.

Jozo's mother lowered her head to the ground. It was his father who spoke. "If the wyrmking allows it, then yes."

"What?" Wataru turned back to the wyrmking. The wyrmking's eyelids lifted slightly, and he looked at Jozo. "Jozo. This will not be an easy battle."

"I understand."

"Even as we speak here, I feel the time of the seal's breaking approaching. Danger is upon us. The demonkin are destructive and powerful. You would still go with the Traveler?"

Jozo shook once from head to tail, then said, "Wataru saved my life. I will go with him!"

"Then it is done," the wyrmking said, lowering his eyelids once again. "Once one is bound to a Traveler, one is bound to duty as the descendant of the great protector, the firewyrm himself."

Those sleepy, half-lidded eyes turned back to Wataru. He could feel their gaze upon him, scalding his skin. "Traveler. Jozo will aid you. Be sure that he returns to the Isle of Dragon at your journey's end."

Wataru swore he would, his fists tightly clenched by his sides.

"Then I wish you luck in battle. May the Goddess of Destiny protect you."

All the dragons gathered and repeated the wyrmking's words in a great chorus, until the cavern was filled with the echoing words of their prayers.

Chapter 48
The Broken Capital

The seven pillars flew in formation, like an archipelago in the sky. They beat their powerful wings with the currents in the wind that flowed far above the sea. Kutz rode on the neck of the dragon in the lead. Jozo, carrying Wataru and the others, brought up the rear. He pushed himself to the limit so as not to fall behind the group.

They were making straight for Solebria, the capital of the Northern Empire. The wyrmking had told them that the Mirror of Eternal Shadow lay in the very center of the capital's palace.

"The Northern Empire protects the mirror not just with the Crown of the Seal but with powerful magical barriers. As it stands, no one without knowledge of these barriers may find it. But your friend—the other Traveler—is a powerful sorcerer. He will do whatever it takes to dissolve any obstacle in his path. Undoubtedly, he will break through to the chamber wherein lies the Mirror of Eternal Shadow. Before he destroys the wall of magic, we will not be able to find it. Yet if we wait too long after he destroys it, we will be too late. Our window of opportunity is brief."

The dragons flew at a tremendous speed. Wataru clung tightly to Jozo's back. *Faster, faster! To Mitsuru!*

Before long, the coastline of the north appeared on the horizon. The calm sea and the ground below them looked as peaceful as it did in the south, yet the sky above them was thin and frozen.

"What...what's that?" Kutz pointed ahead, shouting.

In the distance several lines of smoke were trailing up from the ground into the sky.

"That's the direction of the capital!" one of the seven pillars said. "It's a fire! The city's on fire!"

The dragons increased their speed, and before long, they could see the giant capital city, the walled metropolis of Solebria. It was falling apart. The great gates set into the castle walls had burned down and people could be seen running in panic. Dust and smoke rose from the many-colored roofs of the clustered houses beyond the wall.

"What's going on down there?" Kutz growled, leaning forward over the dragon's head. The dragons pinned back their wings and picked up speed as they descended. They dropped until they were directly over Solebria.

Buildings had collapsed into the streets and flames shot up from the rubble. Smoke flowed through the air like a noxious river. To the right, a section of the castle wall itself had collapsed. Directly beneath them, houses were toppling to the ground. The echoes of destruction and the hot wind blasting past mingled with the people's screams.

"What's going on?" Wataru stuck his head over the edge of Jozo's wing, and spotted several things moving through the vast city below. They looked like people, but they were far too large—larger even than the dragons. Wataru watched, speechless, as the giant gray beings thrashed through the city streets.

What are they? They look like giant robots made out of rock. Their heads were round, their shoulders broad, and their torsos impossibly thick. They swung massive arms and legs and crushed houses with a single swipe of a fist. People couldn't escape getting trampled underfoot. The screams and cries flowed together into a cacophony of noise, all swallowed by the thunderous crash of mortar against cobblestone.

"Those are golems!" Kee Keema shouted. He was looking down at the destruction beneath them with wide eyes. His body shook with rage.

"Golems?"

"Giants of rock crafted by sorcery! Whoever made them is their master—they do whatever he says!"

"I thought those things were from fairy tales!" Meena cried, her face pale. "I can't believe they really exist!"

"Me neither. But they're doing way too much damage to just be a fairy tale!"

The golems looked much like stone statues with smooth, featureless faces. Their hands, too, were more like lumps of rock than anything human. They continued their rampage, ripping the city apart.

"It's Mitsuru," Wataru said, his eyes streaming with tears from the smoke. "Mitsuru made the golems—he's controlling them!"

And he's destroying Solebria. Where are you, Mitsuru? Where?!

Off to one side, a great column of fire rose from the city. The impact of the wind from the blaze made the giant dragon lose his balance, and the tip of his right wing caught on the shell of a ruined townhouse. Meena screamed and nearly fell off his back.

"How many of those creatures are there? I can't even count them!"

"Look at that!" one of the other dragons shouted. "There are even more of them up there! Their numbers are increasing!"

The golems were everywhere throughout the city. Some even stumbled into each other and began fighting. Even when they lost an arm, or their head fell to the ground, they seemed to feel no pain. They continued moving through the city as though nothing unusual had happened. Everywhere Wataru looked new golems continued to spring out of the wreckage with a noise like thunder, one after the other.

"We have to destroy them!" Meena shouted, hitting Jozo's back with her tiny fists.

"Sure, but how?" Jozo shouted back, his voice a half-whimper. He opened his mouth, and flames began to lick past his fangs. Wataru hurriedly crawled up onto his neck. "No! If you breathe you'll roast the people along with them!"

The dragons cast their collective shadows on the chaos below as they circled the city. The people of Solebria were scared to death, yet the golems stood their ground, waiting.

"Help! Help!"

"Mama? Where's my mama?"

The screams from below reached Wataru's ears as they cruised only inches over the tops of buildings. A young man clung to the chimney of a steepled roof, crying for help. Jozo whipped back around, and Wataru reached his hand out for the chimney. Though his eyes were filled with fear, the man extended his arm. Wataru was about to grab the man's wrist when a golem punched its heavy fist through the wall of the house. The roof collapsed and the man flew through the air in an arc. Wataru lost sight of him beneath the wreckage and billowing dust.

Why? Why? Why?

"Traveler, look with calm eyes. The golems make for the palace," one of the seven pillars called out to Wataru. Kutz rode on its back. She was gripping the base of its neck tightly between her knees, brandishing her black whip in one hand.

"Wataru, look!"

The golems had formed a circle as they advanced through the city. As they moved forward, the band tightened. At its center stood the core of the Imperial Capital of Solebria: the milky-white stone palace.

"That's the emperor's castle, the Crystal Palace!" Kutz shouted over the roaring the flames below. She put a hand to the side of her mouth. "Your friend Mitsuru is heading for the Crystal Palace, destroying the city as he goes!"

"A golem-mage cannot stray too far from his creations, lest he lose control of them," one of the seven pillars said. "He must be nearby. We will do all we can to slow their advance. It is up to you to find this Traveler, Mitsuru. Stop the golem-mage, and you stop the golems!"

"R-right!"

Wataru followed Kutz's example and stood up on Jozo's back, gripping the dragon's neck tightly between his knees. A gust of wind blew, rocking him, and the smoke made him cough. Kee Keema moved his body to serve as a shield, and Meena wrapped her tail around his waist to hold him steady.

"Mitsuru! Where are you?"

Jozo flew just ahead of the golems, gliding above the mountains of rubble. More than once a golem's fist nearly clipped him, but he avoided injury by darting and squirming through the air.

"Mitsuru!" screamed Wataru as loud as he could.

Just then, through a curtain of smoke and dust, Wataru saw him. He was sitting on the shoulder of a stationary golem. His black robe fluttered in the wind, and as always, he gripped his magical staff in his hand.

"There!" Wataru pointed. Jozo saw him too and headed in his direction. When they were as close as they could get, Wataru leaped from Jozo's back onto the golem's shoulder. He landed right next to Mitsuru.

"Be careful!" Meena shouted after him.

Wataru stood on shaky legs, to see Mitsuru looking at him with that familiar cold stare. The eyes of the two Travelers met from across the lump of stone that formed the golem's head.

"What are you trying to do here?" Wataru asked

"What does it look like?" Mitsuru spread his arms. "Pretty cool, huh?"

Wataru felt his knees buckle beneath him. *I'm not scared. I'm angry.* "Cool?! This? This destruction?"

"Ah, the great capital of Solebria, home to the emperor himself!" Mitsuru's voice rang out like a song. "Solid as a rock, yet see how it crumbles!"

To their side, another golem was busy destroying a large mansion. The vibrations from the carnage made it hard for Wataru to keep his feet. Yet Mitsuru stood almost leisurely, staff under one arm, hands crossed before him.

"This destruction, this killing, it's pointless! Stop it! Stop it, now!"

"Pointless? On the contrary, it has a point. A very crucial point," Mitsuru retorted. His hair was filthy with the dust and grit that came swirling up from the wreckage beneath them. "This is the only way I can get what I want."

"To possess the gemstone? To break the seal on the Mirror of Eternal Shadow?"

It was the first time Wataru had seen Mitsuru look honestly astonished. "How did you know that?"

"Do you know what will happen if you break the seal on the mirror, and the demonkin come through? Three hundred years ago, during the war..."

"I know about all that," Mitsuru said, cutting him off.

Wataru stood, his teeth clenched. "What?"

"I said I know. The first emperor used the demonkin to wipe out some barbarians who were giving him trouble. From the sounds of it, it was quite effective."

Wataru felt the blood rush to his head. "Quite effective?! If the dragons hadn't come to stop them, the demonkin would've destroyed all of Vision!"

Mitsuru squinted his eyes in the smoke, seeing for the first time the great dragons soaring through the air above his army of golems. "Would you look at that. Since when did you make friends with the dragons?"

"They told me what happened," Wataru shouted over the noise. "Three hundred years ago, the seal on the mirror was broken for only a short time. Even still, that put the whole world in danger. What you're trying to do will destroy it for sure!"

"Probably."

"Are you mad?!"

The golem they stood on was acting like a command tower. While the other golems advanced, it remained perfectly still in the midst of chaos. Beneath it, the ground buckled, and a hot wind blasted past them, making it impossible for Wataru to climb over the golem's head and get to Mitsuru.

Stop the golem-mage, and you stop the golems. If I can take down Mitsuru, I can end this destruction.

But Wataru couldn't even draw his sword. His hand grasping the hilt shook uncontrollably.

"You still don't realize, do you?" Mitsuru said, sounding like a schoolteacher frustrated with a student grappling with a simple calculation. "Remember what I asked you in Sono? Did you come here to make friends with the people of Vision? Did you come here to defend peace in this world?"

But the scene that rose in Wataru's mind was not his conversation on the wharf with Mitsuru, but his late-night talk with Kutz atop the water tower in Gasara. *Even if someone is your friend, if they do wrong, you must tell them.*

"No. We both came here to Vision to change our destinies. But that doesn't mean we can do whatever we want. It doesn't mean we can kill."

Mitsuru slouched his shoulders as he had done so many times before: at school in the real world, on the temple grounds, whenever he met Wataru. He lifted his chin, and cast his eyes to one side. "I think we can. And I do."

And there's nothing more to say...

"You're wrong." Wataru's voice sounded pitifully weak in his own ears. There was no way Mitsuru would be able to hear him over the noise of the destruction around them. "You can't do this. The people here in Solebria, they're alive. We can't just take those lives because it suits us!"

Mitsuru whipped back around to face him. "What? Are you going to recite the code of the Highlanders for me?"

Before Wataru could respond, Mitsuru stamped his foot lightly on the golem's shoulder. "Know what this thing is made of?"

What is he talking about now? "It's rock, right? You made these golems with your magic."

"Yes. They're my puppets, fashioned from dirt and rock. But that's not all." Mitsuru smiled. "One other material is needed: a person. No matter how skilled the sorcerer, a single person is needed to make each golem. How did you think I got so many people? It's quite a large number, you must admit."

Wataru's eyes were fixed on Mitsuru's face. *What is he saying? It's like he doesn't even care. Like he's bored, sitting in the back of the classroom, listening to a teacher drone on about nothing.* With considerable effort, Wataru wrenched his eyes away from Mitsuru and looked out across the city smothered in smoke and flame. There were so many golems he couldn't begin to count them. *These were all once people?*

"If a person should look into the Mirror of Eternal Shadow, they become a shell—a husk without a soul. Turns out the Imperial Family was turning people into shells right and left to suit their needs. They would force them to look into the mirror and then use the mindless automatons they created as slaves to do heavy work in the hinterlands. They did the same to political prisoners and common thieves. It's much quicker than throwing them in prison and trying to return them to society in any meaningful way."

"Are you sure?" Wataru was stunned.

"I heard it straight from the emperor's daughter herself, and I can't see why she'd lie about such a thing. Still, it worked out well for me. I was surprised how readily the shells took to the process of transformation. They made fine golems."

There were many of these shells in the Crystal Palace itself, explained Mitsuru. "You see, you need a person to make a golem, but try as you might, the souls always get in the way. No matter how hideous or bent a man may be, he still has a soul. Use one of them, and you get a golem that just won't listen when you tell them what to do. It's a real pain. But here, the work was all done for me. These shells have no souls, so they made the perfect materials."

Mitsuru continued, "You say I am being cruel. But I wasn't the one who took these people's souls away. It was the emperor. Tell me, what do you think of that, as a Highlander? Hard to forgive, isn't it? So what of it if the emperor's city has to be destroyed? The whole family deserves far worse punishment, don't they? And the people of Solebria—every citizen of this empire—share their crime. They stood by and looked on silently while the emperor did whatever he pleased, and it's been like that for generations. Many even stepped forward and supported him. Why? Because they stood to gain from it. Or maybe they thought they were more important than the people they were crushing. These people deserve their punishment. I would think a Highlander would agree."

The smoke is making my eyesight blurry. The vibrations are making my head throb. The screams of the city as it collapses are making my ears ring.

Which way is right? Where's the justice in any of this?

"You think Vision is important. But this empire isn't as goody-two-shoes as your United Southern Nations. Why, I should think they will thank me for what I've done here. Now there's no worry at all that the North will invade." Mitsuru tossed his head to the side and laughed. "They can make all the powered boats they want, but with their leadership in shambles, you can bet they won't be starting a war anytime soon."

Before he could even form the thought in his mind, Wataru was leaping, lunging at Mitsuru.

And then...

A white flash of light enveloped the ground, the sky, everything. The dragons flying overhead and the golems wading through the town became black silhouettes against a blaze of white.

Wataru reflexively threw his hands up to shield his eyes, hunching over. Then the light was gone as abruptly as it had come.

"There we go," Mitsuru said, a satisfied look on his face.

Wataru lifted his eyes. The light disappeared, but something was different about the city. It was bright—and the light wasn't coming from the sun.

It's the emperor's castle, the Crystal Palace! The looming edifice was glowing from within, as though it was truly made of crystal—from the tops of its towering spires to the great stone foundation at its feet.

"The city is broken," Mitsuru said, looking up at the incandescent palace. "And with it, the barrier."

Mitsuru grunted and waved his staff through the air and disappeared with a flash.

Wataru blinked. He had seen that flash before. *Warp magic! Mitsuru's gone to the palace!*

chapter 41
The Mirror Hall

"Wataru, over here!"

Wataru was still standing on the golem's shoulder when Jozo thundered through the air beside him. Atop his back, Meena reached out with both hands.

A moment after Mitsuru disappeared, the golem underneath Wataru had begun to move. It was joining the rampage with both arms swinging.

Wataru leaped and latched onto Meena. A moment later a powerful stone fist jabbed upward through the air. Jozo flew out of range with an awkward lurch.

"Where's Mitsuru?" yelled Kutz from behind. Her face was black with soot.

"The Crystal Palace!"

"Then that's where we're going! No time to waste!" Kutz grabbed onto her dragon's horns and hugged her body low to its neck. The creature headed toward the Crystal Palace.

"You okay, Jozo?"

"You bet!" Jozo clenched his jaws and followed the larger dragon. Even Wataru could see that the young dragon had taken his share of beatings. The fires had scorched places where collisions with the golems and building wreckage had knocked off some of his scales.

The ring of golems around Solebria was tightening, drawing ever closer to the Crystal Palace. People were running madly through the maze of rubble and burning debris that was their city.

Wataru shouted to the dragons flying near them. "Get the people as far away from the Crystal Palace as you can! Everyone needs to go outside the city walls!"

They all nodded and spun off in concert. Meanwhile, the dragon carrying Kutz was rapidly streaking toward the city's capital building.

Wataru sensed something. It had the distinct flavor of magic, but he wasn't sure what it was. He had felt a similar stirring in the air at the Triankha hospital, and also at the Port of Sono.

"Look out, Kutz!" he screamed.

But just as he shouted, the outline of the Crystal Palace warped. A moment later, a great whirlwind arose from the middle of the castle. The spinning column of wind quickly became a cylinder, growing steadily, enveloping Kutz and her dragon in the blink of an eye.

"Look out!!"

Jozo's wings rippled as the cyclone waves blasted them. Wataru's cry was lost in the roar and they were pushed back from the castle. Tossed like a handkerchief in a washing machine, Wataru and his friends were unsure which way was up or down.

Throughout the city, the golems wavered as the cyclone winds buffeted them. Rubble from fallen buildings lifted into the air, pelting anything that continued to stand. One stone house was ripped from its foundation and tossed afar. Something looking like a fiery watchtower flew through the air directly over Jozo's head. It crashed into the castle walls, falling to the ground in a dazzling pyrotechnic display.

"Hold on!" Jozo screamed. Kee Keema grabbed Meena with one hand and wrapped his other around the edge of Jozo's wing. "Wataru, my leg!"

Wataru reached out, grabbing Kee Keema's ankle with both hands. The winds had pushed him off Jozo's back until he was hanging with nothing but empty sky below his feet. They were falling. The ground came hurtling towards them. *Falling, falling...*

Then, as though a giant hand appeared from below to cushion the fall, Wataru felt them rise once again. Jozo tilted his wings, regained control, and took off toward the sky. In relief, he roared a spiraling ball of flame.

"Is everybody okay? Nobody dropped off?"

"All here, Jozo!"

They had been tossed nearly to the outer city walls. The other dragons were fighting to remain near the cyclone. Wataru could see them beating their wings, railing against the powerful winds. He counted them: one, two…all seven were there. *Which is Kutz's dragon? Where is she?*

"Kutz!" he shouted, but the wind snatched the cry out of his mouth and tossed it away.

"Here! I'm here!" Kutz's dragon came flying down to where they were, one wing dipping lopsidedly as it came. It appeared to be slightly wounded. Jozo descended further. Wataru climbed up his neck until he was directly on Jozo's head. The dragon's eyes were filled with tears.

"That was too scary," Jozo muttered. "What was that?"

"Wind magic. Mitsuru wrapped it around the Crystal Palace so we couldn't come near." Wataru patted Jozo on the head. He felt like crying too.

When they were in flying formation with Kutz's dragon at last, he saw that the staunch branch chief was wounded too. She was covered with burns and soot except for one place above her right eye. The blood from a cut on her face had washed a little bit of the smoky grime away. "No way we can get in there now!" Kutz swore, gritting her teeth. Her whip hand was covered with blood. "Can you do something about that damn barrier?"

"I'm not powerful enough to break it," Wataru said, struggling to steady his breathing. "The only thing I can think of is to use warp magic to jump inside."

Kutz opened her one good eye wide. "If you could do that, why didn't you say so earlier?"

"I can try it, but I'm not sure it'll work. I can't control it like Mitsuru does. I don't know exactly where we'll end up."

"Nothing to do but try then!" Kutz said, lightly jumping from her dragon onto Jozo's back. "Let's go," she said, grabbing onto Wataru's arm.

"Go?"

"You're taking us with you! I'll warp too if I'm holding on to you, right?"

Wataru looked around at Kee Keema and Meena.

"You two help the people down in the city," he said. Then, before Meena could protest, he added, "Kutz and I will deal with Mitsuru!"

Meena's wide eyes reflected the red flames from below. "O-okay."

"You be careful," Kee Keema said, kneeling on Jozo's back. "All right,

Jozo! Once Wataru and Kutz are gone, you can take us down to the city. We'll help get the survivors to safety!"

Jozo gave his wings of a powerful beat. "Gotcha!"

Wataru shut his eyes and mouthed the words to the spell. He felt his body grow light and he could no longer feel the heat of the blaze or the push of the wind. *I'm a magebullet.* He shot into the air, streaking over the heads of the golems and above the capital city of Solebria. He was heading straight toward the Crystal Palace.

Suddenly, reality snapped back into focus. Wataru was floating in the air with Kutz by his side. Right in front of them they saw a large terrace, an elegantly decorated watchtower, and sweeping stone balustrades. It was the palace! The central spire caught the light of the sun, reflecting it back into their eyes.

For a split-second, Wataru saw a garrison of Knights lying upon the ground in the shadow of the arched gates. *Blood, blood, blood.* Gore had been splattered everywhere. Here was a steel boot lying haphazardly on the cobblestones. There was a silver helmet sitting in a fountain, filling with crimson-stained water…

"We're falling!" Kutz shouted. Like a pair of anvils, the two plummeted straight toward the blood-splattered stone terrace.

"Don't interfere!" A voice rang in Wataru's ears. It was Mitsuru. A light flashed in the depth of Wataru's eyes, and suddenly, it was as though they had collided with an invisible wall in the air. Magic impacted with magic, and the world around Wataru warped and exploded.

Kutz shouted with rage and confusion, grabbing on to Wataru's arm.

With a thud, they landed. They were on the ground. Wataru's neck jolted with the impact.

"Where are we?" Kutz looked around. Wataru held his head in his hands until the world agreed to stop spinning around him. He shut his eyes.

When he opened his eyes again, he saw green.

They could still see the Crystal Palace, but it was considerably farther away now. Still, they could see the shining spire and the walls much clearer than when they had been over the city. Thin ribbons of smoke flowed out of the many castle windows.

"I think we're on the castle grounds—this appears to be some kind of garden," Kutz said with disbelief.

Somehow, the two had been transported into one of the many beautiful gardens surrounding the Crystal Palace. A gazebo stood upon a simple stone platform. It was the Garden of Victory, the very place where Mitsuru had spoken with Lady Zophie.

"Quiet here, isn't it," Kutz said, standing and wiping away the blood that had run into her right eye. "Not even a palace guard to greet us."

"I think we're inside Mitsuru's wind-wall." Wataru tried to stand, but his knees gave out beneath him. Kutz held him up.

"So this was spared the worst..." Kutz began, and fell silent. Now that her eyes were focusing properly, she could clearly see that the garden had been ravaged. Flowers were scattered, several trees had been uprooted, and the fence that surrounded the garden leaned at an awkward angle.

In the shadow of one of the hedges, two men appearing to be guards lay with their legs and arms splayed out upon the grass. Their blood stained the dirt an ominous black. Mitsuru's winds had passed through here, with edges sharp as sickles. The storm had slashed through everything made of flesh.

"When we teleported above one of the terraces I was able to peek over the castle walls," said Wataru. "There were bodies everywhere. I saw a severed head, and blood pooling in the courtyard. I think the same thing happened in there that happened out here."

Mitsuru's message was clear:

—I'm going to get the Crown of the Seal and no one's going to stand in my way, be they knight or lady.

Wataru turned his back to the castle and looked out over the capital city. A great wall of wind enveloped the palace grounds, cutting off a clear view of the rest of the city. The light from the surrounding fires glowed like a diffuse crimson aura through the swirling winds.

"Why didn't we just drop on the terrace after we teleported?"

"Mitsuru knocked us away. He knew I was using warping magic, and he used his power to create a wall of some kind."

Wataru saw two drops of blood fall by Kutz's feet. "You're bleeding!" he gasped. "We need to get you some bandages."

"It's nothing," she said. Her right eye was practically glued shut with blood.

"I'm going to try again. Are you ready?"

"Who do you think you're talking to?" Kutz bound her whip tightly at her waist and grabbed on to Wataru's arm.

Wataru closed his eyes. *I can't just think myself there. I need to use the power of the third gemstone...I have to get it to take me to the Crown of the Seal—to the place where the Gem of Darkness lies. I have to listen to the gemstone's voice, I have to let it lead me.*

"Please, take us there," Wataru said softly, and he thought he heard a whispered "yes" in reply. "This is it!" he shouted to Kutz, and the two vanished from the Garden of Victory.

They became nothing but streaks of light, time stopped, and they shot across the sky.

This time they fell farther. Wataru lost all sense of direction. Eventually the two landed on the ground in a tangle.

He must've been knocked unconscious for two or three seconds. When he came to, Wataru was lying face down on a smooth floor. The blue translucence of the floor reminded him of Dela Rubesi. *That icy blue...just like the frozen capital.*

Wataru gasped and thrust out his arms, jerking upright.

He was in a vast hall. Round pillars stood in a ring, and upon each of the pillars was carved a figure wearing robes, a heavy crown upon his head. *Past emperors?* And then he saw Mitsuru.

He was standing alone in the middle of the large hall.

The floor, the pillars, the carved emperors, the high ceiling, everything reflected him standing there in his black robes. The entire hall was a mirror.

Kutz put her hand on Wataru's shoulder, leaning on him once before straightening herself.

Both of them found their gazes drawn inexorably toward Mitsuru. Then their eyes followed his, looking up to one side.

There it was: The Mirror of Eternal Shadow.

It was set between two pillars at the northernmost end of the chamber. It stood as high as Wataru, a perfect circle, tilted slightly upward. And in that mirror, positioned facing slightly upward, was...

Dark.

Impenetrable shadow filled the mirror right to its silvery rim. The darkness seethed, soundlessly surging against its confines.

Mitsuru took one smooth step forward. Then Wataru noticed something: a small star pattern at the mirror's base. Inside the pattern, set at its very center, was a crown. A single gemstone could easily be seen.

The Crown of the Seal, and the Mirror of Eternal Shadow.

The Gem of Darkness, too, was filled with the same burning jet blackness that roiled in the mirror.

Mitsuru lowered his eyes, still looking at the Crown of the Seal. He took another, larger step forward, revealing someone sitting on the floor behind him.

It was a girl. She was wearing an elegant white dress, her hair carefully bound. She sat with someone's head resting upon her lap—a man.

This, it occurred to Wataru, was probably the emperor himself, Gama Agrilius VII. He wore a richly embroidered robe, though it was tattered and ripped in several places.

Tears streaked the girl's face and her dress was soaked with blood. Wataru couldn't tell whether the blood belonged to her or to the emperor.

"L-Lord Mitsuru." The girl called out to Mitsuru in a trembling voice. He didn't even blink. His eyes were fixed on the crown and the mirror.

The girl's face seemed somehow familiar. Wataru thought hard. He had seen someone just like her before. *Who was it?*

"Don't know when to quit, do you?" Mitsuru said. He was still facing the mirror, but his voice was projected directly at Wataru. "Welcome. This is the mirror."

In response to Mitsuru's words, the darkness rippled around the edge of the mirror like water. "And this is my last gemstone, the Gem of Darkness." Mitsuru knelt slowly, one knee on the ground, reaching out toward the crown.

"Please, do not do this. Please!" the girl in the white dress said, sobbing. "Do not remove the seal on the mirror! I beg you!" Her deperate plea totally exhausted her and her body crumpled like a wad of newspaper. The emperor's head slipped off her lap with an awkward thud. She may as well have dropped a sack of potatoes. The emperor was dead.

Before Wataru could even think to do anything, Kutz's whip lashed out across the room. One spiked boot heel kicked against the floor, and her shoulders went back as she leaped.

Without even looking, Mitsuru thrust his sorcerer's staff casually in Kutz's direction. That slight gesture was enough to smack her back through the air like a ball, sending her flying over Wataru's head.

"Best not to waste your time."

From across the room, Kutz moaned softly. Wataru readied his Brave's Sword and fired a magcbullet. Mitsuru swung his staff again. The bullets transformed into fireworks in midair, spraying sparks on the walls and floor.

"Stop!" Wataru lifted his sword and charged. His feet pounded across the slick floor. The next moment he was flying through the air, helpless. He flew head first, crashing into the floor by the girl in the white dress.

"Believe me, I know what will happen when the seal on the Mirror of Eternal Shadow is broken," Mitsuru said, at last turning to face Wataru. His eyes were smiling. His mouth was twisted in a way Wataru had not seen before.

"Why?" The girl said, crying softly. "Why do this?"

"I am a Traveler, m'lady," he said, looking down at her. "If I claim this last gem, the way to the Tower of Destiny will open to me. That is why I came to Vision. How many times must I explain this?"

Across the room, Kutz stirred. She sat up and lifted her whip one more time. Wataru found he had trouble focusing on her. The impact with the floor had left his hands and feet dangling loose like ribbons. It was all he could do to keep a grip on his sword. He saw Kutz waver, dropping her whip, then hurriedly stooping to pick it up. She was cut terribly, and most of her face was lost behind a sheet of blood.

"To change your destiny?" the girl asked Mitsuru, tears dripping from her jaw.

"Indeed," Mitsuru said calmly. Wataru thought he saw, in that instance, something like familiarity in Mitsuru's gaze. "M'lady, with you by my side, I will return the scales of fortune to their rightful position, for they have tilted so very far from balance."

Wataru had no idea what he was talking about. The girl looked similarly confused. *She does looks like someone. I know her.* His searching hands found a fragment of memory tucked away in a corner of his mind.

"Mitsuru's aunt," he said out loud. "She's your aunt. She looks just like her."

I'm only twenty-three. I can't handle this—raising a kid. Tears welling in her eyes.

Mitsuru whirled around to face Wataru.

A fate most unfair, the iron chains of misfortune, a harrowing journey through Vision—could anybody turn back the hands of time? Who had the right to stop something like that? For a split second, deep inside, Wataru hesitated.

In that moment, Mitsuru reached down toward the Crown of the Seal, and softly lifted it from its place within the star pattern. He had never touched anything, or anyone, so gently in all his life—he held it as delicately as if he were handling his own soul.

"Stop!" Wataru's lonely cry echoed through the hall.

Mitsuru's staff was finally complete. Thrusting it into the air he shouted, "I'm giving you a chance to run, as a friend. Now get out!"

Mitsuru began to chant, and a mighty wind wrapped itself around Wataru. His feet left the floor, and he was floating in the air. Wataru thrashed about with his hands, finding the white dress of the girl beside him and grabbing on to it.

"Hold on!"

The hall disappeared around them.

Chapter 50
The Parting

Solebria had collapsed into a smoldering sea of rubble, swallowing thousands of innocent citizens. Those who were lucky enough to find themselves alive trickled from the city like blood dripping from a wound.

In the middle of it all, the Crystal Palace sat quietly.

A single column of light shot from the highest spire toward the vault of the sky above. It left the scarred and broken land below and reached for the heavens. Wataru instinctively knew that the light revealed the path to the Tower of Destiny—the destination of all Travelers in possession of all five gemstones.

Wrapped in his black robes, Mitsuru was flying up the column of light. No one could stop him now. No one could block his course.

Down below, survivors watched until the tiny black figure was sucked up into the blue and disappeared.

At that same moment, the wind died. The great cyclone that had ravaged the palace faded until there was nothing more than a gentle breeze.

The golems trembled ever so slightly before coming to a halt. Their magical switches had been turned off. In the midst of the dust and wreckage, the golems stood silently.

Then, as if by decree, they turned to dust, crumbling like sand castles swept away by the ocean's tide.

Here, one dropped to its knees. A head crumbled, flowing down over its shoulders. A fist evaporated. One by one, the golems disintegrated without a sound or cry, mingling with the wreckage of the city. Soon there was no trace of them at all.

Nothing else moved in the city save the persistent flames. Yet these too faded. The great blazes soon lost their strength, reduced to nothing more than severed tongues of fire searching for nourishment.

Or perhaps it was merely intermission. Those who remained felt the ground tremble beneath their feet. Something was rising from deep below in fits of violent energy—there was a crashing sound of a thousand hoof-beats.

The Crystal Palace once again blazed with a light inspired by the rock it took its name from. The castle began a bizarre transformation. The four square wings collapsed. The main arch sagged. Towers leaned. Terraces warped.

It was collapsing in the most unconventional manner. The entire structure shrank to a single point—that point being the emperor's throne. The shining milky-white rock of the castle was folding into itself, being sucked into a singularity. A thousand mouthlike windows gave off a soundless scream, then they, too, were swallowed.

In the space of only a few seconds, the entire Crystal Palace had disappeared.

In its place, a mist black as night began spreading. It swirled as though it were made of a thousand tiny black birds. In mere moments, it took over the space left by the castle.

The black mist then spread out, forming two wings, rising into the sky. The wings beat slowly, lifting what had slept within the ground higher and higher.

The Mirror of Eternal Shadow.

It hung in the sky like an inverted sun, raining darkness down on the wreckage of the city below. The surface of the mirror shimmered with the joy at its release from eternal bondage. Then, it began to spit a flood of darkness into the sky.

Far away in the National Observatory at Lourdes, Dr. Baksan sat with his spectacles perched upon his nose, poring over the pages of a thick manuscript. He stood on his specially crafted wooden boots, surrounded by the chatter of students busy at their work. A tiny feathered pen moved in his hand, annotating a passage of particular interest—

The doctor's eyes opened wide. The color drained from his face.

"Is something wrong?" Romy asked from nearby.

Dr. Baksan's little mouth was gaping. His eyes swam, looking out the window. "No…" he muttered. Before Romy could catch him, he toppled off his high boots and fell crashing to the floor.

The Spectacle Machine circus troupe had arrived in Gasara several days earlier and set about preparing for their first show. The city was still under the command of the Knights of Stengel. High Chief Gil had been arrested, and the branch stripped of its power. The Knights closely monitored and controlled all movement, not just in and out of the town but within the town itself. People were restless and worried. Troupe leader Bubuho aimed to mend that with the most uplifting performance he could muster, given his limited time and resources. Thus he was engaged in instructing Puck and the other acrobats in the intricacies of a new routine when one of the circus workers ran up. "Bubuho! Granny wants you to come right away!" he said breathlessly.

Bubuho frowned and made his way over to Granny's tent. When he stuck his head in through the curtains hanging over the entrance, he found her seated, staring with narrowed eyes at a crystal ball sitting atop a velvet cushion.

"Something wrong?"

The old woman looked up. "The seal has been broken," she said simply. The faint radiance of the ball shone in her eyes. Her voice was trembling. "The Mirror of Eternal Shadow…the demonkin come!"

Meanwhile, on the Isle of Dragon, the wyrmking stared up at the sky through the Stinging Mist. He saw in the swirling of the fog a sign that no one but he could read.

A shudder of fear and then determination coursed through his ancient body. "Dragons!" said the wyrmking, slowly rising. "The seal has been broken. The Mirror of Eternal Shadow has appeared upon the land. War is upon us. Let us lend our wings of steel to the Goddess, let us rise as defenders of Vision!"

The island, the sea, and even the mist shook as the dragons' howls of rage coalesced into a single oath.

We will rise. We will defend.

Where...are we?

Wataru's cheek was pressed to the ground. He could smell dust.

His eyes opened. The ground he was on was smooth and level. His hands lay before his eyes, covered with grime. His right fist still tightly gripped the hilt of the Brave's Sword.

Wataru twisted his legs around and sat up on his knees. The girl in the white dress was lying beside him on the floor. She was sprawled face down, like a broken doll. One of her shoes had fallen off. The fine silk of her dress was filthy.

Mitsuru had flown out of the mirror hall in the Crystal Palace. Wataru knelt, the world spinning around him, then slumped back down to the floor. He shook his head and tried to stand again.

He could see the city walls of Solebria far in the distance. *How far were we thrown?* He looked around. A sparse forest surrounded them. The grass was dry, and bare ground poked through in places. Rocks lay scattered here and there, as if they too had been thrown from the city.

It's cold. The wind on the north continent was hard and icy. Yet at least it was a natural wind.

What happened to the Crystal Palace? And Mitsuru? What happened while I was unconscious?

Kutz was nowhere to be seen. *Where did she get tossed to?*

The girl in the white dress moaned with pain, and her arms twitched. Wataru hobbled over and helped her rise. "Are you okay?"

The girl's eyes opened drowsily, and after some effort, she managed to focus on Wataru's face. "Where am I?"

"Near Solebria. We're in a forest—I don't see a road."

At the last moment, Mitsuru had told them to escape. *Escape from what?*

"The mirror."

Wataru looked back toward Solebria and swallowed. An inky black mist was swirling in the air over the city.

The dragons were above flying. Actually, they were fighting—they were fighting that mist. As he watched, the fog wrapped around one, sending the winged beast plummeting toward the ground.

Forgetting all else, Wataru began to run toward the city. Lifting his Brave's

Sword up, he fired a magebullet into the sky. "Jozo! Jozo! Where are you?"

After he had fired several more shots, he spotted a red speck low in the sky. *Jozo. He's coming this way—look how fast he's flying.* Directly behind him, a lump of the black mist had broken off from the rest and was giving chase.

"Jozo! Over here!" Wataru ran as fast as he could, waving his arms and shouting, but the next moment he stopped, speechless. He could now see the mist behind Jozo more clearly.

Wings. The mist has black wings. It's not a mist—it's a swarm! Each of the creatures in the swarm was as large as a man. They had sharp talons on their hands and feet, and emaciated bodies. Their skin was the color of night.

Demonkin!

"Wataru!" Jozo shot through the air straight toward him. He came down, flying so low he was only a few feet off the ground. "Get on! Get on! Quick!"

Wataru leaped and landed squarely on Jozo's back. Jozo wobbled in the air with the added weight, his leg nearly brushing the ground.

"The girl! Get the girl!"

The girl in the white dress was still standing where he had left her. Wataru reached out and grabbed her.

He had succeeded in getting half of her up onto Jozo's back when one of the demonkin following them lunged, clutching at her leg with a spiky claw. Slung over the dragon's back, Wataru found himself suddenly face-to-face with the demonkin.

It was a skeleton of bones, black to the marrow. Two holes glared out from above a grinning face. Where there should have been lips gleamed a row of long white fangs. No flesh covered the bones on its hands. It flapped its wings and made a sound like the screeching of twisted metal. Then the thing yanked at Zophie's leg, trying to pull her off the dragon. Turning her head to look at the demonkin for the first time, she screamed.

Wataru sat up on the dragon's back, clutching the girl with one hand while swinging his sword with the other. He aimed it at the thin, filthy hide that covered the demonkin's prominent ribs, thrusting the point in as deep as it would go.

With a grunt, the demonkin let go of Zophie's leg. Wataru was able to pull her all the way up onto Jozo's back this time. He took another slash at the voracious creature.

"Fly up! Shake them off!"

Jozo picked up speed, but the two stubbornly clutched the stump of his tail. Wataru slashed them away with his sword and fired a magebullet at the crowd swarming through the air after them. The bolt of light hit, scattering demonkin in every direction. They had gained a lead, as small as it was.

"Jozo, fire!"

Flame gushed right beside Wataru's face. Bull's-eye. The demonkin were hit square. They fell to the ground, trailing black smoke. Half of the swarm faltered in its flight, and a few of them began to fly away.

"Where's everyone, Jozo?"

"Meena and Kee Keema are with the pillars," he answered between gasping breaths. "I was too tired to carry them much longer. What are we going to do?"

The dragons were still in the air above Solebria. Wataru wondered what had happened to the one he saw fall.

Jozo was clearly exhausted. Blood streamed from cuts all over his body. His eyes swam in tears. He lurched as he flew, his flight path meandering like a snake, occasionally gaining altitude only to drop back down.

The girl in the white dress was rigid with fear. She moved her mouth but no voice came out.

"Take this girl to the forest," Wataru said pointing to a thick stand of trees ahead of them to the right. "You can hide from the demonkin in there. Stay out of sight until I come get you with the others, okay?"

"O-okay. But what will you do?"

"I'll be fine. Now, fly and hide!"

Wataru held the sword in both hands and prayed. *Take me to Meena. Take me to the dragon she's riding on!*

The warp worked. When the world snapped into focus around him again, he was sitting on the back of one of the seven pillars. The dragon was wearing a crown like a rooster's crest atop its head. Meena was holding on to the dragon's neck, but when she saw Wataru she sprang up and jumped through the air to him.

"Meena, are you hurt?"

"No, I'm fine, I'm fine!" She was pale and covered in soot. "Look at it, Wataru, just look at it!"

He looked up to see the mirror being lofted into the air on a pair of giant dark wings. It was a black portal out of which the demonkin armies came streaming, a spring of evil that would never dry up. They blotted out the sky over Solebria, flying to the north, to the south, to the east, and to the west. They would soon cover all of Vision.

The leader of the dragons was bravely flying toward the mirror. He breathed balls of flame and beat the air with his wings. He valiantly knocked away all demonkin that dared come too close. Yet there was no hope against such overwhelming numbers.

"We'll never make it to the mirror like this!"

"Yet we must try—just one breath—I must try!" the dragon's head whipped around, tearing a demonkin off its neck and tossing it into empty sky.

"We must run for now. We can't win against these numbers. We have to protect the people below from the demonkin, tell them to run into the forest. That's where we'll hide!"

"Never!" the dragon roared, spitting jet after jet of flame at the retreating demonkin. Wataru stood on his back, shouting at the top of his lungs. "Everyone, to the forest! Retreat! We'll be destroyed out here!"

"Wataru!" shouted Kee Keema atop a nearby dragon. He held his great axe high above his head. Though his face brightened at seeing his friend again, he had never sounded so disheartened. Behind him several of the wounded from Solebria hung on the dragon's back. The dragon protected them as they clung cowering to its scales, and Kee Keema, howling with rage, cut down the demonkin that came swarming in like insects. "Vermin! I'll send you all back where you came from!"

"To the forest! Get everyone into the forest!"

"Right!"

Enough demonkin now filled the sky to block out sight of anything else. Wataru flew on, occasionally shouting out Kutz's name. He watched the back of each dragon that peeled away from the onrushing black cloud, yet could find her nowhere.

Wataru's eyes swam with fear and anxiety, and he began to worry if perhaps he had already seen her and just not realized it. *Calm down. I have to calm down.* Wataru fended off a tangled cloud of demonkin with a few well-aimed magebullets while Meena gave the dragon directions.

Then, amid the rubble on the ground below, Wataru saw Kutz. She was brandishing her whip, standing guard over two Solebrians. One was lying on the ground, the other hunched over in a ball. They were children.

"Kutz! Up here!"

As they flew by, Wataru fired a few magebullets at the demonkin attacking them. Kutz was dancing on the fallen remains of houses, her whip slashing to all sides, knocking wings and grinning skulls off any demonkin foolish enough to come too close.

Wataru had the dragon fly low and hover next to Kutz's position. He jumped down to the ground. Behind him, Meena deftly wrapped her tail around the dragon's wing, swinging down to scoop one of the children up off the ground. Then she repeated the process with the next. "Got 'em!"

Wataru turned back to Kutz. "Hurry!"

"Just a few more of these to clean up!" Kutz shouted, sending her whip keening through the air to strike the demonkin directly in front of her. Her right eye was completely closed now, and her left arm seemed to be moving awkwardly. In fact, she could hardly move it at all. It must have been broken before when Mitsuru's magic had thrown her across the mirror hall.

"Leave them to me! You have to get on the dragon!" Wataru shouted, grabbing the back of Kutz's vest.

"What are you doing?!"

"Get on!"

The Brave's Sword slashed through a demonkin that flew at them with bared fangs. The dragon spat fire, clearing a path.

Kutz held her whip clenched between her teeth. Her left hand was useless, but she managed to lift herself up onto the dragon's back with only her right. Wataru slashed at demonkin after demonkin, his body drenched in cold sweat.

"Hang on, Kutz. Hang on!" Meena grabbed her arm, when one of the children began to scream. Two demonkin had snuck up from the rear and were climbing onto the dragon's back, their faces leering above its dully reflective scales.

"Meena, behind you!" Kutz shouted, and the whip fell from her mouth.

She stood on the dragon's back, launching herself at the demonkin with her bare hands. A swift kick knocked one of them off. Immediately, she turned and began to grapple with the other. Though she managed to push it back, its fangs flashed, and the foul creature bit deep into her neck. There was a spray of startlingly bright blood.

"Get your teeth off me!" screamed Kutz in a rage. She reached for the demonkin's throat with her right hand. Meena kicked at the demonkin's torso and clawed at its face. Kutz was knocked off balance and fell, and the demonkin came down on top of her.

"In your dreams!" Kutz shouted, twisting the demonkin's neck with her right hand. She successfully wrenched the head from the body. The decapitated corpse slid off the dragon's back. Wataru fired a volley of magebullets into the swarm of approaching demonkin, then leaped on top of the dragon. "Fly!"

The dragon lifted into the air. Meena held tightly to the crying children. Wataru crawled over to Kutz, still lying on her back.

She was still grasping the demonkin's head she had torn off. She took a second to examine it. "Handsome one, aren't you," she spat before tossing it aside. "No one kisses my neck on the first date and gets away with it."

Despite her jests, the cut on Kutz's neck was gushing blood. Wataru took off his shirt, bunching it up, and held it to the wound. The soiled cotton garment rapidly soaked up the blood. "I'm fine," she muttered. "Don't look at me like that."

She was still smiling when she passed out.

The seven pillars were now reduced to five. Jozo lay on his side, sleeping quietly, save for the occasional pained snore.

Several of the refugees from Solebria were hiding in the forest with them. *How many had they saved?* Wataru counted only a dozen or two, no more. *Maybe some escaped to other places.*

A metropolis of one million people reduced to this in merely half a day. It boggled the mind. None among the survivors were unharmed. Some were in such pain it hurt them even to sit up, so they lay on their backs, blank eyes turned toward the sky and unresponsive to questions. Wataru saw a child consoling another child who was crying.

They couldn't treat the wounds properly—they didn't even have medicine.

The dragons, too, were covered with injuries. Heads lowered, they rested their wings and closed their eyes.

Dusk was already turning into night. The only source of light came from a slender crescent moon that hung like a thread in the sky. Inside the forest was like the bottom of the sea. All was quiet under a heavy current of sadness that slowed their movements and dulled their thoughts.

The coniferous trees of this northern forest bristled with thick needles, standing close to one another against the cold. The forest was not as colorful or as varied as the forests of the south. Yet now, it seemed that the trees were reaching out their branches as far as they could, covering Wataru and the others from sight. They hid those who had escaped under their boughs, and turned silent faces to the sky as though nothing were out of the ordinary in the space between their roots and canopy.

Now and then, they would hear the sounds of demonkin wings beating through the air above the trees. But these were only sporadic, and the attacks had ceased completely. Wataru wondered whether the demonkin could move at night. *Did they even need rest? Or would they blend into the darkness, awaiting the chance to strike?*

"Once we've rested and regained our strength, we will head back to our island," the dragons announced to Wataru. "The wyrmking is sure to have sensed the broken seal and will be preparing for war. Some of our kin may be coming this way even now."

"Regardless," said another, "we cannot hope to face them with the few we have here."

Meena and Kee Keema wandered among the injured, talking to them. Meena returned to report that she had found one with some knowledge of the local area. "He says there is a spring nearby, and if we pass through the woods to the west, there will be a rocky hill, where there is a cave large enough to hide us. I wonder if we can't get everyone to the cave before dawn?"

If they were going to move at all, it was best that they did it now during the lull in attacks. This might even be the only chance for the people in the woods here to survive another day.

"Right," Kee Keema said. "We'll take them to the cave, then we'll return to the Isle of Dragon. Then we need to get back to the south. They need to know as soon as possible, so they can get ready to fight the demonkin."

Wataru nodded, but inside he worried whether they would be in time. Worse, even if they were in time to warn the south, what could they hope to do? Even if they were to gather all the Highlanders and all the Knights of Stengel in the south, would they be able to stand against the demonkin hordes?

It's over—the words waited behind his trembling lips. *I couldn't stop Mitsuru from breaking the seal on the Mirror of Eternal Shadow. I failed.*

Mitsuru had won. This time, there would be no coming back.

"Excuse me..." a hesitant voice called out. Wataru looked up to see a short elderly man looking at him. His clothes were in tatters, and his hair was half singed off his head.

"What?"

"Your friend over there..." he looked back at a mound of grass a short distance away. Kutz was sleeping in the weeds. "She says she wants to talk to you."

Wataru put a hand on the tree and managed to stand up. He wobbled, and the old man caught his arm, steadying him.

"Th-thank you."

"Can you walk?"

Wataru couldn't begin to count the cuts and bruises he had endured that day. His left ankle throbbed like it was sprained, though he couldn't remember twisting it.

The old man lowered his voice. "I'm no doctor, but I was a medic with the Imperial Army in my youth. I know what a dying man looks like."

Wataru looked into the old man's eyes.

"Your friend, she's not doing well. I'm afraid if we don't get her help..."

Wataru pulled at the man's elbow, and they stopped. The man patted Wataru's arm lightly, but said nothing.

"Isn't there something you can do? If there's any way we can save..."

"The wound is deep, and she's lost a lot of blood. We can't do much about that. I believe she's aware of the situation herself."

That's why she wanted to see me.

Part of Wataru didn't want to face it. He didn't want to know. He walked slowly, dragging his feet. Yet he walked, and soon he could see Kutz lying in the shadow of a low thicket. Someone had thrown a shirt over her. The wound at her neck was wrapped with strips of cloth. An old woman sat by her side, gently patting her arm.

"My wife," the old man told him. "That we both made it this far is thanks to you."

Kutz's face was paler than the moon. Wataru walked softly over, taking her hand in his own.

"You okay?" she asked, her voice the same as always—perhaps a little weaker.

"Yeah. I managed to make it without getting hurt too bad." He tried to smile. "You too. That's a nasty bite you got, but you're looking good."

Kutz chuckled deep in her throat. "Yeah, well, I'm not so sure about that. I've been hurt before, but never like this." She spoke calmly, quietly. Kutz was never quiet. Even when she was sitting in her chair back at the branch in Gasara, the blood always seemed to be boiling just under her skin. That's who she was. Not this quiet person lying here in the grass.

"Don't give up so easy," Wataru said, trying to sound tough. "Rest tonight and you'll be fine. We'll go back to the Isle of Dragon and get you some proper medicine. Okay? Just got to hold on a little longer."

Kutz released her grip on Wataru's fingers and lifted her hand to his cheek. "I'm sorry," she whispered softly. "I asked the impossible of you, brought you all this way, and it was all for nothing."

"It's not your fault, Kutz." Wataru said, but his voice quivered, and his eyes burned.

"And look at me. Here I am leaving before you...I can hardly ask for forgiveness, can I..."

"Don't say that!"

Kutz smiled and looked at Wataru. She gently brushed his cheek.

Wataru heard footsteps coming across the grass. He looked over his shoulder, thinking it was Meena, and saw instead the girl in the white dress. She was standing, clutching herself with both arms.

"The emperor died, didn't he?" Kutz asked in a hoarse whisper.

"Yes."

"Can't really call it a success, though. Lost my whip too."

Wataru felt Kutz's hand on his cheek, her fingers—so soft. He had never realized how gentle, how delicate her hands were.

"I'm afraid I may have made a terrible mistake. Not just this time, but so many times before."

Wataru wanted to tell her, "No, that's not right," but his mouth remained closed. She wasn't talking to him. She was talking to someone else only she could see. Her good eye wasn't focused on him. She was already back home, in the south, the familiar sound of the busy Gasara streets ringing in her ears.

"You're the chief, Kutz. You're my chief," Wataru said, putting his hand over hers. "You're a great Highlander. You were always faithful to your duty, and you did what was best to protect Vision."

She smiled up at him. "Thanks."

Wataru saw his own face reflected in her eyes. "Wataru. You...you have to make it. Don't die."

Wataru nodded. A tear ran down his cheek.

"Your journey...it's not over. It's nowhere close to being over. Don't even think about giving up."

Her last words were barely more than a breath. Wataru had to lean close to hear. The old man knelt down next to his wife and looked down at the fallen Highlander. "We are Solebrians. You saved us. Can you hear me?"

Kutz moved her head almost imperceptibly, looking in his direction.

"You will go meet with the Goddess now. Until the day you are reborn, you will become a light shining over Vision."

Kutz closed her eyes and took a deep breath, then whispered in a hoarse voice. "Yes. I'm ready."

"Before you leave this land, would you like to give a prayer of atonement? We can help you."

Kutz nodded. Her lips moved, forming the word "please," but no voice could be heard.

The old man held one of Kutz's hands. His other hand he put upon his own chest. Beside him, his wife put her hand to her chest as well. She gently stroked Kutz's forehead with the other.

"We are the children of the Goddess. We leave the dust of the earth, and rise to you." The gentle words of a prayer flowed from the old man's mouth. "Light most pure, source and mother of all, lead us now. Light the darkness at the feet of this traveler who now comes to join you. Wash away her sins, and ready a place for her soul in the heavens."

The old woman brushed Kutz's waving hair.

"Little child, child of the land. Do you repent your trespasses in the Goddess's eyes?"

Kutz, eyes closed, nodded ever so slightly.

"Do you repent your sins as a child of man, the conflict, the anger, the empty struggle, the foolish ignorance?"

Kutz nodded again.

"Do you repent the lies, your own greed, your failure to accept the glory that the Goddess has given unto the children of man?"

Kutz nodded yes a third time. The old man replied with a silent nod of his own. "Here then your penance is done, your sins upon the land wiped clean as you were at birth. Be at peace, child of man, for you will surely be called into that eternal light's embrace. *Vesna esta holicia.* Though a child of man knows time, life itself is eternal."

A single tear welled in the corner of Kutz's eye. Then it trickled up her forehead, falling into her black hair.

At once, the strength went out of her hand that Wataru still held to his cheek.

Wearing a faint smile and looking at peace, despite her many wounds, Kutz died.

The old couple were crying too. The woman stroked Kutz's forehead again and again. Wataru joined their whispered prayer.

Sleep, child of man. Sleep.

chapter 51
The Traveler's Path

Wataru didn't want to see anybody else crying, and he didn't want anyone else to see his own tears. He walked to the edge of the woods, hiding behind a tree from the thin light of the crescent moon. Alone, he wept.

Where had all the sadness come from?

He had been sad when he met his father that time in the park. He had been even more sad when he had run from his mother as she fought with Rikako on the balcony. He had never thought he would be sadder than when Uncle Lou came to drag him out from under the bed afterward.

That's right. I didn't want to be sad anymore. That's why I came to Vision to change my destiny. Yet here I am feeling like my heart will break, crying like a baby.

If this is the way it's going to be, I never should've done anything in the first place. I should've grit my teeth back in the real world if the end result was going to be the same. No matter where I go, sadness follows. No matter how much time passes it won't go away. You get only one heart when you're born, and you can't turn it in or get it repaired. The only thing that fills it is more sadness. I'm surprised there's any room left in there at all.

Wataru cried and cried until it hurt to breathe. He wrapped his arms around the tree and hugged it tight, pressing his cheek to the rough bark, and waited until his breathing slowed.

My destiny…

I tried to change it, and only ran into a new sadness. What will happen if I try to change it again?

What has to change, what needs *to change, is my, is my...*

My what?

What can I possibly do, here in this corner of a Vision just waiting to be destroyed by a horde of demonkin?

Wataru heard soft footsteps coming across the grass. He looked up, quickly wiping his eyes with the palm of his hand.

It was Meena. She had been crying too. "There you are."

"Yeah."

"I...I said goodbye to Kutz."

Her eyes were the color of the night forest. Wataru wondered if his eyes looked the same. Maybe the forest was covering the pain of their loss, and the failure of all their plans, so they wouldn't have to see it in each other's eyes.

"How is everyone else?"

"They're resting."

"Good." Wataru wanted nothing more than to leave this place, and then he remembered he had a good reason. "I'm going to go take a look around before we bring the survivors to the cave. There might be some more who lived out there. I'd hate to leave them behind."

Meena shook her head. "There's no one."

"How can you be sure?"

"How far would you go? It's too dangerous to go back to the city."

"I'll be careful..."

Before he had finished speaking, a large shadow loomed from behind Meena. It was Kee Keema. His face was frozen. He was damp, cold, and exhausted. The lizard-like skin around his eyes was drawn tight with grief.

That's right. It had always been Kutz's passion that kept us going. There were so few like her, with that indomitable energy. There would never be anyone to take her place.

And yet...

"Going on patrol? I'll come too," Kee Keema offered.

Good ears. Wataru sighed. "I was thinking of going back by the city gates. There might be some people there who couldn't walk with the others this far."

"You're right," Kee Keema said, reaching for the axe on his back and pulling it out of its harness. He looked at Meena. "We are Highlanders. Even if

The girl was shivering terribly. Her dress was too thin to protect her from the cold. Her teeth were chattering. "Please, take me with you. There might be someone left—someone from the palace."

Wataru hesitated a moment, then took off his jacket and gave it to her. He would have put it on her himself, but she was taller by a head.

"We were just going as far as the city walls. If it doesn't look like we can go inside, we'll have to stop there."

"That is good enough." Still trembling, the girl drew Wataru's jacket over her shoulders.

Though it had been the gentlemanly thing to do, Wataru was now feeling cold wearing just a shirt in the chilly air. "Didn't you hear what everyone was saying back in the forest? The Crystal Palace is gone. They say it was sucked into the Mirror of Eternal Shadow. I don't imagine anyone in the castle survived."

The girl's cheeks were pale with cold and fear. But when Wataru turned to rejoin Kee Keema and Meena, she followed him.

Now they were four. Meena walked in the rear, staring at the girl in the white dress. "Are you from the castle?" she asked as they walked.

The girl hunched her shoulders and didn't answer.

"That's a nice dress you're wearing. Nobility, are you?"

The girl still said nothing. Perhaps she could hear the barely concealed thorns in Meena's question.

"Well, you must be of high birth, at least. Tell me: when the capital was being torn to pieces, where was the emperor's army? Where are they now? Aren't they even going to try to help their own people?"

Before Wataru could say anything, Kee Keema cut in. "When those golem monsters were tearing the city apart, I saw several groups of Knights come down from the castle. They didn't stand a chance against those things. They were crushed. If any of the troops were left behind in the castle, well, I suppose when the mirror came out…"

Meena was bristling. "Then what about the rest of the army? And what about Sigdora—those special forces? Where were they? What are they doing? You know, don't you?"

From what he had seen in the mirror hall, Wataru could guess who the girl in the white dress truly was. She was none other than the daughter of Emperor Gama Agrilius VII. She was a princess.

And she looked exactly like Mitsuru's aunt back in the real world.

As Wataru had met people that were the spitting image of his father and Rikako, so had Mitsuru met ghosts from the real world too. Wataru still didn't understand the meaning of what Mitsuru had said to her just before he left for the tower. *What did he mean, the tilted scales of fortune?* And that cheating man and woman he had met in the Swamp of Grief were doing the same thing as his father and Rikako were, and justifying it with the same twisted logic. Yet he had never thought of any of them as being particularly fortunate or unfortunate. *Who had Mitsuru met in his Vision,* Wataru wondered. *What did they remind him of? What did they make him think about?*

"Sigdora isn't an army," the princess said in a voice barely more than a whisper. "There's nothing they could do at a time like..."

"They're useless, then?" Meena said quickly, cutting her off. She turned up her nose in disdain.

The emperor's daughter stayed as much in Kee Keema's shadow as she could. Her lips trembled and her body seemed to shrink. "I fear that the palace guards are all gone, if what you say is true. The Imperial Army's elites, led by General Adja, were sadly missing from Solebria at the time the seal was broken. They may be rushing toward the city even now. If they have encountered the demonkin along the way, I expect they are already in battle somewhere out there on the road."

"So you mean to tell me they're out there fighting for the people?" Meena said, pursing her lips with distaste. "Even though Solebria is destroyed? Even though the emperor is gone? Who will take charge of the North? Who will lead the armies now?"

If blood lineage had anything to do with it, the responsibility for the army would fall to Lady Zophie herself. Perhaps that was why she was so desperate to locate Crystal Palace survivors.

"Give it a rest, Meena," Kee Keema gently scolded. "I know how you feel, but now's not the time."

"Give what a rest? I'm just asking her some questions."

"So give the questions a rest, all right? Talk too loud and you'll bring the demonkin down on us."

The remains of the city walls stood before them. The location of the gates were further to the east of where they were now, but they would be easy to find if they decided to follow the main road. Still, none of them savored the idea of walking out on a road or any other open place.

"Maybe we could climb over? Nah…let's just walk around until we find a place with easy access."

This time Wataru took the lead, with Kee Keema bringing up the rear. Lady Zophie cowered behind Wataru's shoulder, walking as close to him as she could without actually bumping into him. Wataru could feel Meena's eyes burning into the small of his back.

"You remember that old couple that prayed for Kutz back there?" Meena said suddenly. Kee Keema and Wataru were busy searching through the wreckage and listening for any sign of people. It seemed that Meena had entirely forgotten their purpose for coming here. Her face was frozen in a scowl, her eyes glaring at the girl's slender back. "They said that about ten years ago their children left for the south, taking their grandchildren with them. They were looking for a way to escape. That's why they said those prayers to the Goddess. It didn't make sense for believers in the Old God to be asking the Goddess for forgiveness.

"Just like my family," she added in a small voice. "For the people living in the Northern Empire life was hard, even for those who were lucky enough to be in the rich capital. The only people living any kind of good life were the royal family and those surrounding them. Everyone else struggled to make it through every day. And now that the seal on the mirror has been broken, not only the North but all of Vision is in danger. What good did the emperor ever do? None! I bet even now he's run off somewhere, worried more about saving his own hide than helping his country."

This was more than Zophie could stand. She whirled around to face Meena. "My father is dead!"

"Father?" Kee Keema's eyes opened wide. "Then you're…"

"Zophie, the daughter of Gama Agrilius VII," she said, standing tall and looking straight into their eyes. "I am the successor to the throne. Now that my father is gone, it falls to me to defend the country and move our armies."

Meena stood dumbfounded. But she quickly recovered, a belligerent gleam in her eyes. "Then what in the Goddess's name are you doing here?! Shouldn't you be off somewhere leading?"

Wataru stepped between the two. "Stop this."

"Stop what?!"

"It's not like you, Meena, to talk this way."

The fire went out of Meena's eyes as though doused with water.

"She might be the empress-in-waiting," said Kee Keema, "but how is she supposed to do anything all alone like this, huh?" Meena turned her back to him, whipping her tail around so fast it slapped into Wataru's side.

Kee Keema looked up at the wavy top of the wall. "How far do we plan to walk tonight? I still think it's too dangerous to go inside."

"It would be nice if we could climb up somewhere—get a view of the city."

"We won't be getting up the wall here. Too high. There must be a place where it's fallen down a bit."

They began walking along the wall again. After a while, they heard a faint noise, like a person weeping. They all stopped and perked up their ears. After a moment they realized it was only the whistling of the wind.

"Still, that's an odd sound. I wonder what it's blowing through. Maybe something up there?" Kee Keema pointed up ahead to a place where rubble had spilled out through the city wall. Burned beams jutted out of the wreckage like leftover fish bones after a meal. "Maybe we can climb up on those?" Kee Keema walked over and tested one with his foot, but it crumbled almost immediately. Though it looked solid, it was like trying to climb a hill of sand.

"That's funny…" If these were the remains of a house or some building, they should be a bit more solid, Wataru thought. *And what's with all the sand and rock?*

Then it hit him. *It's a golem.* This mountain of rubble was the remains of a giant golem.

Mitsuru's words rose fresh in his mind. Each golem required materials: sand, rock, and a person. The stone giants that wreaked havoc in the city were themselves more sacrifices to Mitsuru's cause.

"Wataru," Meena said, grabbing his sleeve. "Do you see something glimmering in there?"

Wataru looked in the direction she was pointing, and there, in between the lumps of sand and earth, he could see a tiny shining light.

Could it be? But how…

Still uncertain, Wataru put a hand on the hilt of his sword. The light flared brighter, shining on his face.

There was no mistaking it. Wataru calmly drew his Brave's Sword and held it up before his eyes.

The spirit in the gemstone spoke to him.

—*Alone I waited a long time in my prison for you to come, Traveler.*

A pure curtain of light began to spread before Wataru's eyes. The curtain opened, and the figure of a tall man stepped through, wearing long-sleeved robes of platinum, and a veil of the same color over his hair.

The fourth gemstone. Even now, when all seemed lost, and Wataru himself was nearing the depths of despair, the gemstones still hadn't given up hope on him.

—*I am the one who honors what is true in people, the spirit of mutual grace and friendship. Though many of flesh and blood lived here in this northern land, they had long forgotten to honor life. They had long forgotten the true path. I was buried in the frozen earth, embraced by stone, and made to sleep.*

Wataru knelt on one knee before the spirit and lifted his eyes.

—*Do not waste your life in vain, or take life in vain. Where there is faith, there is also kindness and forgiveness, and where there is forgiveness, there will you find true balance—the most coveted prize of all. It is easy to stray, misled by one's own greed, or by easy pleasure. Men are weak, and many step off the path never knowing it. It is nothing but a gentle lie to say that most will find heaven when they die. Traveler, by your faith, forgive those who stand in your way. Yet, if they should seek to betray truth, then wield justice to bring their journey to its rightful end.*

The fourth gemstone came down, like an angel descending from on high, and found its place in the hilt of Wataru's sword. The Brave's Sword glimmered once, sending a wave of energy coursing through Wataru's body.

"D did you see that, Wataru?!" Kee Keema gasped, then quickly knelt on the ground and bowed his head low. "It's a sign, a sign from the gemstones!"

Then he leaped to his feet, picking up Wataru in his arms and lifting him high over his head. "Did you see it? Did you see it? The Goddess is still waiting for you! Your journey isn't over yet, not by a long shot!"

Wataru's eyes swirled with the sudden motion. *How can he have so much strength after today?* "Okay, okay! I saw it, Kee Keema! I saw it! Now let me down!"

Kee Keema didn't cry when he heard about the death of Kutz. But now tears streamed down his face.

"You're a Traveler too?" Lady Zophie said, almost staggering in surprise.

"Yes. Mitsuru and I—we come from the same place in the real world. We were friends."

"Then you, too, will follow Mitsuru to the Tower of Destiny?"

Wataru's momentary elation quickly cooled. He still lacked the final gemstone. His Brave's Sword was not yet complete. Mitsuru had already found his—the Gem of Darkness—in the mirror room of the Crystal Palace. If his was there, then where could Wataru's be hiding? Did he even have enough time left to find it?

The wind whistled through the wreckage once again.

Meena's ears shot up. "What's that sound?

Fweeew...

"That's not the wind! That's something calling..."

The four tensed, looking around, trying to determine the direction from which the strange whistle came. On top of the city wall? Beyond the mountain of rubble? Hidden in the night grasses?

Just then a cloud moved away from the moon, and the night brightened around them. Something small and swift darted under the clear moonlight, slicing through the wind.

They heard the sound of wings flapping nearby. But before they could react, a bird of pure white appeared suddenly, perching on Wataru's shoulder.

"Now, now. No need to be so startled," the bird said, its red beak snapping open and shut.

"Wh-what's that? A bird?!" Meena practically shouted in surprise, forgetting where they were. Zophie slid behind Kee Keema's back. The waterkin's big mouth was wide open.

"Why it's me," the bird replied, and the next moment was enveloped in a cloud of white smoke. Wataru leaped back.

Wayfinder Lau was standing before him.

For the space of several seconds, no one said anything. Wayfinder Lau stood with his jaw firmly shut, obviously expecting someone else to break the silence.

"Well, say something," the old man said at last.

Wataru's jaw moved, but no words came out of his mouth.

Wayfinder Lau's long eyebrows lifted, then sank. "Is this all the greeting I get? I would think such a reunion deserving of a bit more fanfare."

"F-f-fanfare?" Wataru squeaked. His heart was doing somersaults in his chest. "Wayfinder Lau? What are you doing here?!"

"What, this old coot is the Wayfinder?" Kee Keema snorted.

"This is the guy who guides all the Travelers?" Meena asked incredulously.

Wayfinder Lau lifted his staff and gave Wataru a sharp crack on the head. "You ask me why I have come? I came because you called for me! But if you've no need of me, I suppose I'll be on my way."

"I-I called you?"

"You wanted to know where the last gemstone might be found, didn't you?"

At once, a palpable tension spread over Wataru and his friends' faces.

"You'd tell me?" Wataru asked, his voice cracking. His heart did another somersault, refusing to settle back into place.

"If you have the will to continue your journey, then I shall," the Wayfinder said almost casually, looking up at the night sky. "Yet you must hurry, or the demonkin will pick up your scent for sure. Now is no time to tarry."

Suddenly, time lurched back into motion. The clock was ticking. Wataru felt a chill run down his spine. "Tell me! please!"

Now that he wanted him to hurry, Wayfinder Lau stopped, staring long into Wataru's eyes. Wataru remembered when he first met the old man at the Village of the Watchers. Then, as now, the Wayfinder had looked at him long and hard, as though judging him, measuring his worth…

The way he's looking at me now, it's even harsher than when I first came here. He's measuring me on a different scale. Have I become heavier somehow? Is the old scale not big enough to measure me anymore?

"Will you confront Mitsuru again?"

"Huh?"

"Listen up, boy. I'm asking if you plan to confront Mitsuru—if you're ready to face him."

Wataru looked back at Meena's face, then up into Kee Keema's eyes. "I am," he answered at last. "I've pretty much already been doing that for a while now."

"It won't be like it was before," Wayfinder Lau said, tapping at the ground with the butt of his staff. "You see, the fifth gemstone, the one you need to transform your Brave's Sword into the Demon's Bane, is none other than the very same Gem of Darkness that Mitsuru has already claimed. Though there may be two Travelers, there is only one final gemstone."

Then how am I supposed to get it? Mitsuru's already left. Why didn't you tell me this sooner?

Wayfinder Lau watched Wataru's eyes, reading his thoughts. His staff connected with Wataru's forehead once again, just as it had in the Cave of Trials.

"It will not do to make such an ill-mannered face at a Watcher, boy. Yes, the final gemstone you need is in Mitsuru's hands. Therefore, should you wish it for yourself, you will need to take it from him. Understand? *Take it from him.*"

Up until now, Wataru's competition with Mitsuru had been a kind of parallel race. He had never had to challenge him directly. He had never tried to take something away from him.

Why does the last challenge always have to be the hardest?

"Then I have to fight him. I have to fight him and win," Wataru said, half asking, half-telling himself. Wayfinder Lau said nothing.

You can win, someone said. For a moment he couldn't tell who it was. It was a voice he had never heard, high, yet firm, and full of resolve.

It was Meena. Her eyes glimmered in the reflected light of the crescent moon. "You can win. I know you can, Wataru. You will win. You have to go."

How can you be so sure? Wataru felt his heart shrink. *I couldn't even draw my sword when we were standing on top of that golem. I can't even win an argument with Mitsuru. How can I win a fight?*

Meena hadn't seen any of that. She hasn't seen the weak me.

"You will go even if you cannot win. You will go because you must. If you do not know this in your heart, I will not open the way for you."

Wataru looked up, into the Wayfinder's eyes. *An old man's eyes, wrinkled and teary. How does his gaze skewer me like that, like a knife going right through my heart?*

Though the old man's mouth was closed, his question rang in Wataru's mind.

—*What will you wish for at the Tower of Destiny? What do you wish for most, right here, right now?*

What do I wish for most? What?

Wataru could hear Kutz's voice as though she were standing right next to him.

—*You're a Highlander. You swore an oath to defend Vision. If you would break that oath, you aren't fit to wear the firewyrm band.*

Wataru looked down at the band, still circling his left wrist. He touched it lightly with his fingers.

What do I wish for most?

Then he saw the meaning behind the Wayfinder's question. He knew what he was searching for. How could he not know? It was a straight path—there could be no stepping off. But once he chose that path, he would never be able to choose another. *Am I okay with that? Is that what I want? Will I not regret it? Will I achieve what I set out to accomplish in the first place?*

Charity and wisdom, bravery and faith, all in the sword.

It isn't my destiny that has to change.

It's me.

Wataru looked Wayfinder Lau straight in the eye. "I'll go. I'll confront Mitsuru and take the Gem of Darkness from him. I have to go to the tower. Wayfinder, open the way for me."

chapter 52
Wataru Alone

A single column of light rose into the night sky.

Even the moon seemed surprised, its light becoming focused as if it were squinting in disbelief. Below, the clouds stopped in their rolling path for a moment. Only the Blood Star maintained its cold composure, glittering red where it hung in the vault of the sky.

A pure circle of light lay upon the ground before Wataru. Just one step and he would be inside. Wayfinder Lau had opened the way for him.

The Wayfinder stood off to the side, leaning upon his staff, watching over Wataru. "Well, will you go?"

Wataru nodded. He turned to look at his friends, Meena and Kee Keema. They wore the same expression: something close to, but not quite, a farewell.

"You're going alone, aren't you," Meena asked, but it wasn't really a question.

Wataru found himself smiling. "Yeah. This time I can't take you with me, no matter how much you kick and scream."

"Was I always that difficult?"

"You were just trying to keep me honest, I think."

"You kept me honest too," Kee Keema said in all seriousness. "And somehow, I think you were always right, Meena."

"Me too." Wataru looked at their faces again and the realization hit. They were not heading out on a new adventure. This was farewell. *From here on, I go alone. No matter what lies in store for me, I'm leaving them behind.*

He wanted to reach out, hold their hands, thank them. But he stopped himself short. *Not yet. I have to finish what I came here to do before thanking them, before saying my goodbyes.*

There was only one thing left to say.

"I'm going."

Meena suddenly launched herself into his arms. She was shaking. "Be careful, Wataru. Please."

"I will."

Wataru hugged her tightly, feeling her warm, slender body in his arms. Kee Keema stepped over and embraced the two of them in a great big bear hug. "Sorry we can't help you anymore."

"No, you can," Wataru said, reaching up to give Kee Keema a friendly punch on the shoulder. "We're all still fighting for Vision—even if we have to do it in different ways now. We're still helping each other."

Meena's eyes, wet with tears, opened wide. "Wataru—wait, what are you going to ask the Goddess?"

Wataru smiled, cutting her off. "It's a secret."

Wataru stepped back from his friends' embrace. "Kee Keema!"

"Y-yeah!"

"Still think I'm good luck?"

"You bet!"

Wataru's smile broadened. "Then let me wish good luck to you. May you win all your battles."

Kee Keema clasped his hands together tightly. "Leave it to me! I'm going to fight those demonkin for every inch of this land, mark my words!"

Wrapped in cold and solitude, Lady Zophie stood apart from Wataru and the others. But when Wataru turned his eyes toward her, she said, "Forgive me." Her fingers were intertwined, her head hung low. "It was I who told Lord Mitsuru the whereabouts of the Gem of Darkness. It was I who told him he could reach the gem if the seal upon the Mirror of Eternal Shadow were broken. And the result—was this."

Her voice was choked with a tide of painful remorse welling up from inside her. The more she said, the more her words pressed upon her with greater and greater weight. "I never imagined this might come to pass. I merely—I sought to ease Lord Mitsuru's sorrow. He seemed so sad, trapped inside the Crystal Palace—so lonely. It grieved me to see him so."

Slowly, Wayfinder Lau spoke. "Mitsuru deceived you. He used you for his own ends."

Zophie shook her head furiously. "I do not think that was the way of it. But—but the end result is the same. I did not perceive Lord Mitsuru's thoughts. In my cleverness, I believed I knew his heart, yet I knew nothing."

He didn't think to offer her comfort, or to console her, yet for some reason, Wataru found himself saying, "You look very much like Mitsuru's aunt in the real world."

Maybe Wayfinder Lau would understand what he was talking about. Wataru turned his eyes to the old seer's drawn face. He nodded knowingly. *Vision is a reflection of the Traveler's heart.*

"When I meet Mitsuru, I will tell him how he's hurt you. I don't know everything that happened between you, but I can see your pain for myself. I will tell him of your loss. He should know."

Zophie buried her face in her hands.

Wataru reached out to touch Meena and Kee Keema's hands one last time, then he smiled. Without a word, he stepped into the circle of light.

So bright.

The column of light went up higher, farther than he could possibly imagine. At first, he could see nothing. Then, while he counted off the rapid beating of his heart, the light coalesced before his eyes into a stairway leading up into the sky.

He began to walk. First one step, then another. Soon he was running, until his breathing became hard, and not once did he look back.

It was the same as it had been with Mitsuru. Wataru rose up the column of light, without hesitating, as fast as he could. He left the clouds below. He caught up to the moon and with the Blood Star. He continued upward, dwindling into the distance.

And then he disappeared.

"He's gone." Meena's whispered words were lifted away on the wind. "I guess that's goodbye."

"No, it's not." Kee Keema shook his head. "You forget what he said. We've all got our own roles to play now. Sure, we may be apart, but this isn't goodbye."

Meena had thought so too, but suddenly her certainty fled. "That's a lie!

We can say whatever we want, but that doesn't make it true. We'll never see Wataru again. We'll never even know what's happened to him!"

Wayfinder Lau took a step toward Meena. "My dear kitkin. Do you truly believe this?"

The circle of light had begun to dim. Slowly, starting at the edges, it melted into the night.

"If Wataru reaches the Tower of Destiny and makes his wish of the Goddess, and should she grant it, you will surely know. I believe that was his promise to you."

"Promise?"

Does that mean Wataru's really going to…?

Meena and Kee Keema watched as the column of light faded into the sky, leaving only a faint trace of an aura before it was gone completely.

"Now, children of Vision, go. Your trials await you."

The two looked back at Wayfinder Lau, but he was already gone. He left the way he had come, suddenly, with the soft sound of wings in the night.

chapter 53
Freedom

Even though he had been running uphill the whole way, Wataru didn't feel tired in the least. His breathlessness was more from excitement than exhaustion. He ran up the column of light, heading ever upward. The shining steps seemed to flow past his swiftly moving feet. Then at last he reached the top of the staircase and stepped into a wide open space.

Is this the top of the sky?

It was no less bright here than it was in the column. A luminous white mist swirled around him. He stuck out his hand and the mist clung to his fingers, sliding over his skin with a soft sensation, like touching silk in a dream.

A dome of fog hung low above his head. Looking down, he couldn't see his own toes. When he began to walk, it was like he was crossing a shallow river, sending ripples through its surface as he took each step. He saw nothing. He was alone. This place was vast, without limits, yet a warm sense of security wrapped around him, and he could feel his pulse steady.

Suddenly, he heard the chattering of birds from somewhere high above.

—*Who has come?*

Wataru's eyes widened in surprise.

—*A Brave has come?*

Though he hadn't heard it then, it was just like the twittering of the birds in the forest when Wataru visited the Village of the Watchers and met Wayfinder Lau for the first time.

—*Who has come?*

This time the sound came from behind him. Wataru looked around and called out into the mist. "My name is Wataru. I've traveled Vision and gathered four gemstones. Wayfinder Lau opened the path here for me."

Somewhere in the mist, the unseen birds began to chirp to one another.

Wataru, Wataru.
You have come far, Wataru.
He bears the Brave's Sword.
Welcome, Wataru.
You have done well, Wataru.

Then, the mist began to clear. Wataru's view widened.

He gasped.

He was standing at the entrance to an entirely new world up here in the sky—a city of crystal. Everything was translucent, shining with a blue radiance.

So vast, so huge. The city was crowded with building after building after building. Their eaves jostled for space, their roofs slanted, and their windows were open. It was like a giant work of art carved directly from a vein of crystal—the largest ever seen anywhere.

In front of him, far in the distance, stood a beautiful tower, poised like a slender woman against the backdrop of the blue sky. It was lofty and magnificent, appearing to have grown out of the crystalline city. Its spire was shaped like two hands clasped in prayer, pointing toward an even higher place.

Now that's *the Tower of Destiny.*

At its very top, where the fingers met, the Goddess awaited.

For a while, Wataru stared up at the tower, forgetting even to blink. It was so beautiful he felt that even to approach it would be sacrilege, yet its elegant form beckoned to him. *Come,* it said. *Here is what you seek.*

He slowly began to walk. Wataru's image was reflected countless times in every direction in the walls of the crystal houses and in the crystal street below his feet. He walked, and his crystalline image walked together with him.

It was not long before he noticed that some of the buildings in the city were beginning to look familiar. He remembered having seen that particular shape of roof, or that particular corner. *I know these places.*

That's it! This street here is Gasara. And there, those flat, connecting roofs are from Tearsheaven. Now that he noticed it, it was all he could see, and he began to run in his excitement. *What's that?* Off to his right stood a cluster of huts just like the ones in the Village of the Watchers. *That warehouse with the broken, hanging rain gutter—that's from Sono.* There was a corral from Maquiba. In the distance, he spotted a building just like the National Observatory in Lourdes, surrounded by the residences of starseers-in-training. Even the eerie form of the Triankha Hospital looked stunningly beautiful, its forbidding walls transformed into pure crystal. This magnificent city in the sky was a collection of all the towns and villages Wataru had traveled since he came to Vision, brought here, rebuilt. The only differences were that everything was made of crystal, and here, Wataru was alone.

Just walking through the city was like a reenactment of his journey. He saw himself reflected in the walls of the house from Tearsheaven. He remembered talking with the girl Sara. Next he climbed a steep street that reminded him of Sono. He could almost smell the sea in the air. And Bricklayer Street in Lyris! Here too, the doors to Fanlon's workshop were tightly shut.

There was only one road he could actually take, and that led toward the tower. There was no risk of getting lost. Wataru walked quietly through the great crystal reproduction of his memories. The farther he walked, the deeper into the city he went, yet he never seemed any closer to the Tower of Destiny. Whenever he looked up at it, it stood alone, dominating the horizon, as far away as when he first laid eyes upon it.

He passed under a small bridge. This brought him to one of the corridor houses he had seen in Tearsheaven. He remembered his surprise when the kind mayor had led him through a house with no furniture—a house built purely for walking through.

He passed through one house, and into another, then another. *Was this the way he had gone when he visited Sara's mother, lying ill in that hospital room?*

But the place where he emerged was no hospital. It was an empty, square room. Something was there, though: a small box attached to one of the walls near the far corner. It was a bird cage, made of solid crystal.

A white bird sat upon a perch in the cage. Wataru approached, touching the cage with his finger.

The bird was about the size of a canary, without so much as a spot on its pure white wings. Its round eyes were the startling blue of the ocean.

The bird twittered and hopped over near to where Wataru's finger was touching the cage. It was staring at him. Then it tilted its head, flapped its wings, and tried to land on Wataru's finger.

"You want out?"

The bird chirped. *It's answering me.*

"Okay. Hang on."

The door was held by a slender bar no larger than Wataru's fingernail. He pushed it up with the tip of one finger, and the door swung open without a sound. The white bird took a hesitant hop out, resting briefly on top of the door. Then up it flew, going in a circle above Wataru's head, before landing neatly on his right shoulder.

Surprised, Wataru took a step backward. The bird was practically weightless, yet it felt warm through the fabric of his shirt.

A scene unfolded in the back of Wataru's mind. It was a vision of home. Wataru was standing in front of the haunted building. It was night. The Daimatsus were there—father and son, both. And there, sitting in a wheel chair next to them, was…

Kaori Daimatsu.

Those black eyes. Always focused on something only she could see. A beautiful girl, without words or any other link to the outside world, shining hair falling haphazardly across her smooth cheek.

Wataru blinked and the vision disappeared. The small bird was looking at him.

This white bird—could this be Kaori Daimatsu? Well, not her…but her soul?

"Have you been in here this whole time?" Wataru hesitantly raised a hand, stroking the bird's little head with a finger. "Did someone trap you in this cage?" Wataru kept patting its head, and the bird closed its eyes. "That's it, isn't it. Kaori's soul was taken from her body and shut away here."

There was no wondering why. Wataru could feel the joy radiating from the tiny bird. That was enough.

"You're coming with me. Let's go home together."

With the little white bird on his shoulder, Wataru began walking again. When he reached the next room, he found another cage. Inside, another bird was waiting.

This bird was as black as the one on his shoulder was white. Even its beak was black. Only its eyes burned a fiery red.

Wataru stood for a moment, thinking. *I wonder whose soul this could be?*

The black bird opened its beak and croaked. Even though it was only the size of a canary, its cry sounded just like a crow's.

A light went off in Wataru's head. *I know who that is!* "Kenji! You're Kenji Ishioka!"

He and his goons had surrounded Mitsuru in the haunted building—Mitsuru had summoned that creature, Balbylone—and Kenji had been left without a soul. Just like Kaori Daimatsu.

"So you were in here too."

Wataru hurriedly opened the door to the bird cage. The black bird shot out like a bullet, flapping crazily around the room, smacking into the walls and ceiling with such force that more than a few black feathers fluttered to the ground.

"Hey, you'll hurt yourself. Come over here," Wataru said, offering his other shoulder. The black bird landed on his head, yanked at his hair, and made a horrible raucous cawing before finally hopping to his shoulder. "You're a troublesome one, aren't you."

The bird pecked at Wataru's ear in reply.

"Ouch! Knock it off." Wataru laughed. *It's Kenji, all right.* "Behave yourself, or I'm not taking you anywhere."

The little black bird blinked dejectedly. Wataru cautiously patted it with his palm. He could feel it trembling.

Oh. "You were scared."

Once again, a scene from the real world unfolded in Wataru's mind. Mitsuru stood, teeth clenched, his cheeks flushed, gazing at the dark creature he had summoned with his magic. Kenji was cowering with fear, his face as pale as ash.

"It's okay. I'll take you home too."

Here, in this crystal city sprawling at the base of the Tower of Destiny, Wataru had found two souls that belonged in the real world. Now they were riding on his shoulders.

He began to walk again, passing through the buildings from Tearsheaven, until he found himself walking down a street in the residential section of Lyris. He remembered when Branch Chief Pam brought him here and how shocked he had been to see the open discrimination at work in the town.

Eventually he came to a small park. There was a bench and some potted flowers. *This must be a part of Lyris too.* Everything was made of crystal, down to the delicate blooms in the planters.

Wataru happened to glance down at his feet, and stopped.

There was a pattern there on the ground, faintly glimmering. It looked as though something hard and sharp had been carved into the smooth surface of the crystal. The more he looked at it, the clearer its outline became.

Can I go back to the real world from here? Come to think of it, he *had* just gotten the fourth gemstone.

But he was no longer standing next to Meena with her piece of the Mirror of Truth. If he stepped on the sigil without the mirror, would it open the Corridor of Light all the same?

The white bird twittered next to his right ear. It was talking to him.

"Wait—of course. I get it." Wataru nodded. "I can take you two home first, can't I?"

At the end of this strange city, Mitsuru was waiting. Wataru would win—he had to win—but what if he failed? He forced himself to think about it.

Okay, then who should I go meet? Wataru didn't have a lot of time. Even as he was walking here, the demonkin were spreading through Vision below. He needed someone he could give the birds to without having to explain all the details, someone he could trust...

Wataru's face brightened. *Of course. How could I have forgotten? Katchan. My friend. My real friend in the real world. I'll go see him!*

Back in the real world, it was evening.

Katchan was upstairs in his room, sitting at his desk. He was swinging his legs back and forth. A textbook and his class notes were open in front of him, but he didn't seem to be studying. He was staring off into space, his elbow on the table and his cheek resting in his hand.

Outside the window, the last glimmer of pinkish light twinkled in the dusky sky. The veranda was empty—his mom must have already taken in the laundry. The warm night air floated steamily through the screen.

He stepped out of the Corridor of Light directly behind Katchan. For a moment, he merely stood there, staring at his old friend's back, the nape of his neck turned dark by the sun. He had probably been to the pool every day over summer vacation.

"Katchan," Wataru said, putting his hand on his friend's shoulder.

Katchan flew out of his chair so fast he knocked Wataru backward. Katchan's eyes were as large as chestnuts. His mouth opened wide.

"Sorry to scare you."

At the sound of Wataru's voice, all color drained from Katchan's face. Even his tan seemed to fade in an instant. "Wa-Wa-Wa…"

Wataru smiled.

"Wa-Wataru, is that really you?!"

He nodded. "Yup, it's me."

Katchan hugged him. Before he knew it, Wataru was crying.

"Where have you been? What happened to you? Where did you go?" Katchan fired question after question at his friend, shaking him by the arms.

"I'm sorry, Katchan. I can't talk about everything right now. I don't have time."

"Huh? What's that?"

Wataru grabbed his friend by the arms. "Look, I need you to do something for me. These birds…" The two birds were flapping their wings, clinging desperately to Wataru's shoulders. He could feel tiny claws pricking his skin. "Can you release them for me—just let them out the window or something? That's all you have to do. You're the only one I can ask to do this, Katchan. Please?"

Katchan's eyes were swimming. He looked like he might pass out.

Wataru reached out to steady him. "Stay with me, now."

Katchan's head wobbled on his neck. When he spoke, his voice was barely a squeak. "Why're you dressed so funny?"

Wataru laughed.

"You look like a character out of *Eldritch Stone Saga* or something."

"I guess I do. Look, I'll explain later—once I'm home for good. I'll tell you everything. I'm just in kind of a hurry right now."

Wataru gently picked up the white bird and held it out to his friend. Katchan loved animals. As disoriented as he was, he picked up the little bird with natural ease. "Where'd you catch this?"

"Actually, I freed it."

Katchan gave the bird a pat on the head with a tan hand. "I think I'm dreaming," he muttered.

"Probably not far from the truth. Open the window, quick."

Katchan shuffled across the room, carrying the white bird on the palm of his right hand, using his left to open the door to the balcony.

He stuck his hand out, and the white bird flapped its wings a few times, then suddenly took off. It swept past the railing and disappeared into the night sky.

"Now this one," Wataru said, holding out the black bird. The bird panicked, missing Katchan's hand and instead flying straight up to smack into his forehead.

"What's with you?" Katchan said, waving his hand around and snatching the bird out of the air.

"Whoa! Watch out! Don't crush it!" Then Wataru laughed. "Well, maybe you can crush it just a little. This one's given us a lot of trouble."

"This bird? Us?" Katchan's eyes were rolling in his head again.

"Yeah. But, we still have to let it go." The black bird didn't fly so well. First it slammed into the railing, then it came to rest on the laundry pole where it strutted and fretted for a while. Katchan leaned out and swiped at the bird with his hand, knocking it into the air. At last, the little black bird took wing and sped off into the night.

"That all you wanted?"

"Yeah, thanks."

Wataru felt a great weight lift off his chest. He took a deep breath, smelling the familiar smells of Katchan's room.

"Wataru…" Katchan began, sniffling.

"Thanks. I-I gotta go back."

Somewhere, far down the Corridor of Light, a bell was ringing.

"Go back? Back where? What's happened to you?"

I'm sorry, I can't say anymore. Wataru felt his resolve strengthen anew. *I have to get back to explain everything to Katchan, to tell him the story of all my adventures in Vision.*

"I'll be back soon, promise. Wait for me."

Wataru stepped back toward the corridor. Katchan reached out to grab him, but then the strength left his arm and his hand dropped. "Wataru!"

Wataru could hear Katchan calling for him all the way back down the corridor.

Back at the sigil, back in the crystal city. Wataru was alone again.
Time to go meet Mitsuru.

Chapter 54
The Last Fight

Wataru walked on through the crystalline collage of all the towns and villages he had seen in Vision. Eventually he came upon a vast ruin that stretched as far as the eye could see.

The Imperial Capital of Solebria.

There was no mistaking the crumbled city wall and the flattened houses. Everything was fashioned from the same crystal, making the broken pillars and the stripped roofs more otherworldly. In a way, the cityscape was even more beautiful than anything he had seen thus far.

If the shapes had been abstract, it would have truly been a work of art. As it was, Wataru lacked the words to express the irony of the view, but he could taste it like a bitter tang in the back of his throat. He hadn't been able to properly process the destruction of the real Solebria—the wounds were still too fresh in his mind. Though the translucent crystal rubble neutralized the feeling of tragedy, it could not lessen the rage, fear, and sadness he continued to feel.

He wondered what Meena and Kee Keema were doing. Did they make it safely to the Isle of Dragon? Had the south been warned about the demonkin invasion?

Wataru lowered his eyes and ran. He ran and ran and ran until something large and looming blocked his path. He had been going so fast he nearly collided with it. He caught his breath and looked up.

It was a large gate. It looked like the front gates to the Crystal Palace. Here, in this precise model of Solebria, the gates to the Imperial Palace stood impossibly unblemished.

For a moment, Wataru recalled the Porta Nectere. These gates were far smaller than the real thing.

The intricate crest carved in the middle of each door was most likely that of the Imperial Family. It looked kind of like a star chart with all the paths of the celestial bodies. Also included were a sword and shield, a night and dragon, and above it all, a single crown.

Wataru pushed and pulled at the doors, but they wouldn't budge. *A dead end.*

He looked around, but saw nothing resembling a way out through the sparkling sea of rubble surrounding him. If he couldn't get through the double doors, he wouldn't be going any farther.

He contemplated climbing the gate, but soon gave up the idea. It was far too slippery for him to get a good grip.

How am I supposed to get beyond this point?

Scratching his head and walking in circles, Wataru felt his anger and frustration grow. He gave the door a swift kick.

Ouch! That hurt. Wataru looked down at his throbbing foot and saw the faint outline of a pattern or diagram on the ground. It vaguely resembled the Corridor of Light star sigil he had seen many times before. But this pattern was only about half the size of a manhole.

Wataru looked around and found others—he counted five in all. They were all laid out in a semi circle in front of the gate.

He tried placing his feet on one of the patterns.

Suddenly Wataru felt an inexplicable joy well up inside his chest. He could hear laughter ringing in his ears. *Who is that? What is this?* He jumped back, startled, and the laughter faded.

He did it again and the same thing happened. He stepped onto another diagram and suddenly he felt angry. And just like before, the feeling disappeared when he jumped away.

The next pattern made him sad. The fourth made him so happy he wanted to skip.

But the fifth pattern did nothing.

Wataru carefully stepped away from the fifth pattern and folded his arms across his chest.

Joy, anger, sadness, and happiness. One emotion for each pattern.

It's just like the huts in the Village of the Watchers! Wayfinder Lau had been mad in the Hut of Anger, sad in the Hut of Sorrow, and gentle in the Hut of Kindness—all so his own mood wouldn't influence how he treated each Traveler who came to him.

Maybe this works something like that. Each pattern has an emotion associated with it. It must be some sort of riddle—but what?

Joy. Wataru stood on the first of the patterns, closed his eyes, and searched his heart. He thought about things that had brought him joy in Vision. Kee Keema loomed in his mind's eye. He remembered meeting him for the first time in the grasslands the day he left the Village of the Watchers.

"Oy! Ooooy! You there!"

That cheerful voice, and the darbaba cart racing across the grasslands, sending up a trail of dust into the sky.

"Don't eat too many o' those baquas now, y'hear?"

How he had been overjoyed when he heard Wataru was a Traveler—his "good luck charm." He picked Wataru up, tossed him in the air. Now that was joy—without a doubt, the first joy Wataru had experienced since arriving in Vision. He had done nothing but worry about what he'd gotten himself into until that moment.

There was a dull clunk, and the pattern disappeared from beneath his feet. Wataru blinked. At the same time, a sliding noise came from the gate, as though a bolt had been released.

I guess I've cleared the first pattern.

The next was anger. He stepped on the pattern, and without even consciously thinking of it, an image came to mind. It was of the two ankha boys who had tricked Meena into helping them steal, then snuck into her hospital room and threatened her. Wataru could feel his skin burn just remembering it. He had dived through the window, forgetting his own safety in order to save her.

Thunk. The pattern disappeared. There was another creaking sound from the door.

Onto the third. *Sadness.* This was an easy one too. His heart was still bleeding from the wound left by Kutz's death. She had tried to console him to her last breath. The feel of her gentle hand upon his cheek.

The third pattern disappeared. Wataru moved over to the fourth.

Happiness. This would be a hard one to narrow down. Listening to Meena singing atop the darbaba cart. The feast of the waterkin in Sakawa. All the good food he'd eaten at various lodgings. The conversations he'd had with his friends on the road. All the memories sparkled in his mind.

Then from among them, one memory stood out—the night he saw the performance of the Aeroga Elenora Spectacle Machine in the mountains outside Maquiba. Meena was a lively girl, but on stage she was incredible. Her high-wire tricks made Wataru fidget with fear even as they thrilled him. And he remembered the close of the show, when all the performers threw flowers. He looked at Meena and thought that she was the most beautiful thing he'd ever seen. He had clapped until his hands were red and raw.

Thinking about it now, all of his happiness and sadness in Vision came from the times he was with his friends.

Thunk. The fourth pattern faded. Another clunk came from the gate, and with a slow groaning noise, it began to open.

I did it!

Wataru thrust his fists into the air. The riddle hadn't been that hard to solve after all.

But what about the fifth pattern? It was still lying there on the ground.

Wataru tried stepping on the pattern again. Nothing happened. Maybe it was a blank, set there to confuse him?

Joy, anger, sadness, and happiness. What other emotions were there? Maybe it wasn't worth worrying about. The gate had opened anyway.

Wataru was running out of time. He turned his feet toward the gate. His heart thumped in his chest.

As he walked through, everything swirled around him. For several seconds, he could see nothing but a dazzling whirlwind of light. When his vision cleared again, everything had changed.

He was in the Swamp of Grief.

It was a perfect replica. The flat surface of the water somehow managed to look just as ominous, even in crystal. He half imagined that somewhere down there was a crystal kalon, waiting for prey, its sawlike teeth bared and menacing. The meager clumps of grass growing around the edges of the lake would cut a man's hand if he wasn't careful. If his feet should catch on a root, and he fell into the water, his body would freeze. The black water of the Swamp of Grief would numb him with its poison, slowly robbing him of life.

Am I supposed to cross this?

Wataru hesitantly took a step and found the surface of the lake to be solid under his foot, as though it were frozen. No matter what shape it took, crystal was crystal after all. Still, with every step, Wataru couldn't help but imagine the kalon swimming somewhere far below. What if it came up through the surface of the lake to claim its victim?

I'm fine, I'm fine. That can't happen. He walked hesitantly at first, but soon regained his confidence. From then on he walked normally. *I just need to make it to the other side of the lake.*

As he walked, he remembered what had happened to him in the real Swamp of Grief. He couldn't help it—the details of the vision he had seen there were etched indelibly into his memory: the other Wataru, the murder of Yacom and Lili Yannu, the stone-baby that had chased him.

Had it all been a hallucination brought on by the toxins in the swamp water? Had poison found a way into his heart when he met the pair who looked like his father and his father's lover? That would explain the horrible outcome of that encounter. He never wanted to go back to the Swamp of Grief again, and here he was walking through it once more.

Let's get this done with quickly. He tried to shut off his memories so he wouldn't have to see the faces of Satami and Sara again. And he especially didn't want to think about that crawling baby that continued to haunt him with every step he took. Wataru had to stop and shake his head to keep the phantoms at bay. He had reached the center of the lake. Seen from the middle, the Swamp of Grief was almost a perfect circle, rimmed by the marsh and thickets of sickly-looking grass.

Suddenly, a strange thought occurred to him. *The circle is like a stage. I'm the only actor in a show of one. And my audience? The sullen swamp air and a few muddy clumps of reeds. Lovely.*

Then he heard a voice.

—*Traveler.*

Wataru tensed.

—*Young Traveler, Wataru.*

The voice was mechanical, flat—if crystal itself could speak, it would probably sound just like this.

—*If you come to kneel at my feet, you must prove beyond all doubt that you are a Brave.*

To kneel? Is the Goddess talking to me?

—As the hand of the mother guides her child from morning to evening, I beseech you—call home the split soul, the wandering one. Call him back to you.

Call what back? How do I prove who I am?

The voice of the Goddess spoke again before Wataru had time to sort his muddled thoughts.

—Now, rise, and triumph!

At a loss, Wataru stood, then he saw it.

Something was approaching from the far edge of the lake—a person, walking toward him, one step at a time. Something about his gait seemed familiar—the shape of the head, the angle of the shoulders. Then he realized why it seemed so unnervingly familiar.

He was looking at his own reflection. It was another Wataru.

His jacket was off, a sword was stuck through the hempen belt at his waist, even the wear on the soles of his weather-beaten boots was identical. The only thing different was his expression. His mouth was twisted into a defiant smirk beneath a pair of eyes that were blazing with rage. The skin of his face was drawn tightly over his cheekbones, and Wataru thought he could see drops of blood splattered across the front of his shirt.

It was Wataru as he had seen him in the Swamp of Grief. Wataru the murderer.

That was just a hallucination. It wasn't real. It was a nightmare. None of that really happened. It's a lie, a liar, a lie!

Trembling, Wataru stepped backward. The other Wataru was rapidly closing the distance between the two of them. He came so close he could see the shadow his eyelashes cast on his face. In one smooth motion, the other Wataru drew his Brave's Sword.

His evil twin opened his mouth, but the voice that he heard was that of the stone-baby who had chased him in the Swamp.

"I've been waiting for you, murderer."

Then Wataru realized. This reproduction of the Swamp of Grief was no stage. It was an arena. A place of combat. He would have to fight this hallucination—this image of himself—right here and right now.

Rise, and triumph!

The other Wataru kicked the surface of the lake with the toe of his boot.

Wataru didn't have time to think. He didn't even have time to reach for his sword. In a flash, his double had closed the distance between them, and the Brave's Sword cut keenly through the air just below Wataru's chin. Wataru's legs buckled and he fell flat on his back, looking up at the sky. The inertia of his fall sent him skidding across the crystallized water.

Unable to change his direction, Wataru slid until he collided with the feet of his double who had run ahead of him. The sword was coming down straight at him. Wataru screamed and rolled off to one side. The edge of the sword bit into the surface of the lake, sending shards of crystal flying through the air.

Wataru crawled away, finally managing to regain his feet. His murderous double was behind him now. The sword swung a second time, coming so close that the wind from the blade's passage through the air was enough to slice into Wataru's ear. Blood trickled down his neck.

He didn't have time to feel pain. The blood was warm on his cheek, and droplets soaked into his shirt. Wataru's head spun with such fear and confusion that he couldn't tell which one of them led and which followed, which was real, and which was merely an image. *Is it him? Is it me?*

Wataru ran, but his reflection grabbed his shirt from behind, and pulled him down. They both fell to the hard surface of the lake. Wataru felt the coldness of the boy beneath him, and it sent a shiver down his spine. *What is this thing?* It felt like it was made out of ice.

But it's real, it moves, even though it's not alive and it's certainly not a ghost.

Wataru's adversary swung his arm, bringing the hilt of the Brave's Sword in his hand down on Wataru's head.

"I'm gonna kill you!" his double screamed, mocking him with his own words. The hatred emanating from his reflection was palpable.

Finally he managed to grab the hilt of his own sword. He couldn't think of any words, he merely prayed. *Fly!*

It was enough. In the blink of an eye, Wataru found himself on his back at the edge of the lake. He hadn't escaped completely, but at least he had time to stand up, catch his breath, and draw his sword. His legs and hands continued to shake and his shoulders heaved.

The other Wataru was still in the middle of the lake, standing straight and calm as though nothing had happened. *Even his posture mocks me.* His face was still twisted in an evil smile. He seemed ready to laugh out loud. This was the hardest thing to believe. *No matter how low I sink, I could never smile like that.*

"H-hey, you!" Wataru said through trembling lips. He lifted his Brave's Sword. It wasn't a fighting pose. He was gripping the hilt of the sword like a drowning man grips a life preserver.

"You're not me! You're not! You don't exist! You're a hallucination!"

Wataru fired a magebullet. His double easily dodged the glowing bolt as it arced over the lake. The next shot he caught with the blade of his sword, sending it straight into the sky like a meteor in reverse.

"You're not real!" With that as his battle cry, Wataru launched himself at his double. His look-alike broke into a run too, coming straight for him. Just when he thought his blade was in reach, the double leaped. His foot came down on the hand in which Wataru held his sword and jumped clear over his head.

Uh-oh! Wataru sensed the kick coming even before it hit him in the back. He went sprawling face first.

He's too fast. There's no way I can beat him like this. Despair and powerlessness morphed into fear. *What do I do now? How do I win? How can I even survive? I need to hide.*

Barrier magic!

Bracing himself against the pain, Wataru chanted a quick spell and moved the tip of his blade in the shape of a cross. His heart was already beating fast. The added strain of raising the barrier made his heart and lungs scream.

Wataru disappeared. His double narrowed his eyes, one hand at his waist, the other hand letting his sword point dangle down toward the lake. He was grinning.

Safe behind his barrier, Wataru began to move, slowly. *If I can only get close enough to strike.*

He could feel his strength draining away. The pain made his eyes pop out of his head. White noise filled his head. His consciousness began to slip.

His double stood straight and tall as if to say *I have nothing to fear from you, little boy.*

His back is turned. He can't see me. Now's my chance. I have to do this, I have to!

Three more steps. Two more. One more step and I'll reach his back.

Wataru lifted his sword, and his double whipped around, an evil grin on his face. "Nice try!"

With a mocking laugh, the double thrust out his sword. Wataru was holding his own blade high over his head—he was wide open. The point of the Brave's Sword slid deep into his chest.

Wataru's mouth snapped open. He had been holding his breath and now he exhaled in one giant heave. Arms still raised over his head, he slowly looked down at the blade sticking into his chest. Blood was seeping out around the blade, soaking his shirt. The mirror-image Brave's Sword was buried deep in his chest.

Wataru felt no pain, but he was freezing. The sword had found his heart and was pouring icy coldness directly into his body.

I'm going to die.

It was a logical conclusion.

My double defeated me. I'm going to bleed, and then I'll die.

His strength left him and his legs bowed. Wataru dropped to his knees onto the surface of the lake. His arms hung limply by his side. His own sword fell loose from his grip, its sharp point hanging listlessly between his knees.

Wataru's conqueror yanked his sword back. Now free of the blade, Wataru collapsed to one side. Laughter rang in his ears. "Pitiful boy. Sad little boy. It's over."

The assailant turned his back on Wataru and began walking toward the far shore. His gait was ebullient—he was almost skipping. Wataru's blood dripped from the tip of the Brave's Sword hanging from his hand as he left.

—*Wataru.*

The gemstones in his sword were calling to him.

—*Steady, Wataru.*

—*Remember what the Goddess said.*

—*You mustn't fight.*

—*Your double is you.*

—*Remember the Goddess's words.*

Blood flowed from his wound, spreading across the crystalline surface of the water. Wataru was lying in a puddle of his own blood.

The Goddess's words?

Wataru hung on the brink of consciousness. He stretched out a hand, desperately trying to retain his grip on sanity.

—*Call him back.*

—*The split soul.*

That double? That murderer?

—*Yes, yes. Because that is you, Wataru.*

Wataru lifted his head. A stream of blood trickled out of his mouth. He had no strength left in him. *I'm drowning in a sea of blood.*

Somehow he mustered enough strength to sit up. The gemstones were all calling for him now.

—*Wataru, Wataru, don't die. Don't give up.*

—*Don't leave your other half alone. Acknowledge him. Accept him.*

After much effort, he was able to sit at the edge of the lake. His double was already standing on the far shore and had begun to disappear through the swamp reeds.

"Hey!" Wataru called out. It took all his remaining strength to do so.

The double stopped, turning around silently, a snake sensing its prey.

"I'm not dead yet!"

The smile faded from his double's face. He lifted his sword.

—*Accept him.*

With a shrill battle cry, his double charged across the lake. He ran with the speed of a hurricane. The tip of his blade gleamed with reflected light from the crystal.

Wataru closed his eyes and quietly spread his arms. He breathed. Fresh blood spilled from his mouth. But he stood his ground. He was calling. His heart was calm.

I have nothing to fear. I'm just calling him back.

Calling back the soul split from me.

Come home!

The double collided with Wataru—and evaporated. He was drawn into Wataru. Two became one.

The force of the impact blew Wataru's hair straight up and knocked him sprawling on his back.

Quiet returned to the Swamp of Grief.

When he opened his eyes, Wataru was looking up at the sky, his arms and legs splayed out in the shape of an X. He could feel the hard surface of the lake; it was solid beneath him.

Wataru gingerly moved his hand, poking at his chest. His shirt was dry. He lifted his head. There was no sign of any wound, nor any blood.

Wataru tried standing. His legs held him up.

I'm alive.

A smile came unbidden to his lips, then a warm wave of relief washed through his body. He put a hand to his chest and felt his heart beating beneath the skin.

Wataru had parted ways with his hatred back in the Swamp of Grief, and now it had come back. It was home in Wataru's body where it belonged. At last, he understood. The gate he had passed through to reach the arena: the fifth pattern *was* the key. He hadn't felt anything when he stood on it because the fifth pattern stood for hate.

Wataru realized that he had spent all this time trying to keep his own hate away. He lied to himself, pretending it wasn't his, not wanting to acknowledge the hate he felt toward Rikako, the hate he felt toward his own father. He didn't want to acknowledge that he could even feel that way. He was deceiving himself.

But that deception had spawned his double and forced it to walk alone, carrying all of Wataru's hate by itself.

"Welcome home," Wataru whispered.

He released one last shuddering breath and stood. He sheathed the Brave's Sword at his side.

It was then that he noticed the mist flowing around him. *Where did that come from?* The area had been perfectly clear only moments before. Soon it covered the entire surface of the lake. It glimmered with a soft light, and the moisture felt like tears on his skin.

Wataru's eyes opened wide.

A black robe was lying in a crumpled heap in the middle of the lake, shrouded in the mist. A boot was sticking out of one side. Loose hairs spilled out of the other.

Mitsuru.

Wataru ran, but it was like running in a dream—he couldn't seem to go forward. His feet slipped on the crystalline water. Burning with frustration, he clawed at the mist with his hands, trying to swim through it.

"Mitsuru!" he shouted, throwing himself forward and finally reaching him. At first he felt nothing, only the mist against his hands. He could see the robes right there in front of him, but they had no substance. It was like grabbing a shadow.

"Mitsuru, Mitsuru!" Wataru shouted again. Suddenly, he was there. Where there had only been an image before, now there was flesh and blood. Mitsuru came into focus.

Wataru lifted Mitsuru in his arms.

Mitsuru's face was pale, his eyes were closed. His cheeks were covered with scars and his arms hung limp at his sides. One of his ankles had been twisted in an unnatural position. It was probably broken.

"Mitsuru! Wake up!" Wataru gave him another shake, and the Sorcerer's Staff fell from the folds of Mitsuru's black robe. It had split clean in two. Mitsuru's pale face, his limp body, the broken staff—they all told Wataru the truth of what had happened here.

Mitsuru had lost.

Mitsuru had faced his own double in this Swamp of Grief, and he had lost.

Wataru understood now. He didn't want to, but the proof was right in front of his face. Mitsuru had let his hate walk alone, too, and it had grown into something far, far greater than Mitsuru himself—too large for him to call back. In the end, his hate had broken him.

What do I care what becomes of Vision?

All I want to do is reach the Tower of Destiny.

I'll do whatever it takes.

That hard determination. That will of steel. That mighty sorcerer's power born by the strength of the gemstones—a power only a Traveler could hope to wield. Mitsuru used it all in his journey. Many were the people he injured, the towns he destroyed, the grief he caused, all leading up to his final act: the destruction of the seal on the Mirror of Eternal Shadow.

Wataru and Mitsuru had been fooled. They both thought Mitsuru knew what he was doing. The destructive will, the desire to kill, the arrogance that led him to trample anyone in his path—these things hadn't belonged to Mitsuru. They belonged to his double, the one that bore all his hate. Yet that hatred was so close to his own heart. He had told himself for so long that he didn't need anything else, that his hatred would see him through. At some point, Mitsuru had become unable to distinguish between his double and himself.

Mitsuru, too, had struggled at first, trying to defeat his double, yet this was the same thing as defeating himself.

Mitsuru's eyelids fluttered, then opened.

Wataru was speechless. It was hard enough to choke back the sob he felt rising in his throat.

Two black eyes slowly focused on Wataru, after much long and painful effort. "You…"

Wataru nodded. Several times. With each nod, a tear fell.

"Why?" He said it like a schoolboy, upset with the teacher at being told to wait after class. *How like Mitsuru.* "I made it so far…how could this happen? What a disgrace." Then he whispered, "I almost reached it." His eyes looked up at the sky. "I could see it, the Tower of Destiny. It was right there. Yet…"

"Don't speak, you'll wear yourself out," Wataru said. He lifted Mitsuru from the hard lake, realizing as he did so that the other boy's wounds were too deep to ever mend.

"Mitani," Mitsuru whispered. Wataru looked at him, into the clear eyes of the other Traveler. "Where did I go wrong? What mistake did I make?"

—Not only the one who runs fastest and first may reach the Tower of Destiny.

The Elder in Sakawa was right.

—The Goddess is still waiting for you.

And Kee Keema, standing before the ruins of Solebria. He was right too.

—Wherever you go, I'll follow.

Wataru was never alone. Meena was always by his side. And when they last saw each other, she held him close and told him to be careful…

I had friends. They watched over my path for me. They didn't let me stray.

But Mitsuru was always alone. The lone Traveler. Even if he stepped off the path, there was no one there to tell him so.

Mitsuru chose his own path. He chose to be alone.

Even so, it seemed too unfair, the conclusion too cruel.

"I'm sorry." It was all Wataru could say. He could have ignored Wayfinder Lau's warning. He could have traveled together with Mitsuru. *But I didn't, and look what happened.*

"What are you apologizing for?" Mitsuru said, attempting a smile. That same imperious smile he had turned on Wataru so many times before. It wasn't working. "You've won. Be happy. Why are you crying?" He shook his head. "Too nice for your own good...down to the bitter end."

"It's not over yet."

"I won't lie to myself," Mitsuru said, his voice softening with a sudden kindness. "I've lost. I'm going to die here. I couldn't change my destiny." Then, after a pause, he muttered, "I brought this on myself." His mind had gone through the same process Wataru's had and come to the same conclusion. "I just...I wanted reach the Tower of Destiny. No matter...no matter what I had to do, I needed to go."

"I know," Wataru said. "Even if no one else will ever understand, I do. I know, Mitsuru."

Mitsuru closed his eyes and smiled. "Get going. Take the gemstone, leave me here, and go."

"No, I won't. I can't leave you here alone, Mitsuru."

"Fool. Let it go." Mitsuru's body twitched. His breathing became congested, rough. "It's...better alone."

Mitsuru to the very end.

Wataru lay him gently down atop the lake in the Swamp of Grief. Lying down, his eyes closed, Mitsuru seemed that much closer to death.

There was nothing left for Wataru to do. Mitsuru wanted to be alone.

Then a memory surfaced in the back of his mind. The quiet forest, where he had said his goodbyes to Kutz...

"Mitsuru."

"What?"

"Can I...pray for you?"

"I don't need prayers."

"Just let me, okay?"

Mitsuru's eyes opened. They fixed on Wataru.

"Please," Wataru said.

"Do what you want."

Wataru reached out his right hand and grabbed Mitsuru's. He placed his other hand on his friend's forehead.

Now do I remember the words?

Wataru began to speak, hesitantly at first. "We are the children of the Goddess. We leave the dust of the earth, and rise to you."

Mitsuru had once again closed his eyes. Wataru gently brushed his forehead.

"Light most pure, source and mother of all, lead us now. Light the darkness at the feet of this traveler who now comes to join you." Wataru grabbed Mitsuru's fingers tightly. "Little child, child of the land. Do you repent your trespasses in the Goddess's eyes?" Wataru's lips trembled, the words came haltingly. Whenever he spoke, the back of his throat burned. *I can't cry, not now*, he commanded himself. There was a moment of silence, during which the only thing Wataru could hear was his own ragged breathing. Then, he saw Mitsuru's mouth move.

"Yes," he said. *He answered the prayer. He said yes. He repents.*

Wataru's vision blurred with tears, and he swallowed. "Do you repent your sins as a child of man, the conflict, the anger, the empty struggle, the foolish ignorance?"

This time, the pause was shorter. "Yes," Mitsuru said again.

"Do you repent the lies, your own greed, your failure to accept the glory that the Goddess has given unto the children of man?"

"Yes."

Wataru could no longer stop the tears. "Here then your penance is done, your sins upon the land wiped clean as you were at birth. Know peace, child of man, for you will surely be called into that eternal light's embrace." Tears like rivers down his face, Wataru finished the prayer. "*Vesna esta holicia.* Though a child of man knows time, life itself is eternal."

Mitsuru's mouth moved slowly. "Those words…"

"Huh?"

"*Vesna…esta holicia.* Do you know what they mean?"

Wataru shook his head.

"*Until you shine through…again…*" Mitsuru muttered, his eyes closed. "Goodbye."

However many times they had said goodbye before, Wataru knew this one would be the last.

Mitsuru slowly began to fade. The mist gathered as it had before. It wrapped around him and covered him in its gentle embrace. Growing pure and luminescent, the mist took in Mitsuru's life.

On his knees, Wataru wept as he watched Mitsuru's outline fade. Then he noticed a single ray of light shining from above his head. It was like the light from a small spotlight, as large as his fist. It shone a pale, warm gold, coming down to the dissolving Mitsuru like a hand reaching out.

Mitsuru noticed its touch. Wrapped in mist, his head moved, his face lifting slightly upward. Half-closed eyelids opened again. A small circle of light shone into his eyes.

This light—could it be?

A sudden realization hit him. Wataru swallowed and a warm feeling of security rose in him.

When we die, we become light. A light shining upon the ground. Until the day we are born again.

This light was surely Mitsuru's sister. His little sister, the one he wanted to bring back to the real world so badly, the one for whom he wanted to change his destiny. She had come back to Mitsuru.

She had come to welcome him.

Mitsuru seemed to understand this too. He smiled faintly. His fingers twitched weakly, moving to meet the light—like he was trying to grab his sister's hand.

"Go with your brother," Wataru said quietly. The golden light winked once in reply.

Soon, Mitsuru had completely disappeared, becoming nothing more than a swirling, glowing cloud of mist. The tiny golden circle of light surrounded it and led it quietly upward.

Still on his knees, Wataru thrust out his arms toward the sky. It was as though he were giving another caged bird its freedom.

To the sky...

When it was done, the mist covering the Swamp of Grief disappeared. A final tear dropped from Wataru's chin.

Slowly, Wataru picked up the fallen sorcerer's staff and rose to his feet.

The gem at the tip of the staff was glowing with a faint purple light. Soon, four distinct points of light appeared within the gemstone. They too, rose into the air, following after Mitsuru.

Only one point of light remained behind, hovering at Wataru's eye level. Wataru drew his sword.

Darkness and light be with you, Brave.

Then the final gemstone found its place in the star pattern on the hilt of the Brave's Sword. A powerful blast of energy ran from the hilt to the tip of the blade. Then it echoed back, traveling up Wataru's arm, infusing him with strength.

The five gemstones were gathered together at last. The Demon's Bane was complete.

Wataru lifted his eyes. He knew what would be there, across the lake, waiting for him before he saw it.

The Tower of Destiny stood with its doors open, revealing a long spiral staircase that rose inside, quietly beckoning.

Chapter 55
The Tower of Destiny

The spiral staircase was barely wide enough for Wataru to walk on. It ran up along the inner wall of the giant, hollow tower as far as his eye could see. The shape reminded him of a model of a DNA double-helix he had seen in a science book.

The Tower of Destiny was made of the same radiant blue crystal as the collage of towns and cities he had just walked through—even the stairway was made of the stuff. After circling the interior of the tower a few times, the translucent steps made it hard for him to judge distance. Wataru ran his right hand along the wall as he climbed so as not to mistakenly step off the edge.

Though the light coming from the crystal was cold, the material of the wall itself was warm to the touch. When he looked closer he could see his own reflection—and someone else's. *Who's that smiling?*

Mom. Wataru stopped. An image of his mother was suspended in the crystal before him. She was much younger than the last time he had seen her. Her hairstyle was different. She was wearing a pastel-colored sweater, and carrying...

A baby? Who is that?

It's me. She's carrying me. The nursing infant in her arms was barely able to hold its own head up. He was trying to touch his mother's face with both hands. She would cover her eyes with a hand then pull it away. *Peekaboo!* The baby Wataru laughed and laughed.

A few more steps up, Wataru saw another image floating into focus in the wall. Wataru ran up the stairs. *Dad.* They were at the local pool on a summer day. He was teaching Wataru how to swim. He was holding on to his outstretched hands, cheering him on as he kicked his legs. His father was walking backward, leading him along. Soon Wataru would be able to cross the pool on his own. *That's it, you've got it!*

More images from the past splashed across the walls. It was like a movie theater built for him out of his own memories. Wataru was transfixed, watching each image intently as he climbed the spiral stair.

Soon, Katchan made his debut. He was wearing the same preschool uniform as Wataru, a yellow bag slung over his shoulder. He was jumping all around, excited about something, tugging on Wataru's shirt until his mother scolded him. *I remember that. It was after the ceremony on the first day of school. We had just taken a photograph by the school gates.*

Wataru's past was playing out before his eyes.

A school trip on a rainy day. Eating lunch right before the track meet. Doing homework by the heater at Katchan's house in the middle of winter. Bringing an abandoned kitten home, and having his mother tell him he couldn't keep it.

More images: Wataru crying on the balcony—he had been particularly bad, and his mother had locked him out. Going to the hospital by ambulance in the middle of the night—he had caught a cold and it got worse and turned into pneumonia. Each scene presented itself clearly. His mother in the ambulance, her face white. Katchan came to visit with his mom when Wataru was in the hospital. He remembered Katchan's mom apologizing. *Katchan's too rambunctious for his own good. He never should have been playing soccer in the rain with your son that day.*

Playing catch with his father in the courtyard of the apartment. *Here comes Mom, carrying an armful of grocery bags.* Dad throws her the ball, she picks it up, tries to throw it, and it goes wild. Way wild. The glass in one of the apartment windows on the first floor breaks, and the three of them go to apologize. Dad's teasing Mom, and she gets mad at him. They sneak away to laugh where she wouldn't see them…

How could there be so many memories in only eleven years? The human heart is a strange, bottomless container. Anything and everything goes in, just waiting to be taken out again someday.

Wataru climbed further and saw an episode with Mitsuru. He was looking grim the day they met at the shrine. This is sacred ground, he told Wataru, sounding adult and knowledgeable.

And there was the priest. Wataru was saying something to him over his shoulder, running off with his bag under his arm. That's right. I asked him if there really were gods, why were they so lazy?

Then he saw her— Mitsuru's aunt. He remembered the silver bangles she wore on her arm. She was worried about Mitsuru, yet looked like a little girl herself. The resemblance to Lady Zophie was startling.

The translucent walls of the Tower of Destiny showed him Uncle Lou too. They were lighting fireworks in the garden at his grandmother's house in Chiba. His uncle was so tan that at night, he could have stepped behind a tree and you'd never have seen him. Only when he smiled would a row of white teeth suddenly appear, floating in the air. Wataru laughed so hard he fell over. It made him smile even now.

But, in the next image, his uncle's face was twisted. He was calling out to Wataru who had crawled under the bed. *Come out, come out*, he was saying. The pain rose in Wataru's chest to see how sad his uncle looked. *I did that. I had no idea.*

What's that, swaying on the wall up there? It's me. He was grabbing on to the collar of a karulakin, dangling perilously far above the ground. He had wandered into a pack of gimblewolves in the Fatal Desert. It was funny to think how little he knew of Vision back then.

Now he was riding on Kee Keema's cart. They were racing across the grasslands. Wataru was holding on for his life, still unused to the rolling ride. Wataru ran farther up the stairs, following the darbaba cart as it raced along the wall.

There, the wall became suddenly dark. But it wasn't night. Black things, too numerous to count, were swarming along the wall. Flying in a great cloud.

It was a swarm of demonkin, so many they blocked out the sky. Long fangs jutted from skull-like faces. He could almost hear the clicking of their claws.

This isn't the past. This is Vision right now.

The shock and horror of the scene made Wataru step back from the wall, his arms hanging slack by his sides. The heel of one of his boots jutted over the edge of the stairs, and he almost lost his balance, which quickly returned him to his senses.

He hadn't realized just how far up he'd climbed. He could no longer see the entrance below. The bottom of the tower was lost in the distance. Only the wind blowing up through the hollow center of the tower served to remind him he was still in a physical space and not some dream world. Once again he began to climb the tower. The images on the wall kept pace.

The town of Gasara. Ramshackle barricades had been constructed everywhere out of furniture, wooden boxes, and barrels. A weary guard was standing on the watchtower, looking at the sky. Captain Ronmel led a group of Knights galloping down Main Street.

In the distance, across the grasslands that surrounded Gasara, a black cloud appeared. As he watched, it grew and swept closer. The Knights drew their swords. As one, they lit their torches. Kee Keema was standing on a rooftop, his legs apart, axe held at the ready. *Meena—there's Meena!* She was helping those who couldn't defend themselves get into cellars and other hiding places for their safety.

The wall twisted and the image blurred. Now he was looking at the Isle of Dragon. A steady stream of dragons were flying up from volcanoes. They looked prepared for battle, and they breathed flames that scorched the skies. Heroically, they blasted their way through the legions of demonkin, and sent them careening into the ocean screeching in pain and anger.

At the port of Sono, boats filled with refugees slowly raised their sails. Demonkin swarmed like ugly ants over the town broken by Mitsuru's magic. Every boat was crammed from bow to stern with people.

All the towns and villages Wataru had seen on his journey through Vision were under attack by the demonkin. Now, at this very moment, the places he had been and the people he had met were fighting a hopeless battle. The walls of the tower burned the reality of it into his eyes.

I have to hurry. The images of battle still tugging at him, Wataru ran up the spiral staircase. Then, quite suddenly, the stairs came to an abrupt end. *Is this it? Am I at the top?*

He was in a hall, the floor of which was decorated with the same pattern he had seen so many times before, the one connecting Vision to the real world. Each point of the star was shining a different color. Wataru walked to the center of the room.

The top part of the pattern was pointing toward a tall, elegant arch. Upon closer examination, it proved to be in the same shape as the top of the tower—two hands clasped in prayer. Perhaps this was the passageway that led to the Goddess.

He took a step toward the arch, when he heard a voice from behind him. "Wataru."

That sweet voice. Wataru tensed and turned around. A girl was standing at the edge of the pattern.

Where did she come from?

"You finally get to meet me."

How many times had she talked to him? In the real world, and even here, in Vision. Wataru had thought she was a fairy—but he had never forgotten what she told him to do on the shore near Sakawa. *"Kill the Goddess."* She had been with him all this time, and he *still* couldn't tell whether she was a friend or foe. And he had never seen what she looked like.

Wataru stared at her, too surprised to even blink. She was the spitting image of Kaori Daimatsu.

Those slender wrists. That graceful neck. Those large, black eyes. A smile graced her exquisite face.

"I'm glad I waited," she was saying. "So glad! I knew you would make it. I believed in you." Speaking gently, she walked toward him. Wataru stepped back, maintaining their distance.

The girl stopped. Her eyebrows lifted, each a delicately curved brushstroke. "What's wrong? Aren't you glad to see me?"

Several questions rose in Wataru's mind at once. He picked one. "Who are you?"

"Me?" she asked, spreading her hands as though in dismay. "Does my appearance not please you?" She grabbed the edge of her skirt and then bent one knee, curtsying like a girl meeting her partner for the first time at a formal ball. But this was no ballroom. And she wasn't wearing a gown. Wataru's memory wasn't clear on this point, but the skirt she was wearing looked like what Kaori had been wearing when he saw her outside the Daimatsu building. The plain, simple attire of a girl in middle school. The real Kaori would have been wearing it as she sat in her wheelchair. Her unfocused eyes hadn't even registered his presence.

Of course not. After all, her soul had been captured in the crystal city—

until Wataru had freed it.

But the Kaori Daimatsu in front of him now stepped lightly across the floor and spun. Her skirt lifted up, her legs flashing beneath it. Wataru had never seen her like this.

Just like Kaori...and yet totally unlike her. Who is she, really?

"You...talked to me many times."

The girl smiled, blushing. "You remembered?"

"How could I forget?" He had been happy at first. Back when he thought she was a fairy. Now he felt differently. "What do you want here? Why have you been following me? What do you want me to do?"

"So serious! You sure know how to ruin a girl's mood."

"Of course," Wataru said, clenching his fists. "How would you act if someone came to you, pretending to be someone else?"

"So you don't like how I look, do you. And I thought you liked her! She's been in your heart all this time."

Was that true? Have I been thinking about Kaori? Me? Wataru didn't think he had been. He had forgotten her—or was it merely that he hadn't been conscious of his own thoughts.

"A stolen, innocent soul," the girl said. "Unfairly injured, the victim of a twisted fate. Yes, just like you."

Is that why she had been in his heart?

Wataru braced, steadying his breath. He had figured out one thing: no matter who this mysterious voice was, no matter how closely she could read his heart or how sweetly she smiled, she was no friend.

"I'll ask you again," Wataru said, his voice gaining confidence. "What do you want? Are you going to tell me to kill the Goddess again? Who are you?"

The girl wrapped her arms around her shoulders as if to fend off a cold breeze. A thin smile still clung to her face. "You want to know who I am?"

"Yeah, I do."

"You're absolutely sure you want to know?"

"Absolutely."

"Then you have to promise me something," she said, her black eyes blazing. "Promise you won't hate me when you see my true form. Promise you won't push me away when you see me as I truly am." Her tone made the words sound like less of a plea and more of a threat.

She didn't wait for Wataru to respond. Suddenly her body began to shrink rapidly. Wataru stared. Where Kaori had stood only moments before, now there was only a small, warped shadow on the floor. Then a slick, black arm came out of the shadow. It was thick and round as a log. A hand like a large fan groped in the air, first to the right, then the left. It was no human hand— though it bore some some similarities. Another arm followed, and together they clutched at the floor, pulling.

"My face..." A large head emerged from the shadows.

Wataru gasped and took a step back.

"My true face. Does it not please you?" Only the sweet voice remained the same. But the mouth was that of a giant bullfrog. Giant lips flapped in the cool air of the tower. Eyes the size of basketballs protruded from its forehead. Ugly warts dotted its forest-green hide.

"Well? Tell me." As it spoke, the frog worked its arms, pulling the rest of its body out of the shadow. A thick hind leg slapped wetly against the floor. There was something oddly familiar in the pattern on its skin. It was like a wallpaper print covered with the moving, writing figures of...

The winged skeletal demonkin. Miniature demonkin writhed all over the skin of the giant bullfrog.

So this is my fairy.

"You seem surprised, dear little Wataru," the frog said, the loose flaps of skin at its throat trembling as it spoke. "Yet this is only what you asked for. This is the truth you dragged out of me. Look well, Wataru. For this is how I truly am."

"Who are..."

"Did Wayfinder Lau not tell you? Do you not know of me? Yes, the very same misfortune you bore in the real world, the same sadness, I have borne here in Vision. My name is Onba." A dark, heavy croaking sound joined the voice of the little girl, making every word a discordant harmony in two parts. "I am the manifestation of all that is ugly, all that is unwanted, all that was cut away as unnecessary by the Goddess at the time Vision was made. I am the darkness where there is light, the negative pole."

The manifestation of everything unwanted...

"My sweet, young Traveler. You who have come this far know the meaning of unwanted. What is unwanted is everything that does not meet the hopes and desires of this world, that falls short of its dreams. It is ugliness where beauty is sought, misfortune where happiness is desired, injustice where justice must be done. All the anger and greed and regret for what might have been—that is me."

Wataru stepped slowly backward, shaking his head, feeling Onba's giant eyes burning into him. "No, I don't understand."

"But you must!" The thick, gravelly voice gained strength, dominating the familiar voice of the girl. *That's what she really sounds like.* "Pitiful child of man. I know the bitter fate you were fed in the real world, I know. That is why I approached you. I knew an unfair fate would destroy what you held precious so that you would curse the real world and come here, to Vision. I knew."

Indeed, the first time the sweet voice had talked to him, Wataru had been living in ignorant bliss, not even knowing about his father and Rikako Tanaka. He had no inkling that the fabric of his daily life was about to be torn in two.

"I pity you, Wataru, I truly do. That is why I wanted to help," Onba said, her voice suddenly switching back to the little girl.

"Stop!" Wataru yelled suddenly. "Don't talk to me like that!"

Then Onba began to laugh, her eyes rolling as her voice dropped two octaves. Soon her great mouth was opened wide, bellowing with laughter. "You should know! Why is one person blessed with happiness, while another must know misfortune? Why must you suffer when it is your parents who have failed? Why you? Why not somebody else? Doesn't it make you angry? Don't you want to use your rage to undo this injustice?"

Wataru merely shook his head. Onba took one lumbering step forward, closing the distance between them. "We are angry when others are given what is not given to us. We are jealous of what we possess when it is given away to others. Our bellies burn with desire and envy. This is our true nature. The negativity that is me should, by all rights, have been scattered throughout Vision, like the shards of the Mirror of Truth. We could have been broken into countless, harmless fragments living peacefully among the masses. Yet the fools wouldn't accept the darkness in their own hearts, they wanted it out. They pretended we didn't belong to them…that they couldn't see us. Like the Goddess before them, they tried to banish us forever!" The great frog's voice crescendoed into a primal howl. "Lost, wandering, we fell into the Dark. Yet the Dark gave us strength, and I was born. I returned to Vision."

So Onba, like the demonkin, had come to Vision from that place, that Dark that hated Vision, and would devour it if it got the chance.

"That is why I wanted someone, a child of man. I belong in your heart. Your heart is my home." Onba's eyes stared at Wataru, her head tilting inquisitively. "Were you not my friend? Have you forgotten how much I helped you?"

Wataru tried to control his trembling, but couldn't. He didn't know if he was scared or sad. If he was sad, he didn't know why—perhaps somewhere in his heart he knew, but he couldn't put it into words. He shook his head, shut his eyes, and clenched his fists. "I didn't know who you were, really. I didn't know what you wanted."

"Who I really am?" Onba's voice was a low, guttural growl. "I am you. I am that unwanted thing, that dark negativity that crouches, hidden deep inside. It is only because I exist within you that you are able to talk to me in this way."

Something unwanted inside me? Wataru had never thought about it—he hadn't really had time. But now that he did, he found that it *was* there. Deep in his heart, a part of him was furious at his misfortune. A part of him wondered, *Why me?*

Just like his hate had become a double of himself, walking free, the negativity within Wataru had called out to Onba. She was the manifestation of all that wasn't wanted, and she was coming home to him.

"Yes, open your eyes. Overturn this world that dealt you your fate. You came here to change your fate? Why not think bigger? Here you are in the tower! Why change only yourself when you could change the entire world?"

"And that's what you want me to do?"

Onba's massive head nodded slowly. "Yes, for that is our victory! The victory of everything unwanted, at last!" Words of rage spilled out of her mucus-laden mouth. A dull black tongue darted between her lips. "We want. We will have our world. We will be God and make all those who hated us and pushed us away kneel at our feet."

Ah, so that's what you want.

"Traveler! I ask you. Do you not wish to destroy the Goddess, and reign together from this Tower of Destiny? Do you not wish to hold both Vision and the real world in the palm of your hand?"

"I do not." Wataru's voice was rock steady. He deliberately forced the chill running through his body to stop. "What you want is wrong."

Onba's large mouth opened even wider, swallowing most of her face, and she laughed from deep in her throat with a sound like rolling thunder. "My sweet, young Traveler. Do you not understand this is your last chance? Merely nod to us here and now, and you will not have to kneel at the feet of the Goddess. No—you will stand on the very top of this tower as lord of all you survey!"

"I don't want that," Wataru answered, his voice clear. "I'm sorry, but I can't help you."

Onba blinked, and her tongue swept across her face. "A foolish choice." A swollen, green hand slid across the floor toward Wataru. Wataru leaped to the side.

"Why? Why do you run from us? Is it our body you hate? Is something so empty, so devoid of meaning more important to you than a chance to sit upon the throne of a god?"

"That's not it," Wataru said, shaking his head. "I don't run because I think you're ugly. I run because you tried to deceive me. You should have told me the truth from the beginning. You should have showed me who you were. Maybe I could have found a way to help you. Maybe we could have made this journey together."

Onba's mouth gaped. "Such sweet lies! Had I appeared before you as I am now, you would have run without so much as letting me speak!"

"I would have been surprised, sure. But if I had only known the truth earlier, if I had known how you truly feel, I wouldn't have run."

"You lie!" Onba spat, slapping the floor with her webbed hands. "Traveler! Betrayer! Your fate ends here! You wish to change your destiny? Fine! I'll crush you into the very dust of the Dark! How's that for a change?!"

With a tremendous roar, Onba's grotesque body lifted off the floor and launched at Wataru. The demonkin in her wet skin rippled with a life of their own.

Wataru drew his sword, leaping to one side to strike at her flank.

Light blazed from the tip of the Brave's Sword. For a second, it blinded even Wataru. The sword felt light as a feather in his hands.

Onba twisted and opened her mouth, releasing a blast of foul air. The force of it nearly knocked Wataru off his feet, and he found it difficult to breathe. His hands and face stung as if he had been burned. *Poisonous breath!*

"How many Travelers have you tempted like this, Onba?!!" Wataru shouted, rolling across the floor to stand a short distance away. "How many Travelers have you stopped here, spouting the same pleas and offers of power? You pity me? No, I pity you!"

"What gives you the right, child of man?!" A sickly-green fist connected with Wataru's side, sending him flying across the room. It hurt to breathe. It hurt even to open his eyes. *The poison is going to get me if I don't do something quick.*

"Your life is dust to me. I will swallow you whole!" Her tongue rose like an independent thing, darting through the air with a wet *thwap* to snake around Wataru's body. He cut it away with his sword at the last moment. Onba screamed.

Light streaked through the air in the sword's path. The power of the Demon's Bane was guiding Wataru's hand.

At last Wataru realized why he needed the Demon's Bane to climb the Tower of Destiny and meet with the Goddess. He needed it to fight this last temptation that stood before him and the completion of his journey. He needed to defeat this unwanted thing that whispered to him of another way. This was the final trial.

Once he realized this, there was nothing to fear. Wataru jumped in front of Onba, feet apart, sword raised. "You cannot defeat me. You cannot defeat the sword."

Onba howled like a wounded beast. The mottled demonkin pattern on her skin swirled like a portrait of madness. "Child!" she screamed, letting loose a blast of foul miasma.

"The time's come to set right all the wrong you've done here, Onba." The Brave's Sword—the Demon's Bane—shone brilliantly in his hand. "It is you whose story ends here! You will not return to the Dark, you will not wander the abyss. Vision is your true home. As you were in the beginning, so shall you return: to fragments, a memory in the hearts of men."

Onba howled with rage and charged. Wataru met her head on, the point of the Demon's Bane aimed at a spot directly between her eyes, which burned red with hate.

For an instant, Onba's entire body gleamed as bright as the sun. The demonkin horde writhed in mortal pain.

And then she exploded into a thousand particles. The pieces scattered, swirling through the air like snowflakes. Not a trace of the giant frog remained. The particles seemed to melt in the air, fading into nothingness.

Only her scream lingered, trailing off through the air until the last particle was gone.

Wataru put the Demon's Bane back in its sheath. He wiped the sweat from his brow with a hand.

"Thank you," he said, though he wasn't sure who he was thanking or why. The words just came to his lips.

Wataru walked across the chamber, stepping over the top of the glowing star pattern on the floor, and passed through the praying hands of the last arch.

Chapter 56
Wataru's Wish

Another long staircase. This time the stairs climbed not in a spiral but in a zigzag.

He could no longer see the walls of the tower around him. The reflections of images from his past were also gone. He was surrounded by a void—the color of the sky just before dawn. At the top of the stairs hung a circular platform that had to be the Goddess's throne. It was like Wataru was floating in space, and the staircase touched the outline of some unknown constellation.

Getting closer, Wataru could see someone sitting right in the middle of the disk. He steadied himself. *Finally—the last step.*

The seat of the Goddess.

A girl was sitting quietly in the middle of that crystal disk. She was wearing a long-sleeved dress of pure white, and she was looking down at her lap. Her long hair was tightly bound on her head, revealing the slender, graceful curve of her neck. An aura of pure light enveloped her body.

She lifted her face and a single curvy strand of black hair fell down upon her forehead.

It was Kaori Daimatsu. Again.

"Wataru," she called. Her lips were the color of cherry blossoms. "You've finally arrived. This is the end of your journey. You have reached the Tower of Destiny."

Confused, Wataru shuffled his feet. He didn't want to step back, yet he was afraid to go forward. Kaori smiled brightly. "As it was with Onba, mine is also a borrowed form. I took her shape from among the people of the real world that you hold in your heart. But I am not Lady Onba. I do not wish to deceive you, nor harm you in any way. Be at ease."

I am the Goddess of Destiny.

It was the same voice, yet filled with an incredible presence.

"Why…" Wataru opened his mouth. He felt like his soul was melting and running down his legs. "Why Kaori?"

The Goddess smiled again. "I believe you already know the answer to that question. Lady Onba told you."

"Because…" Wataru put a hand to his chest. "Because she has been in my heart?"

The Goddess nodded. "She, like you, is an innocent soul who became victim to a cruel fate. As you traveled to save yourself, you wanted to save all those who suffered as you did. That was your true objective, whether you knew it or not."

"'Those who suffered'? Does that include Mitsuru?"

"Of course. He was in your heart as well." Then she added in a whisper, almost too soft for him to hear, "From the very beginning."

"If you speak the wish that is in your heart now, I can make it come true. That is why I'm here. Do you understand?"

"I understand," Wataru replied in a squeaky voice. His forehead felt like it was on fire, and his body was trembling.

The time has come at last. The time when my wishes will be granted.

"Then, come to me," the Goddess of Destiny called to him. "Take my hand, and put your wish into words. Give your wish unto me."

Then those long, slender arms—Kaori Daimatsu's arms—reached out toward him.

All was silent. Wataru found himself wondering at how such pure silence could be so calming. Only his steady breathing marked the passage of time.

One, two, three. His heart beat with each breath. *I'm alive. I'm here. Me. Me…and everyone else.*

Wataru took a jerky step forward, then another. No one had taught him the proper procedure. Even Wayfinder Lau hadn't told him how to behave in the presence of the Goddess. Wataru went down on one knee, took her hand and placed it on his chest, and bent his head.

"My…wish…"

"Yes?" Her soft voice seemed to stroke his hair.

Make your wish into words.

From long before he had realized what his true wish was, Wataru's heart had already known. It had been waiting patiently for this moment. When the words came, they came without a moment's hesitation.

"Goddess of Destiny. With your power, destroy the Mirror of Eternal Shadow. Break it, like the Mirror of Truth, into countless fragments, and spread them through the land. Please, destroy it. Cut off the paths of the Dark and save Vision."

The Goddess's white fingers were motionless in Wataru's hand.

"Is this your wish?"

"It is."

"Do you understand the entire nature of your wish?"

"Yes, I do."

"Do you understand that I may only answer this one wish, this one time. You will never have a second chance."

"I understand."

"Will you not regret this? If I grant you this wish, your destiny in the real world will not change in the least. Can you tell me that you walked the long road to the Tower of Destiny, overcoming many hardships, all for the fulfillment of this one wish?"

The Goddess's words wrapped around Wataru like gauzy ribbons of silk. Wataru grabbed each one of them and held them close.

"You are certain? Even if Vision is saved, your fate will remain as it was."

Wataru looked up. The smile had faded from the Goddess's face, her expression was stern, and her black eyes were focused on Wataru.

"No," he said. "I think you're wrong. Save Vision, and you *will* save me."

The Goddess's head tilted slowly. "On your way here, you saw the disaster that has befallen Vision. You saw the demonkin hordes attacking your traveling companions. That is why these things are burned so strongly into your mind now. You think only to help your friends and save Vision, above all else. But, Wataru, think again. You will never return to Vision. You do not live here. Nor will you ever meet your friends again. You go from here back to the real world. And when you do, you will realize. Once again, you will face the cruel destiny that has found you, and you will find it not a bit changed from when you left. Will you not curse your fate, and be ravaged by regret?"

Wataru managed to smile, surprising even himself. "Like you say, I first came here to change my destiny in the real world. I swore to myself I would do it when I started my journey."

But it's different now. Everything is different. I can see that now. "I was wrong. I was looking at it the wrong way. This Vision, it's *my* Vision. I walked its roads. And as I did so, I created it around me. I made this world. It's me."

Protecting Vision from the demonkin is the same thing as protecting myself. "When I go back to the real world, my fate will be waiting there as it has been this whole time—I know that. But it's not like it was when I left. I'm not who I was before I came to Vision."

"So you say you have grown stronger?"

Shaking his head, Wataru continued. "I don't think I've gotten stronger. In the real world I'm still just a kid. That's why all I could do when things went bad was cry. Because I'm powerless."

And I still am. I can't do anything by myself. I cry when I'm lonely, and I tremble when I'm scared. I fear that what I loved will be taken from me, and I'm afraid of being hurt.

"The time just before I came to Vision, I was sure that I would never be so sad in my whole life. I thought I would never hate another person so much, or get so mad. I wanted to change my fate because I knew then I was the unhappiest I could ever be.

"But, when I came to Vision, I made friends and I had fun—a lot of fun. Sometimes so much that I forgot why I had set out on my journey in the first place. At the same time, I encountered things that were so sad they tore me apart, and times so scary I thought I might die from fright. I cried. I cried out loud. And I shook with fear. Sometimes I was so frightened I couldn't even stand. But I couldn't run away. I still had to continue my journey. I still wanted to reach the Tower of Destiny.

"And now that I'm finally here, I understand. My journey through Vision wasn't to reach the Tower of Destiny at all. The journey itself was the point. It taught me that even if I relied on your power to change my destiny, it would only be this one time. I'm sure that I'll know many more happy times, and many more sad times. I can't avoid that. That's life. And I can't go asking to have my destiny changed every time something sad happens to me."

Wataru never thought he would cry as hard as he did that night he crawled under his bed. But he cried when Kutz died. And he cried when Mitsuru faded into the mist.

And there would be more partings, more losses, more wounds, over and over, again and again. He could change his destiny a hundred times, and each time another loss or separation would be waiting for him on the other side.

As long as there is happiness, there will be sadness. As long as there is fortune, there will be misfortune.

"The joy and the sadness on my journey through Vision taught me that you can't wait around for your fate to change. What's real is something that not even the strength of the Goddess can change. The only one who can change it is me. If I don't change my own destiny, if I don't cut through the obstacles in my path, then no matter where I go, I'll always be standing in the same place, doing the same thing over and over again, for the rest of my life."

That's why I have to protect Vision. That's why I can't let the demonkin win.

"But I—*we* are powerless to defeat the demonkin. Left as it is, the darkness will swallow Vision whole. That's why my wish to you is to save Vision. Give my Vision a future. Give my friends a future."

Wataru stopped talking and looked at the Goddess's face. Her eyes were closed, though her eyelids were trembling, as though they might open at any moment and return his gaze.

But the Goddess's eyes remained closed. Her white hand in his was motionless, without feeling, like the hand of a finely crafted doll.

"Even should this invasion be stopped, it does not ensure that Vision will have a future," she said, slowly shaking her head. "You know this as well as I do. I fear that the Northern Empire and the Southern United Nations will not find harmony. The war will continue. Nor will the discrimination you saw on your travels end easily. Knowing this, would you still use your one chance to change your destiny in the real world to help the people of this Vision?"

Wataru was sure. "Yes. Absolutely."

The endless, foolish, and stupid waging of war, the narrow minds that could only see what they believed and nothing else, impatient hands that reached only for the nearest, most convenient pleasures, all of this was part of

Wataru's Vision too.

It's all in me.

"There's a point to all the mistakes, the comebacks, the rethinking, the living—the living for all you're worth. There's a point to finding our own path. Please, give the people of Vision a chance to find theirs."

Inside, Wataru was perfectly calm. He had said all there was to say. He was now filled with a soul-satisfying contentment.

He bowed his head again deeply.

Then he felt the Goddess's slender fingers tighten around his own.

"Very well."

The Goddess leaned forward and lifted Wataru's chin in her hand. The smile had returned to her face. The aura enveloping her was dazzling to behold. "I shall grant your wish. Stand."

Wataru stood, straightening himself as best he could.

"Give me your sword, the Demon's Bane you have completed."

Wataru drew the sword from the sheath at his waist, handing it to her with both hands.

The Goddess stood without a sound. "Look at your feet."

Wataru lowered his eyes and gasped. Images were swirling across the circular dais beneath them.

Where once the Crystal Palace stood, the Mirror of Eternal Shadow now floated. It was supported on mist-like wings the color of night. Darkness swelled along its edge, and from that portal swarmed the demonkin armies. Even though it was just an image, the sight filled Wataru with unspeakable dread. He found his eyes glued to it, even as he stepped backward.

Demon's Bane in her hand, the Goddess stepped forward, sweeping back the hem of her white dress. She thrust an arm straight before her, holding the blade directly above the image of the mirror. "Traveler Wataru. Here is your answer, from the Tower of Destiny given to the land below." The point of the blade lowered, and the Goddess quietly released her grasp on the hilt. The sword began to fall, falling through the dais, into Vision, toward the Mirror of Eternal Shadow.

Down in Vision, everyone turned their eyes toward the sky.

A single beam of light came down from the heavens. It was the sword of light and it split the sky in two.

Then the piercing light sank into the Mirror of Eternal Shadow.

The great dark wings supporting the mirror flapped twice as if they were desperately clawing at the sky. After that, they began to fade. Without their support, the mirror tilted to its side. And just when it seemed as though the darkness brimming in the mirror might spill out, a bolt of lightning cracked the mirror to pieces.

The residents of Solebria witnessed the Mirror of Eternal Shadow splinter. First into two, then four, then eight, each crack spawning new fissures of its own, until it had broken into a thousand pieces.

The mirror now destroyed, the demonkin hordes were pulled back into the Dark from whence they came—their bodies reduced to black ash falling from the sky.

Everyone saw the source of their terror disappear in the blink of an eye. And before they could react in any way, the dusty remains quickly vanished.

People turned to each other.

They're gone. They've left. The demonkin are no more.

It wasn't long before the cheering began.

Just at that moment in Gasara, Kee Keema was standing on the roof of the branch office swinging his axe. One foul demonkin clawed at his head, another went for his throat, and a third clung to his back. The waterkin thrashed, trying to throw his assailants off, while Meena joined the fray, wielding a frying pan she had taken from the lodge kitchen.

"Off him! Fiend! Hang in there, Kee Keema!"

"Won't these guys ever give up?" he roared. He was covered with wounds, but still fought on, snapping at a demonkin's claws with his bared teeth. "You won't take me down that easy!"

Kee Keema threw a demonkin aside, and Meena smacked it on the head with her frying pan.

And it disappeared.

They all disappeared. The countless demonkin swarming in the skies over Gasara faded away. Kee Keema and Meena stood, covered in black ash, dumbfounded.

"What was that?"

Kee Keema turned, spitting out a black clod of soot that had been a de-monkin claw.

Their eyes met, and both of them looked up. Then they looked higher, toward the tower they knew stood there in the vault of the sky.

"It's Wataru."

By the gates of the town of Gasara, the Knights of Stengel fought for all they were worth. There were elderly and children to protect, and many more demonkin to kill. The gates must be defended to the death.

Looking to the left, a Knight could be seen throwing down his sword and picking up a flaming torch in its stead. To the right, a Knight lay prone, his life slowly ebbing from his body. Everywhere discarded greaves and helms were scattered on the ground.

"Don't give them an inch! Push them back!" the captain yelled to his men. None among them were unscathed. The demonkin were strong and not easily felled. One after another the Knights were crushed by the black wings of death.

"Captain, look out!"

After cutting down several of the demonkin, Captain Ronmel had lifted a hand to wipe the streaming sweat from his eyes, and in that moment, a de-monkin had launched at him. Caught off-guard, the captain stumbled. One of his Knights charged, but he was caught by a dive-bombing demonkin and tossed aside. The demonkin rattled its claws in victory.

"Captain!"

One of the Knights crawled out of the barricade and took off his helmet. He couldn't believe his eyes. Everywhere around him black dust was falling.

What is this?

The demonkin horde had disappeared. All of Gasara hung thick with black soot, as though everyone in town had decided to clean their chimneys at the exact same moment.

But it wasn't soot. It was the remains of the demonkin.

The men stood slack, unable to understand their sudden victory. The Knight who was tossed aside by a demonkin attack was back on his feet. "Captain, Captain!"

Ronmel was nowhere to be seen. All of the remaining Knights were covered in black. Not even the silver of their armor could shine through that dark falling mist. They gaped at the sky, waving their hands to brush aside the swirling particles where their enemy had been. Beneath a layer of grime, the hard expressions on their battle-weary faces softened into smiles.

Is it over?

It's over.

As suddenly as it began.

Someone began singing a prayer to the Goddess. Everyone joined in.

And Captain Ronmel was nowhere to be seen.

The Knight was sure of what he had seen: a demonkin, its fangs buried into the captain's neck, fangs stained red by a spray of blood. But now the demonkin were gone. All around him, the Knights were breathing sighs of relief, and cheering. It was the sound of victory.

The demonkin were gone. But so was their captain.

The Mirror of Eternal Shadow became dust, and the demonkin hordes became ash. Wataru quietly watched as the many particles of darkness found homes in the people of Vision, where they belonged. Blue skies returned to the city of Solebria.

Wataru turned to the Goddess. She was smiling.

"Thank you," he said, returning her smile. "Thank you for granting my wish."

Suddenly the Goddess knelt and hugged him tight. "Thank you," she said, but the voice was that of a girl. *Kaori Daimatsu.* Wataru was sure of it. At once, his heart leaped, and forgetting his restraint and embarrassment, forgetting that this was the Goddess of Destiny, Wataru returned the girl's embrace.

They sat there like that for a long time. In the warmth of the Goddess's embrace, Wataru felt the warmth of so many others—his mother, Meena, Kee Keema, Kutz, and even Mitsuru.

"Now, Traveler. The time has come for you to return to your world," the Goddess said gently, her hand on Wataru's shoulder.

"I know."

"Go the way in which you came. Descend the stairs from my dais. Wayfinder Lau awaits you at the bottom." She stood, smoothing out the folds in her robes. Then she brushed Wataru's hair with the tips of her fingers. "Farewell."

Wataru looked up into her gentle smile and bowed deeply. Unable to find the appropriate words, he silently turned and left.

Wataru felt empty. He was happy and almost dizzy with relief. But with each step down the stairway he felt as though he were walking through a void.

I'm floating. My eyes are open, but I see nothing. I'm just swimming through an endless blue void.

It took him a long time before he noticed the silver boots, their toes covered with mud, and the *clang, clang* of steel-shod feet upon the stairs.

Captain Ronmel was standing on the landing just below him.

He looked up, saw Wataru, and once again resumed climbing slowly. *He's coming toward me.*

Captain Ronmel held his silver helm under one arm. Blood and grit caked his wild blond hair. Several long scratches scored his chest plate. He walked slowly, tiredly, his shoulders hanging low. A wound gaped on his neck, the blood caked and dried.

"Captain Ronmel? Why are you here?"

Ronmel climbed until he was standing on the same landing as Wataru.

"This is the Tower of Destiny...why?"

He took a quiet breath before responding. "I was chosen."

Wataru didn't understand.

"I was chosen. To be the Half. To be the sacrifice," the captain continued, his voice resonating in the empty space of the tower. "The other Half will join me in becoming a Lord of the Underworld, to raise once again the Great Barrier of Light. Together we will protect life in Vision for the next one thousand years."

The sacrifices—Halnera.

"The...other half?"

Captain Ronmel put his grimy, cracked gauntlet on Wataru's shoulder. "*You* completed your journey. That alone should be answer enough."

Oh. Mitsuru.

"I go now to the Goddess. I'm glad we met here. To send off a Traveler from Vision is a great honor…it lessens the burden of sacrifice." The edge of his mouth jerked upward into a smile.

The feel of the captain's hand on his shoulder brought Wataru's sense of touch back to him in a sudden rush. The strength returned to his legs. His blurred thoughts regained their focus.

"No tears," Captain Ronmel said, his blue eyes fixing sternly on Wataru. "This is not a sad thing. Do not cry."

Unable to speak, Wataru merely frowned and nodded.

"You were the one who broke the Mirror of Eternal Shadow?"

Wataru nodded again.

"On behalf of all the people of Vision, I thank you."

Wataru remembered what he had to say. He had so many things to say, but one thing came out first. "Captain!"

No tears.

"I-I couldn't save her. I let Kutz die."

The captain raised an eyebrow then lowered his eyes. "I see."

"She was guarding two children in Solebria. I don't know what happened—but she kept fighting. Even when she dropped her whip she went at those demonkin with her bare hands."

"How like her."

Wataru choked back a sob.

"In Vision, when a person dies, they become light."

"Kee Keema taught me."

"Very well. And you know that eventually, she will be reborn?"

"Yes."

The captain's gaze softened, and the smile returned to his face. "Then I will be watching over the Vision into which Kutz is reborn. That suits me. That suits me quite well."

Wataru knew he was wasn't just putting on a brave face—he truly meant what he said.

"And I hope that when a thousand years are past, and my duty is finally complete, I too will become light. Then I'll be reborn in the same place as her, so many lives later. We never did finish our last argument to my satisfaction."

Now he's posing.

"Tell the truth. You don't want to argue with her again."

The captain threw his head back and laughed. "Go now. I would like to be the last to see you off on your final journey."

For a moment he stood there, looking at the captain.

"Brave Traveler," Captain Ronmel put his fist to his chest in the Knights' salute. "May the Goddess of Destiny watch over you, even in the real world."

"Thank you." Wataru returned his salute, and began to walk. He could feel the captain's gaze on him, pushing him.

He didn't look back.

At the bottom of the stairs, Wayfinder Lau was waiting, just as the Goddess had said. He stood casually with his staff held in both arms. He looked as if he had just sent Wataru on some errand and was impatiently waiting for him to return.

"Shall we?" Wataru said, coming to a stop before him.

The Swamp of Grief and the translucent collage of towns and villages were gone. He now walked through a void much like the one swirling around the staircase. Wataru walked quietly, following behind the Wayfinder. He couldn't even see what they were walking on.

His mind went blank, as empty as his surroundings.

Then the Porta Nectere loomed into view—the giant gate between the real world and Vision, its apex lost in clouds and mist.

It seemed like a thousand years had already passed since he last saw it.

Wayfinder Lau stopped a good distance before reaching the gate. Tilting his head, he gave Wataru an inquisitive look. "You have given the Demon's Bane back to the Goddess?"

"Yes."

"Then to me you must return the pendant that marks you as a Traveler."

As directed, Wataru gave back the pendant. Wayfinder Lau took it and put it in a pocket of his robe. "You journeyed well."

"Thank you."

"Your adventure is your own. No one may ever take it from you."

"Yes."

The Wayfinder's long whiskers swayed. Maybe he was smiling, but even if he was, it was only for a second. Still, for that moment, the loud, ornery old man seemed like a different person entirely.

I'm going home. I no longer belong to Vision. I have to remember there will always be a wall between myself and Wayfinder Lau's world. It is a wall that I will never cross again.

The Wayfinder placed a thin hand like a withered branch of a tree on Wataru's shoulder. "Little child of man who must live in the real world. I shall not meet you again. May your journey through the rest of your life be as fortunate as your journey through Vision."

Wataru nodded. "Wayfinder, I have a request."

The old man's eyebrows twitched.

"What could you possibly want at this end of ends?"

Wataru took off his firewyrm bracelet and handed it to him. "I want you…to take this back for me. Take it back to the people who will know what it means—this will tell them that I have finished my journey successfully and returned to the real world."

Wayfinder Lau made such a sour face that Wataru suddenly became worried. "Did…I ask too much?"

"It is not a difficult request, boy. But I think there is no need. Your traveling companions should already know of your safe return by now."

"Still, if you would. Please, give it to them."

Wataru bowed. Wayfinder Lau stood motionless.

Then Wataru heard a sigh from above his head. "Very well, very well. I shall take the armband. I suppose it can't hurt."

Wataru's heart skipped.

"Mmm?" Wayfinder Lau suddenly looked up toward the sky. "Ah, we'll get quite a good view from here, I should think."

Wataru followed Wayfinder Lau's gaze upward.

High up in the void above them, a glimmering white curtain of light flowed elegantly across the sky. Its radiance was breathtaking, like an aurora of pure light that grew and grew until it filled Wataru's eyes. Its gentle curves softly ebbed through the air, like the fingers of a mother upon an infant's head.

"The new Barrier of Light," Wayfinder Lau said quietly.

The shining curtain swept the sky with a fresh radiance, drawing farther and farther away as it headed for its destination where it would remain for the next one thousand years.

"Halnera is finished. And you saw it happen."

Wataru nodded and reached out to grab Wayfinder Lau's hand. He held it firmly, saying nothing.

Then he turned and looked up at the Porta Nectere.

Without a sound, the great white gates slid open. After Wataru passed over the threshold, they would not open for another decade. When they did swing open again, another Traveler would enter Vision. For Wataru, his journey was over.

"Wataru," Wayfinder Lau called out. "In time, you will forget Vision. You will forget this extraordinary adventure. But the truth shall remain within you."

"The truth…"

Everything I've learned on my journey. I get to keep all that.

"You will have your truth, but only when you leave," Wayfinder Lau said sternly. He then stepped aside, opening the path for Wataru. "Go home now, Traveler. You must live out your life as a child of the real world."

Wataru walked forward step by irreversible step. The gates were open, welcoming him.

What was waiting for him back home? What would he feel back in the real world? How would he live back in his old life?

However I want to.

When he first came here, Wataru was alone. *Now I'm not. Everyone's with me. Mitsuru, and Kutz; Meena, and Kee Keema too. And the Goddess in all her beauty…*

In the National Observatory at Lourdes, Dr. Baksan stood quietly atop his wooden boots and looked out the window. Romy stood by his side.

"Doctor," she called to him.

"I know what you would say. But now, you should be quiet." *And,* he thought to himself, *you should be observing this, my wayward students. All of you!*

"It's disappearing, isn't it?"

The old scholar did not respond. Together, the two stared at the sky in silence.

After a time, he turned to his young student. "The Porta Nectere will be closing now," he said, punctuating his declaration with a sudden, violent sneeze.

Romy quickly reached out, grabbing the old scholar by his collar so he wouldn't topple off his boots and fall straight out the window.

The Spectacle Machine circus troupe had set up its great tent just outside the town of Gasara. But there was no performance. The tent was being used as a makeshift hospital and a refugee camp.

The town doctor was busy. Even if there had been two of him, he would still not be able to get everything done. Meena, who had so recently been fending off demonkin with a frying pan, was helping as a nurse.

She didn't want to stop. She was afraid she might start to think about everything that had happened recently. She kept her mind on the task at hand, and she was grateful that she was needed to deal with emergency after emergency. A child crying over there, an injured man moaning over here. *Where're the bandages? Where's the salve?*

"Meena!" Bubuho stood at the entrance to the grand tent. "Over here. Granny wants to speak with you."

Meena wove through the cots, sometimes stepping over people to get to the door.

"I wish I had five or six more hands, they've got me so busy. Does Granny need me right away?"

"Ask her yourself—she's right outside," Bubuho said, a gentle look in his eyes. "And you need to rest. Even just to catch your breath. I can see the worry swimming in your eyes."

Meena stepped outside. Granny had pulled out a small table and chair where she now sat. She was gazing into the depths of her crystal ball.

Evening had come while Meena was busy tending to patients. The darkening pink of dusk stretched above her head. The evil black shadows of the demonkin were nowhere to be seen.

Wataru saved us. He went to the Goddess and wished the demonkin away.

—*Later, Meena.*

She remembered his words as they stood next to the walls of Solebria.

It had been a promise, one he kept.

What about Wataru's wish? Was this the end Wataru wanted for his journey? All the questions she had desperately tried to keep from asking were now welling up inside.

Meena reprimanded herself. She pushed aside all the other questions, finding the one that resonated the strongest, shaking her heart.

Will I ever see Wataru again?

Then she shook her head. *It's my own fault. He's from the real world. He was a Traveler.*

Granny noticed her footsteps, and hunching over even further, she looked around. "Ah, you've come." Granny gave the crystal ball a light pat with her fingers. She extended her hand toward Meena. "You will not need to look into the ball to see. Here, lend me a hand."

Meena took Granny's withered hand in hers. The old woman tugged at her, leading her farther away from the great tent. Then she looked up. "Do you see?"

Meena's gaze turned skyward. Even the beauty of the sunset failed to stir her. "Granny, there's nothing. Just…nothing."

"It is disappearing," the old woman said, pointing a finger at a quarter of the sky.

There hung a pinpoint of sharp red light. It had been there for weeks. For Meena, sometimes it had seemed even more evil than the demonkin.

But now the Blood Star's light was fading. Even as she watched, it was absorbed into the night sky.

Halnera was ending.

The next thousand years for Vision were beginning.

At the edge of the Swamp of Grief, Shin Suxin took off his glasses and began to massage his knotted shoulders with the palm of his hand. While in Tearsheaven, the gatekeeper stopped sweeping up the remains of the demonkin for a moment and looked up into the sky. By her mother Satami's bed, Sara put a hand on the window.

The dragons were returning to their island. The wounded Jozo sat nestled between his parents, looking up through a crack in the rocks.

Lady Zophie, reunited at last with General Adja's troops, lifted the heavy canvas flap of her pavilion and watched the sky. In her mind's eye, she could still see Mitsuru's profile as he stood in the Crystal Palace.

In the remains of the sula woods where the Triankha Hospital had once stood, a quiet wind blew. Small animals ran over and under the fallen branches. Nearby, a waterkin looked up at the twilight sky from the driver's seat of his darbaba cart.

Halnera had ended.

The Great Barrier of Light was remade anew. *May the Goddess reign in eternity.*

"Meena, Meena!" It was Puck calling her. She looked around to see him jumping to and fro by the side of the great circus tent. Kee Keema was with him, his face looking sad and tired, and his shoulders sagging more than she had ever seen them before.

"Puck, what is it?"

"A white bird just flew by!"

"A white bird?"

"Yep! He stopped right on my shoulder. And then when I looked, he was gone! But guess what, he left something!"

Puck held out his hand. There, in the middle of his palm rested a firewyrm band.

Wataru's armband. Meena put a hand to her mouth.

"This belongs to your friend, didn't it? It's a Highlander band, isn't it?"

"It's Wataru's," Kee Keema said. "He is saying goodbye to us. He's saying he made it to the Tower of Destiny, met the Goddess, and saved Vision for us. And then he left—back to his own world. That's what it means."

I know it, and it's a great thing, so why do I feel so sad, Kee Keema's eyes seemed to ask. He wiped his face with the back of one hand.

Meena took the armband in her fingers and held it to her cheek. She was crying.

"Meena, what's wrong? Why are you crying?" Puck asked, flustered. Meena slowly knelt on the ground, hiding her face in her hands.

Wataru had left. He was gone from Vision.

His journey was over.

"We didn't even say goodbye, did we?" Kee Keema mumbled, his eyes swimming in tears.

Meena gave him a great big hug.

"You don't say goodbye!" Puck shouted, doing another flip. "Meena, weren't you the one who told us not to say goodbye?"

Meena wiped away her tears and looked up. "Did I say that? What did I teach you to say, Puck?"

Puck beamed with pride, sticking out his chest. "Be well, you said! Be well!"

Meena looked at Kee Keema, and the two smiled. "Yes. Those are just the words, I think."

The Blood Star had now completely disappeared from the darkening sky above Gasara. As night's curtain was drawn, the stars began to shine. They began in the darkest point near the top then fell down to the horizon, painting the sky, leading Vision into gentle sleep.

Meena and Kee Keema hugged each other close and looked up. In their hearts they whispered to Wataru, knowing he would hear them.

Our Traveler, and our traveling companion: we wish for your happiness, as you wished for ours.

Be well.

Epilogue

The smell of gas.

He came running from somewhere far away, flying across incredible distances home. Wataru shot up from bed with the momentum of his arrival.

I'm in my room!

School notes and textbooks piled up on the desk. Mom's hand-knit cushion on the seat of the chair. Dictionaries and an encyclopedia set on the bookshelf. Behind the encyclopedias: game strategy guides, a row of comic books, and a secret piggybank with money to buy *Eldritch Stone Saga III*.

My room. My home. But why does it smell like gas?

The air conditioner was turned off. An unpleasant, dangerous stench hung in the air.

Wataru threw off the covers and jumped out of bed. "Mom!" He shouted, running out into the living room. The door to his mother's bedroom was open. A strong smell of gas came drifting from the kitchen.

She left the door open so the gas could fill her room.

Holding his breath, Wataru dashed into the kitchen and almost turned on the light, his hand stopping just before the switch.

Stop, stupid! If the switch lets off a spark this whole place will blow.

Wataru withdrew his hand, then, groping behind the oven, found the main gas valve and turned it off.

Returning to the living room, he opened all of the windows. Nervously, he tiptoed into his mother's room. She was lying there on her side, her face as pale as the moon. Her head was on her pillow and she was facing the ceiling. The summer coverlet on her bed was thin, but even so Wataru could barely see her form beneath it—*that's how much weight she lost in the short time since Dad left.*

But you don't have to die. Please don't die.

The curtains in the bedroom were heavy and thick, and easily slid out of Wataru's hands. He jumped up and grabbed them, but ended up in a heap on the floor when the whole curtain rod detached from the wall. Still, he let his heart give a cheer of victory. Wataru scrambled to his feet and opened the window.

I made it in time! Mom's going to be okay. I'll save her! I can save her!

He had returned from Vision to the real world at the same point he had left—when Mitsuru had come through the Corridor of Light to save him.

The gas smell was thinning. Still, Wataru ran through the darkened rooms, down the hall, running into walls and furniture, until he was out the front door. He hoped the neighbors would wake up in time.

"Can I borrow your phone?! Hello? This is Wataru Mitani, I live next door! I need to call an ambulance!"

It was a dark night in the real world, with no moon. Only the gently flickering fluorescent lights in the apartment hallway watched over Wataru's frantic struggle for help.

Uncle Lou came right away, driving straight in from Chiba. The two sat side by side in the hallway outside the emergency room at the hospital. It was three in the morning.

"You were lucky to have found her so quickly," the doctor told Wataru. "We have to keep a close watch on her until she regains consciousness. But I have every reason to believe she'll pull through just fine. You did well, son."

The doctor was young himself. He had come out to greet the ambulance with a sleepy look on his face when they arrived through the emergency entrance. But when the stretcher came out, he was all business. There was work to be done. *Doctors are a bit like Highlanders in that way,* Wataru thought.

They checked out Wataru too. Spots in your eyes? *No.* Does it hurt to breathe? *Not at all.* Does your head hurt? *I'm fine.*

I'm fine. Is it all right if I stay until Mom wakes up?

So he had sat with his uncle waiting, just the two of them. The bench in the hallway was made for adults, and Wataru's legs swung in the air when he sat up. He kicked them back and forth. *I'm a full-fledged Highlander. Why am I sitting here like a little kid?*

Then he remembered. *I'm not a Highlander, not anymore. I don't have my Brave's Sword. Or the power of the gemstones.*

I'm just Wataru Mitani.

"Municipal gas won't kill you, you know," Uncle Lou muttered. His shoulders were sagging, and his large hands hung limp between his knees.

Wataru had heard something like that before. *That's right, Mitsuru. Municipal gas isn't poisonous enough to be fatal.* But if a spark catches it on fire…

And Mitsuru's gone. Or wait, maybe he's not! What if he's back here in the real world?

"Aren't you sleepy, Wataru?" Uncle Lou asked. He hadn't shaved in a while, and his face was scratchy with stubble. His big eyes blinked sorrowfully.

He looked just like Kee Keema when the big waterkin was in a sour mood. The same giant frame, the same gentle heart.

"I'm fine, really."

"Well, if you get sleepy, my shoulder's all yours."

"Thanks."

He wasn't tired, but suddenly an uncontrollable wave of emotion rose up inside him, and Wataru clung to his uncle's arm. Uncle Lou put his arm around Wataru's shoulders.

For a minute, nobody said anything.

"I'm sorry," Uncle Lou said at last. "You've been put through all this, and it's not your fault at all. It's really not fair. Not fair at all."

His voice trembled and broke slightly, like the unshed tears he was holding inside.

"Uncle Lou?"

"Yeah?"

"Do you remember us meeting?"

His uncle turned and looked Wataru from head to toe. "What are you talking about?" His tired face had a look of honest confusion.

Then Wataru remembered: it had been after he got the second gemstone and passed through the Corridor of Light that he had met his uncle. His mother was already in the hospital then, and Uncle Lou had come in just as Wataru was getting ready to leave. *But she just got to the hospital now. That hasn't happened yet.*

Then Wataru thought, *I'm already here, back in the real world. Maybe it will never happen at all.*

Somehow, the time he'd spent in Vision hadn't registered here in the real world. Finally, the full impact of it hit him. That's what it meant to come back to an apartment filled with gas—the same apartment at the same time he had left it. While he had been running around Vision, here, back in the real world, nothing had happened.

That raised a lot of questions. Where was Mitsuru Ashikawa? What about Kaori Daimatsu? And Kenji Ishioka, for that matter?

Uncle Lou was rubbing his face with his well-worn hands. Wataru felt like he should comfort him somehow. *Really I'm fine. In fact, I'm beyond fine in ways you couldn't possibly imagine.*

But he didn't know how to say it. If he wasn't careful, he might end up crying himself. Not that he was sad—but if he started talking, all the emotion he'd been holding inside would burst out, and he would cry. *Because I'm still a kid.*

Because I'm no longer Wataru, the Brave.

Wataru leaned against his uncle, letting himself be supported by his arm. His uncle was warm and smelled of suntan lotion.

"Uncle Lou?"

"Hmm?"

"I guess I am a little sleepy after all."

"Goodnight, Wataru."

Wataru closed his eyes. The instant he fell into a light sleep, he began to dream. He was riding on the darbaba cart. Kee Keema was sitting in the driver seat, spurring the beast with cheerful yelps.

Finally, the tears came. His first tears back in the real world. They ran down his cheeks and over his lips. They tasted like home.

They stayed at the hospital until morning, but his mother still wasn't up yet, so Uncle Lou took Wataru back to the apartment.

They ate breakfast at a pancake house. The place was empty in the early morning, except for a man in a suit sitting over in the smoking section reading a newspaper. The smoke from his cigarette drifted past Wataru, who was busily stuffing his cheeks with pancakes.

"Wataru."

"What?"

His uncle was looking at him curiously, a Styrofoam cup filled with steaming coffee in his hand.

"What is it?"

Wataru's uncle put his cup on the tray. He furrowed his eyebrows. "You know, you…"

"Yeah?"

"You seem grown-up all of a sudden." There was a hint of surprise in his quiet tone. Wataru realized his uncle had been observing him for some time.

Wataru smiled. A nameless, warm feeling, one part gratitude and one part amusement spread through him. *It wasn't sudden at all. I've just come home from a long journey.*

"I'm just happy that Mom didn't die," Wataru said. "I don't think that's what she really wanted. I don't think that was the right thing to do."

Uncle Lou nodded, unable to speak. His eyes glistened with tears.

School was already out for summer vacation. Even if Wataru went, no one would be there. So, the first chance he had, he made straight for the apartment where Mitsuru's aunt lived.

It was morning, and the doorman was piling up garbage in the waste bin to the side of the apartment. When Wataru arrived, he paid him no notice. But when Wataru came out again, panting for air, he stopped what he was doing and came over, a suspicious look on his face.

"What are you doing here, boy?"

"Uh…I…" The nameplate for the Ashikawa apartment was gone. Right there, on the mailbox in the entrance foyer with the number for the apartment where Mitsuru's aunt had lived was a new, blank nameplate. "Did Ms. Ashikawa move?"

"Ashikawa?"

"Yeah, a young lady, living with a boy about my age. He and I were friends."

The doorman put a hand to his forehead and thought. Then he grunted and rapped his knuckles on his bald spot. "Oh them! They moved."

"When?"

"Just a while ago. Think it was the last day of school."

"Did you see them when they left? Was it both of them? Was the boy with her?"

The doorman seemed flustered by this barrage of questions. He recovered quickly, though—the dour, worldly expression coming back to his frowning face. He glared at Wataru. "What do you want to know for? If you were really his friend, why didn't he tell you?" Glancing back at the mailboxes, he continued, "Say, what did you really come here for? Haven't I seen you around before?" But by that time, Wataru was already out the door and gone.

Wataru wanted to see Katchan more than anyone else. Unfortunately, his good friend didn't have any news about Mitsuru.

But *Yutaro! Yutaro Miyahara.* He was friends with Mitsuru; they were the top students in the class. And they had even been in the same room. *Now where did Yutaro live...?*

Yutaro was busy watering a row of morning glories and sunflowers with his little brother and sister in the small garden behind an old wooden house. His sister was tottering along, carrying a red watering can. Yutaro was busy using a dowel rod to prop up a sunflower stalk.

Wataru put his hands on the steel wire fence around the garden and called out to him.

"Good morning!"

Yutaro jolted upright and whirled around. "Hey there, Wataru. Didn't see you. Good morning. You're up early for a summer vacation day!"

Yutaro walked over to the fence. Wataru mumbled some hasty explanation for his visit. Yutaro's brother and sister stayed in the garden, absorbed with counting the blooming morning glories.

"Hey, Yutaro, you know that kid Mitsuru Ashikawa?"

"Mitsuru? You mean the one in my class?" Yutaro asked without skipping a beat. "What about him?"

Mitsuru does exist! He's here! I didn't just dream him up.

"Do you...happen to know where he is?"

"Where?" Yutaro blinked. "He moved."

This was the answer Wataru had expected. "He was a transfer student, wasn't he? And he already moved away?"

"Yeah. He was in and out of here in a hurry. But I guess with his home situation being what it is and all..."

"Yeah. I was wondering—what was he like?"

Yutaro stared at Wataru for a second. "What do you mean, 'what was he like'?" Yutaro laughed. "Why are you so interested in him, anyway? He wasn't even in your class."

"Well, we were in the same cram school."

"Really? But I never saw you talking to him. He was the silent type, that one."

Wataru nodded. He wanted to know more...but he couldn't think of any questions that wouldn't make Yutaro even more suspicious than he already was.

Wataru was back in the real world now, and Mitsuru was gone. *It's like he was never here in the first place...*

"Wataru," Yutaro called out. "You know..."

"Yutaro!" came his little brother's shout from behind him. "I'm trying to count the morning glories but Mayumi keeps gettin' in the way!"

Back in the garden, the little girl burst into tears. Yutaro hesitated, unsure for a moment whether to be the big brother to his siblings or the friend to Wataru.

"Your sister's crying," Wataru said, letting him go.

"Yeah." Yutaro looked over the fence, and turned toward his sister. Then he stopped and turned back. "The moms at school, they talk too much," he said quickly, as though he was in a rush to get the words out before he changed his mind.

"Huh?"

"There was a PTA meeting before summer break, and this one older lady there loves spreading rumors, and she told my mom..."

Wataru already knew what Yutaro was going to say. For a second, he was afraid that news of his mother's suicide attempt had already made the rounds, but that would have been much too fast. No, Yutaro's mom had doubtlessly heard about the events leading up to that. A couple of kids in Wataru's grade lived in the same apartment complex. They had probably heard something, or the families heard something, and word had gotten around.

Grandma was shouting pretty loudly that night.

"Things are pretty rough at your place, I guess?"

"Yeah." Wataru nodded. Yutaro was as safe a person to talk to about this as anybody. And somewhere along the line, Wataru found he had the strength to talk about it without getting too weepy.

"I know what it's like," Yutaro said, rubbing his lip. "My dad's remarried. Takes a while for things to settle down."

Behind him, his little sister had stopped crying. She and her brother were crouching down by the morning glory patch, digging up something in the soil.

"It was...tough, when it happened."

"Yeah, I know."

Yutaro smiled. "But it got better. I like my brother and sister too. Just wish they were a little quieter."

Now his little brother started crying. His sister was hitting him over the head with the red watering can.

"Yeah," Wataru said. He felt his throat tighten and couldn't say any more.

"So, anyway," Yutaro said, sounding a bit unsure himself. "I guess I, well, you know..." He didn't know what to say either, but his eyes told Wataru enough. *Hang in there.*

"Yeah."

"Yutaroooooo!"

Now both of the kids were crying. Yutaro gave an exaggerated sigh, but he was smiling when he turned around to run back to them.

I wonder how many morning glories there were after all?

On the way back home, Wataru's mind was a blank. He thought of nothing. In his head, there was only a question mark where the face of Mitsuru Ashikawa had been, and in his chest, a lingering feeling of relief from his talk with Yutaro.

He wasn't even paying attention to where he was going, when he saw Katchan walking toward him on the other side of the street. He was wearing a pass to the municipal pool around his neck and yawning. It took him a moment to recognize his friend.

"Ooooooornin'." Katchan waved to Wataru, not even bothering to stifle his yawn.

Wataru stopped, frozen in place, staring at Katchan.

Say, Katchan, you remember that exchange student, Mitsuru Ashikawa?

"What're you doing out here this early in the morning? I know that you didn't come from the pool, I was just there!"

"Gotcha."

"What?" Katchan craned his neck, looking at Wataru. If this early rising was to become a trend, Katchan clearly did not approve.

"Thanks for freeing those birds for me."

"Huh?"

Seeing his expression, it was clear that Katchan didn't know anything about the birds. He never got them, and he never set them free.

"Nothing," Wataru said with a laugh. "Forget about it."

"You look scruffy, man. In fact, you look like you haven't slept a wink." Before Wataru could respond he could see Katchan's brain begin to work double time. "Wait..." now he looked worried. "I hope nothing happened at home, with your old man?"

Wataru knew he couldn't hide the truth from Katchan, but there didn't seem to be any point in telling him the whole story now. *Maybe later, when things have settled down a bit.*

"Katchan?"

"Yeah?"

"Do you know what happened to Kenji...from the sixth grade?"

"You mean Kenji Ishioka? That creep?"

"Uh-huh." Wataru chose his words carefully. "Did he lose his memory or something? Or did he go missing for a while? And when he came back, did he act like his soul was gone?"

Katchan's eyes focused on Wataru's face. He walked straight over to his friend and waved his hand right before Wataru's nose. "Hey! Mitani! Earth to Mitani!"

Wataru laughed. Katchan kept waving. "I know why you didn't sleep last night! You were playing that game, *Detective Meadows: The Case of the Disappearing Client*, weren't you! They say it's the best one in the series! Once

Miyuki Miyabe

✳

811

you pick up that controller, you aren't sleeping until you're done. Well, time to wake up, Wataru. People we know don't go missing. Not in real life."

Wataru laughed while his friend grabbed him by the shoulders and shook him. "Mitani! Mitani!" Katchan was acting like a cop trying to keep a wounded partner from losing consciousness.

"Kenji hasn't gone missing. His memory's fine too, far as I know. Though I did hear that he hasn't been on the warpath lately. Maybe he's gone soft. Maybe somebody took that crooked mean streak of his and straightened it out for him."

Hearing that was enough for Wataru to understand.

It was in the afternoon when the call finally came from the hospital. Grandma had come over from Chiba, and Uncle Lou and Wataru went to the hospital together. Uncle Lou waited in the hallway while Wataru went to see his mother in her room.

Kuniko cried, and Wataru cried. She apologized, and he apologized.

Then, the most unexpected thing happened.

"You know, Wataru," his mother said, "while I was asleep, I had a really odd dream."

"What kind of dream?"

"Well…" his mother began, but just from her expression, Wataru knew. He could see it in her eyes.

"It was the strangest thing. It was like another world—like something in one of those video games you're always playing. And you were there. You were traveling, learning to be a warrior. And you were with this big lizard man, and a girl with cat ears. It looked like you were having fun."

"Do you remember much about my trip?"

If you don't, I can tell you. I can tell you everything. I can tell you what I did, and what I brought back.

"I do! I remember it all. Crazy, huh?" His mother smiled. "Wataru, you made a very dashing adventurer, I must say."

"Mom?" Wataru said after moment. "I think…I think we're going to be okay." *I know now how to not punish myself for what I've lost. I know how to take care of the future.*

"Even if Dad doesn't come home?" she asked in a tiny voice.

"Yeah," Wataru said, nodding. "There's a whole world out there waiting for us."

My Vision. My real world.

In his mother's eyes he saw the blue-gray sparkle of Meena's eyes, and the black eyes of Kutz the Rosethorn. He even saw the clear blue eyes of Captain Ronmel.

His mother hugged him.

Several days later, his mother came home from the hospital, and it was decided that she and Wataru should go to his grandmother's house in Chiba for a while. Grandma had grumbled a bit, wondering if Kuniko wouldn't much rather go to *her* parents' house in Odawara. But her resistance to the idea faded away when Kuniko told her she wanted to talk to her about their future. "I'd really appreciate your advice."

That had been enough for Grandma. The hard lines in her face softened, and she had gone home on the first train to do a little housecleaning before they arrived.

Wataru's father called several times. He saw his mom talking with him on the phone for hours. She wasn't crying or screaming anymore though.

Wataru told his dad he was doing fine.

"I'm sorry, Kuniko, I really am," he overheard his grandmother saying.

Wataru had to tell Katchan the news. If Katchan's parents let him, he could come out to Chiba to play. Uncle Lou said that, if he wanted to, he could stay for all of summer vacation. "Of course, I'll be putting you two to work on the beach!"

Katchan was ecstatic, but he had one request. "I'll go as long as your uncle doesn't force us into a watermelon battle."

"What's that?" Wataru had asked.

"It's like a piñata. You know, when you blindfold someone and they take a stick and try to hit something? But instead of a piñata, you're swinging at a big watermelon. And a lot of people are doing it at the same time. If I played with your uncle, he'd crack me over the head for sure and with those big arms..." Katchan shivered. "Yowch!"

There was one other place Wataru needed to go. Right up until the moment he left Katchan's house, he was half-thinking of inviting his friend along.

He didn't know if he had the guts to go there alone.

But in the end, he said goodbye, and set off by himself.

He began walking in the direction of the Daimatsu building. *The haunted building.*

He hadn't gotten up the courage to come here before today. He guessed that it was probably the same as it always was. Why would it be any different? But for some reason, he was scared to check for himself. He was scared to see that skeleton of abandoned iron girders, quietly rusting beneath faded blue tarps, that rain-beaten sign announcing the plans for the building.

Because when I see that I'll know it's really over. The spell will be forever broken.

So he walked slowly, his eyes cast downward.

He heard it before he saw it: the whine of heavy machinery. Wataru looked up to see a bulldozer and a crane busy at work.

The haunted building was naked, its blue tarp dressing torn to the ground. A long rusted girder was hanging from the arm of the crane.

They're taking it down!

Wataru ran.

He stood watching the steel staircase where he first met Wayfinder Lau. Lost in thought, someone tapped him on the shoulder.

"Well, isn't that our young friend Wataru?"

He looked around to see Mr. Daimatsu grinning at him.

"H-hello!"

"I'll bet you didn't expect this!" Mr. Daimatsu said, waving his hand at the half-dismantled building.

"You're taking the whole building apart?"

"That we are. It sat out in the rain so long, the metal fittings started to disintegrate. So we're razing it to the ground and building it back up from scratch. Finally got all the money in order, this time. It will be a fine building, for sure."

The haunted building was going for good.

Wataru's vision blurred ever so slightly. The roaring of the big tractor drowned out his quick sigh.

Goodbye.

Just then, Mr. Daimatsu turned around and spoke to someone behind him. Whoever it was stood just right so that Wataru couldn't see who it was.

"No need to be shy," Mr. Daimatsu was saying. He smiled broadly and put his arm around the person's shoulder, pulling her around to face Wataru. "This is Wataru…Wataru Mitani. You've met him before, though you probably don't remember."

It was Kaori Daimatsu.

She wasn't sitting in a wheelchair anymore. She wore a knee-length sleeveless white dress that fell down over her slender legs. Her skin was dazzlingly white, and her lustrous black hair was tied in a ponytail that gleamed in the hot summer sun.

"My daughter's gotten much better recently," Mr. Daimatsu said, rubbing her shoulder as delicately as if she were precious jewel. "She came out for a walk and a little fresh air today. Well, Kaori, aren't you going to say hello?"

The girl was staring at Wataru, as though captivated. The look in her dark eyes said that she knew she had met him somewhere, but couldn't remember where. They had spoken, but she didn't know what had been said. *I can't remember how, but I know that I know you.*

Even for Wataru, the memory was fading.

Her soul is back. Her soul was returned.

"I…" Wataru stammered.

The little white bird on my shoulder.

"I once snuck inside this building," he managed at last, "and I tripped and fell. Mr. Daimatsu took care of me."

Once he started talking, Wataru couldn't stop. His voice sounded strange in his own ears.

Mr. Daimatsu laughed out loud. "That's right, I remember that."

Wataru was staring at Kaori. She returned the stare. "Hello," she said quietly.

*Give me your sword, the Demon's Bane…*It was the same voice. Those graceful hands stretched out to Wataru. Those arms that had comforted him in his sorrow at leaving Vision behind. That warm embrace had taken the pain away.

I'll never forget that moment. Never.

You don't remember me, but I remember you.

You were the Goddess of my destiny.

"Well now, you've met again for the first time," Mr. Daimatsu said cheerfully. Kaori Daimatsu looked up at her father and smiled. Wataru thought her smile must have been brighter than the summer sun high in the sky above, the way it lit up her father's face.

"Nice to meet you," said Wataru.

Vesna esta holicia.
Until you shine again.
Into Vision, into the real world.
Though a child of man knows time, life itself is eternal.

Miyuki Miyabe was born in Tokyo and graduated from Sumidagawa High School. After working in law offices and other places, her 1987 debut title, *Warera ga Rinjin no Hanzai* (Crimes of our Neighbors), won the All Yomimono Newcomer Award for Crime Fiction.

Miyabe went on to win the 45th Mystery Writers of Japan Award for *Ryu wa Nemuru* (The Dragon Sleeps) and the 13th 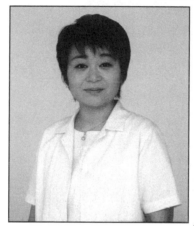 Yoshikawa Eiji Newcomer Prize for *Honjo Fukagawa Fushigi Zoshi* (Mysterious Tales of Honjo-Fukagawa) in 1992.

Her other literary awards include the 6th Yamamoto Shugoro Prize in 1993 for *Kasha* (All She was Worth), the 18th Nihon SF Taisho Award in 1997 for the *Gamoutei Jiken* (Case of the Gamou Residence), the 120th Naoki Prize in 1999 for *Riyuu* (The Reason), the Mainichi Shuppan Culture Award Special Prize in 2001 for *Mohou-han* (Copycat Killer), and the 6th Shiba Ryotaro Prize and the 52nd Minister of Education Award for Fine Arts in Literature in 2002, also for *Mohou-han*.

In 2007, her novel *Na mo Naki Doku* (Nameless Poison) won the 41st Yoshikawa Eiji Literature Prize. In 2008, the English-language edition of *Brave Story* was awarded the American Library Association's Batchelder Award.

HAIKASORU
THE FUTURE IS JAPANESE

THE LORD OF THE SANDS OF TIME
Only the past can save the future as the cyborg O travels from the 26th century to ancient Japan and beyond. With the help of the princess Miyo and a ragtag troop of warriors from across history, O has a chance to save humanity and his own soul, but will it be at the cost of his life?

ALL YOU NEED IS KILL
It's battle armor versus aliens when the Mimics invade Earth. Private Kiriya dies in battle only to find himself reborn every day to fight again. Time is not on Kiriya's side, but he does have one ally: the American super-soldier known as the Full Metal Bitch.

ZOO
A man receives a photo of his girlfriend every day in the mail...so that he can keep track of her body's decomposition. A deathtrap that takes a week to kill its victims. Haunted parks and airplanes held in the sky by the power of belief. These are just a few of the stories by Otsuichi, Japan's master of dark fantasy.

USURPER OF THE SUN
Schoolgirl Aki is one of the few witnesses to construction on the surface of Mercury. Soon an immense ring has been built around the sun and Earth has plunged into chaos. While the nations of the world prepare for war, Aki grows up with a thirst for knowledge and a hunger to make first contact with the enigmatic Builders. Winner of Japan's prestigious Seiun Award!

BATTLE ROYALE: THE NOVEL
The best-selling tour de force from Koshun Takami in a new edition, with an author's afterword and bonus material.

BRAVE STORY
The paperback edition of the Batchelder Award-winning fantasy novel by Miyuki Miyabe.

And soon:
THE BOOK OF HEROES
When Yuriko's brother kills a classmate and then vanishes, it is up to her to journey into the nameless land where all stories are born, to face the ancient evil some dare call...The Hero. From the author of *Brave Story*, Miyuki Miyabe.

YUKIKAZE
In the midst of a war with no end in sight, Second Lieutenant Rei Fukai carries out his lonely missions in the skies over a strange planet nicknamed "Faery." His only companion is his sentient fighter plane, call sign: Yukikaze.

VISIT US AT WWW.HAIKASORU.COM